LIARS' PARADISE

ALSO BY ERIKA FABIAN

BOOKS IN PROGRESS
Stolen Minds (co-authored)
Driver
Acting, Becoming a Character

PLAYS/FILM SCRIPTS IN PROGRESS
The Doctors' Show
Family Christmases
The Stalin Plot.
The Man in Her Closet (Produced by Actor's
Theater L.A.)

PUBLISHED WORKS
Shrink Talk by Dr. Michael Blumenfield (Fabian line and text edited 2021-2022)
Eleven Empty Chairs by Frans Boerlage (Fabian text editor and co-author 2015)
Changing Tracks by Frans Boerlage 2012 (Fabian text editor, co-author)
Making Love Work published in Israel 2000
Maluku, Riches of Land and Sea for Trade, Investment, and Tourism, (the former Spice Islands), 1997
The Travel Photographer's Handbook 1997
The PhD Guide to Photography 1997
Irian Jaya, A New Frontier for Trade, Investment and Tourism (Papua) published in English and Japanese 1994 Costumes of Splendid China 1994
Adventure in Splendid China 1993
Trade, Investment and Tourism in East Java 1992
Sky Riders sold over 100,000 copies, and was translated into Italian, Japanese, and Portuguese, and was "The Book Selection of the Month" in Australia, Publisher: Harlequin 1984
Making Love Work first Publisher Putnam 1980
Making Love Work French translation Les Editions de L'Homme 1980
Making Love Work in paperback Publisher Ballantine 1982
Making Love Work Italian translation, two different editions Publisher Rizzoli 1983

Co-authored with Albert Moldvay (National Geographic Staff Photographer)1980-1982, Publisher: Amphoto

Photographing London
Photographing, Paris
Photographing Rome
Photographing Amsterdam

Photographing New York
Photographing Washington D.C.
Photographing Los Angeles
Photographing Mexico City & Acapulco

As a photojournalist, Ms. Fabian's photo illustrated articles (approximately 200) have appeared in such magazines as the National Geographic, National Geographic's World Magazine, Westways, Peak, Expressions, and the Washington D.C. based, World & I. For five years Ms. Fabian contributed to Albert Moldvay's syndicated columns for the Los Angeles Times, Westways Magazine, and to Garuda International In-Flight Magazine.

For over 20 years Ms. Fabian taught at UCLA Extension and other University of California campuses a workshop entitled Photographing the National Geographic Way, and was honored as Best Instructor of the Year, in 1995.
At present, Ms. Fabian is a public speaker at the Holocaust Museum L.A.

LIARS' PARADISE

A TRUE STORY OF SURVIVAL
UNDER NAZIS AND COMMUNISTS

By

ERIKA FABIAN

ERIAKO ASSOCIATES

LOS ANGELES CA 90291

LIARS' PARADISE. Copyright 2025 by Erika Fabian

Eriako Associates

1380 Morningside Way

Venice, CA 90291

Email:eriakoassociates@gmail.com

FIRST U.S. EDITION 2025

Library of Congress Control Number: 2025946106

Key words for Liars' Paradise: Historical Fiction, Hitler, Stalin, Communism, Satellite Countries, Political Prisoners, Secret Police, Revolution, Antisemitism

ISBN: 978-0-9638417-8-0 (hard cover)

ISBN: 978-0-9638417-6-6 (Paperback)

ISBN: 978-0-9638417-7-3 (eBook)

ISBN: 978-0-9638417-9-7 (audio book)

10 9 8 7 6 5 4 3 2 1

Books are available in quantity for promotional or premium use. For information on discounts and terms please contact the publisher above.

Praise for *Liars' Paradise*

"Erika Fabian has shared her story for many years at Holocaust Museum LA, and we are fortunate to now have her experiences preserved in writing.

Liars' Paradise is a powerful and deeply moving book that highlights an often-overlooked aspect of Holocaust history—the experiences of the youngest survivors. Through the eyes of a child, Erika offers a rare and poignant perspective on a childhood that seems impossible to comprehend. Her vivid memories allow readers to follow not only her difficult experiences, but also the emotions, fears, and resilience that defined it.

Importantly, *Liars' Paradise* reminds us that the Holocaust did not simply end in 1945. For many survivors, liberation marked the beginning of a painful and uncertain rebirth. In Erika's case, growing up under the Iron Curtain added yet another layer of hardship and complexity to her upbringing. This book stands as both a testament to survival and a powerful reminder of the consequences of hatred and bigotry."

—**Beth Kean**, CEO of Holocaust Museum LA

"Liars' Paradise is a taut, humane chronicle of survival—told with the pulse of a thriller and the intimacy of a personal memoir. Gripping, compassionate, and impeccably observed, it's a true story that reads with novelistic immediacy. A mother's ferocious ingenuity: A city closing in—Liars' Paradise is unforgettable. With clear-eyed restraint and remarkable momentum, Liars' Paradise shows how ordinary people improvise courage under extraordinary pressure. Unsparing and tender in equal measure, it restores human scale to history. Scene by scene, the book renders the lethal arithmetic of wartime life—papers, safe houses, impossible choices—without sentimentality or despair.

"Urgent, elegant, and deeply true, Liars' Paradise reads like lived experience: the knock at the door, the breath-held silences, the small mercies that add up to survival. Meticulous research meets intimate storytelling in a narrative that's both propulsive and reflective—honoring resilience without smoothing over terror or moral ambiguity. An essential contribution to the literature of witness."

—**Justin Jampol**, Founder/Executive Director, The Wende Museum

A Tribute to Liars' Paradise

In history's darkest hours,
Erika Fabian's story blooms like flowers.
A memoir bold, in pages deeply sown,
Of childhood's trials, through tyrants known.
Under Hitler's shadow, Stalin's grim reign,
She weaves a tale, with courage as her main.
A life lived on the edge of night,
Escaping death, seeking the light.
In Liars Paradise, truth unfolds,
A story of survival, courage untold.
Skillfully composed, like a novel's art,
It grips the soul, right from the start.
A narrative engaging, impossible to ignore,
Each page a journey, to what lies in store.
Forged in the anvil of a tumultuous age,
In the darkest of days, a way to cope.
So, open its pages, let the story flow,
A story of survival, in a world so cold.

FOREWORD TO LIARS' PARADISE

FIVE YEARS AGO, MY older son, Dan, commented to me, "When you're gone, my children will know nothing about your side of the family. You're a writer, how about writing a book about your family?"

Thus began my long and often painful recollection of my early years of life in Hungary. Describing my survival under the Nazis and then during the communist era was so painful that the only way I could do it was by narrating it as if it were a novel.

The novel format also gave me the freedom to write about my mother's life as she had told me about her early years and marriage, and of other events in her life, without saying "she told me".

Apart from this narrative freedom I had taken in writing this book, all the events and conversations took place as described. This is a true story of my family and my life.

I hope you'll enjoy reading it, more so than I enjoyed writing about some of the events.

Erika Fabian

2025

TABLE OF CONTENTS

CHAPTER 1

THE BANGING AT THE front door of the apartment went on and on. Piry lay in bed, rigid with fear. When the pounding first penetrated her consciousness, she assumed that she was asleep and was having a nightmare. As the hammering continued, it struck her that she was awake, and the reality was worse than a nightmare. A man at the front door really was trying to break it down. Panicked, Piry sat up, clutching her duvet cover, feeling paralyzed as she heard a rough male voice demand, "Wake up, wake up! Everybody downstairs!"

The room was dark; only a streetlight filtered through the wooden shutters. It's not even dawn, she thought. She listened to the kicks at the door. Then she heard a bullhorn coming from the courtyard of the building, instructing all Jewish tenants to gather downstairs. So, they weren't trying to break her door down; they were merely trying to awaken her, she thought with some relief. Suddenly, her bedroom door burst open, and she gasped but quickly smiled as her two daughters tumbled into her bed.

"Mommy, Mommy, someone is kicking the door; why don't you open it?" They demanded, shivering from the cold and fear.

Piry put her arms around Judith and Erika and pulled them close to her under the goose-down duvet. "Keep quiet," she whispered.

What could she tell them, Piry wondered. *That she felt as terrified as they did and had no answers? That they ought to get out of bed instead of huddling under the cover and, obeying the bellowing instructions, go downstairs? Then what? Where would they be taken?* It was late fall, and there were more and more stories going around Budapest about Jewish tenants being evacuated from entire buildings and transported to—God only knew where. Some said to labor camps in Germany. *If only Zoltán were here*—she thought bitterly.

Zoltán, her husband, had been gone for nearly a year. Not a word had come from him in all that time. If she were by herself, she might dress and go downstairs, Piry thought. But what would happen to two small children in a labor camp? No, she wasn't going to abandon her children to fate, as she had been at their age. She peered at her daughters in the dark, their solemn little faces raised toward hers, expecting answers. She smoothed back their hair, Judith's sand-brown and Erika's a wavy honey-gold, so much like her own, and she could see the fear in their eyes.

We are going to stay put, she decided. *Ignore the kicks at the door, the bullhorn, the shuffling feet as families passed along the corridors and down the stairs to the courtyard. It was a terrifying decision.* She knew what would happen to them if the man broke down the front door. It took all her willpower to stay calm as she quietly explained to her children, "They're SS soldiers. Hungarian Nazis called Arrowhead men. Let's stay quiet so the man will go away, and we won't have to go downstairs.

"Why do they want us to go downstairs?" Erika, the irrepressible four-year-old whispered, her luminous hazel eyes filled with fear.

"Can't you hear, stupid? To take us away So, shut up." Judith hissed at her little sister; her seven-year-old heart filled with fear and anxiety.

Erika knew what "taking away" meant. One day, her father stopped coming home from work. Mother then explained that a war was going on, and he had been taken away to a labor camp to work for the war. Erika couldn't imagine what she and Judith would do if they were taken to a camp, but she knew with all her heart that she didn't want to go.

"I'm scared," she whispered, snuggling closer to her mother as the kicks intensified.

"I know you are. I am, too. Shhh." Piry laid back on the pillow, pulling her daughters with her. They lay in silence, rigid with apprehension, listening. Piry felt as if each bang against the door was a boot aimed at her stomach. She wondered why the SS man didn't simply break the glass window in the upper part of the door and enter. Instead, he kicked, then waited, then kicked again. The ominous sound echoed down the long hallway to the bedroom.

They could hear the bullhorn down in the courtyard between the thuds, repeatedly urging people to hurry and gather downstairs. Their apartment was on the first floor, and they could make out every word. The man on the loudspeaker told people to bring only a day's food supply. He promised that they would be provided with everything else. Piry wondered why she resisted the call. *If the Nyilas breaks down the door and find us, he'll just shoot us for disobeying their orders.* This thought made Piry's whole body tremble uncontrollably. Maybe it was best to give up, like the others. *What right do I have to take such an enormous chance with my daughters' lives?* The kicks became louder, and Piry jumped out of bed.

"I'll tell him we'll go in a minute!" she whispered and jumped out of bed.

In that same instant, Judith leaped after her and, grabbing onto Piry's nightgown, pulling her back, whispered furiously, "If you open that door, he'll shoot us!"

Piry looked at the enormous blue eyes staring up at her from a face so young with a gaze so old. When did her daughter become so wise? Their eyes locked in a brief struggle of wills. Then, with a deep sigh, Piry returned to the bed with Judith following her.

"You're probably right, Judith."

What an age we live in, Piry thought, embracing Judith's small shoulders and pulling the child closer to her. *Barely seven years old, and she already knows about getting killed.* The thought made her jump up again. Maybe it was better to join the others. If they went voluntarily, at least they'd have a chance at staying alive.

"They won't shoot if I tell them we're getting dressed."

But hissing, "No, no," Judith grabbed Piry, pulling on her nightgown, and tried to drag her back into bed. Suppressing her sobs, she whispered intensely, "No, Mommy, don't go to the door, don't move, or they'll know we're here. Please, Mommy, you mustn't go to the door!"

Judith was never afraid of anything. It upset Erika to see how frightened her sister was now. She wondered whether they were really going to be shot if the man broke in. But she knew better than to ask. Thus, she just lay in anxious silence, her eyes glued on the dark forms of her mother and sister locked in silent combat in the middle of the room, the sound of the kicks penetrating her till her whole body ached with tension.

She saw her mother free herself and step forward, but Judith lunged after her, wrapping her arms around Piry's knees. In that instant, the kicking stopped, and the bullhorn fell silent. They listened, barely breathing. Piry and Judith stood frozen in mid-motion, Erika rigid on the bed, the three of them waiting for it all to start up again. But there was only a heavy silence in which Erika thought she could hear her own heartbeats. People's murmur and shuffling feet reached them from the courtyard. Piry motioned for Judith and Erika to be still.

Time passed, and then no more sound came from below. Piry waited a bit longer, then padded to the bed and sank down on the edge. Judith did the same.

"They're gone. Let's pray," Piry whispered.

Erika knew the passage by heart, though it was in Hebrew, for her mother had taught it to her as a bedtime prayer. It started with "Sh'ma Yisrael, Adonai Elohenu, Adonai Echad," which meant something about God being the only God and a great God. Erika thought it odd that her mother wanted to pray now after the danger was over. So, she didn't join in.

"You're not praying," Judith accused her.

"I am too," Erika protested and quickly started to mumble the words. Resentment against Judith welled up in her. It's none of her business what I do, she thought. *When I get to be seven, I won't be as mean as she.* Sometimes, she really hated Judith.

After praying, Piry said, "Let's stay in bed for a while to be sure they're gone." They pulled up the duvet again, lying still and listening, but the only sound came from the ticking of the grandfather clock on the wall.

In the dim light of the room, Piry saw that the hands showed five-thirty. It was still so early. Yet, she felt as though she had just passed from one lifetime to another. It was like a rebirth, coming so close to death yet staying alive. She could feel her daughters' bodies next to her lying relaxed, as though they had dozed off. Slowly, she brought a hand out from under the cover and touched her ice-cold nose, then quickly slipped it back into the warmth created by their body heat. It was freezing in the room. The fire in the floor-to-ceiling butter-yellow ceramic stove had gone out during the night, but she had no thought of rekindling it. There was no point to it. They had to leave before someone discovered that they had stayed behind.

I must revise my plans for the day, Piry thought, and the very idea made her want to bury herself deeper under the cover. If only we could have stayed in the apartment three more day, our lives would have gotten on the right track again. But it was not to be. She sighed, thinking if my husband Zoltán were here, he would take charge of everything. *Now I must handle everything.* It wasn't that she couldn't do it; it was just so difficult. All her life she had been taught to rely on men, first her father, then her husband. Now, she was on her own in Budapest and responsible for the children, their livelihood, and everything that remained of their former lives in this apartment.

After Zoltán had been taken to a work camp, new government regulations forced Jewish residents out of their homes in the city, crowding them into designated apartment buildings that had been marked with a large yellow star, the insignia Jews were identified with. They also had to wear a yellow star on their clothes for all to see. This building, on Csanády Utca, was not far from their former apartment on the Nagy Körút, the Grand Ring Blvd. Piry was able to move some of their belongings from their home to this apartment, thinking they could live through the war here. She now looked around the intricately carved cherry wood furniture in the bedroom, at the Persian carpets on the polished parquet floor, and at the windows where cream-colored silk curtains hung in front of the shutters, all purchased over the years with care and love. She realized that she had to abandon it all and flee from this marked building before the Nazis returned for them too.

The sun must be coming up, she thought, as she observed the specks of dust dancing in the shaft of light that poured through the wooden slats like outspread fingers. The fingers of God, Piry thought, the hand of God that saved us. *Now you must continue on your own,* she told herself and couldn't help smiling in the dark. Mentally, she assessed what the day held for them and gently nudged each child.

"Let's get up. We'll each have to pack a small bag and leave here."

"Are you taking me to school today?" Judith asked, still half asleep.

"No".

"I am not going to kindergarten either?"

"No."

"Then where are we going?" Erika nagged.

"I don't know yet, but we've got to get out of here. So, let's get moving". Piry threw the cover back and, sliding to the foot of the bed so Judith wouldn't be in her way, got up.

Erika hated the cold water on her face and hands, but Judith was standing over her in the bathroom, making sure that she washed. In their room, where all the lacquered white furniture had pink edging, and even the sheer white curtains had pink dots, Piry laid out their clothes; wool sweaters, skirts, and long cotton stockings that would only stay up with a garter belt.

"I don't like long stockings," protested Erika.

"You must wear them; it's freezing outside," Piry insisted.

"Don't argue, or I'll hit you," threatened Judith, enforcing their mother's instructions.

Erika gritted her teeth in anger but obeyed, more afraid of Judith than her mother. Judith often hit or pinched her if she was displeased with something about her little sister. Erika never knew when Judith would do that, so she preferred to mind her sister.

They dressed quickly in the freezing cold room and then started to select the clothing they were to carry. Erika wanted to take only things that she liked, regardless of the late fall season, but Piry insisted that both girls choose for warmth.

"We might not be able to return here for a while, and we'll need winter clothes."

"But I don't like these sweaters," Erika argued.

"That doesn't matter, just pack them," Piry replied, exasperated with the child. Taking over from Erika, Piry began to fold her clothes into a small overnight case. As she glanced over to Judith, who seemed to enjoy packing practical outfits into her case, Piry was struck, as always, by the contrast between her two daughters. It was strange how Judith never bothered about clothes while Erika constantly battled over what she was to wear. Then again, Judith resembled her father, and he never fussed about clothes either. Being reminded of Zoltán by the child filled Piry with sudden yearning. But this was no time to feel sorry for herself. She had coped so far and would continue to do so until Zoltán returned. She sat on Erika's small, overstuffed suitcase and closed it.

With the three of them standing in the cold kitchen in their overcoats, Piry quickly spread goose lard on slices of bread and sprinkled them with sweet, ground red paprika for flavor. She found milk in the pantry and poured some into the tea she had prepared. As she watched the brownish liquid become cloudy with the milk, she could hear Zoltán's voice in her head, "Piry, what are you doing? You can't mix dairy with animal fat! It's not kosher!" and he would be right of course. But these were extraordinary times and feeding her children this morning was more important than Jewish

5

dietary laws. What did being observant Jews get them anyway? Zoltán was gone; she and her children were ordered out of their home and were now escaping from this new apartment like thieves in the night. *Thieves indeed, stealing our lives back from the Nazis.* This thought gave Piry a renewed sense of determination yes, they would resist and survive, no matter what it may take. Defiantly, she handed each girl a cup. "Drink this!"

There was no sugar in the house, and Erika grimaced as she tasted the bitter brew. Piry insisted that the hot liquid was good for her and that she must drink it.

"Don't be so difficult or I'll hit you," Judith warned, and for once, Piry was grateful that she had the older child's support. In protest, Erika closed her nostrils with two fingers as she sipped the scalding brew.

After eating, they went down the hallway to the front door, each clutching her little suitcase. Piry stopped them. "I'll check it out first; you two wait until I signal," She cautiously peered through the lace curtains on the front door's glass window, then pulled back as though stung by a bee.

"What's wrong?" Judith demanded, fear distorting her face.

"Mr. Fehér is in the corridor."

"So, we can't leave?" Erika chirped up.

"Shut up, or I'll pinch you," hissed Judith.

Piry was totally exasperated. "Girls!"

They stood indecisively inside as Mr. Fehér's shadow fell on the front door's window.

"Mrs. Fábián, it's all right, they're gone," murmured Mr. Fehér. "I told them you and the girls had left already. That's what stopped them from breaking in."

Mr. Fehér was one of the few non-Jews who had chosen to remain in his apartment, even after the building had been marked with the Yellow Star.

Piry opened the door a crack.

To Erika, Mr. Fehér, with his wrinkled face and hunchback, looked like a dwarf from a fairy tale. Piry must have seen him differently, for she was positively beaming at the man.

"You did that for us?" she asked.

"Of course. We're not all Nazis. But now you must leave." He sized up the trim, dark blonde woman with the warm brown eyes, and the two little girls standing tensely by their suitcases. "Do you have a place to go to?"

"Not yet." Piry didn't tell him, or the girls, that today was the day she had planned to travel to Nyiradon, a small town in northeast Hungary, to pick up birth certificates for herself and her two daughters. These documents would change their identities. They would have new names, and they could register as Christians who had fled from their village because it was near the Soviet border. They chose to come and stay in the capital during the war.

It was her former housekeeper, Kata Polyák, who, before she had left Piry's service, had offered her and her daughters' birth certificates based on her own family's papers.

"I just have to say we lost them and pay for newly issued ones," Kata explained to Piry.

She had been working for Piry for 8 years, since before Judith was born. With the new laws, forbidding Christians to work for Jews, it was dangerous for her to stay on. Either the neighbors or the concierge of the building could report her to the Nazi police. It would get not only her but Piry's whole family into trouble. So, she had to leave.

"I'll be back when the war is over," Kata promised amidst tears.

As the persecution of the Jews grew, more and more laws prohibited them from living a normal life. In the fall of 1943, Zoltán went to visit his and Piry's parents in Debrecen, Hungary's third largest city. He had hoped to persuade them to come to live in Budapest. He felt that with the increasing restrictions against Jews, they would be safer in a larger city than in a town where everybody knew them. But the old couples refused to move. Márton Fábián, Zoltán's father, was the Director of the Jewish congregation in Debrecen. Piry's father, Ignácz Kohn, and his wife Olga, owned a thriving restaurant in town. Although it served strictly kosher food, many gentiles frequented it for its excellent food and service.

"We'll be fine here. We are amongst friends," they all insisted. "And if we need anything, your brother, Tibor, is just a stone's throw away," added Zoltán's mother, Hermina.

Tibor, just a year younger than Zoltán, was a Rabbi at a congregation at the other end of town. He, too, felt that they were safer in a small town where even the gentile community knew and respected them.

At that time, Piry thought, perhaps their parents were right, for they seemed to be fine in Debrecen. Whereas that summer, Zoltán, en route by train from a labor camp to Budapest, had been ordered by Hungarian Nazis to transfer to a different train. She had not heard from him since.

Piry learned about his transfer through a Christian acquaintance, who had been on the Budapest bound train with Zoltán. The man visited Piry at the wholesale hardware store Zoltán and she owned. He told her, as Zoltán was being escorted off the train, he had quickly whispered to him: "Please tell my wife to take care of herself and the children till I return."

Now it was the autumn of 1944, and she had been struggling alone, running the business and caring for her daughters, without any news from Zoltán. Piry wrote to her in-laws and her parents that Zoltán had been deported somewhere by the Nazis, and they replied that Piry and the children should come to live with them. But Piry did not want to leave the capital. She felt safer here, even though the "Jewish Laws" increasingly tightened the web around the Jewish population. They were required to close their businesses or donate them to a Christian. They were ordered to move into designated buildings from which they could go out only between the hours of eleven a.m. to three p.m.

Piry concluded that either she conformed to these new laws or needed to take steps to survive. When the German army occupied Hungary in the spring of 1944, Piry had made her decision. Zoltán owned a small warehouse on the outskirts of the city, in a working-class neighborhood. That is where he stored the stock for his wholesale hardware business in town. Gradually, Piry smuggled as much merchandise out of their store as she dared and took it to their warehouse. She also left some items with Christian friends, turning over to the government only enough merchandise to satisfy the authorities. After all, it was wartime, and they had no idea how much merchandise she and Zoltán still had in the store!

She also thought about her former maid Kata's offer to help and came up with an idea. Nazis could easily pounce on any male on the streets, demand that he pulls down his pants, and if he was circumcised, he was either taken to a labor camp for Jews or shot on the spot. But no one could tell what a female's religion was except by looking at her identity papers. Therefore, she and her daughters needed to have Christian identity papers. Then they could live in the city as freely as wartime conditions permitted—provided no one recognized them. That meant, they needed to move to a district where they ordinarily would not have frequented.

Giving up her store but keeping enough cash to get by for nearly a year, in early summer Piry wrote to her former maid, Kata, and sent her money to obtain birth and baptism certificates for her and her daughters. Kata had a large enough family to be able to get certificates within their age ranges. She also knew which local clerk would provide these certificates for the generous fee Piry had sent.

After weeks of tense waiting, Kata had finally written to Piry that the papers were ready. But due to the uncertainties of wartime postal service, it was not safe to send them by mail. Piry had to go to Nyiradon, a small town in the northern part of the country and collect them. This was the day on which she had planned to go. With the morning raid disrupting their lives, Piry had no idea how she would be able to do that now.

Her original plan had been to have her best friend Irén take care of her daughters while she went to get the papers. Irén was to pick Judith up at her school and Erika from her kindergarten, and stay with them at their apartment, till Piry got back. In exchange, Piry promised to also obtain a birth certificate for Irén. Now, for all she knew, the Nazis had struck every Yellow Star building in Budapest at the same time, and Irén was gone. Even if by some stroke of luck, she wasn't, they needed to make a new plan.

Interpreting the young woman's silence as indecision because they had no place to go to, Mr. Fehér offered a solution. "I heard that a new Swedish Safe House had been opened by the Danube. Why don't you go there?" And he dictated the address to Piry. "Don't come back here, the concierge is a rotten Nazi. I'll keep an eye on the apartment for you."

Piry's eyes filled with tears. "God bless you," she said, wiping her eyes.

"It's all right, I'd hate to see my daughters and grandsons in your situation." His gnarled hand patted Piry's arm.

Erika wondered what he had meant, but there was no time to ask. They grabbed their bags and crept downstairs.

"Mrs. Fábián, how come you didn't leave with the others?" The concierge came through his open door, staring at Piry and her daughters, standing by the large front door that led to the street.

"We're leaving now," Piry said in her most soothing voice and reached into her handbag. When she pulled out her hand, she extended it to the concierge as if to shake hands.

From where she stood, Erika could see that her mother had money folded in her palm. She watched the concierge shake her mother's hand, and when Piry withdrew her hand, it was empty.

The concierge opened the big door and the three of them slipped through it, into the freedom of Légrády Károly Street.

"We'll go to the Nagykörút." Piry quickly guided her daughters down the street, toward St. Steven's Boulevard where buses and streetcars ran, and they wouldn't be conspicuous.

CHAPTER 2

I T WAS A BRIGHT, crisp autumn morning, the kind that quickens the blood and makes one feel glad to be alive.

Piry wondered how it was possible to feel so hunted on a day like this. As they walked briskly along the tree-lined avenue, blending into the crowd, she was full of fear that at any moment someone would recognize her and ask why they were carrying suitcases. She decided that since the Western Train Station wasn't too far, if someone stopped them, she would say that they were heading there. They were going to stay with family in her hometown, Debrecen.

For a second it crossed her mind that going there might not be a bad idea, but instantly she knew that it wouldn't work. She had not heard from her parents or her in-laws for months. Wartime mail being sporadic it could have been that their letters got lost. Or, for all she knew they had been collected like the people in her apartment building. So, Debrecen was not a place to go to.

We're like the leaves on these trees, she mused bitterly, her eyes following the flight of the withered yellow leaves that drifted in the breeze slowly, reluctantly to the ground.

Down the street she spotted an old man with a large broom, clearing the sidewalk. If I'm not careful, we'll be swept away like these leaves. She raised her chin stubbornly into the wind. Not as long as I have a breath left in me.

She could take the children with her to Nyiradon, she thought, but as it was close to the Russian border; traveling there might prove to be difficult or even dangerous, especially if one was a Jew. Alone, she could move faster and handle problems that might arise. But before going, she had to find a safe place for her children. She spotted the lemon-yellow frame of a phone booth and walked over to it, with Judith and Erika in tow.

"Wait out here," she commanded her daughters as she stepped in and closed the door.

Irén Stern answered on the first ring, "Where have you been all morning?"

Piry quickly explained then asked, "Do you think your building is safe?"

"Based on what you just told me, maybe till tomorrow, or the day after."

"Then you'd better pack a bag and meet me at the new Swedish Safe House," Piry suggested and gave her the address.

"What about the papers you were going to get?"

"We'll talk about that when I see you."

"You want me to go into the Safe House with you?"

"Why not? It beats moving into the Ghetto or being deported. Besides, two heads can think better than one."

"I'll be there as soon as I can."

Irén Stern was Piry's closest friend. It might be easier to cope together with the life they were now facing, she thought. She smiled at her daughters who were standing by the glass walls of the phone booth strangely subdued, waiting for her instruction.

"Let's cross to the streetcar stop," Piry said as cheerfully as she could muster.

Among the regulations for Jews were several that Piry had simply defied. One required all Jews to wear a yellow Star of David on their outer clothing. Although Piry had obtained the yellow stars from her synagogue, she had never sewed them onto their clothes. Instead, she carried them in her handbag, ready to be attached with safety pins if someone stopped them. After all, neither she nor her daughters "looked Jewish" and she saw no reason to advertise that they were.

Another rule was that Jews were not allowed to use buses or taxis; they could travel only on the last carriage of streetcars. Piry used public transportation as she needed to and never took the last carriage. She knew that streetcars were raided periodically but had decided early on that she would take that chance. Once again, with her two daughters in tow, she made that choice. It would take too long for them to reach the safe house on foot, and a streetcar would take them there in just a few stops.

They got on, choosing the middle carriage of the streetcar, not the first or the last. It was crowded; women with wicker baskets filled with vegetables were on their way home from shopping at the markets, men wearing fall coats and hats were holding on with one hand to the overhead leather handles, reading the morning paper with the other.

Warily, Piry noticed a couple of young men wearing armbands that identified them as SS, Hungarian Nazis, sitting at the far end of the carriage. But they were busy talking to each other not looking around. Nevertheless, Piry breathed easier when she and the girls got off at the stop just before the streetcar crossed the Danube on the Margit Bridge.

She guided the girls down the Korzó, the elegant promenade alongside the Danube, searching for the address. This street was full of memories for her. As newlyweds, this was where she and Zoltán used to come and sit in the stylish coffeehouses, sipping espresso and eating pastry. This was where Zoltán had proudly paraded a baby carriage with their first child, Judith, on Saturday afternoons. Now Zoltán was gone, and she and their daughters were running for their lives. Piry took a deep breath and swallowed the air as though to push down the bitter feelings rising in her. She couldn't afford them.

There it was! Since mid-summer of 1944, a Swedish diplomat, Raoul Wallenberg, who came from a wealthy family in Sweden, had taken over several office and apartment buildings, and designated them as "safe houses," where Jews could live under the protection of the Swedish Government. Wallenberg also spearheaded the issuing of "Safe Passes," called Schutz-Pass by the Germans. Whoever had them was supposed to be under the protection of the Swedish Government.

Piry had obtained passes for herself and the children as soon as she had heard about them. Now she was about to use them. She wasn't sure whether this was her best move—to own up to being Jewish—but for the moment this seemed to be the only solution. They needed shelter, at least until she could figure out her next move. Before going into the building, she pinned the yellow stars on their coats. If they were going to admit being Jewish, they had to wear the star.

The concierge came out of his glass booth and examined their passes. He was a tall, thin man with a droopy mustache and a wrinkled face from which small watery blue eyes peered at the newcomers. "You are the first ones," he commented. "We've just opened this building." He handed the Safe Passes back to Piry, "These seem to be correct, so they give you the right to stay here," he explained.

"I am also expecting a friend," Piry said. "Do you mind if we wait here?"

"Go ahead." The man waived them to the bench across from his booth. They sat down.

"I'm bored," Erika declared as they sat in silence.

"That's tough," Judith responded.

Piry could hear malicious joy in her voice. Judith was jealous of Erika, and much to Piry's dismay, enjoyed taunting her.

"Please, Judith, be nice." she pleaded. "Why don't you teach Erika to write some new words." She dug into her handbag and came up with a pencil and a piece of paper. "Here."

Judith had started school at age six and to help her learn to read faster, Zoltán had hired a private tutor. Three-year-old Erika liked to sit in on these sessions and soon she too could read. When Piry proudly mentioned this to their pediatrician, the good doctor was alarmed,

"Keep her away from books, she will strain her eyes! A child at this age is not ready for reading," he warned.

Piry tried but it was impossible to keep Erika away from books. She would steal them from Judith and hide with them in the dimly lit pantry off the kitchen. Finally, Piry gave up and let her read openly so that at least she wasn't ruining her eyes in the dark.

"I already know that one!" Erika declared as she saw Judith laboring to write a long word.

"No, you don't!"

"I do too."

"Then write it!"

Erika did, flawlessly.

"How about this one?" Judith dictated another word.

Erika knew that one too. Judith felt challenged and for a while the two girls were absorbed as if they were playing a game.

It was nearly mid-morning and Piry began to wonder if anything had happened to Irén when she finally came huffing through the main door. She looked as mousy as ever; Piry thought to herself, happy to see her friend. Irén was a stocky woman in her mid.-twenties, whose large glasses were hiding a plain face that was actually quite pleasant. She was dragging a large suitcase with her.

"I couldn't decide what to pack but I think you'll like what I finally brought," she said with a disarming smile. "What's the procedure here?"

"Check in with your Schutz-Pass, then we'll go upstairs and find us a place."

There was an enormous room on the first floor, with mattresses stacked on one side and no other furniture. The tall windows faced the street, painting elongated rectangles of sunshine onto the polished oak parquet floor. Piry spotted a small door at the far end of the room and crossed over to investigate what was behind it.

"This is perfect," she declared as she surveyed the narrow room that could have been a storage closet, except for a sink by the window. She tested the faucet—it worked.

"We'll settle in here," she declared.

"Why do that when here's all this space?" Irén protested.

"Because we won't be the only people here for long and I'd rather stay in a small room on our own than in a large one with a crowd. Besides, the sink and faucet in there means that we'll have water."

"There are two floors with bathrooms and toilets down each hallway" Irén insisted. "If, as you say, the place will fill up, we're going to have to walk through a crowd to get to the toilets."

"I still think we should stay in there" Piry closed the discussion and began to pull mattresses off the pile. Reluctantly, Irén helped her. Piry called to her daughters, "Judith, Erika, grab the other ends."

Under Piry's instructions, they piled the mattresses on the floor and against the wall, like a sofa, and were settled in the little room. Then Irén opened her suitcase and pulled out bread, salami, green peppers, and hard-boiled eggs.

"Where did you get all this?" Piry was amazed.

Irén grinned. "I traded silver trays for food."

Piry laughed. "We make a great team."

By mid-afternoon, the room next door had begun to fill and by evening there wasn't an empty spot on the floor. Several people opened the door to the little room to see if they could join Piry's group, but he told them, the children had a possibly contagious disease, and the seekers would quickly close the door.

At ten o'clock at night the concierge had shut off the lights in the entire building. Curled up on their mattresses in their overcoats, for the room was chilly despite the central heating, Piry and her group attempted to sleep.

"How long do you think we'll stay here?" Irén whispered in the dark.

"If we see it's safe, you and the girls will stay here, and I'll go to Nyiradon to get the papers. After that, we'll have to look for a new place. Let's get some sleep now. We'll know more in the morning," Piry whispered back.

Actually, she had no idea whether her plan would work. She needed to get those papers, but she wasn't sure which would be the lesser of two evils, leaving her daughters and Irén behind or taking them with her. But she didn't want to discuss this with Irén till she made the decision.

She must have fallen asleep for it was into a deep and timeless darkness that the sounds had reached her. Something was happening in the next room.

Erika, also a light sleeper, heard it too, so she reached over to touch her mother, "What's that noise?"

"I don't know, sweetie, just stay still."

They listened. It sounded like people were moving about. A shaft of light swept under their closed door.

"Looks like a flashlight," Irén whispered in the dark. "Should we look?"

"No, let them find us," Piry's tone was cautious but defiant.

"The soldiers again?" Judith asked with fear in her voice.

"We don't know what it is. Let's just listen." Piry put a protective arm around Judith's shoulders.

Irén stared at the fluorescent dial on her watch. "It's three a.m. What could be happening?"

A bullhorn blared in the other room. The male voice ordered everyone to hand over their safe passes so they could be processed overnight. They would be returned in the morning.

Someone cracked open their door and shouted inside "Passes, hand over your passes!"

"Stay still," Piry commanded and peering through the opening she saw that it was pitch dark in the other room except for the flashlights of three men in shiny black coats and tall black boots, looming ominously over the people spread on the mattresses. They waved their lights around the room and Piry could see that everyone was searching for their documents. She noticed that the men didn't bother to look at the papers that were handed to them.

They just threw them into the satchels they were carrying. She pulled the door closed, feeling that something was remiss. These men are Nazis. Who had authorized them to collect the Swedish Safe Passes? What proof would anyone have of giving them the papers in the middle of the night? she thought and decided against obeying.

"Let's just fold up four pieces of paper from my notebook and hand those over. We're keeping our Safe Passes."

"What if they verify all the passes and ours isn't among them?" Irén worried.

"In this dark? Let's just take a chance."

The men were gone in an hour, and everyone settled down to sleep again. Except Piry. She was worried and needed to think over their situation. She didn't know what it meant that everyone in the building was now without passes, but she knew that she no longer felt safe about staying. Irén could have been right; based on the concierges' registration book, by morning they could match the papers to those present and easily identify those who did not submit their passes. She waited until she could hear the even breathing of the people in the next room and then softly shook her daughters and Irén. could hear the even breathing of the people in the next room and then softly shook her daughters and Irén.

"Wake up, we're leaving," she whispered.

"Now?" protested Judith, half-asleep.

"Yes, now."

"Why, Mommy?" Erika wanted to know.

"Because I say so."

Erika sighed. When her mother used that tone, it was best not to argue.

They gathered their small cases in the dark, splashed some water on their faces, more out of habit than for cleanliness, and with great caution picked their way through the prone bodies in the next room.

Erika could hardly keep from giggling as she juggled her case over the heads and feet of people, and once she almost fell across someone after she had bumped into his mattress. But Judith, who always kept an eye on her, hissed at her, "Shush," cutting off her laughter.

It was a miracle that they got out without anyone waking up or asking where they were going. In the dim light that illuminated the staircase, Piry looked at the tired faces in her charge.

"I'll go ahead and see the concierge about opening the front door. Wait for me here."

With that, she disappeared down the stairs. It took her a while to return. "Let's go, fast," she whispered, and holding on to the banister they followed her without a word.

The concierge stood by the front door. He opened it noiselessly. Piry was the last to leave and by the light of a streetlamp on the sidewalk Erika saw that as her mother walked through the door, she slipped something into the man's hand.

The street was freezing cold outside and so still that it was hard to believe that they were in danger. They stood in the doorway, staring into the dark winter dawn.

"Now where to?" Irén asked.

"Let's just walk very quietly away from here. But wait," said Piry.

She unpinned the yellow stars from their coats, then in one swift gesture ripped Irén's off her coat and handed it to her.

"What are you doing?" Irén was aghast.

"Put it away. We can't move around with these on. Let's go."

Irén shook her head in dismay. Piry was right but if they were caught, they'd be shot for breaking the rules. Sometimes she wondered about the audacity of her friend. But this was no time to argue.

Hugging the walls of the buildings they melted into the dark shadows of the early dawn, themselves more shadows than real as they followed Piry in single file down the street, turning corners, heading toward the "Inner City," the central district of Budapest.

Irén moved from behind the girls next to Piry.

"You're hiding something," she whispered.

"The concierge told me that the Nazis said they would return at six and all those who didn't have their safe passes will be lined up by the bank of Danube."

"What do you mean lined up?"

"You know what I mean. Those who are able-bodied will go to labor camps, the children and the old people will be shot and fall into the river."

Irén shook her head in disbelief. "How come he let us get away?"

"I showed him that we still had our passes. Then I promised to pay him if he let us leave."

Irén reached out and squeezed Piry's hand. "You've saved our lives."

"Not yet," Piry smiled. "But we've got another chance. The question is, where do we go from here?" Once again, it crossed her mind to head for the train station and travel with all of them to Nyiradon. However, if Jews were picked up even at the Safe Houses, it could be worse on a train. They might get trapped. It was imperative for her to find a place for Irén and the girls to hide while she alone went to Nyiradon. Suddenly, an idea occurred to her, and she smiled brightly,

"C'mon, I know who might help us." She looked at her watch, it was nearly six a.m. "Traffic will start up pretty soon, let's just keep walking till then to keep warm."

They walked and stopped once in a doorway so Irén could get some bread out of her small suitcase because they were all hungry. Then they walked again, and only when the streetcars and buses began to carry full loads of passengers, did Piry risk getting on a bus with her companions.

"If someone asks why we have travel cases, say that we just got in from Debrecen," she instructed them.

However, no one asked. At this hour no one cared. The bus rolled across the Lánc Bridge to the Buda side and halfway up the Gellért Mountain before they got off. Clutching their bags, they followed Piry up a winding, cobblestone street, lined with stately villas.

◉◉◉

Chief Surgeon Miklós Nagy had had a bad night. He couldn't decide on what gift—a bribe in fact—to give the district chief of the Hungarian Nazi Party, called Arrow Cross. The kind of present he had in mind would be discreet but expensive enough to ensure that his hospital would not be raided and deprived of its many Jewish doctors. But he had limited funds for this and knew only one man who could come up with the right object, Zoltán Fábián. But Zoltán was gone, had been for some time, and Dr. Nagy did not know where else to turn. It wasn't that Fábián was the only goldsmith in town, but he was the only one who could always deliver exactly what was needed. He was a rare talent, not only a wholesale merchant of hardware but also a sculptor who could listen to an idea and shape it into the most exquisite work of art in gold.

Damn the Jewish laws, Nagy cursed softly to himself as he puttered around in the kitchen in his blue terry bathrobe and slippers, putting a pot of coffee on the stove. He was a tall and gently balding man with incisive gray eyes, in his late forties. He was the youngest Chief Surgeon in Budapest and by reputation the best. But these days being the best surgeon didn't count. One also had to be a politician to survive. He wondered if Zoltán's wife, Piry, would know of someone who could make or find for him the right present. It was too early to phone her yet, but he would do so before he left for the hospital.

He had met Zoltán and Piry Fábián through the athletic club to which they had all belonged. Zoltán was on the kayak rowing team, and they had trained together. Later, when Zoltán's younger brother Dennis, wanted to get into medical school, it was Nagy who helped him, despite the quota that allowed only a limited number of Jews into the department. At the time, Zoltán had presented him with an exquisitely sculpted head of Hippocrates. Carved in gold, the four-inch statuette revealed a talent that had impressed Dr. Nagy.

"You should give up your hardware business and become a sculptor," he urged Zoltán.

"And who would support my family, and pay the university tuition for my brothers?" Zoltán replied, smiling.

Nagy just shook his head. *Jews were different. They had a sense of obligation to family members, rare among his Christian friends. Of course, that was a generalization.* Zoltán's brother Dennis, for example, could not get into medical school in Budapest because the Jewish Laws restricted him in Hungary, so he moved to Prague. There, his tuition was paid by Zoltán, and he also got food supplies once a week from a cousin, Feri Shatz, a journalist who lived in Prague.

Once he graduated, he did not return to Hungary but left for South Africa where he had been promised financing for opening his own medical practice after he married the daughter of a wealthy merchant. He didn't worry about his family obligations!

Zoltán's youngest brother, Eli, a physical education teacher, became a Zionist and had left for Palestine in the early 1930's, accompanied by his girlfriend—also a renegade family member. On the other hand, Nagy, a Catholic, had harbored several Jewish doctors at the hospital, with false identity papers claiming they were Christian.

"Miklós, didn't you hear the doorbell?" His wife, Helen came into the kitchen, stopping his musings. She was wearing a flannel robe, and her hair was disheveled from sleep. Her blue eyes reflected concern. "Who could it be at this hour"?

"We'll find out." He smiled at her. She always imagined the worst.

Trailing after him, she tugged at his dressing gown. "Ask first."

He ignored her and opened the front door. For a fleeting second, he merely registered the face of a pale young woman with two little girls and another woman standing behind them, all looking lost. Then recognition lit up his face, "Why Mrs. Fábián, I've just been thinking of you, and you appear!"

"Dr. Nagy, this is my friend Miss Stern, and my daughters, Judith and Erika."

"Welcome, come right in!" He ushered them through the hallway into the warmth of the kitchen, wondering what sort of trouble made Piry come to him with this entourage so early in the morning. "Take off your coats and sit down."

They eased themselves down on the chairs around the table as they were told, and while he prepared cups of coffee for them, he saw that Piry had leaned back in her chair and closed her eyes as though she were exhausted and on the verge of tears.

He wondered why Helen had left the kitchen, as he set out bread, butter, and a large wedge of Ementhal cheese. Then he sat down and gently placed his hand over Piry's.

"What happened?"

Piry told him, her voice tight as she fought back tears throughout her narrative. "So, I came to you, thinking, you might have an idea how we can proceed from here…"

Dr. Nagy knitted his brows in an effort to think through the situation. During the past year, he had seen Piry a number of times, but the shoe had always been on the other foot. After her husband had been recruited into forced labor service, Piry had enough talent to continue their business and had contributed generously to Nagy's funds when he told her he needed to harbor Jews at the hospital. Now it was her turn to ask for help.

His cool gray eyes traveled around the kitchen table, from Piry to her friend Miss Stern, to the little girls, and back to Piry. *Yes, they could pass for Christians*, he thought. But where would the children and Miss Stern stay while Piry went to get the new identity papers for them? And once Piry got back even with their new papers where would they live? My own wife, Helen, wouldn't come into the kitchen during the discussion, probably because she wanted to know as little as possible.

Their housekeeper would be arriving in an hour, and she knew Piry was Jewish. There was no way he could hide them at his house even for a couple of days. Harboring Jews would mean losing his license at best. No, he could not endanger his work, his family, and all the people at the hospital. Some other way had to be found. He rose and patted Piry's hand.

"I have to be getting dressed. Why don't you settle in the sitting room and make yourselves at home. We'll find a solution somehow."

With an encouraging smile he ushered them into the living room, then disappeared down the hall to his bedroom.

Helen was waiting for him there. "I didn't want to interfere, but I couldn't help overhearing her story," she began. "I've got an idea for you."

"What?"

"How about my brother's apartment?"

"What are you talking about?"

"János is in the army, his wife and kids are in Eger with her parents. How about letting these poor people use their apartment? We have the keys to it."

Miklós stared at his wife. They had been married twenty years, but he had never loved her more than at this moment, when with a simple offer she so completely embraced his cause. He put his arms around her and looked down at the classic features that were beginning to show her forty-two years of living.

"Helen, if I had to do it over again, you're the only woman I'd marry."

She laughed, delighted by this unusual burst of tenderness. "The same goes for me, Miklós. Now take the apartment keys and get these people out of here before the maid shows up. I know she's the world's best cleaning woman, but I'm not sure that she is the most charitable Christian. Maybe you could drive them there on your way to the hospital."

Miklós suddenly felt sick to his stomach as a realization struck him. "Your brother's apartment is in an all-Christian building. When they move in, they'll have to register with the police. As you know, religion is listed on the form."

"You'll just have to secure some papers for them," Helen smiled, patting his hand. "It wouldn't be the first time…"

19

Miklós shook his head. "That's not the problem. Piry in fact has papers available for them but she has to pick them up in Nyiradon. Where could her kids and friend stay until then?"

Helen shrugged. "At the hospital. Surely, you can hide them for a couple of days. But go talk to Piry, my dear, because you've got to be going."

In the living room, Piry and her group sat stiffly, silently, like people condemned. Piry had no idea what Dr. Nagy could do for her, especially with the children. But she was hoping that a discussion with him might open up some alternatives.

When he returned to the room and made his offer, she was elated. Never in her wildest dreams had she imagined that Nagy could provide an apartment for them.

"I can sneak Miss Stern in at the hospital as a charwoman till you come back. As for the girls, I think the best thing might be to hide them at the Children's Hospital that's run by the Red Cross." He saw Piry grow pale. "We don't have a children's ward, or I'd keep them with us."

"Could I go with them?" Irén asked.

Nagy shook his head. "That would be suspicious. I will give you a prescription that the girls are to be taken in under observation for tuberculosis. They don't look Jewish; nobody would suspect anything."

Piry sighed. I'll do my best to get back by tomorrow evening."

She knelt down in front of her daughters and held on to each one by a shoulder and looked into their eyes. "Do you understand what we're talking about?"

They nodded.

"You're sure, Erika?"

"Yes. You have to go somewhere, and we have to wait for you in a hospital."

"Good." Piry hugged her children, feeling their little bodies clinging to her in quiet desperation. Then she rose. "Judith, take care of Erika. I'll be back as soon as I can and after that we'll live in a nice apartment and won't have to move around anymore."

"We'll have an apartment to live in?" Judith wanted to hear it again.

"Yes." answered Nagy. "But now we must get going." He led the little group out to his car. He hoped that everything would work out as they had planned. He would ask Piry about the gift after they were settled in their new place. She had other things to worry about till then.

CHAPTER 3

E RIKA WAS UPSET. SHE hated being in the hospital. They had been put into beds next to each other, alongside a lot of sick children in a huge room. The beds were lined up in two rows with headboards against the walls and feet toward the middle of the room, where nurses and doctors could come and go. They lay on cold sheets under a thin blanket, all smelling of disinfectant. The nurse who showed them to their beds instructed the girls to remove their coat and shoes but keep their clothes on because there was no heating in the room.

"If we don't pretend that we are sick, we'll be in big trouble" Judith whispered to Erika. "We must stay in bed, just like the others, till Mother comes for us. Do you understand?"

Erika heard the tension in Judith's voice. She knew that she had better obey her sister, or she'd get pinched by her. So, she nodded. "I do."

They lay side by side in their beds and were quiet for a while. Then Erika began to fidget. "I'm bored," she whispered to Judith. "Tell me a story."

"Later," Judith hissed as she spotted doctors and nurses at the end of the long row of beds.

A doctor, an intern, and a nurse walked slowly by the foot of the beds and looked at each child. They stopped by some of the children, the doctor their foreheads for fever, and stuck a thermometer under their arm, instructing them to hold it tight. Others, including Judith and Erika, they just asked how they were feeling. When the children answered "fine," they were instructed to stay in bed and keep quiet so as not to disturb those who were feeling worse.

After the doctors' rounds, they were brought breakfast. Erika was repulsed by the thin, saltless caraway soup and only picked at the chunk of dry bread that came with it. The enamel of the soup cup was chipped and as her lips tasted the tin with the soup, she pushed it away, grimacing.

"If you don't want your bread, save it for later but you must drink the soup," insisted Judith. "Mommy says, a hot drink is important in the morning."

Erika obeyed, remembering that their mother told Judith to take care of her. She didn't wish to make her sister angry. She forced the soup down, feeling like throwing up with every sip but she swallowed and made herself keep it down by taking a couple of deep breaths after each gulp.

Once she had eaten, she felt better. She gave her bread to Judith, who put it into Erika's little suitcase that had been placed under her bed.

"You can take it out when you're hungry," she told Erika.

Many of the children in the room were crying. Others lay quietly, just staring at nothing.

"Can you tell me a story now?" Erika begged.

"Come over to my bed," Judith commanded.

Then she began telling Erika a story, and slowly, the children nearby came to sit at the end of their beds, listening. It pleased Judith to have an audience and she did her best to make the story fun.

For lunch, they were given potatoes cooked with fried onions and green peppers but with no meat in it, and more of the caraway soup. They were all ordered to nap after lunch.

When they awoke, those who were feeling up to it, were told to get up and walk along the corridors of the hospital for about half an hour, to get some exercise. Then it was back to bed, and Judith told another story. This time more of the children who had walked with them came to listen. They sat on the beds or on the floor, happy to have some diversion. Erika was enormously proud of Judith's popularity.

"She is my big sister," she informed the children around her.

Dinner was a watery soup of pinto beans, and another piece of bread. The doctors and nurses made their rounds, and then it was lights out.

"Do you think Mommy will come for us tomorrow?" Erika whispered to Judith in the dark. She had slipped out of bed and leaned close to Judith's ear so the others wouldn't hear her.

"Maybe. Go to sleep." Judith whispered back.

"Thank you for the stories. Everybody loved them." Erika quickly kissed Judith's cheek.

"Go to bed!" Judith ordered. She didn't react to the kiss because she didn't want the others to be jealous of her having her sister there.

◎◉◎

Very early the next morning, they were brought breakfast by the nurses, the thin caraway soup and bread. They were told to eat fast because after their meal everyone had to put on their coat and shoes and go downstairs. They were to line up outside the building to be taken somewhere else. The hospital was being "evacuated."

Even learning a new word didn't thrill Erika. "How will Mommy find us when she comes back?" she asked Judith, quite worried.

For once, her sister didn't have an answer. Neither did the nurses.

While gulping down her breakfast, Erika thought, *I just want to stay in bed and wait for mom to come for us. After all, Judith and I are not sick; we are just pretending to be sick. But Judith said we can't tell the truth because then we would be in even bigger trouble.*

Erika whispered to Judith, "I wish all these horrible things would stop happening and Daddy would come home, and I could go back to kindergarten again."

"Quiet!" Judith ordered her and Erika knew to obey.

As soon as they were done eating, the nurses rushed them to get dressed and go downstairs. "Go out the door and line up in pairs along the wall of the hospital," they instructed the sick children who could barely follow their orders.

It was cold and still dark outside. Erika shivered in her overcoat as they waited to be told what to do next. They had been too upset to eat their ration of bread, and just like the day before, Judith had put it into each of their suitcases. "Like Aunt Irén," she grinned, "we'll carry our own food."

"It'll just make the suitcase heavier. I won't eat mine anyway."

"You will when you get hungry."

"Maybe by then Mommy will come for us."

Judith looked at her little sister's face, the cute, upturned nose, her large hazel eyes staring at her with so much hope and felt uncomfortable. She wasn't at all sure that their mother would come back or that she would find out where they were being taken. She often wondered if all their troubles weren't caused because their daddy had been taken away and their mother didn't love them as much as he did. Why else would she have wanted to open the door to those Nazis? Or leave us at this hospital where now we will be taken somewhere else? Yet, she had to believe, like Erika, that their mother would find them. Until then, she was in charge of Erika.

"Whenever she comes, we have to be well, so I will take care of us," she said with a confidence she did not feel.

When there was a line so long that Erika couldn't see the end of it, they were told to follow the man in the black uniform up in front. He walked fast and there were other men along the line in black leather coats, shouting at the children who couldn't keep up.

"Move faster or go to the end of the line. "

Erika would have liked to do that, but Judith wouldn't let her.

"Those are the really sick kids," she whispered to Erika. "We should stay here."

"Why?"

"Because I say so."

"You're not my mother."

"Mommy told me to watch over you. So, you do what I say."

Erika didn't reply. Her sister's face was pale, her big blue eyes dark with determination. Erika didn't feel like fighting her. Walking fast in the dawn light and dragging her suitcase along was hard enough. A light snow began to fall, making the road slippery and slushy as they trudged along. Erika kept her face down, drawing her scarf around her neck tighter so the snow wouldn't get under her coat. She kept switching hands in which she carried her suitcase and saw that Judith was doing the same.

"Are you tired?" she asked Judith.

"A little."

"Me too."

"Maybe we'll stop soon." Judith was trying to console her sister.

"No talking!" One of the men came over to them and prodded Judith's ribs with the stick he was carrying. "No talking. Just move!"

In the silence, Erika could hear the heavy breathing of their companions and realized that they too were becoming exhausted. The air was getting colder, and she could see her breath as she labored along. The wind rose, blowing wet snow into their faces, making it harder to walk. But the men didn't seem to care, nor did they seem to have any intention of stopping for a rest.

Morning turned to noon, a gray light illuminated the streets till noon became afternoon, and it was getting dark again. They were marching without a stop. Some of the children could not keep up and they had been left behind with the men at the tail end of the line.

Erika thought she heard a couple of sharp cracking sounds, like when bullets were fired, but Judith did not seem to have heard it because she just continued to walk, her head bent into the wind. So, Erika trudged on but found it increasingly hard. Her cheeks burned in the biting gust, and she had to squint against the wet snow assaulting her face. Her calves ached, she could barely lift her legs, and time and again she stumbled over the cobblestone paving.

"Watch your step," warned Judith, grabbing Erika to keep her from falling.

"My suitcase is too heavy," Erika complained making sure she was not overheard by one of the uniformed men. "I want to leave it on the road."

"You can't, Mommy wouldn't like that," whispered Judith, her face pale, her lips pressed into a thin, determined line.

"But I can't carry it anymore," Erika whispered back, feeling helpless, afraid to leave her suitcase because of Judith, yet knowing that she would collapse if she had to carry it another step further.

"Give it to me."

"Then you'll have trouble walking!"

"Just for a while."

Erika felt so sorry for Judith that her stomach hurt as she watched her sister trudge on, carrying both their cases. But she couldn't help herself. Her whole body ached, her neck and face were wet from the snow that kept flying at her. Her soggy scarf no longer kept the water from seeping down her back, making her feel both hot and cold. As the streets turned dark, she was becoming so exhausted that she had trouble putting one foot in front of the other. Then, just when she thought she could not take another step, they were told to stop at a building in front of them.

"Go through the door," their Nazi uniformed guards ordered them.

Inside, was a small entry hall, with a warm air that hit their faces.

"Keep going through that other door," the guards yelled.

Past that second door was a gigantic hall with a great glass dome that the evening sky painted indigo blue. It was already full of children. But the exhausted sick group from the hospital pushed their way in and crumpled to the ground making spaces for themselves among the others in the hall.

Judith pulled Erika with her and carefully stepping around the other children, made them settle against the wall at the far end of the room. "It's warmer back here," she told Erika.

Except for their breakfast at the hospital, they had no other food all day, and it didn't look as though they were going to be given any dinner. Now that they were seated, Erika's stomach gave a loud growl. Judith heard it.

"We have those breads from last night and this morning," she triumphantly reminded Erika.

"We'll wait till it gets really dark, and then we'll eat only the older piece, and save today's bread for breakfast," she declared.

Erika was too exhausted to argue. When the room grew silent and they began to hear the even breathing of the others, they pulled the stale chunks of bread out of their suitcases and sat close together in the dark, munching.

"It's better than being hungry," Judith said with satisfaction.

"Yes." Erika could feel her stomach calming down and she was grateful that Judith had insisted on saving their bread. Around them, many of the children lay in exhausted sleep, but some were crying. They have no food, Erika thought, and she felt relieved that in the dark they were not seen eating.

"How will Mommy find us when she comes back from her trip?" Erika whispered.

"I don't know, but I'm sure she will."

Secretly, Judith wasn't sure about anything. She knew that not only adults, but children were taken away by the Nazis to labor camps and she feared that this was where they were headed. But she didn't want to alarm Erika.

"I am glad you're sure," Erika said warmly.

For the first time in a long time, they were getting along. Together, they arranged their suitcases to use them as pillows and lay down hugging each other in the dark unheated hall, as much for warmth as reassurance.

"Do you think we might be taken away before mommy can come for us?" Erika whispered.

Judith's heart leaped with fear. How could Erika guess at what might happen to them? "No, she'll come before that," she replied without much conviction. "Now go to sleep" she ordered, just to keep Erika from asking more questions. But she herself found it hard to fall asleep. She worried that their mother may not return in time or may not be able to find them, and that she might not be able to take care of her little sister if they were forced to march on in the morning.

◎◎◎

The same day that Judith and Erika had left the hospital, Piry, exhausted but triumphant, arrived by midday at the Western Rail Station in Budapest. Not wanting to transfer from streetcar to streetcar, she took a taxi from the train station to the Red Cross Children's Hospital to pick up her daughters.

She was carrying in her purse legitimate birth certificates for all four of them. At the last minute, Kati, her former maid, had managed to obtain—for a significant sum of course—yet another birth certificate for Irén. She had officially become a cousin, with Polyák as the new last name for all of them.

Kati had enough family to closely match their dates of birth to a variety of cousins and their children. The girls' ages remained the same, but Piry became a year younger, and Irén turned two years older. Their birthdays fell on different dates too, but this was a small enough change. In addition, for fear that Judith's name sounded too Jewish, it had been changed to Anna, while Erika's remained the same.

Piry did not really mean to name her second daughter Erika. During her last month of pregnancy she had gone to her dressmaker to pick a robe the woman had sewn for her. While waiting for last minute adjustments to be done, Piry spotted a beautifully dressed doll on a chair, with long blonde hair. A label on the doll read: Erika.

Her second daughter came into the world unusually fast, and when Piry was asked to name her, still in semi-stupor. Piry whispered 'Erika'. Her orthodox in-laws hated the name because it sounded so Christian. But life had a strange way of twisting things around. Her in-laws, with their strict Jewish ways, were God knows where at the moment. Piry had not heard from them in a couple of months. Whereas Erika, with her Christian sounding name, was safe in Budapest.

All Piry had to do now was to pick up her daughters at the Red Cross Children's Hospital and take them to the apartment whose keys she had been given by Miklós Nagy. She would telephone Nagy afterwards and ask him to send Irén directly to them. Then, she'd have to think of a present for Nagy and his wife. She still had a small stock of jewelry hidden in their warehouse, and with various Christian friends. She'd find something unusual for Nagy as soon as they were settled in the apartment.

It was incredible what freedom those pieces of paper meant. From being condemned to the ghetto or death, she felt like they had a passport to life again.

"Here we are Miss," the taxi driver pulled up in front of the hospital. Piry paid him and with buoyant steps entered the building. The porter's booth was empty. She rang his bell and while she waited, she became aware of the deep silence around her, as though no one was around. Then she heard steps.

She first saw the black boots, then the hem of black leather overcoats, and finally the faces of two young men in black SS caps, coming down the hall toward her. Her heart leaped into her throat, but she pulled herself together. She was in no danger, she had legitimate papers in her handbag.

The men saw the attractive young woman standing by the porter's booth and stopped.

"Are you looking for someone, Miss?" the taller asked politely. He had pleasant brown eyes, and a bit of sand-colored hair showed from beneath his cap. The shorter man had small blue eyes, tight lips, and a rougher demeanor.

Piry's instincts told her something was drastically wrong. She forced a smile on her face.

"I had been given this address as a children's hospital. I thought I'd come by to see if they needed some volunteers. You see, my husband is on the front, and I was looking for something useful to do."

The men's faces softened by a fleeting smile. The taller one said, "This had been a children's hospital, lady, but it has come to our attention that they were harboring Jewish brats. So, unless you've got an interest in Jews, we don't think you'd have wanted to volunteer here."

"All those brats had been evacuated this morning," the second Nazi added.

For the hundredth time since the war had begun Piry had inwardly blessed her luck in having been born with a typical 'Hungarian look'—a slightly turned up nose, dark blonde hair and warm brown eyes. Nobody ever took her for a Jew unless they knew her family. These men didn't even ask for her papers. They just assessed her by appearance. She gave them a shy but charming smile.

"Thank you for telling me I'm in the wrong place. Did you say this is no longer a hospital? What is it now?"

"We'll probably use the building for our own brave soldiers. You can come back to nurse them," the shorter man grinned at Piry.

Piry felt her knees grow weak. She leaned against the wall for support.

"Are you all right, Miss?" The tall man stepped over to her and reached for her arm.

"I'm in my third month." Piry told him, wondering where that came from, "So occasionally I get a little dizzy." Then, realizing the foolishness of what she had said, she quickly added, "My husband was on home leave, he doesn't even know it yet." Somehow, she managed to turn her face away as though she were hiding her blushing.

The two men laughed a little, like bachelors who had been told an intimate marital secret, and it embarrassed them.

"Would you like us to escort you somewhere?" The leader of the two offered solicitously.

No thank you." She moved away from the wall, giving them a brave smile. "It's gone now. I'll be fine walking in the fresh air. Good day, gentlemen."

"Heil Hitler," they saluted.

"Heil Hitler," Piry repeated and pulling herself erect, left the building.

Her head felt as though she had been clubbed. She moved quickly down the street, looking for the nearest phone booth. Then she changed her mind. Those two could be following her. She turned into a main street and hailed a taxi. She gave the driver the hospital address where Dr. Nagy was in charge.

Once again, luck was with her. Nagy was just coming out of the operating theater when she arrived. He looked tired but broke into a broad smile when he spotted her.

"You're back! Does that mean you've got the papers?"

Piry nodded. "I did. But now we've got a bigger problem."

"Let's go into my office" he said quickly.

He had a large, comfortable office. A heavy Biedermeier desk dominated the center of the room, a large glass case against the wall contained leather bound books with gold lettering, and off to one side he had a conference area set up with comfortable leather chairs and a coffee table full of magazines. He pointed at one of the chairs for Piry.

"Have a seat, my dear." He sat down, facing her: "What's the problem?"

Piry told him about the evacuation of the Children's Hospital. He immediately rose, went to the phone and dialed. It took him several calls to track down where the children had been taken. He came back, sat down and looked directly at Piry.

"One of my colleagues who had worked there had been phoned by the administration and told not to go in today. When he had asked why not, he was told, the children were going to be taken to the Eastern Market Hall in Óbuda, and from there they will be transported by train to a hospital in Germany."

Piry and Dr. Nagy stared at each other, both knowing that it wasn't a hospital the children would be taken to but to a death camp.

Piry could hardly breathe. "When?" she finally squeezed out the words, feeling like the sky was caving in on her.

"Most likely tomorrow morning."

"I've got to get them out of there today!"

"The question is, how?" Nagy knitted his brows, and they sat in silence, trying to think of a feasible plan to get two healthy Jewish children out of a group full of sick ones. Piry wasn't sure which was worse, trying to rescue healthy children or Jewish ones.

Suddenly, Nagy started to laugh. Startled, Piry stared at him wondering whether the stress had finally gotten to the man since he must have clearly gone out of his mind.

"I've got a brilliant idea," he said, when he finally got his laughter down to a chuckle. "Two of the people at our hospital posing as doctors, are actually actors. Jewish of course. Let's go talk to them.

Erika awoke because she was cold. At first, she didn't know why she lay curled up on the ground, with her back against her sister's, and her body stiff from the discomfort. Then she heard breathing all around her, and crying here and there, and it all came back to her. The long march from the hospital, being put with all the other children into this cold, dark hall without supper, and how Judith told her to take a nap till their mother came for them. But now she was awake, chilled and hungry. The room was still pitch dark, and their mother had not come. Afraid to wake Judith, she gently pulled away from her so she could sit up.

"Are you up too?" whispered Judith as she also sat up.

"Yes. What are we going to do?"

"What do you mean?"

"Mommy hasn't come for us."

"Maybe she is not back yet from her trip. She will."

"What if she can't find us?"

Judith was quiet. She had thought about that. She didn't know whether to discuss it with Erika. After all, no matter how smart she was, Erika was only four years old.

"I don't know where we'll be taken, but I think Mommy will find us, wher-ever we are," she reassured Erika, though inwardly doubting her own words.

"Why can't we just tell them we are not sick, and they should let us go home?"

"Home to where?"

"Oh, yeah." Erika remembered that only a day or so before they had to leave their home. She was scared. "Where could we go then?"

"We just have to wait. Let's go back to sleep till morning."

Silence fell between them; there was nothing more to discuss. Judith felt helpless but she knew that no matter what happened to them, from here on, she would have to watch over her little sister. The thought did not make her feel any better.

Erika wondered what would happen to them in the morning. Maybe they would get breakfast, and then? She hoped that they wouldn't have to march again.

"C'mon, lie down," Judith urged her. "Are you cold?"

"Yes."

Judith put an arm over her sister. "Here. Let's snuggle to keep warm."

They must have dozed off because suddenly both of them woke with a start as they heard their name being called out. A man was walking around the room, shouting their name. Children around them stirred from sleep but none answered the call.

With a sudden surge of hope, "That's us!" Judith whispered to Erika. "Hurry up, we're being called." She pulled Erika to her feet. "Here, take this." Judith handed over one suitcase, and picking up the other, she pushed Erika ahead of her toward the exit door.

Silhouetted in the light streaming in from the open door, they saw a tall man in a Nazi uniform, calling their names into the dark room.

The uniform startled Judith and for a second, she grabbed on to Erika's coat to hold her back. She remembered that a few nights before, at the Swedish Safe House, her mother wouldn't obey the Nazis' orders about handing over their papers. Maybe this was another trick, and it would be better for them to keep quiet and wait till morning. But the man called their names again and Judith decided that anything was better than staying in the hall with the sick children. After all, if they alone were being called. Maybe it was their mother who had sent this officer for them. Grabbing Erika's hand, she walked with her to the man, and said, "I am Judith Fábián, and this is Erika, my little sister."

The Nazi officer looked at the two little girls in the light of the doorway. The older, a light brunette with deep blue eyes, the younger a golden redhead with bright hazel eyes. They fit the description he had been given.

"Good, come with me, both of you. And don't talk."

He led them out of the hall down a narrow corridor into an office that was warm and crowded with desks and papers.

Erika blinked in the bright light as she spotted a man wearing a gray uniform, sitting at one of the desks, almost buried behind stacks of papers.

"These are the children," the tall Nazi stated. He handed some papers to the man behind the desk.

The man took them, studied them, then picked up a sheet of paper on his desk, and said, "Sign here for them."

The Nazi officer did, and the man behind the desk returned the documents the Nazi officer had given to him before.

"That is all, you can take them," he said.

Erika opened her mouth to ask where they were going but Judith pinched her arm on the tender underside. She didn't cry out with the pain because the look on her sister's face warned her to keep quiet.

"Let's go," the Nazi said. "I'll carry those suitcases for you."

Before Judith could protest, he took both cases and went ahead of them. Erika gave Judith a quizzical stare, but the older girl just shrugged, indicating that they had no choice but to follow.

Outside, it was still dark, the snowfall had turned into soft drizzle, and the pavement glowed with the reflections of store windows. It was warmer on the street than it had been inside the hall.

"Just walk with me," the Nazi instructed them quietly.

After a while, Erika finally whispered to him, "Where are you taking us?"

"To your mother," came the answer.

"How come she sent you?" Judith's tone was full of suspicion.

"Because of my uniform. They wouldn't have released you to her."

"Are you a friend of hers? asked Erika.

"You might say that" he smiled.

He had such a nice smile, it made Erika feel good. "That's good then." She was satisfied, and to show it she tried to slip her hand into the man's but realized that she couldn't because he was carrying their suitcases.

He noticed her gesture. "You can hold on to my coat sleeves. Both of you."

It was easier to walk holding on to him.

"Listen," he said quietly, "We will now get on the streetcar. We'll take it many stops. Don't talk while we're on it. You understand?"

"Yes." They answered.

Neither of them really understood why they couldn't talk but perhaps there was some rule they didn't know. They waited only a few minutes before the yellow streetcar pulled up to the stop with its usual clang. They got on, and he directed them to sit opposite him.

The conductor came around and he bought their tickets, saying, "three please," pointing at the girls. Erika studied the man's face in the golden light of the coach. He had dark hair and intense dark eyes, and she decided that despite the uniform, he was very handsome.

After what seemed a very long ride, the Nazi said, "This is our stop. Let's get off.

Once on the street again, he bid them to hold on to him as before and kept them walking down a still empty street as briskly as they could manage. It was barely dawn.

Erika, reminded of their earlier march, became worried. "Is it far yet?"

"We're here." He stopped in front of an apartment building. "You two go inside. Your mother is waiting for you in the concierge's room. If for some reason she is not there, come right back. I'll wait here till all three of you come out. In fact, I'll hold on to your suitcases, so you won't have to drag them in and out. Now go!"

The entryway was dark but on their left the concierge's room was brightly lit. Through the door window they could see inside. Leaning against the wall, stood their mother. They burst into the room and into her arms, all three of them crying and hugging each other.

"I was so afraid they'd take us away before you got back," sobbed Judith, feeling a great sense of relief.

31

"They made us walk in the snow all day, and I was so tired," Erika told her mother.

"It's all right, it's all right, my darlings, from here on everything will be fine."

But no words could reassure them for a while, so they just stood there hugging each other, Piry gently rocking her daughters in her arms. She was thinking that they were the most precious things in the world to her. With Zoltán away, the only reason she had for fighting to stay alive.

Finally, wiping their eyes and hers, Piry sat down on a chair behind her and taking both girls' hands, looked into their eyes. "Now listen to me. There is something very important both of you must learn. We can't leave here till you do so. Are you listening?"

"Yes," they echoed each other eagerly.

"Judith, from here on, your name will be Anna. Erika, yours is fine as it is. And our last name is Polyák. Can you remember not to call each other by any other name?"

"I like my new last name," laughed Erika. "Erika Polyák is nicer than Erika Fábián."

"Didn't Mommy just say we don't have another name?" Judith turned on her sister in a sudden temper. "Forget Fábián!"

"I will," Erika assured her, "but we won't really forget it. We'll just put it away and use our new name till Daddy comes back, right Mommy?"

Piry couldn't get angry at Erika, she had such charm. "Right, Erika, but you must remember never ever to call your sister anything but: what?"

"Anna!"

"Good. Now here is something else. If anyone asks where your father is, you say that he is fighting in the army on the Russian front. We are refugees from Nyiradon and are living in the apartment of a friend of your daddy. Can you repeat all this?"

They did, with Piry drilling them, asking over and over again where they came from, where their father was, and what their names were. Then she said: "Now comes the last and most important part. If anybody, and I mean anybody, asks, 'what is your religion,' you say, we are Protestants. What are we?"

There was a moment's silence as the two girls looked at her and at each other, then Judith quickly said: "Protestants." Erika's eyes lit up with understanding and she repeated after her sister, "We're Protestants."

"What is your religion, Anna?" Piry asked again.

"Protestant."

"And yours, Erika?"

"Protestant."

In rapid-fire succession, Piry asked all the important questions again, mixing up the sequence, forcing them to think quickly on their feet, but neither girl made a mistake. In the span of a half an hour they were reborn; They were now two Hungarian Protestant children, with their heroic father fighting on the Russian front. They were ready to walk out of the concierge's room and step into a new life.

From now on, all I have to worry about is surviving the rest of the war, Piry thought, as she led her daughters out to the street. The young man in the Nazi uniform was leaning against the wall, a cigarette between his fingers glowing in the dark.

"Is everything all right?" he asked Piry quietly. "I think so."

"Just to be safe, I'll accompany you to the apartment."

Piry didn't object. It lent her a certain sense of security to have a man walking with them. Ironically, his hated uniform was an added source of protection.

It had started to snow. At this early hour the streets were empty, and their steps echoed softly on the wet pavement. After a twenty-minute walk, when they got to Mester Street 12, Piry took out a key to the front gate.

"I don't know how to thank you," she told the Nazi officer. "What is your name?"

"Andor Sáradi at present." He suddenly reached into his pocket. "Before I forget, Dr. Nagy sent this to you and wished you luck."

Piry took the small black book from his hand. "Thank you, Mr. Sáradi."

It was a Protestant Prayer Book. She laughed. "How considerate of him."

A moment's silence fell between them, then he asked, "May I come to see you once in a while?"

Piry hesitated. She felt deeply obliged to the young man. She was also a married woman. But what harm was there in his paying a visit to her? She looked into his warm brown eyes.

"Of course. Come for dinner. Any time. Tell Dr. Nagy I'll be in touch with him shortly."

He raised her hand and kissed it. "You're a very brave woman."

"You're a very brave man," she said.

His eyes caught hers as she looked up at him and for a moment Piry felt a strange electricity course through her body. Disturbed, she looked away.

"I will come to see you," he said.

Piry wondered why suddenly his words made her blush. She gave him a weak smile and said lamely, "We had better go in now."

Handing Piry the children's briefcases, he left. Piry, after locking the main gate, led her children upstairs to their new home on the second floor. They stepped into the kitchen and saw Irén turn to them from the stove where she had been cooking potatoes for breakfast.

"Welcome home," she said with a broad smile as the girls rushed to her, hugging her like a long lost relative.

CHAPTER 4

I N THE MONTH THAT followed, Piry and Irén had adjusted to coping together with wartime survival. They got along well. Irén was grateful for not having to be alone during these difficult times, and Piry appreciated her friend's help with her daughters and the running of the household. Fact was that Piry grew up with maids and had both a maid and a nanny during her marriage. She would have had a hard time managing alone.

Irén was calm and efficient. She had been a bookkeeper for a large law firm before the war. Supporting her aged mother who lived with her, and two younger brothers through university, gave her no time for romance or so she felt. Besides, she did not consider herself attractive enough to try. She was five foot five, somewhat heavy-set, and had a round face surrounded by mousy brown hair. Her best feature was her dark brown eyes but hardly anyone noticed them because they were hidden behind thick glasses. Irén didn't mind. Her family gave her enough love to not worry about her lack of suitors. She believed that when the time came, the right person would somehow walk into her life. When the war broke out, her brothers had been ordered to go into a forced labor camp, and her mother had decided to join her older sister in Szombathely, a small town, in Northern Hungary. Irén opted to stay in their apartment in Budapest, even though when the law forbade Christians to employ Jews, she had been officially dismissed from her job. Unofficially, the company paid her to work from home till that morning, when Piry's call alerted her that her life was in danger.

She and Piry had met when Irén, moonlighting to earn extra cash, did bookkeeping for Zoltán. Piry's forwardness and Irén's low-keyed personality seemed to complement each other, and the two women became fast friends. Irén vicariously enjoyed Piry's family and for Piry, Irén represented the friend she could always count on. Even during their current living arrangements, they divided responsibilities between them quite comfortably. It was Piry who went out to do the difficult tasks, such as finding milk, sugar, or extra bread through the black market. Irén stood in line for staples like potatoes and beans or took care of the girls while Piry was out. When the siege of Budapest began in early December, food became increasingly scarce. Both women had to spend long hours to obtain what they could.

This particular morning, Irén and Judith had been standing in line for nearly two hours, stamping their feet in the snow to keep warm as they awaited the opening of the butcher shop. Early in the day word had spread in the building like wildfire that at mid-morning horsemeat was going to be available. Irén volunteered to go.

"You want to come with me?" she asked Judith whom she favored over Erika because of the child's quieter disposition.

Judith jumped at the chance. She loved standing in line and listening to all the gossip around her. Most of it she didn't really understand but the war news she did.

The women, bundled into heavy overcoats and woolen headscarves against the bone piercing cold, covered their lips with the corner of their scarves and whispered about the advancing Russian army and the retreating Germans. Both Irén and her mother had warned Judith never to ask anyone, apart from them, about the Soviets or the Germans. Judith noticed that although the women whispered about the Russians, they only talked about battle news. Nobody admitted to rooting for them.

Irén explained to Judith in private, that this was because the Germans still dominated the city and the more desperate, they became about the possibility of losing the war, the more dangerous they were. A person saying the wrong thing could be reported by an informer and this still meant deportation or death. So, Judith stood in silence, eagerly listening to whatever the women had to say because she had heard that a Soviet victory would end the war. The end of the war meant to her that she could be called Judith again and her father would return.

Judith adored her father. Her mother was someone she depended on, but her father represented all the fun things in her life. When he was still at home, she would crawl into his bed early in the morning and just sniffing his familiar scent made her happy. At night, when he came home from work, she would run to the door and he would lift her high into the air and ask, "How's my favorite girl?"

Even after Erika was born, and their father spent time with her too, Judith felt that she remained his favorite. He took her kayaking, saying, she was old enough to learn; he took her to the circus; when she turned five, he bought her a bicycle and taught her to ride. At night, it was her dad who read her a bedtime story. Now he was gone, and Mother never did any of these special things with her.

"This brat is Jewish!"

Judith heard the shout and at the same moment felt a strong hand grab her by the arm and yank her out of the line. She felt her heart leap into her throat as she looked up at the smooth-shaven face of a blond youth wearing a Nazi arm band.

"Are you crazy?" she heard the women shout all around her.

"Don't touch this child!" Irén grabbed Judith's other arm, pulling her away from the youth. But he held on to her arm and so did Irén.

I am Anna, Judith thought frantically to herself. My father is at the front, I am Protestant. Her large blue eyes stared at the Nazi youth, but she was so terrified that she couldn't utter a sound.

"Just look at her nose!" the Nazi pointed at Judith's nose, which was perfectly straight with a softly rounded tip. It wasn't a particularly Semitic nose, but neither was it turned upward as that of so many Christian Hungarian children.

Judith's heartbeat wildly, her eyes surveying the women who were shouting and upset.

"What nonsense! Now we're going to arrest kids by their noses!"

"We know this kid; she lives in our building!"

"Let her go or you'll get into real trouble with us!"

"Why don't you pick on someone your size! Go fight on the front instead of picking on innocent children!"

"Get out of here or I'll squash you!"

Judith saw Mrs. Pataky, a giant of a woman from her building step forward to confront the young man, hands on her hips, thrusting her face an inch away from his.

"Let go of that child and get lost! My son is fighting at the Russian front, and this is what you do? How come you're not at the front?"

He reluctantly released Judith's arm, "Have her for now. But I'll keep an eye on her. And you, too, Jew-lover!"

One of the women bent down and picking up a handful of snow quickly formed it into a ball. A few others followed her example. The youth retreated, backing away from the irate women but he might still have gotten bombarded with snowballs had not the butcher appeared, opening his shop.

"The little bastard," the women muttered indignantly as shuffled closer to the door.

"Don't you worry, sweetie," Mrs. Pataky patted Judith on the cheek, then rushed back to her place in line.

Both Judith and Irén were pale and shaken to the core as they inched their way forward in the line.

Irén felt like going home instantly, but she knew that would be a grave mistake. Judith was not in danger for the moment, but their sudden departure would provoke a discussion among the women. By staying, they wouldn't have a chance to talk, and the incident would soon be forgotten. Then, too, her little adopted family needed that kilo of meat desperately. They were subsisting on a diet of pinto beans, lentils, dried peas, and bread. Thus, whenever meat became available, sometimes pork but mostly horse, they lined up from dawn to dusk to get a kilo or two, as though it were the greatest delicacy. Irén knew that for the two young children it was essential that she bring home what she could obtain.

Holding Judith's hand tightly for reassurance, she pulled the child into the middle of the line, sandwiching her between herself and the other women. She was secretly praying that they would get served and reach home in case the young Nazi had a chance to return with reinforcement.

◉◉◉

When they got home, and told Piry what had happened, she hugged Judith for a long time. Then said, "From now on, if you go out on the street, wrap a kerchief over half your face as though you had a toothache, or because you're cold. But it would be best if you didn't go out of the building."

"Can I go play with Józsi now?" asked Judith, dismissing her morning scare.

"If you'd like. But only at his home. Will you be all right?"

"Yes."

"Don't tell him what happened."

Judith made a face. Did her mother think she was dumb? "Of course not!"

"Lunch will be ready at two."

Judith picked up her coat. "I'll be back then."

Erika, who had been silently listening to the story, observed her mother's face as she watched Judith leave. Her mother seemed upset, and Erika decided it would be best if she, too, made herself scarce.

"I'll be drawing in the living room," she informed Piry, and going through the kitchen door went down the hallway. Their apartment consisted of a kitchen with a direct entrance from the building's corridor, as well as a main door into a hallway. Along this hallway were the living room and a bedroom to the right. A bathroom and a separate toilet room were on the left.

At night, Piry and her daughters slept in the bedroom while Irén made her bed on the living room couch. During the day, they all used the living room. All the furniture in the apartment was made of dark walnut, with cushions in beige. Cream colored lace curtains on the windows softened the dark, hard lines of the furniture. Erika liked the lace curtains. Sometimes, if she stared at them long enough, she could discern faces and animals in the pattern. She tried to draw these and then color them with the new set of crayons Piry had given her on her fourth birthday.

In the kitchen, Irén brought out a bag of pinto beans to clean while Piry picked up the meat that came in newsprint. She slowly unwrapped it over the sink and washed it. Then placing the meat on a wood board, began cutting it with a butcher knife into bite size cubes. She forced herself to concentrate on the task, but her hands were shaking, and tears were rolling down her cheeks. She stifled the sobs that were raking her body but couldn't suppress the sound completely. Irén was at her side immediately, putting an arm around her shoulders.

"I almost lost her for a kilo of meat," Piry whispered through her tears. Without a reply, Irén stood by her and let her cry because sometimes one needed to do just that.

And Piry cried about Judith, and the unbearable loneliness of coping without Zoltán, and the fear that despite her efforts they might not live to see the end of the war. Then, having spent her tears, she blew her nose, washed her face, and giving Irén a half smile, said, "I'm all right now."

They had to survive. Simply had to.

◎◉◎

Judith did not go to her friend Józsi. Instead, she waved at him as she passed by their apartment window and continued along the corridor till she reached the staircase. She climbed to the sixth floor, at the top of the building. She walked to the railing and looked down.

The apartment building they lived in had a large main door leading from the street to an entry hall. From there, one could go out to a central courtyard or take the elevator or the staircase up to the different floors. Apartments were reached by walking along corridors that circled the courtyard.

From where Judith stood, the floors circling the courtyard looked like layers of a snail's shell. She saw a woman come through the main gate of the building, carrying a basket and go to her ground floor apartment. Judith pulled back from the railing, not wanting to be seen. When the woman was gone, she poked her face out again over the wrought iron railing.

She couldn't get the young Nazi out of her mind. She felt the terror of it again, her helplessness as he grabbed her arm. *If Dad had been there, this would not have happened*, Judith thought, and her little heart ached with longing for his strong arms. She loved the way he used to pick her up and swing her around in the air, laughing and asking, "Who is my favorite girl?" And she would squeal, and laugh, and throw her arms around his neck, giving him a big hug, rubbing her face against the rough stubble on his face at the end of the day.

He left because I look Jewish; and he will never come back, she thought, and her heart sank at this idea. She looked at the courtyard. It was so very far down. *If I climbed over the railing and fell, I would die, and nobody would care. Because nobody really loves me. Only Daddy loved me, but he left me. This would teach him that he shouldn't have done that*, she thought, and put a leg over the railing.

◎◉◎

In the living room, Erika tilted her head to hear better. There was a high-pitched whining sound coming from the kitchen, as though someone was crying.

She was about to go and investigate when the doorbell rang. She ran down the hallway, shouting, "I'll get it!"

It was Józsi, a tow-headed, blue-eyed boy, Judith's favorite playmate. He looked pale. "You had better come with me, quick!" he whispered.

"What for?"

"Just come. Now!"

"I'm going to Józsi's!" Erika shouted in the direction of the kitchen not sure anybody heard her. Grabbing her overcoat off a hook by the door, she ran outside. "Where to?" she asked.

Józsi pointed upward: "Look!"

"Oh, no!" Erika raced up the back stairs of the building, with Józsi following. I hope she'll wait for me, Erika prayed, filled with anxiety. This was not the first time that Erika had to beg Judith not to jump. Each time Judith got upset, she would go up to the sixth floor and threaten to kill herself. The trouble was that she had really meant it and Erika knew it. It was up to her to convince Judith not to do it because Judith had warned her, if Erika told their mother about it, she would jump.

Panting, Erika bolted down the corridor till she reached Judith. She was sitting perched on the black iron railing, looking down at the dizzying depth of the cement courtyard.

"Please, Anna, get off the railing," Erika pleaded. Despite her fear, she did not forget to call her sister by her wartime 'Christian' name.

Judith laughed. "I'm going to jump. You want to watch?"

"No! I beg you, Annie, please don't" Erika used her nickname to show that she was loved, and Erika was frightened for her.

Judith leaned gently forward, and Erika grabbed her arm. "I'll lend you my coloring set for as long as you want if you come off the railing!"

This was the most precious thing she could offer, and Judith knew it. She looked at Erika's pale face and large hazel eyes pleading with her. At times, she hated Erika for being so cute, and because everyone seemed to like her. But the fear frozen on her sister's face touched Judith. *Maybe Erika really cared.* Judith swung her legs over to the inside of the railing and hopped off.

"Now remember, I can use the crayons as long as I want."

"Yes," Erika heaved a great sigh of relief.

"Bring them to my place, we'll play there," Józsi piped up, cheered by the turn of events.

◎◉◎

When Erika delivered the coloring set, Judith invited her, "You can stay and play too."

"I heard someone crying in the kitchen before," Erika began, "do you think it was Mommy?

"No, silly, why should Mommy cry?"

"It was the horse meat you got this morning." Józsi nodded wisely.

"What are you talking about?"

"Don't you know that when horse meat is being cooked it cries?"

"I don't believe you!" Erika shouted.

Judith took Józsi's side. "It does, Erika, everybody knows that."

Erika looked at them, their faces perfectly serious, and shuddered. "That can't be."

"I'm telling you the truth," Józsi insisted.

Erika felt awful. She loved animals and it was as though she could feel the horse's pain. How could her mother cook it, and worse, be in the kitchen listening to that poor animal crying in the pot! Unless of course Józsi and Judith were lying. She studied their faces, but both of them stared back at her without blinking an eye. If they are right, I will never, never eat meat again. Not any kind, Erika vowed to herself.

"I'm going home to ask," she declared, heading for the door.

"No, you're not," Judith jumped between Erika and the door. "We were just kidding. You're so stupid, you believe everything!"

"I didn't really believe you! And I am going home! I don't want to play with you two."

"All right. Let's make peace. We won't tease you anymore. Let's all draw till lunch and then we'll go home together," Judith offered.

Easy to appease, and eager to play, Erika accepted the offer. But as she reached for the red crayon, Józsi snatched it away from her. "I want this one, take another."

Erika saw the two of them exchange a glance and grin. Furious, Erika shouted, "You asked me to stay! I can use whichever color I want!"

"Stop yelling or I'll hit you!" Judith warned her.

"Give me the red one!" Erika lunged toward Józsi, but Judith pushed her back. Erika hit her leg on the corner of her chair. With tears in her eyes, not from the pain but the indignity of being pushed around, she ran out of the room, shouting, "Go to hell, both of you!"

Blinded by tears, Erika grabbed her coat and dashed through the front door to the corridor, bumping straight into a boy a head taller than her. He put his arms out to soften the impact.

"Ho, ho, where're you running to?"

"Oh, Peter, it's you!" Forgetting her anger, Erika looked up at him with adoring eyes. "Edith and Józsi were teasing me again. Come and play with me!"

"I can't right now, I'm going for cigarettes to the tobacco store."

"Can I come with you?"

"Ask your mom's permission."

"She thinks I am at József's with Edith, so it doesn't matter," Erika shrugged.

Peter looked at her, thinking it over. "All right, just this once because I have to get back quickly. But put your coat on."

Erika realized that she was still just holding her coat. She slipped into it and looked up at Peter. "Let's go!"

Peter was ten years old, and Erika idolized him because he always defended her against Judith and her gang. He had also taught her to play checkers, and had even tried to teach her chess, though Erika had a hard time learning strategy. Yet she insisted on playing, for she enjoyed the challenge of the game. Instinctively, she also knew that Peter would spend more time with her if they played chess instead of checkers. "I wish you were my brother," she would say to him as they sat together over a game or a book.

"I am like a brother to you," he would reply, smiling.

His saying this made Erika happy.

Now, as they stepped out into the street, they saw that a crowd had gathered down the block just before the intersection.

"Let's go see what's happening," Peter suggested.

They walked as briskly as they could but the snow on the sidewalk was impacted, and slippery.

"Hold on to my hand," Peter told Erika.

When they reached the ring of people, Erika and Peter were small enough to slip between people's legs till they found themselves facing a wheelbarrow. On it lay a man; his face covered with newspapers. A gust of wind suddenly lifted the papers and Erika stared at the man's face—at the awesome stillness of death.

"What did he die of?" she heard a woman ask behind her.

"Who knows? Probably hunger. He just collapsed on the street," replied the man standing next to the woman, and they both continued to stare.

Erika couldn't take her eyes off the dead man either. He was not old, but his face seemed curiously wizened and yellowed, as though he had been carved out of wax. There was a rigidity and a density to him the likes of which Erika had never seen before.

"Why is he so still?" she whispered to Peter.

"Let's get out of here, then I'll tell you."

They worked their way through the crowd again.

"Tell me," Erika demanded.

"After a person dies, they become rigid like that. That's because their soul leaves their body."

"Do animals have a soul too?"

"Some people think they do."

"Horses?"

"I'm not sure."

"Do horses cry when they are cut up and put into a pot to cook?"

They had been walking slowly toward the tobacco store, now Peter stopped and stared at Erika. "Where did you get such an idea?"

"Józsi and my sister told me. Afterwards they said they were just joking but how can I be sure?"

"One of these days I'll get that little bastard," Peter muttered. "No, Erika, nobody feels anything once they're dead. Not even animals. And they certainly don't cry in the pot."

"Oh, I feel so much better," Erika beamed at him.

Peter smiled at her and put his arm around Erika's tiny shoulders as they walked. Something about Erika always made him feel warm and protective.

The tobacco shop smelled of cigarettes and stationery. Erika and Peter watched the surly owner, who sported a bushy, brown mustache, make the cigarettes. He took into his yellow-stained fingers a copper tube and opened it along its length. Then he carefully filled the tube with loose tobacco and closed it. From beneath the counter, he took a packet of white cigarette papers and wrapped one thin sheet around the tube. He pushed a stick into the tube and as he pulled it out, the cigarette was rolled. He glued the edges of the paper together with a wet sponge, and now it was ready. When he had six of them laid out, Peter fished some coins out of his pocket.

"Make it seven."

The man looked at him and said nothing. When this last cigarette was done, he wrapped all seven in a newspaper and handed them to Peter.

On their way home, Peter pulled Erika into a doorway. "Don't tell anyone," he warned her, "but the seventh is mine."

He pried open the package and pulled out his cigarette. "I saved my pocket money for it." He took a small box of matches out of his coat pocket and lit up. Erika watched him in silence.

"Want to try it?"

Erika's eyes sparkled. "Yes."

He handed her the cigarette. "Don't wet the edge. Just put it between your lips and suck in as if you were taking a breath. But don't swallow the smoke or you'll get sick. Just hold it in your mouth."

Erika followed his instructions. An acrid taste filled her mouth, and she gagged.

"Take it." She handed the cigarette back to Peter, not liking it at all.

Peter took a few more puffs, then extinguished the cigarette on the wall of the building. Touching the smoky tip between his fingers, to made sure that it was no longer hot, he slipped it into his pocket. "It's got to last," he grinned.

Like a pair of conspirators, they took a roundabout route back to their building so the fresh air would clear the smell of smoke that hung about them for a while.

◉◉◉

Until the siege of Budapest began in earnest in December of 1944, life had been relatively smooth for Piry and her little family. Their identity had been accepted without undue questioning by the other tenants in the building. Even the concierge and the police had made no fuss when they registered as new residents. They didn't question their story of being refugees from Sárospatak and using their friends' apartment. Judith and Erika had made friends with the other children in the building so during the day they kept themselves entertained for the most part. They had found in the apartment a pantry well stocked with canned fruits and vegetables and had been told by Dr. Nagy to feel free to use up the supplies. Piry was grateful, for it supplemented nicely the staples she and Irén obtained elsewhere.

Together with Irén, Piry managed the children and the necessities of their little household quite well. Without Irén's help she could not have gone out as freely to hunt up their essential food items and the much-needed kerosene, which they used for lamp fuel when the electricity went off. During winter it got dark by three in the afternoon, so they needed the lamps, since due to the heavy bombing the electricity was going off more and more often. With the increased bombing, fear returned to haunt Piry.

Each apartment building had a basement that came to be used as a bomb shelter. Tenants were supposed to go down there as soon as the sirens began to warn of an oncoming air raid. But ever since the incident between Judith and the Nazi, Piry was afraid to take her children into a large gathering of people. It wasn't so much that she was concerned about Judith's looks as of the danger that if someone were to ask a leading question one of the children might make a mistake and reveal their true identity. Thus, even during heavy air raids she had kept them upstairs in their apartment. She insisted that Irén go to the shelter, but Irén refused to leave.

"It wouldn't look right for me to go down there alone," she explained.

Piry on the other hand felt it was safer for them to stay in the apartment. Despite the ear-splitting noise of the sirens that had set her teeth on edge, figured that if their building was hit, they would have a fifty-fifty chance of survival, but if one of her children said the wrong thing in the shelter, they wouldn't survive at all.

While listening to the distant and sometimes near thud of bombs, she would whisper to herself the same Hebrew prayer that she had taught her children in earlier times as their bedtime prayer. Sometimes, when they thought that Erika was asleep, Judith would join her.

"I know you two are praying in Hebrew," Erika had whispered to them one night between two hits that rattled the windows. "But you don't have to worry, Mommy, I won't tell anyone."

Piry hugged Erika and said, "I know you wouldn't. But try to forget what you have heard." Secretly, she was angry at herself for not having prayed in silence. She hadn't even realized what she was doing till Erika pointed it out. *Old habits die hard*, she thought. From early childhood she had been taught that Jews didn't pray in silence, they actually said the words so that the sound of their prayer would ascend to God's ears.

All praying aloud did, she now thought, *was to bring up the past in the child's mind and put us in possible danger. Or maybe not. Maybe it's just the opposite. After all, if Erika had not forgotten her former identity, yet had been able to keep it such a deep secret all these months, then probably we would be all right, and a lot safer in the shelter.* Thus, Erika's overhearing the prayer became a turning point in their lives. They joined the others in the shelter, sleeping almost every night on the hard canvas cots allocated to them. It was cozier down there and the bombs seemed a lot farther away.

Christmas was approaching and despite its state of siege, the whole city seemed to burn with a holiday fever. Magically, more food began to appear in stores and somehow people were kinder to each other. Irén came home one day with a Christmas tree. At first, Piry was greatly disturbed by the tree as the symbol of the birth of Christianity. How could she celebrate that, she thought bitterly, when Christianity had brought nothing but pain to her and her family?

"We could have pretended to be too poor to get one," she argued quietly with Irén.

"Everyone in the building has one," Irén pointed out.

So Piry resigned herself to accepting the tree as one more compromise needed for survival. She had even managed to obtain colored construction paper so they could decorate it.

Judith and Erika learned to make glue, by mixing water and flour, and together with their friends in the building the two girls kept busy for days, pasting strips of colored paper into rings to form chains, and making stars to hang on the tree. Even Piry had to admit that once it stood in the living room in full holiday decor, the tree looked lovely.

The aroma of baking wafted from every kitchen into the central courtyard. Piry managed to get hold of some sugar and make cookies. One night, while they were sitting in the shelter through another interminable air raid, a woman had offered Erika a cookie. The shelter was full, everyone sat on benches and cots along the walls, and some had brought folding chairs to sit in the middle of the long passages that ran under the building. There was always a musty odor down here but with the heat of the bodies, the cold wasn't too bad. The tapers and flickering kerosene lamps that people had brought down with them cast a warm light over their drawn faces as they sat wrapped in blankets.

Not content to just sit, Erika often broke into a spontaneous performance, singing and doing a Hungarian folk dance, or reciting a poem for anyone who would listen. This night she had recited the Lord's Prayer, a particular favorite of hers, because it asked God to give them their daily bread, and Erika had found this a very sensible request. After the prayer, she genuflected and then looked around, for people often rewarded her with a piece of bread or a carrot, or at least a smile or praise, and that too pleased her.

It was at this point that the lady from the first-floor apartment had been so charmed that she called Erika to her. She handed Erika a large, star shaped cookie, and watched the child bite off one of the peaks. "Do you like it?" she asked with a broad smile.

"Oh, yes, thank you so much," Erika beamed at her. However, she wasn't going to eat the whole cookie. After that bite, she was going to take the rest to share it with her family, when the woman asked, "Does your mommy make this kind of Christmas cookie?"

Erika froze. Her family had never made any kind of Christmas cookies. In fact, they had never even celebrated Christmas before. She had almost said so, but then she glanced at her mother who sat nearby, and Erika knew immediately that this would be the wrong thing to say.

"We don't make these kinds in Nyiradon where we come from," she finally replied.

"You're a smart girl." The woman smiled and gave her a couple more cookies. "Here then, eat yours, and take these to your family." Piry crushed Erika to her in an embrace, and she knew that it wasn't because she had brought them cookies.

◎◉◎

Dr. Nagy came by the day before Christmas. Piry was alone in the apartment, Irén had gone out to stand in line for potatoes, and both Judith and Erika were playing somewhere in the building with their friends. Piry had not seen Dr. Nagy since she had delivered to him two expensive gold statuettes, shortly after they had moved into the apartment. One piece was a Diana, goddess of the moon and hunting, and the other Mars, the god of war, which Dr. Nagy needed as a gift for somebody.

"Diana is for you and your wife to keep," Piry explained, and would not accept money for either of the statuettes. "What you have done for us is priceless, and so are these pieces," she explained. They were the last two Zoltán had left her.

Dr. Nagy came with cans of meat and condensed milk, items Piry had not seen since the escalation of the war.

"Patients give these in lieu of payment," he explained. "Helen and I thought you would enjoy them. Of course, the children could use the milk, I'm sure."

45

Piry sat him down and offered him "ersatz" coffee, the wartime chicory drink that had been substituted for the real thing, and some Christmas cookies she had made. Then, as he sat in the kitchen with her, she brought out a bracelet and asked him to take it to Helen. But he wouldn't accept it.

"You may need it later to trade for food," he explained. "From what we hear, things will get a lot worse. The Russians have surrounded Budapest, and the Germans intend to defend it building by building. Have you had any news of Zoltán?"

"Not a word. What about Helen's brother?"

"Since I know you can keep a secret, I can tell you, he sent word that he expects to be in Budapest in January."

"You mean he is coming back to the apartment?"

"No, he is coming with the Red army."

"What is he doing with the Soviet Army?"

"At the start of the war he and some of his friends slipped into Soviet Russia and joined the Red Army."

"Is he a Communist?"

"I don't know if he is as much a Communist as he is anti-Nazi."

Piry had been so taken aback by this revelation that the importance of Dr. Nagy's news had just hit her. "Did you say the Russians will be able to take Budapest in a month?"

"That's the message we got. Whether they'll make it or not remains to be seen. They are pouring into the country from the East and the South and despite the fierce resistance by the Germans the Soviets are gaining ground on all fronts." He rose to leave. "I thought it'd make your Christmas to know that the war will be over sooner than the Germans claim. And for sure, they won't be the victors."

Piry sighed. She hoped Dr. Nagy was right. "I feel like we're living on borrowed time, so for us a Russian victory can't come soon enough," she confessed to him.

"I'm sorry to have missed your daughters," he said as he was heading for the door. "Are they well?"

"Fine." Piry smiled. Then she could not help asking, "Incidentally, is Andor Sáradi, who got them back for me, still with you?"

Dr. Nagy sighed, "He also decided to slip into Russia. I haven't heard from him since. I hope he made it."

Piry nodded. "I hope we'll all make it."

Dr. Nagy left, and Piry sat down again at the kitchen table, savoring this rare quiet moment, wondering about her husband, and daring to hope that as soon as the war was over, Zoltán would also return.

Christmas passed, followed by a bitter cold January. Tenants from all the buildings were ordered out to shovel the snow off the streets so the German regiments could pass with greater ease. Those who were stronger, also had to help build barricades against the approaching Soviet army. But rumors had it that the Russians held an unbreakable ring around the city, and that slowly they were winning their way into the heart of Pest. Day and night airplanes screamed through the sky, and as buildings collapsed around them, Piry and her family hid, with all the other tenants, in the bomb shelter. There was no sense risking getting killed now when the end of the war seemed so near.

When all able-bodied adults in Piry's building were ordered out to shovel snow, Piry put a warm kerchief over her head, and wearing her heavy black overcoat went to the district headquarters of the Hungarian Nazis, the Arrow Cross. Being a very attractive young woman, she was well received by the young Arrow Cross men.

"What can we do for you?" "My family is very sick, I have two young children and my cousin living with me, and they're all seriously ill. I'd like us to be exempt from shoveling snow. We've survived the war so far, please help me, my family will die without my care," Piry begged.

The young officers looked at each other, evaluating the pretty woman's tears, and her obvious distress. They nodded at each other, and one of them said, "Don't cry, we'll give you a release paper you can show the concierge of your building."

Piry could hardly contain her sense of victory as she presented the official Nazi document to the concierge, who shrugged and stopped calling on her and Irén for snow removal service.

◎◉◎

At the end of January, the cold intensified and so did the anticipation that the Soviets would reach the 9th district where Piry and her family were living. Talk in the shelter turned to blaming the Germans for the war and anticipating liberation by the Soviet Army. Piry and Irén remained silent. It was safer to not take sides until victory was final.

However, secretly she obtained a Russian pocket dictionary and during the day when they could be upstairs in their apartment, she and her family started to learn the Russian words for hello, bread, kerosene, and thank you.

District by district Pest was won. On January 27th the Germans officially surrendered Pest, but the fighting continued on the Buda side of the city. Buda fell in a fierce two-day battle on February 13th with both German and Soviet troops suffering enormous casualties. Budapest lay in ruins. A great many buildings were either destroyed or damaged, including historical treasures such as the Parliament Building and the Castle on Buda. The five magnificent bridges spanning the Danube had been blown up by the retreating German army. Transportation between Pest and Buda was managed by pontoons, bridges quickly put together with Soviet help, and by private boats. Despite the destruction, people began to venture out on the streets. Shops began to open, and food lines formed everywhere when news spread that some victuals were available.

In the middle of February, Irén came home laughing and crying. "The Russians are here! I saw people stop by a Soviet tank where soldiers were standing, so I went over too, and they pressed this into my hand." She set on the table a cone shaped bag made from newsprint. It was filled with sugar, something they have not seen for weeks.

"Where are they?" Piry asked, excited by the news.

"Just over on Mester Street."

"Let's go see them."

Judith was out with Józsi, but Piry and Erika grabbed their coats and ran the couple of blocks till they spotted the tank. Three men, dressed in quilt khaki uniforms stood by it. Holding Erika back, Piry slowed down but one of the soldiers spotted them and a bright smile lit up his face.

"Devushky, idyi suda," (girls, come here) he called out to them and waved for them to come closer. When they did, he bent down and lifted Erika up in the air, then seating her in the crook of his arm, he gave her a warm smile. "Ya derzhat devushka kak ty" he said, kissing her cheek.

"He says he's got a daughter like you," a woman translated it next to Piry.

Then the soldier lowered Erika to the ground and reached into his pocket.

Erika watched with fascination his huge hand and dirt encrusted fingernails as he pulled a large chunk of bread out of his pocket and extended it to her. "Chleb."

Because of her daily practice, she knew he had said "bread."

"Spasiba." She thanked him, as her mother had taught her, and this created a roar of laughter among the three soldiers. They crowded around Erika and made her repeat the word, one of them showing her the proper pronunciation with the accent on the second syllable. When Erika repeated it after him, he pulled a piece of chocolate from his pocket to reward her.

In the ensuing weeks, Erika lived in a dizzying world of success. Russian soldiers loved children and as her Russian improved, Erika was able to say hello, ask in full sentences not only for bread and sugar, but kerosene as well. The soldiers melted at her charm, kissed her cheeks, and commented on her beautiful eyes while generously giving her the things she asked for.

Erika took these gifts seriously. With the streets safe again, she went out each morning as though she were heading for work. By noon, she would run home with food and a jar full of kerosene. Spreading these treasures out on the kitchen table, she would proudly pound on her chest exclaiming, "Now I am the breadwinner of the family!"

Judith observed Erika with envy. After her terrifying experience with that young Nazi, she had become shy, afraid to go out on the street, much less go around on her own asking anyone for anything. She insisted on still being called Anna in public, afraid of being called a Jew. Erika was too happy to notice any of this. She gladly shared with her sister the pieces of chocolate she received, and loving her own sense of importance, was ready to run out again for more.

Piry was busy too, visiting ministry offices in the hope of getting information about her husband, and their families' whereabouts. She got no help, the officials claimed that no one knew anything yet about the people who had been taken to Germany or even to forced labor camps. Piry wondered how long it would take for those who survived to return home.

◎◉◎

One morning, while Erika and Piry were out, and Judith went over to play with Józsi, Irén heard movement in the apartment. Thinking Judith had come back, she continued to make the bed in the bedroom. Suddenly the door swung open. A tall, stocky Russian stood in the doorway, his gun slung casually over his shoulder, his quilted clothes reeking of unwashed months of war.

Irén let out a small cry of surprise and fear.

"No afraid," he said in broken Hungarian, as he smiled and stepped into the room.

She backed away from the bed. Somehow, this triggered a reaction, a spark as old as man, a primitive instinct in the soldier upon the sight of a lone woman at the end of a long war. He smiled and talked to her in Russian as he slowly advanced. Irén put up her hands in protest, backing into a corner. His eyes gleamed as he reached for her and when she let out a scream, he put a large, callused hand over her mouth. Irén struggled fiercely, she cried and begged him to let go of her, but he pushed her over the bed and holding her down with his weight, unbuttoned his fly and pushing up her skirt, forced open her legs.

Irén felt a piercing pain course through her body, but the soldier continued to muffle her cries with his palm. He thrusted and thrusted and she couldn't breathe. Her world turned black.

When Irén came to, he was gone. She was lying on her back, a warm, sticky fluid oozing out of her. Irén felt humiliated and wanted to die. She had survived the war only to lose her last hope for a normal life ever again. Hungarian men married only virgins. All these years, when she was taking care of her family, Irén held on to her purity because she knew that someday she would meet a man who would value that in her. She had no beauty, no money, only this great gift that she could give to a man: her untouched body.

Now this too had been taken from her by the war. She felt a pain, such a deep seated, searing pain that she just wanted to die. Somewhere in her rational mind, she knew she had to get up and hide her shame. If I get up now, no one will know, she thought. But she couldn't. She curled up into a small ball, and felt her body grow rigid. She was cold but didn't have the strength to pull the cover over herself. Her eyes stared expressionless at an empty spot on the wall, but her mind ran on a frantic racetrack of denial, reality, and rage.

Piry found her in this position when she returned.

"Irén! What happened?" She noticed the pool of blood and wet spot on the sheets, the smell of semen hitting her nose, and guessed. "Oh, my poor baby," she crooned, and wrapped her arm around Irén's shoulder. "How did this happen?"

Not getting an answer, she said, "Irén, come on, sweetie, you know this is happening all over town to women—don't take it so to heart." Still not getting an answer, she continued, "Come on, let's clean you up before the children get home. C'mon, let's clean you up and no one will know. I certainly won't tell…."

This seemed to have penetrated Irén's mind. Piry was right. I shouldn't just lie here and further expose myself to shame. No one must know… she thought frantically, and looking at Piry, rolled off the bed.

"I'll change the bedding, you go wash," Piry instructed her. Without a word, Irén ran for the bathroom. Piry gave her a little time, then followed. Irén, now dressed, was standing over the sink, sobbing. Piry dropped the soiled sheets and held her friend.

"He just appeared out of nowhere," Irén sobbed. "And I had no place to run. What will happen to me now?"

"Nothing, absolutely nothing," Piry assured her. You will heal. And we'll never talk about it again. We'll pretend it never happened."

"But it did. I'll never be the same."

"None of us ever will be after this war. I hope this is the worst thing the war has done to you!"

Irén pushed her friend away and looked into her eyes. Piry's attitude, bitter but practical was like a salve on her soul. After all, married women were not virgins, and it didn't show on their forehead like a stigma. Besides, why should she worry about marriage? She was now too old and marred, even to think about it.

And if she never married, no one besides Piry, would ever know of her shame. Piry was right. When her parents and brothers returned from the war, this would become a matter no importance. Certainly, they must never find out.

"I'll wash the sheets," she said.

CHAPTER 5

O N APRIL 4th OF 1945, all of Hungary was officially declared liberated by the Soviet Army. In the thawing spring weather people danced in the streets and strangers hugged each other with joy. The war was finally over. Piry looked at her daughters and her friend Irén, and said, "Time to go home and become ourselves again."

Judith was overjoyed at the prospect of being able to go home again. She had been wondering how her daddy would find them on his return if they were living at their present apartment. Erika on the other hand suddenly felt a great sense of loss at the thought of leaving the building where Peter lived. Irén wondered what she had to go home to, but she did not share her thoughts with Piry.

They had survived the war, and that was good enough for the moment. From here on life would sort itself out. A new sense of hope pervaded the very air they breathed. Each of them, child and adult, expected that with the war over nothing as bad as what they had lived through could ever happen again.

They didn't know that new troubles were just beginning.

◎◉◎

Starting mid-April 1945, men were returning from the war zones. Battle-weary soldiers along with tattered, starved men from forced labor camps, dismounted trains that arrived from the Russian front to the Northern Station.

Piry went there daily, because as far as she knew, Zoltan had been sent to a forced labor camp at the Hungarian Russian border. But after a futile week, she stopped one of the emaciated men to ask where he was returning from. He told her that toward the end of the war many of the people at forced labor camps had been transported to Germany.

So, she switched her daily trips to the Western Station to await the arrival of trains from Germany. She watched as soldiers streamed in from the European front, and surviving Jews from Nazi concentration camps clambered painfully off the same trains. They were walking skeletons, their eyes dead, except for a vague glimmer of hope as they looked around at the station, hoping to spot a familiar face. Yearning to find a family member who might still be alive in the cities and villages they had called home before the war. A familiar face that would justify their return to the country that had sent them to die.

Piry scanned with anxious eyes the incoming survivors as they dragged themselves by her. An army of ghosts with large, feverish eyes that studied her face then passed her by. She wasn't sure she would recognize Zoltan if he looked anything like the rest of the returning Jews—she would have to rely on him to call out her name—but he never did. As the weeks passed, and she stood on the arrivals' platform studying the unfamiliar faces going by her, she felt a hard lump in the pit of her stomach grow larger and larger, till she turned on her heels and headed home.

One night, Piry awoke from a horrific nightmare. She sat upright in bed, putting her hands on her wildly thumping heart to calm it.

Irén, now also awake, whispered, "What's wrong?"

"Zoltan. I dreamt about him. He was in the middle of a black lake, a lake like tar, that was pulling him down. He was drowning. He was getting sucked down deeper and deeper, with one arm in the air, struggling to stay afloat, but he couldn't. As he sank, his head went under, then his arm, and only his hand was still visible reaching for help.

Then I woke up"

"It was just a bad dream," Irén said gently. "Probably comes from your train station visits. I think it's time for you to stop going there."

"But he won't know where to find us if I'm not there!" Piry protested.

"Of course, he will! Move back with the girls to your own apartment. Surely, he'll go straight there when he arrives!" Then she added something she has been afraid to say, "Look, Piry, I need to go home too. We all need to get back to our own lives. What if my family returns and can't find me because I'm not where they expect me to be?"

"You're right," Piry sighed, feeling defeated and emotionally spent. "First I'll get us some food supplies, and then we'll all move."

◎◉◎

Despite the end of the war, food was becoming increasingly scarce in the city. Even Piry had trouble finding it, regardless of her ability to pay for it. That's because as spring finally arrived, the farmers stopped bringing their meager winter vegetables and scrawny livestock on their horse-drawn carriages into Budapest. Instead, they began to use their animals to plow and plant their fields.

Piry knew that Irén would have an even harder time finding food that she did. So, she decided to stock up for both of them before they moved. Leaving her daughters in Irén's care, Piry went to the station once again, but this time to board a train bound for the southern part of Hungary. She assumed that villages there were less affected by the war than other parts of the country and might have food supplies to sell. She wasn't sure where she would get off the train but trusted her instincts to decide it out along the way. She carried little money because she figured that the peasants would need something far more useful. She could barter with the tools that she carried in her little suitcase.

Much of the stock stored with friends from Zoltan's wholesale hardware business was gone. Trusted friends, at whose homes she had hidden some goods, shrugged their shoulders and apologized for the missing merchandise. "The Russians took it," they would all say, and give her the meager leftovers. Piry only half believed their stories. It was more likely that they had been selling the tools, piece by piece, to sustain their own survival.

But she said nothing. She thanked them for their help, and took whatever leftover merchandise she was returned, appreciative of their kindness. Zoltan will know how to get started again, she consoled herself. Meanwhile, there was no point in making enemies of old friends. Besides, she had another resource—provided the war or thieves had not taken it.

Now that peace returned to the city, and taxis began to circulate again, she felt safe enough to hire one and go to the small warehouse on the outskirts of the city where Zoltan stored the merchandise for their wholesale business.

When the Jewish laws made him close his shop, with Piry's help they secretly put in their warehouse as much stock as they thought wise—before giving some to friends for safekeeping and let the government take enough so as not arouse suspicion about their possessions. Considering the loss of goods by their friends, Piry had little hope for the warehouse. She expected the building to be either bombed or sacked. But she had to go and see for herself.

Her heart skipped a beat when the taxi turned the corner, and miraculously, she saw the warehouse standing intact. She asked the taxi to wait for her and walked to the front door. With hands trembling with excitement, she opened the lock and stepped in.

Joyful prewar memories flooded her mind. While stocking the shelves, or picking up merchandise for their customers, Zoltan was also teaching her about the tools—their names, uses, and prices—both wholesale and retail.

"If I ever become ill, you'll need to know this so you could run the business," he told her.

She laughed when he had said that. He was five foot eleven, weighing 200 pounds, and a sportsman in top physical condition. He participated in kayak races that went from Budapest to Vienna, a distance of more than 200 kilometers. He was also a champion amateur wrestler, with many trophies to prove it. Nothing could ever happen to him, she thought, but wanted to learn the hardware business anyway, because she enjoyed working in business more than at home.

Housework was something her maid could do. She hired a nanny for the children so she could spend several hours a day at the shop's office, working alongside Zoltan. He didn't like Piry to be in the shop, but she insisted. Now she was glad. The merchandise, piled on the shelves by categories, was going to be their salvation; the key to rebuilding their lives. Her heart flooded with gratitude that Zoltan had taught her about the tools. She could manage sales till he got back.

She felt a momentary pang in her stomach as her thoughts flashed on the skeletal men slowly descending from the trains. *Will Zoltan be just like them*, she wondered. But she shook off the fear. It didn't matter, as long as he returned. He would have time to recover, she could run the business while he did. She took another look at the shelves and decided to carry just some important pieces with her in the small case she had brought along. She didn't want to reveal to the taxi driver what she had in storage. She would come back later, after she found the truck driver who used to work for them and take more.

Outside, in the brilliant spring sunshine, her heart felt light, and she flung her small case onto the back seat of the cab as if that, too, had no weight. Perhaps their lives would get back on track after all.

When she boarded the train at dawn, she carried in her suitcase carefully selected equipment that would sell well in the villages. Items farmers had not seen since the beginning of the war and needed for making repairs. Axes, nails, saws, and hammers, whatever she could fit into her case. Each piece would become currency for food.

She sat on the train, a frail blonde woman, surrounded by tired soldiers traveling back to their villages, and men and women who looked thin and hungry, like her. *Were they all going for food*, she wondered and worried—*will there be enough for everyone to bring back? Where will I find a farmer willing to sell me food for hardware? How will I do it? Go from house to house, knocking on doors? Where? In what village?*

Then she chided herself, *Oh, what's the point of worrying? When I get there, at whichever village I'll get off, I'll find a way.* She leaned back against the hard wood of the seat and let the clickety clack of the wheels dull her anxiety as she stared out the window at the barren fields, decimated forests, and farmers pushing their ancient plows into the black earth, hoping it would sustain them once again, as it had for hundreds of years.

At mid-morning, most of the passengers brought out their small packets of food, wrapped in red-checkered cotton dishcloths or newspaper. For some, this was breakfast, for others a snack, or their midday meal. Piry, too, reached into her handbag and slowly unfolded the clean towel into which she had wrapped the end piece of a loaf of rye bread—her meal for the day.

She knew she should preserve this bread till she got really hungry but with everyone around her eating, she also knew that she could not just sit there. Others would notice that she had no food and pity her. She could not bear that idea. As she bit into the hardened, dry piece, her nostrils tingled with the smell of smoked salt bacon nearby. Slowly, surreptitiously, she followed the scent with her eyes. It came from the man sitting opposite her. It wouldn't do to look directly at him or his food. According to custom, staring at someone eating was impolite because it implied that the viewer "coveted the food out of the other's mouth." Piry was well mannered. She would rather die than reveal her aching hunger by peeking.

But the stocky, elderly peasant sitting across from her, knew. He was a tall man, wearing a lamb-fur lined winter jacket, and thick, dark grey wool pants that were tucked into his black leather boots. He had a weatherworn, kind face, and warm brown eyes now fixed on her. Then he looked down at his food, cut a chunk of bacon from the slab and a thick slice of bread from the home-baked loaf of rye before him. He placed the bacon on top of the bread. Piry watched, mesmerized, as his stiff, work-thickened fingers reached out toward her, offering the open sandwich: "It's not much, Miss," he said with the characteristic modesty of country folk, "But I'd be happy to share it with you."

Piry felt such a rush of saliva under her tongue that she could barely get the correct, polite response out, "Thank you so much but you won't have enough for yourself then."

"Oh, there's plenty for both of us," the man insisted, smiling. "You look like you could use a square meal, if you don't mind my saying so." With that, he leaned forward, pushing the food so close to Piry that she had to take it.

"I don't know how to thank you," Piry murmured with eyes moist over this unexpected kindness, holding herself back from wolfing the food down. For a moment she held the man's gaze in hers and saw that he understood her. This farmer, probably not old but prematurely wrinkled from a harsh life and hard work in the fields, could see into her very soul. Piry knew that he could read her hunger, her desperation, her sense of being lost in the world, yet fighting for a foothold with all her might. Aloud, all she uttered was the customary saying before a meal, "Good appetite," and when he responded with "To you too," she bit into the bacon and bread.

To Piry, no food ever before had tasted as good as this meal. She ate it slowly, savoring it, honoring the country folks' custom of not talking during the meal. But her thoughts ran wild. She ached for not being able to share the food with her daughters and Irén, yet she knew that saving it for them would be pointless. It would go bad by the time she got home. Besides, she needed sustenance right now, so she could negotiate without hunger pangs. I'll bring them baskets of food, she promised herself.

As the meal soothed her hunger, she thought, with a mischievous inner smile, Father and mother would have a heart attack, not to mention my in-laws or even Zoltan, if they could see me now. She relished the rich, greasy, crunchy texture of the bacon and sourdough taste of the bread. A perfect combination, yet this was the first time in her life that she had tasted bacon. Bacon was not kosher. Observant Jews were forbidden to eat pork—any part of a pig. Yet, eating it now, she felt like God sent it to her directly, to save her life, to infuse her with the strength she needed to succeed in her mission.

The constant ache of hunger abated as she filled up with the much-needed nourishment. Eating enough for the first time in months, brought color to her cheeks. What did it matter that bacon wasn't kosher? Who cared about dietary laws when food had become a survival item, not a matter of choice? Yes, she would observe kashrut again when she could afford it. Right now, she ate to gain strength. Her children needed her, and who knows in what condition Zoltan was going to return? He might be a walking skeleton, like the others—not a man to take the helm on arrival. She swallowed her last bite with a tightened throat.

"Another piece?" asked the farmer, his knife ready to slice her more food.

"Thank you, I couldn't eat a bite more", Piry smiled, patting her stomach.

"Maybe for the road then," he said, cutting the bacon and bread. "Take it for the road, don't be shy" he insisted, handing it to her.

Piry accepted it, and wrapped it into the same towel the dry piece of bread was buried in. "I don't know how to thank you," she whispered.

The man wiped the bacon grease off his pocket-knife with his red checkered towel, and clicking it shut, carefully slipped it into his coat pocket. Then he packed up the food into the wicker basket by his side, and ignoring her gratitude as good manners dictated, asked, "So where are you going Miss?"

Piry smiled at him. "Actually, I'm a married woman, with two children. My husband is not back yet from the war, and I'm going to a village to trade."

The man's curiosity was aroused. "My, you don't look a day over eighteen, Miss, if you don't mind my saying so. How old are your children?"

"Eight and the younger one almost five. I'm not as young as I look, Uncle." She smiled at him, using the customary title of respect to one's elders that was friendlier than addressing him as "Mister".

"So, if you don't mind my being nosey, what are you bringing to trade?"

"We were in the hardware business in Budapest. So, I'm bringing some things to exchange for food."

His dark brown eyes under bushy brows looked at Piry with increased curiosity. "Things like what?"

"Tell me what interests you, maybe I have it," she said, her natural merchant's instinct turning him into a buyer, rather than offering him what he may not want.

"I could do with nails, and a good new hammer, and maybe some other things too."

"I have all those," Piry nodded.

His face lit up, his eyes studied Piry more carefully. "I'll tell you what, young lady, if you haven't a specific village to go to, why don't you stop at ours. I'm sure my Mrs. could put you up for the night, and maybe we could do some business. I also have friends, so what I don't need, maybe they will." He smiled at Piry, awaiting her response.

Piry felt as though a great weight had fallen off her shoulders. She wouldn't have to search for a village or a place to stay. Nor would she have to go knocking on doors with her suitcase full of goods. She took a deep breath, making it look like she was weighing his offer, hiding her overwhelming joy and relief behind a sweet but reserved smile.

"Why, Uncle, that sounds like a very nice offer. Perhaps I'll take you up on it. But what will your wife say when you show up with an unexpected guest? I wouldn't like to burden your family." Her protest was the customary polite reticence, and they both knew it.

"Oh, she'll be glad to have you. Especially if you're also bringing some female items, like underwear."

Piry smiled, and said, "I'm afraid not on this trip. But I can, next time, if she tells me what she wants."

"That's settled then" he said and gave a little twirl to the ends of his bristly mustache, obviously pleased with himself.

"Where is your village, if you don't mind my asking," Piry smiled at him.

"It's a very small place, called Kakucs. The train will stop at Inárcs, a neighboring village, only four kilometers from Kakucs, and my wife will meet us at the station with our horse and buggy. Is that all right with you, Miss?"

"Of course it is," responded Piry with a broad grin. "I am honored to be invited by you."

"Oh, the honor is ours," said the man and leaned back on is seat, pleased at their arrangement.

It was mid-afternoon when the man said, "Here we are."

While the train slowed to a halt, he pulled his suitcase and Piry's off the rack and offered to carry it along with his own.

"Here, you can take this," and he handed to Piry the wicker food basket.

His wife was waiting outside the train station, sitting high in the driver's seat of a wood carriage drawn by two sturdy horses. She was a stout, middle-aged woman, dressed in typical country style clothes—a flowery flannel shirt with billowy sleeves, a warm body-hugging sheepskin vest over it, and multiple layers of pleated skirts, one on top of the other, that came down to the edge of her fur lined boots. She stared for a moment at Piry, walking alongside her husband, then loosely wrapping the leather straps of the harness to the front rail of the carriage she clambered down. She stood there, a stately figure, facing them; relaxed but expectant.

"Hi Ilonka," he greeted his wife. "Look what the train brought us!"

Then, turning to Piry with a smile said, "We never did properly introduce ourselves, Miss. My name is Paul Miko, and this is my wife, Ilonka."

"How do you do, Ma'am," Piry bowed her head politely while her mind was racing. Should she call herself by her wartime name or the real one? "I'm Piry Polyák, she finally blurted out, realizing that she had to keep her name the same as her travel documents.

Miko quickly explained to his wife that he had invited Piry to stay with them.

With customary country hospitality, Ilonka said, "God brought you, you're very welcome. We don't have much, but we'll be happy to share it with you."

"Thank you so much, I'm honored to stay with you," Piry responded as was expected.

With that, Miko put their luggage in the back, and the three of them climbed up to the front seat of the carriage. It was a work vehicle. The front part had a long wooden seat with a canvas roof against the elements, and the back part had high sides for carting farm tools, produce, or animals to the market. Normally, only two people would sit up front—but if needed, three could squeeze in together. Miko took the driver's seat, his wife sat next to him, and Piry sat on the end.

Miko gently tugged at the leather straps and made a clucking sound with his tongue. The two chestnut-colored horses began to trot at a brisk pace, their hooves clip-clopping on the hard ground, like a special set of drums, that set the tempo for the journey. Piry leaned against the wood back support with an enormous sense of relief. These were good people, and she was on her way to accomplish her goal. Someone 'up there' is watching out for me, she thought with a deep sense of gratitude.

The Mikos lived indeed in a small village. Their home, just like all the others on their street, was built with a side of the house facing the street, while the long main façade opened into their front yard. On approach, Piry and Mrs. Miko got off, so the latter could open the wide wood gate to let her husband drive the carriage to the back of the yard where the stable was.

Piry observed that in the middle of the front yard was a well. Away from the main house, at the back of the yard, were three smaller structures. One was a pigpen, the other a chicken coop, and the third, smaller building, she guessed to be the outhouse. Even in the fading light, Piry could see that this was not a poor household. They had animals and their own well. A large haystack towered against the fence at the rear of the yard, no doubt feed for the animals. A stately red rooster and several gold-red hens ran towards Ilonka, clacking as if to greet her.

Ilonka bent forward, her hand extended to the fowl, her fingers moving as though she was throwing them feed. "I'm back, my sweets," she said, "I know, you want your supper. Just wait a minute, you'll get it." She straightened up and smiled at Piry. "They are like part of the family," she explained.

Inside the house, Mrs. Miko led Piry into the "good room," as villagers called their living room. "Make yourself at home here, if you don't mind, you'll be sleeping in here, so just settle in. We'll make up the bed for you later, on the sofa."

"This is lovely, thank you," Piry said, looking around at the carved chairs and sofa, all decorated with hand embroidered doilies. "I can't thank you enough, for putting me up."

"Oh, don't mention it," Mrs. Miko said with well-mannered modesty, then added, "The facilities are outside. We've just a humble home, not like in the cities where you have it indoors."

"It's just perfect," Piry laughed. "I am not completely a city girl; I grew up visiting relatives in a village." She cut herself off, realizing, she had said more than she wanted to.

Oh, where?" came the natural response.

"Near Debrecen," Piry replied, suddenly uncomfortable. She didn't want to talk about herself or her family.

But she was in luck. Mrs. Miko didn't question her further. She nodded, and said, "I guess with the Russian troops there, you wouldn't want to go visiting now, would you?"

"That's right, I wouldn't."

They looked at each other, two women, from very different walks of life, but both familiar with the reputation of Russian soldiers concerning women. Piry found it interesting that news about the Soviet soldiers' behavior had reached even these untouched villages in south-central Hungary—but she thought it best not to elaborate on the subject.

There was a knock on the door, and Paul Miko walked in, carrying Piry's suitcase. He put it down and said to his wife, "Are you cooking dinner or just enjoying the company while you starve her and your poor husband to death!"

"I'm going, I'm going," laughed Mrs. Miko.

"I'll light the fire for you, so it will be nice and cozy by the time you go to sleep. Just let me know when I can bring in the wood."

Piry looked at the tall ceramic stove in a corner of the room. It was light green, and each tile had a raised flower design. "Any time. Though I can sleep with my coat on, and you wouldn't have to waste wood for me," she offered.

"You're my guest, I wouldn't dream of it," he said with pride. Then he left to bring in a basketful of logs.

Dinner was a simple fare but to Piry it felt like she was eating at the best restaurant in the world. They had vegetable soup with small bow-tie noodles, followed by a dish of paprikash chicken, richly spiced with red paprika, and accompanied with mashed potatoes. Piry had not eaten food like this since Budapest had become a war zone nine months ago. A part of her felt guilty for dining on such rich fare while her children and Irén were probably eating dry bread and weak tea. But it wouldn't have helped them if she had refused the food, so she gratefully ate and made a promise to herself that her children, too, will soon have such meals again.

During dinner she tried to steer the conversation away from her hosts' queries about her family lest they ask something she could not easily answer. Instead, she asked her hosts about their survival during the war. They had a son who was in the army, and they expected him to return from somewhere in Italy, soon. Their daughter was married and lived nearby. They had seen no fighting in their own village but had heard stories about the liberating Soviet army behaving worse than the Germans when they marched through the nearby villages and towns.

"After they left," Miko commented, "villagers would say, 'Yes, the Russians liberated us—from everything they could lay their hands on.'"

"So, let's hope they'll go home, and we can get on with our lives like before the war," sighed Mrs. Miko, her words sounding like a prayer.

"It's late, let's turn in," said Miko after dinner. Sated with good food and a couple of glasses of home-made red wine, he was feeling tired.

"We'll deal with business in daylight," he winked at Piry.

In the warm room, under a down filled cover, for the first time in a very long while, instead of fear and desperation, Piry felt hope rising in her heart. *I'll be able to get food for goods till Zoltan comes back, and then life will start all over again*, she thought, as she fell asleep listening to the soft crackle of the dying embers in the fireplace.

The next morning, after a hearty breakfast of bread, cheese, and a glass of milk, Piry spread out her merchandise on the central table in the living room. Miko looked with appreciation at the stock. There were wrenches, screwdrivers, a couple of hammers, a small jigsaw, files of various shapes and lengths, and three small bags, one filled with nails, the other with screws, and the third with nuts and bolts.

Watching his face, Piry could tell that these were items Miko had not seen for some time. She waited in silence while he hungrily eyed each tool, carefully picking some up and examining them from every angle. Finally, he selected tools and nails and asked how much she wanted for them.

"I don't know what food costs around here," she said quietly, so make me an offer.

Item by item, they bartered; hammer and screwdrivers for meat and potatoes; chisels for eggs; nails for cheese. Mrs. Miko threw in a large loaf of bread to seal the bargain.

Then, Miko offered to walk over to his neighbors and let them know what was still available.

By noon, all the hardware in Piry's suitcase had been replaced with food. Hams, cheeses, pork chops, some beef, and a whole plucked, eviscerated chicken, all carefully wrapped in old newspapers, nestled against fresh carrots, onions, and a good size bag of pinto beans. In the end, Mrs. Miko even gave her a wicker basket, packed with a second loaf of rye bread, more ham and cheese, and a bottle of red wine—so she wouldn't get hungry during her trip home.

"You can bring back the basket on your next trip," she told Piry.

Miko and his wife drove her to the train station in Inárcs. Carrying a list of requests for her return, Piry felt she had made important new friends in Kakucs village.

It was nearly midnight by the time the train pulled into the Southern Station in Budapest. Worn out but excited about her success, Piry caught the last bus to their apartment. Could this be the last time she took this route, she wondered. Before her next trip, she would have to move with the children back to their old apartment and let Irén go home to her own place.

Suddenly filled with anxiety, she wondered—will our apartment be there? Did it escape the bombing or is the building lying in rubble as so many others in the city? Will Zoltan be back by the time I need to make another trip for food? If not, with Irén gone, who will watch the children while I am away? She could feel a knot forming in the pit of her stomach again.

The bus pulled to her stop. As she got off, carrying her bags filled with food, she straightened her shoulders and thought, tonight we'll celebrate. Tomorrow will be time enough to worry about tomorrow.

Judith was ecstatic about the move back to their old home. She helped enthusiastically with the packing, and couldn't stop repeating, "Daddy will be there, Daddy will come home now."

Listening to her, Piry's heart lightened. Perhaps the child was right, it will all work out once they are back at their own place.

By contrast, Erika was profoundly unhappy about the move. She went to see Peter.

"We are leaving, and I will never see you again," she complained to him, her large hazel eyes filled with tears.

"Oh, I am sure we will see each other again" he consoled her.

"How?" Erika cried, tears rolling down her cheeks.

"You'll give me your address, and I'll come to visit you" he said brightly, though he wasn't entirely sure that this would be possible. Master Street, where they now lived, was on the outskirts of Budapest, and he was too young to travel alone to the inner city, where Erika's family was moving to. Patting her awkwardly on her shoulder, it broke his ten-year-old heart to see her cry.

"I'll ask my mom to take me there, don't worry," he tried to calm her.

"Are you sure?" she sobbed.

"Of course," he said with more confidence than he felt. Then, on an impulse, he bent down, and gently kissed Erika's cheek.

Erika instantly stopped crying. Her small fingers touched her cheek where his lips had been, and she stared up at him as though in shock. Kissing was for parents and relatives, but Peter was none of these. When his lips touched her skin, she felt a warm tingle go through her.

His brown eyes were looking at her with such intensity, that even four-and-a-half-year-old Erika recognized the look of love.

"Promise you will always be my friend," she demanded.

"I promise," Peter said, solemnly. "Now let's go to your house and ask your mom to give me your address."

◎◉◎

When moving day arrived, all they had to do was pack their small suitcases with their clothes and meager supplies into the hired car. Piry and Judith were excited about leaving but Erika felt sad and upset, as though something very important was being torn from her. She sat squeezed between Irén and her sister in the back seat of the taxi; Piry sat up front with the driver.

While the others were happily discussing the bright days ahead, and how they were going to restore their former lives, Erika sat with arms wrapped tightly around herself, watching their rush toward the inner city through tear-filled eyes. Yet she suppressed the urge to cry with the utmost willpower. She thought that she needed to hide her sorrow—lest she'd be ridiculed for crying over the loss of a friend instead of looking forward to the future. Little did she know that this was just another lesson in learning to conceal and control her feelings—an essential skill for the life that awaited them.

A few days later, after Irén helped them to settle in, she was ready to leave for her own apartment. She had visited it the week before, and much to her relief had found the building and her place intact. It was so, because, thinking that Irén had been deported by the Nazis, the concierge allowed her two sisters to move in from the countryside. When Irén showed up, they were all very apologetic and offered to leave within a few days. Now they were gone, and Irén could go home. She was hoping, that just as she had remained alive, so have her parents and brothers. That it was merely a matter of time before they would show up at her doorstep.

"We'll miss you terribly," said Piry and her daughters echoed her.

"It's not as if we're never going to see each other again." Irén was deeply touched but bravely put on a cheerful face. "We can visit each other as often as we like."

"I can't thank you enough," whispered Piry, holding back tears. "

"For what?" Irén protested.

"If it weren't for your help, I couldn't have gone through the war" Piry said, looking into her friend's eyes.

"And without you, I'd probably be dead, so we're even," responded Irén, pretending to be very matter of fact about their parting, to stop everyone from crying.

For a moment, both women's thoughts flashed through their struggles to survive, including Irén's rape, then skipped over it, like over a pebble on a sandy beach. They bravely smiled at each other, with a sense of shared victory.

"We did great together. Good luck to you. Keep in touch," Piry said, mustering up her fighting spirit.

They all hugged one last time, and then Irén was gone.

After locking the door behind her, Piry suddenly felt forlorn. A quick chill made her shudder, and she felt goose bumps rising on her skin. Time stopped for a moment and there was a deep silence in her head as if the world was gone and she stood alone in a dark and soundless space.

"Mommy, we're hungry, what's for dinner?"

Judith's voice brought her out of her strange reverie. She looked at her daughters, both standing in front of her by the door, waiting for her to take care of them. At least I've got them, she thought, and bent down to wrap her arms around each child's shoulder. "I don't know, let's go to the kitchen and see."

In their absence, the apartment had been occupied by the concierge's cousin and his family. They assumed that Piry and her family had perished during the war, and when she showed up to let the concierge know that they were alive, ready to move back in, Mrs. Fodor almost keeled over in shock. Apologizing, she explained how she had to allow her cousin to move in so no one else would take over the apartment. But now that Piry was back, naturally, the cousin and his family would be returning to their own home. When on the agreed upon day Piry moved in, the place was clean and ready for her. But much of her expensive furniture and beautiful Persian carpets were gone. So were many of her kitchen utensils, and expensive dinnerware.

"The Russians took it," Mrs. Fodor said, shrugging her shoulders, "You know how those people were, my dear. They just went from apartment to apartment, collecting everything they could lay a hand on. God only knows how they will haul all that loot back to Russia!"

Since Irén had the same experience at her place, Piry decided it was better not to argue with the woman, nor care whether it was the Russians or her family who liberated Piry of her belongings. It mattered little at this point. They were alive and back in their home. Losing some things was the least of her concerns. With the concierge's help, she managed to get beds, and a table and chairs for the kitchen. That's all they needed for the moment. When Zoltan returned, they'd recoup their losses.

There was still no word about him and now, without Irén, she had two children to take care of alone. But she was young, and strong, and full of optimism. They had survived the worst—now it was just a matter of time for life to become normal again.

◎◉◎

It was the end of May 1945. Trees were in full bloom on the wide boulevards of Budapest. Dark winter clothes were switched for lighter spring colors in beiges and greens. There was still no news of Zoltán, or her parents, or any of her other family members. Piry was apprehensive but the daily care of her children kept her too busy to do anything about it. Although she kept up her hope that one day Zoltán and the rest of her family would return, she began to wonder how she could make a living till they did—and sometimes hesitantly added—if they did. In any case, she needed to find a job or start a business for steady income. She did not feel she could continue the wholesale hardware business—that was a man's job. She needed some work that would allow her to also be there for her children.

She required time without the responsibility of caring for the girls to get their lives unto a normal track again. She found a summer camp for Judith and a different one for Erika, for her age group, both starting the first week of June. It promised to be a good summer for the girls, as both were going to be at resorts in the Sáros Hills north of Budapest. Lots of fresh air and activities awaited them in the country which was at peace again.

On a warm, sunny morning, she took Judith to meet the group of children and their Camp Leader near the Western train station and was relieved to find that Judith joined them without a protest. However, when she took Erika to the meeting point near the Eastern Station, there was a large truck waiting to transport the two dozen or so children, and Erika screamed and refused to get on the truck.

"They will hurt me!" she cried, desperately clinging to Piry.

"No one will hurt you, darling," Piry assured her."

"Mommy, please, please don't let them take me away," Erika screamed, as she was hoisted on the truck by a hefty young man, one of the counselors from the camp.

"She'll be all right once we get going," he assured Piry. "Just leave, Ma'am, and she'll calm down."

With a heavy heart, Piry followed the Counselor's advice. On her way home on the streetcar, she suddenly thought of a reason why Erika might have been so afraid of getting hurt. It wasn't her wartime experience of "being taken away," as Erika called it, for Piry had carefully explained to the child what summer camp was. It was an earlier memory, in kindergarten that must have caused Erika's fear.

In 1943, before the war had totally disrupted their lives, Judith had been attending first grade in a private school, and Erika was enrolled in an exclusive kindergarten, run by two well-educated German ladies.

Many cultured Hungarians spoke German, and Piry thought it a good idea for Erika to start learning the language at an early age. She had done the same for Judith, who had then continued to study German as a second language at her elementary school.

Erika loved kindergarten. Since German was the only language spoken there, she began to understand and speak it in just a few weeks. Her teachers gave Piry high praise for Erika's intelligence but complained that the child simply would not sit still. During playtime Erika was fine, for she could run and skip to her heart's desire. She got along well with the other children, especially with the boys who challenged her to all sorts of games. One of these was to climb on chairs stacked high on top of each other, and then competing to see who could jump off and land the best. With a muscular built like her father, Erika could well hold her own and had often won. This earned her respect among the boys but the envy of her girlfriends.

The two teachers acknowledged that Erika was a tomboy. They also recognized that she was quick at learning skills, like tying her own shoelaces or using wood blocks to build structures. However, when it came to story time, Erika became a discipline problem.

This was a period when the children had to sit on their small wooden chairs and listen to a story read aloud by one of their teachers. When the reading was finished, the children had to show their comprehension of the story by answering questions and engaging in a discussion.

Erika's hand was always raised; she wanted to be called for the answers and had little patience for the others who were slower or hesitant to speak. When she was ignored by the teachers, Erika fidgeted on her small stool, and at times would whisper the answer or shout it out loud, mostly out of boredom while the other children stumbled over words and phrases.

The strict German teachers reprimanded Erika when she did that. They ordered her to sit still when she rocked in her chair, and Erika would try to obey but simply could not. One day, during a particularly slow response by a little girl, Erika got so agitated that she fell over, chair and all. The other children burst into raucous laughter, but the teachers were not amused.

Frau. Klaus, who ran the kindergarten, shouted loudly, "Stop. All of you stop! This is not a laughing matter! Back to your story! And you Erika, if you can't sit still on your own, we will have to teach you how."

Then, while Fraulein Ingeborg, the younger teacher, continued the discussion, Frau Klaus picked up Erika's chair, and set it down behind the other children. She motioned Erika to come and stand by it. Frau Klaus took a large jar of wood glue and smeared it on the seat. She ordered Erika to sit down and to not move till she was permitted to do so.

When the story discussion was over, it was time for the children to get ready to go home. Erika was told she, too, could rise. When she did, the chair rose with her.

It was glued solid to the back of Erika's naked skin, since she had lifted her skirt before sitting down, to keep it clean. No one expected her to get glued to the chair. The children laughed, the teachers gasped, and Erika cried out in pain as the weight of the chair, small as it was, pulled on her skin.

"Sit down!" commanded Frau Klaus.

Erika sat down again, relieving the pain. The teachers tended to the other children who were being picked up by their parents or nannies—then turned to Erika.

"We must help you to get unstuck, before you are picked up," said Frau Klaus, looking at Erika with considerable distaste.

Then the two women got to work. They asked Erika to lean forward and stand up halfway, while each woman slowly pushed and tried to lift her skin off the chair, inch-by-inch.

"It hurts!" Erika shouted, as they struggled to pry the back of her thighs off the chair.

"Just be patient, we're doing our best," growled Frau Klaus. Fraulein Ingeborg said nothing. She was slowly, carefully pulling away Erika's skin, trying not to tear it. But it was hurting, and Erika kept crying out.

At that point, Erika's nanny, Kata, arrived, to take her home. "What's wrong with Erika?" Kata asked, seeing the two teachers bending over her.

Frau Klaus turned to Kata, explaining somewhat apologetically, "The child is glued to the chair, we'll get her off in a minute."

With that, she reached with one hand for Erika's shoulder, and with the other grabbed the back of the chair. With one swift motion she pushed Erika forward and yanked the chair off.

Erika screamed. Large patches of her skin had stayed on the seat, and she was now a quivering, crying mess, as the backs of her thighs were raw and bleeding.

"Get some wide bandages! Quick!" Frau Klaus ordered. Fraulein Ingeborg ran to their office and returned carrying a First Aid Kit. With skilled hands, Frau Klaus wrapped the gauze thickly around Erika's thighs, and tearing the ends into halves, she tied the bandages.

"There, now, you'll be just fine," Frau Klaus said, satisfied with her quick rescue work.

Erika was not only in great pain, she was also seething with anger. She grabbed her school bag and walked out the front door without a word, ignoring even Kata, who followed her speechless. Erika knew she should have said good-bye, she knew she should have thanked Frau Klaus for bandaging her. But she also knew that something terribly wrong had been done to her, and she was never going to return to this place—no matter what her mother would say.

Kata decided to take a taxi home with Erika because the child could barely walk and certainly wouldn't be able to sit in a streetcar. Erika lay on her stomach across Kata's lap in the back seat, trembling with tension and pain. She hobbled into their apartment, fell into her mother's arms, and burst into a heartrending sob. She was crying so hard, that it was Kata who had to tell Piry what had happened. Piry was outraged.

"I'm taking you to a doctor right now," she told the crying child. "And tomorrow, I'm going to have a little talk with Frau Klaus!"

It took weeks for Erika's thighs to heal. All that time, she had to sleep on her stomach, for she could not tolerate anything touching the back of her legs. When the gauze bandage had to be changed, it had to be moistened so as to get it unstuck. Erika endured this daily ordeal gritting her teeth in agony, because even the cool water caused a burning sensation on the back of her thighs. But slowly the wounds healed, and despite her misery, Erika missed kindergarten.

She missed playing with her friends there, and the story sessions, hard as it had been to sit through the discussions afterwards. To stave off utter boredom, she asked Piry's permission to sit in on her sister's tutorial sessions that took place in their living room every afternoon during the week. Judith was getting mediocre grades at school in math and reading, so Piry had hired a private tutor, Stefán, a charming young man, to come and work with her.

Piry suspected that Judith was missing her father, and it was affecting her interest in learning and everything around her. She often found her daughter morose, sitting quietly in her room, staring into nothing. Piry thought, that apart from needing the lessons, the presence of a male figure in Judith's life would be a good influence. Judith was a slow and methodical learner. She had to be carefully explained each step of the reading process and the math tasks of multiplication and division. Erika sat spellbound, quietly listening, and learning.

One day, when Judith was having a particularly difficult time reading a word aloud, Erika burst out, "No, Judith, it's "frontier, not forntier".

Stefán was stunned but hid his reaction. Instead, he told Erika, "You must keep quiet, or you will have to leave the room."

When the session was over, Stefán asked to speak with Piry.

"I think Erika is learning everything I'm teaching Judith, faster than her sister. Is that all right, Mrs. Fábián?"

Piry was taken aback, thought for a moment, then said, "I think it is. Why not, if the child is capable of learning? Just make sure it's Judith who is really making progress!"

Thus, Erika learned to read and write alongside her older sister, and as much math as she could comprehend at age three. She could spend her time reading while she was recovering. The big picture books Stefán had left at their home seemed to soothe Erika's restlessness better than any other activity. But by the time Erika's skin healed completely, the siege of Budapest began, and all schools had closed down.

Piry, recalling this as Erika's dreadful experience at the kindergarten, called her summer resort director. She explained to the Director over the phone why the child might have a problem adjusting to being there. Piry told the Director, "Once Erika sees that she is being treated well, she will enjoy the company of the other children and the camp activities. But please contact me if Erika indeed has a problem with being there."

With her children away, Piry was free to travel to Kakucs village a couple of times, and with Mikos' help sold all the hardware she could carry there. But she knew that by the end of the summer, when her children returned from camp, she would have to have established a regular income in Budapest.

The building where their store used to be had been hit by a bomb and was a now just a pile of rubble. Piry thought, she should start looking at new locations, so when Zoltán returned, he could make the final choice. But another week passed, and Piry was beginning to feel as though she were living in a vacuum concerning Zoltán and their families.

So, she came up with a new idea. Wearing her most attractive pre-war summer outfit, a green linen dress that showed off her trim waist and displayed her shapely ankles, she slipped her small feet into a pair of white, high-heel sandals. She took time to brush and shape her shoulder length dark blonde hair and added just a hint of rouge to her sallow cheeks and lips. It doesn't hurt to look good when one goes to see officials, Piry thought, as she took a final look at herself in the bedroom mirror.

Streetcars were running again, and she could take one that left her off just a few blocks from the Ministry of Interior Affairs. Once inside, she quickly glanced at the directory by the porter's desk, and asked to see Mr. Andor Szegedi, listed as the official in charge of citizen registration.

"You can't do that, Madam, without an appointment—or have you got an appointment?" the clerk asked, opening the appointment book on his desk.

Piry sized up the man's pale, tired face, and the lines under his eyes. He wore a threadbare jacket, his shirt was frayed at the neck, and his hands were gnarled, likely, from a lifetime of hardship. He was obviously a low-ranking clerk, working for starvation wages.

She reached into her handbag, pulled out a few bills, and discreetly slipping them under the open registry book, saying with a smile: "I am his cousin. This is meant to be a surprise."

The clerk carefully lifted the book, glanced at the money, squinted at Piry, and shrugged.

"Don't blame me, if his secretary throws you out! Third floor, his office is to the right, elevator is not working."

"Thank you," Piry smiled at him sweetly, and straightening her shoulders just a bit more, headed for the stairs. In the hallway on the top floor, handwritten card pasted on the white French doors read: Andor Szegedi, Ministry of Interior, Registration Office.

Piry knocked lightly, then pressed down the brass handle, and entered. A surprised, middle-aged woman looked up from the paperwork on her desk and was about to protest the intrusion when Piry gave her a bold, brilliant smile.

"Pardon the interruption," she said quickly, but I am here to see Mr. Szegedi."

"Is he expecting you?" the secretary asked in a cautious but not unfriendly manner. These days all sorts of people came to see Mr. Szegedi, and he didn't always inform her as to their identity. She had to be really careful to protect him but at the same time, not to offend a possibly important visitor.

Piry didn't want to answer that question. Instead, she replied, "Please tell him, Piry Fábián is here to see him on an urgent matter. She had no idea how he would react to this message. She used her name, simply because she figured, he was a man, and on hearing that a woman wanted to see him, he might be curious. The idea was to get her foot in the door.

As the secretary knocked, a man's voice shouted, "Come in!".

"Piry Fábián!" he exclaimed, grabbing her hands and pulling her into the room. Neither of them even noticed the fast retreat of the secretary, as she softly closed the door behind them.

"How did you find me?!" Andor asked, his voice betraying joy and wonder, holding her at arms' length, drinking in her face.

"I had no idea it was you!" she responded, feeling shaken, hardly believing her luck. Now, as when they first met that dark night, he seemed to exude a power that deeply affected her. She felt like falling into his arms, she felt like kissing him wildly, and felt the sharp irony of the purpose of her visit like a knife in her chest. Their eyes locked for a fleeting moment, and she knew, he too, was feeling the same electric connection. Yet, with enormous self-control, he let go of her and retreated a step.

"How are the girls?" he asked lamely.

"Fine, they both survived, thanks to you."

"So glad to hear it. But then, if you didn't know it was me you were coming to see, what brings you here?

Piry looked at him, and reading her expression, he stopped her from answering: "Let me guess. You simply came to the ministry because your husband has not returned, and you wanted to know…"

Piry nodded. "I've been at the train station for months, and nothing. Nothing at all. No news whatsoever," she explained, awkwardly stumbling over the words.

His expression turned solemn. "I'll look into it if you'd like."

"Thank you," she whispered, unable to move, just staring at him.

"Where will I find you, once I have news?"

"I moved back to our pre-war apartment. I also go by my real name now Piry Fábián. Is yours real—the one on the door?"

He gave her a wry smile. "It'll do for now."

Piry laughed, then on an impulse asked, "Would you come for dinner—with or without the news? After all, you never did during the war. Dr. Komlos told me you had gone to Russia."

Surprise flashed across his face as he studied her, and then he said with a strained smile, "I'm rather busy these days. Not much time for dinner. But perhaps for you…"

She jotted down her address and his eyebrows rose slightly as he glanced at it. It was one of the most elegant locations in the city…St. István Boulevard, next door to the Comedy Theater, and just a few blocks from the Danube. He studied his calendar. This was Monday, perhaps he could free himself later in the week.

"Would Thursday at 8 p.m. suit you?"

"That would be fine," Piry said, hardly able to breathe.

A silence ensued as their eyes met, and he suddenly pulled her into his arms, his lips touching hers. She felt herself responding with an eagerness that deepened their kiss, as Piry felt a powerful current run through her body. Were it not for him holding her close, her knees would have buckled.

Sensing her feelings, he stopped, gently pushing her away. "Go now." His voice was husky.

Piry had no idea how she made it down the stairs of the Ministry, stopping along the way, pressing a palm over her pounding heart. This was totally insane. She had never had this reaction toward a man. Not even for her husband, certainly not when she had first met him.

It was a bright June morning in 1933, in Debrecen, the third largest city in Hungary, where Piry and her family lived, that she went to visit her best friend, Bertha at the latter's home.

"My cousin is here from Budapest." Bertha sounded excited.

Piry was curious. This cousin seemed to be the "odd man out" in the illustrious Fábián family. Ferenc Fábián was the Secretary of Debrecen's Jewish Congregation—a euphemism for being its president. Piry knew him and his wife, Hermina, and three of their sons, because once in a while they came to dine at her father's restaurant. But she had never met their fourth son who had moved to Budapest.

Bertha and her visiting cousin were sitting on the porch at her house. Bertha saw Piry approaching and waved to her to come directly up the stairs. Piry ran up, her long dark blonde hair flying, her face flushed by the summer heat. She was wearing a white cotton dress with small, multicolored flowers printed in a random pattern on the collar and the skirt. A crocheted white scarf was swinging in her hand. She brought it along in case she needed to cover up her bare arms on meeting a religious elder.

They rose when Piry reached them. Bertha said, "Piry, meet my favorite cousin, Zoltán."

He stood at about 5'11", built like an athlete with a stocky, muscular body. He had wavy black hair and dark brown eyes. He was a good-looking young man, with a warm smile that revealed even white teeth.

"Fábián Zoltán, at your service," he said, as he extended his hand.

"Kohn Piry." She shook hands with him and couldn't help noticing how strong and padded his palm felt against hers.

Bertha brought out glasses of cold lemonade, and they settled on the porch in comfortable wicker chairs, with a small round table in front of them.

During a half an hour of polite conversation, Piry learned that Zoltán was staying for a week. He was single, and his wholesale hardware business was located in the center of Budapest. He knew that Piry's family owned the largest kosher restaurant in Debrecen.

Finally, Piry stood up. "Sorry, I must leave. I am expected at the restaurant."

"I'll walk there with you," Zoltán quickly offered.

There was a fleeting smile on Bertha's face as she said, "I'll see you both later."

Zoltán used the walk to ask Piry about herself. For some reason, she felt compelled to talk about her life, something she normally would not do. "I was 5 months old at the outbreak of World War I in 1914, when my father was recruited to fight at the Russian front. He returned at the end of the war, in

1918, to find that my mother, his beloved wife, had died of typhoid fever but his 4-year-old daughter, I, had survived that terrible illness.

My mother was the oldest of ten sisters, all of whom doted on me, their orphaned niece. My father remarried when I was five years old. I've got a half-brother and two half-sisters, but being the eldest, I'm the one my parents expect to help out at their restaurant. I hate doing it. I would have much preferred to study and become a gym teacher." Piry's voice trailed off. She had no idea why she told all this to a total stranger.

Zoltán smiled at her. He told Piry, he himself was heavily involved in sports. Rowing and amateur wrestling—prize fighting—in Budapest. So, he could easily understand her love of gymnastics. Before they reached her father's restaurant, Zoltán said, "I'd love to see you again. Is that possible?"

"I usually have a couple of hours free in the mornings," Piry replied. She liked him. He was older than the students who came to her father's restaurant, and that appealed to her. He also seemed mature, more like a man than the boys who tried to court her. That, too, attracted her. To top it off, she liked his looks.

They spent a couple of hours together every morning that week. They walked through the forest that bordered the west side of Debrecen, and talked about themselves, their dreams, and their goals in life.

Zoltán had grown up in Budapest, where his father had been the Chief Rabbi of a large Jewish temple. When he decided to retire, he was invited to become the Secretary of the Jewish Congregation in Debrecen. But Zoltán did not want to move there. He was the second eldest of four sons, and from the time he was a young boy, he had a love of tools and hardware. When he turned fourteen, instead of going to High School, despite his father's strong objections, Zoltán insisted on becoming a smith's apprentice. He learned to work with metal and bend it to his will, making tools. He also learned to work with gold and silver, preferring to make small sculptures of the precious metals, instead of jewelry.

On Friday morning, he said to Piry, "I am leaving for Budapest early Sunday, and would like to see you before I go. But tomorrow morning I'll have to go to the synagogue, and since it will be my last day in town, I'll have to spend the evening with my parents. So, would you be able to meet me Saturday in the afternoon?"

Piry had mixed feelings about meeting with him. They had gotten to know each other quite well during the week and now she didn't know what to expect. She had no idea what compelled her to have spent the week meeting with him every morning. She wondered what she could hope for when he was leaving and clearly had no intention of returning soon. Nor could she just go and follow him to Budapest, her life was set in Debrecen. So, what was the point of meeting again—just to say good-bye? Yet, she agreed to see him.

Zoltán waited for her as usual, around the corner from her home. Piry didn't want him to come for her at her house; didn't want to introduce him to her parents. After all, what could she say about this new acquaintance? She knew that people in town had seen them walking together but she didn't care. He was leaving, so what was there to gossip about? At home, she merely made excuses, saying, she was going out on errands, or seeing a friend. Her father was always at the restaurant, and Hermina, her stepmother, treated her with care but not a lot of affection.

Many years ago, when Piry was still a small child, and her stepmother was new to her, Piry did something Hermina didn't like. She advanced toward Piry with her hand raised to slap her. But she tripped and fell forward, twisting her right arm so badly that she wore it in a sling for a week. Believing that perhaps it was Piry's dead mother who had caused her to fall, Hermina never raised her hand at Piry again. Nor did she ever get close to Piry. She was good to her, but Piry never felt the love and concern Hermina showed towards her own children. Thus, close as Piry was to adulthood, it was easy for her to come and go as she pleased.

Zoltán looked solemn in his black Sabbath suit and tall hat. Piry, though she had not attended services that morning, was also dressed formally, in a light blue, long sleeve blouse with a small, checkered pattern, and a navy skirt. She smiled at Zoltán as he joined her, both of them walking in a comfortable rhythm toward their usual path in the forest. They spoke little till they got to a clearing, where an empty bench awaited them.

They sat down, and Zoltán turned to Piry.

"Since I am leaving tomorrow, I'd like to take this opportunity to have a serious talk with you," he said rather stiffly.

Piry tilted her head a little and looked at him expectantly. "Go ahead."

"I think we've gotten to know each other fairly well this week, and I really like you. I am a very serious man, as you might have gathered that by now. So, what I wish to say to you is not done lightly. My situation is that I have three brothers, all of whom are studying at a university. And although my father is still working, he does not have the means to pay for their tuition. I do. I will be finished paying for their education in three years. I would like to ask for your hand in marriage, but I cannot get married for the next three years. You're a beautiful young woman, and it may not be fair to ask this of you—but would you wait for me?" He stopped abruptly, his eyes pleading with her.

Piry's heart was pounding. She closed her eyes for a moment. I like him more than any other young man I had met so far. But how could I decide on him now, I had just met him, and he is asking me to wait for three years? I'll be an old lady by then, I'll be twenty-one. And yet, and yet. He is handsome, hard-working, obviously very responsible. He would take good care of me once I marry him.

Bertha implied during one of our discussions, that he is quite wealthy, a great catch. Marrying him would mean a life in Budapest, away from this provincial town, away from my father's restaurant, my stepmother, and the small-town mentality I so hate. Definitely, he might be the best husband I could ever hope for…and here he is, asking me to marry him.

Piry opened her eyes, and looking into Zoltán's dark eyes, nodded, "I'll wait for you."

He lifted her hands, and kissed each one, whispering, "Thank you."

It was the end of May 1935. The three years of waiting was over. Piry and Zoltán stood side by side in the temple under the chupa, the canopy set up for the marriage ceremony of Jewish couples.

The temple was full, practically the entire Jewish community of Debrecen had attended the wedding. Hermina, Piry's stepmother, looked pleased. Her three children, Lilly, sixteen, Peter, fourteen, and Judith twelve, were all dressed up for the occasion, and seemed genuinely happy for their half-sister's good fortune. As Piry and Zoltan slowly walked down the aisle, after their vows had been made, Piry hugged Lilly by the exit door of the temple, and whispered to her, "You're next!"

All nine of Piry's birth-mother's sisters had attended with their families.

Zoltán's parents, his three brothers, Tibor, László, and Dénes, and numerous aunts and uncles had come with their families, plus many friends. Even some of the restaurant's Christian clientele had been invited. After all, the children of two important families in Debrecen were getting married, and the town came out to celebrate this happy event.

Piry's father had closed his restaurant to the public so they could have their wedding feast there after the ceremony. While everyone was still enjoying the food and the music, at midnight, Piry and Zoltán slipped away. They changed into travel clothes and took the dawn train to Budapest to start their married life together.

They arrived in the afternoon at Zoltán's newly rented apartment on Saint István Boulevard, one of the most prestigious locations in the city. Piry was impressed and overjoyed by her new home. It was a spacious corner apartment, on the first floor, with three bedrooms, maid's quarters, kitchen with a pantry, and even a laundry room. The living room and master bedroom faced the main boulevard, the other two bedrooms had windows to the quiet courtyard. It was sparsely furnished, and Zoltán explained, "It's waiting for you to furnish it the way you want."

They settled in, unpacked, and at Zoltán's suggestion even had some pastry and coffee till early evening set in. Then Zoltán led Piry to the bedroom. Seeing the large double bed, Piry suddenly stood very still, feeling apprehensive. Zoltán, picking up on her feelings, discreetly left the room, allowing Piry to prepare for bed. She quickly changed into the nightgown she had brought with her, and pulling the door ajar, slipped into bed, then called out to Zoltán, "You can come in!".

He entered, already in pajamas, and slipped under the covers next to Piry. He leaned over Piry, gently took her into his arms, and started kissing her. Piry responded, but when his hands slid under her nightgown, she stopped him.

"Please give me time…I'm very tense. This is all so new to me, I'm scared."

Much as he desired her, Zoltán decided to be patient. He wanted their marriage to start off the right way. He understood that his bride was shy, and of course afraid, even embarrassed. So, he gave her time.

A week passed, and Piry was still pushing him away when it came to consummating their marriage.

During the day he went off to work, Piry went shopping for food, for furniture, draperies, and all the necessities of setting up a new household. She hired a maid to help her. The young girl, Kata Polyák, came from a Hayduhatház, a small village in northern Hungary, to earn her dowry by working as a maid. Being almost the same age, the two young women got along well, and enjoyed establishing a household routine. Kata cleaned and cooked, Piry did the shopping and teaching Kata how she liked to have things done.

At night, after an excellent meal, they left Kata to clean up and Zoltán would often take Piry for a walk around their neighborhood, familiarizing her with the city. Piry was happy and adjusted easily to their new, shared lives, except for the end of the day. Each night she would allow Zoltán to kiss her and hold her, touch her with increasing intimacy but could not go through with their union. He would try, and she would pull away from him, saying, "It hurts!"

At the end of the week, Zoltán suggested that they spend Sunday at his yacht club. He introduced Piry to his friends there and took her kayaking on the Danube. After lunch, it was customary for club members to retire to their own cabins to rest for a couple of hours in the heat of the summer day.

It was here, on the narrow cot in Zoltán's cabin, that they finally consummated their marriage. Later, Piry would tease him, saying, "The only reason you could get me was that the walls were too thin, and I couldn't scream."

Actually, it took some time before Piry began to experience the pleasure of their union but once she did, it became a cornerstone of their marriage. It was ritualistic, following orthodox Jewish practices. At the beginning Piry found this absurd but later learned to appreciate it. When she had her monthly period, Zoltán wouldn't even kiss her. Piry found it insulting and ludicrous that Orthodox Jews considered a woman 'impure' during her menses. But Zoltán was profoundly religious, and she had to go along. After her last day of bleeding, he insisted that Piry go to the ritual bath, the Mikvah, to be 'cleansed'.

Piry could have died she was so embarrassed by this ceremony. Two elderly hags greeted her and led her to a dressing room. There they asked her to strip all her clothes, and naked, led her to the bathing room. She was told to step into a tub. Then the women dunked her from head to toe under the hot water that filled a small, but deep tub. She would come up for air, then they would push her under again, three times in a row, ending the ritual with a prayer. Then they handed her a towel to go and shower before getting dressed again.

Piry could just imagine the lascivious comments they would make after a young wife's bath. For after a woman had been 'cleansed,' she was once again allowed to make love with her husband.

The women at the Mikvah kept a list of their clientele, and God save the woman who did not show up for her monthly ritual bath, for it was a strict observance that nothing should stop except pregnancy.

At first, Piry, was so resentful of this 'public ceremony' of her private life with Zoltán that she carried her anger to him as well. He patiently explained to her, "The waiting makes me hunger for you all the more. If we could make love at just any time, all the time, it would soon become a routine act. This way, having to abstain for more than a week, makes me anticipate the joy of our union. Knowing that we have a time limit, makes my desire for you more intense."

Although she was too modest to admit it, she agreed with him, and loved him all the more for teaching her the wisdom behind the custom. Slowly, she learned to ignore the public aspect of her monthly baths and to eagerly anticipate her nights with Zoltán.

He was also willing to teach her about his business, and the cultural life available to them in Budapest. They went to plays, concerts, and art exhibits. She began to read famous secular authors and truly enjoyed the evenings of entertainment Zoltán and she attended.

Despite his liberal interests in cultural events, in some ways Zoltán remained extremely conservative, much to Piry's annoyance. One night, on their way to a play, as they stepped out of the apartment, Zoltán noticed that Piry had put on a light shade of lipstick.

"Take it off immediately," he demanded.

"I will not," Piry countered stubbornly.

"We're not going anywhere till you do," Zoltán announced and planted himself solidly against the railing of the corridor outside their apartment.

Piry, realizing, that they will arrive late to the show unless she concedes, dutifully but angrily rubbed off her lipstick.

"Happy now?" she pouted at him.

"I won't have my wife looking like 'a woman of easy virtue'" was his response.

On Sundays Piry joined Zoltán at his sport club. With his encouragement, she finally had a chance to explore her gymnastics abilities by working with a trainer he had hired for her. She had never been happier in her life.

Then, six months into their marriage, Piry woke up one morning with a headache and nausea that would seldom stop for nine months. She was pregnant and miserable. Her maid, Kata, tried to alleviate Piry's nausea by giving her every folk medicine known to in her village, but to no avail.

Zoltán also tried to help Piry. He brought her any food she desired, mostly pickles in the middle of the night, soda water by the gallon, and he seemed to suffer with Piry, in empathy. Finally, after nine agonizing months, she gave birth to a daughter. At first, she thought Zoltán would resent that their first child was 'only a girl,' for most Hungarian men, even Jewish men, wanted a boy. But she was wrong. Zoltán was ecstatic. They named her Judith, and their parents and all their siblings came for a visit to celebrate the birth of the first grandchild in the family.

Judith was not a pretty child. She had large blue eyes, and a very ordinary round face with a pug nose. But to Piry, Zoltán, and their large family, she was the most precious thing alive. Zoltán would rush home after work to bathe her. He also fed Judith the late-night bottle, change her diaper and then put her back to the crib. Piry, despite Kata's help, was exhausted and grateful for being relieved at night of breastfeeding as her motherly duty.

Wanting to help Piry to recover, Zoltán hired a nanny for the baby. Six weeks after Judith was born, Piry went to the Mikvah, and their lives resumed with the added joys and complications a child brought to them.

On March 13, 1938, the world around them grew more complicated. Judith was only six months old when Germany annexed Austria. By the time the family celebrated Judith's first birthday at the end of August, Germany had swallowed half of Poland. Encouraged by the German Government's unpunished activity, the Hungarian Government made demands to recover the territory it had lost after World War I. Acting as arbitrators, the German and Italian Ministers of Foreign Affairs returned to Hungary a portion of what was at that time Southern Slovakia.

The acquisition of this territory increased the Jewish population of Hungary. Since the 1920s Hungary had instituted a quota for the number of Jewish students accepted at universities. Encouraged by the "Anschluss," the union of Germany and Austria, in May of 1938 the Hungarian government passed a new law, restricting Jewish employment in all professions and industries to a mere twenty percent.

Since Zoltán owned his own business, he was not affected by these laws. Nor was his oldest brother, Tibor, since he was a rabbi. However, his two university student brothers, were. Dennis, the third brother, was a medical student, and had to move to Prague to finish his training as a physician. László, the youngest one, studying at the Faculty of Physical Education in Budapest, was told that he could no longer attend.

He and Zoltán were not close, for Lászlo was not an observant Jews and lived a totally secular life. Furthermore, he belonged to a Zionist organization, advocating emigration to Palestine as their true homeland.

Soon after being thrown out of the university, Lászlo came to say goodbye to Zoltán and Piry. He and his girlfriend, Beatriz, were leaving for Palestine.

"If you were smart, you'd come too, with your whole family," Lászlo said fervently to his older brother. "The situation is going to get a lot worse here."

"Nonsense," Zoltán replied. "On and off, there have always been waves of anti-Semitism in Hungary. This, too, shall pass."

The brothers wished each other luck as they warmly embraced. They had no way of knowing that this would be the last time they did.

László's predictions came to be true. Starting in 1939, the Hungarian government instituted a forced labor service for all Jewish men of military age. Zoltán and his brother Tibor were past this age, and for a time they continued living as normally as it was possible with what felt like a tightening noose around the Jewish population.

Zoltán began to teach Piry in earnest about his business. "Should I be called in for service, you'll need to know everything so you can carry on and support the family," he told her.

Piry loved the opportunity to learn. She had a good head for business and enjoyed working with inventories and figures. Zoltán had to admit that his wife was not a typical "rich man's wife".

"You forget that I helped out in my father's restaurant since I was fourteen," Piry reminded him. "I like working in a business."

"You're also a mother, and should be at home with your daughter more," he gently reminded her."

"She is too young to know the difference," Piry responded. The Nanny has more patience for her at this stage than I. When she gets a bit older, I'll spend more time with her."

It was a tense and sad Christmas season in 1939 in Budapest. The war was raging in Europe, and everyone knew it was merely a matter of time before Hungary would be forced to get involved. Yet, life went on almost in a normal way. Piry and Zoltán took their young daughter to Debrecen to be with the family over the holiday season. They returned to a bitter cold snowy January 1940 in the capital, but business was still good and Zoltán thought they would somehow weather the political situation unscathed.

CHAPTER 6

IT WAS MID-JANUARY OF 1940 that Piry began to wonder about her period. They had been very light for the past few months, and this month she had no sign of it at all. Normally, being quite regular, she went to see their family doctor. He examined her and told her to dress and meet him in his office. He sat behind his desk and peering over his glasses at Piry, sitting across from him, he said, "I don't know how to tell you this."

Piry's heart jumped, expecting him to tell her that she had a deadly disease. But she sat still, waiting for the doctor to continue.

"You seem to be more than three months pregnant," he finally blurted out.

"Is that all?!" Piry exclaimed, flooded with joy.

The doctor stared at her as if she had lost her mind. "Mrs. Fábián, these are very hard times. Most women start crying in this office when they hear of bringing a child into this world, with the war and all…"

"Doctor, you don't understand, I'm so happy that I'm pregnant and not sick! I don't even care about the war! Piry explained.

"That is wonderful," he sighed with relief. "According to my calculations, your baby will be due at the end of May or early June."

Zoltán was as happy as Piry with the news. They bought another crib for the new baby and wrote to their parents about it. Zoltán's mother and father wrote back that Piry should come with Judith and finish her term at their home." they wrote.

Piry wouldn't hear of it. She was overjoyed that her pregnancy caused her no morning sickness this time and wanted to continue her work with Zoltán as long as she could.

Secretly, she was also determined to have both her children born in Budapest. Whoever heard of Debrecen, she thought to herself, I wouldn't have my children explain for the rest of their lives where that is. The whole world knows where and what Budapest is. That's where my children belong." She knew she had aroused the ire of her parents and her in-laws' by stubbornly staying in the capital but she didn't care.

On a hot June night, just as they had fallen asleep, Piry was awakened by a searing cramp in her lower belly. She shook Zoltán awake, "It's coming!"

He called the doctor, and they were instructed to meet him at the maternity ward of the hospital. Both maids, the housekeeper and the nanny were awakened, and wished them luck, as they helped Piry gather her overnight case, while Zoltán called for a taxi.

It was just past midnight when they arrived at the hospital's reception area. By this time Piry was experiencing severe cramps that made her double over in pain. The gynecologist and a young intern were already there, waiting for her. Zoltán took care of the paperwork, while Piry was placed on a gurney and wheeled toward the labor-room. That is where she would have to stay until it was time to go into the actual delivery theater. As she was being wheeled toward the room, Piry began to feel a series of fast cramps and an excruciating pain and shouted, "It's coming, it's coming!"

"Madam," the doctor tried to calm her, "relax, and take a deep breath, your labor has just begun, it might take hours…"

"No, it won't," Piry screamed as she pushed down despite herself, feeling her lower body ripping apart.

Something in her voice alerted the doctor. He swiftly instructed the attendant to push the cart into an available operating theater.

"Hold it," he shouted to Piry. "Don't push!"

"I can't help it!" she screamed.

They barely had time to place Piry on the birthing table, and a quick exam electrified the entire staff. Her clothes were pulled off, and white stockings were rolled up her spread-eagle legs; another nurse guided Piry's arms through a hospital gown. By the time a cap covered her hair, Piry was screaming, the doctor administered an injection to calm her, but shouting "push, push," and then it was all over.

With a great sense of relief Piry was out of pain. Through the haze of the tranquilizer, she saw a nurse holding up a bloody little body, and it took only a couple hard pats on the child's bottom before it burst into a lusty cry.

Piry was exhausted, felt totally enervated, couldn't move a muscle. Hearing her child's cry, knowing he was all right, she closed her eyes, relieved. The pain was gone, and that's all she cared about for now.

"Piry, what will you name her?"

She heard the doctor's gentle voice as he leaned over her, placing his ear near her lips so she wouldn't have to strain, speaking.

Piry said, "Gábor."

"No, Piry, it's a girl," the doctor responded.

Piry heard him through a fog, and whispered, "Péter".

"No, Piry, you have a little girl!"

Bitter disappointment swept through Piry's consciousness. She so badly wanted to give Zoltán a son! Then the image of a large doll floated into her mind. She had seen it sitting on a chair at her dressmaker's home, just a couple of weeks before. It had long blonde hair and large blue eyes and embroidered on its blouse was the name Erika.

"Erika," she whispered.

Satisfied, the doctor stood back up. "Erika it will be," he said and patted Piry's arm. "You did fantastically. Now rest."

◎◉◎

Erika was such a beautiful baby that whenever Piry and Zoltán walked with their daughters, people would stop at the stroller and admire Erika. Then look at Judith and add kindly, "she'll grow up."

Judith was aware of the change of tone and looks of pity instead of admiration and developed feelings of animosity and jealousy toward her little sister. What saved Erika from being completely hated by her sister was that Judith knew, her father still loved her 'best'. She was clearly his favorite; he paid more attention to her and called her his little angel. He never did that to Erika. In fact, while he hardly ever scolded Judith, but when Erika did something wrong, he didn't hesitate to spank her. This knowledge was not lost on either child.

Erika was two years old when during the summer her whole family had gone to Debrecen on vacation. Zoltán's parents put a large basin out in their yard and filled it with water so Judith and Erika could play in it during a searing hot afternoon. Judith soon got tired of splashing water on each other with Erika. She went into the house that was cooled by the shades that had been drawn. She lay down on her bed in the room she shared with Erika and read the story book she had brought with her.

In other bedrooms, the men were taking a nap. The women were busy in the kitchen, preparing dinner. Erika, alone in the garden, spotted a flock of baby chicks as they strutted together, pecking at the ground.

'They must be very hot,' she thought, so she walked over to them and one by one, dunked each chick into the basin of water, holding it by the neck. She then took the limp, thoroughly wet birds and carefully placed them on the ground in the sun, to dry.

Piry, wondering about the silence in the yard, went out to look and gave a shattering scream as she spotted the little yellow bodies laid out neatly in a row.

"What are you doing?" she shouted at her daughter.

"I'm giving them a bath," Erika said proudly.

"You've killed them!" Piry yelled at her, and grabbing the child dragged her away, preventing her from killing the last of the chicks. She was aghast. It didn't even enter Piry's mind that Erika had no idea of what she had done. No concept of having killed the birds by her action. Instead, Piry was seething with anger, for she knew, these chicks were being raised as food for her in-laws. The economy was terrible and people even in rural towns, like Debrecen, had to grow their own vegetables and raise animals for food. Now Erika had destroyed months' worth of meat. In her anger, Piry called to Zoltán, who came running, hearing the distress in his wife's voice. It took only seconds for him to assess the situation. Without hesitation, he sat down on a nearby bench, put Erika across his knees, and whacked her behind several times, quite hard. "Look what you have just done!" he admonished her, "You killed those poor chicks!"

"I didn't know," Erika cried.

Zoltán let go of her. "Promise you'll never do anything like this again!"

"I promise."

As Erika was marched into the house, she was full of anger. She felt like she had been punished without her knowing that she had done something wrong. *Father is not fair, he simply doesn't love me*, she thought. *He would have never hit Judith.*

Another incident with Erika had also involved chickens, or rather, this time their precious product, their eggs. By now, Erika was nearly three years old, an inventive, active, curious child. She was a happy child, who ran instead of walking, danced instead of standing still.

Passover was coming and Piry shopped for all the items needed during the eight-day holiday. She bought a hundred eggs, for it was a staple food during Passover, as well as an important ingredient in making matzo balls with special, kosher flour. She bought enough flour to also make the matzoh, the unleavened bread they were to eat for the week, and several chickens for soup and roast. The meat was stored in a cooler box with ice, and the eggs in a huge, oblong wicker basket, along with the rest of the materials, in the pantry just off the kitchen.

One day, while Piry was preparing lunch, she kept hearing Erika's laughter but in a strange, intermittent rhythm. She would laugh, followed by silence, then laugh again. Piry wondered what the child was laughing at but was happy that Erika was busy and didn't want to disturb her fun. Then, as she turned around in the kitchen to get a plate from a cupboard on the wall, she noticed a yellow liquid oozing from under the pantry door. Then came Erika's laughter from behind that door. Piry turned the knob and her heart sank. Erika was standing next to the egg basket. She happily reached into the basket, took an egg, raised it, and then dropped it unto the tile floor. The egg broke with a thud, its content flowing around Erika's feet like a yellow river with transparent foam. Erika gave a shriek of delight, drowned out by Piry's shout, "Stop! Stop right now!"

Erika froze as she looked up at her mother. She had no idea that what she was doing was wrong. But that did not prevent her father from giving her a spanking when he came home for the midday meal.

It was in the Spring of 1943, that Zoltán began to think of leaving with his family not only Hungary but Europe as well. His youngest brother, Dennis, after becoming a full-fledged doctor in 1941, did not return from Prague. Instead, he notified his family that he was emigrating to Johannesburg, South Africa. Through a marriage broker he had arranged to marry a wealthy young woman, whose family also promised to set him up with his own medical practice. Zoltán wrote to Dennis, asking his advice. Dennis wrote back that his marriage had not worked out. The girl's parents never provided the dowry they had promised so he divorced his wife and was now struggling on his own to establish a practice. "You can come," Dennis wrote, "but I won't be able to help you financially. It might be difficult for you to start a new life here, burdened as you are with a wife and two children."

It was around this time that the newly formed Hungarian Fascist Government revised its emigration laws. Jews could only leave the country if they donated all their possessions to the government. After receiving the discouraging letter from Dennis, Zoltán did not wish to expose his young family to untold difficulties by moving to a different country, penniless. He was an optimist, and believed that despite the difficulties and the war, they could manage their lives better at home. He had plenty of money, and it could still buy almost anything, including immunity from persecution.

When six months later, in the fall of 1943, Zoltán was called in to join a forced labor camp on the Eastern border of Hungary, he still believed that once the war was over, their lives would normalize. After all, the Germans had been defeated in the Soviet Union and were now waging a desperate war to survive. It could not last much longer.

Erika barely missed her father. Her memories of him were tainted by the anger she had experienced coming from him. Judith on the other hand, pined for his love and attention. She would not turn to Piry for these, she wanted her father to come back.

Piry, being left on her own, tried to contact both their families in Debrecen but could not get a response. After March 19, 1944, when the German soldiers marched into Budapest in orderly rows, their boots hammering with a frightening thud on the pavement, there was nothing more she could hope for except trying to survive. And that they did.

Tonight, she would perhaps find out whether her husband did as well.

Piry spent the rest of the week preparing for the dinner with Andor. She was not used to doing household chores alone. A typical well-to-do family in Hungary had at least one live-in maid who worked from morning to night, cleaning, doing laundry, and cooking for the family. Piry, during her married years, could also afford to hire a laundry woman to come to her apartment a couple of times a week, and a live-in nanny for her children.

While in hiding during the siege of Budapest, her friend Irén shared the household duties with her. Now she had to clean, shop, and cook alone. She carefully planned the menu and cleaned her apartment until all the rooms were spotless. When she shopped for food, what she couldn't find at stores and wholesale markets, she obtained through a thriving black market. It was a matter of being able to offer more money. When she did, the vendor would reach under the tablecloth that covered the display table, and offer Piry the "good" vegetables, flour, and sugar.

For the first course, she cooked a vegetable soup. The main course was a slice of kosher beef braised and served with two side dishes. One was sauerkraut, cooked with caraway seeds and paprika for color, the other potatoes that had been boiled in water then combined with sautéed onions and lightly fried. For dessert, she baked an apple tart. While she was cooking, she silently blessed her father for insisting that she learn at his restaurant's kitchen how to prepare dishes that combined well and provided a balanced "home style" but elegant dinner.

Andor arrived punctually at eight, looking rather formal in his black suit and a white shirt with a rust-colored tie. He seemed a bit nervous as he stepped in saying, "I came straight from work".

"Then I hope you're suitably hungry," Piry smiled at him, thinking, how odd their small talk was.

"Where are the girls?

"Oh, they're both at summer camp," Piry said airily. "They needed the fresh air and the sun, and I needed the free time to put our lives back together," she explained, as she led him from the hallway into the living room. Then she added, "Please excuse the lack of furniture, we've been 'liberated' from most of it by the people who occupied the apartment during the siege, and also of course by the armies."

He laughed. "I'm familiar with the phenomenon. It won't take you long to get new things, I'm sure."

She shrugged, "It depends…" and let the rest of the sentence fall off for she couldn't say, it depended on her husband's return.

But he understood. He reached into his briefcase and pulled out a bottle of Egri Bikaver, a full-bodied Hungarian red wine, impossible to obtain even after the war.

Piry gasped, "Where did this come from?

"Oh, we have our connections," he gave her a wry smile. "Would you like me to open the bottle?" he asked, avoiding Piry's unspoken question lingering between them.

"Yes, that would be lovely," Piry responded, postponing the 'moment of truth'.

She led him into the dining room, where she took a corkscrew from a drawer in a China cabinet spared by the intruders and opening its glass doors pulled out two ordinary water glasses. "This is all I could buy for the moment. All my crystal glassware is gone."

He smiled, "Those are superficial things, Piry. Of course, it's nice to keep formalities, but I'm just as happy without them."

He poured, and they clinked glasses, looking into each other's eyes, "To your health." they said, almost simultaneously, and laughed a little at this, taking a sip of the precious wine.

"Ummmm, this is so good," Piry acknowledged his gift.

A silence fell between them. Piry could sense that he was somehow ill at ease and decided to play it safe by not asking before dinner whether or not he had brought her news. Instead, she said, "You must be starving, coming straight from the office—shall we eat?"

He put his glass down and gently took the glass from Piry's hand as well. Then, holding her hands, faced her, looking into her eyes.

"Piry, I'm afraid I have some bad news."

She froze, and steeling herself whispered, "Tell me, please".

"The allies found Zoltán in the Bergen Belsen camp. They hospitalized him with double pneumonia and typhoid fever. The medical staff did their best, but he didn't make it."

"Oh, God," Piry cried out and shutting her eyes put her palms above her heart to still the sharp pain that seized her.

"I'm so sorry." Andor pulled her into his arms.

Piry burst into tears, sobbing against his chest. "He died when the war was over—how could he!?"

"He was emaciated. His system couldn't handle the double illness. He weighed 45 kilos when he died. He weighed 90 kilos when he arrived at Bergen Belsen."

"How, how do you know all this?" Piry stammered between sobs.

"I spent the last few days searching for him. The Nazis kept very accurate records I'm so, so sorry. Come, let's sit down."

Andor half pulled half led Piry to the sofa. He eased her down next to him. Piry buried her face against his chest, desperately needing to be held while she was coping with the news. She felt that her whole world had just collapsed within her and without. All these months what sustained her and helped her move forward was awaiting Zoltán's return. The thought that he never would, brought on another wave of uncontrollable sobs.

Andor gently caressed her hair with one hand, while the other held her in his embrace. He let her cry.

"What am I going to do now?" she asked, feeling desperate. "How will I go on? What will I tell the girls?" she sobbed.

Finally, when Andor sensed that the greatest storm in her was subsiding, he said in a soft voice, "You will know what to tell the girls. And you will manage—and you won't have to do it alone."

Lifting her tear-streaked face to him Piry looked into Andor's eyes, and he answered her silent question by gently touching her lips with his.

Piry pushed him away just enough to be able to study his face. She saw a promise, a gentle, protective love, and as though a dam had broken within her, all her pent-up yearning and pain burst forth.

She wrapped her arms around his neck and pulled him close to her. They kissed and couldn't stop. With their lips exploring each other, she reached to loosen his necktie and unbutton his shirt. He threw off his jacket, she pulled off his shirt, he slid his hands from her shoulders to her breasts. She gasped and let him remove her blouse. They were exploring and caressing each other wildly, like two lost souls, grasping at straws to stay afloat.

Piry continued crying softly, but clung to Andor, letting him pull her clothes off, letting him lower her to the Persian carpet on the floor and possess her body. With eyes closed, she held on to him, not really to him but to life itself. She didn't want to think, only to feel, to disappear in his desire, to meld with him into a sphere of nothing but acute pleasure; a pleasure that was surpassing the horrible darkness she felt at her core.

He, too, must have needed this passion and forgetting, for he held her and made love to her for most of the night. They finally fell into a light sleep, then awoke as the first rays of the sun came through the shutters. She lifted her head from his shoulder and smiled at him. Then, recalling the start of the night and his news, Piry asked, "What now?"

"As I told you, you're not alone unless you don't want me."

"I do," Piry sighed. "Truth is, I've wanted you from the time I first met you."

"Same here. And now you've got me," he said with a gentle smile. "Strange, how life is. One door closes and another opens." He planted a soft kiss top of Piry's head. "Do you think we could have some dinner now? I'm starving."

◎◉◎

After he left for the Ministry, Piry locked the front door and crawled back into her bed. It had happened all too fast. Her feelings for Andor were unmistakable. She was in love with him, though she knew nothing about him. Or was it just lust? Did it matter? Zoltán was gone—she could barely fathom it. The pain of this new reality made her bury her face in the pillow.

She recalled her dream about Zoltán in the black waters and wondered whether that was the night on which he might have died. *He left me—he gave up*. This thought filled Piry with fury. *He was such a strong man, why couldn't he hold on, he must have known the war was over, why couldn't he heal? Didn't he remember his wife and daughters?*

The anger flooding her was overwhelming. *I waited three years for him, lived with him for merely seven; ten years out of my life dedicated to him, and he left me! Left me with two young children! How am I going to support them now? How will I earn a living, when my own father refused to let me to go to school long enough to become a teacher? Am I going to spend my life selling hardware because that's the only thing I've learned in my years with Zoltán? At least, I have that,* she thought, her natural optimism rising within her.

Agitated, she got out of bed. The living room, the dining room, and the kitchen were a mess with remnants of the night and the hastily eaten dinner for breakfast. She needed to clean up and put her home and her life in order.

The mail in her mailbox later that morning, much to Piry's surprise, brought a postcard from Erika. It read: "Mother, I'm starving here. Please take me home. Kisses, Erika."

Piry was stunned. Could Erika be telling the truth? A part of her got upset because she had barely managed to place the child into a summer camp. To bring her home would mean that she would no longer be free to look for a way to start earning a living. Wondering about Andor's reaction also crossed her mind but she dismissed that—he knew she had responsibilities beyond him. Right now, she just had to investigate the situation with Erika.

She quickly finished the house chores, then called Andor's office. He was at a meeting. Piry left him a message that she had an errand to run and wouldn't be back until evening, asking him to call her then. Life was becoming complicated, she thought, as she quickly dressed for the trip to the cool Zugló Mountains.

On sheer instinct, she put into her purse a couple of Almond Joy bars. She had been given these by HIASZ, the Jewish post-war organization in Budapest, sponsored by the Americans to help Jews put their lives back on track in war-torn countries. She had been saving these for when she planned to visit her daughters at their summer camps. Now seemed like a good idea to take them along.

When she arrived at the Zugló Children's Resort, in the hills of Buda, she was ushered into the Director's office, a middle aged, emaciated looking woman.

Piry showed her the postcard from Erika.

The woman glared at Piry over her glasses and with defensive attitude. "This is just a few months after the war. Of course, we have a limited amount of food. But none of the other children are complaining. Erika seems to be a the only one."

"You're right, Erika is demanding." Piry agreed, just to ease the tension between them.

"Well, we have nothing more to provide her at the moment but what everyone gets."

"Could I talk to my daughter?" Piry asked.

"Why of course." The Director went to the door and called to the secretary, sitting just outside her office, asking for Erika to be brought to her.

The few minutes it took for Erika to arrive, the Director and Piry spent in small talk, expressing their hope for better times to come now that the country was at peace again. Piry was grateful that the woman didn't ask about Erika's father. Perhaps she would have, but Erika burst into the room, almost leaping into Piry's arms, shouting, "Mom!".

Thin during the war, Erika seemed to have lost more weight. She did not look healthy.

"You came for me!" Erika was overjoyed. "Please, please, take me home."

It took little time to gather Erika's belongings, and they were on their way to the fogas, the cog-wheel tram that would take them downhill, back to the city. As they settled on the wooden bench inside the noisy tram, Piry asked: "Are you hungry?" and watched Erika devour both Almond Joys as if she had not eaten in weeks.

According to Erika, she had not been given enough food. In the morning, they were served a thin caraway soup and a piece of dry bread; for lunch and dinner the same soup, usually followed by a dish of mashed yellow peas, which Erika hated and could not swallow. Some nights they served mashed potatoes, and she could eat that but first she had to scrape off the standard garnish on top, which was a spoonful of chopped, fried onions.

"The burnt smell and greasy taste of those onions, or just a bite of the yellow peas-purée made me nauseous," Erika explained.

Piry listened, speechless. What could she do with this child who was so picky about her food that she would rather starve than eat something she didn't like. *If Zoltán were around, she would eat it*, Piry thought, and felt tears well-up in her eyes. She blinked and hid them. This was not the time to tell Erika that her father was gone forever.

◎◉◎

Piry had a trying week, juggling her time between caring for Erika, dragging her to explore business locations, and then to the park so she could get some sun and fresh air, and being with Andor late at night, when he had a chance to spend a few hours with her.

Within a week, again through HIASZ, Piry had found another summer camp, located at one of the nicest hills above the city, on Hárshegy. Erika was apprehensive, and sullen on the way to the camp, but Piry explained to her that she had to go.

"Judith is at camp and has been sending only happy postcards, so likely, you would find this new camp better. In any case, you'll have to try it because I can't go around looking for work with you at home."

The summer camp, overlooking a vast valley, pleased even Erika. She also took a liking to the headmistress, a lively blonde in her thirties. She greeted them warmly, and had Erika whisked away, promising her that she will like her campmates.

Relieved, Piry returned to the city. She visited business locations, went to see Dr. Nagy, asking his opinion about her opening a hardware store, and saw as much of Andor as his time permitted. He was heavily involved with work, much of it of political nature. He didn't like talking about that part, and Piry, though resenting his secrecy, didn't want to push him. She was happy that she had him in her life. It prevented her from facing her terror of being left alone in the world with two daughters and no other family.

It was eight o'clock in the morning, just a few days after Erika had gone to her new camp, when Piry's phone rang. It was the headmistress at Erika's camp.

"Mrs. Fábián, sorry to disturb you so early but could you please come to see us?"

Piry's heart skipped a beat. "Has something happened to Erika?"

"No, no, we don't mean to alarm you, but we do need to talk to you."

The woman sounded polite, but definitely evasive and tense.

Piry sighed. Erika was in trouble. "I can come this afternoon."

"That would be wonderful," the phone clicked off.

She called Andor at his office to let him know that she had to go to Erika's camp again.

"It's all right." He sounded distracted. "I've meetings until late tonight. I'll call you when I'm done."

Her sixth sense told Piry that something was not quite right with Andor, but she didn't want to question him. She knew he had a very difficult job, and she was careful not to add to his troubles. She sometimes wondered what they had in common besides their wild physical hunger for each other. She put him out of her mind, and after tidying the apartment dressed for her visit to Erika's summer camp.

It was mid.-afternoon when Piry got there and was immediately ushered into the director's office. The tall, blonde woman greeted Piry warmly and invited her to have afternoon coffee with her on the terrace.

"The children have just come back from a hike and are having their afternoon snack. We'll call for Erika just as soon as we've had a chance to get acquainted a bit. Please, have a seat."

Coffee and cookies were served by an assistant, and Piry was grateful, for she had become quite hungry during the journey. The director chatted about the activities the camp offered to the children, and the importance of normalizing their lives after the war. Then she finally came to the point about requesting Piry to come to see her.

Mrs. Fábián, forgive me for asking, but how did your little girl get into our program?"

Piry was surprised by the question. "Through HIASZ of course…"

"But that's not possible. The HIASZ, is a Jewish organization, they only work with Jewish families, and Erika told us you were Protestants. She insisted that she wasn't Jewish and recited the Lord's Prayer to prove it."

Piry stared at the Director and burst out laughing. "Oh, my God, that is too funny." Then she stopped laughing and serious now, added, "Or would be if it weren't so sad."

The Director stared at Piry, "Please explain."

Piry told her about their survival with Christian papers, and how she had taught her daughters to pray like Protestants.

"I told Erika after the war, when we got back to our own apartment, that it was okay for us to be Jewish again, but I guess she didn't believe me."

"Why don't we talk to the child now?" The Director asked her assistant, a young woman, to bring Erika out to the terrace.

When Erika spotted her mother, she ran to her, throwing her arms around her wildly begging, "Mother, I want to stay here, I'm having lots of fun, but they keep asking me if I am Jewish, and I keep telling them I'm Protestant! Please tell them!" and she winked, to emphasize to her mother that she knew what she was supposed to say.

Piry couldn't help feeling the tragedy of the situation. Here was her five-year-old child, so terrified of being killed as a Jew that even when she had been told it was all right to admit it, she couldn't. *What kind of a world did Erika live in? How long will it take for her to get over the lies and fear of the war?*

"Erika, it's all right, my sweet, nobody is going to take you away or want to kill you any more for being Jewish. That was only during the war. The war is over, you know that. Now it's all right to admit it. Everyone here is Jewish."

Erika looked up at her in amazement. She knew, if her mother said so, it must be true.

"Yes Erika, we're all Jewish here," confirmed the Director.

"Mother?" Erika looked at Piry with big question marks in her eyes. She thought perhaps she was just being tested.

"Yes, Erika, it's all right. We can be Jewish again, believe me."

Erika slipped off Piry's lap, and asked, "May I go play now?"

"Yes, you may." said the Director, and the two women watched the child run off, as light as air.

◎◉◎

"Your cousin, Laci is back." Andor told Piry one night, when he had been able to get away from work and had come to see her.

"Oh, my God, where is he? Maybe he'll have news of the family," Piry was ecstatic.

"I'll arrange a meeting for you, though it might have to be at his office at the Ministry of Interior. He is pretty busy these days, working for Péter Gábor."

Piry was a little taken aback by this information but made no comment. Péter Gábor was the head of the AVO, the Hungarian State Defense Office, a new organization that had been formed just a few months after liberation to replace the old fascist national defense system.

Rumors had it that this new security organization was backed by the Communist Party and the Soviet Government. But then again, these were politically troubled times, with several parties struggling for control. The two strongest parties emerging from a multi-party political medley to govern the country were the Independent Smallholders' Party supported by a majority of the population, closely trailed by the Hungarian Communist Party, that was backed by the Soviet Union. The third contender was that of the Social Democrats' Party. Piry's friend, Irén, had been a member of this party even before the war, and was now quite active in it. She tried to persuade Piry to join as well.

"I don't like any kind of politics," was Piry's response.

"If everyone felt this way, you know where this country would be? Right back in the hands of the Hungarian fascists!" Irén exclaimed.

However, their different attitudes did not affect the friendship between them. Both were still waiting for news about their families and Piry thought, since Irén was single, politics were her way of "belonging," and coping with the lack of news about her family.

Piry's reasons for living were her daughters and to some extent her involvement with Andor. But much as she loved the nights spent with him, she realized that Andor was not discussing a serious commitment between them. Only once did Piry suggest, as though in jest, that he "make an honest woman out of her".

Andor's immediate response was, "That would be impossible at the moment."

Piry never broached the subject again. She figured, he wanted to take his time to decide about a wife. She was a woman with two young children, perhaps not his choice for the future. For the time being she knew how to keep him interested in her, and that was enough. Her prime concern had to be figuring out whether or not she could set up a business to make a living for her daughters and herself.

The reunion with her cousin Laci was exciting and joyful, though a bit tense. Piry thought, *it must be due to the circumstances of the meeting*. She had been ushered into his office by two young men dressed alike in dark suits, white shirts, and red ties, both acting more like security guards than office personnel.

Laci and Piry had been close friends as children. Now they hugged affectionately, then studied each other at arm's length, smiling broadly. Laci was a head taller than Piry. He wore his dark brown hair smoothed back, making his intense brown eyes even more striking. He was a handsome, charismatic man, with an aquiline nose and even white teeth in a round face, often lit up by a warm smile.

"You're looking good, but a bit thin," he commented.

"The war," Piry shrugged.

Laci was only a couple of years older than Piry, His mother was one of Piry's eight aunts. Laci told her, his mother, Irén, survived being in a concentration camp, and was now recovering at a sanatorium. He knew about Zoltán and expressed his condolences, adding, "Now that I'm back, I'll work on finding the whereabouts of the rest our family."

They sat down in the reception area of Laci's office, sinking into large, leather armchairs. Over freshly brewed espressos brought in by a male secretary, they talked about themselves.

Laci had spent the war years in the Soviet Union. He had recently returned and was now working for Péter Gábor, as his assistant. They had also worked together for the Soviet Government in Moscow. Now they were setting up a new Hungarian security system, called the ÁVO (State Defense Department). One of the new agency's functions was finding Hungarian Nazis and informants who had collaborated with them betraying Jews and communist sympathizers during the war.

"Will you continue working with Péter?" Piry asked.

"For a while. When life normalizes again, I plan to attend the Technical University and become what I've always wanted to be, an engineer," Laci grinned. "Come, I'll introduce you to Gábor."

Piry did not feel at ease with Péter Gábor. Something about him sent a chill down her spine. He was a short, slim man, with shifty hazel eyes under thick, straight brows. He had a long, sharp nose and a bushy moustache that covered his thin upper lip. To Piry, he seemed like a heartless man. He wore a dark suit and a white shirt with a red tie, that by now Piry realized identified him, as well as those in his office, as belonging to the Communist Party. Piry was sure he sized her up just as quickly, but his face showed no signs of it. He shook hands with her and gave her a quick smile that faded immediately as he expressed his condolences about her husband. Then he muttered a few words about hoping for a better future and apologized for being too busy to spend time with her and Laci. He never offered them a chair.

Piry had the impression that Laci had prearranged this brief meeting with his boss and that is why Péter Gábor knew about the loss of her husband. It was clear to her that the two men were close. But she did share her thoughts with Laci. He escorted her to the building's exit. When they said good-bye, Piry left with a glimmer of hope that the rest of their family might be found with Laci's help.

During this summer of 1945, with her daughters away in summer camps, Piry had also taken several more trips to Kakucs Village. With Miko's help she expanded her business to surrounding villages as well. The economic situation in the country was bad and getting worse.

The value of money was declining daily and Piry began to think that there was little hope for her to be able to open a business on her own. Instead, she concentrated on liquidating the rest of her merchandise for cash or food, and whenever she could, for gold coins of any denomination.

Dr. Nagy advised her to do this. He came to visit Piry after she moved back to her apartment, acting like a big brother, once he learned of Zoltán's death.

"You should try to obtain either U.S.A. dollars or gold coins," he told her. "As you well know, the pengő is becoming worthless. Convert whatever cash you can."

He gave Piry the name of a man who would be able to exchange Piry's paper money for American dollars or gold coins and advised her to keep the information to herself.

Piry thought, *even if I sold all the remaining stock from our former store, if I have hard currency, I could always buy new merchandise, should I want to open a store.*

Her daughters were due back from summer camp in a week, and Piry wondered how she was going to take care of them and continue her travels for business, as well as keep up the affair with Andor. She need not have worried about Andor. Returning home from one of her village trips, she found a letter from him in her mailbox.

"Dear Piry,

I have been given an assignment outside Budapest. Must leave immediately. Thank you for everything. You were the best thing that has happened to me in my whole life. Take care of yourself and the girls.

Embracing you,
Andor"

Good thing I'm sitting down, Piry thought, reading and re-reading his note. The shock of his sudden departure took the strength out of her legs and the breath from her lungs. So, it is over. A few months, and he is gone. *Disappeared without a forwarding address.* She wondered whether he had known all along that this would happen. She wondered whether her cousin Laci had known about their affair. *Surely, he must know Andor's whereabouts.*

Piry picked up the phone to call Laci but put it down quickly for the doorbell rang. She considered pretending that she was not at home. Then thought better of it and forced herself to go and open it. In the doorway stood her sister, Lilly, the oldest of her three siblings, seven years younger than Piry.

"Lilly!" Piry cried out and hugged her with overwhelming joy. "Come in, come in!"

Pulling Lilly by her hand, Piry led the way to the living room, babbling, "You're alive, you're alive!" Gone were her despair and sense of abandonment. She was no longer alone in the world; she had a sister back. *Perhaps even more family members?*

"Tell me where you have been all this time?! Do you know where others of our family are?" Piry was so excited, she was bombarding Lilly with her need to know. Then, remembering her manners, she added, "Are you hungry? Come, let's get you something to eat."

"It's all right, I'm not hungry," Lilly tried to calm Piry down. "Let's just catch up with each other."

"How you have grown!" Piry exclaimed, as she studied her little sister, who at 24, was a striking beauty. Jet black hair curled around her heart-shaped face, her coal-black eyes were not large but brilliant and lively. Her even row of white teeth took the focus away from her nose, which was slightly curved and a bit lumpy. She was slender but had full breasts, and moved gracefully, displaying shapely legs under her short skirt.

Piry just couldn't resist the inbred custom of serving food to a visitor. She pulled Lilly into the kitchen so she could prepare a quick meal for her before they would settle down to talk. She piled on a plate cold cut, bread, and dill pickles. Then, carrying the food and plates into the living room, they sank into the sofa, facing each other.

Lilly told Piry, "When all Jews were ordered in Debrecen to gather and march to the train station for transportation to some German work camp, I snuck out with the help of a young Hungarian officer. With his help, I took the train from Debrecen to Budapest. I came to your apartment, but the concierge told me you were gone. So, I contacted a couple of our parents' Christian friends, and one family offered to temporarily hide me at their home.

"They then provided me with a new birth certificate and school records, using a duplicate set from one of their daughters, who was twenty-one, just like me. With these documents in hand, I got a job as a nanny in a wealthy Catholic household, taking care of their two young children, a boy and a girl. Then I got connected with the Jewish underground, and during my days off I worked with them, printing Christian identity papers to save Jews.

"After liberation, I spent time looking for our family members who might be returning from the concentration camps. Then I found out through a friend at the Interior Ministry that our sister Edith, and our parents, died in Auschwitz. Our brother, Péter, died serving in a forced labor camp for the military."

Here, Lilly stopped and wiped her eyes. Piry sat numbed by the news, with tears rolling down her cheeks. Lilly cried with her. Then Piry reached out and held Lilly's hand, letting their grief subside.

Lilly sniffed, wiped her nose, and continued, "No one knew your whereabouts. Devastated and in mourning, I continued working as a nanny for the same family. Since I could get no information about you and yours, I finally took matters into my own hands. My first logical step was—knowing where you had lived before the war—to come and look for you at this apartment on St. Steven's Boulevard. This was the third time I had come. On each previous occasion, the concierge told me that she had not heard anything, but that the apartment was still there, waiting. And finally, you had moved back, and I had found you!"

"The girls and I survived by hiding with Christian papers. Zoltán is gone. I just found it out recently." Piry's voice broke off as Lilly cried out, "Oh, no!" and she began to cry again.

Dusk settled like gray gauze over the room as the sisters dealt with their grief.

Piry buried her face in her palms, stunned by the pain and horror of envisioning her parents, her siblings, aunts, uncles, and cousins, all the people she loved, being forced into freight trains for transportation to death. Lilly, who has had some time to deal with her own grief, sat in silence, allowing her sister time to process their loss.

Meanwhile, Lilly was coping with the death of her beloved brother-in-law, Zoltán, and what this must have meant for Piry and her children.

Finally, Piry took a deep breath and broke the silence. "Please eat something."

Lilly, just to be polite, made an open-face sandwich with bread and slices of salami, topped with a pickle.

"You eat, too," she urged her sister, who looked drawn and thin.

Piry gave her a wan smile and put a slice of salami on a piece of bread, just to be polite and not have her sister eat alone.

"Are you still working? Or do you want to quit and come to live with me till you find out what you really want to do with yourself?" Piry asked her younger sister.

"There is something I didn't tell you yet," Lilly said, blushing.

"Boy matter?" Piry guessed with a teasing smile.

Lilly nodded. "Met him a few years ago when I was visiting you. Do you remember that Friday evening when you couldn't go to temple because both girls were sick with a cold, and Zoltán took me with him anyway? I met some friends of his after services at the temple."

"Vaguely."

"Well after the services Zoltan introduced me to some of his friends, among them the three Hollis brothers, and their sister, Violet. The middle brother, Donát became interested in me."

"And?"

"We met again recently, and have become quite serious…"

"How serious is 'quite serious?"

"We're just waiting to find out who of our family members have returned and then set a wedding date." Lilly smiled shyly.

"That's great news! And, as your older sister, may I ask, how he is planning to support you?"

"He and his brothers own three large factories. They manufacture paints, chemicals, and pharmaceuticals. In fact, all three factories operated even during the war, because the government needed the materials they produce."

"Ah, so he is rich!"

Lilly smiled modestly, "You might say so".

Piry hugged her sister, "That's fantastic! It's the best news I've heard since I don't know when!"

She fell silent for a moment, thinking of Andor's letter, then pushed the pain away.

"So, would you like to live with me and the girls, till the wedding?"

Lilly's face lit up, "Thank you so much for the offer, but I want to keep working till we get married".

"If you're working for a trousseau, I'd be happy to provide it for you."

"No, they've been so good to me during the war that I promised to stay there till my wedding. They're almost like family by now. But I could come and stay with you on weekends if you'd like."

"Of course I would! I'd be happy to have you! And the girls will be thrilled to get to know you. It's settled then."

◎◉◎

Just before summer camp was over at the end of August 1945, Piry had determined that she simply could not handle full time care of her daughters while seeking a way to earn a living. For the new school year, starting in September, she had found a boarding school run by a Zionist organization that was gladly accepting Jewish children. She promised her daughters that this would be a temporary solution, just until she established a way to support them.

She had not had the courage to tell them about the loss of their father and all their grandparents, and likely, many other family members. Instead, she merely told them that she had to continue to travel for a while, and therefore they needed to be in a safe and stable environment so they could go to school undisturbed. She reassured them that, "Of course, you will come home as per school rules, every other weekend."

It broke Piry's heart to have to leave them at the boarding school. But now that Zoltán and their parents were gone, and even Andor had left her, she had no one to turn to and felt a desperate need to secure their financial situation. Apolitical as Piry was, she was aware of the governmental and economic turmoil around her. Common sense told her that the war in Hungary may be over, but their lives were far from stabilized.

Her friend, Irén Goldberg, still had not heard from her family, thus got a job again as an accountant. She was also deeply involved in politics. She visited Piry one evening, and over dinner complained to her that "The Communists are manipulating the government even though it was the Smallholders' Party that had won the elections and are officially running the country."

"How are the communists doing that?" Piry asked.

Irén explained, "In the last election, my party, the Social Democrats, had received the same number of votes as the Communist Party. Yet, the Communists have gained many more seats in the government. And they are pushing members of the other parties out of power by accusing their leaders of treason and having them removed from their posts.

It's not looking good for the future of our country."

All Piry could do was to listen to Irén's angry description of what was going on in the government. It was obvious why with all the political infighting, the economy was getting worse. One had to carry a suitcase-full of paper currency to buy a loaf of bread.

"Just be careful with your role in the party," she cautioned Irén.

Irén shrugged, "I'm small fry. Not important enough to be noticed." Irén was downplaying her actual position. She was a board member of the leadership of the Social Democratic Party in Budapest.

Piry knew this but didn't want to contradict Irén. "You are my closest friend, I don't want anything to happen to you," she said to Irén as they hugged good-bye for the night.

Piry knew that Irén was right about their country. Her own common sense told her that there was no way to predict the difficulties they might face in the future. That is why she had to make sure that she had the means with which support her little family's daily necessities. She couldn't explain any of this to her young daughters. All she could do was use the time while they were at boarding school to build a future for them.

CHAPTER 7

JUDITH DID NOT PROTEST about going to boarding school. In her father's absence, nothing much mattered to her. She was convinced that their mother didn't love her and Erika. That is why Piry had sent them to a camp during the summer, and now to a boarding school.

Erika missed her mother, but she was not unhappy at the boarding school. Sleeping in a large room with five other girls was fun. They would talk at night or tell stories before falling asleep. During most of the day they were in classes, which Erika loved. She eagerly participated in question-and-answer sessions and especially loved learning Hebrew.

Having learned some German in kindergarten, she now found it fun to learn a different language. Hebrew had strange, guttural sounds, its alphabet was nothing like Erika had ever seen, and she found all this challenging and exciting.

Officially, first graders had to be six years old, and Erika had only completed her fifth birthday in June, just two months before school started. So initially she was placed into a pre-school class. But she could read and count, thus she was allowed to sit in for these subjects in the first-grade classes, as well as in all the arts instructions. During their bi-weekly singing lessons she was happy to learn melodic Hebrew songs that spoke of friendship, and pride in the land of Israel, from where all Jews originated. She learned to dance the Hora, a line dance imported from Israel and found joy performing in plays and skits during Jewish holidays.

Being a strong-willed child, she aimed for the lead roles in these plays and discovered that if she put a lot of energy into her reading during casting auditions, she invariably landed the role she wanted. Some of her schoolmates were jealous or angry because she always won the lead roles, but she didn't care. Playing a lead character made her feel important and that's all that mattered. She had a close circle of friends who were proud of her and admired her.

Generally, these girls also excelled in their studies and looked upon Erika as their leader. The rest of her classmates, who got lower grades, or were less talented in Erika's eyes, did not matter to her.

She seldom saw her sister, since Judith was in classes three years above her. They met on the weekends when twice a month they were allowed to go for a home visit. Piry had given Judith detailed, written directions on how to reach their home, almost an hour's walk from the boarding school.

Winter came early that year, and on their second visit home, at the beginning of October, it was snowing heavily as they started out from school on a Friday afternoon.

Halfway home, Judith said to Erika, "I need a toilet."

"But there isn't any here," Erika pointed out, looking at the empty streets and locked gates of apartment buildings.

"Wait for me here," Judith ordered, pointing at a doorway as they were walking by a bombed-out apartment building. Before Erika could protest, Judith disappeared along a wall still standing on the left as one entered the gawking ruins.

Judith must have gone deep inside, for Erika could not see her from the doorway. She stood waiting, feeling the snowflakes landing on her hair, on her face, and inside the scarf around her neck. She was getting cold, and increasingly worried, for Judith seemed to be taking forever. "Googo," Erika begged, calling her sister by the nickname she had used when she was a baby and couldn't pronounce Judith's name, "Please, please come back!"

No sound came from the ruins. Erika began to panic. *What if Judith fell into a bomb hole and died inside—would I find my way home or even back to school?* and knew the answer was "no" to either place. Judith was the only one who carried these addresses. Erika called out again, now with tears streaming down her face, pleading, "Please, pleeaase come out."

Finally, laughing, Judith emerged. "What are you whining about? Let's go."

The relief Erika felt made her forgive her sister's cruelty—for she was sure that Judith had deliberately not responded to her calls, just to worry her. She was merely glad that Judith had reappeared and that they would soon be at home with their mother.

◎◉◎

Judith and Erika found that not only their mother but Lilly, their beloved aunt, was also there. It was a joyous reunion, for Lilly stayed the whole weekend. She took the girls to the nearby Saint Steven's Park to play, something they hadn't done since before the war. They threw snowballs at each other, and Lilly stopped Judith from hitting Erika with balls that were formed too hard, so it was fun. This was a happy time for the children, though their mother seemed rather preoccupied.

On the second evening at home, Judith asked Piry, "When is Dad coming back?"

"I don't know what to tell you," Piry replied.

Judith clung to her mother and told her, "I don't want to go back to school!"

"Me neither," Erika piped up.

But Piry explained that during the week both she and Lilly were out working, and no one would be at home to take care of them.

"It won't be long now, I'll find a way for you to come home to live with me, I promise," Piry assured them, though in reality she wasn't sure about the timing.

Both Piry and Lilly accompanied the children on their return to the boarding school. Judith became sullen and barely responded to the hugs she received before her mother and aunt left. Erika suppressed her anxiety by thinking of her friends, and the things she loved doing at school.

It wasn't until the end of the school year, when her daughters returned home for the summer, that Piry had worked up enough courage to tell her daughters about their father's death.

"You mean he will NEVER come back?" Judith asked, aghast.

"That is what dying is—it's going to heaven forever," Piry said sadly.

Judith sat stunned, then burst into a sob so heartrending that all Piry could do was to hold her tightly in her arms and let her cry.

Erika cried, too, but could not feel the same deep sorrow as her sister. By now, her father was just a vague memory. She was used to living without him. She left her mother and sister to their grief in the living room and went to the bedroom she shared with Judith. She sat down on her bed to think about her father, but except for a bit of sadness, she felt nothing more. Instead, she put on her pajamas, got under the duvet cover, and reached for the book on her night table. She buried herself in a fairy tale.

Piry entered the room with Judith, who, spent from crying, was ready to go to bed. Seeing Erika reading, Piry's first instinct was to take the book away from her and try to discuss how Erika felt about her father's death. Then she thought the better of it. Clearly, Erika's way of coping was to occupy herself with something other than the current reality.

Judith was the one who needed all the love her mother could give her. Piry waited for Judith to get into bed, and sat by her side, gently stroking her hair. After a few moments Judith pusher her mother away.

"I want to go to sleep now."

"Would you like to sleep in my bed next to me?" Piry asked Judith.

"No, I just want to stay here and sleep." Judith shut Piry out by rolling over to face the wall.

"Come to me if you change your mind," Piry told Judith with the most soothing tone she could muster. She felt helpless, watching her child suffer. She turned to leave, and saw that Erika had put the book down, and lay motionless, staring at the ceiling.

"The same goes for you," Piry said to Erika, leaning over to kiss her good night. "Just come to me if you feel like it."

"Thanks Mom," Erika replied, and closed her eyes, making it clear that she didn't want to talk either.

She had a hard time believing that her father would never come back. The story she had just read, was about twelve princesses, whose evil stepmother turned them into swans. They became princesses again with some smarts and magic by twelve princes. Erika imagined that her father was perhaps hiding somewhere, and that someday, by some magic he would reappear. She fell asleep with that thought.

Piry had left the door of her daughters' room ajar. She knew how hard it was to cope with the loss of a loved one. She hoped that her daughters will recover emotionally as she had to and go on with their lives.

At the end of the school year, the same Zionist organization offered to keep the children at their institute for the summer. Most of the children living there had suffered the loss of one or both parents and relatives. The surviving family members were grateful to be able to have a safe home for their children while they were trying to rebuild their lives.

Piry still had merchandise to sell at the villages and decided to let Judith and Erika also stay at the Zionist boarding school. The principal there assured Piry that the children will be taken on excursions into the hills on the Buda side and will be well cared for through a variety of activities. They could still go home every couple of weekends.

Both Judith and Erika were subdued on these home visits. They had accepted spending the summer at their boarding school since all their friends were there as well. When the next school year started, Erika officially entered first grade, and Judith went into fourth.

The sisters seldom saw each other but one day Erika heard through the school grapevine that Judith had gone with some friends to the roof of the building and told them to watch her jump off. Erika broke away from her friends and ran as fast as she could, upstairs.

She found that Judith's friends, terrified, were holding her sister back. Judith, on spotting Erika arrive, pulled back, and pretended to have been just joking. She told her friends never to mention it to any of their teachers. When Erika questioned her during one of their home visits, Judith also ordered her to never talk about it to their mother. She claimed, it was just a prank.

Having remembered Judith's wartime attempts at jumping off from the top floor of their building, Erika knew it wasn't just a prank. But she did not want to create a concern for her mother, so she decided to keep quiet about it. She was good at keeping secrets.

When their school year was over, for the summer of 1947, Piry secured places in two different vacation camps for her daughters. Both camps were in the hills of Buda and promised to provide lots of outdoor activities in the sun. Piry felt, this would be healthier for her daughters than remaining in the city during the hot summer.

By this time, she had managed to sell the entire stock from the warehouse. Besides gold coins, she had turned part of her earnings into American dollars. Despite her success financially, Piry felt rudderless in a life without Zoltán. She decided that the money from the sale of their stock needed to be kept hidden as savings for emergencies. She was hoping she could find some sort of a job during the summer and perhaps hire a maid again so she could work and also bring her daughters home in the fall.

On occasions, when Piry got together with Irén, the latter reiterated her concern that Hungary was becoming a country dominated by the Communist Party. "It is backed by the Soviet Union, whose army is still here to keep Hungary under their control." Irén explained.

She saw this as a threat to every citizen's freedom. By now Irén had learned that her brothers and parents had perished in Nazi concentration camps. Now living alone, Irén filled her days working as a bookkeeper and as a political activist. She complained to Piry that slowly all political parties were being integrated into the Hungarian Communist Party. Those who did not join seemed to be treated more and more like "the enemy within."

During one of their dinners together, Irén advised Piry not to return her daughters to the Zionist run boarding school in the fall.

Irén explained, "You must be aware, that there are negotiations going on among the 'powers that be' about the establishment of a Jewish State. The Soviet Union is hoping that the new State of Israel will join the communist fold. But if they decide to join the West, the Zionists will become black sheep, and our government will be looking askance at the Zionists' loyalty in Hungary. It's not a good idea for you to be associated with their organization at this point," Irén warned.

Piry thanked her and wondered where she could place her children in the fall if she didn't manage to get a job.

In the meantime, Erika was in trouble at the summer camp. For some reason, she often ended up in the infirmary, either with an upset stomach or having a cold with high fever. During one of these occasions, when Erika was ready to leave the sick ward, and return to her activities the next morning, she came down with a cold again. So, instead of playing outside, she was reading in bed for days. Her friends at the camp came to visit her when they could. They were not allowed into the sick ward, so they would come to the window of her room.

As Erika began to feel better, she would get out of bed and lean out the open window visiting with them. The afternoon before she was to be released, a new doctor came into her room and explained to Erika that she was to get an injection against a dreadful new disease called Polio.

"It won't hurt," the doctor promised. "It will protect you from becoming very sick and not being able to walk or run." He injected her and left.

Erika had to admit, the doctor was right, the sting wasn't bad.

The next morning, Erika woke early, ready to jump out of bed, so she could dress and leave the sick ward. Except that she couldn't. Both her legs were bent at the knee, just the way she had curled them up when she fell asleep, lying on her right side. Now she rolled onto her back but could not straighten her legs.

The nurse came in, bringing breakfast, and cheerfully saying to Erika, "Finally, you'll get to have some fun outdoors with your friends."

"I can't straighten my legs, so I don't know how to get up," was Erika's response.

The nurse put the tray down and examined Erika's legs, gently pushing down on her knees.

Erika winced, "They won't go down."

The nurse shook her head. Just stay put till I ask a doctor to look at you."

Erika rolled onto her side, wondering what would happen to her now. The worry about not being able to get up killed her appetite for breakfast; but she did have to use the toilet. She rolled out of bed, falling on all fours, ignoring the pain her fall had caused her. She found that she could move her legs, she just couldn't straighten them.

Thus, she managed to make her way on her hands and knees to the bathroom. With great difficulty, for her legs seemed to have lost most of their strength, she pulled herself up with her arms, and twisting and turning, managed to seat herself on the toilet.

She didn't even wonder how she would get back to her room. She rolled off the seat, more carefully this time, and moved like a small cat, on all fours. However, she couldn't pull herself up onto the bed. When the doctor and a nurse showed up some time later, they found her lying on the floor, curled up into a ball.

The doctor lifted her onto the bed. Erika began to tremble with apprehension. He ignored this as he surveyed her bent knees.

"Do your legs hurt?" he asked.

"No, they're just stuck," Erika explained.

"Can you straighten them?"

"I've tried, but I can't."

The doctor lifted Erika's right leg by the ankle and pushed down hard on her knee. Erika screamed in pain. He let go of her leg, looking upset.

"We'll have to keep you here till your legs straighten out," he told her, and left.

The nurse helped Erika sit up by placing pillows behind her back. With the help of an attendant, they rigged up a table over her bent, frozen knees, so she could eat sitting up. They brought her books and games to play with, and assured her, in a day or two she'll be all right.

But she wasn't. Days went by, and Erika's legs were still in their cramped, folded position. Twice a day, doctors from the infirmary would visit her, try to straighten her legs, but give up when Erika screamed in pain.

A week passed with Erika still in bed. Her friends came to the window and Erika crawled onto a chair, kneeling, to talk to them. She entertained them with the stories she had read, and they talked about their activities. Their visits were the highlight of her days.

A physical therapist came daily, and gently tried to pry Erika's legs straight, but that didn't work either.

Piry came to visit a couple of times, but that was all she could do. "There is no point in taking you home," she explained. "Here you are under 24-hour care, something I couldn't do for you at home. Please be patient and I promise I'll find a solution if you're still not walking by the time camp is over."

Erika understood her mother's explanation, but each time Piry left, she felt forlorn and abandoned.

At the end of the week of her paralysis, a new doctor arrived. He was a tall, strong-looking man. He examined Erika briefly, asking whether she was in pain.

"Only when I try to straighten my legs," Erika explained.

"I'll do it for you," the doctor said, and picking up Erika's right leg. With a swift motion he pushed down hard on Erika's knee while with the other hand lifter her foot high up.

Erika screamed at the top of her lungs because it felt like the doctor was ripping her leg off at the knee. He quickly let go, and ignoring Erika's reaction, bent over her, to get a closer look at the leg. Erika, in absolute fury, lifted her knee and struck him in the face.

The doctor was shocked. Erika must have hit his nose, for he put his palm on it, seemingly in pain. Then he let go of his nose, and shouted, "You brat!"

He turned and left the room without another look at Erika. Despite her anger at the pain the doctor had caused her, Erika felt a great sense of satisfaction at being able to fight back. By now, she hated being in bed and had no patience for doctors who couldn't do anything but torture her. She lay back on her pillow and thought, maybe I'll always be like this. How will I go to school then? For the first time, her condition terrified Erika.

◎◉◎

The next morning, a lovely young woman in a white coat came to see Erika. She had large brown eyes and curly brown hair which framed her longish face. She sat on the edge of Erika's bed and looked her in the eyes.

"Erika, my name is Miss Vera, and I need to ask you something. Do you wish to spend the rest of your life in bed, and never go outside to play or go to school like your friends?"

"No, no!" Erika shouted. Miss Vera was voicing her very own fears.

"Well, if we can't straighten your legs, that's what will happen. You won't be able to walk. You will have to sit in a wheelchair all the time and miss out on a lot of fun you could have if your legs were straight. What do you think of that?"

"That's horrible! I'd rather die!"

"Then help me to help you. I will come every day, and we will work together on straightening your legs. It might hurt but if you won't put up with some pain, you might never walk again."

Her gentle tone, her calm and straightforward manner, touched Erika's heart.

"I will work with you," she promised, her eyes filling with tears.

Thus began an arduous physical effort on both their parts. Each day, Miss Vera came at mid-morning, and again in the late afternoon. She gently pulled on Erika's legs or pushed her knees down while Erika tried sliding her heels forward on the bed. She winced and groaned but she understood that without this effort she would be paralyzed forever. So, Erika bore the pain bravely. She even continued to push down on her legs in between the therapy sessions.

After a few days, both of them noticed that Erika's legs began to yield. This encouraged Erika to such an extent, that now she was spending hours in bed working on her legs, instead of reading. By the middle of the second week of treatments, she was able to slip off the bed, and walk with her knees still bent, but about half as much as before. By the end of the third week, her legs were almost completely straight, and she could walk.

Miss Vera gave her exercises to strengthen the muscles that had atrophied some during the long bed rest, and Erika did them with determination. Being able to use her legs again was thrilling. She felt like she had been released from a terrible bondage. Walking was something Erika would never take for granted again.

Just two days before summer camp ended, and Erika was to be released from the sick ward, she came down with a cold again. Terrified, even with a fever of 39 Celsius, (102.2 Degrees Fahrenheit), she would move her legs, straighten them in bed, pull them under her by the heels and slide them out again, slowly, controlling the motion, tensing her muscles to make them strong.

When Piry came to the sick ward, to take her home, she praised Erika for working through the healing process. Piry had no idea of the inner strength her daughter had gained by learning that she could heal herself with some help and a great deal of willpower and effort.

The orphanage for Jewish children, where Piry had placed Judith and Erika for their new school year, was a nightmare existence for Erika. One of the rules was that in the morning older children had to help younger ones to dress, supervise their breakfast, and get them ready for school.

Judith took it upon herself to care for Erika. Each morning, she insisted on combing Erika's hair that had reached almost to her waist. Judith liked weaving it into two pigtails down Erika's back, "as mother likes it," she told the younger girl. The trouble was that Erika's light auburn hair easily tangled, and Judith had little patience. She would pull and yank Erika's hair with a rough brush to straighten the strands before weaving them into tight pigtails.

"You're hurting me!" Erika would protest.

"Shut up or I'll hit you," would be Judith's response.

At times, Judith experimented with Erika's hairstyle, folding the pigtails into various convoluted designs.

"I look ridiculous," Erika would protest. "I'm not going to school looking like this!"

"Of course, you are," Judith insisted, admiring her creation.

Erika was embarrassed by her elaborate hairdos and hated Judith for forcing her to wear them. Even after she got to school, she was too afraid of Judith to dare change her 'hairstyle of the day'.

Meals at the orphanage were another ordeal for Erika. The food was plentiful, but she disliked most of it. She ate the potatoes, beans, and lentils in soup or as a vegetable dish. But could not swallow a bite of pureed yellow peas that was served for dinner at least twice a week. The smell of the fried onions that garnished the plateful of pureed peas made her nauseous. On those evenings, she made sure she sat away from her sister, and close to the huge fireplace in the room. When no one was looking, Erika would toss the contents of her plate into the live coals. She grew thin and was often sick with a cold or an upset stomach, resulting in frequent stays at the orphanage's infirmary.

Her one joy was the institute's library. While other children played, Erika spent her time reading once she finished her homework. The librarian was an older, heavy-set woman, with wavy white hair in a bun. She recognized Erika's hunger for this escape and treated her kindly. Whereas other children could check out books only once a week, she allowed Erika to get another book as soon as she finished reading the one, she had borrowed. Erika read two or three books a week.

She usually read in the large "common room," where the children spent their after-school hours doing homework and then playing. On one occasion, Erika sat near the brick fireplace with her back against the wall, completely absorbed in 'Treasure Island' by the English writer, Robert Luis Stevenson.

It had been translated into a fluid, easy-to-read Hungarian. Erika didn't understand everything in the book since it told a tale of a strange world with very odd people in it. But she was absorbed in the narrative with an intensity that it made the room disappear around her.

Finally, at a lull in the exciting adventure story, she stopped reading and realized that the room where she was sitting was completely deserted. She felt like she was emerging from a profoundly silent bubble and wondered where everyone had gone. She shut her book and went upstairs.

To her surprise, she discovered the usual noise of everyone busily getting ready for bed. The bathrooms were full of laughter as children toweled themselves down after a shower, while others were at the sinks, brushing their teeth. She wondered why they were already preparing for bed when she hadn't even had dinner. She spotted her best friend Ildikó at one of the sinks.

"What happened to dinnertime?" She asked Ildikó.

"That was hours ago!" the freckled brunette replied. "Where have you been? Miss Hannah, two caregivers, and your sister were all looking for you!"

Miss Hannah was one of the supervisors at the orphanage.

"Why?" Erika was dumbfounded.

"Duh…you were missing at dinner! You'd better let someone know you hadn't run away!" Ildikó advised her.

Miss Hannah was the kindest of the supervisors, so Erika bolted to her office.

"Where have you been?" The pretty, young woman cried out when Erika slipped through her door.

"I was reading in the common room by the fireplace, and no one let me know we had to go to dinner," Erika explained.

Miss Hannah laughed. "You are a strange one."

She was forgiven. The floor supervisor brought Erika for dinner a large slice of bread, smeared with garlic and cooking oil, and told her to eat fast, then wash up and go to bed with the others. Her friends near her in the dormitory greeted her as if Erika had been lost. They laughed when she told them it was a book she had gotten lost in.

Just before falling asleep, Erika thought about her experience of 'falling into a deep silent space' while reading. She loved her disappearance into it and wondered whether she could ever do it again, at will.

When the leaves turned to red and gold in the fall of 1947, Lilly's long-awaited wedding took place. Lilly and Donát got married in an elegant ceremony at the Dohány Temple, the largest Jewish temple in Budapest, in fact, in all of Europe. Nearly two hundred people came to celebrate it, since Donát and his brothers were important factory owners and prominent members of this congregation.

Judith and Erika were allowed to spend the weekend at home so they could attend the wedding. They were the bridesmaids, and wore pink taffeta dresses, white gloves, and matching pink socks inside their black patent leather shoes—all provided by their Aunt Lilly.

In the large temple, the bride and groom's relatives were directed to sit the first row. Next to Piry sat Donát's sister, Violet, and her husband, Vidor, plus Donát's two other brothers, Elek and Harold, with their wives. All the other invited guests were asked to sit in the rows that followed. Once the guests were settled in the pews, the Rabbi and the Cantor entered from a side door. A chupa or canopy, had been erected in front of the bima, the altar. It was a white damasque roof stretched over four sturdy white metal posts, wide enough for the bride and groom to stand comfortably under it. The canopy symbolized the new home of the couple.

Once the Rabbi stood facing the congregation on the bimah, the groom was led from the back of the temple to the chupa, flanked by his two brothers, Elek and Harold. When they reached the chupa, the brothers stepped to the side, Donát went under the canopy, and turned toward the center isle where his bride was now slowly walking toward him. Because her parents and two of her siblings had died in the war, Lilly was led by her closest surviving relative, Piry.

Judith and Erika followed behind them, carrying small bouquets of Lilies of the Valley. Erika thought that Lilly looked like a fairy tale princess in her shimmering white satin gown and flowing gauze veil. It was held in place by a crown of Lilies of the Valley over her cascading jet-black hair. Donát wore black tails, a white bow tie, and white gloves. He looked very solemn as he awaited his bride.

Once at the chupa, Erika and Judith were directed to stand by Piry's side, where they got a clear view of the ceremony.

The Rabbi now faced the bride and groom, as well as the congregation and started by reciting a prayer in Hebrew. Then the Cantor sang and encouraged the congregation to sing with him. Then the Rabbi asked Donát "Do you, Donát Halász take Lilly Kohn as your lawful wedded wife to love and cherish till death do you part?" After Donát said, "Yes," the Rabbi repeated the question to Lilly, but of course asking if she wanted him as her husband.

After Lilly whispered "Yes," the Rabbi instructed Donát to place a ring on Lilly's finger.

Donát's older brother, Elek, handed him the ring, and Donát smiled as he slowly put it on Lilly's ring finger on her right hand.

"You may now kiss the bride," said the Rabbi.

Donát carefully lifted the veil off Lilly's face and planted a gentle kiss on her lips.

A moment of silence followed, while Donát's younger brother, Harold stepped forward holding in his hand something wrapped in a white napkin.

He put it on the floor in front of Donát's feet. Everyone in the temple watched as Donát raised his right foot and brought it down powerfully over the object. As the sound of shattered glass filled the temple, everyone broke into a loud shout, "Mazel Tov!"

The Cantor and the guests burst into a jubilant song, clapping the rhythm, and Erika could feel that the whole temple was filled with a sense of joy.

Then the Rabbi held up his hand to quiet people down, and after several more blessings, invited the guests to the sumptuous reception at the temple's social hall. Erika and Judith sat near their mother at the long table filled with guests, relishing the dishes. It was 'real food' versus the fare at the orphanage. However, they were whisked home by their nanny soon after the wedding cake was cut, when Piry caught each girl sipping a glass of champagne, their eyes looking a bit too bright.

Piry learned that four of her aunts and several cousins did return either from hiding or concentration camps. In the late fall of 1947, two cousins, Ernő, and his younger brother, Elemér, looked her up, and asked if they could stay with her till they got their footing back.

Piry was glad of their company. They were pleasant, smart men. Before the war, their families owned a grocery store in Debrecen. Their parents were now dead, and they decided not to return to his hometown, but to start a business in Budapest. Able to live at Piry's apartment, it took them only a few months to set up a tiny store in a central location.

Learning that Piry was not going to continue her hardware business, they invited her to work with them. She tried it for a while but did not enjoy it. She did not like dealing with retail customers, and the scent of groceries brought back painful memories of her parents' restaurant.

Ernő sensed that Piry did not enjoy working at their store. He asked Piry to have dinner with him on a Saturday evening at the Csárdás, a fancy restaurant in the center of the city. During the delicious main course of "fogas" a fancy Hungarian fish, accompanied by roast potatoes and green peas, they talked casually about the business and Piry's children. They were due to come home for a visit the following weekend.

After the desert of a richly layered chocolate cake, Ernő put his fork down and said, "Piry, I don't know how to do this, so I'm going to come straight to the point: "Would you marry me?"

Piry was completely taken aback. She liked Ernő, had known him most of her life as her cousin, but could not imagine him as her husband. He was a short, slightly built man, with curly black hair and warm brown eyes. Not bad looking, but Zoltan's memory made Piry wish for a man taller and more muscular, similar to her husband. She did not want to hurt Ernő's feelings by rejecting him, so she replied tactfully, "Ernő, I am honored that you should ask me to be your wife. But Zoltán's memory is still too fresh for me. I am not ready for another marriage; I don't know if I ever will be."

"Is that a definite no, or should I wait for you?" Ernő was a man of quick decisions.

"Don't wait for me."

Shortly after Piry's rejection, Ernő and his brother Elemér came to a drastic decision. They would sell their—by now profitable—business and emigrate to America.

"Look at the political situation of this country!" Ernő pointed out to Piry. "All the political parties that still exist are fighting for power. We still have the Soviet Army stationed as 'peacekeepers,' eating us out of house and home. That new 'home security' organization, the AVO, is arresting members of Parliament as though they were common criminals. I'll bet you my bottom pengő that soon the Communist Party will take over. I don't want to be here when we become ruled by Russians."

"You are exaggerating," Piry protested. I saw Laci not long ago. He is working with Péter Gábor, the head of the AVO. I even met Péter! He didn't seem like a monster to me."

"You'll see! Though I'd rather you didn't. Marry me, and we'll take the children with us to America. I think we could all have a happy life there."

But Piry could not overcome her lack of physical attraction for Ernő. She smiled at him with warmth and charm, but still said, "I can't go."

After Piry's repeated refusal, in the following few months the two brothers sold their business. They obtained their passports and visas to America and said good-bye to Piry.

"Thank you for having us with you," they told her. "Remember, you'll always have a home with us in America."

Ernő added, "Should you change your mind, you and the girls will always be welcome."

◎◉◎

Not long after Ernő and Elemér left, Piry was introduced to Ferenc Haydu. Feri, as he preferred to be called, owned a prosperous fabric store in a Budapest suburb, named Ùjpest. He also had a large residence there in a good neighborhood of private homes. Soon after they met, he asked Piry to come and look at his home. The property consisted of a spacious three-bedroom apartment and a separate one-bedroom apartment occupied by one of his brothers, Imre and his wife, Magda. In the center of the dwellings was a garden filled with a rainbow of colorful flowers. Beyond the garden was a separate long structure of four storage rooms. Piry was impressed.

Újpest was not considered a particularly elegant part of town. Many working-class people lived there, and not far from Feri's house was a giant medicine factory, the Chinoin. But Piry overlooked these details because she was falling in love.

Feri was a head taller than she, had a muscular, stocky build, similar to Zoltán's, and a tough, handsome face, framed by wavy brown hair. His smallish blue eyes under bushy eyebrows seemed somewhat shifty at first but Piry soon accepted them as part of the clever, but quite inarticulate personality of the man. Feri's wife and three-year-old daughter perished in a Nazi concentration camp. He had survived the war on the eastern front, in Transylvania, slaving in a forced labor camp.

Feri was eager to marry again and told Piry he loved the idea of getting two daughters in exchange for the one he had lost. He introduced her to his three brothers and their wives, and to his friends. Some of them subtly hinted to Piry that Feri had not been a very nice husband during his first marriage. Piry's own close friends urged her to think twice about rushing into this marriage.

Lilly, busy settling into her own new life with Donát, simply asked, "Are you in love with him? Will he make a good father for your daughters?"

Piry replied, "I'm crazy about him, and I believe he'll be a great father."

"Then don't listen to gossip and envy. Marry him, and be happy," Lilly advised.

Before making her decision, Piry brought home her daughters for the Christmas weekend, so they could meet Feri. She wanted to see how they interacted with each other. To observe Feri's reaction to her daughters as well as assess her children's response to him.

Piry had also done this when Ernő asked her to marry him. Even if she wasn't in love with the man, she didn't want to rule out the possibility of providing a home for her daughters. Erika liked both Ernő and Elemér, but then Erika liked most people. Judith was hostile and told her mother, "I will never accept Ernő as my father."

Eleven-year-old Judith's attitude definitely influenced Piry. If Judith won't accept Ernő, and I'm not in love with him, why would I marry him? she thought. But Feri was a different matter. Piry was in love, and no friends or daughter could dissuade her from marrying the man. She told herself, Judith will never approve of any man as her new father so I should do as I see fit. All Piry could hope for was that eventually Judith would accept Feri as a stepfather who took care of them as a family.

The wedding was held on February 10th, 1948, in a quiet ceremony at the large, beautiful Jewish Synagogue of Újpest. Attending was Lilly and Donát, Feri's three brothers and their wives: Imre and Magda, the youngest brother Lajos and his wife Ica, and Vince, the oldest brother, a widow.

A number of Piry's relatives and friends, who had survived the war, had also come to celebrate the occasion.

For their honeymoon, Feri took Piry to Kékestető in the Mátra mountains, a beautiful vacation spot during the summer, and a popular ski resort in the winter. After a week's honeymoon, they moved into his house in Újpest.

It was mid-February, and Piry figured, by the end of the school year, in early June, she will be able to get her daughters out of the orphanage because she could provide a home for them. There were two schools in the neighborhood, both walking distance to their new home. All seemed perfect.

Except that a mere three weeks into the marriage, Piry knew she had made a terrible mistake. Feri was great in bed but that was where his attributes ended. Day by day, even during their honeymoon, he had been changing from the man who had courted her with flowers and sweet words, into some primitive, uneducated boor, whose table manners were poor and conversation crude.

Piry now recalled all the warnings by his and her friends but felt helpless. She was too ashamed to leave him. Somehow, she could not admit failure. It would have been too humiliating, and besides, she had given up her apartment in Pest. She had no place to go and no way to support her daughters.

She thought, *perhaps in time I will be able to change him to be the man with whom I fell in love, not the man he is with his mask off. Besides, his house is large and wonderful, and my daughters need a home and family life again. Somehow, I will manage.*

The first weeks after moving in, Piry felt like her life with her second husband had taken her to another planet. Instead of living in the elegant apartment building in central Budapest, her new home was in a suburb called Újpest. In this part of town, acacia and chestnut trees lined quiet streets of spacious private homes, like Feri's. But this was only in the "better part" of Újpest.

Much of the district consisted of tiny houses which had only a kitchen and a living room, and perhaps one bedroom, or of two-story buildings with similarly small apartments. These were for the workers who lived near the large pharmaceutics manufacturing firm, Chinoin. It was located just six blocks from Feri's home. He did not point this out to Piry when showing her his home before they got married. Since she had moved in, she discovered that at times the acrid stench of chemicals puffing out of the tall factory chimneys permeated the whole neighborhood.

Piry wondered why she had never considered the surroundings to which her marriage would take her. *Because I didn't want to be deterred by anything,* she admitted to herself. *I was too in love to care or to listen to any advice. Now I have no choice but to make the best of it. Besides, the school year will be over in just a couple of months, and my daughters will be able to have a real family life again, Piry consoled herself. Until then I have plenty to do to make Feri's house home for them.*

The apartment's interior needed painting. All the parquet floors needed refinishing. The worn linoleum flooring in the kitchen, bathroom, and entry room had to be changed. Piry had to find suitable tiles and a skilled laborer to lay them, as well as a painter for all the walls.

She also wanted to have curtains made for all the windows. Feri could supply the fabrics from his store but for everything else she had to do her own shopping and hiring of workers.

Piry discovered that in Újpest there was only one shopping street, Árpád Út, with streetcars running along it to make the many businesses lining the broad avenue accessible. Feri's fabric store was centrally located on Árpád Út.

Depending on the weather, Feri either bicycled or walked to his shop, to open it by ten a.m. and close it at six p.m., six days a week. He was an observant Jew and attended temple services on Friday nights. But he kept the shop open on the Sabbath, much to Piry's chagrin.

"I do more business that one day than sometimes the whole week. I can't afford to close it. I don't tell you how to run the house, don't tell me how to run my business", he snapped at Piry, barring any objections from her.

Proprietary as Feri was about his store, he was the opposite concerning his house. He gave Piry free hand at fixing it up and making it a home to her liking. The building was a one-story, L-shaped duplex. From the street, all one could see was the long front façade, with four large windows. Inside, the house contained a large four-bedroom apartment, and another, one bedroom apartment, at the short end of the L.

Entrance from the street to both apartments was through a ten-foot-tall solid metal door, at the end of the building, past all the windows. It was painted apple green to match the stucco color of the exterior walls. It was kept locked at all times. Visitors had to press a small, white button on the wall next to the metal door, that rang in the main house. Ten-foot tall, thick stucco walls separated the neighbors' houses on all sides of the property, providing complete privacy. From the front gate, one proceeded down a tree lined walkway that led to a surprisingly lovely garden and to the front door of each apartment.

Feri's third brother, Imre, and his wife, Magda lived in the smaller apartment that sat at the short end of the L. Their living room and kitchen windows overlooked the garden. A long hallway led from their front door to their living room, bathroom, and bedroom. Their bedroom looked out on the street through the fourth large window of the building.

The long side of the "L" was home to Feri and his new family. Its front façade was facing the garden, which had two round flowerbeds in its center, full of the season's colors. Feri loved to garden and had an artist's eye for arrangements.

He had won several first prizes for his window displays at his fabric shop. Piry realized that it was this artistic side of his that had attracted her to him originally. It was also this aspect of Feri that enabled him to make his store successful. He instinctively knew what fabrics to stock and how to present his merchandise to make it irresistible to customers.

Clothes for both men and women were all custom made, with ready-made clothing barely entering the post-war market. Thus, hardly anyone left Feri's shop without buying. The interior of his house however, had been sadly neglected and now Piry took it upon herself to make it as beautiful as Feri's store.

The main entrance to Feri's apartment was through a front door with a glass window. It opened to a bright, square shaped room with a large window overlooking the garden. The only indication of its being the entrance was the tall hat and coat tree by the door. To the right of this room was a long, narrow kitchen with a window to the garden. On the opposite side of the room was a long walk-in pantry.

With money generously provided by Feri, it didn't take Piry long to change the linoleum floors of these areas to cream-colored ceramic tiles. She did the same thing with the floor of the next room, a dining and family room, and also with the bathroom floor next to it. Piry figured, these were the rooms the family and guests would first enter from the outside, and during rainy or snowy days, tile floors would be easy to clean.

She bought a vermillion red table and four chairs for the entry room, so during the summer they could eat there. For the winter dining room, she found a golden oak table and chairs which fit it perfectly. This was the room in which they would spend a lot of time during cold weather. A hazelnut-colored round ceramic stove nestled in a corner of the room, to keep it warm when needed. Piry also placed a comfortable armchair in the winter dining room. Re-upholstered in muted orange corduroy, it sat by the window through which light streamed in from the entry room.

This window's niche housed Feri's sophisticated radio. He could listen on it to all Hungarian stations. Even though Hungarian news were censored and broadcast only what the government wanted the population to hear, he could almost read between the lines and interpret as to what was really happening in his country and around the world.

Once these rooms were renovated, Feri begrudgingly admitted that he would never have thought of turning them into such attractive living quarters. Piry realized that this was his way of complimenting her on the work she had done and was happy to have pleased him.

From the winter dining room, a glass door opened into a spacious living room, and from here one continued through double doors to two of the bedrooms. These three rooms had the large double pane windows facing the street, matching the one in Feri's brother's apartment. The third bedroom which completed the long L shape of the house had no window but a large a glass door to the garden.

Piry had all the walls painted a light cream color, and all the parquet floors sanded, stained, and varnished a golden oak tint. The last step in Piry's home-decorating was to buy the right furniture for the rest of the rooms. By now, she knew that Feri was a taciturn, stubborn man, who listened to no one but his own counsel. If she wanted something from him, she learned not to ask for it outright.

Instead, she would say, "My Dearest," putting her arms around his powerful neck and nestling into his lap like a purring kitten, "yesterday I saw the most beautiful living room furniture. Do you think you could come and look at it with me?" and she'd suggest a time she knew he could spare by closing the store for a couple of hours.

"You know I don't have any help at the store, how could I leave it?" Feri would growl.

But Piry knew how to be patient and persistent in the sweetest possible way till she wore down his resistance, and he would agree to go and look with her. With such cajoling, Feri eventually paid for two antique sets of furniture, one for the living room and the other for the master bedroom.

The living room furniture was made of cherry wood, in a delicate Louis XIV style. It consisted of a sofa, a chest of drawers, two small, exquisitely carved armchairs, and a coffee table to be placed between them. The pièce de résistance was a tall linen closet with glass paneled double doors. Delicate serpentine carvings embellished the façade of each piece.

The master bedroom furniture was of the same period, made of golden walnut and decorated with inlaid tortoise shells, in thin brass frame around each. They glowed like jewels when the sun came through the large bedroom windows.

The second bedroom, its double windows also facing the street, was to be her daughters' room. Before they came home from boarding school, Piry went out of her way to find suitable furniture for them. This was a long room but narrower than the master bedroom, so the pieces had to be narrow as well. She discovered a set in a consignment store that consisted of a single bed, a long, narrow table with a matching chair, and a tall closet, with two sides for clothing separated by bookshelves in the middle.

All the pieces were painted a semi-gloss ivory with gold trimmings. A small vanity with a full-length oval mirror and a padded chair completed the set. Piry also bought a mattress that was to be placed on the floor every night for Erika to sleep on. During the day it could be stored under the Judith's bed. The last piece Piry bought was an oak school desk and chair that fitted perfectly under the window. Piry figured, one of the girls would use the desk for doing her homework, while the other could work sitting at the table in the middle of the room.

From the girls' bedroom a solid wood door painted cream color like the walls, led to the last room. This one had a door to garden, as yet another entrance to the home. Piry had placed luxurious Persian rugs to cover the floors in all the rooms, except this last one. This was to be the maid's room. Piry furnished it with a single bed, a cotton throw rug in front of it, a night table, plus a tall double-sided clothes closet, all made of pine and varnished in light beige.

All the windows had the typical Hungarian wood roll-up shades that darkened the rooms at night but were raised during the day. Piry hung cream-colored, translucent curtains in front of the shades to block curious eyes from the street during the day. She hung paintings and placed on the living room table the silver menorah (a six candles holder) that she had been able to rescue from her pre-war life. Her father had given it to her but originally it belonged to her birth mother, so it had special sentimental value for Piry.

Once the house décor was completed, Piry asked Feri to walk through the rooms with her for a look. He had tolerated the upheaval all the renovations had brought into his house but wasn't pleased with it. However, now he reluctantly granted Piry a smile, saying, "The whole house looks a lot nicer than with my previous stuff."

"Thank you for letting me do all this," Piry acknowledged, enfolding him into her arms.

Then it was time to bring her daughters home.

◎◉◎

Judith grudgingly admitted that having a home of their own after years of hiding and then being in boarding schools was wonderful. When they were alone in the children's room, she said to Piry, "I love this room; You did a great job on the rest of the house too—but do we also have to put up living with Feri?"

"Hush!" Piry reacted, even though she knew Feri was at the store. "You'd better treat him with respect, or you'll make trouble for all of us. And call him Apu (Dad). That's the least you can both do."

"Don't worry, I know." Judith opened her suitcase and went to arrange her clothes in her side of the closet.

Erika raced through the house, ecstatic about the space, the décor, the garden.

"Do I really have to share the room with Judith?" she whispered to Piry in the dining room, voicing her only concern about their new home. "After all, I don't even have a regular bed, just a mattress on the floor. I don't mind sleeping on the floor on it but I'm kind of worried about sharing a room with Judith. I'd rather be in the maid's room," she pleaded with Piry.

"Just try to get along," Piry scolded her, then added, "Maybe after a while, if you make friends with the maid, she'll let you take your mattress to her room. But for now, stop fussing and be happy with what you've got."

Erika grew quiet. There was no way to argue with her mother when she used that tone and ordered her to be grateful. *I'll just have to manage,* she concluded.

Shortly after Piry moved into Feri's home, she hired a maid to help her run the household. The young girl was fresh from a village in southern Hungary, and for a while Piry was also busy teaching Boriska housekeeping the way she liked to have things done.

Boriska—Bori for short—wore a triple layer of pleated skirts over her knee length cotton bloomers, and low cut, tight bodices that pushed up and displayed her ample bosom. She plaited her long blonde hair into two braids and pinned them on top of her head into an intricate design, like a golden crown.

After Piry introduced Bori to her daughters, both Judith and Erika made fun behind Bori's back about her blatant display of her "charms". As pre-puberty girls, they were bashful about their own bodies.

But they learned that this was how women dressed in Bori's village and soon got used to her appearance. She spoke with a heavy regional accent, which Erika found fascinating while Judith declared that she sounded "like a peasant".

"Of course she does!" Erika defended Bori's accent. "She is from the countryside."

Ignoring Judith's opinion, Erika endeared herself to Bori by helping her make beds, or cleaning vegetables in the kitchen for their main meal of the day. Breakfast was always just a cup of coffee and a slice of rye bread with butter and jam smeared on it. Lunch, eaten around two or three p.m., was the main meal of the day and needed hours of preparation.

At their boarding school, the two girls never gave a thought as to where the food had come from when it was served to them at mealtimes. At home, it was different. When possible, they were enlisted to help with pealing vegetables or setting the table. Erika always preferred to help in the kitchen, while Judith liked setting the table.

Their midday meal consisted to their meals of a first course, which was some kind of soup, or salad during the summer. Then came a main course, which always had a large serving of potatoes, or rice, or pasta, plus a vegetable, and a small portion of beef or chicken. When a dish had been prepared with a dairy product, such as sour cream or cheese, then the protein was either an egg or fish, since Piry ran a kosher kitchen and could not mix meat with dairy.

One of Erika's favorite foods was "layered potatoes." Sliced, boiled potatoes were layered with sliced hardboiled eggs, each layer doused with melted butter plus sour cream, then topped with breadcrumbs, and baked in the oven.

Feri loved a very simple dish, buttered spaghetti generously sprinkled with finely ground poppy seeds, heavily sweetened with powdered sugar. He would devour a heaping plateful of it the nights Piry prepared it especially for him.

Erika didn't particularly like spaghetti but watched with fascination how her mother made it. Piry kneaded the dough, then with skilled fingers flattened and folded it several times. Then sliced it at lightning speed into long strips and dumped it into boiling water.

"It helped growing up with parents who ran a restaurant," Piry commented smiling at Erika. "Now you can learn from me how to do it."

"I don't think I could ever do it as well as you," Erika laughed.

CHAPTER 8

SINCE IT WAS SUMMER, there was an abundance of fresh vegetables: peas, green beans, carrots, cauliflower, and spinach. This latter, Piry always prepared creamed. Meat dishes were served with a "sour" side dish: either a cucumber salad vinaigrette, or pickled cucumbers, or sauerkraut sautéed with onions and braised with laurel leaves and caraway seeds.

Piry and Erika also added a hot green or white pepper to their meals, that burnt the tender inner skin of their mouth, but they loved it. By contrast, Judith and Feri never touched hot peppers. Feri claimed it gave him heartburn; Judith simply didn't like them.

Actually, Feri ate his main meal at night when he came home from the store. During the day, he just had a sandwich that Piry had prepared for him each morning to take along. Whether it was Feri's need, or Piry's idea, but ten minutes after Feri got home, his meal was on the table, piping hot. He always ate everything with relish but never complimented Piry on her cooking. While he ate, Piry sat by his side, making small talk about the day's events, to which he responded in monosyllables.

Judith and Erika were usually sitting at the table as well. But having had their main meal in the early afternoon, they were either eating just a piece of buttered bread, or fruit, or were quietly reading.

"Never talk to a man about anything important till after he's had his meal," Piry would advise Judith and Erika, while they were helping her with meal preparations.

Every evening it was Bori's job to take off the bedcovers and prepare the beds for sleeping. Erika liked to go and help her, because while they were working, Bori would talk about her life in her village; her fiancé, and their plans to get married. She confided to Erika that she was only staying till the fall.

"I have to go home to help with the harvest," she said. "By then I'll have saved enough to buy me a new dress for my wedding after the harvest."

Erika knew she should let her mother know this, but Bori had asked her not to, so she said nothing. She knew instinctively that it was important to keep a secret if she had been asked to do so even if it meant not informing her own mother.

All summer long, Piry and Bori went to open air markets very early in the morning and returned with enormous baskets full of seasonal fruits and vegetables. Cherries, apricots, peaches, pears, and sour cherries, which was Erika's favorite fruit. Green beans and peas followed. Piry enlisted her daughters to help prepare the fruits and vegetables, so she could make them into preserves.

After each morning's shopping, Erika and Judith sat in their garden, facing the beautiful flowerbeds created by their stepfather. They had enormous bowls in front of them. It was their task to pit, peel, and slice the fruits and vegetables, and then toss them into the appropriate bowls. They even saved apricot pits to be dried out in the sun, for they had delicious nuts inside. Once dry, the hard shells were cracked, and the nuts eaten as a snack.

"I don't hear you!" Piry would shout to the girls through the open kitchen window, "Either talk or sing," she'd order them while they were working with the sweet, delicious fruits.

The girls would just laugh. They knew, Piry told them to do this so they wouldn't fill their bellies with so much fruit that later they would have cramps.

Each type of fruit and vegetable required a different way of preparation. The most complex were the apricots and peaches. These had to be cooked with sugar till they became a thick, spreadable jam. Then they were poured into sterilized jars and cooked again in a double boiler that had a special basket so water wouldn't get into the jars. This done, Piry would sprinkle a white preservative powder on the surface of each marmalade in the jar. The final step was to seal them by pouring a layer of hot wax on top which soon turned solid. Specially designed covers were fitted airtight over the jars. When they cooled, they were labeled and carried into the pantry and placed on the shelves in neat rows.

"You'll be very happy with these in the winter" Piry told her daughters, as they were eyeing the increasingly crowded shelves.

Sundays were Bori's day off, and the family's day to go out together. During the summer, Piry rose around six a.m., and packed two enormous baskets with roast chicken, salad, bread, pickles, fruit, and cake or cookies. She filled two huge bottles with juice made from her own raspberry syrup diluted with water. She carefully wrapped glasses into kitchen towels before placing them in the food baskets. Two large cotton blankets completed their supplies for the day. By eight o'clock, the whole family was ready to leave. Feri and Piry carried the heavy baskets, and each girl a blanket plus a bag with bathing suits. They took a streetcar to the Margit Bridge in Pest and then transferred to a bus that went to the jewel of city, Margit Sziget, (Margit Island) in the center of the Danube River.

◎◉◎

In the early history of Budapest, the island was called "Rabbits' Island," due to its enormous rabbit population. It was not inhabited by people. In 1241, King Béla made a pledge that if God helped him to successfully defend

Hungary against the Tartar invasion, he would bequeath his daughter, Margit, to the service of God. He was victorious over the Tartars, and true to his promise, built a church and a cloister on Rabbits Island. In 1251, he moved his nine-year old daughter to live there. She died in 1271, at age 29, but the religious order remained until 1354, when due to a Turkish invasion of Hungary, all the nuns fled from there to the city of Pozsony, in northwest Hungary. The island remained unused until 1838, when the Danube flooded Budapest. After the water receded, like a miracle, the ruins of the church and cloister were revealed. The government began a restoration project, making the island a recreation facility for the city. Like another miracle, twenty years later, Margit's grave was found. She was canonized and the island was renamed after her.

In modern times, Margit Sziget had become the most popular public park of the city. A deluxe hotel, the Nagyszálló, (Grand Hotel) stood at one end of the island, an outdoor summer theater held shows ranging from opera and ballet to comedies and children's plays. But the favorite daytime fun was provided by the Palatinusz, a public spa with seven swimming pools.

One pool was Olympic size, with 6 lanes. There were two natural thermal pools, one of which had been designed like a maze, with built in seats for soaking. The bottoms of two pools were raked from two feet to five feet in depth for children and non-swimmers. However, the crowning glory of the Palatinusz was the "wave pool". It was half Olympic size and had built-in wave-making machines. All day long, fifteen minutes before each hour ended, a bell chimed, and the motors got into action. For ten minutes, the pool would become a raging ocean. So many people would run to the pool and jump in to enjoy being bobbed by the waves that every summer at least one cartoon in a newspaper featured what looked like an ocean composed not of water but of a solid surface of human faces and heads.

Surrounding all the pools were fields of manicured grass for sitting, picnicking, and sunbathing. On arrival, after buying their day tickets at the box office, Piry and her daughters disappeared into the female dressing rooms, while Feri went to the men's section. They changed and placed their clothes into lockers with padlocks.

Emerging in their bathing suits, they sought out a spot partly in the sun partly in shade; for Piry and her daughters loved baking in the sun, but Feri liked to lie in the shade. Often, they met acquaintances and would place their blankets on the grass next to them. Since this was still just mid-morning, Judith and Erika would run off into the pools, while Piry stretched out in the sun, and Feri went to the thermal pools. He loved to soak his aching joints. They had been damaged during the winters he spent in a forced labor camp in Transylvania during the war, working in the snow and sleeping in unheated barracks without adequate clothing or food.

This was a time for all of them to relax and Erika loved it. At the start of the summer, wearing a rubber ring around her chest for swimming, she paddled in the shallow waters, and watched Judith being taught to swim by an instructor Piry had hired. He also offered to teach Erika, but after one lesson, during which he floated her in the water by putting a hand between her legs, she refused to continue, without revealing the reason. But she knew the strokes because Judith had shown them to her after her lessons, so she practiced them on her own.

There was a huge clock in the center of the spa, and Piry had told them to get back to her by noon, so both Judith and Erika showed up on time. Feri came out of his spa as well, and Piry served them lunch. After their early breakfast, and the swim, the food tasted delicious.

"No swimming for an hour after eating" Piry declared. She spread a generous amount of tanning lotion on each girl and ordered them to lie down and rest. She didn't have to tell Feri what to do. He was already napping, his joints relaxed, his belly full. Piry felt content; this was her reward for all the hard work she had been doing since she got married; having her daughters with her, being a family again.

During one of these Sunday afternoons, Erika went back to the children's pool and feeling safe with her rubber swim ring on, lay on her stomach in the water and started practicing the breaststroke Judith had taught her. Without noticing it, she had swum clear across the pool to the deep end. Thrilled, she turned around and swam back to the shallow side. It was not until she had stood up that she realized that she had forgotten to put on her swim tube. She had been wearing it all morning, and the memory of its pressure had made her think that she had it on but in fact, she had swum the length of the pool and back, without it.

Thrilled, she ran to Piry, "Mommy, I can swim! I just did it, without the tube!"

"Really?" Piry got up, hugged her, planting an affectionate kiss on her cheek, "I'm so proud of you! Come, show me."

Judith went along as well, and after Erika climbed out of the pool, she said warmly, "Now we can have fun in the water together! I won't have to worry anymore about you drowning!"

Erika felt proud and happy.

In the late afternoon, for the spa closed at six p.m., they all washed off the pool chlorine at the outdoor showers and went off to change into their street clothes. With much lighter baskets, and a light heart, they headed for home.

◎◉◎

Feri and each of his three brothers, were all two years apart in age. The oldest brother, Vince, a widower, lived in the countryside, where he owned a farm.

He grew vegetables and had a vineyard full of red and green grapes. Feri was the second oldest. The middle brother, Imre, and his wife, Magda, were the ones living in the second apartment on Feri's property. The youngest brother, Lajos, had an attractive but nagging wife, Ica, and a two-year old daughter, Anni. They lived not far from Feri but never invited him or his new wife and daughters to their place. Among the four brothers, Feri was the only "shop keeper," his two other brothers, Imre and Lajos made a living as truck drivers. Each one owned a large carriage made of sturdy wood, with front seats for the driver and a companion and the back section was for carrying whatever they were hired to do. The carriages were pulled by one or two horses, depending on the job load.

When Erika got to know better her new Uncle Imre, at times he invited her to the stable where he kept his horses after work. She watched him take off their harness and helped him load hay into the trough in front of them. She was thrilled, when guided by Uncle Imre's hand, she could stroke the velvety noses of the horses. They snorted and breathed hot air into her palm, and Erika loved it.

Uncle Imre also kept two goats in the stable. Each day, before going home, he set down on a small stool by the side of the female goat whose udder was swollen with milk. He placed an enameled blue bucket with white interior under the goat's udder and began to rhythmically squeeze two teats at a time. Erika saw with fascination the milk squirt in powerful streams from the tiny holes of the teats into the bucket.

"Can I try milking it, please," she begged her uncle.

"Here. Sit down." Uncle Imre got up and let Erika take his place. "Now hold on to each teat tight, and squeeze evenly but real hard, without pulling on them."

Erika tried. The teats felt soft like rubber tubes in her little hands. She squeezed but nothing happened. "I can't get any milk out," she looked up at her uncle.

"Yeah, it looks easy but it's harder than you think. When your hands get a little stronger, you'll be able to milk her." He sat down again, and as he quickly and efficiently milked the udders, he asked Erika, "Want to taste?"

"Yes!"

"Grab a cup."

He had a couple of enameled cups on a shelf and Erika brought one to him.

"Hold it under a teat" Imre instructed her.

She did, and he filled the cup halfway.

"Good enough for a first try," Imre laughed, and watched as Erika first smelled the milk and then took a sip.

"I like it!" Erika exclaimed. "It's so different! It's warm and smells and tastes of goat!"

"Well," Imre laughed, "That's just what you're drinking, goat's milk."

Then they bicycled home, with Erika sitting behind Imre, her legs stretched forward and away from the back wheels, her hands holding on to her uncle's waist. The small, round aluminum container with the goat milk was swinging from the handlebar as Imre pedaled them home.

◎◉◎

In late August, Uncle Vince invited them to his farm for the grape harvest. On a searing Sunday, they all got into Uncle Imre's carriage pulled by two of his horses, and he drove them to Uncle Vince's farm just north of the city.

Uncle Vince was a short, sturdy man with a handlebar mustache and small, laughing eyes under bushy brown brows. He welcomed them with freshly made cold lemonade.

"You can come and help, or stay cool in the house," he suggested, looking at the women and children.

"I can't stand all the bugs and the sun," Judith fussed, as she swatted at a couple of flies.

"I'll stay in the house with you," Imre's wife, Magda offered.

Piry and Erika followed Feri, who chose to go and help the harvesters.

Vince led them to a large field, where Erika saw children running around happily, while a group of women, their head covered with kerchiefs, and men wearing hats against the blazing sun, were walking amongst the vines. They were cutting off clusters of grapes and placing them into the large baskets they were carrying with them.

Vince turned to his brother and Piry, "Come, I'll show you how it's done. Erika, you can join the children."

Erika eagerly ran off, and it didn't take long before she was playing hide-and-seek among the walnut trees with the local children, three girls and two boys. After a while, one of the boys suggested, "Let's climb a walnut tree and pick some."

The boys held their hands together, so the girls could use them as a stepladder. They could place one foot in a boy's hands, held high, and lift the other leg to reach the lowest branch on the tree. Pulling themselves up on the branches, they all managed to end up in the largest tree. Climbing from limb to limb was not difficult. Erika had never been so high up in a tree and was a bit scared, but pride prevented her from telling the others. They each selected a limb to straddle and started picking walnuts that were all various shades of green.

"Get the darkest ones," one of the boys instructed them. "Those are the ripest."

"But it's more fun to pick the green ones," countered the other boy. "When you break those, the walnuts are milky inside and taste sweeter."

Erika noticed that as she broke off the green walnuts, her palms were getting green.

"Look," she held up her hands for the others to see.

"Yeah, you'd better not touch your dress with those hands, because the green won't come out in the wash," one of the girls warned her.

"Just throw the nuts to the ground," ordered the other girl. "We can't climb down holding them."

They watched as a small pile of walnuts was growing beneath their tree.

"That's enough," said the boy who seemed the oldest among them. "Let's climb down.

That was a bit difficult for Erika, but the others instructed her where to place her feet and, in the end, the oldest boy among them jumped to the ground first and caught each girl as they leaped off the last limb. Then they sat on the ground and using sharp stones they had picked up from around the tree, set to crack open the walnuts.

Erika could feel the green outer husk spray her face as she hit the walnuts and realized, not only her hands and face but also her clothes were splattered with the green juice. But she was having too much fun to care. Peeling off the yet soft brown shell, the semi-ripe walnut inside tasted sweet and milky. *So delicious*, Erika thought.

After a while, she noticed that at the end of the grape fields, several adults were doing something really strange. The men had rolled up their pants high, and the women gathered their skirts up and tucked them into their waist to make them into shorts. Then both men and women removed their shoes and climbed into huge vats, where they began stamping their feet in a dance without music.

"What are they doing?" Erika asked her new friends.

"Oh, they're making must," explained one of the boys.

"What is that?"

"It's the first step to making wine. The grapes have to be crushed so they release their juice. And the best way to do this is by stamping on them. Then they take the grape juice and pour it into barrels, to let it ferment till it becomes wine."

"So that's how wine is made?" Erika was amazed.

"Yeah. And they mix the grape skins with the food for the pigs," laughed one of the girls, "and then all the pigs get a little drunk."

"No, silly, they don't get drunk, the skins don't get fermented, because they give it to the pigs fresh," countered the other girl.

"Come, let's taste the must! I'm pretty thirsty after all those nuts!" suggested the younger boy.

They all rose and ran to the vats where the men and women were stomping. One of the men offered the children to taste the must, handing them small glasses with the red liquid.

Erika felt uncomfortable, holding the glassful of the juice that had been made by the bare feet of the workers. But when she took a sip, she changed her mind. The drink was sweet and smooth like the best juice she'd ever tasted. It was also a bit fizzy, as if someone had mixed it with soda water.

They ate lunch close to mid-afternoon, and Erika had a few more glasses of must with the fried chicken and roast potatoes the women had served. By the time she climbed into the back of Uncle Imre's carriage at dusk, she felt strangely lightheaded.

"How many glasses of must have you had?" Piry asked her.

"Don't know."

"Didn't someone tell you, it's fermented, and you can get drunk on it?"

"I guess not," Erika grinned, feeling mischievously happy.

"And look at your hands and clothes!" exclaimed Feri. "Don't you realize how much soap it will take to get you cleaned up? Soap costs money, you know!"

Erika shook her head, "Sorry, I didn't think of that."

In reality, she didn't care. *Apu is being stingy and doesn't understand anything. This is the best summer I've ever had, and I am just feeling happy. I won't let him spoil it.*

◎◉◎

The only sad note of the summer was when true to her word, Bori had said good-bye to them late August. To her surprise, Erika didn't miss her as she had thought she would. Perhaps it was because she took an instant liking to the next maid her mother had hired just a few days after Bori had left. She was a young gypsy girl, and her name was Vica.

Vica was pretty. She had coal black eyes and long black hair that she pulled back into a ponytail, tying it with a red or yellow ribbon. She was small and slim, and always wore a tight-fitting blouse over long, ruffled skirts that hung to her ankle. She liked to walk around barefooted, but as the weather got cooler, she did slip on her small feet black patent leather shoes if she had to go outdoors.

The first week of September both Judith and Erika started school again and had homework to do in the afternoons. But Erika still found time to befriend Vica by helping her make the beds at night. Vica usually talked to her about men. Erika didn't understand everything in her stories, but she liked hearing about Vica's love life.

"There was this real handsome gentleman," Vica confided in Erika, "... and he was so generous with me. He took my virginity, but I was glad for him be the one who deflowered me. He gave me some money and a real nice set of gold bracelets. See?" Vica raised her right arm to show off the two thin bangles she was wearing.

Erika had no idea what "virginity", or "deflowering" meant but she knew from the way Vica talked about it that it was something precious.

"Of course, I never saw him again but there were some others who hung around longer." Vica looked nostalgic. Erika kept quiet so she would hear about the other men. It seemed that they all loved Vica and gave her money and presents but did not stay with her for long.

Then one Sunday, as Vica was leaving for her day off, Piry came into her daughters' room and caught Vica red handed, collecting hair ribbons and sweaters from the girls' closets.

"Just what do you think you're doing?" Piry thundered at the maid.

Vica grinned, "Oh, Ma'am, you don't mind if I take just a few of these for my family."

"I most certainly do! Let me see what else you're taking in your bag!"

Piry grabbed Vica's large handbag off the floor and looked inside. She pulled out the silver *menorah*, her six-prong silver candle holder, the only thing that Piry inherited from her birth mother. It was beautifully designed, with a dragon head decorating each side, and Piry cherished it for its artwork as well as for the memory of her mother. She had it stored with Miklos Nagy during the war, and now she had almost lost it. Piry, who never raised her voice, was now shouting: "Out! This instant! Get out of my house!"

She took Vica's bag and dumped its content on the floor, but there didn't seem to be any other stolen item in it. Piry wondered whether on previous occasions Vica had taken any of her jewelry but didn't want to reveal its hiding place by checking on it. Instead, Piry warned the girl, "If you had taken any other thing from this house, you'd better return it, or I'll send the police after you. I know where you live! I'll have your whole family put in jail!"

Terrified, Vica backed away from Piry's fury. "I swear, Ma'am, this is the first time I've taken anything. This is all I took. I don't know what possessed me to do that when you and your family have been so kind to me!"

"Out! NOW!" Piry pointed at the door.

"Can I just get my things?" Piry watched as Vica collected her few belongings. Since she had already been paid for her week's work, Vica left through the door that led from her room to the outside gate.

"Open the gate and give back the house keys" Piry ordered her.

Judith and Erika had witnessed the scene in Vica's room, and then followed Piry and Vica, as the girl hurriedly left, too intimidated, to say good-bye to them.

"Good riddance," Judith complimented her mother, as they returned to the house.

"I'll miss her," Erika said, "She was so nice, I had no idea she was stealing."

"All gypsies steal," Judith declared victoriously because her theory had just been proven.

"I can't believe that" Erika countered. She had an innate trust in people and refused to judge all by the actions of one. "Maybe Vica was just very poor."

"All right, girls, we don't have a maid anymore, come and help me make lunch," Piry announced, putting an end to their discussion.

◉◉◉

In the ensuing weeks both Judith and Erika had to help their mother with household chores. Erika didn't mind making beds and washing dishes, while Judith preferred to dry the dishes and dust and vacuum. Piry did all the shopping, cooking, and sandwich preparations as she made sure that Feri didn't feel the absence of the household help. But Piry did, and she knew, her daughters did as well. She started looking for a maid.

Two weeks passed, and one day, when Erika returned home from school, she found her mother sitting in the summer dining room, talking to a very elegant woman, who looked to be about her mother's age.

"Erika, come meet Mária. She will be our new housekeeper." Piry beckoned.

Erika walked forward, and shook the woman's small, bony hand extended to her.

"Hello. I hope we will be great friends," Mária smiled, showing her even white teeth that were marred by ridges across them.

Erika stayed in the room and listened to her mother and Mária's discussion about the daily chores of housekeeping. She observed that though her smile was friendly, there was something odd about Mária. She had short brown hair and was wearing a small box hat coquettishly slanted across half her forehead. Her well-cut, light gray suit displayed a slender figure, and shapely legs. She wore high heel shoes with straps wrapped around her slim ankles. She seemed more like a visiting countess than a maid.

It's her eyes that give the impression of her not being quite 'there,' Erika concluded. She had large, sky-blue eyes that seemed to have an odd, distant stare even while talking to Piry directly.

Judith arrived home, and she, too, met Mária.

After the introductions, Mária stood up. "It's all settled then, Mrs. Haydu. I shall return tomorrow with my belongings." She smiled at the girls, "I hope we shall be great friends as I was with the daughters of King George the VIth," and she walked out with Piry.

When Piry returned from letting Mária out the gate, both Judith and Erika burst out, "Mommy, you can't be serious about her! She is not a maid! And what was that nonsense about King George? She is clearly crazy!"

"I admit, she is a bit odd. But not crazy. She lived in London during the war, and it seems that the heavy bombing there affected her mind a bit.

But I spoke to her at length, and she seems just fine otherwise." Seeing her daughters' skeptical grins, Piry added, "Really. And she needs a job and a home, and we need a housekeeper, so we'll give it a go. Please be nice to her!"

Judith and Erika rolled their eyes skyward, but there was nothing more they could say. They didn't know then, what a pillar of their lives this strange woman would become.

◎◉◎

On September 6th, 1948, Judith and Erika started school in Ùjpest. Under the socialist government's educational system, all children went to "General School" from age 6 to age 14. After that if a child was not a good student, he or she was encouraged to attend some sort of technical school to learn either an office or a manual skill. The better students could go on four more years to a "Gimnázium", which was a preparatory high school for continuing education at a university.

Judith, who was 11 years old, was placed into the sixth year of the General School, and Erika into the third year. The sisters barely saw each other at school since the upper grades studied on the second and third floors and the lower ones on the first.

There were thirty-six children in Erika's classroom. Three rows of two-seat desks lined the room. Seating was arranged by the homeroom teacher, based the child's grades from the previous year's report card. Good students were placed in the front rows of the classroom, average students in the middle, and those with poor grades toward the back. Seating was assigned for the entire school year.

Erika's homeroom teacher, Mrs. Boda, taught classes in Hungarian literature and grammar. For all other subjects, different teachers came into the classroom for the hour, several times a week, depending on the subject. Math was taught daily, literature three times a week, grammar, geography, and history twice a week. Much to Erika's chagrin, drawing and music lessons were also taught only twice a week.

Studying the Russian language was instituted that year. In Erika's class it was taught three times a week by a former German language teacher. She seemed to be learning Russian just one step ahead of her students. Erika enjoyed acquiring this new language, her third in her eight years of her life. She found it amusing that her first new language was German during her ill-fated kindergarten experience, and the Germans had lost the war. Her second was Hebrew at the Zionist boarding school, which she also had to leave for political reasons. Now she was learning Russian, and it looked like this one may have the strongest staying power.

All classes lasted fifty minutes, with a ten minute-break before the next one started on the hour. The only time students went to another location was for their bi-weekly gym classes. The school had a large gymnastics room on the first floor of the three-story red brick building. Prior to entering their gym classes, students were required to change into gym clothes and gym shoes in the locker rooms by the gymnasium.

Because Erika had been an "all five" student in her previous schools, with five being the highest and one a failing grade, just like in the Soviet Union's school system, she was assigned to sit in first row, along with three girls and two boys—the other top students. She thought it interesting that no one ever commented as to why good students were placed closest to the teacher's desk—but they all knew. They were the "smart" group, to whom the teachers directed their lessons.

It didn't matter that the rest of the children were struggling to understand everything that was being taught. The "five" and "four" grade students were the only ones who seemed to matter. The children knew they were the ones who would be accepted to institutions of higher learning. Those with average grades, or lower, would either have to transfer at age fourteen to a vocational school or simply quit school and get a job.

Erika's classmates, having been together the first two years of elementary school, all knew each other. They looked at Erika with some hostility at first but soon accepted her because Erika knew how to ingratiate herself with her naturally friendly manner.

In the ensuing months, she also gained her peers' and teachers' respect because she excelled in all subjects, though her favorites were literature, grammar, and the arts. She loved to draw and paint and also joined the school choir where she was able to sing in a wide tonal range.

She enthusiastically participated in the strenuous gymnastics' classes. During class breaks, before the gym class started, she frequently clowned by effortlessly wrapping both her legs around her neck behind her head and walking on her hands.

"You ought to join a circus!" her classmates would shout, laughing.

"I'd love to, but my mother would never let me," Erika would respond as she walked around on her hands to entertain the others.

She was speaking from experience. Once, when she was performing a solo dance at the school assembly during her years at the orphanage, Piry had come to see it. After the show, Erika was allowed to run to her mother, and while Piry was hugging her proudly, two men in dark suits approached them. They introduced themselves as scouts for the Hungarian National Ballet, and said to Piry:

"Your daughter seems unusually talented in dance. Would you consider enrolling her in our school?"

"What school is that?" Piry asked.

"It is a combination of academic studies plus dance and music education. Only exceptionally talented children are invited to study there—like your daughter."

"And where is it?" Piry asked cautiously.

"In Moscow, Ma'am. It is the world's best ballet school, the Bolshoi Ballet Academy."

"I thought you said you were from the Hungarian Ballet Academy."

"We are. But students, who seem to show remarkable talent are selected to study at the Bolshoi. It provides the best training possible for students to become the world's greatest dancers."

"So, she would be taken to Moscow?"

"Yes."

"For how long?"

"Until she turns eighteen. Of course, she would be allowed to come home for visits during winter and summer school breaks."

Erika froze as she listened. She understood that the men were asking to take her away somewhere far, to study dance. A part of her really wanted to go but she was also terrified of being away from her mother again. The Bolshoi school seemed very far away, and, surely, if she had to live there, she would see her mother even less than she could now.

Erika wondered, what if this is just a trick to take me away and kill me because they know I am Jewish? She listened with great apprehension to her mother's reply.

"Your offer is very flattering, and I'm happy that you see so much talent in my daughter. But you must forgive me, I didn't rescue her from the Nazis to now give her up for schooling in another country."

"Madam, don't you realize, your daughter could become a world-famous ballerina?"

Piry stood firm. "Thank you for your offer. I may send her to ballet school here in Budapest but in no way will I allow her to leave the country."

Erika breathed easier, infinitely grateful to her mother for not sending her away. The orphanage is bad but at least I can go home on some weekends, and Anyu had promised to take me home as soon as she could do it. Going to that place, Moscow, seems like the end of the world. Erika watched the men taking their leave very politely but obviously disappointed. One of them gave Piry a name card to contact them if she changed her mind. Erika clung to Piry with both arms around her waist, feeling very happy.

Erika did not tell her classmates about this experience when they praised her agility, for she felt it would have sounded like she was bragging. Being accepted by them, and her scholastic achievements, made Erika content with her school. She wanted to belong and be liked.

◎◉◎

As the school year progressed, the only thing bothering Erika was the awareness that her homeroom teacher did not seem to like her. She did give high grades for Erika's compositions that had to be written and turned in three times a week. But she seemed to avoid asking Erika to read aloud in class or choose her to answer questions during the lessons.

Erika put up with Mrs. Boda's hostility until the day when a city-wide story competition had been announced at her school. All students were given an hour to write a story as to why—with Comrade Stalin's help—their lives had become better than before. One story was then selected at each school from each grade level to compete for first prize.

Erika wrote about her life during the war; the hunger and the fear of bombs, and how now there was peace, and enough food—all thanks to Comrade Stalin. She knew that she had written the best story, for afterwards each child in her classroom read his or her work aloud, and Erika could compare their stories with hers. Yet, her teacher had selected another student's composition to send in. It did not win, and Erika was furious about having lost the opportunity to compete. When Erika saw her mother that evening, she complained to Piry:

"Mrs. Boda hates me. Probably, because I'm Jewish. I'm the only Jew in my class, and she seems to treat me differently."

"What makes you think so?" Piry responded cautiously.

"She never calls on me to read aloud or answer a question, even when I can see that I am the only one who knows the correct answer. She'll let two or three kids answer, and even if they're only partially right, she says, "Fine, let's move on." Also, she deliberately ignored my composition for the contest."

"Maybe the other story was better?"

"No, I know mine was the best. I know how to write the best story."

"I'll look into it," Piry's promised.

◎◉◎

To get to their school, both Erika and Judith had to walk two blocks on Virág Utca, (Flower Street) their acacia tree lined home street, to a street called Nyár Utca, (Summer Street) turn left and walk for another fifteen minutes to get there. During the fall, because their school was in the same direction as Feri's fabric store, he often offered to take one of the girls there on his bicycle. Judith, with her intense dislike of Feri, always declined his offer. Erika frequently accepted the ride.

She sat sideways on the horizontal bar in front of Feri between his seat and the bike's handles. Secured by Feri's extended arms, Erika held her schoolbag on her lap with one hand, while with the other she gripped the handlebar. She enjoyed not having to make the long walk in the mornings.

But as the weather turned cold, Feri could no longer use his bike due to the frequent rain. Thus, he took a direct route to his store, and Erika walked to her school. She and Judith did not go together, for the older girl had made friends with whom she met along the way and did not invite Erika to tag along.

One of the students Erika befriended in her class, was Ildikó. She lived on the same route Erika had to take. Once Erika started to walk to school, the two girls would meet up and go together. At the end of the day, with Piry's permission, Erika often stopped at Ildikó's house to do homework together. Ildikó was better at math than Erika, but not better in composition and grammar. So, the two girls would help each other with their respective "best" subjects.

Erika came to love Ildikó and her family. Ildikó was slightly built, her silky blonde hair fell straight to her shoulders, and she had large blue eyes that seemed sad, although she always appeared to be happy. But Ildikó was actually a sickly child; she said her heart was too frail to do sports. She carried a medical excuse and usually sat out gym class with a book in her hand. When she finished reading it, if she liked it, she would lend it to Erika. She read voraciously, after finishing her homework, before and after dinner, or at night, till Judith ordered her to put the book down so she could shut the light off and go to sleep.

Erika often read even while walking on the streets. Once-in-a-while she would abruptly stop and apologize, sensing that she was about to bump into a person then look up and see that it was just a lamppost. Judith and Piry made fun of her reading habit, but Erika didn't care. Books took her to worlds that were amazing. Many nights, when Judith ordered her to go to sleep, she would lie motionless under the goose down duvet and weave her own stories.

Her favorite was about a girl whose father had disappeared during the war. Then one day, when she was most miserable at school, for her homeroom teacher scolded her for talking during a lesson, the door opened, and her father walked in. He was wearing a magnificent golden cape and a crown. He told the astonished teacher that he had been away to rule a kingdom but now he had come back to take his daughter, Erika, with him.

This story often comforted Erika into sleep. At times, while sitting in her classroom, feeling frustrated, she would stare at the door and fantasize that her story would turn real.

One morning, Ildikó was not waiting for her at the usual time in front of her house. Assuming she had gone ahead, for Erika was a little late, she just hurried on. But Ildikó was not at school either. Erika stopped by her house on the way home.

"She is very ill," Ildikó's mother explained. "You can go in to just say hello.

Ildikó lay in her bed, under a white duvet. On the night table next to her were bottles of pills, and books. The room had a large white bookcase against one wall, full of books, and a small closet full of clothes. A small while desk with a chair completed the furnishings."

Erika pulled up the chair next to Ildikó's head, so her friend could see her without straining.

"Get well, soon, school is boring when you're not there," Erika told her.

Ildikó gave her a wane smile, "I'll try," she whispered.

Erika was pained to see that Ildikó could hardly get the words out she was so short of breath. Yet, she did not seem to have even a cold.

"Don't talk, just nod, if you want me to tell you about the homework?" she told Ildikó.

Ildikó shook her head. "Just sit with me a bit."

Erika felt an overwhelming love as she looked at the pallid face of her best friend. Her skin was almost transparent, even on her hands.

"I love you so much," she whispered. "Please get well."

Ildikó nodded "I'll try."

Erika missed Ildikó at school the whole week. She stopped by her home several times but was told by her mother that her friend was too sick to receive visitors. With a heavy heart, Erika would leave, wishing Ildikó a speedy recovery.

◎◉◎

A couple of weeks later, Erika's homeroom teacher, Mrs. Boda, announced that the entire class was invited to a mass for Ildikó, who had passed away. Erika burst into tears at the news, as did several other girls in the classroom.

"Fábián, control yourself," Mrs. Boda hissed at Erika, using her last name for emphasis.

Erika was shocked: *How could Mrs. Boda not understand the pain and loss I feel?* She stared at her teacher's face, her eyes narrowed, her lips pressed tight and felt the woman's hatred like a wave coming at her. Erika took a deep breath and made herself stop the tears. But not her feelings of anger and resentment towards her mean teacher.

It was freezing cold in the catholic church of Ùjpest, where the funeral Mass was held. A large crowd had gathered to say good-bye to Ildikó. Erika was seated in the isle toward the back, with all her classmates but could see Ildikó's family in the first two rows, near the altar.

Between the pews and the altar lay the open coffin on a pedestal. Rows of mourners rose, walked up to the coffin to look at the girl lying inside, crossed themselves, then slowly filed back to their pews. When it was Erika's row's turn, she shuffled slowly forward with her classmates, till she reached the coffin.

Ildikó had never looked more beautiful and more at peace. She wore a white lace dress. On her head was a lace veil, crowned with flowers, and her blonde hair cascaded smoothly to her shoulders. Her eyes were closed.

To Erika, the still figure seemed more like a wax effigy than the warm, smiling friend she had known. She suddenly recalled the strange, rigid appearance of the man she and Peter had seen lying dead in a wheelbarrow during the war. Tears began to silently roll down her cheeks. As she slowly walked back to her seat, she thought, *I've lost Peter, and now Ildikó.*

She had no notion that coping with these losses would steel her for handling future ones. All she knew was that suddenly there was a feeling of emptiness in her heart.

◎◉◎

On a chilly Sunday morning in early October, Erika saw with amazement Uncle Imre's carriage arrive at their front gate. Her stepfather opened both sides of the gate, and Uncle Imre, turning his two horses around to face the street, backed his carriage into the entrance. It was loaded with coal, looking like black eggs piled mountain high.

"Get out of the way!" Feri snapped at Erika.

She moved aside but watched as her stepfather and Uncle Imre, plus two other workers, loaded the coal into wheelbarrows which they had brought with them. Then they rolled these to the first of the four sheds that lined the far wall of the garden, built against the wall between their property and the neighbor's. Feri opened the shed door, and they poured the coal in.

Piry came running out of the house, "Oh, great!" she exclaimed.

Erika caught Feri's dismissive expression, as if he were saying, 'This isn't your business,' though he didn't utter a sound. She also caught a shadow of pain cross over her mother's face. Then it was gone. Piry glanced at Erika and smiled. "We'll be warm this winter," she said.

"Let's watch how they do it," Erika suggested, inviting her mother to stay with her.

Standing side by side they watched the men work. Erika now understood why three of the four sheds have stood empty all summer long. The fourth contained Feri's old furniture and gardening tools. Now, when the first shed had been filled with briquettes to the top, the workers also filled most of the third shed. Then, all the men piled into Imre's wagon and left. They returned after a while with the carriage loaded with long wood logs chopped into triangles, about two feet long. They set to work, neatly piling the logs into the second shed and filled the leftover space, in the third.

"Why are they putting only half and half stuff in there?" Erika whispered to her mother, when they came out of the house once again to watch the men work.

"That's for Uncle Imre and Aunt Magda. They have a smaller place to heat."

"Ah."

After the men were done loading the sheds, Piry brought out a pitcher full of water, and a bottle of wine, with Erika carrying glasses. The workers politely accepted the drinks.

Magda had also come out of their apartment by this time, so Imre informed her, "We'll drive with the men to return the horses and carriage to the stable. Then Feri and I will walk home. We won't be long."

Erika liked the considerate way Uncle Imre spoke to his wife. She observed that her stepfather merely nodded good-bye to her mother, while Piry just gave him a little smile. They did not speak. *They look so strained*, Erika thought, but said nothing out loud.

◎◉◎

Along with the start of the regular school year, Piry had also enrolled her daughters in Hebrew school at the Újpest's Neolog Synagogue.

Hungarian Jews divided themselves into three categories: Orthodox, Neolog, and Status Quo. The Orthodox Jews were ultra-religious and celebrated major and minor holidays throughout the year. The Neolog Jews were moderately observant, many kept a kosher home but did not bother with minor holidays. The Status Quo people showed up in temple only on high holidays, if at all.

With Zoltan gone, Piry could not imagine herself keeping up with Orthodox practices. She certainly had no intention of ever returning to the ritual baths after her monthly period was over. But neither could she totally abandon the religious observances of her upbringing. She felt comfortable joining a Neolog Congregation. She continued to keep a kosher kitchen, as well as observe the lighting of candles every Friday night at the start of the Sabbath.

Had it been up to Feri, he would not have cared about keeping kosher or going to temple except maybe on the High Holidays. All his brothers ignored religious practices, especially Lajos the youngest, whose wife Vica had converted from Catholicism in order to marry him but had little interest in Jewish religious practices.

"My parents were not observant," Feri explained to Piry. "Besides, with all of them having been killed by the Nazis—even my formerly Catholic wife and child died in a concentration camp—so I find it strange to continue praying to a God who let this happen."

"Most of my family had been killed, too," Piry gently reminded him. "But we're not to judge why it happened. Just go along with me on this, please," she pleaded.

He consented. After closing his store on Friday nights, he went to temple, and to early service on Saturday mornings before he opened his shop. To Piry's amazement, he could read fluently the Hebrew prayer book and was familiar with all the holiday rituals.

◎◉◎

Friday evenings became special for Piry, because when he got home after temple, she would serve a lovely dinner, with her two daughters also participating. Meat was expensive and somewhat scarce these days, but Piry always managed to make a chicken or goose soup, and a main dish using the fowl from the soup, accompanied by potatoes and a green vegetable. Desert was home baked pastry, usually a fruit tart.

In wintertime, Piry used one of her homemade apricot, cherry, or plum jams to make the cake. She enjoyed using the skills she had learned at her father's restaurant to create these wonderful meals despite the severe economic shortages in the country.

She and Feri had a glass of wine with their dinner, diluted with sparkling water. The mood around the table was usually jovial, each of them telling some funny story about their week's events. These were times when Piry felt she had made the right decision marrying Feri and creating a new home for them all.

CHAPTER 9

On Thursday afternoons both girls attended Hebrew language and Jewish religion lessons at their temple. It was nearly a half an hour's walk from their home but both Judith and Erika could get there comfortably in half that time, by going there directly after school.

The temple resembled a Turkish mosque with its colored brick façade and two turrets. Erected in 1866 and renovated after it was partially damage during WW II, it was a grand building. The interior contained a thousand seats, including a gallery where the women sat on both sides of the nave. Above the altar was a small balcony for the choir with a view of the entire interior of the temple. There was a separate building for classes, not nearly as fancy as the temple but Erika loved glimpsing at the splendid façade of the temple on her way there.

"You are eleven now, and when you turn twelve, you'll have your bat-mitzvah, so you need to know the right prayers, and learn what to do during the holidays," Piry explained to Judith. "Besides, you might meet some nice new friends there."

Judith did, and so did Erika, who liked the idea of studying Jewish history and learning Hebrew again. On Saturdays, after lunch, because it was "the day of rest" and Piry forbade them to do homework, each girl went to visit their Jewish friends who were also observant.

Erika particularly liked going to the home of one friend, Noémi, because the affection and harmony she observed in their home made her feel good. Noémi had an older brother and a younger sister. They were so orthodox that Erika could not ring even their doorbell for that would generate electricity on the Sabbath. She had to knock.

"Come in, come in," Noémi's mother would open the door, and usher Erika in. They lived on the second floor of a three-story apartment building, on Árpad Utca, the busy shopping street. Although Erika was aware that they were poorer than her own family, she also noted that they seemed happier. They spoke to each other in gentle, loving voices instead of the tense tones at her home. Noémi and Erika were allowed to go for a walk, or as the weather turned cold and rainy, they would stay in and sit in Noémi's room, munching cookies and talking about school, or books they had read, or at times about their activities.

"I couldn't stand sitting with my mother upstairs in the women's section, during services," Erika told her friend. "So, I went downstairs to sit with my stepfather. But that was even more boring. He just sits there murmuring in Hebrew, and if I as much as look around, he hisses at me to behave. So, last week I signed up to sing in the choir."

"Our temple is so ultra-orthodox, we don't even have a choir," Noémi replied wistfully.

"Then who sings the songs during the service?"

"We have a cantor, and he does, or we all sing together."

"That must be fun."

"Not really. We just do it."

"Can I come visit your temple during the High Holidays, and see?"

"Of course."

Noémi attended a small orthodox school in Újpest. Erika was curious what Noemi's opinion was concerning their secular, socialist education.

"Yesterday, the biology teacher said there is no God. Life just happened on earth. There was no God to create it. He said, people invented God because they were afraid and could not explain many of the things happening around them. So, they decided there must exist a very powerful being who had created it all," Erika told her friend.

"Our teacher said the same thing, but he added that this is just Soviet communist theory. He said, we can believe what we want. But then he added that Judaism is centuries old, and we have observances that have kept us together as a people—that is what being Jewish means. But I think there is a God, and our observances were dictated by God," Noémi countered with conviction.

"But where is God?"

"Everywhere. That's what they teach us in Hebrew school. You just started there, so it may be all new to you. Just listen, and you'll get it."

But Erika didn't get it because at her school, her history teacher, Mr. Kovacs, told a very different story about "the origin and purposes of religion".

"Religion was invented to make people behave correctly. It became organized by people who claimed to have a special connection to a creator, God. They named themselves his emissaries, priests, and established an organization called the Church. And then it became the job of the priests to collect money from the people and send it to the Pope, the head of the Church. People were told they not only had to obey the Church's rules, but they also had to donate money to the Church so it would save them from going to hell after they died.

Kings enlisted the help of the Church to rule the population. The people were taught that if they worked hard on this earth, and obeyed their rulers and the church, they would be rewarded in the afterlife by going to heaven. Religion is nothing but the opiate of the masses."

One of the boys raised his hand and asked: "What's opiate?"

"It's a drug people can take to feel good," said Mr. Kovacs, adding, "praying also makes people feel good. So, it's like a drug. The Church and the King collected money from the people they ruled and thus made them stay poor. But today, with the help of the Soviet Union, our government is working hard to build a better life for everyone. To help people live well here on earth, without having to give money for it to the Church." Mr. Kovacs stared at his students with a happy smile. "So, you people are lucky to be growing up today in Hungary under socialism."

Erika would have liked to believe Mr. Kovacs, but in her everyday life she found many contradictions to his teachings. One day, she watched her mother return home frustrated, angrily dumping a basketful of potatoes on the kitchen counter exclaiming, "Before the war, we fed this kind of potatoes only to animals! Now we're the ones who must eat them because we can't get the good ones—those are shipped to the Soviet Union!"

Erika was also aware that her mother often had to go out very early in the morning to stand in line at stores, because later they would run out of both milk and vegetables. Erika thought, *maybe under socialism "building a better life" is different from living one.*

◉◉◉

In Hebrew School, Erika learned that the Bible was essentially the recorded history of the Jews. And subsequent religious books were the written discussions and interpretations of the laws that governed every aspect of Jewish life.

Erika thought, *Mr. Kovacs's said that the Catholic religion was used to keep people in line, and here the Rabbi is saying the Talmud prescribes how Jews must live. So, the two religions are not that different. Both dictate people how to live. Mr. Kovacs is right; religions just want to control people.*

This thought made Erika feel uneasy. Then, as she learned to translate the Hebrew prayers into Hungarian, Erika was surprised that they were nothing but praises of God. By contrast, the Catholic prayers always asked God and the saints for help. When Ildikó, Erika's best friend was alive, she went to Church on Sundays and at times Erika was allowed to go with her. Thus, she was familiar with the mass and the prayers. She thought, *Jewish prayers are absurd, especially, if Mr. Kovacs is right that God doesn't exist. At least the Catholics pray to Jesus and to saints who were real people at one point and are supposedly in heaven now, so they can help.*

Erika's life at home contributed greatly to her thinking that all religions were just rituals that only had power over people if they submitted to those beliefs. According to Jewish laws, a Jew could never eat certain foods; pork being highest on this list of prohibitions. One Sunday, her uncles Vince and Lajos arrived in the latter's horse drawn wagon, and walked a very large, very fat, loudly grunting pig into the yard. Both Uncle Imre and Feri also came outside. The four brothers laid tarps on the grass to protect the garden, and Magda brought some bowls out from their apartment.

Piry came out into the yard, watching their preparations with disgust. She quietly pulled Feri aside and asked, "You're doing this here?"

He yanked his arm away and said in a terse voice, "Go inside. This is none of your business."

Judith never came out of the house, but Piry stayed in the doorway, and Erika, standing by her mother's side, watched with horror and fascination as three of the brothers held on to the pig, while Vince, using a long, sharp knife, slit its throat. The animal stood frozen for a few seconds, its legs splayed, blood squirting from the wound. Then it collapsed onto its side. It gave a deep shudder and grew very still.

"It's dead." Erika whispered to Piry.

"Shsh. Go inside." Piry murmured back.

"No, I want to see what they do."

Piry looked at her daughter, shrugged, and left her standing there while she disappeared into their house. Erika watched as Uncle Imre grabbed one of the bowls and held it under the pig's neck to catch all the blood. This really surprised Erika. She knew Jewish law dictated that when an animal was killed all the blood had to be drained from its body and discarded, before the meat could be used.

Erika had gone once or twice with her mother to the special person, the shochet, who had been trained to kill animals in this "kosher" way. She had watched as the shochet, dressed in a white lab coat and his head covered by a white round hat, took the chicken they had brought to him, and tied its feet together. He hung the bird upside down by the rope around its feet on a hook over a trough. Then he took a long, wide, sparkling clean knife and tested its sharpness by slicing a strand of his own hair in two with one swing.

"Good," he muttered, and said to Erika, "It has to be super sharp so as not to cause pain."

Then he walked over to the chicken and quickly plucked some feathers off its neck. He lifted the knife, and with one swift motion cut across the chicken's neck. The blood from the wound flowed to the bottom of the trough, which had water running into it from an opened faucet. In a few minutes, even the last drop of blood was gone, washed down the drain. Then, and only then did the shochet lift the chicken off the hook, and wrapping it into a piece of butcher paper, handed it to Piry.

By contrast, in their yard, the men collected every drop of blood into the bowls, and then handed them to Magda, who took them into her kitchen.

"What will you do with the blood?" Erika asked her aunt as she passed by her.

"Use it to make blood sausage."

Erika didn't have time to ask Aunt Magda how this was done, for she got distracted by the next procedure. She watched as her uncles systematically carved up the pig. Its intestines were collected and washed in a big bucket of water, and once again, were handed over to Aunt Magda. She looked at Erika and said, even before the child could ask, "We use the cleaned guts for making all kinds of sausages."

"Can I see how?" Erika asked. In reality, she was more curious about what was happening than feeling sorry for the slaughtered pig or being affected by the carving up she had just witnessed.

"Just come on in," Aunt Magda invited her.

Once the three brothers divided up the meat among them—Feri wouldn't take any pork meat—Vince and Lajos left, taking their share of the meat and the leftover remains of the pig.

It took most of the afternoon for Imre and Magda to grind up different parts of the meat on a home meat grinder. Erika watched with fascination as the ground meat was divided into batches, and after adding various spices to each batch, they were cooked separately in large pots. In the meantime, the guts were being filled with water from the sink faucet and emptied, and filled again and again, until the water flowing out of them was colorless.

When Magda and Imre deemed all was ready, Imre set up a special grinder. He placed one end of the intestine over the opening of the grinder and Magda fed the meat into the machine. A lever she turned filled the intestine while Imre was shaping it into a solid tube. Periodically they would stop grinding, and tie strings around the newly filled intestine at even distances, creating a whole line of mid-sized sausages. They did this with all the variety of meats they had prepared.

"When we're done, we'll have to take it all to the smokehouse at the butcher shop, and it will be ready to eat only after it's cooked again by smoking it," Imre explained to Erika.

"Can I come over and taste it then?" Erika asked.

"It's not kosher," Imre teased her.

"So what?"

"I think your mother is calling you," Magda interrupted.

Indeed, Erika could now hear her mother's voice. She thanked her aunt and uncle for "the look," and ran home.

"Aren't you ashamed of yourself," Piry scolded her, "watching that disgusting pork being processed?"

Erika shrugged, "It was interesting. Most people eat pork in this country, why shouldn't I know how they prepare it?"

Piry couldn't answer her daughter. Erika was far wiser than her years.

◉◉◉

In late November of 1948, Piry announced to her daughters that their cousin Miri, and her mother Batya were arriving for a visit and would be staying with them. Batya was Uncle Eli's wife. Piry explained that Uncle Eli was their father Zoltan's youngest brother, the gymnast. He was a Zionist, changed his name from Laci to Eli, and went to Israel in 1936. So, this would be the first time Judith and Erika would meet their cousin Miri.

When Batya and Miri arrived, Piry set up the maid's room for them as the guest room, and asked Maria, the maid, to sleep in her daughters' room. Erika loved the commotion while Judith became cranky about what she called "crowding" her room.

But in fact, Maria came to sleep late in the night, very quietly, lying on a mattress on the floor near the door to her room, and was the first one up, before anyone was awake. She left the children's' room noiselessly, to go to the kitchen to prepare breakfast and sandwiches for Feri and the girls to take with them.

Because the guests had come during the week, the children could only see each other after Judith and Erika returned from school. Then they would play together for a while before Judith and Erika had to tend to their homework. On one of these afternoons, the three girls went for a walk, while Batya and Piry stayed at the house, to talk.

It was cold outside; the streets were blanketed in snow. Judith suggested throwing snowballs at the trees as a game. Miri, the cousin who was just three months older than Erika, had never seen snow before, and loved the idea.

"Scoop up the snow with both hands and make it into a hard ball by pressing it between your palms, Judith instructed Miri. "Then we each throw our ball one after another, and the one whose ball falls apart least, is the winner." Judith declared.

They had fun playing in the street, till dusk set in.

"Last turn," Judith announced. She had been steadily winning, but the younger girls didn't mind, since they were having fun just throwing snowballs.

"This time though, we'll throw the last balls at that door" Judith declared, pointing at the wood door of the house in front of which they had been playing.

"What about the people inside?" Miri asked.

"They won't know it" Judith stated offhandedly. "We'll all throw together and then run home."

Erika, used to Judith's bizarre sense of humor and occasional mischief, held her snowball back and let Miri and Judith throw first. Miri's snowball flew at the front door, which had suddenly opened, and the snowball struck the proprietor, a stocky woman, in the chest. Surprised, she stepped forward and slapped Miri's face. It had all happened in an instant. Miri cried out, but Judith grabbed her arm, and began to run with her toward their house, just up the street. Erika was quick to follow.

"You brats!" the woman shouted after them, "If I catch you again throwing snowballs at my house, I'll wring your necks!"

Judith was laughing so hard when they finally reached their own gate, that she had trouble fitting the key into the lock. She finally did it, and pulled the two younger girls inside, hurriedly locking the door behind them. Miri was not amused. In fact, she was furious and ran into the house to find her mother. When Batya heard the story, she confronted not only Judith and Erika but Piry as well.

"My daughter had never been slapped in her life!" Batya shouted indignantly. "What kind of manners are you teaching your children? Really! I demand an apology!"

"Judith? Erika?" Piry's voice was menacing.

"I'm sorry," Erika came forth immediately and Judith seconded her, "I'm sorry, too. We didn't know the lady was going to come out."

"But what kind of behavior is this, throwing snowballs at people's houses!" shouted Batya.

"We did that just once, for fun," Judith tried to explain, feeling very threatened.

"Some fun! Doesn't your mother teach you better?" Batya hammered relentlessly.

"Yes, they know better but they're children!" Piry interceded. "So, once in a while they step out of line. I'm sure they won't do this ever again. Right girls?"

"Right," Judith and Erika chorused.

"All right let's have some tea and cookies" Piry suggested, as she led her disgruntled sister-in-law and the children into the warmth of the winter dining room.

The real cause of Batya's anger was not this incident, although it added fuel to the fire. She had spent all afternoon trying to convince Piry to allow her to take Judith and Erika with her to Israel at the end of her visit.

"You are clearly not happy with Feri. Eli sent me to tell you, you should let the girls come with me. Divorce Feri, and you'll follow. The government will let you out because your children will already be in Israel. I've brought all the necessary documents to take them with me as our 'adopted orphans'. Our Zionist organization in Budapest will facilitate their exit permits. There is talk of having the borders shut between the Western countries and those taken over by the Soviet Union. This might be your last chance to get them into a free country and then giving you a reason to follow."

"I am not sure the government would let me go. I will not take a chance on losing my children, even if they'll be safe with you in Israel."

"Can't you see the handwriting on the wall, with the Soviet Army staying in Hungary and the Communist Party taking over the government?"

Batya asked angrily. "You will have a Soviet style dictatorship in this country within a year! They have already nationalized all the big industries; how much longer do you think it will be before they take over the small industries and all privately owned businesses? A year? Two years? They have already nationalized all the schools this year, so what do you think they're teaching your daughters? The Bible or the Communist Manifesto? What kind of future will your daughters have under a government that despises capitalists, with their father having been a capitalist merchant, and their stepfather the same?

Just like in Russia, they'll only allow working class kids to get higher education! In Israel, your daughters will be free to study and choose any profession they want! They'll have a free life!"

"I can't let you take them without me. That's not why I saved our lives during the war." Piry countered.

"Wasn't the war enough for you? You like being 'Jewed down' in this country as long as you live? In Israel everyone is Jewish, so being a Jew is not an issue! It's the only country in the world where Jews are simply citizens, with all rights. Wouldn't you like your daughters to grow up like that?"

"Yes, I would. But I wouldn't like them to grow up without me. I lost my husband, their father, and most of my family—they're the only close family I've left. There is no way I'll let them go without me."

"As I told you, we'd be practically smuggling them out as orphaned children who are being adopted by their father's brother! We could hardly take you along! But we will help you get out later, I promise!"

"I repeat, they're not going anywhere without me."

"You're just being selfish! Don't you trust us to help you to follow them?"

Piry looked at her sister-in-law's face. She saw a woman with dark, short, cropped hair, skin tanned by the sun, a square-set jawline, and angry brown eyes staring hard at her, and she shrugged, "Frankly, I don't."

"You were always impossible," Batya exclaimed. "The whole family thought that, and you're just proving it true."

"I know that none of Zoli's brothers liked me, least of all you and Eli. So why would I trust you to get me out of Hungary later? I think you and Eli would be happy to just forget about me after you got hold of Zoli's children!"

Batya stared at Piry, completely taken aback. Was the woman clairvoyant? How did she sense their plan? But all she said was, "In that case, Miri and I are leaving in two days. Let me know if you change your mind."

Piry didn't and Batya did not bring up the subject again before they left.

They parted with strained hugs and kisses, Piry and her daughters wishing Miri and Batya a safe trip home. As Piry watched them get into a taxi and disappear from view, she felt a small pang of regret, wondering whether she had made the right decision, keeping her daughters in Hungary. She looked at them, smiling up at her, and felt that she had. *No matter what the future will bring, at least we're together, and I can take care of them*, she thought.

◎◉◎

On a freezing cold night in February 1949, Feri came home late from his store, in a rather agitated state. He slammed the front gate and entered the house, also shutting the front door rather forcefully, turning the key in the lock as if he were afraid.

"What's going on? I was getting worried about you?" Piry exclaimed, as she helped him out of his overcoat.

He quickly went into the winter dining room, sank heavily down on his usual chair near the ceramic stove, and said, "Don't bother with dinner. I'm not hungry."

"What happened?" Piry insisted.

"This morning, when I got to the store, I found the display window broken, and most of the fabrics decorating it, gone. They must have gotten scared away somehow, because they didn't actually enter the store. But I had to spend the whole day first boarding up the window, then going to the police station to file a report. Then I went to find a glass supplier to replace the window. It cost my week's earnings to put in a new window!"

"I am so sorry! Why didn't you give a kid five forints and sent him to me to let me know! I could have gone there to help you."

"There was nothing you could have done."

"I could have minded the store while you were away."

Feri waved his hand in the particular rigid way he moved. "Nah…the butcher next door kept an eye on the store. It's all right. I'm getting a dog tomorrow. It's late and I'm tired. I'm going to bed."

"Don't you want to eat something?"

"No."

With that, Feri got up and with his lumbering gait left the room.

Piry stayed for a while, sitting alone, wondering why she felt so forlorn. She knew she should follow Feri to the bedroom. Instead, she waited till she could hear his even breathing with an occasional snort to indicate that he was deep in sleep, before she slipped into bed next to him.

◎◉◎

The following evening, Feri came home and shouted into the house, "Everyone, come on out!"

Piry, the two girls, and even Maria grabbed their coats and ran into the yard, to see Feri holding on to a strong rope. Tethered to it stood the largest dog anyone of them had ever seen. The dog's dirty white fur cascaded in ringlets down its sides to his feet, so when he moved, it looked like he was wearing a blanket. His head reached up to Feri's chest, and his tail, with its long, curly fur resembled a gently waving flag. His eyes, peering through the ringlets that covered his massive head, were looking straight at the family. Only his big black nose was not covered by ringlets.

"Oh, my God, you got a Komondor!" Piry cried out.

"Now we'll see who's going to break into the store!" Feri exclaimed with satisfaction.

"He is beautiful! Can I pet him?" Erika asked.

"Go ahead. But first walk up to him slowly, and hold out your hand, palm up, close to his chin. But don't touch him. Let him come to you and smell you first." Feri instructed her.

Erika was just a bit afraid, but she bravely stepped forward, her right hand extended toward the dog's chin. He lowered his head, smelled her palm, and with a swift tongue licked it.

"Oh!" Erika cried out happily, "He licked me!"

"That means he likes you. Now you can pet his head."

Erika reached up. The dog was so tall that she was face to face with him. She gently patted his head. The dog stood very still, then pressed his nose against Erika's arm, clearly with affection.

"He is great!" Erika beamed.

"He won't bite?" Judith asked.

"Not if you do like Erika. He has to get to know you first," explained Feri.

One by one, each member of the family followed Erika's example, acquainting the dog with their smell and their touch.

"Where will he sleep?" Erika asked.

"Out here in the corner of the garden. He's got enough of a coat to keep him warm. Tomorrow Uncle Imre will bring him a doghouse. Make sure he always has a dish full of water within his reach," Feri instructed them.

Maria immediately disappeared into the house. She returned with a large aluminum bowl filled with water. In the meantime, Feri led the dog to his designated corner, and tied his makeshift leash against a piece of wood he had hammered into the ground like a post.

"Get a blanket," he ordered them. Piry went into the house and quickly pulled their oldest blanket out of her linen closet for Judith to take outside. Feri took it from her and laid it on the ground after he had scraped away the snow there.

"Isn't he going to freeze out here?" Erika was concerned, looking at the dog.

"Not with all this hair on him! These dogs sleep in the Puszta on the snow, guarding cattle, sheep, or horses, all winter long?"

"I didn't know that." Erika and Judith both responded with amazement and respect for their new dog.

"Yeah, a shepherd will spend his whole year's salary on a dog like this; that's how good they are at guarding! So, we can all sleep safer tonight" Feri grinned at the girls.

"So how much did you spend on him?" Piry asked.

Feri grinned at her. "I lucked out. Somebody didn't want him because he bit a neighbor, and I was at the police station when they brought him in. I volunteered to take him off their hands. They were happy not to have to shoot him, and we got just the dog we needed."

When they went into the house and Piry served Feri's dinner, the girls sat with him and Erika asked, "What is his name?"

"What do you want to call him?" Feri asked magnanimously.

"He looks like a polar bear. So, let's call him Maczkó" Judith suggested.

"That's a great name!" Piry seconded it.

"Maczkó it is then," Feri said. "He'll stay at home during the day but in the evening, I will take him to the store and let him sleep there."

Thus, Maczkó's life settled into a well-established routine. Feri came home for dinner, and Maczkó was fed as well. Then Feri and Maczkó would walk back to the store, regardless of the weather, and he would lock the dog in there and return home. The store itself was dark, but the window display was always lit, so passersby could admire Feri's imaginative décor.

As long as the passersby just stood there looking, all was quiet inside the store. However, if any of them pointed at a fabric by touching the window even lightly, Maczkó would jump up and give them a show. He would rise to his full, formidable height, and hurl himself against the window or door inside the store, barking wildly, and baring his impressive row of white teeth, with a menacing growl.

Few people lingered at his display, for it was obvious, if the dog kept jumping against the window, eventually it would break. And no one in his right mind would want to tangle with a komondor. All Hungarians were familiar with the breed and knew its ability to defend whatever it was guarding, even at the cost of his own life.

On the great Hungarian flatlands, the Puszta, herdsmen kept two or three of these dogs with them, all year around. Three Komondors could easily kill a wolf stalking the herd they were guarding. Komondors were also trained to keep the animals together, or herd them as needed. A mere human was certainly no match against the strength and fighting ability of this dog, weighing around 60 kilograms (125 lbs.) or more. Feri could sleep in peace at home, there would be no more break-ins at his store.

In the mornings, before he opened the store, Feri now first stopped at the butcher's next door and bought a kilo of raw meat, cut into chunks.

Then, as soon as he opened his store door, Maczkó would first greet him then run out to the sidewalk to take care of nature's call. When done, Feri would unwrap the paper around the dog's "breakfast," and lay it down before him on the pavement by the store entrance. Maczkó would sit patiently, watching his master.

"Eat!" Feri would command him, and the dog, in one swift motion would stand up and lower his head over his food. He practically inhaled it, then sat again, looking at his master.

"Go home." Feri would order the dog.

Maczkó would take off like a bullet, his long blanket-like ringlets flying and Feri would start the routine of opening his store for the day.

Fifteen minutes after Maczkó left the shop, he would show up at his home. During summertime, he had an easy way to let the household know that he was there, for in the morning all the windows were open to air the rooms. Maczkó could just stand up on his hind legs and bark into the room till someone would acknowledge him and open the gate for him to come in.

But during the winter, regardless of the weather, he would sit in the snow or rain by the locked gate, looking pitifully forlorn at any person passing by. They would usually get the idea, and say to him, "Oh, you poor dog, you've been locked out? Want to go in?"

Maczkó would wag his tail and look hopeful. It was a mystery how he could make his face so expressive, but he did. At this point, the kind passerby would look for the bell and ring it. Now came the drama. If the person just rang the bell and went on his or her way, all was well. However, if he or she decided to stay and wait for the gate to be opened, the moment it was, Maczkó would turn on the person with a wild bark, warning him or her, to "not even think of entering".

It would take grabbing his collar by the household member who had come to the door, and vigorously ordering him to calm down, before Maczkó did. Then he would stand tense and alert, while the household member thanked the Good Samaritan and apologized for the dog's behavior. Maczkó eased up only after the person had left, and the gate had been locked. Then he very calmly walked to his own corner, drank some water, and settled in front of his large doghouse disregarding the weather, to keep an eye on his territory.

Contrary to his behavior toward strangers, he was sweet and obedient with all household members. He seemed specially love Judith and Erika. They could sit on his back, pretending to ride him, or even take a bone out of his mouth. He would let them, and wait till it was given back to him, looking at them lovingly with his intelligent, brown eyes through the curtain of ringlets covering his face.

Later, during hot summer days, Feri would invite Erika to go with him and Maczkó to the shore of the Danube, not too far from their house. Feri and Erika would ride on his bicycle, while Maczkó would trot alongside them on his leash. Erika would watch as Feri would pull into the water a very reluctant dog, for a bath. But he would tolerate the thorough soaping down Feri and Erika gave him and then swim with Feri to wash the soap out of his coat.

Erika loved watching Maczkó scramble up the shore and shake his ringlets, the sparkling water showering her and everything around him.

Imre and Magda had a dog as well, a small female dachshund, and the two dogs became friends. The little dachshund would often run out of his home and greet Maczkó on his morning arrivals, and they would spend time together, playing, or just lying peacefully side by side.

In late spring, much to everyone's surprise, Tuba, the dachshund, gave birth to three tiny dogs, all white with some brown patches, short haired but unmistakably resembling their father.

Erika liked to go over to Aunt Magda's apartment and watch the puppies greedily nursing while their mother lay patiently on her side, letting her pups tug at her.

Aunt Magda said to Erika, "We cannot keep three more dogs, so Uncle Imre is threatening to drown them, unless we find another solution."

"Oh, no!" Erika protested. "He can't do that! I can ask my schoolmates who wants a puppy! Or I can sell them at the Sunday outdoor market!"

Erika knew that a few blocks from their home, every Sunday a street was turned into an open-air market from Spring to Fall, and one could buy anything there, from food to used clothes, and even pets.

"Is that a promise?" Aunt Magda demanded.

"Yes. I give you my word," Erika said solemnly.

"They'll open their eyes in about ten days, and we'll let them to grow a bit, but after that...."

"I'll do it. Promise." Erika insisted.

As it turned out, both brothers, Lajos and Vince took a male puppy, and the last one, a female, was given to a cousin of theirs, Ede, and his wife Aniko. They lived in a small village, about an hour's train ride from Budapest and had come for a visit to meet Feri's new family.

As was customary, out of town guests were given the master bedroom to sleep in, while Feri and Piry took the living room couch. During such visits Piry and Maria worked twice as hard, to make sure they served the best foods available, and that their visitors were made to feel at home.

Generous hospitality was an inbred Hungarian custom. It was also customary for guests to bring a gift. These guests, because they owned a bakery in their village, had brought several loaves of rye bread with them—a staple of Hungarian diet. At the end of their stay, while they were enjoying a dinner of chicken paprikás, and a rich dessert of apple strudel, Ede spoke up.

"Feri, Aniko and I would like to thank you and Piry for your generous hospitality. We really enjoyed being with your new family. And this coming summer, when their school is out, we would like to invite the girls to come for a vacation with us."

Piry and Feri looked at each other, and their daughters. Judith was solemn, Erika was beaming.

"Well, would you girls like to accept this wonderful invitation?" asked Piry.

"I would!" Erika jumped at the opportunity.

"I thank you, Uncle Ede and Aunt Aniko, but I need to stay in Budapest during the summer, so I could study for my Bat Mitzvah," Judith explained.

"It's all settled then," Uncle Ede declared. "I will come back after school ends and take Erika with me; and if she likes being with us, and if she behaves herself, maybe she can stay the whole summer." He winked at Erika.

"I can hardly wait," was Erika's response. She had no idea what it would be like to spend a summer at their home, but she thought, *it might be better than staying at home.* Their home life was becoming increasingly tense, and Erika was happy at the chance to get away.

◉◉◉

Erika's and also Judith's feelings of being unhappy at home were caused by witnessing the frequent discords between Piry and Feri. Piry would broach a subject and Feri's response was always curt, sometimes rude. Most of the time it left a tense silence at the end of their conversation. It got to the point that when Feri came home from the store, Erika and Judith would scatter with one excuse or another into their bedroom. But they could hear their parents' voices and feel the tension in the air when they had to cross the winter dining room to go to the bathroom.

The conversation between their parents wasn't always an argument. Sometimes, they would discuss household or store related issues. But Feri's tone was always dismissive or a sarcastic put-down of whatever Piry had said. Once in a while, Erika could hear her mother crying late at night, when she thought everyone was asleep. Yet, in front of her daughters Piry pretended that all was well and ran the household with devotion and a positive attitude for the most part. Piry's loyalty was such, that even though she listened to her daughters' derogatory comments about Feri's stubbornness or unpleasant remarks and difficult nature, she would stop them from saying anything truly nasty about their stepfather.

She would admonish her daughters, reminding them of their difficult years in boarding schools. "He has given us a home and is working hard to keep us warm and well fed. Nobody is perfect. Just be grateful you're here instead of at the orphanage!"

At that point, both Judith and Erika would fall silent, for they knew, no matter how much they resented and feared Feri, their mother was right.

By winter of 1949, their lives seemed to settle into a routine, with Feri trudging through snow-filled streets to his store, the children crunching their way to school, and Piry and Maria managing the household. Except the routine kept getting interrupted by unexpected events.

In the severely cold weather of early March, Piry's Aunt Margit arrived for a visit from Debrecen with her daughter Ibi and the latter's husband, Sam. Aunt Margit was one of the ten sisters of Piry's birth mother. As was customary, guests who came to stay, were given the "big bed" in the main bedroom, while Piry slept with Feri on the sofa in the living room.

Aunt Margit and the young couple stayed an entire week while awaiting their passports and immigration documents from the Canadian Embassy. They were all survivors of Auschwitz, in fact, Ibi and Sam had met at that concentration camp. Sam, originally from Poland, helped save the women's lives by smuggling food to them from his own rations. He learned to speak Hungarian at camp, and he and Ibi fell in love. Sam was twenty-two and Ibi merely sixteen at the time. When the war was over, Margit and Ibi returned to their hometown, Debrecen, in Hungary, and Sam chose to go with them. After regaining their health, Ibi and Sam got married. Now they were all emigrating to Toronto in Canada. None of them could stand living in the European countries that tried to kill them merely for being Jewish.

Once again, Piry came under pressure from her relatives, especially from Aunt Margit, to divorce Feri and follow them to the new world.

"Can't you see that the Communists are taking over the country? Your children will have no future here," Margit warned Piry.

"He won't go anywhere, and I can't leave him," Piry responded. "But we'll start studying English, and maybe we'll follow you to Canada in a couple of years."

"While you're making up your mind, let's talk about an idea I've got," Margit said, pulling Piry into the privacy of the master bedroom. "Listen to me. I don't foresee things getting better in Hungary either economically or politically. So, I want you to seriously consider emigrating, and before you do so, prepare for it financially. Here is how I suggest that you do it:

Just as we have cousins and other relatives in Canada—which is why we are able to go there—I will meet others there who have relatives here in Hungary. These relatives in Canada might want to send money to help support their families in Hungary. But the official rate of exchange is ridiculously low and I'm sure it will get worse.

"Therefore, this is how we can make a smart business out of this. The people in Canada will give me the money they want to send to their relatives in Hungary. I will write to you and ask you to take to those relatives gifts of food, such as flour, beef, chicken, duck, goose, or rice, potatoes, or apples, or a combination of any these items. Each of these foods will have a certain monetary value. For example, a kilo of flour will mean 100 forints. A kilo of beef will be 200 forints, a kilo of chicken 300, duck 400, and goose 500. Each apple will be 10 forints, and so on.

However much money they'll give me in Canada, I'll write to you that we have had a party, and I prepared X kilo of potatoes, chicken, or beef, or whatever, and you will figure out the total weight of each of these items. You will then convert those weights into money and take that amount of forints to the designated family. I assume you still have some funds in reserve. The equivalent money you give here will be saved for you in Canadian dollars by me, as given to me by these families. I will take ten percent of their orders to cover my time for doing this. The rest will be yours, safeguarded by me."

"I don't have a lot of reserve left. When I run out, where will I get the forints to give to the people here?" Piry asked, evaluating this deal.

"That's the other side of this business. There will be people in Hungary who will want to give you forints so that their relatives in Canada could convert their money into savings for them. You will accept these forints and use these funds to give money to the people whose relatives in Canada want to send them money in Hungary.

Then you'll write to me naming the food items you had 'bought" for such and such a family, as a job they've asked you to do or for a party. I'll know how to pay the people in Canada and put money aside for you. Also, I have friends in the diplomatic corps and other government jobs, who can travel between Western countries and Socialist ones. They will bring you 'gifts,' such as nylon stockings, Western made clothes, and even food items you can't get here.

You'll sell these things to earn cash.

"I will send you a letter, saying, 'My cousin so and so will be coming to visit you on such and such a date. Please call them to confirm that you'll be at home or set up a different meeting time and place with them.' When you meet, they'll not only bring you merchandise, but they'll also give you names and addresses of people who will take the stuff and pay you for it."

Piry was amazed, "Where did you come up with all this?"

Margit grinned. "I didn't spend a year in a concentration camp in Auschwitz without learning how to survive. We all had to deal and trade— food for services—and God knows what. One learns. How do you think we managed to make a living since we got back? You will learn too when you need to feed your children. Just be super cautious. Don't talk about this to anyone. Not your sister, not even Feri. One day you'll be glad you kept it to yourself."

Piry's sixth sense told her Aunt Margit was right. "I promise. And thank you."

"You're my dead sister's baby. I've got to take care of you."

They hugged, to seal the deal.

◎◉◎

With Erika's friend, Ildikó gone, another girl was seated in her place, and Erika offered to do homework with her, as she had done with Ildiko. The new girl, Zsófia, was not as good in sciences as Ildikó had been but Erika still found it more fun to study with a friend than alone.

Zsófia lived in the opposite direction from the school than Erika, so to do their homework together they stayed at school after classes. One day, as they were finishing their Hungarian literature compositions, and Erika was helping Zsófia with her last sentence, Mrs. Boda walked in.

"And just what are you two up to?" Mrs. Boda asked in her most menacing tone.

"We were just doing our homework together," Erika explained.

"And who told you that you can stay here after school?"

"Nobody. We just thought…."

"Erika, you're a troublemaker!" Mrs. Boda shouted at her and grabbed Zsófia's composition book off their desk. "I'll bet you wrote this for Zsófia, hadn't you?"

"I did not," Erika protested.

"She did not," Zsófia piped up, indignant at the accusation.

"You're both lying!" shouted Mrs. Boda. "I will keep this, and if I recognize as much as one sentence as Erika's writing, I will flunk both of you in Composition for cheating! Now out with you two!"

The girls quickly gathered their schoolbooks and throwing them into their briefcases, left the classroom. Zsófia was so upset, she was shaking.

"Don't take it personally," Erika tried to calm Zsófia once they were outside the building. "Mrs. Boda has it in for me because I'm Jewish."

"What has that got to do with anything? We're not supposed to have any religion at all! So why would she hate you for something you don't even have?"

"Because we still all know who has which religion and I'm the only Jew in her class."

"Well, I don't care what you are. You are my friend, and you will always be my friend."

"Thank you," Erika hugged Zsófia, before each of them went on her way home.

Erika could hardly wait to tell her mother about this latest incident with Mrs. Boda. She now knew for sure that she had to change schools for she wouldn't survive another year with this homeroom teacher. Everything at school depended on their grades. If Mrs. Boda lowered her grade in any subject, Erika would not be able to go to high school. Only top students were accepted there. Being Jewish and middle class, instead of working-class, were all bad qualifications. Erika knew that her only chance for being admitted into a high school was to be an 'all five' student. *The Nazis robbed me of my father. This anti-Semitic teacher isn't going to rob me of my future,* Erika swore to herself.

Piry listened to Erika's complaint again and promised to take care of the matter before the next school year began.

◎◉◎

Summer came, the school year ended, and in mid-June, true to his word, Uncle Ede showed up, ready to take Erika with him for a village vacation. Piry and Erika packed a small suitcase for her: summer clothes, underwear, pajamas, and a bathing suit. Although there was going to be no place to swim, children did wear a bathing suit on hot summer days, just to get a tan.

Erika packed her favorite book as well, The Last of the Mohicans by the American writer, James Fenimore Cooper, in Hungarian translation. This book was a surprise birthday gift from Feri. Erika's birthday, on June 6th, had been celebrated quietly. Piry gave her an envelope with twenty forints, which was a lot of money for Erika, and she was surprised and grateful for it. Judith handed her a novel she had finished reading. Maria made Erika's favorite snack, slices of rye bread quick fried in cooking oil and then rubbed with a garlic clove. Feri's was the most surprising gift. He had placed the large picture book on Erika's pillow while she was still asleep, then went off to work.

When Erika awoke, she felt the hard edge of the book. She opened her eyes and was amazed at how beautiful it was. Its shiny cover displayed a handsome native American Indian carrying the limp figure of a blonde girl in his arms, with a big moon over them in a deep blue sky. It took Erika no time at all to read the book.

Then she went to the local library and borrowed all the books they had in Hungarian translation by Fennimore Cooper. But those were books she had to return to the library. The Last of the Mohicans was her very own, and she cherished it, reading favorite sections over and over till she knew them by heart, yet read them again. That whole world was so different from hers that it held a fascination she could not shake.

Piry packed a small wicker basket for them with some fruit and sandwiches.

"It's only a two-hour train ride," Ede protested.

"You can get hungry anyway, so it's best if you have some food with you," Piry insisted.

The Western Train station was a streetcar's ride from Erika's new home in Újpest. Uncle Ede insisted on carrying Erika's suitcase but let her bring the food basket. He said to her, "Hold on to my hand when we get into the train station. I don't want to lose you."

Erika felt a bit peculiar putting her hand into Uncle Ede's; after all, she was nine years old, she could look out for herself, but she did as she was told.

The stairs up into the train were steep, and Uncle Ede, after hoisting up Erika's suitcase and food basket, simply lifted her under the arms and placed her into the train. Then he climbed up as well. Erika was keenly aware that when he lifted her, he had held her only under the arms and made no attempt to reach lower toward her chest. She was relieved.

They found a compartment with two empty seats next to each other just as it began to rapidly fill up with other passengers.

"Take the window seat," Uncle Ede instructed Erika, "that way you can watch the scenery along the way." He put her suitcase on the shelf above their heads but kept the food basket under their bench.

Erika was excited about the trip, though a little nervous about staying with strangers in their home. But deep down she trusted that it will be fine. She heard the train's sharp, loud whistle, then felt a lurch as the train rolled out of the station. She smiled at her uncle, and he patted her hand, saying, "I hope you'll enjoy your stay with us."

Erika watched the streets and houses thin out, and fields with growing crops come into view. Uncle Ede put his head back against the compartment wall and closed his eyes. The cabin was full, people were busy talking to each other, and no one paid any attention to the little girl who presumably was traveling with her father.

Shortly after the train made its first stop, the cabin door slid open and an elderly woman made her way into their compartment, carrying a small basket on her arm. She searched for a free seat just as the train was starting to roll. There were none to be had, and the woman stood looking ill at ease as she tried to keep her balance while the train speeded up.

Ede, who woke up during their stop, nudged Erika and said, "Let's move over a bit so the lady could sit down?"

The woman overheard, and said to Ede, "That would be most kind of you, I am only going one stop. My daughter lives in the next village, and I am taking new ducklings to her."

"Of course," Erika responded, eager to be of help, and squeezed herself tightly against the window. But there still wasn't sufficient space for the old woman to sit down.

"For just one stop you can sit on my lap," Uncle Ede declared.

Erika obediently stood up, Ede slid over to the window seat, and picking Erika up by her waist, placed her on his knees sideways, so she could still be facing the window.

"I can't thank you enough." The old woman gave them a toothless grin as she was trying to keep the basket level on her arm, while slowly lowering herself unto the aisle seat. "Want to see the ducklings? They've just hatched about a week ago."

Erika jumped off Uncle Ede's knees and stood staring with amazement as the old woman uncovered her basket to reveal the eight tiny, yellow birds inside.

"Can I touch them?" she asked.

"If you're very gentle."

Erika reached inside, her fingertips feeling the soft, cottony puffs of feathers that barely covered the skin and bone ducklings.

"I must cover them now, because they can easily catch a cold," the old woman said.

"Thank you for the look," Erika said politely. A vague memory of the chicks she had drowned when she was very young floated into her mind, but she dismissed it. That happened such a long, long time ago, in a whole different world.

Once again, she turned toward the window, feeling comfortable to be sitting on Uncle Ede's knees. "I'm not too heavy?" she asked him.

"Nah, you're light as a feather. We'll have to fatten you up a bit with good village food," he joked with her.

When the old woman got off at the next stop, and Erika regained her seat, Uncle Ede pulled up the food basket from beneath their seat. As the train rolled on, they ate the salami sandwiches and an apple each, prepared by Piry for them. Then Uncle Ede said, "Trains make me sleepy, so don't mind me if I doze off. It's not your company," and he grinned at her.

"Feel free," Erika smiled back, feeling more and more at ease with him.

True to his word, Ede leaned his head back, and Erika could hear his gentle snoring while she stared out the window at the ever-changing landscape. Green fields separated villages, and occasionally she saw a river run alongside the train. In the distance horses were pulling buggies with families sitting on them. It was all so new and so very beautiful. Watching the countryside go by, Erika felt at peace.

Even during this short time that they had spent traveling together, she could tell that Uncle Ede was a very different man from her stepfather. He seemed at ease with people and the world around him. Apu was always like a taut string, ready to snap at the slightest thing he didn't approve of. Uncle Ede was not talkative, he only spoke when he had something to say or explain. But when he did talk, he did it nicely. Above all, Erika just knew that he would never treat her the way Apu did.

CHAPTER 10

IT HAPPENED EARLIER IN the year, after Aunt Margit's visit that Piry informed Erika, "Apu has decided to continue sleeping in the living room. So, from now on you and I will be sharing the big bed in the master bedroom."

Erika was surprised at the news but didn't question why. She knew. It was obvious that her mother and stepfather were not getting along. It will be nicer to sleep in the bedroom with mother, than in the room with Judith who always orders me around, even at night, Erika thought.

Judith was happy that from then on, she had the "children's room" all to herself, at least at night. Clearly, they both had to study in the same room. But now she could shut the light off when she wanted to go to sleep, without having to order Erika every night to stop reading.

When it came to sharing the big bed, Erika told Piry that she would be more comfortable sleeping "footsies". So Piry lay as customary, with her head at the headboard beneath the window, and Erika slipped under the duvet cover with her head at the "foot" of the bed. This way they also had more room, which they needed, since Erika was a restless sleeper, turning frequently, and spreading her arms out while she slept.

Nobody in the family ever commented about this new sleeping arrangement. The adults never gave any explanation, and Erika and Judith knew that their parents didn't really get along. So, things were just the way they were with nothing to discuss.

Then came the night Erika would never forget. Judith needed a couple of new skirts, so one evening, she and Piry went to the dressmaker. There were no ready-made clothes or shoes to buy in Hungary. When new clothes or footwear were needed, people had them made. They would select the leather and the color they wanted for the shoes. Ankle-high winter shoes, regular shoes for warmer weather, even sandals had to be custom made by the shoemaker.

For clothes, people bought fabrics for tailors and dressmakers to make them into outfits. That is why Feri's store was so successful. Everyone needed to buy fabrics at some point, and Feri knew how to find good quality but not very expensive materials.

Of course, because he sold fabrics, the women in his household got theirs from him. But with Feri nothing was a simple procedure. When any of them needed a fabric, it was Piry or Erika who had to beg for it. Erika learned quickly from her mother how to sidle up to Feri in the store and using the diminutive nickname for father, say to him sweetly, "Daddy, that wool (or cotton) fabric over there would be perfect for the new dress (or skirt or blouse) that I need for the holidays (or school)." Whatever the occasion was, Erika would point at the fabric on the shelf.

Feri would look up, and says, "Haven't you got enough clothes?"

Then would come the explanation for the need, such as "Everyone will be wearing new clothes then" followed by a series of fawning compliments about Feri's generosity, and how good the new clothes will look for the needed occasion.

At times, it would take over an hour to cajole him to cut the necessary yards of fabric. Piry and Erika would then put their arms around his neck and kiss his cheeks, thanking him for his generosity. He would bend down with seeming reluctance to let them kiss and hug him. Judith would simply thank him, and he would nod, barely looking at her.

He would then fold the fabrics with professional skill and wrap them in brown paper so they wouldn't have to carry them openly on the streets.

That particular time Judith had received two different fabrics from Feri, one for school wear, and one for her upcoming bat-mitzvah. Piry had two dressmakers lined up. One who lived in the center of Budapest, sewed haute couture, and charged accordingly. The other, whom they visited that particular evening, lived walking distance from their home, and charged a lot less.

While they were out, Erika had finished her homework and continued to sit in the winter dining room reading. Feri went to bed as usual, around nine o'clock. Maria, the maid, having finished cleaning up after their dinner, had gone to her room as well. The house was quiet. Erika got sleepy and decided not to wait up for her mother and sister. After changing into her nightgown and using the bathroom, she quietly tiptoed through Feri's room to get to her bedroom.

Unexpectedly, Feri called to Erika in his low, tense voice, "Come here."

Erika obeyed, and he lifted the duvet for her to get into bed with him. Erika thought nothing of it, though it seemed odd for her to do this. But she didn't say anything because she was somewhat afraid of him.

Suddenly he rolled over her, weighing her down by pressing against her pubic bone. Erika was stunned but not knowing how to react, she stayed silent and very still.

"Open your legs," he ordered her, as he pulled up her nightgown.

Erika always slept with panties on, as she felt cold without them. Feri did not pull her panty off but pushed it aside, and Erika felt something round, hard, and warm press against her crotch. She immediately realized that he was rubbing his penis against her, but she felt completely helpless and lost as to what to do. She didn't have the courage to scream and also didn't think it was a good idea to alert the maid as to what was happening to her. Her mother was out, what could the maid do?

She lay there, tolerating the pressure of his quick movements against her, trying to breathe under his weight. What a swine, she thought to herself, and wondered how long he would be doing this. Suddenly he let out a deep sigh and slumped over her.

"I can't breathe," she protested, and pushed at his shoulders with both her hands.

He rolled off and kissed her gently on her temple.

"Can I go now?" Erika asked feeling enormous discomfort and resentment.

"Yes."

She climbed out of his bed and went to the bathroom where she washed herself carefully, filled with disgust, humiliation, and fury. She was totally at a loss as to what she could do about what had just happened. She knew what he had done. When she was six years old, at one of the summer camps, a boy asked her to play "doctor" with him. He made her lie down in the grass behind a bush and lay on top of her. He rubbed himself against her and she felt her panties get wet.

"You pig, you pissed on me!" she shouted, tossing him off.

He laughed, and Erika ran off, furious at him. She had to go and wash her skirt and panties and sit in the sun till they dried. In some way, she knew that what the boy had done to her had to be kept a secret, even though she wished she could talk about it at least with her girlfriend at camp. But she couldn't bring herself to talk about the humiliation of his peeing on her. It was so disgusting. Why would he do such a thing? She never spoke to that boy again. It was a year or two later that she learned, through conversations with other girls, that Erika learned that the fluid had not been urine, but something that came out of boys' and men's penises. She never mentioned her experience to any of her friends, even during their intimate discussions. But now, what her stepfather had done was an even bigger secret, and even more disgusting.

By this time Erika knew it was a thing adult did with each other, that's how they made babies. *But an adult shouldn't be doing it with a child. Especially not a man who is supposed to behave like a father!* She waited in the dining room till she heard Feri's even snoring and then crept soundlessly across his room to her own bed next door. She lay under the covers as tense as a violin string, until she heard her mother's and Judith's voices. They have come home, Erika finally relaxed, and closed her eyes, pretending to be asleep.

When Piry crawled into her side of the double, Erika wished she could tell her mother what had happened. But somehow, she couldn't. She felt so ashamed that no matter how scared she would be from now on about being alone with Feri, she could never reveal it to her mother, or anyone else. *I will just have to find a way to avoid him if we are left together without Anyu or Judith in the house.*

The train slowed to a halt, and Uncle Ede opened his eyes.

"I dozed off, didn't I?" he smiled at Erika. "We're almost there. Next stop is ours."

When they got off the train, Uncle Ede said, "We'll walk from the station to my house. It's not far."

As Erika kept pace with Uncle Ede through the village, she had found everything around her amazingly different from her surroundings in Budapest.

Instead of apartment buildings, there were only small, private houses with whitewashed adobe walls and red tile roofs, along the tree lined, unpaved streets. From the street, one could see only the side of each home, and the yard in front of it. Meter-high picket fences, mostly painted white, had gates that were wide enough to drive a horse drawn carriage through them or for cows to come into the yard.

Aunt Aniko and Uncle Ede lived on the main street. It was wide but also unpaved and lined with homes behind trees and fences. Aunt Aniko was expecting them, and as soon as she heard the gate squeak open, she came to greet them with a warm smile, "Welcome, welcome." She first hugged her husband, then Erika, saying, "C'mon in and make yourself at home."

"You show Erika around, I'll check on the breads," Uncle Ede said, and pointed further down the yard, "The bakery is there," he explained to Erika as he left.

Their home spread far into the yard, with many doors, but the interior was actually quite small. The main entrance was through the kitchen, and from there one could continue to three mid-size rooms that served both their daytime needs and as bedrooms. The kitchen was cozy. It had a small table with four chairs, and a large, old wood-burning stove for both cooking and heating in the winter.

The walls held shelves displaying plates, and cabinets for pots and pans. A couple of plates, painted with wildflowers and green leaves decorated the free spaces on the walls.

The first room off the kitchen was the "best room," or living room. It had colorfully embroidered fabrics hanging from the walls, and hand crocheted white curtains covering the two windows that overlooked the yard. A large sofa stood against the far wall, plus an armchair cattycorner to it, both covered with embroidered doilies. There was a fireplace and near it was a small stand with a ceramic bowl on top of it. On the floor next to it was a bucket with water and a cup hanging off its edge. The center of the room was empty, allowing traffic to flow through to the next room.

"Pssst…" Aunt Aniko put her finger to her lips, "The baby is taking a nap".

Surprised, Erika whispered, "I didn't know you have a baby!"

"Yes, she is a year old. We also have my auntie living with us. She helps me with the baby and the work around the house. She is napping too. She is getting on in years and gets tired by the afternoon."

They peaked into the room and Erika saw on a narrow bed the small figure of an old lady, curled up on her side. In a crib next to her slept the baby, covered with a light blanket, despite the summer heat. Actually, the rooms were cool, probably because the house is built of thick adobe, Erika thought. A sewing machine with a small chair sat below the window, and a dresser and a closet stood against the other walls.

Aunt Aniko cautiously closed the door, taking Erika with her. "Let them sleep. The third room is nothing special, it's just our bedroom. Are you hungry?"

"No, thank you, we ate sandwiches on the train. But I would like to use the toilet," Erika replied.

"Oh, of course, come I'll show you."

To Erika's great surprise, Aunt Aniko led her out of the house, down the courtyard. She pointed to a small wood cabin opposite the house, at the far end, where a fence separated the front yard from a larger yard beyond it.

"We don't have indoor facilities," Aunt Aniko explained. "We use the outhouse. Do you know how?"

"Not really."

"Come, I'll show you."

Aniko walked to the outhouse with Erika and swung the latch up on the door. "You just open the door and step up on the floor inside. This long box that looks like a bench but has a lid in the middle, is the toilet. You just lift the lid and sit down. When you're done, use the paper we keep here on the side. Throw it in the toilet and close the lid. We don't have a fancy flushing system like you have in the city. But we do just fine, and you'll get used to it, too."

"I'm sure I will," Erika smiled, eager to be pleasant and hide her shock.

Aunt Aniko left her.

Erika closed the door and opened the lid. A strong odor hit her, and she quickly pinched her nostrils closed for the smell made her nauseous. But then she saw that the walls of the outhouse were made of planks of wood with narrow slits that allowed for ventilation. So, she slowly released her nostrils and breathed through her mouth, allowing herself to get used to the smell while catching fresh air through the walls.

When she came out, she spotted a bucket of water and a small pan with a long handle just outside the door. Aunt Aniko was standing on the other side of the yard, and called out to her, "Dip the pot into the water to rinse your hands over the grass."

Erika did as she was told and then joined her aunt.

"Come, I'll show you our bakery" Aunt Aniko said to her.

Located just past the fence that divided the yards, was a large room where at the far end its entire wall was a giant oven. It had a dome shaped roof, and coals were burning in an open pit of the floor. On a rack above the coals, neatly lined up, sat large round and oval shaped loaves of bread.

Uncle Ede, wearing a white apron which covered him from shoulders to toes, was leaning into the oven, balancing a long wood pole, with a flat shovel at its end. He straightened up as he heard their voices. "I am about to pull these loaves out. Want to watch?"

Without waiting for their reply, he turned toward the oven and deftly maneuvered two loaves unto his shovel. He swung around, and as Erika jumped out of the way, Uncle Ede slid the steaming hot loaves unto a large wooden rack in the middle of the room. The aroma of fresh, hot bread filled Erika's nostrils. There is no better scent in the world, than freshly baked bread, she thought.

"The people who ordered these will be picking them up in about an hour. By then they've cooled down," Aunt Aniko explained to Erika. "But of course, we'll also keep a couple of loafs for ourselves."

"Do you bake every day?" Erika was curious.

"No, just three times a week. About half these loaves are brought in as dough by people in the village, and we just bake it for them. The others we make and sell to people who place orders for them. We don't bake for stores, only for the villagers and ourselves. We used to sell at the village's general store, but now we have been told by the local government that we can't do that anymore."

"Why not?"

"We're not allowed to have a private business."

"You're not?" Erika was surprised.

"It's a new government regulation. It's considered a 'capitalist business practice' and now all production has to be done by a government owned bakery." The sudden tightness in Aunt Aniko's voice indicated that she was upset about it but didn't wish to discuss it any further.

Erika got it. She was not to ask more questions.

Aunt Aniko said, "Come, let's go into the house. You've had a long trip; you'll see the rest of the farm later."

Uncle Ede handed Aniko a large round loaf. Wrapping it into a towel, for it was steaming hot, she carefully carried it into the house with them.

Erika, who had been eating only store-bought bread at home, could hardly wait to taste the fresh, home baked bread.

During dinner, she met the old lady, Auntie Marci, and the baby. As a good guest, Erika offered to play with the little girl, Kata, any time they wanted her to do so.

"That's very sweet of you," Aunt Aniko responded. "But we want you to feel free to meet other kids your age, and play, not become a nanny."

"You're so nice, but I really don't mind helping with whatever I can," Erika responded.

"We'll see how it'll go," Aunt Aniko smiled at Erika.

Auntie Marci said nothing. She sat at the table smiling and holding the baby in her lap, even during dinner. She had gray hair, dark eyes, and almost no wrinkles, though she seemed very old because she had no teeth, and her lips caved into her mouth.

"Auntie Marci washes her face every morning and evening with water into which she pours a bit of vinegar. That's why she hasn't got any wrinkles," Aunt Aniko explained to Erika. The old lady, pleased with the compliment, nodded, smiling, but said nothing.

People in the countryside went to bed early. After the simple supper of bean soup with pieces of ham in it and a thick slice of the freshly baked bread, dipped into sunflower oil for flavor, Erika's bed was made up on the sofa in the "best room." Her suitcase had been brought in earlier by Uncle Ede, and she was given a drawer and space in the closet to store the clothes she had brought with her.

While Erika was getting ready for bed, she discovered that there was no running water in the house, not even in the kitchen sink. Aunt Aniko pointed at the washbasin on the stand in the room, and the bucket with the small pot on the floor beside it.

"Pour some water from the bucket into the bowl to wash your hands and face and use the towel hanging on the rack of the stand. In the morning, we'll heat up water so you could bathe. And here is a glass for water to rinse your mouth after you brush your teeth. You can also take a glass of water from the bucket by kitchen sink, and keep it next to your bed, in case you get thirsty at night. And by the way, I put a potty under your bed, in case you have to go at night. It's perfectly safe for you to go outside, but I think you'll be more comfortable if you don't have to do it in the middle of the night. Besides, the dog might bark at you since he doesn't know you."

"Dog? I didn't see a dog when we came home."

"That's because it was out in the pastures guarding the cows. But now the cows are at home in the stable, and the dog is in the yard. You'll see them all tomorrow."

Erika nodded, feeling as though she had been dropped unto another planet. She was learning about a whole different way of life, and she found it amazing. At the same time, she just accepted it without fuss or comparing it to the comforts of her home. She now said, "If I can use the outhouse now, before I go to sleep, I won't have to go again till morning."

"That's fine, go ahead," Aunt Aniko smiled at her. "The dog's name is Zorka, so if she comes to sniff you, which she will, just say her name and stand still while he does."

"We've got a Komondor at home," Erika reminded Aunt Aniko, "so I'm not afraid of dogs."

Uncle Ede, who had come into the room to say good night, now said, "Don't you remember, we got Zorka when we first came to meet you? Your Aunt Magda's dachshund had puppies with your komondor."

"Oh, I can't wait to see what she looks like now!" Erika exclaimed.

Indeed, Zorka, a tan and white curly haired mid-size dog was in the yard. Her tale up, she was moving slowly toward Erika, who waited, held her hand out for Zorka to smell, and then patted her on the head. "Zorka, we'll be good friends," she informed the dog in a gentle, low tone. Shaking her tail, the dog let Erika go to where she wanted.

When Erika finally slipped into bed under a sheet and a wool blanket over it, Aunt Aniko came in to say good night.

"I hope you'll like staying with us. I know all this must be very new to you, so if you have any questions just feel free to ask. I think you'll get used to our ways quickly and will have a great summer."

"I'm sure I will. I love it here. Thank you for inviting me."

Aunt Aniko kissed Erika's cheek. "You're very welcome. We're happy to have you."

◎◉◎

Erika adapted to life with her relatives in the village with ease. They had two cows in a stable at the end of their long yard, and every morning at dawn Uncle Ede went to milk them. If Erika woke up at that time, she would take a cup from the kitchen and paddle barefooted down the yard to the stable. As with the goats in Budapest, she tried milking one of the cows and failed. But she was invited to hold her cup under the udder while her uncle filled it with foaming, hot milk, smelling of cow.

Erika learned to draw water into the bucket which hung on the side of the well that stood in the middle of the yard. It had a roof, supported by four posts, to keep things from falling into the water. Erika, amazed by the depth of the well, would frequently lean under the roof to stare at the water that was so far down that she could barely see it.

To get water, she used a pully to lower the bucket till she could hear it plop. She could see the bucket fall sideways, then get weighed down with the water that rushed into it. At that point, Erika would yank at the cord. Carefully, slowly, using all her arms' strength, Erika would roll the pully to bring up the full bucket. It took quite a bit of strength to unhook it and lift it without spilling the water back into the well. But Erika learned to do it and then to carry the fresh water into the kitchen.

She also learned that each day the fresh milk was "put to rest" in a cellar located in the yard across from the house. After a day or two, the cream rose to the top in the large milk buckets. It got ladled off and stored in a separate container in the cellar. When enough cream had been collected, Auntie Marci went to sit in the yard on a stool with a tall, round bucket between her knees. Inside this wooden bucket was a thick screw like tool with a handle at its top. Aunt Aniko poured the cream into the bucket and would slowly turn the handle, churning the cream sometimes for an hour, till it became the best butter Erika had ever tasted on a slice of fresh rye bread.

Once a week, Uncle Ede had to carry a portion of the milk, and some of the cream, to the village Commune Office. All villagers had to turn in a portion of their milk production to this office, run by the District Government. The amount of milk was determined by the number of cows a family had. The Village Council provided tall, cylindrical enamel containers for the milk. They had lids with clamps to keep them tightly locked while being carried. Smaller, similar containers were given for carrying the cream.

Erika accompanied Uncle Ede the first time he delivered during her stay and offered to carry the cream containers. From then on, she would go with him each week, to be of help.

"Why do we have to take these to the Commune Office?" Erika asked as she walked alongside Uncle Ede.

"It's like a tax or something. Or maybe they just don't want us to have too much milk, so that we couldn't sell what we don't use for ourselves. Before the war, we never had to donate milk to the government, but times are different now." Uncle Ede explained, none too happily. "But please don't repeat what I've just said to anyone. It might get me into trouble."

"I won't," Erika promised, and added with a smile, "I'm good at keeping things to myself."

Erika participated in her hosts' lives in other ways as well. Every morning, Aunt Aniko sent her gaggle of eight geese with a couple of village girls to the fields where the wheat had already been mowed. The geese grazed all day, pecking at the leftover greens and seeds. The girls, who herded not only Aniko's but also other families' geese, lounged around in the wild grass, keeping an eye on their charges.

Aunt Aniko introduced Erika to them, and she joined the girls several times a week. But Erika did not enjoy just lazing around. She asked the girls to teach her their favorite songs, and in turn she taught them hers. Some of their songs were lively, with a quick rhythm, that made Erika want to dance. So, she did, asking her new friends to join in. The village girls had been taught folk dancing at their school, as part of their 'heritage education'. Villagers passing by would watch with broad smiles the three young girls dancing and singing in the fields, surrounded by a cackling flock of white geese. During these times, Erika was filled with joy and wished the summer would never end.

Another of Erika's favorite activities was to climb up on a ladder that was laid against the one-story high pile of hay in their yard. She would lie on her back on top of the warm and scratchy hay in her bathing suit, getting a tan, while watching the cumulous clouds float by. This was a serenity she had never known before. Voices from the house seemed distant, an occasional dog bark would break the silence. But in the middle of the afternoon heat most people were indoors, and Erika loved the solitude and stillness of the world around her.

Once a week, she sang and danced her way to the village post office, to send a postcard to her mother. On some days she would be invited by neighboring children to play "hide and seek" at their homes or to climb a fruit tree. They ate apples or sour cherries that were beginning to ripen in mid-summer, right off the branches.

Erika felt carefree, like the child she had never been before. She also experienced how much love there could be in a home when everyone was kind and appreciative of each other. She never wanted to go home again. But the third week of August Uncle Ede packed a basketful of fruit, loaves of bread, and butter to take with them, and Erika packed her suitcase.

"Come back next summer," Aunt Aniko told her, as she hugged Erika good-bye.

"I will if you'll have me! Thank you so much for everything," Erika hugged her with tears in her eyes.

◎◉◎

The moment Erika walked into her home it felt like she could cut the tension with a knife, but she ignored it.

"So, how was it?" Judith asked, her voice full of disdain, fully expecting Erika to report how boring it had been, and how she hated every minute of her summer.

Erika didn't honor her with a reply, instead she asked, "How was your summer,".

"Great," Judith boasted, "I went swimming every day with my friends, and we went to the outdoor theater on Margit Island. It was fun. But the most fun was that you weren't here to bug me."

Erika walked away; she had nothing to say to her sister. She had just realized that she had felt the same way about being away from Judith. No one was teasing her and ordering her around all summer long. That alone had been worth being at the village.

She did tell her mother, while she was helping with dinner preparations in the kitchen, how much she had enjoyed her summer. Maria was pleased as well to hear that Erika had had a nice time. When Feri came home from the store, Erika thanked him for sending her to his relatives. He grunted and gave her his usual strained smile, obviously pleased that he was instrumental in providing her with a good summer.

◎◉◎

School started the first week of September. Piry, true to her promise to transferred Erika to the other school in their district, did so. It was the same walking distance as the first one but in an entirely different neighborhood. The first school was attended mostly by middle class children; in this one most students came from working-class families.

Erika felt a bit out of place until she met her homeroom teacher, Mrs. Mandel, who asked the students to call her Aunt Emma*.

This was the first meeting of the class. Aunt Emma did a roll call, assigned their seats, and gave them the class schedule for the term. She was a slim woman of medium height; short, black hair framed her face, she had dark eyes, and full lips. Her most prominent facial feature was a small hook nose.

"Look at her Jewish nose," Erika heard a classmate whisper behind her just as they settled into their seats. Sitting in the front row, due to her excellent report card from the previous year, Erika winced at the comment. *Maybe being a Jew at this school will be just as difficult as it was at the previous one*, she thought. But at this point, all she could do was to make the best of the situation.

As it turned out, her apprehension was unwarranted. In the ensuing weeks, her classmates were friendly and curious about her. They seemed to like and accept Erika. Aunt Emma, who turned out to be her teacher for Hungarian literature, grammar, and the Russian language, seemed to subtly favor Erika. *Perhaps she knows I'm also Jewish*, Erika wondered.

◎◉◎

Two weeks after school started, during one of their homeroom sessions Aunt Emma explained that all students had to join the "Little Drummer Organization". This was the elementary school level of the Pioneer Organization. First created in the Soviet Union, it had now spread to all the Soviet satellite countries, including Hungary.

Children from age seven to ten were recruited as Little Drummers. At age ten, they joined the Pioneers, until age eighteen. After that, those who merited it, would be accepted into the Communist Youth Organization. The greatest honor was to be inducted into the Communist Party as a young adult.

Aunt Emma handed each child a sheet of paper that spelled out the rules of conduct for the Little Drummer, and then read each point aloud to them:

169

- The little drummer is a loyal child of the Hungarian homeland
- The little drummer loves and honors his/her parents, educators, comrades
- The little drummer studies and works with diligence, helps his/her comrades
- The little drummer tells the truth and acts correctly
- The little drummer exercises his/her body and guards his/her health
- The little drummer lives life so as to become worthy of the pioneer's red neck kerchief

Hearing the rules, some of the children snickered but stopped when Aunt Emma announced, "You must memorize these points by tomorrow. I will test you on it." She went on to say, "As you are seated in three columns of double benches, in ten rows, in a couple of weeks we will elect leaders for each column, and one leader for the whole class. By then you'll have had a chance to get to know each other."

That same day, Aunt Emma also distributed their 2nd year Russian language textbook and gave the first lesson. It consisted of reading aloud a simple story in the Cyrillic alphabet, while also learning the pronunciation of words and even the letters. Some of these were real tongue twisters, such as combining d, z, and s, into one sound. This created lots of laughter as the rowdier boys were spitting out the sounds as if sneezing. Erika observed that Aunt Emma had a difficult time controlling the merriment in the class, and she appeared relieved when the bell rang for the ten-minute break between classes.

◎◉◎

In the late afternoon, when both Erika and Judith were sitting in the winter dining room, doing their homework, Judith turned to Erika,

"What do you think of us having to learn Russian?"

Erika shrugged, "It's just another language".

"What I mind is that it's being forced on us," Judith objected.

"Don't you ever say that to anyone!" Piry shouted, overhearing Judith's comment while she was ironing next door, in the summer dining room.

"Why? What would happen if I did?" Judith asked.

"They could take me away from you as a bad parent, for not teaching you proper communist dogma. They could jail me and put both of you into a reform school. We are supposed to love this new government, and love everything they do. And don't you two ever forget this if you don't want to cause trouble for us all."

Piry sounded very serious; Judith and Erika looked at each other, grinning.

"We hear you!" Judith assured her. She turned to Erika, "We have the same Russian language book. Want to study the first lesson together?"

They sat at the table, reading the story aloud, and bursting into laughter at each word that was a tongue twister.

"This is a dumb language, and the school is dumb for forcing us to learn it," concluded Judith when they were done with the lesson.

"Just keep your opinion to yourself," Erika whispered to her sister, smiling. "I know."

◎◉◎

It was the strangest thing; Erika observed at school that all the children knew that they were not supposed to say some things to anyone, anywhere. Adults of course knew it too. They had guarded conversations with friends and even family members. Erika thought, *maybe the parents had warned their children, as Mom did us. This knowledge seems to have filtered into every adult's and child's consciousness, perhaps from the radio, and newspapers, and through government propaganda. Maybe it's the way teachers talk to us during classes, praising the Soviet Union, Comrade Stalin, and of course, Comrade Rákosi, the leader of the Hungarian People's Republic,* she concluded.

Erika liked the upbeat atmosphere at school. She liked hearing that everything in their lives was improving and getting better and better each day. At the same time, there was a quiet voice inside her that knew the truth but also knew that it was not to be discussed. Her parents worried every day about money, about food scarcities, about the rise of new regulations in their lives, and their future. Erika could sense the tension all around her.

One evening during a dinner they had at their house, she overheard her parents, Aunt Lilly and Uncle Donát talk about the "show trial" of László Rajk, Hungary's former Foreign Secretary. He had been arrested and charged with treason. Erika didn't understand the term "Show trial," but knew it was a bad word. She wasn't supposed to repeat it at school where her history teacher also talked about the Rajk trial as a good thing.

"It will cleanse our government of traitors," her teacher had said.

Erika also learned at school about the nationalization of big industries and the establishment of collective farms in the villages.

"Large industries, held by one owner or a group of capitalists will now belong to the people, under government leadership," their history teacher explained in Erika's class. "Farms are also being nationalized," he continued. "They are taken from their owners and pooled into one large farm to increase food production. The farmers will work together in the cooperatives and receive a portion of the produce for their own households as part of their pay. The rest of it will go to feed the nation or will be exported to the Soviet Union."

As her teacher explained this about the farmers, Erika had a hard time seeing its benefit. *In effect, it's the Soviet Union who will benefit from this,* she thought. Erika knew about this nationalization of the farms.

One evening, she had overheard Piry tell Feri, "I found out today that the Mikos' farm had been taken away from them and put into the collective. These poor peasants who had their own farms for centuries are now being told to work as a collective! And for their backbreaking work they will receive only some of their own produce. The government will take the rest and do what they want with it.

"On top of it, the Mikos were arrested and jailed as "kulaks". They could hardly be considered "kulaks," wealthy landowners, who 'exploited their poor neighbors by hiring them to work on their land. They were just farmers who had given a job to their more needy neighbors. I am heartbroken."

"You can't do anything about it, so just forget you even knew them," was Feri's response.

Erika knew the Mikos were the villagers who had helped her mother after the war by buying her hardware merchandise. She felt sorry for the Mikos, sorry for her mother's pain, but kept quiet.

She wasn't even supposed have heard their conversation. So, she pretended she had not, and next morning went to school to praise every move the government made for the improvement of their lives, including the formation of agricultural collectives and factory nationalizations.

◎◉◎

Aunt Emma announced in October, during one of their Hungarian literature classes, that they would be electing the leaders for their Little Drummer organization this day. She asked the students to vote for three leaders, one for each column of seats. They could only choose from their own column. They were told to write the person's name on a piece of paper, then fold it and throw it into one of the three corresponding boxes Aunt Emma had placed on her desk.

This was challenging, for none of them had voted for anything before, but the buzz in the room showed that they all found it exciting. Erika covered up her little piece of voting paper and scribbled on it the name of her desk partner, Kató. She was a small, friendly girl, with sandy brown pigtails down her back, large brown eyes, and a cute, turned-up nose. Her teeth were crooked, but her smile was sweet. She had offered to help Erika on her first day at school with anything she needed to know about her new surroundings, and Erika felt Kató would be a good leader.

After each student had walked up to the teacher's desk, making a dramatic display of throwing his or her vote into the correct box, a tense silence ensued in the classroom. Aunt Emma took the third box and walked over to face the third column by the window. She called on the student sitting in the last row, "Peter, come up here."

Peter, a lanky boy with tousled brown hair, wrinkled clothes, and dirty shoes, reluctantly ambled up to the teacher.

"Help me count the votes," Aunt Emma commanded, and Peter and she unfolded each piece of paper. Aunt Emma piled repeated names on top of each other on her desk.

"Here, count whose name was written the most," and added, speaking to the class, "This is how people get elected in a true democracy."

Peter counted the most votes for Boriska Kovács.

The class erupted into loud congratulatory shouts and applause as the girl, whose name had been called, stood up by her seat. She had been seated into the middle section of her column, so clearly, she was just an average student, but her classmates seemed to like her. She had dark blonde hair, and blue eyes. Her large front teeth needed her face to grow up around them. She stood smiling shyly and didn't know what to do next.

"Come up here," Aunt Emma ordered her. Then she repeated the same selection process with the other two columns, till all three newly elected leaders stood by her. The middle column had elected a boy, Imre Tóth, a popular student with flaming red hair, freckles, and dark green eyes. To Erika's joy, her seatmate, Kató became the third leader.

"Put your right hand on your heart," Aunt Emma instructed the new leaders, "and repeat after me, saying your own name where it's appropriate, "I (name) solemnly swear to uphold all six principles of the Little Drummer, and to serve my fellow Little Drummers, and my whole class, and my whole school, and my nation to the best of my ability."

A deep silence fell upon the class as they listened to the solemn commitment of their classmates who had now become their leaders. When the three children finished their oath, the rest of the class broke into enthusiastic applause.

"You may go back to your seats now." Aunt Emma instructed them, smiling.

Erika gave Kató a big grin as she slipped into the seat next to her. Feeling a great sense of solidarity with her classmates' enthusiasm, deep within Erika wondered what the leadership of the three would really entail. Her thoughts were interrupted by Aunt Emma's voice.

"And now, we shall nominate the leader for all three Little Drummer columns of this classroom. My suggestion is that we choose someone who is an outstanding student, who is friendly to all of you but has no special friends in the classroom so she will be fair to all and favor none. I nominate for the Class Leader Erika Fábián. All those in favor raise your hands."

Erika was shocked, her thoughts racing. *How could Aunt Emma nominate me when I barely know my classmates and I'm still so new to the school? Won't this set these kids against me for being placed as their leader?* But to her amazement, almost everyone's hand shot up into the air.

"How many against her?" asked Aunt Emma.

Erika sheepishly cast her eyes around the room and didn't see a single hand raised.

"It's all settled then," Aunt Emma declared with satisfaction. "Erika, c'mon up here."

Kata gave Erika's hand a quick squeeze as she scrambled out of her seat and went in front of the class.

Turning to Erika, Aunt Emma said, "When I gave the class the Little Drummer's rules, I had asked everyone to memorize it. Can you, as our new class leader, recite it for us?"

Erika looked at her teacher, and thought, *how does she know that I can?* Feeling good that indeed she could, she nodded. She stood up very straight, facing both her teacher and the class, and with all eyes on her, recited each point with as much dramatic flair as she could muster. The experience had moved Erika, and she swallowed hard when she had uttered the last words.

The class broke into spontaneous applause. Erika felt suffused with happiness. For the first time, she felt accepted and part of a group. Except that she soon discovered that she wasn't truly a part of the group. She was their leader. She learned that she was the one who had to schedule and attend their once-a-week column meetings; head the once-a-month class assembly; and gather reports from the column leaders on their activities to write a monthly report about their meetings. All this made her feel somewhat set apart from her classmates. Except for a couple of students who befriended her, she was their leader, not part of the crowd.

The school held monthly assemblies that all the students had to attend. They lasted an hour—or longer—if there was an observance of an important event. The assembly usually consisted of the principal of the school giving a pep talk about working hard and being citizens of value to their People's Democracy. Then the pioneer choir sang some patriotic songs, often joined in by the entire student body at the prompting of the vice principal, or the choir master. Toward the end of the assembly, selected students were called to the stage to give a speech or recite a poem.

As the school year progressed, Erika found herself often called upon to read a composition she had written in class about an important event, or to recite a patriotic poem by heart, always to thunderous applause when she was finished. She was never sure whether the clapping came because the students knew that they were supposed to praise the message, or it was personal for her performance. Whatever it was, it pleased her.

Her recitals made her known to the entire student body. Therefore, she felt obligated to always be on her best behavior at school. She didn't find it hard to do so but she felt like she was constantly acting because she was being observed and judged.

After a while, knowing how to comport herself in public became second nature to her. She just imagined herself as always being on stage. When she actually was performing on stage, she felt like she was just playing a different role, for everything in her life was just a role. She also learned that she had to watch what she said not just to her schoolmates.

One Saturday morning, she stopped by Feri's store after Hebrew school, to pick up Maczko and walk home with the dog. But first Feri sent her next door to the butcher shop to get the dog's breakfast. While waiting for the butcher to chop the raw meat into bite-size pieces, the man said, "I hear you're the class leader. That's really excellent".

"Yes, we all act like we're big communists, but I think we're all just pretending," Erika blurted out. Somehow, she felt she could trust this man because he was her father's friend.

The man stopped the cleaver in mid-air, and looked at her sharply, "Don't repeat that to anyone!" he warned her.

"Don't worry, I won't," Erika shrugged, then waited in silence as the butcher finished cubing the meat. He wrapped it in a newspaper, and handed it to Erika,

"Be a good girl now and watch what you say!" he cautioned her again as she left.

That night, during dinner, Feri brought up the subject.

"The butcher told me what you had said to him, and warned me to remind you, you mustn't say things like that to anyone, anywhere, any time. Don't ever say anything bad about whatever is happening in our country, or at your school, or whatever the government leaders are doing, or you'll get all of us into big trouble! Kapish?"

He used the Russian word he had learned during the war in forced labor camp, to emphasize that he wasn't joking. His guards there used this word to make sure their prisoners followed orders. It meant "You understand?" Erika nodded. "I understand."

It never ceased to amaze Erika how Feri could have so many faces. He could behave like a caring but strict father who provided for them and loved them. Yet, whenever he found the opportunity, which fortunately was not often, he would order Erika to come to his bed at night. It happened only when both Piry and Judith went out somewhere together.

Erika suffered through these occasions, obeying Feri's commands and tolerating his disgusting rubbing against her. She hated him for this but feared him enough never to be able to turn to Piry or anyone to talk about it. Instead, she avoided him as much as she could and put up with him when she couldn't. *Life is just one big lie, and the trick is to navigate through it safely day by day,* Erika thought.

CHAPTER 11

I**N LATE** S**PRING,** P**IRY** announced that they had a new family member. Aunt Lilly had given birth to a little boy, Nándor. They all went for a visit once mother and child were home from the hospital.

Lilly lay on the sofa-bed in their living room, the tiny baby, wrapped tightly in swaddling clothes, lay nestled in her arm. The proud father, Donát, sat at the other end of the L shaped sofa, beaming.

"Why is he wrapped up like a silkworm?" Erika asked and the adults burst out laughing.

"What do you know about silkworms?" teased Donát.

"I learned about them in school. They weave a cocoon around themselves with their own saliva and hibernate there till they become butterflies. Except when they're bred for silk, the farmers who raise them unravel all the silk thread that covers their cocoon, and all the poor larvae inside die. But people get to have silk fabrics. So why is Nandi wrapped up in that cocoon?"

"You were wrapped up too, and so was Judith, and so is every newborn," Piry responded. "The bones of an infant are still soft, and the wrapping ensures that their legs grow straight while they gain strength."

"How long do babies stay in the cocoon?"

"For about three months."

"Oh." Erika said, thinking, how uncomfortable that must be for the baby, not to be able to kick his legs around. She couldn't, of course, recall her own discomfort, so she stopped worrying about it.

"When he gets older, I'll come and play with him; and when I get older, I'll babysit for you," she offered to Lilly and Donát.

"That's very sweet of you, Erika. I will remember your promise when the time comes," Lilly smiled at her.

◎◉◎

Piry got a postcard from her friend Irén Goldberg, asking her to come for a visit. She hasn't seen Irén for several months. Thus, while her children were at school and Feri at the store, Piry went to Irén's apartment in the center of Budapest. Since liberation, as the post-war era was called, Irén lived alone in the two-bedroom apartment that she used to share with her mother. The living room and both bedrooms had large windows overlooking the street. The kitchen had a small dining room next to it. Irén and Piry had coffee and poppy-seed strudel there, while they chatted about Irén's secretarial work, Piry's children, and her married life.

After they finished their snack, Irén said, "Let's go for a walk, I need to air my head."

Piry wondered what was wrong with Irén. The late fall weather was quite chilly and the gathering dark rain clouds in the sky were hardly conducive for a stroll. But after they put on their warm coats and left the building, Piry quickly learned that Irén's headache was just a pretext for taking the walk. Irén had been heavily involved in politics and the governmental elections that took place from the end of the war to the latest one in 1949.

She was a leader in the Smallholders Party, which had been the majority party in the new post-war government. But her party, along with other smaller ones, was now being forced to dissolve. As they walked, she told Piry in a low voice, "I fear that I'm being watched by the State Protection Department, (ÁVO), and my apartment may have been bugged. I needed to tell you this but couldn't while we were there."

"You must be kidding," Piry was incredulous. "Why would they bother with you if your party is being dissolved anyway?"

"I don't know," Irén replied, then added, "but I do know that they are rounding up people of political opposition to the Worker's Party, and as a high functionary, I might be a target too. You must have been aware of the Rajk Lászlo trials!"

"Of course, I was. My first cousin, Laci, works for Péter Gábor at the ÁVO, and Rajk was the big boss when the ÁVO was formed. The whole Rajk trial was a sham but there is nothing we could have done about it. It was an internal power struggle among our 'beloved' leaders. However, you my dear friend, are more like a family member. Would you like me to go to Laci and ask for your protection?

"I wouldn't dream of it!" Irén exclaimed, vehemently. "My situation may be bad, but you mustn't make it worse by calling attention to me. You can't trust any of those people—and pardon me—that may include even your cousin!"

Piry shrugged, "I don't know about that, but you could be right. I won't say a word."

"Don't you realize that with this last election we have become a puppet nation of the Soviet Union?"

"What do you mean?"

"Let me explain."

Irén took Piry's arm and led her down the quietest street she could find, casting furtive glances around to make sure that they were not within anyone's hearing distance.

"This year, all parties, including mine, *The Independent Small Holders*, have been pressured to either merge with the Soviet backed Hungarian *Workers' Party* or dissolve as 'ineffective and out of step' with the current political goals of the country. The *Social Democratic Party*, the only significant competitor of the Workers' Party, came under heavy pressure to join forces with them. They finally did, thus forming a majority voting power. In the most recent elections, this fortified Workers' Party was able to grab key government positions for their communist party candidates, thus essentially taking over the government."

"I am confused," Piry interrupted. "You are talking about the Workers' Party as the strongest, and then you say it's the communist party candidates who have taken over the government."

Irén smiled. "They're one and the same. The name Workers' Party is actually a cover name for the communists. At this point, in this country, nothing is being called by its true name. You might have heard that the new government came up with a new constitution but of course they didn't advertise that it is a copy of the Soviet Union's constitution. Just wait and see how this new system will affect all our lives."

Piry protested, "Of course, I am aware of the change in government and that the country has been renamed "The Hungarian People's Republic." I just don't know what all these political maneuverings have to do with insignificant people like us. Maybe you have a rightful concern because you've been politically active. But the rest of us?"

Irén laughed bitterly, "This is why I wanted to see you. To warn you. You must be aware that they've been steadily nationalizing the mines, electric plants, heavy industry, factories, and banks. Now, with this new government, they'll probably take over everything else, large or small. They have no private property in the Soviet Union—I'll bet you we'll become just like them in the next few years."

"C'mon, just because they closed down all the other political parties, and took over big industries, it doesn't mean they'll interfere with the lives of individual citizens.

Irén shook her head. "Mark my words, if I were you, I'd warn my sister's husband, because he and his brothers are mid-size industrialists. Down the line, I would even worry about Feri's business. And be very careful with what you say and to whom. Warn your daughters and Feri as well. Nobody is safe anymore."

Piry parted from Irén with a heavy heart as she watched her friend stealthily look around before slipping into her apartment building. She didn't know whether to believe Irén or dismiss her warnings as based on her own failed political life.

But she was to find Irén's words prophetic.

◉◉◉

During the winter of 1950, the government nationalized all three factories owned by Donát and his brothers. Piry and her family had come to visit Lilly and Donát a couple of weeks after it had happened.

"It was shockingly simple," Donát described. "Two men came into my office on that Friday, wearing dark suits red neck ties, and presenting their identification card from the Department of Industry. They stood in front of my desk, refused to sit down. One of them said, "You can leave this office taking nothing with you. Or you and your brothers can choose to donate your factories and continue as employees of the State. The three of you will remain the Directors of each factory but you will work for the State and receive a salary from the Government, like everyone else."

"There really was no choice," smiled Donát, shrugging his shoulders. "Now we work in our factories as hard as before but with all the profits going to the State. And we're grateful to have been able to keep our jobs. On top of it, they had warned me that my wife also must work, because every able-bodied person in the country has to have a job and get paid for it. The new slogan to live-by is: "You don't work, you don't eat." So, because our son, Nandi is still small, we were allowed to start a 'home based packaging service'. Want to see it?"

Lilly led Piry and her family into the former maid's room, where boxes and sheets of brown paper were piled high on several tables and even on the bed which now had a board covering it.

"I have to wrap these small instruments and deliver at least a hundred boxes a day or they will take away this job and put me to work in a factory," Lilly explained.

"What about taking care of your son?" Piry asked, aghast.

"They offered to put Nandy into a state-run nursery from 8 a.m. to 6 p.m. so I could work. Over my dead body! I hired a woman to come in during my work hours. She is happy to have a job at a home instead of a factory. I put her to work on the boxes so I could take care of Nandy."

Piry shook her head in disbelief, then added, "I wonder when they'll swoop down on Feri's business."

"Don't worry, it'll come," Donát predicted with a wry smile.

Feri was nobody's fool. Witnessing the nationalization of large and small industries got him concerned about his own business. He felt he should protect himself despite reassurances by the government that it will keep small businesses of less than a hundred employees private because they supplemented the government-run businesses.

Several nights a week, he would lock up his business as usual and go home. But after he had walked Maczko to the store, he would stay there till late, watching his street, Árpád Út, empty of people. While waiting, he wrapped brown paper over a couple of valuable bolts of fabric and then carried them home under his arms. He figured, even if someone stopped him and asked where he was taking those bolts, he could say, his wife and daughters wanted them for new outfits.

One spring night, Erika was out in the garden with Maczko, when she saw Feri and her mother carrying bolts of fabric through the basement door.

"Upstairs," she heard Feri say.

He was suggesting the attic. It had a slanted roof, and only the tall central part was being used for hanging the laundry there to dry. Now, Erika realized, it would also be a hiding place for some of Feri's merchandise.

When her parents came into the house, Piry went over to Erika who was sitting in the winter dining room, reading.

"You didn't see anything and know nothing," Piry whispered, her voice cutting the air like a steel knife.

"Of course not! What is it I'm not supposed to have seen or know?" Erika smiled at her mother, shrugging her shoulders.

Piry hugged her.

◎◉◎

This strange duality pervaded all aspects of their lives. Trials for high government officials accused of treason were regularly reported in the most important daily newspaper, the Szabad Nép, (Free People) and discussed even at the elementary school in Erika's classroom. It was hard to understand why these men, who were educated in the Soviet Union, and brought communism to Hungary after the war, were suddenly declared traitors and "Dogs of the USA, spying for the West."

The West meant all the countries that did not belong to the Soviet bloc. Countries under the Soviet Union's socialist system were labeled Eastern European. But Marshall Tito, who was the leader of Yugoslavia, and part of the Soviet Bloc, was their dear comrade-in-arms until one day he declared his independence from the Soviet Union. Then he was declared "The lackey of the West, and the Enemy of all the People's Republics" even though his political system was still socialist.

Despite these political storms, daily life went on; classes were taught, Judith and Erika regularly attended Hebrew School, and on holidays went to temple with their parents.

Prior to some of the holidays, the Hebrew School teachers put on plays for the congregation about the story of that particular event, casting their students. Erika auditioned for each play and found that by putting a great deal of energy into the role she wanted, she would get it. She usually aimed for the lead female role, or an important character in the play.

The other students, and even the teachers, recognized Erika's intense desire to get the best role, and few would stand up to her competitive spirit.

During spring, she got the lead role in a play that was being prepared for Purim. The holiday commemorated the saving of the Jews from imminent destruction in the Persian Empire. The Persian King, Achaswerus, had a prime minister, Haman, who had sought the annihilation of all Jews in Persia. Esther, Achaswerus's Jewish wife, cleverly brought to her husband's attention Haman's edict, thus preventing the minister from carrying out his evil plan.

Erika loved the role, loved wearing the elaborate costume and the little crown that defined her as the queen. Her dress was made of pink taffeta, the crown was papier-mâché covered in gold foil, but to her it was as real as her occasional fantasy of her real father being a king and coming to take her away. Being queen for a night on stage, and receiving applause and praise afterwards from her peers, was a great way to feel far-removed from her life at home.

It wasn't just the occasional sexual demands by Feri that made her miserable. Her sister Judith's moods were like a weathervane, and she was taking out on Erika her own unhappiness. When Judith was in a bad mood; she would make nasty comments about whatever Erika was doing or wearing. When in a good mood, she would insist that they play a game after both were done with their homework.

Erika had to comply but would usually end up playing it wrong, according to Judith, who then would hit her or slap her. At times, Judith would hide the book Erika was reading and only return it after Erika's extensive begging and promising to do something for Judith, such as her Russian homework. Erika felt defenseless in the presence of her sister. At times, when Judith was really mean to her, she would complain to their mother, who in turn would punish Judith. But later Judith would retaliate.

Once, after Erika spent hours on a drawing for the next day's class, Judith grabbed it and tore it in half because Erika didn't answer fast enough her question about a character in a Soviet book they had both been assigned to read as homework. Drawn to the room by Erika's screaming, Piry had witnessed Judith throwing the torn page at Erika and demanded an explanation.

"Aren't you ashamed of yourself? How can you do this to your little sister?" Piry shouted at Judith, who now sat at her desk in defiant silence. Her apology was, of course, useless since Erika had to redo her homework, which took the better part of the evening. So, Erika tried to stay out of the way from both her stepfather and her sister.

This brought her closer to the company of her mother, and their maid, Maria. She helped Maria with cleaning, and when her mother was at home, Erika stood by her side while Piry was either cooking or ironing. Invariably, Erika would be asked to help with what the women were doing but she didn't mind. She was learning from Piry to iron and to prepare food, and in exchange, Piry would tell her stories about her own childhood. Maria usually talked nonsense about the King of England, but Erika liked that better than Judith's sarcastic comments about whatever Erika said or did.

Erika made two friends at school. Ibolya lived two blocks from Erika's house, close to the Chinoin drug factory. Both her parents were employed there. Ibolya was having trouble with her grades in literature and math. Rózsi, the other girl, lived on the way to Erika's house. She needed help her with Russian and geography. Their home-room teacher, Aunt Emma suggested that Erika spend a couple of hours a week, after school, helping each girl to improve. Thus, Erika would stop at Rózsi's home once a week and go to Ibolya's house once a week in the late afternoon. After her teaching each girl, they would chat or play a board game. As the two girls' grades improved, they became not just Erika's friends but almost like her disciples. Judith frequently teased Erika about this.

"You don't have friends, you have followers, like little dogs," she would say. "Now my friends and I are my equals, and we do fun things together, not just schoolwork!"

"I like my friendships," Erika shrugged, not wanting to get into an argument with Judith. She certainly was not going to point out to Judith that none of her friends were nice or even pretty. Judith had once told her that she chose friends who were less attractive and worse students than she because she didn't want to compete with her friends.

"You're dumb, because your friends are just as attractive if not more so than you, and with your help they are getting better grades, too. Maybe one day they'll pass you, and then you'll have to sit in second or third row at school, especially because they're working class and you're a middle-class Jew."

Erika had a hard time understanding her sister's self-centered attitude but found it easier to just shrug her shoulders without answering Judith. She liked to have attractive friends and was happy to help them become better students. In turn, they gave her appreciation and friendship.

◎◉◎

When Spring arrived, there were several holidays that were solemnly observed by the entire nation. March 15th was the anniversary of the 1848 uprising by Hungarian patriots against the Habsburg domination of their country. One of the leading poets of the era, Petőfi Sándor, wrote a poem that became the rallying cry of the revolution in 1848.

Under the new socialist government, every year on March 15th this poem was recited at all institutions, all schools, and at all public celebrations. Erika's school observed the holiday by gathering the student body into the gymnasium that had been decorated with the red, white, and green national flag, and with ribbons of the same colors all around the walls. Speeches were delivered by teachers and students, with a senior student selected to recite this poem during their assembly.

April 4th was Liberation Day that commemorated the official end of World War II in Hungary. It was the day when the German Army finally surrendered to the Soviet forces. Erika's school was among those selected to partake in the celebratory march on this day. Erika had not forgotten how right after the war she had gone around asking for bread and sugar from the Soviet soldiers. She was happy to partake in the march.

All students were to wear their official pioneer or little drummer uniform. It consisted of a dark blue pleated skirt whose length was just above the knees, or slacks for the boys, and a white, long sleeve cotton shirt with a button-down collar. Tucked under the collar was the prized triangular red scarf of their movement, knotted into a two-pronged tie, decorating the front of the shirt.

"You look adorable," Piry kissed Erika on the forehead after she helped to properly tie the knot of her red scarf. She held out a blue sweater for Erika to put on.

"I can't take that, we're supposed to all look alike," Erika explained. "We'll be marching, so I won't be cold."

Students were all gathering at their schools and were transported in trucks to the center of the city, to the Hösök Tere, the Heroes' Plaza. Erika, who had never been in this part of Budapest, found the area beautiful. Majestic buildings surrounded the large open square that had a lake and a castle at one end. At the other end a semicircular colonnade displayed magnificent equestrian statues of the leaders of the nine Hungarian tribes, and the head of all the leaders of the tribes, Árpád, who had led his people in the 10th century to the territory of current Hungary. The horses and men were all so vibrantly sculpted that to Erika they seemed alive.

She was thrilled to feel the excitement of all the marching groups coming into the plaza along with her own schoolmates, in three column formations. All the marchers wore uniforms; soldiers in various hues of green, workers in blue overalls, and the many school children in pioneer outfits.

Section leaders, like Erika, were handed small Hungarian flags with the new emblem at its center. The old Hungarian emblem contained on the right half the three major hills that belonged to Hungary prior to World War I, with Hungary's first king, St. Steven's crown on top of the hills, and red, white and green stripes on the left side, chosen by the king as Hungary's flag colors.

The new flag had the three colors, but the original design had been replaced in 1949 with a Soviet emblem: a circle made of two wreaths of golden wheat stalks had a five-pointed red star at the top. A hammer and a wheat stalk in a blue field was in the center; all supported by a Hungarian tricolor ribbon as the base.

"As you march, keep in step with the music and with everyone in your group," warned the tense teachers as they ran alongside their students who now stood in formation, ready for the events to begin.

It was a beautiful spring day, with a soft wind fluttering the flags that shone brightly in the mid-morning sun. Erika felt her blood quicken as a band way up front struck up marching music to the beat of large kettle drums. It felt to Erika like hundreds of hearts all beating together. Waving their flags, the groups began to move to the tempo of the drums. Way up in front, a marching choir's voices drifted back to Erika and her schoolmates as they were briskly keeping step with the procession.

Erika felt the emotional power of the columns of marchers. There was a certain euphoria in the air, as though together they were exuding strength and joy. It was an amazing feeling. Yet, deep inside, Erika was keenly aware that a part of her was merely observing it all with an objective eye; recording the colors and feelings as though she were not actually there but outside of it. It was a somewhat similar feeling to her being on stage, where on one hand she was a different person in another world, on the other, her inner self knew she was acting and needed to remember the lines and actions of her character. Here, she was the pioneer leader of her schoolmates, marching in celebration of their country's liberation day. At the same time, she felt like all this was just a play, in which they were pretending to be one big happy nation.

◎◉◎

In addition to Liberation Day celebrations, April also brought the complex and work intensive Jewish holiday, Passover. A week before the start date, Piry and Maria turned the house upside down and inside out, cleaning even the remotest corners of their home that may contain something made with flour. Erika and Judith were also enlisted to help remove every crumb.

"Bring all cookies you might have stored anywhere in your room," Piry ordered them.

Food was too expensive to throw away but according to the laws of kashrut, the special dietary laws of observant Jews, during the week of Passover they had to get rid of anything containing wheat or even rye flour.

Aunt Magda, next door, did not keep kosher, so she was happy to be the recipient of all these items. Both girls remembered Piry creating this same upheaval the year before, but then they were too young to help. This time, after school, they had to assist with packing and boxing up all the dishes, utensils, pots and pans, and carrying them out to the storage shed till after Passover. Piry had an entirely different set of kitchen utensils, dishes, and cutlery for both dairy and meats to use only during Passover.

Personally, Erika thought it absurd that just because during the Exodus Jews didn't have access to leavened bread, now they couldn't eat it either. But there was no arguing about this with Piry or the Hebrew teacher. "The law is the law," they said.

So, Judith and Erika obediently followed their mother's instructions without expressing their opinion—which for once they shared. They also watched their mother gradually bring boxes with eggs into the pantry. Eggs were expensive and hard to come by these days. One could obtain only six at a time. Somehow, Piry managed to buy them all over the city, so by the time she was ready to make their first Passover night's meal, she had nearly a hundred eggs in a large oval basket.

They were to be used throughout the upcoming week for making matzo balls, breakfasts with scrambled eggs, hardboiled for snacks between meals, or made into deviled eggs, always eaten with matzo instead of bread. It was during this time of feverish preparations that looking at the basket of eggs with Erika at her side, Piry asked her with a nostalgic smile,

"Do you remember when you broke nearly half the eggs one Passover?"

"Not really. Only the story that you had told me."

Piry sighed, "It was easy to get more eggs then, and we didn't have to worry about money either."

"Then why did my father spank me for breaking them?"

"To teach you not to do it again."

"Oh! When I grow up and have children, I'm not going to spank them. I'll explain to them what they did and why they mustn't do it again."

"Not at age two!"

"I probably would have understood it at that age."

"You barely understand now when I tell you not to do something," Piry teased her.

Erika shrugged. It wasn't a matter of not understanding her mother. Sometimes she just wanted to do what she wanted to do. Then her mother would get angry and her way of expressing it was by a quick slap on Erika's face or butt. It was just the way it was between parents and children. There was no point in discussing it, only finding a way to avoid it by doing one's best to either obey or not get caught. Judith never got hit, only scolded or punished by being sent to her room. Erika had the impression that her mother was always trying to avoid conflict with Judith. They seemed to have an uneasy peace between them instead of the closeness Erika felt with her mother. But then again, Judith was unpredictable to be with, even for Piry, and certainly her relationship with their stepfather was just a truce.

A while ago, Judith talked back to him, and he slapped her. Since then, Judith stopped talking to him altogether. If Feri asked her something, she would reply in curt phrases but other than saying hello when she needed to, she never spoke to him. Piry pretended that they were a happy family and ignored Judith's behavior.

Erika followed her mother's example because it was smart to do so. But she was keenly aware of the tension in the room as soon as Feri arrived home in the evenings. Judith simply clamped up. Erika and her mother acted toward Feri with charm and warmth even if it was fake and in reality, they were afraid of him.

◎◉◎

Since Lilly always celebrated Passover evenings with her husband's family, Piry invited Feri's brothers and their family for the first two nights and the last night, a week later. It was traditional to observe the holiday first by telling of the story of the Exodus followed by an elaborate dinner. Piry and Maria spent days preparing the big Passover meals since there was to be no cooking during the first two days once the holiday started the evening before.

To start with, they prepared the traditional Passover plate items: the grated bitter radish, as a reminder of the bitterness of slavery. There were leaves of parsley, and hard-boiled eggs, again as a reminder of the foods they ate in Exodus. Then Erika's favorite, a mixture of apples and celery marinated in sweet wine, representing the mortar used by the Jews in Egypt to build the pyramids. Erika could never figure out why the so-called mortar was sweet, but she loved eating the mixture. There was also a silver tray with three pieces of matzoh, each wrapped in a hand-embroidered white doily. The matzoh played an important part in involving the children in the evening's ceremony.

All this was placed on the dining room table that was covered with a gleaming white tablecloth with lace edging. Although time consuming and labor intensive, these small items were an essential part of the telling of the Passover story. Jews all over the world spend the evening the same way we are, Erika always thought as she sat through the event.

It was the first part of the evening that Erika and Judith abhorred. The whole family had to sit quietly while Feri, at the head of the table, recited the story of Passover. The trouble was, he was reading it in a singsong voice in Hebrew, and nobody around the table understood a word because none of them spoke Hebrew. Not even Feri. But this was the way his father had conducted the Seder ceremony, and this was the way he was going to do it whether anyone liked it or not.

Around the table sat Feri's oldest brother, Vince, who had come with the youngest brother Lajos and his wife Ica. She had converted from Catholicism to Judaism when she married Lajos. Their two-year-old baby girl Anni had been given supper earlier and was now fast asleep in a rocking crib they had brought with them. Lajos, like his two older brothers, was a horse-drawn truck driver, so it was easy for him to bring his family and the baby's bed in his vehicle.

He had parked the truck just inside the gate, with the horse facing into the yard. Lajos had placed a feed bag under the horse's chin, the bag's long handles hooked over its ears, so it could eat at leisure during the evening. At first, Maczko barked and rattled his chain. But when he saw that the horse wasn't coming to trample him, he settled down, keeping a watchful eye on the calm, four-legged giant.

The other guests were Imre and his wife Magda from next door. They smiled at Erika and Judith noticing that the two young girls were discreetly sighing and rolling their eyes during what seemed like an interminable reading of the Passover story. It didn't help Erika's interest that as the youngest at the table, she got to ask the four questions about why Passover was being celebrated and thus initiated the telling of the story of the exodus. Erika knew the story since it was taught in Hebrew school. In fact, she loved to hear of the Jews being liberated from slavery and successfully escaping from Egypt.

But Feri's recital of it is incomprehensible and boring. Enough to want to stop any religious observance, Erika thought.

By the time the 'storytelling' was over, and dinner served, both Judith and Erika were sleepy. But this was one of the few family occasions when they had to stay up till the evening was over. Piry beamed as everyone commented on her excellent cooking, feeling like this had made her hard work all worthwhile. Even Feri gave her grunts of acknowledgement as he dug into each dish.

The first course was chicken soup, with a huge matzo ball floating in the middle of everyone's plate. Next came a roast goose, accompanied by sweet-and-sour red cabbage and sliced potatoes sautéed with caramelized onions. For dessert, a layered chocolate cake made of matzo meal, plus apples and sweet liquors were served.

The interesting part of the evening for Erika came after dinner, when she had to look for the afikomen, a piece of matzo that her stepfather had hid at the start of the prayers. They could not finish the Passover dinner without it turning up for the final prayer and the last glass of wine. Traditionally, all the children would look for this hidden piece of matzo, and the one who found it could ask for a present in exchange for returning it.

But Judith at age eleven, deemed it beneath her to look for it, so it was only Erika who clambered under the table, lifted corners of the tablecloth and finally, with a victory cry, found it under the baby's blanket.

"I'd like money for two movie tickets," she announced, holding the napkin-wrapped matzo in her hand.

"Why two?" Feri teased her.

"So, Judith and I can go together," Erika replied saucily, smiling at her sister.

"Judith could work for her own ticket," Feri taunted her. "She could wash the dinner dishes."

"We have to do that anyway. So, it's two tickets or no afikomen and nobody gets to go home," Erika countered.

"Oh, all right, we'll all chip in," Imre cut in good naturedly. Feri laughed, and said, "No, it's all right, you can have two tickets," and Erika handed over her precious bargaining chip.

It was nearly midnight by the time they all got to bed.

"Thanks for getting me a ticket too," Judith whispered to Erika as she headed for her room. "We'll pick a movie together," she added magnanimously.

Erika felt good. For once, Judith had acknowledged something she had done for her.

◎◉◎

When the spring sun slowly melted the snow on the streets, Maria started to open the double windowpanes while cleaning the house. As a result, at least once a week some young man, wearing a dark suit with a red tie, would stop by. He would peer through the window into the rooms and knock on the window's glass to catch someone's attention inside the house.

While her children were at school, Piry usually went out, either to shop for household needs or on errands she never talked about. She didn't want Feri to know about the financial exchanges she was conducting as it had been set up with her aunt Vica, who was now safely living in Canada. Left alone in the house, Maria wouldn't dream of letting any of these young men come in. When she heard their knock, she would stick her face out and ask, "Hello, what do you want?"

"Can I come in to talk to you?"

"What about?"

"Our country and Comrade Rákosi"

This always triggered an angry reaction in Maria. She would shout, "Don't even think of it! I saw the King of England last weekend, and he told me not to allow any strangers into the house! You want to get me into trouble? Get away from here!"

Hearing this, each young agitator, as they were commonly called, would recoil, for clearly the woman at the window was out of her mind. She looked it, too, her face turning red, her blue eyes bulging in their sockets. They would leave, muttering,

"Sorry to bother you, Comrade."

However, on one occasion, Piry was at home and felt that she had better invite the young agitator in, or he could take it as a 'hostile attitude.' If he reported something like that to his superiors, she could be in real trouble. She could be hauled in for interrogation about her political beliefs, or worse, they could simply arrest her. So, she smiled, and led him into the living room, apologizing for the disorderly state of the room and herself, explaining, "I'm in the middle of Spring cleaning."

Indeed, she had a navy kerchief with white polka dots covering her auburn hair, tied neatly at the nape of her neck, and wore an old, beige shirt over a spotted brown skirt. Her feet were in worn out slippers. It was obvious that she was indeed in the middle of major housework. In fact, she was glad that the man had found her dressed so poorly. Considering the luxurious décor of the house, it was best to have it in disarray along with her looks. As she led him into the living room, she called to Maria and asked her to bring them coffee and pastry.

"Have a seat, please," she gestured, pulling one of the small armchairs toward him.

He sat down, looking a bit ill at ease.

Piry smiled at him, and pulled her chair up to face him, "So, what can I do for you Comrade?"

"We are canvassing the neighborhood to find out what people think about our leaders and our new lives."

"Why, all is just fine," Piry replied cheerfully, hoping she sounded sincere, while her stomach twisted into a knot. She had a drawer full of contraband nylon stockings from Vienna. If for whatever reason, the young man asked her to open the dresser drawer so he could take a look, for sure she would end up in jail without parole.

Maria tottered in, looking equally ragged, bringing two small cups of espresso, small sugar cubes, and pieces of Piry's freshly baked poppy-seed strudel. Piry jumped up to take the tray from her.

Maria glared at the young man, and said, "You are wasting our time, soon the children will be back from school, and we won't be finished with the cleaning. Last week Comrade Rákosi rode on the same streetcar with me, and we had a nice chat. There is nothing new you can tell us."

Piry saw the shock of surprise on the young agitator's face, and then his difficulty in suppressing a grin.

"Maria is my relative," Piry quickly explained to him, sounding as if she were sharing confidential information. "She lives with us. Please, help yourself to the strudel."

"It's very kind of you," he muttered, without reaching for the food. It was obvious that Maria standing there and staring at him made the young man nervous.

"Eat up and then please leave, so we can get on with our work," Maria barked at him and briskly marched out of the room.

Piry smiled apologetically. "She is not quite right in the head. She was affected by the bombing during the war, so often she talks nonsense. But she is harmless, and we love her."

Piry placed a piece of strudel on a plate and handed it to the young man. She pushed the espresso cup in front of him and asked, "How many lumps?"

Embarrassed, the young man took the plate from her. "Two please".

He seemed to be at a loss for words then, as he ate and sipped the coffee, said, "This is very kind of you. It's not often that I get a treat while trying to discuss politics."

"Oh, it's fine with me," Piry shrugged. "We love our government, love our country. My first husband died in the war for his country." She paused and delicately dabbed her eyes with her napkin. Silence ensued between them for a moment. Then Piry added, "My current husband served on the Eastern Front, and I have a cousin who works with Péter Gábor."

The young agitator nearly dropped his cup on hearing the name of the dreaded head of the Secret Police. As fast as it was politely possible, he finished his food.

"Clearly, you are one of us," he managed to say in a deferential tone. "I won't keep you any longer. You don't need to be re-educated."

He rose, and Piry walked him out of the house, along the garden, and down the long passage to the front gate. Keeping a comfortable pace, yet with her stomach still in knots, she could barely suppress her relief at his departure.

He stopped at the gate, and saluted Piry with the word that has become the accepted greeting upon meetings or departures, "Liberty".

"Liberty," Piry echoed and locked the gate after him.

Her knees nearly buckled under as she rushed back into the house.

◎◉◎

One day, Rózsi asked if she could come to study at Erika's house because she had forgotten her keys at home, and her parents would not be back till after their workday at the factory. So, she couldn't get into their apartment till then.

"Of course," Erika said, and walked home with her.

Maria served them lunch, and after that they set to study. Piry came home, and Judith as well, and Rózsi was still there. So, she got invited to have dinner with the family as it was time for their evening meal.

Finally, around eight o'clock, just as Feri was arriving home, Rózsi said, "I think my parents will be home by now. Thank you for the hospitality, I'll go now."

"Don't mention it," Piry patted her on the shoulder. "You're welcome here, any time. Did Erika really help you?"

"Yes, very much," Rózsi smiled.

◎◉◎

A few months later, Erika was lining up her classmates for an assembly in the gym. The three sections of the class had formed three columns. Before leaving the classroom, Erika had to make sure that all their red pioneer kerchiefs were neatly tied around their necks. When she got to Rózsi, she saw that hers was askew.

"Straighten your tie, please," Erika asked her.

"What's the difference," Rózsi snapped. "I'm in the middle row, who's going to notice if my tie is crooked?"

"I just noticed. We're Little Drummers and it's our duty to look as neat as we can," Erika responded, somewhat sharply.

"You live in a big house and have a maid, so just shut up. You don't' have the right to tell me what to do," Rózsi said acridly.

Erika looked at her without revealing the shock the comment had caused her. She recognized the jealousy and anger that lay behind it. She also knew the danger she could bring on herself and her family if she didn't handle this right. All Rózsi would have to do is tell her father to report them for "living in luxury," and they would be promptly deported. She knew how easily that could happen.

A few weeks before, around four o'clock in the morning, Erika awoke to see her mother kneeling in their bed at the window, peeking through the slits in the shutter.

"What are you doing?" Erika whispered.

"Shshsh…" Piry responded.

Erika clambered from her end of the bed next to Piry and looked through the slats.

She saw a black, windowless van standing in front of the beautiful home diagonally across the street from them. Three uniformed ÁVO men stood by the van, watching the family residing there come out of their house. They were flanked by two other ÁVO men. Erika did not know the family but had seen them come and go. A nice-looking couple and their two sons, who seemed grown-up to Erika. They were probably around eighteen and twenty years old.

Piry and Erika could not hear what the ÁVO men were saying but could see the family being instructed to get into the van. They carried small bags but no other luggage. Two of the ÁVO men got in the front seats, one of them was the driver. After the family clambered up into the back of the van, the three other ÁVO men got in with them. The doors were shut and silently the van rolled away.

"Mom, where are they taking them at this hour?" Erika whispered as they sank back onto their bed.

"I have no idea," Piry shrugged. "Maybe they're just going on vacation. Maybe he is an ÁVO man. Don't talk to anyone about what you've seen! Do you hear?"

"Not even to Judith?"

"Nobody."

"You're going to tell Apu?"

"I may mention it to him, though probably he had seen it too, unless he slept through it. But we're never going to talk about this, to anyone. If Judith was awake, fine. If not, don't mention it to her. You understand?"

"Yes."

For about a week the house across the street stood empty. Then, early one evening, Erika saw a couple coming out of the house; obviously they were living there. They must have moved in very quietly.

They walked briskly, like a young couple. Erika could not see their faces but saw that the woman was wearing a long, dark fur coat, and under her Soviet-style matching fur hat her curly blonde hair tumbled to her shoulders. The man wore an ÁVO uniform, the cap keeping his face in shadow.

The memory of that family's deportation flashed through Erika's mind now, and she knew she had to smooth over the situation with Rózsi. "It's your choice," she said in a softer tone. "We should all look our best because we're Little Drummers; that's all I meant." Though she felt weak in her knees, she walked with determination to the head of the three columns, and faced them: "Are we ready to go?" She could feel the release of tension as her classmates shouted,

"Ready!"

Erika turned face front to lead her group down to the gymnasium. She knew she had handled the situation right and felt an enormous sense of relief. *I can never invite any of my 'proli' classmates to my home, ever again*, she thought, as she led her Little Drummers to the assembly, with a bright smile on her face.

One Friday night, Feri got home earlier than usual. He burst into the house, briskly threw his jacket on the coat hanger in the entry room and went into the dining room. He sat down heavily in his chair without uttering even a "good evening".

Piry bustled about him, concerned, "Are you okay? How come you didn't go to temple after the store? Should I bring you dinner now? It'll take just a few minutes to warm it up."

"It's over," he uttered.

Piry froze. "What's over?"

"I handed the store keys to the government men. They gave me a certificate that I had 'gifted my store to the People's Republic of Hungary'. Merchandise and all. That's what I've worked for all these years—so I could make it a gift to the government!"

Piry and the girls stared at him, astonished. His tone was bitter, his face distorted with pain. This was an aspect of him none of them had ever seen. He was hurting and said so. He appeared to be a broken man.

"Don't take it to heart so," Piry went to him, and putting her hands on his shoulders, gently kissed his cheeks. "We knew this was coming. At least you look good because you gave it to them, instead of having them nationalize the business, like they did with Donat and his brothers' factories. Are they going to keep you there to run it?"

"No. They also took over the butcher shop next door. They'll probably give both these businesses to be run by their own buddies."

"So poor Maczko will never go to your store again or get food from the butcher!" Erika interjected.

Feri looked at her and couldn't help giving her a wry smile. "That's right. He'll stay home from now on, and you'll have to feed him leftovers. Or if you haven't got enough of that, you'll have to buy extra meat for him. At least you don't have to feed him kosher meat," he added with a broader grin.

"That's the least of our problems, now" Piry shrugged, annoyed at Erika's interruption, and turned back to Feri, "So what will you do now?"

"I am to report Monday morning to a furniture factory."

A stunned silence fell on them, finally Piry blurted out, "What do you know about furniture making?"

Feri shrugged. "I'll learn."

"Apu, I'm so sorry," Erika went over to him, and put her arms around his neck, hugging him. It was quite natural for Erika to do this. In their daily life Feri had always acted as a father, and Erika as his loving daughter. There was never even a hint of inappropriate behavior by Feri except on the occasional night when Piry would go out with Judith and the maid was asleep. Erika hated to be called to his bed and did her best to avoid it. But when it did happen, after she was able to leave him, feeling a deep sense of disgust, he simply went to sleep. He never referred to their secret, not even when they were alone. Erika considered his duplicitous behavior no different from their everyday public lives.

Everyone is a liar; we live not in a socialist paradise as the government tells us, but in a liar's paradise, Erika concluded.

Feri patted her on the back. "It's okay. Life is full of changes. Now let's stop mourning and have dinner!"

"Right away," Piry scurried out of the room, ordering briskly, "Girls, get your books off the table and come help me bring in the food."

◎◉◎

Within a month, Feri learned the ins and outs of the furniture factory. He worked long hours; left around 7 a.m. and often didn't get home till 7 at night. In three months, he was promoted to a supervisory position because the party members who ran the factory recognized an intelligent, hard-working man when they saw one. This meant a small raise in Feri's salary.

Of course, as Piry blurted out one day to Erika, it wasn't nearly enough to pay for all the expenses of their household. Piry covered the costs by spending more of her time drumming up business, selling nylon stockings and transferring money for people through the arrangements with her Aunt Vica. At times, she enlisted Erika's help in her transactions.

"Go visit Aunt Irén after school today," she would tell Erika. "And on the way, stop at this address," and she would hand Erika a street address and an apartment number, near Irén's home. "Memorize this address and throw away the paper. You'll be carrying a small package, which you'll have to hide under your books in your school sachet.

If anyone stops you when you enter that building and asks who you're looking for, just tell them one of your classmates lives there. If they follow you to the apartment, ring the bell, and when someone comes to the door, ask for your classmate. Obviously, they're going to say you've got the wrong address, so you apologize and leave. Then come home immediately.

If no one follows you, when the person answers the door, ask if Dorotea is home. If they say yes, you can go in. If they say no, say 'thank you, Piry sends her regards,' and leave.

If they invite you in, tell them, you are bringing a gift for Dorotea, and just give it to them. Then leave and come home directly."

"Don't they have to give me money for what I give them?" Erika asked.

"No, it's all taken care of in advance."

"Oh. And don't I get to visit Aunt Irén?"

Piry looked at her daughter, thinking it over. "If all goes smoothly, and you're done early enough, you can. If not, come straight home."

◎◉◎

Erika loved to visit Aunt Irén. Her apartment had been subdivided, separated by a thin makeshift wall, and was now occupied by a couple and their two children. Irén was confined to the maid's room, which luckily had a private bathroom. So now she lived as if she had only a one room flat, but she told Erika that she didn't mind. She put a small Bunsen burner on top of a filing cabinet in her room, on which she could prepare simple meals. She used the bathroom sink to wash the dishes.

Whenever Erika stopped by to see her, Irén prepared tea and served cookies.

"I could live like this," Erika commented to her at one time. "I could even live just in the bathroom. I could sleep in the tub and put the Bunsen burner on the sink counter if I needed to cook. Then in the morning I would roll up my bedding, take a bath, dress and go to school. Of course, besides a hook on the door, I don't know where I would hang my clothes."

And they laughed, for Erika loved clothes and Irén knew it.

"Do you still give your mom a hard time about what to wear?" Irén teased her.

"Yes, every Monday. I can't help it. We must wear the same thing for the whole week, and when Mom selects my clothes, I throw a tantrum, because I want to wear something else. But she always wins. So, I go to school every Monday feeling upset and thinking that I look ridiculous. Then some girl in my class will say, "Oh, you look so nice," and I feel a lot better. By the end of the day, I'm happy with what I've got on. So, when I go home and tell that to Mom, we make peace, till the following Monday." Erika grinned.

"You're such a difficult child! Why can't you just put on the clothes without making a fuss and see what your classmates say at school. Then if they don't like what you're wearing, you can always change the next day."

"No, you see, that's just the thing. We have to wear the same clothes the whole week! That way we're not "showing off". So, I've got to feel good about it at the start."

"Does Judith also give your mom a hard time about her outfits?"

"No. Never. She just puts on whatever she is given."

"You see? Why don't you learn from her?"

"We're very different. I can't help myself," Erika admitted. "I don't even know why I am the way I am."

"Someday you'll understand yourself. Till then, try not to give your mom such a hard time. She's got enough to cope with."

"I know."

Both of them would fall silent at this point, not wanting to discuss Erika's home life.

◉◉◉

It was different when Piry came to see Irén.

"I admire the fact that you never complain and just accept life as it's doled out to you," Piry would comment, as she looked around her friend's modest quarters.

"What's the point? I can't change anything, so why fight it? I'm just biding my time."

"You scare me when you say that."

"It's my reality. I have no family and can barely make a living. Since my party was dissolved, I'm just waiting for the other shoe to drop," Irén whispered, and added, "You know they've jailed some of my former party members. I'm just wondering why they haven't come after me yet considering I was pretty high up in the party."

"I hope they never will!" Piry hugged her friend.

Irén laughed. "I hope so too. Now, to your problems: if you're so unhappy with Feri, why don't you divorce him?

Besides her sister, Irén was the only other person in whom Piry confided that her life with Feri was less than ideal. "He is so crude and hard to talk to.

We have nothing in common, except that I need him for providing a roof over our heads." Piry wiped away her tears. "This is not what I expected but then I was a fool not to listen to everyone's advice. Now I'm paying for it. But if I divorce him, I've got no place to go with the girls. So, I want to ask you something." Piry fell silent and looked around the room, including up at the ceiling.

Irén immediately understood and turned on the radio so even their hushed voices could not be overheard by any of her neighbors, or a recording device possibly hidden somewhere in the room by the ÁVO.

Piry then whispered, "If I leave Feri, it would be to escape from the country. Would you know of anyone who could help?"

Irén replied by picking up a piece of paper from her table and wrote: "I know people who might help you escape with the girls. I'll give you some contact names. You must memorize them and then we'll burn this paper."

"Of course."

Irén scribbled down a couple of names and phone numbers. She then handed the paper to Piry, and for the next ten minutes they sat in silence, as Piry memorized the information. Then Irén lit her Bunsen burner and turned the paper into ashes.

"You are as close to me as my sister," Piry told Irén when they hugged goodbye. "Please keep in touch. I worry about you."

"I am careful, as you can see. Don't worry. What will be will be." She gave Piry a wry smile. "We've been through worse than this. Someday, this too shall pass."

Piry always felt better after her visits with Irén. Then one day, when she came knocking on Irén's door, to have come to see her, the neighbor stuck her head out her front door and said, "She's gone."

"Gone where?"

"We don't know. Last week two ÁVO men came for her around five o'clock in the morning and asked her to go with them. She hasn't been back since."

"Thank you," Piry held on to the railing as she inched down the staircase of the building, feeling like another piece of her heart had been cut out.

She thought of visiting her cousin, Laci, to plead with him to rescue Irén from the clutches of the ÁVO. But she didn't dare. She had gone to see him at his invitation, a few weeks before. He was charming, served her espresso in his office, and told her he was about to marry Péter Gábor's sister, Kató.

"It will be a very quiet civil ceremony, no guests, except Gábor and my mother as witnesses. But I wanted to tell you about it in person."

"How wonderful! Congratulations! Do I get to meet your bride before the wedding?"

"I don't think so. She is busy with her own work at the Ministry of Interior. But you'll have plenty of chances to get to know her once we live under the same roof. You'll all come for visits. Now tell me how you are and what's new with your family?"

Piry looked him in the eyes, then asked, "Can I talk to you about something very private?"

"Of course! You can always confide in me."

"My marriage to Feri is not going well. I'd like to leave the country with my daughters. Can you help us do this?"

Laci's face suddenly changed into a stone mask. He came out from behind his desk, pulled Piry out of her chair and with his face touching hers, whispered with clenched teeth:

"I love you, but don't ever ask such a thing of me or you will force me to report you to the authorities."

Piry blanched. She pulled away from Laci and looked into his eyes, dark, unfathomable, like pieces of onyx. She realized that she had made a huge mistake. Not only was her cousin a devout communist, for all she knew his office might be bugged, and she might have put him as well as herself, and her family, in enormous danger.

She said in a clear loud voice, "Please forget what I said. I didn't mean it. It's true my marriage is not a happy one. But the rest—I don't even know why I said it. I guess, I'm just so desperate to get away from Feri, I'll say anything."

"That's better," Laci leaned forward, and kissed her lightly on the cheek. "All is forgiven, just watch your tongue and don't make bad jokes. You know I don't have a sense of humor when it comes to loyalty."

When Piry left Laci's office, she wondered how she could have been so foolish as to confide in him. Of course, family was family. But he did spend years in the Soviet Union and now held one of the highest positions on the staff of the most dreaded and powerful man in Hungary. On top of it, now he was marrying Péter Gábor's sister!

As she was leaving the ÁVO building on Andrássy Út, one of the most beautiful, tree lined avenues in the city, she felt like the time when she had escaped the Nazi officers at the Red Cross Hospital. She walked to the streetcar stop, upset and sad. Sitting on the hard wood bench as the vehicle lurched along the long road to Újpest, she reflected on what had just happened.

We live in times when politics are more important than family, and fear rules. I'm just lucky that he didn't call his henchmen to haul me away! I can't afford to alienate him, but I can't trust him either, ever again. I wonder if his mother knows what he has become. Well, I'm certainly not going to ask her. It seems that only the uniforms have changed not the way ideologies are enforced. But at least now it's not just the Jews they're after—it's everyone who is different from them, she thought smiling to herself.

◎◉◎

To comply with the government regulation that all able-bodied citizens must work, Piry went to the local government office that gave jobs to women who wished to work from home. She received a week's training on a sweater knitting machine and was given the equipment to take home.

She and Maria moved her bed around so the knitting machine and the accompanying table for the finished pieces could be placed in her room. Piry was to knit the five parts of a sweater, two fronts, one back, and the left and right sleeves. She had to produce ten complete sets each day and deliver them to the commune office at the end of each week. The Commune Office supplied the yarn. It was cotton, mixed with a little wool, always a dull blue or gray color.

"I won't be able to produce as many pieces as they want delivered each week, unless you help me," Piry declared to Maria and her two daughters.

"I have too much homework to help," Judith responded immediately.

"I can help," Erika offered. "I'll work after I finish my homework, late afternoon or after dinner."

Piry hugged her, "Thanks."

"I can help, too, after I'm done with the housework," Maria promised.

"I'll pay you extra for the pieces you do," Piry promised.

CHAPTER 12

FOR SEVERAL WEEKS MARIA's room smelled of the knitting machine oil, and yarns. It looked like a mini warehouse with the finished pieces stacked high on the new table. Maria never complained, she accommodated herself to the new arrangement. After cleaning the house in the morning, she spent a couple of hours knitting. Piry, too, found time to knit after she cooked the day's meal. She even ran her errands, usually in the late afternoon, before she had to serve dinner. But life became too hectic for her, and she sought a way out. She went to see the nationalized health service doctor. She complained of headaches, caused by the smell of the materials, and joint ache in her wrists caused by the repetitive movement of sliding the knitting needles across the railing of the machine.

"I can't continue doing this, Doctor, it will ruin my health completely," she told the middle aged, balding general practitioner. He sat in his white coat behind his desk, staring at Piry.

"What would you like me to do?" he asked her.

"Can you please write a certificate that I am injured and cannot work? You know what to say!" She reached across his desk and placed an envelope in front of him. "Here is a description of my symptoms. I thought I'd write it up for you to make it easier."

He peeked inside the envelope. His face didn't move a muscle at seeing the five hundred forints Piry had put in there with the letter. He gingerly pulled out the letter and read it.

"It's very well explained, Mrs. Haydu. Just wait in the reception area and my assistant will bring you a letter that you can take to the Council Office. I'm sure they'll accept it."

"Thank you so much for your help, Doctor!"

Piry practically floated out of his office. *Communism or not, money still speaks louder than words*, she concluded with a sense of victory. She knew she had taken a chance by putting the money into the envelope. But if the doctor hadn't wanted it, he simply could have read the letter and given it back to her with the envelope saying, he couldn't do anything for her. However, he took the money and provided her with the certificate she wanted. Now she was free again to pursue her next goal—finding a way to leave the country. Summer arrived, and with it a letter of invitation for Erika to return to the village home of Uncle Ede and Aunt Aniko.

"Do you want to go?" Feri asked.

"Yes, yes, please," Erika jumped up and down to show her enthusiasm.

"Who's going to help me with making the preserves this summer if you're on vacation for two months?" Piry teased Erika.

"I don't know, I don't know but want to go!" Erika chanted, jumping up and down.

Piry looked at Feri, "I guess we'll have to manage without her, if you agree." Feri nodded, "Yes, let her go."

Once again, Erika had received an 'all five' top grades report card. Both her parents acknowledged it only as "this is what we expect of you." As usual, Judith's report card was mostly '3'-s. She did get 5's in Hungarian literature and grammar, but the rest of her grades made Piry less than happy. Feri wouldn't even comment since he and Judith still avoided talking to each other. In a way, Erika was made to feel that she was being rewarded with the vacation.

Uncle Ede arrived to pick Erika up a week after her school year ended. Staying in the village with Ede's family was the best time Erika could ask for. She sought out the children whom she had befriended the summer before, and they were happy to see her. Like a small gang, they ran barefoot through the dusty, unpaved streets of the village, climbed trees together, guarded geese in the fields, and took Erika with them up into the Church tower, to watch the bell ringer ring the big bells for Sunday service.

However, there were some changes for Erika. She could no longer run around in a mere sunsuit, which consisted of shorts with a rectangular piece of fabric attached to the front of the pants. The front was held up by strings tied around her neck and covered her midriff but not her nipples. And Erika had begun to grow breasts. They were small mounds, not a significant rise, but enough for her to feel self-conscious and insist on wearing a blouse tucked into her shorts. She also noticed that the boys in her group began to look at her differently. They would stare at her chest then look away when she caught their gaze. But they were still willing to help her up or down trees, or up into the church tower to listen to the bells.

In her hosts' home, Erika felt a different sort of change. Although they were as loving and kind toward her as ever, she sensed a tension that had not been there before. But clearly it had nothing to do with their little girl, Kata. By now she was running happily on her chubby little legs around the house and yard, always followed by Aunt Marci. The old woman would shout after Kata to be careful but could no longer keep up with the child's speed. Aging had slowed her down significantly.

The uneasy change Erika perceived had to do with discussions between Uncle Ede and Aunt Aniko. Erika could hear but not understand them because they lowered their voices when they thought she was around. Erika figured that they were in some sort of trouble. She worried that perhaps she was in their way, but they were too polite to ask her to go home.

Finally, she brought it up to Uncle Ede, for she felt closer to him than to his wife. She sought him out in the stable when he was doing the evening feeding of the cows. She watched him pick up great bunches of hay with a pitchfork and toss them into the trough in front of the two waiting bovines.

"Uncle Ede, am I overstaying my welcome?"

"Now what makes you think that?"

"I noticed you and Aunt Aniko are often talking like you don't want me to hear, so I'm wondering."

Uncle Ede stopped tossing the hay; he held the pitchfork high up in the air while he stared at the little girl standing before him with such a pained expression.

"Erika, my sweetie, our talks have nothing to do with you." He tossed the hay before the cows and then squatted down to be on level with Erika, looking into her eyes.

"Adults have their own problems, and we've got lots of them this year. That's what we're discussing, trying to find the best solutions."

"Like what problems? Can I help with anything?" Erika offered.

"You're very sweet, but these are government caused problems, not personal ones. The Village Council declared that we could no longer run the bakery, because that makes us capitalist businessmen, and in our People's Democracy there is no room for private businesses like ours. So, we must close it down or face God only knows what punishment."

"But if you close the bakery where will people find an oven to bake their bread?"

"That's a very smart question, Erika. It turns out, the village chief has a cousin who manages a state-owned bakery in the next village. So, people will have to go there."

Erika thought back to the night when she had watched the ÁVO van take away the people across the street from them. She didn't tell Uncle Ede about this but now said, "It's better to do what the government wants. My father, Feri, as you know, had to give up his business, too. He now works in a factory. What will you do after you give up the bakery?"

"Maybe I'll offer it to the government, and they'll let me run it for them."

"That would be better than people having to go to the next village to bake!"

"You're a smart girl, Erika. It will all depend on the mayor of our village. And he doesn't like Jews. We're the only Jews here, so we'll see what he decides."

"Uncle Ede, how come you are the only Jews in the village?"

Ede's face turned grim as he answered, full of pain in his voice, "They had all been deported and killed in the Nazi concentration camps! I survived because I served on the Eastern Front, same as your stepfather. Aunt Aniko and Aunt Marci miraculously survived in the Jewish Ghetto in Budapest. But they suffered a lot. Aunt Aniko's mother died during the war. She and I married after the war. Aunt Marci is Aniko's mother's sister. She came to live with us because there was no one left of our immediate families."

A momentary silence ensued between them. Then one of the cows gave a deep mooohh, and Uncle Ede said, "I've got to finish feeding these animals."

Erika put her arms around Uncle Ede's neck, "I'm so sorry about what happened during the war, and what is happening to you now."

He smiled at her, "Thank you. Please keep this conversation between us. I think Aunt Aniko would consider you too young for me to tell you all this."

"I will." *He has no idea how good I am at keeping secrets*, Erika thought.

She went back to the house, while he continued to feed his cows, wondering, how long it will be before the government will also 'nationalize' his livestock.

◎◉◎

While Erika was away, Judith spent her summer being tutored in mathematics and other sciences by a private teacher Piry had hired for her. "You must get your grades up high enough to get into high school. I'm willing to help you but you must also make an effort to learn," Piry urged her daughter.

She knew Judith hated these extra lessons. To give her an incentive to study, Piry agreed that after the mornings spent with the tutor, she could join her friends at the big public pool run by the city of Ùjpest. It was a clean, beautiful recreational park with green grass surrounding two pools. One was a half-Olympic size for advanced swimmers and the other a smaller and shallower pool for younger children. A play area had several swings and a large sandbox. Parents could stay with their children, spreading blankets on the grass. Teenagers would come on their own, since the city also provided supervision. There were attendants in the male and female dressing rooms, and a lifeguard for the pool area, who sat in the shade and kept an eye on everyone at play.

Judith met up with her girlfriends in the afternoons. They swam, sunbathed, and flirted with the boys from their own school, and with others from different schools in Ùjpest. Judith, at thirteen, was becoming attractive. Her deep blue eyes sparkled in her round face, her figure was slender with small, high breasts, and she had long, shapely legs.

All girls wore the current fashion's two-piece bathing suits, and Judith knew she looked good in her small, blue-and-white polka-dot suit. The boys confirmed it by chasing her around the pool. It was an accepted way of flirtation among teens that boys would chase a girl around the pool, and when they caught her, they would grab her by the ankles and wrists, and swinging her over the water, toss her into the pool. The more a girl was chased and tossed, the more it confirmed her appeal to the boys. This, in turn, raised the esteem of her girlfriends.

For the first time in her life, Judith was feeling generally liked and admired. With Erika away, she had no competition for attention either at home or socially. It made her so happy that she cried when she had to stay home because it rained, or she had her period. She simply loved this summer and felt content for the first time in a long time.

◎◉◎

With both her daughters occupied during the summer months, Piry set her mind to forging a future for them. She was making enough money with her illegal financial transactions, and the sales of nylon stocking from Vienna, to supplement the household expenses so they could live without want. She was also increasing her savings with her aunt Vica in Canada. Because of her friend Irén's disappearance, Piry had not contacted the leads Irén had given her. She was afraid that they might be under surveillance as well. Instead, she went to visit Doctor Komlós, not at his house but at the hospital where he worked.

"How nice to see you!" he exclaimed, and added, "This calls for a celebration! Come, I'll take you out for coffee."

He removed his white coat and told the head nurse that he would be absent for an hour. He led Piry out of the hospital to a nearby hole-in-the-wall cafe. "I needed to get away from there a bit" he sighed as they settled across from each other into the tiny chairs by the tiny marble top table.

The waitress came around, and he ordered two espressos and a "krémes" and a "dobosh" the most typical Hungarian pastries. The krémes consisted of super thin pastry at top and bottom, and the middle was filled with vanilla pudding. The dobosh was built of six thin layers of sponge cake, and each layer was filled with chocolate cream as thick as the pastry. Then it was topped with a hard, golden caramel crust.

"We can share half of each pastry, and that way we can have the best of both worlds," he told Piry with a grin. He looked tired and seemed to have aged considerably in the time that she had not seen him. He, too, was studying her face.

"You look wonderful," he declared, "life must be good to you."

"What about you?" Piry asked.

"Eh, it could be better. I'm overworked and underpaid in our great new socialist system," he whispered, smiling.

They fell silent as the waitress brought their coffee and pastries.

"With your leave," Dr. Komlós expertly sliced the pastries in half, and placed the halves on their plates. Then reached for his espresso. "Piry, my dear, to what do I really owe the pleasure of your visit?"

Piry found it ironic that in the midst of eating such sweet pastries, they should be talking about the bitterness of their lives. She sat with her back to the front counter, and there were no customers near their table. Still, she lowered her voice as she blurted out, "I am not happy with Feri, and I also feel that I made a mistake staying in this country after the war." She paused a minute, wondering whether she should continue, then decided she could trust Komlós. "My daughters would have a better future in places where my dead husband's brothers live. Each had promised to help me raise them. You have many contacts, so I was wondering perhaps you might be able to help us to get out. The girls and I would go first, and Feri might follow us."

"Oh, my dear, my dear," Dr. Komlós shook his head. "If only it were that simple! But I'll do what I can. I will look around for an opportunity for you. However, unless you want Feri to go with you at the same time, the first thing you must do is to divorce him."

Piry was startled. "That has never even occurred to me. Why would I do that?"

"Well, just think about it. First, because you are unhappy with him and therefore should leave him behind anyway. Second, if you have an opportunity to leave and he won't go with you, and he is still your husband, his fate will be sealed. He'll be considered a collaborator and guess what'll happen to him?"

Piry was aware of a new law that went into effect on July 12, 1950, that could impose a life sentence on those caught crossing the border in an attempt to illegally leave Hungary. The law would also penalize those who were complicit in aiding the escapees or knew about their plans to escape and did not report it. They were all guilty, whether the escape was successful or not. Piry's blood ran cold as she thought of the possible consequences to Feri.

"If we got out, and he didn't go with us, for sure they'd take his house away, and he would be jailed or deported to a labor camp. Who knows what else they would do to him for not reporting to the ÁVO what we were planning. I can't do that to him, you're right. Even if I asked him to come along, I am not sure that he would. But if we divorce and the kids and I don't leave right away, where would we live?"

Dr. Komlós smiled, "My dear, with the current housing shortage, you would stay right where you are. His house is big enough to allow unrelated families to live there. In fact, if you and the girls moved out, don't you think the State would move another family right in? His house is too big for one person. No housing agency would tolerate that. If you and the girls stay, and you and Feri are divorced, if anyone asks, you can simply explain that you no longer live as husband and wife but you're still sharing the household for practical reasons.

Lots of unrelated families are forced to live under the same roof these days because not enough apartment buildings have been built or repaired since the war. So, you and the kids can stay where you are, regardless. That's all."

That evening, Piry asked Feri to have a talk. Tired as he was, he sensed the seriousness of her request and stayed in the dining room after dinner to hear her out. Piry did not tell him how unhappy she was in the marriage. She merely talked about their future.

"There is nothing for us here. My daughters won't be accepted into the higher education schools because we are considered bourgeoisie, bad political elements. Why should the state waste classroom space on my daughters instead of giving a chance to some working-class kids? That's the future we're looking at for them. You are a talented businessman yet look what you're forced to do with your life! I also only know how to conduct business, but if I'm caught doing the way I'm earning money, I'll be jailed. This is no way to live."

Feri listened quietly, then asked, "So what do you propose we do?"

"I went to see Dr. Komlós today. He will help find a way for us to get out."

Feri became motionless and withdrawn into his own thoughts, as if evaluating what Piry had just told him. Finally, he nodded and looking at Piry said, "Let's see what Komlós comes up with. One thing I know though, even if he comes up with a perfect plan, if we all leave together and get caught, we won't have a house to come home to. The government will jail us and take over my house. You want to risk that?"

"Of course not. But what would you suggest?"

"That whatever plan Komlós comes up with, you and the girls should do it first. If you succeed, I'll follow you. If you don't, you'll all have a home to come back to."

Piry stared at Feri; she didn't expect him to be such a sharp planner. She said with a wry smile, "Komlós had the same idea. He suggested that if we divorced, and the girls and I go first, you won't be held responsible even if we manage to escape."

"I always knew he was a smart man," Feri smiled at Piry.

They made fervent love that night on Feri's sofa bed, and afterwards Piry whispered, "Which of us should file for divorce?"

"Both of us. For incompatibility."

Then he made love to her again.

◎◉◎

When summer was over, Erika came home from the village deeply tanned and content. After all the tutoring, Judith had felt more confident about her knowledge of math and grammar, ready to tackle the new schoolyear. Her summer experience by the pool among friends gave her enough self-confidence to look forward to returning to school.

Piry was content that her daughters had a good summer. Hers had been full of anxiety concerning her preparations toward a different future. She and

Feri had quietly filed for divorce and were waiting for a court date with a judge to officially terminate their marriage.

Piry had not heard from Dr. Komlós but assumed that she would when he had news for her. She and Feri decided not to inform the girls of their impending divorce. Their lives returned to their daily routine. Feri was going to work at the factory, Piry kept house with Maria's help, and Judith and Erika were back at school the first week in September.

"Guess what?" Judith turned to Erika one night, when they were getting into pajamas in Judith's room, "the children's room".

"What?"

"I got my period this summer," Judith said proudly.

Erika knew vaguely what that meant, because she had overheard her mother talking with Aunt Lilly about having cramps during her period, but she wasn't absolutely certain what "a period" was. She didn't want Judith to know this, lest her sister would regret sharing what was obviously an important secret. Instead, she asked, "Does it hurt?"

"I feel funny just before I get it. My belly sort of aches, but once it starts, I'm fine."

"I'm glad. How long does it last?"

"About four days."

"Oh. Will I get it too?"

"Of course, you will. All women have periods and usually get it at around age 12 or 13. So you have something to look forward to," Judith grinned.

Erika did not dwell on the subject further. She figured she'd learn more about this mysterious period when in a few years' time she would get hers.

◎◉◎

One evening, three weeks after school started, Judith and Erika were in the dining room doing their homework. Piry was out somewhere and so was Feri. Maria was in the kitchen, cleaning up and keeping the food warm for when the parents got home.

"I'm done," Erika declared, putting her pen down and closing her composition book. "I'm tired, I'll get ready for bed."

She went into the bathroom, which was just off the dining room. Once she got through her routine of washing, brushing her teeth, and changing into pajamas, she came out, holding her panties in her hand.

"Judith, there is this funny brown stuff on my panties—it's definitely not number two—what do you think it is?"

Judith put her book down and looked. "Hey, I think you've got your period!"

"What are you talking about, I'm only ten!"

"Go wipe yourself again in the bathroom and look at the color of the toilet paper."

Erika did as she was told and was amazed at the dark red spot on the paper.

"Well???" Judith shouted through the door.

"I think you're right!" Erika shouted back. She pulled up her pajama pants and came out of the bathroom, "Now what do I do?"

"You get a hug first, because now you're a big girl, like me." Judith folded Erika into her arms, in an unusually affectionate gesture from her, and gave Erika a peck on her cheek.

Erika was touched. Judith does care about me, she thought.

Releasing her sister, Judith said, "And now I'll take care of you. Wait here." She went to her room and came back in a few seconds with a clean, white cotton rag.

"You wear panties under your pajamas to hold this cloth there. It will absorb the blood that will come out. When Mon comes home, we'll ask her for more cloths so you could change this out when it gets saturated. As soon as you remove it, you must wash it in cold water with soap. Otherwise, the blood will stain the fabric, and it will be really icky to reuse. Don't ever use warm water because the blood will taint the fabric. It must be cold water."

"Why can't we just throw them out and get new cloths?"

"Because they cost money, Dummy!" Judith fell into her usual mocking tone.

"Oh." Erika stopped asking further questions. She figured, she'll find out from her mother what more she needs to know.

It was past ten o'clock when Piry got home, and found her daughters waiting up for her, reading in the dining room.

"Why aren't you two in bed, you have school tomorrow!" she exclaimed.

"Guess what, Mom," Judith grinned at her.

"What?"

"Erika got her period!"

Piry stared for moment at her younger daughter, then exclaimed, "That's wonderful!" and took her in her arms. "Congratulations! Now you're a woman."

"But I'm only ten," Erika protested.

"Well, it happens sometimes that girls get their period at an early age."

"I took care of her," Judith declared.

"That was very good of you," Piry hugged her too. Then she said, "Erika, I'm going to tell you the same thing I told Judith when she got her period. Once you have it, you can have babies. And there is only one way to get pregnant, and that is when a boy sticks his penis into you. It starts with him wanting to kiss you and that will get you to feel all excited because kissing is nice. But then he'll want to touch your breasts, and then touch your butt, and the next thing you know he'll want to stick his penis between your legs. You can't get pregnant from hugging or kissing. But that can lead you to losing your self-control and he can get you pregnant by doing what he really wants."

"Mom, I don't even have a boyfriend!" Erika protested. "I just turned ten! Why are you telling me all this?"

"Because you're a girl who just got her period, and therefore you can get pregnant. Either one of you. So, I want you to be aware and mindful of what you are doing out in the world among your friends. And now it's time you both went to bed." Piry kissed them good night and waited for Feri to come home so she could tell him the big news.

Feri took it in without a comment. His face retained the blank expression he always had when he was presented with something new. But his mind was racing. So, she's become a woman. Now I'll really have to watch how I touch her in the future. Getting her pregnant could land me in jail.

Piry didn't wait for him to respond. She went to the kitchen and brought out his dinner. She sat with him while he ate. He took large forkfuls of the thick noodles mixed with cottage cheese that had been sweetened with powder sugar. He chewed, swallowed, and finally said with his half smile, "This is woman's stuff. I won't comment to her. You just make sure she knows what it means." And he felt that he had done his job as a father.

◉◉◉

Piry got a letter from an old family friend, Elek Gyula. It was a brief note.

"Dear Piry,
I haven't seen you for a while. Please come to my shop for a visit any time during regular working hours on any weekday.
Fondly,
Gyula."

When Zoltán was growing up, his family lived in Budapest, and his father was the Chief Rabbi of a large Jewish congregation. Elek was a wealthy supporter of that temple. Then Zoltán's father retired from his post as a Rabbi and became the head of the Jewish Community in the town of Debrecen. But Elek continued his contact with the family through his friendship with Zoltán, who had moved back to Budapest when he finished high school.

Elek was actually more than a friend. He became Zoltán's mentor when the young man decided to open his own wholesale hardware business, for that was Elek's business as well. That is how Elek had made a fortune, and he was more than willing to teach Zoltán how to conduct his business to make money with it. Now Elek was retired and supposedly lived on the small pension he and his wife received after he donated' his business to the government.

But Piry suspected, that just as he had successfully managed to hide himself and his wife during the war, escaping the Nazi persecution, he most likely had also hidden enough of his money for them to live comfortably in their old age.

Actually, Elek wasn't completely retired. He had a small office and a shop on the outskirts of Buda, where he trained young men in the craft of iron-smithing, just as he had once taught Zoltán. He had no children of his own but derived great pleasure from teaching young people his craft. At the same time, this justified his ability to maintain his home, a lovely villa in the Buda Hills, because the Ministry of Heavy Industry provided him with a salary to run his valuable training program.

Piry knew where his shop was. Going there brought up many fond memories of visiting Elek with Zoltán. Now she came alone, wondering why Elek had sent her the note. Knowing him as well as she did, she figured, it wasn't for just a casual visit. From the bus stop she climbed the steep road to his shop and knocked on the office door which faced the street directly.

"Come in," shouted the familiar hoarse voice.

Piry pushed the door open. She was shocked at seeing how much Elek had aged since she had last seen him. His hair was thin and totally white, his face full of deep lines.

He broke into a broad smile, "Why Piry, what a pleasure to see you!" He came out from behind his desk. He seemed to have shriveled into a thin, short man since Piry had seen him, nearly a year before. But his spirit was still bright as he came to embrace her, planting kisses on her cheeks.

"The pleasure is mine," she returned his hug.

"Come, come, sit." He pointed at the chair by the side of his desk. "What can I get you? A coffee?"

"No, thank you. Maybe a glass of water."

He went to the pitcher that stood on a small table near his desk and poured water into a tall glass. He placed it in front of Piry and went back to sit behind the desk, not taking his eyes off her face.

"So, you got my note," he stated, as he watched her taking a sip of water.

"Yes." Piry put the glass down and looked quizzically at him.

"A little bird brought me news that you and Feri were getting divorced." Elek was wasting no time with niceties. "What's next for you? Have you met someone else?"

"No, not at all."

"Well, then?"

Piry did not reply. She wasn't sure whether she should talk about her plans with Elek, for she did not want to get him into trouble. The fewer of her friends knew about it the better off they were, in case they were questioned later by the secret police.

He was watching her face, then stretched out his arms, "Come here."

Piry went to him, and he pulled her close, making her sit across his lap, as though she were a little girl. He put one arm around her waist and caressed her hair with his free hand. "You know you can confide in me." He turned her face toward him and gently kissed her lips.

The old letch, Piry thought, *he still wants to get into my pants, I hope that's not why he dragged me here.* After the war, she had occasionally visited Elek to seek his advice about selling Zoltan's merchandise. He was always helpful, taught her what some of the tools were used for when she wasn't sure, and told her how to price them when taking them to the villages. In exchange, he would ask her to let him hold her, kiss her and fondle her breasts. Once or twice, he asked her to sit astride on his lap, and move a bit, so he could come. He was always very sweet and gentle about it and raved about her beauty and desirability.

Piry didn't have the heart to turn him down. But now she was not in the mood to play.

"Is this why you asked me to come to see you?" she deliberately sounded astonished.

"No, my dear, this is just my bonus. I can't resist holding you when I see you," he said smiling, and slipping his hand under her skirt between her legs.

Piry ignored his hand. "If this is the bonus, what's the main prize?"

"Iren Goldberg had come to see me and asked me about an escape route. When I questioned her closely, she said, she wanted it for you. I told her I'd look into it. And then she disappeared. But I haven't forgotten my promise to her, and as soon as I knew of something, I contacted you. Oh, this feels wonderful!" He closed his eyes and slid his fingers inside her panties.

Piry felt a jolt in her belly as he breached the walls of her private parts, touching the soft, moist flesh inside. She arched her back and opened her thighs slightly to allow his fingers to penetrate her. She put her arms around his neck to stay securely sitting in his lap. She closed her eyes, suffused by pleasure throughout her body.

"What if someone comes in?" she asked as she leaned further back on his lap so she could spread her thighs wider.

"Yes, we ought to lock the door," he murmured, his breath hot over her lips.

Piry gently reached for his hand and pulled it away. She rolled off his lap and smoothing down her skirt, went to the door and turned the key in the lock.

Whatever he has to tell me, can wait, she thought, as she walked back to him with a provocative smile on her face.

He had turned his desk chair so Piry could straddle him across his lap. She felt his penis harden beneath her and raised herself slightly to reach down and unzip his pants. She freed his organ, and pushing her panties aside, allowed him to penetrate deep inside her. *He isn't as hard as he used to be*, she thought, *but it's still great. For a short man he's got quite a tool,* flashed through her mind, as she moved on it, at first slowly, deliberately, as if massaging herself on its length. Then as her pleasure intensified, she moved faster and faster, no longer in control but impelled by an inner need to gyrate and go up and down, till a hot cloud of pleasure suffused her from her core all through her being. She collapsed over him, her arms around his neck, her face pressed against his. His cheek was moist with sweat; she could feel his penis pulsating inside her. They stayed motionless till she could feel him shrinking and slipping out of her. Then she rose, lifting herself off him.

"The bathroom is the door to your left," he said in a hoarse, sated voice.

By the time she came out of the small vanity room, her clothes were neatly arranged, and so was her face, except for the flush on her cheeks and the glow in her eyes. He had also put himself back together, and sat primly at his desk, as if nothing had taken place between them. Only his warm smile betrayed what did.

"Now we can talk business," he said in a naughty tone.

"I'm all ears" Piry sat down opposite him, and putting her elbows on the desktop, cupped her face into her hands, looking like a flower in its calyx.

"I found an escape route for you," he said simply, matter-of-factly, picking up the conversation from the time she had first sat down.

Piry marveled at his ability to dismiss their lovemaking as an incident come and gone, without a glance or a touch of tenderness in its wake. When Feri made love to her, he at least held her for a while, putting gentle kisses on her face and eyes, still caressing her body. But Elek was all business now, so she quelled the tremors she still felt in her guts like aftershocks, and paid full attention to what he was saying.

"It's done by going on vacation to Romania, and from there to Yugoslavia, where they don't care if you slip through their border to Italy. Once there, you ask for asylum at the consulate of the country to which you wish to go, and you're on your way."

"It all sounds so simple, so uncomplicated," Piry responded. "I know Romania is a sister communist country, but how do you get a passport to go even there, not to mention from there to Yugoslavia?"

"You first meet with the man who is the tour guide for this little trip. He will tell you the date of his next tour and instruct you every step of the way how to get on it. He is a state certified tour guide, so you shouldn't have any trouble going on vacation with him. And taking your daughters with you, of course. Maybe when Erika has her birthday in June, you could claim it's a gift for her. By that time your divorce should be final."

◎◉◎

Piry and Feri received their divorce court summons at the Ùjpest Courthouse. The Judge was a no-nonsense man in his mid-fifties. He had sparse, graying hair, thick glasses, and a wrinkled, tired face. His robe seemed to hang on a skeletal body. He first questioned Piry, then Feri as to why they wanted to dissolve their marriage.

Piry, visibly uncomfortable with her answer, said, "My husband has abandoned all his marital duties for the past year. So why be married?"

The Judge turned to Feri, "How do you respond to this statement by your wife?"

"She is telling the truth. I have no objection to her statement."

"Do you then mutually wish to dissolve your marriage to each other?" The Judge asked.

"Yes, Comrade Judge," they each answered.

The Judge scratched his head, read their written statements, and pronounced the marriage dissolved due to mutual incompatibility. Within a few minutes the court clerk handed each of them their official divorce document stating that as of this date they were no longer husband and wife. Piry was allowed to retain her married name as her last name. But since she had not asked for alimony, there was to be no future obligation whatsoever between them.

They walked out of the courtroom together, having a hard time suppressing smiling, hiding their sense of glee at accomplishing this first step toward their future plans.

"I've got to go back to work, see you at home," Feri said, as he took the streetcar in the opposite direction from Piry, who was heading back to their house.

"I'll have dinner ready as usual," she smiled at him.

◎◉◎

It was early October when Piry received a postcard without a return address. But she knew it had come from Elek, for the typed message read, "Be at the Western Station at 10 a.m. on Thursday, the 11th to observe a group leaving for vacation."

Piry dressed in her most conservative dark gray suit, with a navy blue felt coat over it. She pulled her dark blonde hair back from her face and tucked it under a steel blue beret to be as inconspicuous as possible. She arrived early at the Western Station and stood by a post on the train platform that was clearly marked for Cluj, Romania as its final destination. A train stood there with its doors open, ready for boarding.

She saw nothing out of the ordinary as she watched people come and go, carrying large and small suitcases. There were couples, older and younger people, children holding on to their mother's hands, all with a harried expression on their faces, looking for their train compartment to board. To her right, a little way down, her eyes caught an older man hurrying to the window where suitcases could be stored for a brief period before one's journey.

He handed over his luggage ticket and waited. In a few minutes the clerk came back to him shaking her head while saying something. The old man became visibly agitated as he answered.

Piry slowly moved toward the scene so she could hear them.

"What do you mean you can't find my suitcase?" the old man raised his voice, upset.

"It must have been misplaced. Give me a bit of time, for sure I'll find it!" The clerk replied.

"I don't have time! shouted the old man, "My train is leaving in fifteen minutes!"

"Well. I'm alone here at the booth, so I can't just go looking; I have to tend to the other passengers…" the clerk responded, her head indicating the line forming behind the old man.

"You MUST get MY suitcase first, my train is leaving, I can't miss it! and I can't go without my suitcase!"

His loud voice echoed under the glass dome of the cavernous station. Piry saw a policeman head toward the luggage window.

"If you can't find it, let me go in and look for it!" The old man shouted. "Don't you understand how urgent this is?"

"I do, Comrade, but I'm not allowed to let you into the luggage area. You'll just have to be a bit patient," the hapless clerk responded, as she took a piece of luggage from another passenger and handed over the tag for it.

"My train is leaving in ten minutes!" the old man shouted, now desperate.

"Why don't you take the train, and we'll ship your suitcase to you tomorrow. We'll have it delivered directly to your hotel in Cluj. Just tell me where you'll be staying." the clerk suggested.

"I won't leave without my suitcase!" The old man exclaimed, exasperated.

By now the policeman was standing by them, "What is the problem here?"

"This incompetent comrade can't find my luggage, and my train is about to leave. I must board it with my suitcase!" the old man shouted.

"I offered to send it after him," the clerk explained.

"Let me have his receipt" the policeman ordered the clerk. She handed it to him, and without asking her permission, the officer went through the door to the luggage room. He returned within a couple of minutes, carrying a small but heavy case, "Is this it?"

"Yes! Thank you so much officer!" the old man reached for his case.

"Just a minute," the policeman held on to the suitcase, "Let's see why you made such a fuss about getting it."

He placed the suitcase on the ground, flipped open the lock, and stood staring at the content utterly amazed. It was filled with a large canvas bag, closed with a string neatly tied in a bow at the opening.

"This doesn't look to me like clothes for a vacation trip!" he policeman exclaimed and pulled open the cord. He reached inside and brought out a handful of gold coins. "Well!" He stared at the old man, who looked like he was about to collapse.

Suddenly, the officer was shouting to a uniformed train attendant, "Stop the train to Cluj! Tell the conductor to wait until I say he can go! Run!"

The attendant didn't have to be told twice. He broke into a swift run toward the front of the train. The policeman once again turned his attention to the old man.

"What is this? Are these yours? Who else is traveling with you to Romania?"

Before the old man had a chance to reply, the police officer waved down a bypassing train attendant, "Comrade, Come here!"

The attendant stopped in his tracks and obediently came to the officer.

"Go to your Station Master on the double and tell him shut all the doors of the station. Nobody leaves, and nobody should come into the station till we clear up this matter. And have the Station Master send me a couple of police officers who are here at the station to guard this man while I go and call my superior officer."

He didn't have to repeat himself; the attendant saluted like a soldier and ran off.

Piry, overhearing the policeman, didn't wait to find out the fate of the old man caught in the web of law and order. Nor did she care about the fate of the other passengers heading for the Romanian vacation. She calmly turned around and headed for the nearest exit before the station doors got locked. Once on the street, Piry moved briskly, taking the first streetcar, she could get on, regardless of its directions.

She took it two stops, then got off and figured out which streetcars she should be taking for the fastest route home. While she sat on the streetcar with no visible sign of distress, her mind was racing. *Because of that stupid old man, now the whole operation will be exposed. Those poor people who were on that trip! I wonder whether the leader was on the train too. He must have been. I must go see Elek right away, to let him know. Or maybe not, just in case he may also get implicated.*

Somewhere up there, someone is watching out for us. The girls and I could have been on that train or something like this could have happened on the next train, the one that we were planning to take. There must be a way out, but certainly this wasn't it.

Piry sighed with a deep sense of relief entering the gate of her home. As she turned the key in the lock, securing their privacy, she felt a deep sense of gratitude toward Feri for providing her and her daughters with this haven of safety and beauty. Yes, beauty, which she had been able to create, making their home elegant and comfortable. *Maybe life here isn't so bad. Perhaps I should stop fighting and accept what is,* Piry thought.

◎◉◎

Feri came home from work a few days later, fuming. He tossed a propaganda flyer on the dining room table and exclaimed to Piry, "Those bastards! As if it weren't enough for us to work for a pittance, now they are asking us to donate from our meager wages to something they just cooked up, a 'Peace Loan!' It's supposed to help fund the rebuilding of our economy, but I don't see how we can donate when our salary is barely enough to buy food! Besides, they'll be sending that money to support the war in Korea; not a penny will go to help our poor country!"

"Calm down," Piry hushed him, "you don't want the kids or the maid to hear you!"

"I don't give a damn anymore! I'm sick of all this," Feri muttered lowering his voice.

Piry hugged him. "Don't worry, one of these days we'll find a way out of all this."

He looked at her sharply "You got another escape plan?"

"Not yet," she grinned. "But I'm working on it. I'll let you know."

He didn't question her further. She brought in his dinner, and he ate with gusto the large bowl of spaghetti heavily garnished with poppy seeds, sweetened by powdered sugar. As if by venting to Piry he had gotten rid of his anger.

"Join me?" he asked Piry as he prepared for bed after his meal.

"I will," Piry acquiesced, glad that he had settled into a better mood. Since they slept in separate rooms, he on the living room sofa and she with Erika in the master bedroom, she seldom visited Feri of her own accord. She waited for him to ask her and never refused him regardless of how she felt. Because Piry considered making love as the principal glue by which their relationship was held together. Feri was a good lover, and they were both in a better mood the day after they had made love. Sometimes, Piry spent the whole night with him, at other times she slipped away once he began to snore. She enjoyed the quiet comfort of the double bed she shared with Erika, who never snored.

CHAPTER 13

URING THE FALL OF 1950, there had been lectures in all the schools about the war between North and South Korea that had started in June of that year. Judith simply ignored the indignation with which teachers spoke about the capitalist countries' aggression toward poor North Korea.

Erika felt like a whole new world was being presented to her when her geography and history teachers displayed a map showing where Korea was located in Asia. Photos of Korean soldiers were posted on the bulletin boards in their classrooms.

Erika found the look of the Korean people amazing. In Hungary people had a range of hair and eye colors that varied from black to blonde hair and from blue, hazel, and brown to black eyes. But all Koreans seemed to have black hair and almond shaped dark eyes, which Erika thought was exotic. But she had little understanding of the cause for the war. Her teachers said, "The imperialist South Koreans attacked the peace-loving Socialist North Koreans." But it wasn't clear to Erika why this had happened.

Erika, along with all the other students, was ordered by their literature teacher to write essays about the 'imperialist invaders', and how it was the duty of all socialist countries to support their Korean comrades.

They also had to write about the meaning of Stalin's declaration in Pravda, the most important Soviet newspaper, in which the great leader stated, "If the warmonger agitator nations succeed in deceiving peaceful nations with their lies, we might all be swept into a new world war."

Their Hungarian literature teacher explained the meaning of this declaration, along with a resolution created during the 2nd Congress of the Hungarian Workers Party. She quoted, "We must sharpen the class warfare against the country's enemies and strengthen communist iron discipline at the workplace and in all of society."

Erika quickly learned the slogans and expressions used by her teachers. Although she did not fully understand their meaning, she knew how to use the words to write inflammatory essays in the approved flowery language against the "…Evil imperialist forces, held at bay only by our great leaders, Comrade Stalin, and Comrade Rákosi."

She was selected to read one of her essays at the school assembly on the following Friday. After the thunderous applause for her reading, Erika sat modestly among her classmates during the rest of the program. She knew that despite the accolades for her "outstanding writing," it was best to put on a humble face. It prevented her classmates from attacking her for being "middle class." She was clearly proving with her essays that she was part of them—the great proletariat.

But at this day's assembly, Erika's mind was elsewhere. Her thoughts wondered back to the joke her father had told them during dinner the night before. He came home in his usual taciturn mood, now fueled by tension at his workplace. The men feared that another world war was brewing, this time originating in Asia, where there was fighting not only in Korea, but it had also spread to Vietnam.

It was risky to discuss these wars except at the weekly political meetings that were held in the factory's assembly hall. There, of course, they had to mouth the party line, "We'll fight against the imperialist pigs till death, to defend our democracy!"

No one could utter a word publicly against the foolhardy possibility of getting involved in this war in distant Asia while their own country was still suffering from the economic ruin of World War II. Instead, all workers at the assembly supported the party line of the day.

Each night, after dinner, Feri felt obligated to listen to the news on either of the two official radio stations, so he could be up to date the next day at work. Privately, he found the broadcasts full of propaganda. They praised Stalin and "his strong hand in maintaining the peace against the possibility of the escalation of the Korean war into another world war by 'capitalist, imperialist forces.'

Erika, listening to the news with him, observed, that it just put Feri into a worse mood. But last night, while they sat around the dinner table, he broke into a broad smile.

"I heard a good one today," he said, and the three women around the table stopped eating to listen.

"A worker at the factory says to his best buddy during their cigarette break, "You know, I work my tail off, my wife works her tail off, but we still can't afford to buy a baby buggy for our three-month-old son."

His friend shakes his head and says, 'But we're working in a baby buggy factory! Listen, I have an idea for you. After each workday, take home one part of the buggy in your lunch bag. No one will notice if you're careful. After a couple of weeks, you'll have all the parts to put together a buggy for the kid!'

"That's a great idea, I hadn't thought of that," the man says.

"Three weeks later, the work buddies meet again during their cigarette break. "Well, did you manage to put a buggy together?" the friend asks.

"I don't know what's going on," the other man answers, "As you suggested, I took home every single part we make in the factory but each time I put the parts together, no matter how I did it, it turned into a machine gun."

The three women at the table broke into laughter, and even Feri was laughing with them.

Now, as the words of the assembly's speakers registered with Erika about the war, she thought of the real meaning of the joke. They all talked about supporting their comrades in Korea and clearly, guns were being shipped there from Hungary. The teachers who spoke, encouraged the students to study hard so they could grow into "Valuable members of our socialist society, who will defend their homeland against imperialist invaders." *I hope we'll never have another war in Hungary*, Erika thought, recalling her years of hiding and hunger.

◎◉◎

After the assembly, on the way home, Erika was followed by three boys, schoolmates, who wouldn't stop teasing her.

"You think you're such a hot shot," one of them called after her while another grabbed hold of her long braids and pulled on them.

Furiously, Erika swirled around swinging her school bag and hitting not one but two of the boys.

"Oh, she is feisty!" the third one cried out, and grabbed at her arms, as if to restrain her. Erika kicked the boy in the shin and shouted, "Get lost, all of you, or I'll tell on you tomorrow to your home room teacher!"

They let go of her, intimidated by her threat, for they knew that this would not sit well with their teacher, or their parents, who would hear of it for sure. Good behavior was very important at the school and within the Pioneer organization. Erika was a Pioneer leader; it was not wise to provoke her. They didn't even know what made them do it.

"You're just a stupid girl," they shouted at her as they ran off.

Erika straightened her jacket, smoothed down the pleats of her skirt, and feeling upset despite her victory, walked swiftly the last part of her route home. She was aware that boys were drawn to her, but they seemed to prefer fighting with her instead of admitting their attraction. She didn't know what she could do about it except to chase them off and threaten to tell on them.

She wished she could do the same with Feri, who still grabbed her on occasion for his own pleasure.

Since it was winter, and heavy snowfalls and bitter cold kept Piry home at nights, he didn't have the opportunity to call Erika to his bed. But when he could, he made use of their cellar.

From the gate, before entering the house through Maria's room, there was a door to a staircase that led up to an attic and down to a cellar. They hung the laundry in the attic to dry, stored fabrics from Feri's former store, and used the spacious cellar to keep apples, potatoes, and onions. It was cool in the summer and warm enough in winter not to freeze the fresh supplies. At times, Piry would ask Feri to bring up a basketful of vegetables or apples. In turn, he'd call on Erika to come and help him gather the stuff.

On these occasions he would order Erika to face him, and pulling up her skirt, stick his erect penis between her legs. Holding her hips tightly to himself, he would move back and forth till his member would pulsate and then go limp. Then he would quickly pull his handkerchief from his pocket, wipe himself, and hand Erika the kerchief to do the same. Erika could smell a musty odor and feel a disgusting sticky liquid between her legs as she wiped her thighs. The whole thing would take just a few minutes, and afterwards they would quickly and wordlessly gather the items Piry had asked for.

On the way up, carrying the baskets, they acted as if nothing had taken place between them. Once in the house, Erika would take the first opportunity to go to the bathroom to wash and change her underwear. Feri's action disgusted her, but she thought there was no way she could reveal it to Piry, and certainly never to her sister. She could not confide in Judith, and she was afraid to say anything to her mother, for she didn't know how Piry would react or how Feri would retaliate. So, it was best for her to keep quiet.

Young as she was, Erika was keenly aware that the duplicity of her own life seemed to be the way of life in general, for most people. Maybe they didn't have a sexually predatory stepfather, but everyone had problems, and everyone always had to lie and hide their true feelings. In public, people talked as though their lives were wonderful, food plentiful, and their salaries enough to live in comfort. Yet everyone knew that most people's lives were exactly the opposite. They barely existed on their meager paychecks, barely had enough food, and resided in crowded quarters. Many unrelated families had to share an apartment because there was a lack of new housing.

However, members of the Communist Party, depending on their rank, were given apartments and homes of the formerly well-off. Or, they were lucky, as her family was, to somehow escape scrutiny and able to own a private home. Her Aunt Lilly's family could also keep owning their apartment because they worked in essential occupations. They manufactured needed chemicals. The Government rewarded the people they found useful.

Erika realized that even though 'Equality for All' was supposed to be the principle on which their lives were now built, there was no equality among them at all. She was well aware that most of her classmates were poorer than she, their parents were low-paid factory workers, and they lived in tiny apartments. But the oddest thing Erika experienced in their daily lives was the constant demand for praising their government, be it at work or at school. They all knew that if they ever made a critical comment about the political system, or the government, they would be arrested and jailed as enemies of the people.

Everyone had become so skilled at pretense that it easily carried over into their home-life as well—at least at Erika's home. Her mother pretended that Feri was a wonderful husband, Feri pretended to be a good father, and Erika pretended to be his loving daughter. Judith was the most honest person among them. She loathed Feri and never showed any affection for him. Feri in turn avoided her. They only spoke to each other if they had to, thus creating a tension between them that Piry and Erika simply ignored in order to keep the peace. Maria, the maid, was the only one who seemed always to be happy. She appeared unaware of the family dynamics. She was friendly to them all, and they all treated her with love and appreciation.

Erika thought, were it not for Maria, their lives would be in total disarray. Her mother was often out in the afternoons, doing God knows what business, and it was this slender, slightly crazy woman who happily worked from dawn to dusk to keep their home clean and have food ready when they returned from school or work.

Being the youngest, Erika was often the first one to arrive home. Judith was usually at her friends' till shortly before dinner time at eight. After Erika had changed into "home clothes," so she could keep her "school clothes" clean for the week, Maria was ready to serve her lunch. Later, around five o'clock, after Erika had done her homework, she would go to the kitchen where Maria was busy cooking dinner, and announce, "I'm hungry."

"I can make you a couple of fried toasts," Maria would offer and a few minutes later she would bring the snack to Erika, who was sitting with a book in the day room.

"I learned to make this in London," Maria said, the first time she prepared it for Erika.

"I used to make it for the King's children. It's so easy to do, you should learn how. Just take a piece of bread, rub it with garlic and quick fry it on both sides in a little bit of cooking oil."

"I like it when you make it," Erika patted Maria's hand, dismissing her remark about serving it to the royal children, as part of her mental illness. "Thank you. I'll come and help you when I'm done eating."

"It's all right, you just study," Maria would respond and return to the kitchen.

This was Erika's favorite time of the day when she could lose herself in a story and be somewhere totally different from her own life.

◉◉◉

On a Friday in November, Piry had received a postcard from Dr. Komlós, to come to his hospital office on the following Wednesday, at 2 p.m. It was a bitter cold day, and Budapest was blanketed by a sad gray sky. Piry pulled her black wool coat tightly around herself as she got off the streetcar close to the hospital where Komlós worked. She knew that this time was his usual lunch break, so she hurried into the building. He was just coming out of the elevator and met Piry at the nurses' station.

"How nice to see you!" Dr. Komlós exclaimed, as if it hadn't been at his invitation that she had come. Without letting her remove her coat, he added, "Let's go have lunch." And he led Piry out of the hospital to his favorite restaurant nearby.

"You look lovely," he observed, when she removed her overcoat to reveal a smart light blue wool suit, with a body-hugging jacket and matching skirt. She kept the small, blue-gray hat on top of her dark blonde curls.

"You don't look too bad yourself," Piry smiled at him, noting that he had left his white doctor's coat at the hospital, and was wearing a well-tailored dark brown suit. His hair was turning salt and pepper, making him look distinguished.

"Why, thank you," he smiled. Although there had never been any kind of sexual overtone to their relationship, they admired each other, and over the post-war years had kept up a comfortable friendship. After they settled at their table, he ordered stuffed cabbage, which was this restaurant's specialty; large cabbage leaves filled with ground beef and rice that had been stewed with sauerkraut and bay leaves to give it a tangy flavor. It was accompanied by boiled potatoes to balance the sourness.

"Oh, I forgot, you eat only kosher meat," Dr. Komlós exclaimed after the waiter had left and he saw Piry eyeing the food.

"It's okay, you can have the meat, I'll eat the cabbage and potatoes," Piry smiled at him, and skillfully unrolled the cabbage leaves, placing the meatball on his plate. "I assume you didn't ask me for lunch just to see me," she added, during her maneuvering the food.

"Why, you know I would do that, but actually you're right," he grinned at her. "This time I also have some news for you."

They started to eat, first chatting about their families as was the polite thing to do, and then Dr. Komlós asked, "Are you still thinking about getting out?"

Taken by surprise, Piry quickly swallowed her food, as she replied, "Yes, if we could do it safely."

"I met a Hungarian born American citizen who has come back to look for a wife. He is setting up a business in New York and needs capital. I told him about you and your girls, and he was very interested."

Piry smiled pensively, "For a fee of course."

"Yes. Of course."

"How much?"

"Six thousand dollars for the three of you."

Piry swallowed hard, "That's probably my total savings abroad. Would he accept payment in forints? I could easily do that here."

Six thousand dollars converted into forints was more than a year's salary for a factory worker. Piry did not flinch at offering such a large sum and Komlós did not ask how she had come to have that much cash. People, even friends, never asked about each other's finances, because they knew if people had money beyond the meager salaries the state paid them, they had to be involved in some sort of "black marketing". Just knowing about it and not reporting it to the authorities could land a person in jail, not to mention the fate of the one who actually engaged in illegal transactions. By not discussing it they knew nothing, and all were safe.

"I'll find out for you before I'll introduce you to him." was all Komlós said.

◎◉◎

A week later, Piry told her daughters to come back from school directly, because she wanted them to meet a friend of hers. When Judith and Erika got home, their mother was sitting in the living with a stranger, talking in low tones. He stood up immediately, and smiling, extended his right hand to shake hands with each girl. Erika noted that he was so tall he had to stoop his shoulders to be able to look them in the eye. He had nice blue eyes and very black hair. Judith judged his smile as pleasant but somehow phony.

While they shook hands, Piry made the introductions, "This is Mr. Antal Molnár, and these are my daughters, Judith and Erika."

Then they all sat down, with the girls looking at Piry for an explanation as to why they had to meet this man.

"Mr. Molnár lives in America. He is visiting here." Piry said.

"Would you like to go to America?" he asked them with a broad smile.

Judith and Erika exchanged quick glances, as if saying to each other, *"Is this man out of his mind? Who, in Hungary would say anything good about America openly, much less express a desire to go there?"* and kept silent, staring at him.

Piry, quickly realizing the reason for her daughters' reaction, said soothingly, "It's all right, you don't have to answer that…how was school today?" She skillfully led the conversation to neutral topics, such as the courses they were studying.

But as if totally ignorant of the political situation in the country, Mr. Molnár asked, "What foreign language are you two studying? English, I hope?"

The girls exchanged glances again before Erika blurted out, "No, we're studying Russian! English is not taught at school. It's the language of capitalist countries!"

Now it was the adults who exchanged glances. An awkward silence ensued, then Piry said, "All right, you two, run along, go start on your homework."

She stayed in the living room, continuing talking with Molnár in low voices.

He explained, "I wanted to leave Hungary in a couple of weeks. But if you could wind up your affairs and come with me as my wife, I could wait another two weeks for you and the girls."

"This is a bit sudden for me," Piry responded. "I'd have to look into marriage laws and getting passports for us to go with you may take more time. I'm not sure what story the government would believe about our sudden marriage."

"We could always cook one up, like we met as children and loved each other, and now meeting again, we fell in love again!" He grinned.

"We'd have to have met during the war, when I was in hiding with the girls with Christian papers, or the whole story could be researched and proven false," Piry said pensively.

"Or we met now, during my current trip, and fell madly in love," he countered. "The simpler the story, the better, I think."

"You may be right."

"We'll have to start seeing more of each other."

"Yes," Piry replied, her mind racing over her obligations for the coming weeks.

He handed her a business card. "Here is my name and local phone number. Call me when you have time to meet, and I'll make myself available. Or do you have a number that I could call?"

"No, ordinary people like me don't have home phones yet. I'll look into the legal proceedings, and as soon as I have the information, I'll call you."

He looked a little uncomfortable as he said, "You know of course, that the funds would have to be deposited into my bank account before we get married."

"Of course." Piry looked at him, feeling somewhat uneasy about this aspect of the arrangement, but she did not let on. "We can discuss the details next time we see each other. By then we'll also know more as to how to proceed."

She escorted him out of the house without asking the girls to say good-bye to him. At the gate, he suddenly leaned down and gave Piry a quick kiss on the cheek.

"Just for good measure," he grinned.

Piry locked the gate after him and leaned against it, to think over the situation before she went into the house. *I wonder if this will work. I wonder if I can trust him. He accepted taking the forints so easily; I wonder what kind of government contact he is working with here to make this happen. How do I know it's not a trap? He'll take the money from me as proof and then denounce me, so I get arrested as an "enemy of the people." I'll have to find out more about him from Komlós.*

◎⦿◎

Piry didn't have to contact Komlós about Molnár because while out on an errand, she saw a headline at a newsstand in the daily paper, Népszava. It read: New Marriage Law. The article explained that a new law had gone into effect as of that week, concerning marriage between a Hungarian citizen and a foreign national. They could marry, and the foreign citizen spouse could choose to stay in Hungary or depart to his or her homeland. However, the Hungarian citizen spouse would not be allowed to leave Hungary.

Piry was thunderstruck. Once again, a promising escape plan had fallen apart. She walked down the street to a corner phone booth and called Dr. Komlós.

"I saw today's paper," he said immediately on hearing Piry's voice.

"What do I do now?"

"Thank your lucky stars that you haven't paid him a cent yet and go on with your lives till there is another opportunity."

"He already knows?"

"Of course. He has booked his ticket back to America. He'll just have to find a rich widow or divorcée over there."

Piry could hear the grin in his voice. "Thanks again, and please don't give up on me."

"Me? Give up on you? Never!" Komlós reassured her.

◎◉◎

January and February of 1951 were unusually harsh winter months with snow piled knee high by the curbsides. Despite the freezing weather, most people could find little coal to heat their homes. Piry was grateful to Feri for stockpiling both coal and wood the summer before, through the contacts his brothers had in the moving industry. At that time, she felt like they were overpaying for the heating materials. Now she was glad they had bought them in time, for this winter people couldn't buy heating supplies at any price. Rumors had it that all the good coal went to the Soviet Union, leaving little for Hungarians.

There were other shortages as well. Soap for washing clothes was hard to come by. The usual large brick shaped pieces for household use suddenly disappeared from the stores. As of February, the government introduced the rationing of lard and sunflower seed oil, both staples of Hungarian cooking. Meat was also scarce and expensive. Kosher meats cost nearly twice as much as the regular meat prices. Piry came up with a plan.

"Could you please clean up a part of the storage shed for me this weekend?" she asked Feri. "I am going to learn how to force-feed geese and buy a couple, so we could continue to have meat on the table. That's the only way we'll manage."

Feri grunted a reluctant "Yes," thinking, *Piry is nuts but resourceful.*

Two weeks later, despite the bitter cold, Piry and Feri took a streetcar to St. István Boulevard, and then a bus across the Margit Bridge to Battyányi Square on the Buda side of the city. Located directly opposite the Hungarian Parliament building, across the Danube, Battyányi Square was named after Count Lajos Battyányi, Hungary's first Prime Minister. The square was a popular tourist attraction, due to the Roman Catholic Church of Saint Anna.

Built by the Jesuits between 1740 and 1762, it was one of Budapest's most beautiful baroque churches.

But Piry and Feri were not going sightseeing at the square. Their mission was a visit to the market hall, also located on Battyányi Square. It was renowned for selling livestock, such as chickens, ducks, and geese.

They returned home by taxi, carrying two wicker baskets, each with a young, snow-white goose sitting inside, under a cover. They had also bought several large bags of husked yellow corn to feed the geese.

Before bringing the geese home, Piry had bought two large enamel bowls to use as feeding dishes. Once the geese were settled into their individual cages in the storage shed, Piry went into the house to prepare their food. In her kitchen, she filled the bowls first with corn, then drizzled cooking oil over the corn, mixing it by hand to make sure all the kernels were coated. Then she filled the bowls with water to soak the corn overnight.

"The corn will soften and puff up and will be easier to digest," she explained to Erika, who watched her mother's activity with interest.

The next morning, Piry got up at 5:30 a.m. She put on two wool pullovers and wore over them a lamb fur-lined beige leather vest. She had also bought this at the market, for she knew, it would be bitter cold outside at the early hour she had to feed the geese. In the shed where the geese were, she sat down on a small stool she had set up earlier and placed one of the corn-filled bowls to her left. Then she opened the cage and lifted the first goose into her lap.

Prior to buying the geese, Piry had gone for several days to the market to learn from the woman who would sell her the geese, how to "force feed" them. The woman had explained to Piry that "Without force-feeding, the geese would not fatten up. Plus, they would need a grassy field to roam on to find their own food."

So, Piry learned how to force-feed. It wasn't easy. First, she had to position the goose securely in her lap, holding it tight against herself with her right arm. Then, with her right hand she had to hold open the goose's beak. Taking a handful of corn with her left hand, she had to find the right opening in the bird's throat. She had to make sure that the corn went down its throat to the gullet, not the trachea that led to its lung. If that happened, the bird would not be able to breathe and would choke to death.

Jews were not allowed to eat animals that died unless they had been killed ritually by the shochet, a man, especially trained for the job. So, if the goose died mid-feeding, it would have be sold or given away. Piry wasn't thrilled about force-feeding the geese, but this was the only way she could ensure her family's meat supply in these trying times. Oddly, the geese didn't seem to mind. The woman at the market warned her that once a goose had been fed this way, it would not eat again on its own.

Erika came to watch the evening feeding and Piry explained to her how it had to be done.

"I'm sorry, I can't let you try it, because geese are expensive, and we can't risk making a mistake with their feeding."

"I understand," Erika said, but stayed to watch. "How do you know how much corn to give it?"

Piry showed Erika a bulging pocket inside the end of the goose's neck. "It's called the crop, and the corn first goes in there, so when it's full, like this one is getting to be, then I stop."

"Why is it going there first?"

"Geese have this extra pocket, so they can store food there, like a pantry, and pass it down to their gizzard, or stomach, to be digested slowly. This way they can survive if they don't find food all the time."

"That's fascinating! I can write about this for my biology class homework," Erika grinned, then added, "of course I won't say that I learned this because my mother keeps geese at our house."

"Tell them you read about it," Piry smiled at her daughter.

"You're amazing," Erika said, as her mother had finished feeding the birds, and then let them walk about in the garden for a few minutes before returning them to their cages.

"Actually, I don't enjoy doing this. But I do what is necessary," Piry responded gravely.

The lesson was not lost on Erika.

◉◉◉

On a chilly Wednesday in March, when there was still snow on the ground, Piry and Maria heard a frantic ringing of the bell at the gate. It was not even eight o'clock in the morning. Feri had gone to work, and the children had left for school a half an hour before. Piry and Maria had just began cleaning the house together. They froze, and Piry cautiously peered out the living room window.

"It's my sister!" she exclaimed, surprised. "Keep working," she told Maria, and rushed to the gate.

Lilly stumbled through the opening, shaking, looking totally distraught. Piry wasn't sure whether her sister was merely cold or upset about not being heard sooner.

Lilly hugged Piry tightly and whispered into her ear: "They took Károly last night, and I can't stop trembling."

"Come inside!" Deeply shocked, Piry wrapped her arm around her sister's shoulders and led her into the warm dining room. "When? Tell me what happened?"

"I can't get over it," Lilly collapsed into a chair and burst into tears burying her face in her palms.

Piry waited patiently.

Lilly lifted her tear-streaked face. "You know, we used to joke that if someone rang the bell at 4 a.m. and it was the milkman, it was good news. Well, when the bell rang at Károly's house at 4 a.m. it wasn't the milkman. Two AVO men stood there and gave him half an hour to gather his things and say good-bye to his wife.

As soon as they left, Klara called Martin and Donald, and they both told her to stay calm, they'll do what they can. But she couldn't give them any information, since she had no idea where they had taken him or why—they wouldn't say, no matter how many times she asked before they left with Károly."

"Now what?" Piry urged Lilly to go on, completely shaken by the news.

"Donald told Klara to go to work and act as if nothing had happened. As you know, Klara works as a dental technician and Donald warned her, not to spread the news among her co-workers. He told her that he and Martin will also show up at work as if nothing had happened. But that was a good thing, because through their contacts at the Ministry of Industry, they could make discreet inquiries as to where Károly had been taken.

As soon as Donald left for work and the maid showed up so I could leave Timmy with her, I came to see you." Lilly's eyes filled with tears again. "I'm terrified that tomorrow or the next day they'll come for Donald, or Martin, or both. What do I do?"

Piry noticed the time on the wall clock in the dining room. It was only 9 a.m. It crossed her mind that maybe Lilly was being watched and followed to her house, thereby endangering them as well. But she didn't say this out loud; instead, she pushed the concern out of her mind and said to Lilly:

"You'll do exactly what everyone else in the family is doing. You go home, get to work, and pretend that nothing had happened."

Lilly stared at her older sister. "You're crazy! How can we pretend that nothing had happened when we all know what did!"

"Come, have some coffee and a krémes and you'll come to your senses without me having to explain things."

Lilly sipped her double espresso, and filled her mouth with the delicious pastry, as if she had never eaten before. Then she shook her head and said, swallowing hard, "We must all be crazy in this country."

Piry shrugged. "Only if you don't know the difference between reality and pretense. As long as you know that to survive, pretense is the spoken reality, and the truth is not to be discussed, you're okay. Lilly, you've got a son at home. Make sure he grows up with you, instead of in a state sponsored institute while you're serving a sentence somewhere. Go home and take care of him."

Lilly forced a bitter smile. "Thanks, big sister."

Four months later, in early June, Klara got a postcard from Károly. He was at a work camp about an hour's train ride from Budapest. "You can come visit me next Sunday," he wrote.

Károly's two brothers, Donald and Martin, their wives, and even his sister, Violeta, all helped Klara put some practical food items together, such as 'winter salami' and cheese both of which could be kept for a long time at room temperature. Klara also packed a change of clothing for Károly.

The brothers escorted Klara to the train station and smiled as she waved through the window when the train began to move. That was the last they saw of her, or their brother, or even knew of their whereabouts for the ensuing three years.

By now everyone was whispering about the 'resettlement program' the government instituted in earnest. What happened to Károly and Klara, or to the neighbors across the street from Piry's house, were not isolated incidents. The Hungarian government had begun a systematic 'resettlement' of formerly wealthy people, labeling them "exploiters". The AVO came for them mostly at night, and took them either to a work camp, or forced them to live in villages. There, they were crammed into the homes of formerly well to do farmers, whom they also labeled "exploiters of the people". Since even wealthy farmers' homes consisted only of a 'best room' and a bedroom or two, when peasant families were forced to take into their homes these "undesirable city families," living conditions became extremely difficult for all of them. To top it off, there was a social stigma attached to both the host families and the newcomers, due to their undesirable political classification."

Piry often wondered whether the Mikós's, her postwar village family, met the same fate as other well-to-do peasants. But there was no way for her to find out. She was afraid to write to them lest she bring disaster to her own doorsteps. If they were under surveillance, or house arrest, their mail would be opened and read by local communist party commissariat personnel, before it arrived to them. Then even if she had put no return address, they would ask the Mikós who sent them the postcard. If he didn't tell them right away, they would torture him till he confessed even sins he never committed, let alone Piry's name. *This is just like hiding from the Nazis, in plain sight, she thought, the best we can all do is stay low, and hope to survive. Better to just tend to the family's needs and forget the outside world as much as it's possible,* Piry concluded.

Piry's foremost concern during June was Erika's health. Since Piry had been able to give her a home instead of keeping her at the orphanage, Erika's health had improved greatly. She had suffered less often from colds and almost never had an upset stomach. The one exception was her frequent complaint about a sore throat. Gargling with hot salt water and an aspirin or two could always cure that. However, just before her final exams for the year, at the end of June, she came down with a serious bout of sore throat, this time accompanied by high fever. Alarmed, Piry took her to the family doctor, who looked at her throat and declared, "Her tonsils must come out. They're full of puss and will affect her heart if we don't remove them."

"Can't I at least get through my exams," Erika croaked, "I'll have to repeat the year if I don't take the exams."

The doctor looked at Erika's pleading expression, then at Piry, and shrugged.

"I guess a week or two won't kill her." He scribbled a prescription, and handed it to Piry as he said, "Make an appointment at the hospital for the day after she's done at school."

He instructed Erika to take the medicine he prescribed and to continue her routine of aspirins and gargling every chance she had, so her condition wouldn't worsen.

Erika's proudly brought home an "all 5" report card. But her celebration of the end of the school year was overshadowed by knowing that the following morning she was due at the hospital by 7 a.m.

It was a large, antiseptic-looking building. The white tile floors were immaculate, nurses walked around in white dresses and white aprons with white starched kerchiefs covering their hair. An elderly, heavyset woman sitting behind a reception desk asked about their business.

Piry explained, and the woman put a checkmark by Erika's name on her list of patients to be admitted for treatment that day. Then a nurse came for Erika and told Piry to leave. She wasn't allowed into the wing where the surgery was to take place.

"She'll be in the recovery room by noon," the nurse informed Piry.

After a quick hug, whispering to Erika, "Be brave," Piry left with a heavy heart. Since the war, she never felt at ease when Erika or Judith was away from her, though she knew she couldn't tether them to herself. They were growing up and soon will be teens with their own need for indepence. But Erika was only eleven years old, and being on her own for this surgery could not be easy for her. Piry had made no other commitments for the day, so that she could return to the hospital by noon.

Left with the nurse, Erika was directed into a small changing room. She was told to remove all her clothes except her panties. She was handed a white hospital gown to put on, that closed in the back with several strings to be tied into knots. Then the nurse had left. When Erika was ready, she sat down on a bench against the wall and waited. It wasn't long before another nurse, dressed in all white, with a facemask hanging from a string around her neck, came for her. The nurse was pretty, with large blue eyes, but she had pulled her chestnut brown hair into a tight bun so that not a hair was out of place, and it gave her a humorless look. She held a tablet with a piece of paper on it.

She looked at Erika, "Tell me your name,"

"Erika Fábián"

"Your age?"

"Eleven."

"Birth date?"

"June 6, 1940."

"Your address?"

Erika gave it to her, wondering why the nurse was asking all these questions. "My mother had provided all this information already when she had checked me into the hospital," she blurted out.

"We just want to be sure you're the right patient," the nurse finally smiled at her. "Now come with me."

She led Erika gently by her shoulder into a large room that to Erika smelled horrible with some pungent odor. It was also freezing cold in the room. The nurse directed her to the far end of the room and told her to sit in a white leather chair that had a tall back and arm rests. It also had wide leather straps. The nurse put a strap around Erika's waist and another over her thighs and fastened them tightly but not uncomfortably. She tied Erika's wrists to the chair's arm rests.

"Why are you tying me up? Erika asked with considerable concern.

"This is so you won't move around during surgery," the nurse explained as did a final check of the tightness of the straps.

There were a couple of other nurses moving about the room. Some were by the glass cabinets along the walls, taking things out. One of them came over to Erika, holding up a syringe with a long needle. She was a tall, skinny woman, and her dark hair was also pulled back into a smooth bun.

"Good morning," she said cheerfully, "I'll be giving you an injection which will ensure that you won't feel anything during the surgery. I'll be injecting it into your throat," she explained breezily. "You will feel just a little sting and then nothing. So, put your head back, sit very still, and open your mouth for me, wide."

Erika did as she was instructed. The nurse leaned forward, and her fingers forced Erika's mouth to open more as she thrust the needle into Erika's throat in the back. The pain was excruciating, and Erika let out a blood-curling scream. The tall nurse quickly pulled the needle out. The other nurses in the room froze for a moment, as they turned to stare at Erika.

"I'm sorry," said the nurse, then quickly turned toward the others in the room and shook her head, "It's nothing, she'll be fine in a minute."

A doctor arrived and headed directly to Erika. He looked to be around forty, his head was covered with a white cap, and he wore a long-sleeved white coat. His intense black eyes smiled at Erika, "Were you the one letting out that awful scream?" he asked, almost jovially.

"Yes," Erika whispered. "The nurse hurt me."

"Well, of course an injection will hurt. But the stuff in the injection will numb your throat, and then it won't hurt any more. We have to give you three more injections, the one in the back you just got, and one on each side of your throat, so we can take those nasty tonsils out that always make you sick. So be a good girl and open your mouth wide."

Erika did as she was told, feeling intimidated by the doctor's powerful presence. He took the syringe from the nurse and helping to open Erika's mouth wider with his fingers, swiftly stuck the needle into Erika's throat. Again, the pain was excruciating, and unable to control herself, Erika screamed. Startled, the doctor quickly pulled the needle out of her mouth, leaned back and stared at Erika. Then he said coldly, "You scream again, and you'll see what will happen. Now open your mouth."

Erika sniffed a bit but obeyed. Her throat was burning from the fluid they had injected worse than the pain from the infection. The doctor took the next syringe from the nurse, and stuck Erika in the throat, hard. Erika screamed at the top of her voice. The doctor quickly pulled the needle out, and snapped at the nurse, "Get this brat out of here. I can't work like this."

The nurse swiftly unlatched all the ties around Erika. It seemed as if she were barely able to hide a smirk as she said, "We'll take you to your room now, and the doctor will decide what to do with you."

At noon Piry had arrived at Erika's room. Erika was lying in bed, reading a novel she had brought with her about Soviet pioneers during World War II. Except for a very sore throat, she was comfortable and did not care that the doctor had thrown her out of the operating theater.

"How did it go? Are you in pain? Look, I brought you vanilla ice-cream. Your favorite," Piry chattered cheerfully.

"I didn't have the surgery," Erika croaked. Her throat felt really raw, and she preferred not to talk.

"What happened?" Piry was shocked.

"The doctor threw me out of the operating room because I screamed when he was injecting me in the throat. He was really hurting me."

Piry looked pensively at her daughter. "Was he going to take out your tonsils with just numbing the area?"

"I think so. That's what they told me. That it wouldn't hurt after the injections took effect. But it did even after the first injection.

Piry grinned. "Well, eat the ice cream anyway. I'll go talk to the doctor."

Erika recognized her mother's tone. Piry was not going to take "no" for an answer. She wondered whether her mother had a spare envelope in her handbag or was just going to slip a few of hundred forints into the doctor's palm as she shook hands with him, assuring that he would perform Erika's surgery in the most painless way possible.

The next day, a nurse woke Erika early in the morning and walked her back to the operating area. After she had changed from her pajamas into the white hospital gown, the nurse said, "We're putting you to sleep today, so you won't feel a thing when the doctor takes out your tonsils."

She was instructed climb up and lie on her back on a hard, padded table. They put a light blanket over her body and a freezing cold mask over her mouth and nose.

"Take a deep breath," the nurse's voice instructed her from what seemed to Erika, a great distance away. She inhaled the pungent smell of the mask and exhaled.

"Again," she heard the nurse's voice from even further.

By the third breath Erika was barely conscious, and by the fourth she no longer felt anything. Her last conscious awareness was sinking into a deep, freezing cold, black space.

Then she came to, in the bed of her hospital room. As Erika opened her eyes, she saw Piry sitting by her side, smiling, "It's all done," she assured Erika.

Erika wanted to say she didn't remember a thing, but her throat felt like the raw meat they used to feed Maczko for dinner at Feri's store. Except that this raw flesh was in her throat, hot and burning. The acute pain made her gasp for air.

"It's all right, don't talk," Piry soothed her, caressing her arm. I brought you more ice cream."

Erika shook her head and closed her eyes. She couldn't swallow a thing.

"You sleep now," Piry said gently. "I'll have them put the ice cream in the icebox and you can have it when you wake up."

Erika squeezed her mother's fingers and shut her eyes. She slipped into sleep unaware of when her mother had left.

The feeling of raw flesh and burning pain in her throat made Erika cranky during her first days in the hospital. She refused to eat anything but cold pudding and ice cream, since she found swallowing an ordeal. Even liquids, such as cool chamomile tea and cold milk hurt her as she slowly drank, being watched by a nurse. *How does she know that I would toss it right down the sink?* Erika thought. But by the fourth day her throat felt better, and by the time Piry came to pick her up on the sixth day, her throat felt almost normal.

"Now you won't get those horrible colds anymore," Piry said with satisfaction, as they sat on the streetcar on their way home.

CHAPTER 14

WHAT WILL I DO THE rest of the summer? Am I going to Uncle Ede's village again? Erika asked.

"We haven't heard from them at all, not even a postcard," Piry replied. She didn't share with Erika her thoughts as to why this may be.

Erika was smart, though at times careless. "Maybe they were moved from their village," she whispered.

"Hush," Piry snapped at her.

Erika gave her a knowing glance, and they continued the rest of the journey home in silence.

Erika didn't know what her mother had in mind for her, but trying to envision a summer without being in the village was difficult for her. However, she didn't have to worry too long. Two activities awaited her for this summer. One was the usual demand by Piry to help clean fruits and vegetables so they could be preserved for the winter. The other was a welcome new activity. She was allowed to go to the same public pool Judith had been enjoying with her friends.

The first few times Erika tagged along with Judith, so she could familiarize herself with the streetcar route that took them there. Judith also helped her obtain a season pass and showed her where the changing rooms were. They had lockers with locks in which they could leave their street clothes. Once in bathing suits, with their towel hanging over their shoulders, Judith led her to the pool area.

"There is the wading pool for younger kids and non-swimmers," she pointed to her right, "and there is the big pool for swimmers," she indicated to her left. "Make sure you wash your feet before entering either pool; the lifeguards are really strict about that and will throw you out if you forget to do it. Now I'm going off to meet my friends, and you'll probably find some of your school friends here somewhere. I'll meet you in the changing room at 4:30. After we get dressed, we'll head home together. The pool closes at five."

Erika felt a bit intimidated being left on her own in this vast playground with pools. But at the same time, she was relieved to be out of her sister's domineering presence. She felt confident that she could swim in the big pool and headed toward it.

"Erika, hey Erika! Here!" she heard laughing voices calling her and to her delight she spotted two of her schoolmates waving at her. They were sitting on a blanket on the grass by the large pool. Erika headed for them.

"What are you doing here? We've never seen you at this pool before!" they said in greeting and moved over on their blanket to make room for Erika.

"Szervusz, (Hi) Dora, szervusz, (Hi) Ida," Erika greeted them enthusiastically. "So glad to see you here! I'm spending this summer at home, not with my relatives in their village."

"Nice. How come this is first time you've come?"

"I had my tonsils removed right after school ended, so I couldn't come till I healed."

"Now you'll be here every day? We are! Can you swim?"

"Yes. Not terribly well, but I can."

"Oh, Erika can't swim terribly well! I'm shocked that there is something you don't do terribly well," Dora teased her. "

"In her case it's probably just false modesty," Ida teased her, grinning.

They laughed, and Erika protested, "No, really, I am not a good swimmer!"

"Well, by the end of the summer you will be, because all we do here is swim and play in the water," Dora assured her.

Erika found not only Dora and Ida at the pool over the summer but also several of her other schoolmates. They met daily, and she no longer depended on coming with Judith, but arrived on her own, at prearranged time with her friends. They swam, played games in the pool, and lay in the sun till they were tanned bronze. It was a happy, peaceful time for Erika.

Boys from their school also came to this swimming pool, and Erika even found their daily teasing harassment kind of exciting. There were several boys who followed Erika and her girlfriends, sprinkled them with ice cold water when they were lying in the hot sun or bumped into them on purpose in the water when they were all swimming laps. Secretly, Erika really liked one of the boys.

He was tall, slim, had a shock of curly brown hair, and a very attractive face with large brown eyes that occasionally locked into hers. When they did, Erika felt a small bolt of electricity go through her body. She had no idea why this happened but was keenly aware that this boy stood out from his group, at least for her. He was not one of her schoolmates but was friends with the ones that were. Erika heard them call him Tomy. That's all she knew about him but seeing him around made her afternoons by the pool exciting.

One afternoon in August, as Erika and her friends were about to jump into the pool, Tomy, and two of his friends, rushed to them and grabbing Erika, Tomy locked his powerful hands over Erika's arms, and the two others grabbed her ankles. They lifted her off the ground and stepping to the edge of the pool swung her, shouting, "One, Two, Three," and tossed her into the deep end. Sinking to the bottom, Erika flayed her arms and legs wildly to surface for air.

She was both shocked and infuriated by the surprise assault. By the time Erika surfaced, her girlfriends, as well as the three boys, were circling in the water to make sure that she did come up unharmed. When Erika saw them, she leapt straight for Tomy, shouting, "You bastard!"

He let her catch him, and they wrestled in the water, amidst encouraging shouts from his friends and hers. Erika felt frustrated by Tomy's superior strength but also exhilarated by the physical contact with him. He effortlessly pinned her arms behind her, and as their legs treaded water to stay afloat, he pulled her close, so their bodies were touching.

"Let me go!" Erika clamored, struggling against him, keenly aware of the excitement she felt by the contact with him.

"What did you call me?" he asked, holding her closer.

"I called you what you are, a bastard," Erika responded.

"Take it back or I won't let you go!"

"Oh, yes, you will," Erika protested, "all three of you are bastards, how dare you throw me in!" She leaned her head forward and bit his shoulder.

He let go of her, "You're a little wildcat!" he exclaimed, as he clutched at his shoulder.

"You deserved that!" Erika shouted and quickly swam away from him.

The others around them laughed, and Erika's girlfriends encircled her, as if to protect her.

The boys surrounded Tomy. "C'mon, she's not worth fighting," one of them said, and pulling Tomy along they all swam to the other end of the pool.

The girls clambered out of the water.

"You are so brave!" Ida patted Erika's shoulder.

"I had no choice," Erika shrugged, secretly proud that she was able to defend herself.

◎◉◎

Then Erika got her period and had to stay at home for four days. She was glum those days and just wanted to sit with a book in the coolness created by the semi-closed blinds of the 'children's room'. The following week it rained every day, and Erika's mood got worse.

Observing her Piry, asked Erika to come and watch her iron the sheets and tablecloths from the week's laundry. "You need to learn how to do this," she told Erika.

"I don't care," Erika shrugged as she stood there observing her mother skillfully rotate the iron around corners, smoothing out even the slightest creases.

"So, who is the boy?" Piry asked, not looking up from her work.

Erika blushed to the roots of her auburn hair, "What boy?"

"You must be in love, or you wouldn't be so miserable about not being able to go swimming," Piry explained in an even tone.

Erika fell silent. Her mother's words hit on a truth that had never even entered her mind. She read about being in love in books. But it had not occurred to her that her own mood swings of elation and despair might mean that she was in love.

She was able to return to the pool the last two weeks of August. Erika and her girlfriends and the group of boys eyed each other but stayed at a distance. It was a curious thing, as if having thrown Erika into the pool had broken some sort of spell among them. There was no more teasing, just keeping an eye on what each group was doing but not joining their activities. When the girls were swimming, the boys sat at the pool's edge, watching. When they came out of the water, the boys jumped in.

At the end of the month the pool was shut down for the season.

◎◎◎

The girls and the boys all started school the first week in September. Tomy attended a different school, and Erika became too busy to even think about him. Her mind was on her studies and to comply with the socio-political demands by her school in order to stay on the top student list.

Erika liked being back at school. She and her classmates had been moved to a different room from the previous year, but her homeroom teacher, Mrs. Emma Weiss, stayed with them. It was customary to keep the same homeroom teacher from age 6 to 12, throughout all the elementary school years. Once again, at the start of the school year a welcoming assembly was held for the entire student body.

Erika was assigned to read a patriotic poem about their homeland. She also had to write a brief introduction before reciting the poem by heart. Now she stood on stage, glanced at her introductory note, and then at the audience. The entire student body and faculty had their eyes on her. She smiled at them and began:

"First, we give thanks to Comrade Rákosi and Comrade Stalin, our wise leaders, for giving us the opportunity to receive such a great education; a privilege we must not take lightly. These years at school will prepare us for becoming productive, useful members of our great socialist society."

She was about to go on to recite the poem but had to stop because of the thunderous applause that followed her introduction. She modestly looked down but could barely keep from grinning because a joke she had recently heard had popped into her head while she waited for the clapping to stop. She knew that the applause was not for her delivery but the flowery words she used to praise their leaders, and the political system under which they lived.

The joke she overheard Feri tell Piry, was about watching a film at a movie theater. It was customary to show a half hour of news on a variety of subjects, before the feature film. The joke went: "One of the newsreels was about the opening of a new factory, attended by Comrade Rákosi, the prime minister of Hungary. When he appeared on the screen, the whole audience erupted into applause, except for a short, bald man, sitting in the center. He had just turned to his wife next to him, and whispered, "See, how my people love me?" when he felt someone tapping on his shoulder. The man sitting behind him whispered, "Hey, baldy, you had better clap too, or they'll haul you away!"

This applause is just like the one in the joke, Erika thought, as she listened to it dying down. Just as it did, she delivered the poem with her well-rehearsed performance. Then she quickly left the stage during the enthusiastic applause. Were her schoolmates applauding her delivery? Some of them might have been.

But mostly it was for the poem, praising their wonderful life which they had to applaud.

Erika felt comfortable with this "double think," saying one thing and thinking something totally different. The phrase had been coined by someone and had spread like a swift underground river.

In the fall of 1952, a new dress code had been introduced in grade schools, and Erika was happy about it. All girls had to wear a dark blue apron that covered the outfit which they wore to school. Plus, all students, over the age of ten, had to wear their red pioneer scarf, like a necktie. The apron was obligatory so as to eliminate any kind of clothing rivalry among the girls at school.

Erika loved its equalizing effect because she was keenly aware that her custom-made clothes were better than most of her schoolmates. She knew it was wiser to blend in than to stick out among her working-class companions. Proof of how well Erika played this role was that soon after school began, Erika was elected once again as head of the three pioneer units of her classroom.

Her school always participated in the observance of honoring the Great October Revolution which had given birth to the Soviet Union. But due to the heavy rainfall this day, students at her school did not march to the Heroes' Plaza at the center of Budapest. Instead, they held a formal assembly.

Erika sang in the choir and recited a poem praising the Soviet revolution which in turn gave Hungary a chance to become a part of the Union of Socialist Republics. She enjoyed performing and loved the fervor the celebration created. The 'secret observer' of her mind wondered how they could all keep a straight face while praising their oppressive government—but they all did.

In October, on another cold and rainy day, a different kind of celebration was held by Piry and Feri. Radio Free Europe began to broadcast in Hungarian. Nightly, when they thought Judith and Erika and the maid Maria, were asleep, they shut the doors to the dining room and huddled by the radio, listening to "real news" that came crackling through a short-wave station.

"Let's not forget to always return to Radio Kossuth or Radio Petőfi, when we're done" Feri warned Piry, while he tried to fine tune the station for better sound.

It was through these late-night broadcasts that they learned about the terrible labor camp of Recsk, where six hundred people were being held prisoners as "politically undesirable". Additionally, over four thousand "politically unreliable" young men in their twenties had been conscripted to serve in army supply units for heavy labor.

The broadcast also described the methodical resettlement of "former exploiters." The radio reporter explained: "There are three kinds of resettlements. The mildest form is when they order the apartment owners to get out and find another place to live because the government deemed them unworthy of their present home.

"The second type is more punitive; the family has to leave not only their home but also give up residing in Budapest. The third is the hardest. They actually arrest the hapless owners, and either send them to a work camp, or if their case is milder, place them into villages. They must live there under a deliberately created "social stigma." They are assigned to move in with so-called "kulak" families, (formerly rich peasants) thus punishing those people as well.

The peasants and their new tenants are forced to live under crowded conditions in the tiny village houses. These generally consist of a kitchen, a "good room," which is used for visitors, and one or two bedrooms where everyone sleeps. There are no indoor toilets or even running water in these houses. They're lucky, if there is a well in the yard.

"The so-called "exploiters," now sharing peasant homes, had been the top industrialists, professionals, and intellectuals of the country. Now they are considered "enemies of the new working class" society. In Budapest alone more than twelve-hundred people have been forced out of their homes."

Piry and Feri would sit in stunned silence at hearing these detailed reports. It wasn't as if they had been unaware of what was going on in the country. Their neighbors across the street had been "taken away." So were their own relatives, Károly and his wife, Klára. But when Radio Free Europe talked about what was going on, these were no longer isolated incidents or guesswork. '

"I wonder where poor Károly and Klára are," Piry sighed, as they re-set the radio to the official Kossuth station before shutting it off.

"Be glad you're here and not with them" quipped Feri, with his usual gallows humor.

Piry nodded and gave him a smile. She thought about her friend Irén Goldberg, who had disappeared from her apartment, and of her friends the

Mikós in Kakuk Village. But it was better not to dwell on these thoughts. She had geese to feed early in the morning, and bread to bake to supplement the meager supply they could buy with their ration cards, in bakeries. It was best to get a night's sleep.

◎◉◎

Early December, in a surprise move, the government ended the rationing system. Once again people could buy as much food and bread as they wanted, provided they could afford the new, increased prices.

"If they don't screw you one way, they find another way," grumbled Feri to Piry, as he swung his lunch bag over his shoulder.

"You're right," Piry smiled appeasing him, then added, "But look at it this way: now that we can buy enough bread at the bakeries, we have one less thing to deal with. We're saving on the gas it took to bake bread at home, not to mention having had to buy the flour on the black market."

"You always have a sunny way of looking at things," Feri grumbled, and left for work.

"I loved the bread you baked," Erika piped up as she was leaving for school. Grabbing her "10 a.m. snack bag," she added, grinning, "But I also love the sourdough the bakery makes."

"You'll have to put on the stove when you get home," Piry reminded her daughter. "Maria will be out this afternoon."

"Yes, Mom," Erika skipped away, locking the big gate behind her with her own key.

There was a new government regulation that everybody had to have a job, or as the slogan said, "If you don't work you don't eat." Thus, two days a week, Maria went to work somewhere else, so she could register as having a job.

Erika didn't ask where Maria worked. All she knew was that when she got back from school, and no one else was at home, it was her job to light the fire in the ceramic dining room stove. Thus, by the time household members drifted in, that part of the house was warm.

Even in the dead of winter, with heavy snow on the ground, and minus 24 degrees Celsius, (-11.2 °Fahrenheit) during the week they only heated the dining room that served as the "day room." They slept in freezing cold bedrooms where even their faces had to be covered with their goose down duvets to keep warm. In the mornings, when Piry rolled up the wood shutters, Erika liked to see the fantastic flower designs created by the frost on the windows, like lace curtains. Looking at it, she didn't even mind shivering as she slid out of the warm bed into the freezing cold room to get dressed for school.

In the afternoons, when she got home, she would go into the house, drop her school satchel and head for the shed where the logs were stored. But first she would stop at Maczko's house, where the dog would emerge from inside, shaking his long ringlets, and trying to lick Erika's face. Then, after sufficient petting, she would open the padlock on the shed door.

For some months in the late fall, she had watched Feri chop wood, and eventually he taught her how to do it. Now she picked a log that was not too big and set it vertically on a huge round log that served as a platform for chopping. She lifted the axe sitting by the chopping block, and with careful aim for the center brought it down on the selected log. Most of the time she was able to split it in half with one strike,

then halve it again, and again. She kept cutting wood till she deemed that she had enough kindling to start the fire. She also chopped a few logs into thicker pieces, for once the sticks had burnt midway through, she had to start loading thicker pieces to keep building up the fire.

She had learned from Piry at what point she should add one or two shovels of coal to the burning wood. Thus, eventually the entire fireplace became fueled by coal that heated the room while it turned into glowing embers. Erika took pleasure in doing this work, it made her feel good that she could provide warmth for the family when they got home.

Once she got the fire going, she warmed up her lunch that had been left on the kitchen stove by her mother or Maria. Then she settled down to eat with a book propped up in front of her, to read during the meal. She usually got through at least half her homework by the time any household member showed up. These tranquil, solitary times in the house always made Erika feel at peace, ready to cope with the tension that arose once Judith and Feri came home.

Even if they didn't talk to each other, Erika could feel the stress in the air, and it made her cringe inside. She and her mother had always tried to get along, to create at least a seemingly loving atmosphere among them. They chatted about the day's events, school, or some plans for the weekend.

But as soon as Judith opened her mouth to say something, usually putting Erika down, or Feri made a critical comment about something someone was doing, the mood shattered like glass on which they all had to tiptoe so as not to get hurt. It was a relief for Erika to be sent off to bed at 10 o'clock, for then she could hide under the duvet in the cold, dark bedroom, and weave stories in her head till sleep took over.

◉◉◉

On a snow-covered Sunday morning in mid-December, right after breakfast, which they all ate together in the warm dining room, Feri looked at Erika and ordered her: "Go put on a nice dress and be quick about it."

"Why?" Erika asked, surprised.

"I'm taking you somewhere special. But get moving or we'll be late."

Erika caught the upset expression on Judith's face, and said defiantly to Feri, "I'm not going unless Judith can come too."

Surprisingly, Feri smiled at Erika, and barked, "All right, but hurry, both of you!"

Judith put on a blue velvet dress that matched her eye color, warm beige stockings, and her ankle high brown snowshoes. She slipped on her navy wool overcoat and put a blue kerchief over her head, ready to go in just a few minutes. Erika fussed about what to wear till Piry picked out the emerald green velvet dress that was one of Erika's favorites. She tied Erika's long pigtails with green satin ribbons that matched her dress color.

Then Erika declared, "I'm not wearing those horrible beige stockings" and Piry responded, "Then you're not leaving the house!"

So, Erika succumbed, because by now Judith and Feri were standing in the doorway, and Feri was shouting, "Come now or I'll leave you at home!"

Erika knew her stepfather meant business. So, she quickly pulled on the stockings. And tied the laces of her ankle high brown snowshoes. She slapped a white beret on her head, wrapped her white wool scarf around her neck, and slipped into her gray winter coat as she ran to catch up with her sister and stepfather at the gate.

They headed with quick mincing steps toward the streetcar stop, for despite the day being sunny, the streets were covered with icy snow and walking on it was slippery. After taking two different streetcars, Feri said, "Let's get off, we're here". Both girls were speechless as they gazed at the majestic building of the Opera House on the Nagykörút, the Grand Boulevard in the center of the city.

"Hurry," Feri urged them, as he rushed ahead to the box office where he had to exchange his two tickets and buy a third one for Judith so they could all sit together. For once, he didn't grumble about the cost as he led them to their box seats midway above the orchestra. They sat in the front row of the box, and Erika couldn't help leaning over the banister to gawk with amazement at the audience streaming into the theater, filling every orchestra and balcony seat.

The theater itself was a marvel to see. It had plush red velvet covered seats and carved banisters covered in gold. It looked all so elegant as people took off their coats and sat down in their Sunday best. The audience was composed mostly of children and one or two adults with them, probably their parents. *I wish Anyu could have come too*, Erika thought, but didn't dare ask Feri why she had not. Instead, she asked him, "What are we seeing?"

"You'll find out when it starts," he replied, with a teasing smile.

"Yeah, just be glad you're here," Judith snapped at Erika, for once, in support of Feri.

"Do you know what we're seeing?" Erika asked, ignoring her sister's nasty tone.

"Yes, I can read," Judith mocked her. "Didn't you see the posters as we came in?"

"I guess not," Erika admitted.

"Then wait and see."

Erika gave her sister a deprecating look and leaned back against the velvet cushion of her seat. The audience had settled down by now, and the crystal chandeliers that hung high above them were dimming. A bright spotlight illuminated the red velvet curtains that covered the stage. The orchestra pit became alive with musicians settling in; violinists gently testing their bows over the strings of their instrument. The audience fell silent, then burst into applause as the conductor came into the orchestra pit. Stepping up on his rostrum, he briefly bowed to the audience, then turned to face the musicians.

You could cut the silence with a knife, Erika thought, as the theater grew hushed with anticipation. The orchestra members were looking at the right hand of the conductor who had raised a small baton. Then the baton swung down, the conductor's left hand pointed at the musicians, and Erika recognized the opening tunes of The Nutcracker. *I've heard this on the radio a million times*, she thought, *are we going to sit here and just watch the orchestra play it?* Slowly, the red curtains glided open, and she gasped as on stage was the most marvelous living room she had ever seen. It had beautiful furniture, but what dominated the scene was a huge Christmas tree, fully decorated with gold, silver, and red balls. Erika watched as dancing children and their parents twirled on toes into the room, and she understood.

"We're seeing the Nutcracker ballet!" she whispered to Feri.

He put a finger across his lip to indicate that there was to be no talking.

Erika was transfixed by the show. She sat motionless, her eyes drinking in every step, every lift, every graceful extension of legs and arms. She had never seen anything as beautiful as this three-hour performance of a story that was part dream, part "real".

During intermission, when Feri asked if they wanted anything to eat or drink. Judith went with him to get a drink, but Erika shook her head. She didn't want anything to distract her from the vision in her mind of the dancers swirling, long after they had disappeared behind the curtain.

Somewhere in her memory she recalled an event, a time when she was dancing on stage, and a man asked her mother to let Erika go with him and study ballet. *So, this is what he wanted me to learn, how to dance like that,* she ruminated and felt a profound sense of loss for not having been permitted by her mother to go with the man. *One day I will find a way to learn to dance like that,* she promised herself and felt better.

After the theater, Feri took them to Lily and Donat's apartment, just a short streetcar ride from the Opera House. Piry was already there, and they had the main meal of the day together. Feeling high after the show, Erika entertained the family by skipping around the room, imitating the prima ballerina's movements. Her cousin, four-year-old Nandi, laughed loudly each time Erika leapt up or whirled around. This, of course, encouraged Erika to go on, till Feri finally said,

"That's enough, sit down and eat."

◎◉◎

Erika obeyed, though not without resentment for having her stepfather spoil her fun. She found it hard to understand him. First, he was so kind as to have taken her and Judith to see a ballet. After they came out of the theater, he clearly enjoyed the outpouring of thanks from Erika, and even Judith's terse "Thanks". But now his voice was raspy and harsh as he had ordered her to stop.

Erika ate quickly, then asked to be excused from the table, so she and Nandi could go and play together. Her offer seemed to please Lilly and Donald, so they let her go. In the next room, Erika gathered Nandi into her lap, and asked, "Want me to tell you a story?"

They settled down, cross-legged, on the large Persian carpet that covered the parquet floor, and Erika told Nandi a simplified version of The Nutcracker, occasionally getting up to show Nandi how each of the characters moved. He was a receptive audience, and they were happy in each other's company. Then Lilly came in, to put Nandi to bed, for it was getting late. The winter evening had set in.

"Oh, it's so dark outside," Erika exclaimed, glancing out the window as Lilly lowered the wood shutters.

"Yes, and your parents want to leave," Lilly smiled at her. "You and Judith have school tomorrow." Lilly picked up Nandi, and they walked back into the living room where Piry was holding Erika's coat for her to put it on. They all hugged and kissed, then Erika and her family headed home. They walked to the streetcar stop, with a bitter cold wind in their faces. But despite the stinging winter air, Erika felt warm inside. For once, she has had a perfect day.

◎◉◎

In early spring, Aunt Emma, her homeroom teacher, asked Erika to go to the principal's office.

"Did I do something wrong?" Erika asked as Aunt Emma walked with her down the long hallway.

"Don't be afraid, it's nothing bad, you'll see," Aunt Emma whispered.

"Come in, come in," the principal called out as his secretary ushered them into his office. He was a tall man with friendly blue eyes, and a bulbous nose above his thin lips. He combed his thinning brown hair across the top of his head to cover his balding. Erika found that amusing. He wore a dark suit and a wide red tie over his white shirt.

"Sit down, please," he indicated the two chairs in front of his desk. Then he interlaced his long fleshy fingers over the desktop, and said,

"I called you in, Erika, to give you a very big task, and I've asked Comrade Emma to come with you so she could help you with it if you need it."

Erika soundlessly heaved a big sigh of relief, and leaned forward, to pay close attention.

"I don't know whether or not you've heard of a terrible thing that is happening in that cruel, capitalist country, America. A couple living there, Ethel and Julius Rosenberg, have been accused by the American government of spying for the Soviet Union. They have two children, Michael, who is 9 years old, and his brother Robert, who is only 5. So obviously the parents would not endanger their children's future. They are completely innocent. But the American government needs scapegoats so they can rile up their people against socialist countries. They will then allow their government to wage war, like the one in Korea. Remember you wrote a letter to Comrade Stalin about the war in Korea?"

Erika nodded, and he went on: "This time we want you to write a letter in the name of all the children at our school, asking the President of the United States to save the lives of those innocent parents of two young children. Just imagine how you would feel if your parents were put in prison or executed, and you would never see them again! Who would bring you up then?" the principal's voice was full of emotion.

Erika's eyes filled with tears. "Strangers," she shrugged. She recalled how forlorn she felt when she lived at the orphanage, even though she knew her mother was alive.

"I see you understand the kind of letter we want you to write," the principal said with a faint smile.

"I do," Erika assured him.

"Can you do it in a week?"

"Or less. I'll get on it right away, after I do my homework."

"That's a good pioneer talking!" the principal exclaimed.

"What an honor!" Aunt Emma gently patted Erika's shoulder as they walked back to the classroom. "Can you stay a bit after school, so I could fill you in on the Rosenberg's story? It might help you to compose your letter?"

"I'd be glad to. It will really help me to know about them and what's happening to them now."

They sat in the empty classroom, and Aunt Emma explained Erika, "The Rosenbergs had been accused of stealing from the American Government the secret of making an atom bomb and passing it on to the Soviet Government, so they could build their own bomb. Their supposed action had been reported by co-workers, and both Rosenbergs had been given the death sentence. Because the Rosenbergs were the only ones convicted to die, and all other collaborators got only prison terms, people all over Europe and in the Soviet bloc countries have been protesting and asking for clemency. Your letter will be sent to the American President, along with letters from many other schools. The voices of children are important to raise because of the Rosenbergs' children."

Erika felt the weight of this responsibility, "What if I don't write a good enough letter?"

"You will. I'll help you phrase it," Aunt Emma reassured her.

A week later, Erika's letter was read to the general assembly at school and wildly applauded by her fellow students. This was one time when Erika, though outwardly showing modest embarrassment, knew that she had every right to feel proud of her writing.

That summer, just before school ended, Piry received a letter from the school:

"For Erika Fábián's outstanding scholastic achievement as well as her significant contribution to many other school activities, we are awarding her a two-week vacation at our exclusive Pioneer Camp in Jánoshegy, just northeast of Budapest, from July 15 to the 30th. You will receive detailed instructions for her preparation for this honor, given only to the best of students from around the entire country."

It was signed by the principal. Piry handed the letter to Erika and let her read it before she grabbed her daughter into a bear hug. "I'm so proud of you," she whispered into her ear.

Erika felt, her mother's praise was the best birthday gift she had been given on this 12th year of her life.

◎◉◎

Erika loved the pioneer camp. The campers roomed in dormitories, grouped by age, and went mountain climbing, or walking through dense forests gathering wildflowers for their mess-hall tables. In the evenings they gathered around campfires and sang folk songs and patriotic songs, created by Hungarian and Soviet musicians in praise of the regime. While marching through thick vegetation, they sang:

Mint a mókus fenn a fán,	Like a squirrel in a tree
Az úttörő oly vidám,	A pioneer is so happy,
Ajkáról ki sem fogy a nóta.	Songs just never leave his/her lips.
Ha tábort üt valahol,	While setting up camp somewhere
Sok kis pajtás így dalol,	The many buddies sing this song,
Fújja estig kora reggel óta.	Nonstop from dawn to dusk.

| Fürgébb, mint a könnyű szél, | Faster than a light wind, |
| Gyorsan jár és messze ér, | The pioneer moves briskly and gets far, |

Nincs túra, ami kifog rajta.	No road can defeat him/her,
Hívja erdő nyári rét,	As woods and summer fields call him/her,
to	

Vígan marsol, jól kilép,	He/she speedily marches with joy,
És a szemét mindig nyitva tartja.	Vigilant wherever he or she goes.
Mint testvér, vagy hű barát,	Like a sibling or good friend,
Megsegít, ha bajban lát,	He/she aids you if you're in trouble,

| Munkában alig akad párja. | At work he/she hardly has an equal, |
| Hol szöget ver, hol meg főz, | Whether he/she hammers a nail or cooks a meal |

| Mindent megtesz, amit győz, | He/she does whatever he/she can, |
| És a helyét mindenütt megállja. | And does it all with excellence. |

Évek szállanak a nyári fák alatt,	Years fly by beneath the summer trees
Oly vidám az ének.	Our song is so full of joy
Boldog dallama így önti dalba ma:	This happy melody pours into words:
Csuda jó, gyönyöru az élet.	How great and wonderful our lives are.

Erika put her heart into the song; she loved its positive message and marching tempo. For this brief period in her life, she stopped "the observer" in her head from criticizing and just went along with the activities. What enchanted Erika most about the camp was a group of visiting Chinese students. They were about her age and roomed in the same building as her group.

There was one girl in particular whom Erika liked. The feeling seemed to be mutual, for they sought each other out during evening campfire sing-alongs and sat together. The girl, Lien was slightly built and about Erika's height, 5'2 inches. She had shiny black hair cascading down her back, and large almond shaped eyes under thin, gently arching eyebrows. A small nose with no ridge emphasized her exotic eyes. Her full red lips looked like a cherry.

Erika thought she was beautiful and felt joyful just being with her. They could not speak each other's language, but Lien taught Erika to count to ten by holding up her delicate fingers and naming them one by one. Erika imitated her words, and taught Lien to count in Hungarian. They laughed a lot together as they corrected each other's pronunciation.

They touched each other's hair and marveled at the differences. To Erika, Lien's hair felt thick and not unlike a horse's mane. When Lien touched Erika's auburn hair, which streamed down her back to her waist, rubbing the strands between her fingers, Lien indicated that she found it very fine. With a deep, guttural sound Lien said, "hao". Their interpreter told Erika, it meant "good".

The two weeks of camp went by like a dream. On the last evening, they sat around the campfire and sang Hungarian, Soviet, and Chinese songs. To Erika, the Chinese songs sounded plaintiff but sweet. She and Lien exchanged addresses and promised to write to each other. Through their interpreter they agreed that maybe one day Lien would come back to Hungary to study, or Erika might have a chance to visit her in China. Both countries were "social democracies," so travel could be possible.

It was with a heavy heart that Erika returned home. But her the camp experience made her hope that someday she would be able to get away from her unhappy family life.

◎◉◎

School began with the usual ceremonies and Erika's participation in them. Once again, her classmates elected her as their leader. Erika worked diligently to keep up her grades, tutor classmates whose grades needed improvement, and silently tolerated her homelife.

A couple of times a week she was able to visit Aunt Magda and Uncle Imre, her stepfather's brother and his wife, who lived next door them. It gave Erika a chance to get out of her own home. They kept their cat and small dog indoors, and Erika liked to play with them. Her own mother would not let even Maczko's tail inside their house, and it was a limited time that Erika could spend petting Maczko in their yard. So, she enjoyed her aunt and uncle's animals.

Because her school activities occupied so much of Erika's time now, she had no time to go to the stables with Uncle Imre. But visiting their house was also fun. Her aunt and uncle genuinely liked each other and never seemed to argue. They often offered Erika a piece of their home-made sausage or some other food saying, "This is not kosher, are you sure you want it?"

Erika would respond, "Of course I do. It's delicious."

"Just don't tell you parents," Uncle Imre warned.

"You know I wouldn't!" Erika protested as she stuffed her mouth.

"I don't get what you see in those people," Judith would comment whenever Erika got home from her visits.

"I like them," Erika would shrug.

Judith just shook her head, "They're nothing but peasants."

"I like peasants," Erika would counter.

"What do you to talk about with them?"

"Aunt Magda reads lots of books and she tells me about the stories in them."

"Ah," Judith would nod, and add, "I can just imagine the kinds of books she reads."

"They are by English writers, like Dickens, and C.S. Lewis, and French writers, like Alexandre Dumas. She has them in Hungarian translation."

"Oh. And are you caught up with your school reading list?" Judith could never resist lording over Erika, monitoring her activities as the older sister.

"Yes. Except for this one," and Erika would pull a book out of her schoolbag and open it to read, to cut off further discussion with Judith.

"I'm reading a very good novel; Once I'm finished with it, you can borrow it if you behave," Judith would add.

"Thank you. Let me know when."

Erika knew, if Judith offered her a book to read, it would always come with a price. She would have to do something for her sister, like shining Judith's shoes a couple of times, or mending her stockings, or doing her Russian homework. But if the book looked interesting, it was a small price to pay. Besides, exchanging favors preserved a kind of peaceful interaction between them and Erika liked to have peace in her life.

◎◉◎

Piry was often out till just before Feri got home. Judith never commented or asked where she had been. Erika didn't have to ask. She knew that Piry was busy with her black-market deals, selling nylon stockings and other goods, smuggled in from the West. She knew, because occasionally Piry still asked her to deliver packets to the people who bought these items.

If Feri had some inkling that Piry spent a lot of time out of the house while he was at work, he only accused her of it when they got into an argument over something. Late at night, when they were in his bed, sometimes he would accuse Piry of cheating on him. Whether she did or not he would never find out because Piry knew how to appease him with sex and keep her own activities private.

Actually, Piry was busy looking for another escape route. She felt that she was working way too hard just to maintain the household; shopping, cooking, and earning money with deals that could land her in jail.

All this, because Feri's salary couldn't cover more than their daily rations of potatoes, bread, and milk. Meat, clothing, Maria the maid's salary, and all other expenses of running their household at a relatively comfortable level, she had to provide. Piry did not complain, she simply conducted her businesses and kept a cheerful face at home, hiding her unhappiness.

Her only escape would be to find a way to get out of the country. She and Zoltan had relatives in America who would help her and her daughters to get on their feet and create an easier, successful life.

◉◉◉

The Jewish High Holidays, Rosh Hashanah and Yom Kippur came at the end of September in 1952. Feri sat all day in the men's section on the main floor of the synagogue, and Piry was in the balcony with all the other women.

Judith escaped services by spending time in the courtyard of the temple with her friends. As far she was concerned, religion was useless. If God had cared, her father wouldn't be dead. Therefore, she did not care for God.

Erika occasionally sat with her mother, and she was young enough to sit with Feri where only men and children were allowed. The view of the altar was better from ground level. But Erika had an excuse for not sitting and praying with either of her parents. She was a member of the choir that had its own balcony above the altar. Erika enjoyed singing in the choir.

She also loved gazing at the rich Byzantine style architecture of the temple's interior, and at the colorful flowers of the stained-glass windows that decorated both sides of the interior. The dual tablets of the Ten Commandments were carved into one of the windows.

Every year, during the hour-long reading of the Torah, when the choir was not needed, Erika escaped to her friend Barbara's Orthodox temple nearby. She liked seeing all the women there covered in white from head to toe, their feet in white socks. The men's section could only be viewed through a wood lattice fence that separated males and females. Peeking through the holes in the fence, Erika could see that all the men covered their heads with their tallit, a wide shawl with black and white stripes and black fringes at both ends. Under the tallit each man wore a white cotton robe that when the time came, would become his burial gown.

"They wear this in case God decides to take them during the holidays," Barbara explained to Erika, when they went outdoors during the Torah reading at her temple.

The only time Erika and Judith joined their mother during services was when it came to saying Yizkor, the prayer for the dead. Judith sat on one side of Piry, and Erika on the other. The girls murmured the Hebrew words along with Piry, asking God to remember their father, their grandparents, their mother's siblings, and all their relatives who had perished in the Nazi concentration camps.

Judith murmured the words suffused with pain over the loss of her father. She saw her mother surreptitiously wipe her tears, and her eyes filled up as well. But Erika didn't cry. She was too angry to cry. *How could all those people just obey the Nazis instead of rebelling against them?* This was a question that had often haunted her. *I would have preferred to get shot rebelling than to be tattooed like cattle and marched into a gas chamber,* Erika thought, her anger growing with every name she had to mention in her prayers.

She recalled her long march with Judith toward deportation and was proud of their mother's ability to rescue them. *My mother fought back, she didn't just let us be deported,* she thought, glancing at Piry. She reached out and put her hand over Piry's, giving it a gentle squeeze. Piry turned her head and smiled at Erika. She appreciated Erika's touch and felt really close to her as they continued praying for their dead.

Erika was conscious of the fact that they were oppressed under their current regime, and lived in constant fear of the government, of their neighbors, even of their friends. They had to be on the alert at all times concerning what they said and to whom they said it. A wrong word, and someone could report them to the secret police. But at least they were not persecuted or killed just for being Jewish.

The communists are right. Religion is the opiate of the masses. Were it not for religion, they would not have been killing Jews. So much killing, all for a belief in one God or another—what difference does it make whether you call God Yahve or Jesus? Erika mused listening to the murmur of collective prayers. Still, when it was over and she could escape to the choir, she sang with gusto and fervor, for the haunting melodies of the prayers touched her soul.

◉◉◉

A couple of weeks before the annual celebration of the "Great October Revolution," Piry received a letter from her cousin, Laci. They saw each other occasionally, at times Laci and his wife, Kató, invited them to their villa for a Sunday dinner. But that was the extent of their relationship. Since Laci made it clear to Piry that as a member of the ÁVO he would not help her leave Hungary, she never brought up the subject again and was leery of commenting to him about anything of political nature. But it was important for her to pretend that nothing had changed between them.

In the letter, Laci wrote:

"Dear Piry,
Since this year the anniversary of the Great October Revolution will fall on a Friday, and your daughters won't have school that day, would Judith and Erika like to spend the holiday weekend with us? You could bring the girls on Friday morning, and they could go home Sunday afternoon. Let me know by telephoning my office. If I'm not there, just leave a message with my secretary as to whether or not they will come.
With love,
Laci."

"I'm not going to those commi bastards' house" Judith declared when Piry read the letter to her daughters.

"I'd love to go!" was Erika's response.

CHAPTER 15

O N THE APPOINTED DAY, Piry and Erika set out late morning for the latter's weekend visit. After taking two different streetcars and crossing the Danube from Pest to Buda by bus, Piry and Erika, trudged up the Rózsadomb (Rose Hill) ankle deep in snow. Erika, carrying her small overnight case, didn't mind the cold and the stinging wind blowing in her face. She was excited about spending the weekend at her uncle's house. She liked Laci and his wife, Kató.

Family gossip had it that Kató was about ten years older than Laci, but nobody dared to ask. They whispered that she had seduced him, and Laci could not avoid marrying her because he was working for her brother, the dreaded Péter Gábor, head of the ÁVO. Euphemistically named State Protection Department, it was actually the Secret Police.

Once, Piry angrily blurted out to her sister Lilly, that Laci would never have joined the ÁVO, were it not for his wife's insistence. Kató told him, that he had a better chance of being accepted at the university, to study engineering, if he belonged to this prestigious organization. That was a couple of years ago, and by now the family had made peace with what Laci had become. Erika had heard all the family gossip but didn't care. She liked the couple, liked visiting them, and appreciated the things she could learn from them.

During the summer, when the whole family had been invited for a Sunday afternoon meal at their villa, Uncle Laci took Erika out to their beautiful garden behind their house and taught her to shoot a gun. He picked a lightweight one off the rack of guns he kept in a cabinet in his study. He showed Erika how to hold it, how to aim, and how to react to the "kick" the gun made against her shoulder after she fired it.

"You've got a good eye and rock steady hands!" he exclaimed, when after just a short practice Erika could hit the bull's eye. Erika grinned with pride.

Given that their garden would now be covered with snow, Erika secretly wondered what activity her uncle would devise to keep her entertained over the weekend.

"It's exhausting to go uphill in this snow," Erika sighed, as it crunched under their boots. They were passing one villa after another, all looking alike under the thick blanket of white on their roofs. She was getting tired of having to put ever so carefully one foot after another so she wouldn't slip and fall with her overnight case. The rubber snowshoes she had to wear over her ankle-high leather shoes felt heavier and heavier.

"We're almost there," Piry assured her. Then added, "Behave yourself with them, and be careful of what you say."

"I know!"

No matter how nice Laci and Kató were, Erika had to be cautious and keep to the "party line" just like at school. *All is well; there is nothing to complain about the way our wonderful leaders are running the country.*

Somewhere in the back of her mind Erika remembered overhearing her mother and stepfather whispering about the villas on Rózsadomb. They had formerly belonged to rich people, many of them Jewish. But the government had appropriated these homes and awarded them to their own high-ranking officials. Laci's wife, being Péter Gábor's sister, of course got a villa when she married. *But this was not the time to be thinking such thoughts.*

"Here we are," Piry stopped in front of a tall wrought iron gate. A thick layer of snow sat on top of each curlicue, and icicles hung beneath the curves. To Erika, it looked like a fairy tale gate to a magic castle. Piry pressed a small white button on the black gatepost.

In a couple of minutes Laci opened their front door and came to the gate in high black boots, and his fur lined ÁVO overcoat. Clearly, he had just come home from work.

"Welcome," he shouted, and hugged them both after he guided them into the house.

It was warm inside, bright lights gave the rooms a golden glow, and Erika was delighted to be there. The large living room was furnished with rosewood sofas and armchairs with soft cushions; the dining room had an oblong table with eight carved chairs around it. The kitchen was big too, it had white cabinets, a white gas stove, and a large icebox in a corner.

Kató led Erika upstairs where the bedrooms were, to show her the room in which she would be staying. It had a double bed with a blond-wood headboard, a dresser, a closet, and the usual bassinette on a stand for conveniently washing one's face and hands in the room. The toilet was down the hall, and next to it was a separate bathroom with a tub and sink. As they passed a couple of closed doors, Kató pointed to one and said, "That's our bedroom; if you need anything at night, don't hesitate to come and knock."

They would not let Piry leave without first sitting down to a light snack of espresso and pastry. Aunt Kató served it in the dining room, on a beautiful set of Rosenthal porcelain dishes. They made small talk about the family, and assured Piry that they will take good care of Erika. They invited Piry to bring Feri and Judith on Sunday, to have a meal together before taking Erika home.

"Come early, so you could get home early enough for Erika to prepare for school the next day," Kató said, with a smile.

◎◉◎

A surprise for Erika came when evening fell. She had spent the time after her mother left sitting with Uncle Laci in his study, talking about school, and about her summer camp experience. He seemed pleased with her, and said, "You continue this way, and you'll go far in this county."

Around eight o'clock, Aunt Kató called them to the dining room for dinner. As they heeded her call, the front door opened. A young man entered, shaking snow off his green military coat and cap, and stamping his boots on the mat in the entry hall.

"Good evening," he shouted.

"You're just in time, Árpád," Kató called out to him. "Leave your coat and boots in the hallway. There are slippers by the wall that you can put on and join us."

They introduced him to Erika as Árpád Gombós, a young soldier whom they had invited to spend the long weekend with them.

"His family lives in a small village, too far for him to travel there for just a three-day holiday, and we didn't want him to be alone in the barracks," Aunt Kató explained, patting him on the shoulder lovingly. Then she said, "And this is Erika, our niece".

Árpád nodded to Erika, and said to their hosts, "I'm sure we'll get along just fine."

Erika didn't find out till next morning just what Árpád had meant by his comment.

It was still dark when Erika heard voices outside her room. She quickly rolled out of bed and throwing her white shantung robe over her green pajamas, went looking for her hosts. Piry had given her the robe for her 12th birthday, and Erika was proud to bring it along for the weekend because she found it beautiful. She saw her aunt and uncle standing in full uniform downstairs in the hallway, talking to Árpád. When they spotted Erika at the bottom of the stairs, Aunt Kató came to rest her hand on Erika's shoulder and said,

"So sorry, sweetie, but Uncle Laci and I have to go into work. Didn't want to tell you yesterday, so as not to spoil your evening with us. But it's just for the day. We'll be back for dinner. In the meantime, I'm sure you and Árpád can entertain yourselves. Make breakfast—sorry we can't sit with you—we're late as it is. Árpád knows which cabinet in the living room is full of games, chess and other board stuff. You can play with whatever you like." Both of them gave her a peck on the cheek, left.

A sudden silence filled the air as Erika and Árpád faced each other.

"I can make us some eggs," Árpád offered and walked to the kitchen.

Erika followed him. "That's fine." She was wondering why she felt this strange tension between them, and whether or not she should shower and dress first. But he did not seem to be bothered by her night clothes.

"How would you like the eggs?" Árpád asked.

"Scrambled or sunny side up, whichever you prefer."

Erika made toast and set the table with butter and jam, milk, and a glass carafe filled with coffee, which had been left for them by Aunt Kató.

During breakfast, they chatted about school life and his life in the barracks; all the training Árpád had to go through. While talking, Erika thought, he is incredibly attractive. He was tall, slim, with broad shoulders, had brown hair, hazelnut color eyes, and well-shaped, full lips. The only thing that marred his features was his skin. It was rather pockmarked.

He noticed her eyes on his face, and said, "I had very bad acne during my teens and my skin never recovered."

"It's okay," Erika shrugged, "you look fine". She blushed a little when she realized that she had just paid him a compliment.

"Why, thank you!" he exclaimed, a bright smile lighting up his face. "You look fine yourself, Comrade," he added, as if to diffuse the compliment.

After they cleared the breakfast dishes, an awkward silence fell between them again.

"Now what?" he asked, breaking it. "What would you like to do?"

"I should get dressed, and then we could play some games if you want to," Erika suggested. "We could even take a walk in the snow and see the neighborhood."

"Why don't you stay as you are, we'll play some games, and then you could go and change so we could take a walk before Laci and Kató come home?

Erika liked the suggestion. With a sure feminine instinct, she knew that he found her desirable. Her robe was half open, displaying her pajama top, which had an open V neckline to just above her breasts. She felt tension and pleasure as his eyes traveled to her décolletage. She let him stare for a brief moment at the rise of the soft cotton pajamas over her breasts, then shrugged, "If you don't mind, I don't care. Let's play."

He collected himself and headed for the cabinet where the games were kept.

She stared at his broad shoulders and tight derriere in the moss green military slacks as he reached up to open the cabinet door. He is so well built, she thought.

He turned back to her, and must have caught the look in Erika's eyes, because he swallowed hard before he asked, "What shall we play?"

Erika had the distinct feeling that his question had a double meaning. That it implied they could play games other than board games. But she pretended not to notice his subtler meaning and said as casually as she could, "Chess, or checkers. I'm better at checkers. How about you?"

He pulled the checkers box off the shelf. Erika's eyes traveled to his muscular arms under his khaki shirt sleeves and wished they would enfold her. But she was careful to make no move to make it happen.

"We'll start with this, then we'll graduate to chess." He removed that too off the shelf. "I'm not great at chess either, but maybe we can teach each other some new tricks."

Erika's stomach spun and she could feel her heartbeat faster. She knew when a man made a sexual innuendo, and that he was implying something far more than board games. But she chose to ignore it and gave him a wry smile.

They settled on the living room carpet and set up the checkers between them. As they played, Erika was aware that every time she leaned forward to make a move, his eyes were plastered to her chest. She found this exciting.

They played several rounds of checkers, and occasionally, as they reached for their pieces, their fingers would touch. When that happened, Erika felt a current race down her body, and she wondered whether he had felt it as well. He gave no sign of it.

He was funny, and made her laugh a lot, commenting about the way they played the game, and telling her stories about his life in the barracks. He described how his mates tried to cheat on tests, and how tyrannical the officers were. He seemed to know he could trust Erika not to repeat his tales to their hosts.

When the story was funny, Erika laughed boisterously, leaning back, with arms outstretched behind her, supporting herself on her hands. She knew that displaying her body this way was provocative, but she couldn't help herself. She could feel him staring at her, his eyes traveling over her body, but he said nothing, just waited for her laughter to abate, and then urging her, "C'mon, let's play."

After a while they got tired of checkers, and he set up the chess set. The mood between them changed from jokes to thoughtful moves, as each of them was trying to win the game. He won the first round, then taught Erika the moves that allowed him to do it. She applied his techniques in the next round, but he won again. Again, he showed her how he did it and how she could avoid the mistakes she was making. The next game, Erika won. She wasn't sure whether he had let her, or she truly played a better game, but she was thrilled. So, they set up the next game.

"I'll tell you what," he said, "let's start playing for prizes. If you win, you can ask me to do something. If I win, I can ask you."

"Like do what?"

"I don't know. Whatever the person thinks of asking."

Erika realized that this was a dangerous but very exciting challenge. Throughout the game she kept wondering what she would ask of him if she won. *Money? Certainly not. Then what? A kiss*, floated into her mind. She looked at his shapely lips and felt a tension in her body; her breasts ached with a desire she had never felt before. She was so distracted during the game that he won with just a few moves.

"Now what?" Erika asked, sitting back on her haunches, her robe draped in a circle around her on the carpet. Their eyes met, and Erika knew that he wanted her but was afraid to say so.

"What do you want to give me?" he finally asked, smiling broadly, his even white teeth glistening between his lips.

"What do you want?" Erika responded, her heart pounding as she sat up on her knees, facing him.

"A kiss" he said, his eyes traveling to her lips.

Erika's heart was beating wildly. She had known that's what he would ask for because the pull between them was so great that only a kiss could ease it. Erika was dying to kiss him, she wanted to feel his lips on hers, yet she now protested, because that was the proper thing to do. A girl couldn't kiss a guy she barely knew. It just was not done.

"Don't you think that's a bit much to ask?"

Her experiences with her stepfather never included kissing. In her mind, he was just a pig who rubbed against her his unseen but painfully hard penis. She hated every minute of it. But for the first time in her life, she was feeling something totally different. Even though she recognized it as a prelude to sex, which she certainly didn't want, a deep inner turmoil drew her to Árpád. She wanted him to take her into his arms, the way she never wanted anyone else ever to touch her. She wanted to feel his lips on hers. But she could not bring herself to honor their bargain. Nice girls didn't kiss boys, let alone a stranger.

Árpád was studying Erika's face, waiting. Their eyes locked, the air became heavy between them. Erika could hardly breathe. Árpád reached out and pulled Erika to him, pressing her body against his. Holding her tight, he brushed her lips with his.

"Oh," Erika sighed, looking up at him.

"All right?" he asked, smiling at her.

She nodded, and then all of a sudden, his lips were on hers, his tongue inside her mouth, touching the tip of her tongue, then gently sucking her tongue into his mouth, all the while his lips pressing hers with increasing intensity. She nearly swooned from the force of her own wild, internal response; all the muscles of her thighs tightened, and her breasts ached to be touched. He must have known, because his hand now cupped a breast, and gently squeezed her nipple.

Erika gasped with a pleasure that felt almost like pain. She pulled her lips away from his and pushed his hand away, sitting back on her hunches.

Árpád's eyes were glazed, he was panting lightly.

"Are you all right?" Erika asked, staring at him.

"Sorry, I got carried away. It's all your fault. You are so sexy!"

Erika laughed a little. She knew men found her so but had no idea why. "I should go change," she offered without conviction.

"Yes, you should. But not yet."

He pulled her to his chest again and kissed her. Erika responded instinctively, enjoying the feel of his firm body against hers. His fingers traveled to her pajama buttons and started to undo them. Erika pushed his hand away.

He stopped kissing her, and begged, "Let me see your breasts".

His request startled Erika. She felt bashful. "No way," she said firmly.

He held on to her wrists, facing her, "I won't let go of you till you show them to me. You're so beautiful, I want to see all your beauty."

"Forget it!" Erika exclaimed and tried to extricate herself from his hold. She now felt scared. Since she started growing breasts, at age nine, she had never let anyone see her naked, not even her mother or sister. She changed clothes in the only room that she could lock—the bathroom. Now, here was this stranger, asking her to reveal herself to him. No matter how drawn she was to him, she wasn't going to do it. She tried to pull away from him, arching her back, pushing at his chest to release her. Instead, he let her fall back on the carpet, falling with her, pinning her under him.

"Get off of me!" Erika shouted, pushing him away.

"I will. But first let me see you just for a moment."

Erika closed her eyes. Then suddenly she pulled up her knees and rolled onto her side, her move taking him by surprise but only for a moment. He grabbed her by the waist and pulled her close. She could feel his hot breath as he kissed her neck, and her body involuntarily reacted by pressing against him. She knew she should fight him off but what he was doing to her was so, so exciting. When he lifted his head from her neck, she turned toward him, and pleaded, "You must let me go," though she knew she wasn't very convincing.

"I will, as soon as you do what I ask."

Erika knew when she was beaten. The desire to reveal to him what he wanted was stronger than her resistance. "If I do what you ask, will you let me go?"

"I promise." His voice was husky, his face flushed.

"But what if you don't keep your word?"

"I will. Soldier's honor," he smiled at her.

"All right then."

She faced Árpád, and he gently unbuttoned her pajama top and opened it.

"You are so beautiful," he murmured, drinking in the sight of her small round breasts, her torso tapering into a tiny waist. He reached out to cup her breasts, but Erika pushed his hands away.

"You said, look. No touching!"

He stopped short, taken by surprise, and she quickly folded her pajama top over her breasts.

He sat back on his heels and watched her scramble to her feet. "You are a clever girl," he said, his eyes glued on her as she pulled her robe together and tied the belt around her waist.

"I'm going to dress now," she announced, apprehensive that he may not let her go.

"Go!" he replied, sitting back on his haunches, watching her as if mesmerized.

By the time Aunt Kató and Uncle Laci got home around six p.m., Erika and Árpád had had lunch and afterwards stayed in their respective rooms. Erika was reading a novel and didn't know what Árpád was doing. He knocked on Erika's door an hour or so before their hosts were expected to return and suggested that they play a game to put a semblance of sobriety into their relationship. They had not discussed their earlier activities, pretending that all was normal and casual between them. They sat demurely at the dining room table, playing a board game called "Mill".

Each player had to lay twelve pawns onto a board that had three rectangles drawn equidistance from each other. The goal of the game was to move their pawns from point to point horizontally or vertically so three of them would align, to form a 'mill.' Then the player could remove one of the opposing party's pawns. The player, who was left with at least three pawns so as to be able to build a 'mill', was the winner. Erika had a special talent for this game. After her second win in a row, Árpád said, staring at the board, "You've won again!"

"I'm not going to ask you to show me your chest," she whispered, smiling.

"Sorry about that, I lost my head," he grinned back at her sheepishly. "It won't happen again."

Chuckling, Erika's eyes flashed toward the sound of her arriving relatives, "I should think, not."

◎◉◎

Aunt Kató prepared dinner with Erika helping her to peel vegetables and setting the table. They spent the evening in quiet conversation about movies and books they had read, and life goals they had. Árpád wanted to become a mechanical engineer after he served his term in the army. Erika said, all her literature teachers suggested that she consider becoming a writer.

"You know that we value artists in this country," Uncle Laci said, obviously pleased with Erika's plan.

They all retired early for the night, but Erika was too keyed up to fall asleep. She tossed and turned, reliving the excitement of her tousle with Árpád, regretting not to have allowed him to kiss her again. It was nearly dawn when she fell asleep, exhausted.

◎◉◎

The next day, after a leisurely brunch, Erika packed her carrying case and got ready to leave. Her parents arrived around 2 p.m. to take her home.

"Judith couldn't come, she had to do homework for tomorrow," Piry apologized for her older daughter's absence. "But she sends her love," she added, for good manners.

As was customary, they had brought an elegant dobosh cake with them as a thank you gift. Kató put it on the table and insisted that after the meal they cut the cake for dessert. So, after lunch, they all sat around sipping espresso and eating dobosh while chatting pleasantly, till Feri got up and said to Erika, "Let's get your bag. We should leave before dark."

He followed Erika to the room where she had been staying, and before picking up her case, he turned to her, saying, "I know that soldier did something to you. I can see it in your face. What did he do?"

Erika was shocked, how could he see? she thought, but she just shrugged and said, "Nothing. What are you talking about?"

"I know what I'm talking about" Feri insisted. "Did he force himself on you?"

"Of course not!"

"Then what?" Feri suddenly lifted her braided hair off her neck, and pointed at the red spot on Erika's neck, "What's this?"

"What's what?" Erika pretended, realizing with inner horror that Árpád's kiss had left a mark there.

"This is a hickey! He kissed you there! What else did he do to you?"

"Nothing!"

"Don't lie to me!"

The pressure he exerted frightened Erika. "Okay, so he kissed me there! It was the prize for a chess game he had won! So what?" she practically shouted at him, furious.

"I knew it!" Feri exploded. "What else happened between you?"

"Nothing!"

Feri turned on his heels and marched into the dining room, where the whole group was sitting and laughing at something. He pointed at Árpád and said, "You! Can I see you for a minute? I need to ask you something in front of Erika."

Árpád rose, obviously alarmed, but followed Feri. So did the others.

"You bastard, you violated my daughter!" Feri shouted at Árpád as they entered the room where Erika was standing by the bed, frightened, not knowing what to expect.

Árpád, visibly upset, protested, "I did nothing of the sort!"

"Look!" Feri grabbed Erika, turned her violently, and showed the red mark on her neck. "What else did you do, you son of a bitch! This is a twelve-year-old girl you have abused!"

Árpád gasped, "I thought she was fifteen, going on sixteen!"

"So, you admit abusing her!" Frank shouted, and grabbing Árpád by the shoulders, raised his knee to the young man's groin.

Árpád, being quick on his feet managed to pull back just enough to soften the blow, and shouted, "Comrade Laci, I didn't do a thing to your niece! Help me!"

Laci, as if coming out of shock, stepped between Árpád and Feri.

"Feri, violence won't solve a thing." He turned to Árpád, "What really happened between you?"

Árpád protested, "Nothing. We played chess, and some other parlor games all day."

Laci turned to Erika, "How did you get that hickey on your neck?"

"We played for a prize in one of the chess games. I lost, and that's what Árpád wanted as a prize…a kiss. That's all." Erika glanced at Árpád and knew she had said the right thing in the right tone, making light of the whole situation.

A stunned silence followed Erika's confession. Then Laci said, "Árpád, you're practically a grown man, how can you ask for such a thing when we trusted you with our niece in our home?"

"Like I said, I had no idea she was so young."

"I saw how flirtatious your daughter is," Kató broke into the conversation. "Even this morning she was running around in that seductive robe during breakfast. If Árpád didn't know her age, you can't put the blame only on him."

"He could have asked!" Feri bellowed.

"She looks older, and he is nineteen, why would it occur to him to ask? Kató countered.

At that moment Erika felt an overwhelming surge of hatred toward her aunt. She realized that by putting the blame on her, Kató was defending not just Árpád but also herself and Laci for having left the two of them on their own. But Erika kept her silence. If she ever wanted to be invited back, she had to let the adults sort this out as they wished.

Feri also thought for a moment about Kató's argument, and said, "I will send Erika with Piry to be examined and if your protégé has damaged my daughter, he will spend the rest of his life behind bars!"

"Let's just go, Feri," Piry put her hand on his arm to soothe him. She turned to Laci and Kató, "So sorry that your wonderful invitation had to end like this. Thank you for your hospitality, you really had nothing to do with this. Kids can't always be under our control. So, please, let's all calm down till we have real reason to worry."

She hugged Laci and Kató, and taking Erika by the arm, walked toward the front door. Erika turned to her hosts. "Sorry for causing all this trouble. I really didn't mean to. Thank you for your hospitality, and please don't be angry with me. Or Árpád. We really didn't do anything."

Laci and Kató seemed surprised at Erika's farewell speech and smiled at her. "It's all right. We still love you," Laci said.

Feri, exuding anger, wordlessly followed, carrying Erika's travel case.

On the way home, Erika sat next to Piry on the streetcar, away from her stepfather, and wouldn't look at him. She felt humiliated, furious, and deeply upset at Feri as well as at herself for caving in under his pressure. She now recalled another incident when he questioned her when they were at the Palatinusz pools on Margit Island. She had joined Feri in the hot spring waters, and he asked her if the man sitting on the other side of her had tried to touch her. She remembered her feelings of indignation and disgust at his suspicion.

She also thought of all the times she had overheard her parents fighting, and how during some of those arguments Feri had accused Piry of cheating on him. *Son of a bitch*, she thought, *he is blaming everyone of doing what he actually does to me, and who knows to how many other women! I shouldn't have admitted a thing. Lucky, I didn't tell him what really happened between Árpád and me.* As she was able to analyze what had transpired and why, she felt better about the situation but despised Feri more than ever.

◎◉◎

The following Tuesday morning, Piry said to Erika, "I'll pick you up after school. We're going to a doctor."

Erika just nodded. She had no idea that this doctor's visit would be one of the most humiliating experiences of her life. Piry took her to a gynecologist and waited in his office while a nurse led Erika into the doctor's examination room. She instructed Erika to remove her shoes, stockings, and panties, and place these on a chair, and left the room. Erika did as she was told. Then someone knocked on the door a few minutes later, and Erika, smoothing down her skirt and standing barefooted, shouted, "Come in".

The doctor entered, wearing a white coat and a smile. He wasn't a bad looking man, about forty years old, with thinning brown hair, warm brown eyes, and a fleshy hook nose. He asked Erika to lie down on her back on the hard, narrow bed in the middle of the examination room. "I'm just going to take a look at you, don't be afraid," the doctor said. "It won't hurt."

Erika wasn't afraid of him; she was just uncomfortable about what she was told to do.

"Put your heels in the stirrups," he instructed her, "and then slide down toward me so your knees are bent, and your buttocks are at the end of the table."

Erika obeyed his instructions, feeling more and more ill at ease. The doctor sat down on a small rotating chair between her legs. Although Erika's skirt, stretched over her knees, covered her view of him, she knew that the doctor was looking at her private parts and she was ready to die of embarrassment.

"I am going to examine you," he now said, "it won't hurt. The lamp might feel a bit hot but the whole thing will take only a few minutes".

Erika didn't reply. Her whole body was rigid with tension as she felt the doctor's fingers gently separate her most private part and shine the lamp at it, which did feel hot, but it was tolerable.

He then touched her no further, took the lamp and shut it off. He rolled his chair away from her and said, "You can get dressed now. See you in my office," and left the room.

Erika sat up, quickly lifted her feet out of the stirrups, and jumped off the table. She grabbed her panties and stockings and pulled them on. Then stepped into her ankle high winter shoes and after lacing them up, she poked her head into the hall.

Her mother was waiting for her outside the door, holding her coat and cap. "Come with me."

They went into the doctor's office, where he sat behind his desk and motioned them to take the chairs facing him.

"Mrs. Haydu, your daughter is just fine. You can relax. Nothing is broken."

Piry let out a deep sigh. "Thank you doctor, I'm very grateful to you for checking."

She put an envelope in front of him on the desk. Erika knew that her mother had just given the doctor money.

She had seen her mother slip envelopes to the nurses when she was in the hospital having her tonsils removed. For sure Piry had also paid extra to the doctor who did the surgery. Another lesson learned, Erika thought, and pretended not to have seen the envelope placed on the desktop.

The doctor leaned back in his armchair and smiled at them. "Have a nice evening."

On the way home on the streetcar, Erika did not tell her mother how she felt about being looked at by the doctor. Instead, she asked, "What was all that about?"

Piry looked at her daughter surprised, "You really don't know?"

"Know what?"

"About being a virgin?"

"You mean like Mary, Jesus' mother?"

"Something like that. You didn't know that every woman is born a virgin?"

"I know the word, but I don't exactly know what it means."

So Piry spent the ride home quietly explaining to her daughter, "There is a membrane, called the hymen that covers the opening of the vagina. It's supposed to stay intact until a girl gets married. When she has intercourse with her husband for the first time, he breaks the hymen as he enters her vagina with his penis. There is usually some bleeding when the hymen breaks, but this just proves to him that she hasn't been with any man before him.

In other words, this is a very important thing a bride brings to the marriage—her innocence. When a girl has no dowry to give her husband, it is even more important. Your purity, your virginity, is your gift to him. So, if you had done something really stupid with that soldier, your chances of finding a good husband might have been greatly reduced. Once the hymen is broken, it's broken. And men want a bride with whom they are the first and only one. That's why Apu and I were so worried."

Erika nodded. Now she understood what all the fuss was about. She also understood why when she was forced to lie beneath her stepfather, he used her by just rubbing himself against her but never entering her—whatever that meant. She now hated Feri even more for the hypocrite that he was. He could do to her what he wanted but created a scandal after forcing her to admit even the smallest thing of what Árpád and she had done.

"Were you a virgin when you got married?" She asked her mother.

"I was, indeed," Piry smiled proudly. In the time left on their journey home, she told Erika how she had lost her virginity at their sports club, practically a week after the wedding. "I am telling you this story to impress upon you the importance of keeping yourself pure until you get married," Piry concluded, as they trudged through the snow in the dark winter night from the streetcar stop to their home.

Erika wondered how she could work up the courage to confront her stepfather and stop him from touching her ever again. But she didn't have to do that. Fate did.

◎◉◎

On December 2nd, 1952, an arctic cold Monday evening, Erika and Judith sat in their cozy winter dining room reading. Their homework done, this was a rare time of peaceful coexistence. Each girl was buried in her novel, enjoying the quiet of the house and the warmth radiating from the ceramic stove.

They could hear Mária softly puttering in the kitchen, but their stepfather and mother were out. The girls didn't know, nor cared where Feri was. They knew their mother had gone to a meeting at Judith's school and didn't expect her home for another couple of hours. Suddenly, their serenity was broken by Maczko's fierce barking in the garden.

Mária stuck her head into the room, "Someone is ringing the bell at the gate. Shall I go see who it is?"

"I'll go with you," Erika offered, wondering who it could be.

"Yell for me if you need me," Judith called after them.

Friends, even family members, would not come without previous arrangements unless it was really bad news. Erika's school friends, even the ones who lived nearby, would not just drop by, and Judith's friends simply never visited. If it was the ÁVO, the Security Police, it was best not to have

Mária receive them. She behaved normally enough in daily life, but if she was in any way riled, she would start shouting that she was a friend of the King of England. That would not sit well with a communist security policeman, even if Mária proved to be insane. Erika grabbed her coat off the hook by the front door and quickly followed Mária through the snow-covered yard to the gate.

"Who is it?" Erika called out with Mária standing by her, vigilant.

Over the wild barking of Maczko, a deep male voice replied, "I'm a friend of your mother, my name is Viktor."

"She is not home at the moment. Was she expecting you?" Erika asked through the locked gate, and then shouted at the dog, "Maczko, hush!" The dog obeyed and in the silence Erika and Mária heard,

"It is very urgent that I see her. Would you mind if I came in and waited for her?"

Erika looked at Mária and saw her nod. "I guess it's all right."

She fiddled with the key in the gate, a bit apprehensive, and hoping that what she was doing will be all right with her parents, but the decision had been made.

Facing her in the open gate was a man of medium height looking very dashing in a dark gray winter coat and a gray lamb's wool ushanka style hat.

"Thank you." He flashed a smile at Erika and Mária, showing a row of even white teeth.

Erika took a quick glance behind the man, making sure that he was alone, and that this was not some sort of Security Police trick, a harbinger of her mother's arrest. But the street was empty, blanketed in white. So, she and Mária let him in, carefully locking the gate again. Maczko barked wildly, straining against his chain, but stopped after they had entered the house.

Viktor removed his overcoat which was lined with a soft gray fur. He hung it up together with his hat on the coat rack in the summer dining room. It was unheated and served as the anteroom in the winter. Mária returned to the kitchen and Viktor followed Erika into the warm room where Judith was already standing, curious as to who the visitor was.

As he said hello to Judith, Erika thought that his black, wavy hair and narrow moustache made him look like her mother's favorite American actor, Clark Gable. He wore a dark suit and a blue tie over his white shirt. He was elegant and dashing.

"Sorry to barge in on you like this," Viktor said with an engaging smile, "but I need to talk to your parents rather urgently. Do you know when they'll be home?"

"Can't tell about Apu but my mother should be here a little before ten," Judith replied.

The man glanced at his wristwatch. "It's only 7:00. Is there any way you could get hold of your mom? It's very urgent."

The girls looked at each other. Erika shrugged, "If it's really urgent, we could go and get her. She is at a teachers-parents meeting."

"That would be wonderful."

Judith eyed Erika. "I can't go. Mrs. Csernok, my homeroom teacher, hates me." She didn't add that it was because she was Jewish, and her teacher was anti-Semitic. Everyone at the school knew it.

But Judith had to put up with her because that was the only middle school in their district. Instead, she simply added, "I can't interrupt the meeting. She'll take it out on my grades."

Erika understood the real reason for what her sister was saying. Lowering Judith's grades would mean that she would not be accepted into a high school after finishing middle school. Without a high school education, she could not go to university. For the rest of her life, she would have to work at low-paying jobs because she would lack the higher education for a profession. The sisters were so well trained in the requirements of their educational system, and the future that would await them should they fail to get top grades, that they thought this through in a flash.

"I'll go!" Erika offered. "Make yourself at home, I'll get my mom".

He walked out with her to the anteroom and while Erika was putting on her coat and hat, he said, "Please tell your mom—when no one else can hear you—that a mutual friend sent me from Vienna. Be very careful when you say this to her."

Oh, another code, Erika thought, but to the man she merely nodded, "Got it."

Erika knew that her mother used different code words and phrases for the black-market businesses she was involved in. She just wondered what this man was bringing to her mother, since he had come without even a briefcase. She didn't need to ask. She had a sixth sense about these things. She was on a secret mission to get her mother home as soon as possible.

Though it was early evening, the town was completely deserted. Erika raced down the familiar streets to Judith's school. For the most part, people going home after work had crunched the snow down but sometimes, she had to kick the icy mounds that had accumulated with the wind so she could cut a path through them.

Judith's school, a three-story building, occupied an entire city block. All its windows were illuminated tonight as the quarterly teachers - parents meeting was being held there. It looked like a beacon in the silent, snow-covered world she had just traversed.

Erika had been in this building before and now figured that her mother would be attending the meeting in Judith's home classroom on the third floor. By the time she got upstairs, she had stomped all the snow off her ankle-high winter shoes and quietly stopped at the closed door. She peeped through its glass window and sure enough, there was Mrs. Csernok, in front, talking to the parents who were sitting at the student desks looking as if they were getting a lesson.

Erika spotted her mother in the third row, listening attentively. She softly knocked on the door and when Mrs. Csernok turned to look, Erika pushed down the handle and slipped inside.

"Please excuse the interruption, Aunt Csernok," Erika said bravely and loudly, "but a relative arrived at our house and urgently needs to see my mother."

Taken aback by Erika's verve and charm, Mrs. Csernok, gave her a little smile, "And who is your mother, little comrade?"

"Mrs. Haydu."

"Oh." Mrs. Csernok lost her smile as she turned toward Piry, who had risen from her seat.

"Well, Mrs. Haydu, it looks like you're urgently wanted at home," the teacher said, with a hint of sarcasm in her voice.

"It seems that way, Comrade Csernok," Piry replied as she hurried toward Erika. "My apologies for having to leave. I shall make an appointment to see you about Judith's progress."

"You do that," said Mrs. Csernok in a tone that was almost a command and turned to face the rest of the parents.

Piry and Erika slid out of the room shutting the door behind them as quietly as they could.

No one commented on Piry's sudden departure, but the parents, even the teacher, had trouble resuming the meeting for a few minutes. Such urgent need for going home could mean anything; an arrest; a serious threat to a family member; one never knew. A child would not come to collect a parent from a meeting unless it was a very serious matter. Were it so, the child certainly wouldn't reveal it in public.

The remaining parents all took a deep breath and let out a sigh before they could pretend that they were not worried about their own lives and could proceed with the business at hand.

◎◉◎

"Who came? Tell me!" Piry demanded as she followed Erika rushing through the corridors and down the stairs.

Erika put a finger over her lips till they were outside, then quietly said, "You have a visitor. He said a friend of yours sent him from Vienna."

"Oh. That was smart of you, not to say that in the classroom!"

"Mother! What do you take me for?"

"I'm just glad you know better," Piry smiled.

She glanced at her daughter as they plowed their way through the snowy streets, thinking how sharp twelve-year-old Erika was. Piry also knew why

Judith didn't come for her. She wouldn't have felt comfortable hiding the real reason. That was why Piry would never dream of sending Judith on the black-market delivery errands that Erika could so easily accomplish.

Maybe it has to do with the difference in their personalities and ages, Piry thought. *Judith is always solemn and never lies. She prefers to not say anything rather than lie. Also, Judith had been just old enough to recognize the danger of every situation we were in during the war and after. Perhaps she now just wants a life without complications,* Piry concluded. *Erika, on the other hand, is fearless and obviously good at lying. Her success at school is a clear indication of this. For sure, she would be inventive if confronted with an unexpected situation, just like she had been this evening. Maybe it's due to her young age, not fully realizing the danger she might be in. Or it is just the way she is. She is just like me,* Piry mused, casting a glance at her daughter as they hurried home in the dark night, their breath like puffs of clouds ahead of them.

CHAPTER 16

WHEN PIRY AND ERIKA arrived home, they found Feri already there in deep conversation with Viktor, while Judith sat quietly at the table, listening. Viktor was explaining that "Vienna was a city divided among the four nations that had won the war. Several sectors belonged to each of the conquerors: the Americans, the British, the French, and the Soviets. However, the center of the city, "District One," belonged to all four nations. Therefore, it changed hands at the end of each month by rotation among the four powers. It was a ceremonial occasion, with the outgoing nation's soldiers marching out and the new troops coming in with their own marching bands.

"In the rest of the city, to cross the demarcation lines of the occupied zones, residents needed an identity card issued by the Allies. It was in all four languages (German, English, French, and Russian) and contained eleven stamps of approval.

"Soon after the establishment of the zones, it became easy to cross the division lines among the Western powers. However, entering the Soviet Zone was like going on a trip abroad.

"If you wandered into their sections of the city, and did not have your identity card with you, the Soviet might accuse you of being a spy. Arrest you and ship you off to one of their forced labor camps in Siberia." Viktor was saying.

"So, you really have to know the city," Feri concluded.

"Are the demarcation lines clearly marked for each section?" Judith asked.

"Yes, there are signs that say, 'Now you're entering such and such a zone'. But you could easily miss it if you don't know what that means."

"That's scary." Judith said.

"It is, till you get used to it." Viktor jumped up to introduce himself to Piry. She and Erika had been quietly standing in the room, listening, because when they stepped in, Piry said to their visitor, "Please just continue your explanation."

Now Viktor turned to Piry, "My name is Viktor Nemec. Mr. Katz from Vienna sent me to you. He is a friend of your former brother-in-law, Tibor Fábián, the rabbi who lives in America."

Piry nodded and extended her hand. Viktor took it and bent over to kiss her hand in the pre-war manner. Piry smiled at his old-fashioned courtesy.

"Please, have a seat. Would you like some coffee?" she asked.

"Thank you, but I'm afraid it's getting a bit late for me. I must get back to the inner city. Can we just have a word privately?" he asked lowering his voice and glancing at the two young girls who couldn't take their eyes off him.

"Of course," Piry smiled, "Judith, Erika, please go to your rooms and get ready for bed."

There was no arguing with their mother's tone, no matter how much they would have liked to stay. Both girls politely said good night and marched off to their freezing cold bedrooms. For despite the sub-zero temperature, the bedrooms were heated only rarely. It had to be a special occasion, such as for visitors, or a holiday observance during which they used all the rooms. Fuel was expensive and hard to get. What Feri was able to stockpile with the help of his brothers, had to last the entire winter and this was only early December. Their goose down duvets kept them warm while they slept.

Mária had also left the kitchen. She took the garden route to her bedroom, out the front door, and walking through the freezing cold yard.

Alone with the couple, Viktor got down to the purpose of his visit. "My understanding is that you would like to leave the country. I'm here to help. I'm the one who took your friend Mr. Katz to Vienna, and now I'm ready to do the same for you."

Piry and Feri sat up straight, stunned by Viktor's offer. Finally, Piry spoke up, "Could you please give us the details of how you plan to do this for us?"

"You say nothing to anyone, not even your closest relatives, so you don't put them in jeopardy. You pack just a briefcase for each person, with what you deem essential to take. You leave everything else behind. We will leave on Friday at dusk. Winter is getting severe, and this will be my last run for the year. So, you must decide now whether you are ready to go or not."

"But how do we get out?"

Viktor gave her a wry smile. "That's my business. I'll give you the details if you tell me you will leave with me on Friday afternoon."

"To where exactly?" Feri asked.

"Enough to say for now that after crossing the border into Austria, I will take you into the American sector in Vienna. When we get there, the Americans will be in charge of the center of the city, Zone 1. From there, you must make your own arrangements to go wherever you wish to live—America, Israel, not my business."

"And how much will it cost?" Piry asked.

"Eight thousand dollars for the family. Half to be paid at the start of the trip, the other half once you're in Vienna."

"That's a lot of money," Feri remarked. At the current conversion rate into Hungarian Forints, that was a year's salary for him.

"I'm taking great risks and must pay off a lot of people to succeed" smiled Viktor.

"What is our guarantee that we will succeed?" Piry asked.

Again, a smile danced on Viktor's face. "My skill and experience are the guarantees. I've done this many, many times. But this will be my last trip, so I'll make bloody sure that we all get across safely. Of course, nothing is a hundred percent sure. Not even your lives here. So, you'll just have to take a chance."

"Can we talk it over and then let you know?" Feri asked.

Viktor withdrew a piece of paper and a black Montblanc pen from his jacket pocket and scribbled down a phone number. Then he meticulously replaced the cover on the nib and put the pen away, handing the paper to Feri, "Call this number tomorrow morning, before eleven, and say 'Aunt Tilly is better' if you are coming. Or 'Aunt Tilly is worse,' if you decide not to take the risk. And now I must leave."

He rose briskly, and shook hands with Feri, extending his hand to Piry as well.

"I'll walk you out," Piry said, and led Viktor to the anti-room, where he put on his coat and hat. As they walked to the gate, Piry said, "I hope you understand that this is a very big decision for us and you're not giving us much time."

"I'm sorry, I must leave Budapest on Friday whether you come with me or not." He once again took Piry's hand and brought it lightly with his lips.

Then he slid like a cat through the gate and disappeared into the night, a shadow on the snowy street.

◉◉◉

Feri was in his usual chair when Piry returned. She sat down facing him.

"What do you think?"

"It's not up to me," he shrugged. "You're the one who has the itchy feet."

"It's for the girls' future. There is no life here for them. They have uncles in the West who will help me bring them up. They'll pay for their schooling. The whole world will open up to them. Here they are nothing but Jews with a bad upper middle-class background. One wrong word, or a teacher's dislike, and they'll be put at the bottom of the pit, into menial jobs."

"All right, then go, if that's the way you feel."

"Go? What about you?"

"I'm not going anywhere. I can live on what I earn, I don't have a bright future ahead of me. Just need to survive here with what I've got. Besides, what if something goes wrong, and you all get caught? You'll need a home to come back to."

Piry sat stunned at Feri's logic and forethought. He was right. Where would they go if their escape failed, and they had to come back to Budapest?

"If we get through, will you follow us?"

"If you send for me," he smiled at her. "For all I know, you'll find yourself some rich husband there."

"Not on your life!" Piry jumped up, sliding into his lap and kissing him.

They made love that night as if it were for the first and last time.

◎◉◎

The next morning, as soon as Feri left for work, and her daughters went off to school, Piry threw her coat over her goose feather filled feeding jacket, pulled a hat over her forehead, and walked to the public phone booth, a block from her house. She dialed the number Viktor had given her. She recognized his voice but asked anyway, "Viktor?"

"Yes."

"This is Piry. Just wanted to tell you, Aunt Tilly is better."

"That's wonderful. Then I'll come for a visit Friday at 4 p.m."

"But only 3 of us will be there. Feri will be at work."

"I see."

"I assume the cake will cost less?"

A silence followed, she could hear his breathing on the line.

"Will six forints do?"

"Fine."

"See you Friday."

The line went dead. Piry stood in the phone booth for a moment, watching her breath fog up the frosty windows. Her feet felt stuck to the wood planks of the booth, as though she had become a statue inside the glass walls. She couldn't move. *This is it. We will finally get out of the country.* The thought both thrilled and terrified her.

What will our new lives be like? Should I listen to Viktor and not call even Lilly to say good-bye? Would it indeed endanger Lilly to know, or would she be a good enough liar to deny having known anything about her sister's plans? Leaving on a Friday night!

Friday night was always reserved for the Sabbath, the lighting of candles and prayer, and absolutely no travel on any vehicle till the Sabbath was over on Saturday evening. *How could I commit to doing this on a Friday night? Maybe it's a mistake. No, despite Viktor's warning I have to consult Elek Gyula, because it requires traveling on a Friday evening.*

And I have to tell Lilly. We can't just disappear. Lilly is smart enough to keep a secret. She survived the war; she would know how to deny any knowledge of our actions. After all, we live so far from each other. Lily in central Budapest, we on the periphery, in Üjpest! We don't see each other that often. Besides, I don't have a home phone so I can't just call her.

The government only provided phone lines to people with essential occupations. She and Feri couldn't get one. Still, she had to let her sister know.

Piry lifted the receiver in the phone booth and dropped in a coin. She dialed Elek's number first and made an appointment to see him at midday. Then she called Lilly and asked if she could stop by for a few minutes at mid-afternoon, on her way home from an errand in town.

"Is something wrong?" Lilly asked, immediately concerned about this unexpected visit.

"No, just want to see you," Piry said in as calm a tone as she could muster.

"Fine. I'll be home."

Having made these calls, Piry felt better. She returned home to get dressed for her visits.

"You're as beautiful as ever," Elek commented as he rose from his desk on Piry's arrival. "But what's wrong, my dear?"

Piry gave him a quick hug then putting a finger to her lips, whispered, "Can we please go for a little walk?"

"Of course," he grabbed his coat and hat off the hook on the door and escorted Piry through the front reception area, commenting to his assistant, "We're just going for an espresso."

Elek's office was on Fortuna Street in the business district of Buda, full of shops, passersby, and buses and trolleys rolling in both directions.

Despite the subzero temperature on the snowy streets, Piry stopped him from entering a coffeehouse and said, "I need to ask you something that can't be overheard. So, we'd better keep on walking, if you don't mind."

"Of course," Elek responded, and linking Piry's arm into his, led them down a side street.

In a low voice that Elek could barely hear, Piry told him of their impending escape plan.

"I trust the man, but the thing that worries me is that we must travel on a Friday evening. That's his schedule and he can't alter it."

"Are you sure you can trust him?"

"Yes. He also said this will be his last trip this year. So, this is really our only chance."

"Then you must take it." Elek thought for a moment, pulled his hat lower on his forehead, and said quietly, "You know, it's a Jewish law that if a life has to be saved, you can break the rules of our observances, like kashrut or travel. It seems to me, this event is a life-saving situation for you and your daughters. So, you must consider it as such and go ahead with it."

Piry felt as if a heavy stone had been rolled off her heart. She stopped, lifted her face, and kissed Elek's cheek. "Thank you. I shall miss you so—."

They both knew that this was likely the last time they would see each other. He and his wife were too old to attempt an illegal border crossing, and there was no other way to leave Hungary. He held Piry's face between his palms and looked into her eyes. "Be careful. You have no idea how much I shall miss you. But above all, I wish you success. Write, once the dust settles, but of course don't put your name or return address anywhere inside or outside the envelope. Since Tibor is a rabbi, he can correspond with other rabbis and will know how to get your address to me once you're settled."

"I'll do that." Piry smiled at him.

They were both so well trained by the socialist regime, that they knew, if she did put her address on a letter coming from America, he might be interrogated by the ÁVO. They opened all foreign correspondence. He could be accused of being a spy. If they recognized her name on the return address, for sure he would be accused of having been an accomplice to her leaving the country. Thus, he couldn't resist reminding her to be cautious.

"Don't come back to the office with me," he said, and once again leaned forward and kissed her cheeks.

"If we succeed, Feri will know because he'll be on his own at the house." Piry said. She turned on her heels and left quickly, without looking back. He had been very important in their lives before and after the war. Walking away, she felt she had severed that tie.

◎◉◎

Lilly opened the front door on Piry's first ringing of the bell.

"Come in, come in. If you don't sit down for a minute you'll give me nightmares tonight," Lilly laughed, quoting an old superstition.

"Can we talk privately?" Piry asked, looking around uneasily, knowing that her sister had an assistant working in the kitchen.

"Let's go to Nandi's room, he's in kindergarten today. Settle down, I'll get us some coffee."

"No Lilly, I just came for a few minutes."

"You can't come to my house without eating or drinking something!"

Piry sighed. "Go ahead. Bring me an espresso."

Once they settled down, both women sipping the hot, thimble size coffee, Piry explained to her sister the change that was about to happen in their lives.

"So, if anyone asks, I was running errands in town and stopped by but said nothing to you about my plans. You understand?" Piry drilled her sister as if she were still a teenager.

"Yes, of course, I do." She gave Piry a toothy grin, "If it works, send him back for us."

"Gladly. Now I must go, I've got a million things to do before Friday."

They embraced, holding each other tightly, and Lilly whispered, "God be with you."

◎◉◎

While Piry and Judith were quietly discussing what they needed to pack in the briefcases that Viktor said each of them could take along, Erika was secretly saying goodbye to everything around her. The snow-covered trees along the way to her school, and at home she touched her favorite books, some of the clothes she liked, then walked through each room of the house, taking leave of all she loved. Above all, she spent time every remaining day, petting Maczko.

"I'll really miss you," she whispered to the dog. Of course, I'll also miss my relatives and friends, but those people I might see again. But I'm not sure I'll ever see you again. I hope you'll live a long, healthy life and not miss us too much." Tears welled up in her eyes. She buried her face on top of Maczko's head, while the big dog stood patiently, enduring this outburst of affection, gentry wagging his tail.

Piry told her daughters, "We must take two sets of warm clothes. We'll wear these layered on top of each other under our coats. Look through your closet and decide what you want to wear for the next couple of weeks, till we can buy some new things."

"What can we carry in our case?" Erika asked.

"In your case, you'll probably take books," Judith grinned.

"Stop teasing her," Piry snapped. "This is very serious. We'll each take our important personal documents with us, like birth certificates, identity cards, and yes, an extra set of underwear. That's about it. Now get packing."

◎◉◎

Thursday was Erika's last day at school. She attended the classes with a strange sense of detachment. Her body was there but her thoughts were floating into an unknown future ahead. She was keenly aware that their upcoming journey was going to be dangerous. So, on this last day at her school, she was secretly searching for an omen to reassure her that they would get across the border all right. Her last class was choir practice. They had been learning a new song, and this song, which until now had no particular significance, suddenly became the omen she had been looking for. Erika stood by the grand piano among her chorus members, and sang:

"Don't fear, go,
With a song in your heart,
When new life,
New adventures
Call you,
Go and take part.
Just look around you,
Winter is gone,
Spring has arrived.

A shiver ran down Erika's spine. *The song says, "Spring has arrived," but it's December! We're heading into winter, not spring,* she thought, suddenly concerned. *Never mind, this is just a dumb song, not an omen, she reassured herself. It doesn't matter that it's winter now, spring will follow. And by the time it arrives, we'll be in America."*

They finished packing on Friday morning, telling Mária that they were going to visit an aunt in Debrecen.

"Take good care of the house and Feri while we're away. You know what to do," Piry said to Mária, and slipped a hundred forint note into her hand. "This is just for you, Feri will pay your salary while we're away—but in case you need anything extra."

Surprised, Mária thanked her, for this was a lot of money. Then went off to prepare supper for Feri.

"Aren't we telling Aunt Magda and Uncle Imre that we'll be away for a while?" Erika asked Piry.

Piry shrugged, "They'll find out soon enough from Apu, after all, Imre is his brother. He is bound to let them know why we haven't returned from visiting our relatives." She smiled at Erika, "Go finish packing."

Erika felt uncomfortable leaving without saying goodbye to Magda and Imre, so she ran over to their apartment for a few minutes. Only Aunt Magda was home.

"We're going to Debrecen for a week or so," she lied smoothly. "Just wanted to let you know."

"Well, have a safe trip. It's even colder there than in Újpest," Aunt Magda said, and added, "but you'll be fine. I'll lend you a new book when you get back."

They hugged. Erika knew that although she liked being with them, her mother was not close to them. Thus, Piry didn't feel the need to let them know that they were going on a trip. But Erika felt better for having done this.

Feri came home around 3 p.m., looking grim. He and Piry spent time talking alone in the living room. When they came into the dining room, Piry put on the table her four silver Sabbath candlesticks with long white candles in them. Judith and Erika stood by silently, watching their parents. Their small leather school briefcases, packed with the essentials they were taking, had been placed by the front door, along with their coats. Even Piry had bought a similar leather case for her things.

They all felt the weight of the moment, and none of them spoke. Feri covered his head with his prayer shawl, lit the candles, and prayed, his voice breaking as if he were suppressing a sob. Then he turned from the candles, opened his arms and gathered the three women into his embrace. In a subdued voice, he chanted a blessing for travelers. Then, laying his hands over Piry's head first, then on Judith's and last on Erika's head, he blessed each of them with yet another prayer in Hebrew. He finished by saying, "May God bless you, give you a safe journey, and may we reunite in the Holy Land."

He pulled out a large handkerchief from his jacket pocket, dabbed his eyes and cheeks and blew his nose. Erika was surprised to see tears rolling down her stepfather's face. She never expected him to feel so deeply as to cry. That he could actually show love for them, and how sad and hurt he was about their departure. She felt sorry for him. This was an utterly new sensation for her concerning this man. He was the father for whom she felt love at this moment, and the man she hated most in the world. Even Judith relented and kissed him lightly on the cheek. He and Piry embraced tightly, just as they heard Maczko's bark and the bell ringing at the front gate.

"You get your coats on, I'll let him in" Feri said, still sniffing, his voice hoarse.

Viktor came into the anteroom wearing his dark coat and hat, looking as dashing as the first time. But he was in a much more subdued mood, as if he understood the pain of parting this family was going through.

"Ready?" he asked, then added, his voice a bit husky, "Piry, we just have one more thing to settle before we leave."

"Oh, yes, girls, stay here, Viktor, come into the dining room please."

The three adults closed the door to the dining room. Judith and Erika could see them talking and Piry handing him an envelope.

"How will I know that all went well?" Feri asked, quietly.

"A friend here in Budapest will send you a letter within two weeks. Once you get it, read it and burn it. Then contact the relatives and ask how much longer Piry and the girls plan to be there. After they reply that they are not there, go to the police and report that your wife and daughters went to visit relatives and had not returned. Tell the police that the relatives claim they had never arrived there."

"Got it. And what happens if for some reason—God forbid—you don't make it?"

Viktor smiled wryly, "Don't worry, you'll know it because the ÁVO will come knocking on your door. They will question you. Stick with your story that as far as you know they went to see relatives in Debrecen."

Feri gave him a piercing look, "I hope that won't happen".

"Me, too," Viktor flashed a devilish smile.

They went back into the anteroom and put on their coats and hats.

Hearing them, Mária came out of the kitchen for a good-bye hug, and to wish them a pleasant visit. Feri let them out the gate and locked it again, walking back to the house with a heavy heart. After four years of having a family, and celebrating Friday evenings together, the candle lights seemed to flicker sadly, and the room as well as the whole house felt empty.

Mária came in to ask if she could bring him dinner. Oh, I'm not completely alone, he thought. Although he had no appetite, he told her she could. He turned on the radio and listened to the standard news station, his mind miles away. His heart was thumping as if in rhythm with the train on which his family will be riding toward their freedom.

Dusk was darkening the sky; the snow glistened golden under the streetlamps as Viktor and the women walked in silence to the bus stop that would take them across the city to the Northern Train Station.

The irony didn't escape Piry, as she sat on the bus tense with anticipation, that had they been going to the town of Debrecen they would have taken the streetcar to the Western Train Station. But they were heading northwest, toward the town of Komárom, not far from the Austrian border.

It was a good thing that Feri had not accompanied them to the train station. When questioned about their disappearance, he would be able to say that as far as he knew they had gone to Debrecen. He was a poor liar, and in any case, the ÁVO's men had their ways of getting information out of people. Under torture people confessed even things they hadn't done.

Everyone knows this, Piry thought. *It will be best for him to tell the truth, that he hadn't gone with us to the train station, so he had no idea which train we had actually taken to where. That would be as much as he could say not to be implicated in our escape.*

Judith sat on the bus, with eyes closed, leaning her head against the window. Erika was staring out into the growing dark, watching the familiar houses disappear one after another. An icy feeling gripped her at the thought that this was the last time she would see these streets, these buildings, all that until now comprised her world. It gave her a tinge of smile to imagine the surprise of her schoolmates and teachers when they learned that she had escaped. *They would learn about it because word got around about all true and secret things despite the cap the government kept on it.* She glanced at Viktor's handsome profile and felt a surge of confidence rise in her. *He is going to get us through,* she assured herself.

The train station was big and noisy. People scurried back and forth, carrying large and small suitcases. They shouted, laughed, cried, hugged each other good-bye, and climbed the narrow metal stairs up into their train compartments. Viktor left them waiting in the main concourse while he went to buy their tickets. When he returned, they were just in time to board the train for Komárom.

Their compartment consisted of facing hardwood benches, each seating two, in ten rows. Piry and Viktor quickly found seats, and took the isle ones, letting the girls sit by the window. They watched as people leaned out to wave kerchiefs and shout their last good-byes. Erika, too, stuck her head out the window, although she had no one to say farewell to in the crowd. The array of travelers fascinated her.

Soon the train gave a sharp, loud whistle, white smoke billowed from beneath it, and slowly the long metal snake set into motion. A few minutes later it was rolling through the city and passengers got busy pulling up the windows to stop the sharp winter air from blowing in.

Erika watched the lighted windows of buildings stream by with increasing speed. Then the lights became sparce as the train traveled through the outskirts of Budapest. Soon all the lights were gone. The train barreled across the countryside in vast darkness, with occasional village houses lit up in the distance. Erika buried her face in her coat sleeve and went to sleep.

The others sat in silence, none of them felt like talking. After a while, Judith and Viktor also decided to nap. Piry sat staring at the black world outside, with reflections from the interior of the train swimming by on the windowpanes. As time passed, she too, closed her eyes but couldn't sleep. She wondered how she was going to contact her ex-brother-in-law Tibor in America once they got to Vienna, and how they were going survive in America while learning to speak English. Then she had a dreadful thought, what if we get caught crossing the border, either into Slovakia or into Austria? She gently nudged her daughters' arms whispering into their ears, "Wake up, I need to tell you something."

Judith and Erika opened their eyes, grumpy at being awakened for probably some unimportant detail.

"What?" Judith asked, leaning her head back with her eyes still half closed.

"Just listen carefully," Piry ordered, looking at Erika who sat with her head bent down, "Are you up?"

"Of course, I am," Erika grumbled. "What's so important?"

Piry glanced at Viktor; he was asleep and gently snoring. She turned to her daughters and whispered, "We will most likely get to Austria with Viktor's help. But if things go wrong and we don't make it, either at the upcoming Hungarian border or crossing into Austria, this is what you must keep in mind: if we get caught, we'll be questioned by the secret police. They will want to know why we wanted to leave Hungary, and where we were planning to go. Regardless of what they ask you, or how they threaten you, you must say that we were going to your Uncle Eli in Israel. That you had lost your father in the war and miss him terribly. Uncle Eli offered to be like a father to you in Israel and this is why you wanted to escape. To go and live with him. Do not, under any circumstances, say a word about wanting to go to America. Is that clear?"

Piry didn't have to explain to either girl why they had to say this. Both knew, America was the evil empire, the capitalist hell. Anyone wanting to go there was an enemy of their socialist paradise. They understood that wanting to have an uncle as a father substitute was not an unreasonable excuse for what they were doing. It was not against their regime or country; it was merely a child's desire for close family ties while growing up. They nodded, and Piry sighed with relief.

She expected for everything to go as planned, but should anything go wrong, her daughters were prepared. Hiding as Christians during the war and lying in their daily lives under communism taught them how to act under stress. It was good to be ready for all eventualities. Piry leaned back and seeing her relax, Judith and Erika closed their eyes again.

Although it was an express train, time again it stopped at cities along the way. But Viktor and his little group slept on. Then, after several hours, as the train came to a stop at yet another station, as if by instinct, Viktor opened his eyes and reached over to gently touch Piry's hand, "Next stop is Komárom."

Piry nudged Judith and Erika awake.

"Where are we?" Erika asked, her voice husky with sleep.

"We'll be getting off at the next stop." Piry replied.

They clambered off the stairs from the warmth of the cabin into a biting cold night. Even in gloves their fingers grew stiff around the handle of their briefcases.

"How long are we staying here?" Judith asked, her teeth chattering.

"Just a couple of hours," Viktor replied. "We arrived a bit early for our next transport, so we'll just wait it out."

Piry and Erika followed Viktor as he took Judith's arm and told them they would be just walking around in the train station for a while. Then the station quieted down and the last of the passengers left with the 10 p.m. train. No more trains were running till morning.

Viktor directed them out into the freezing cold night, illuminated only by the snow covering the streets. Ignoring the weather, Viktor took Judith's arm and began to stroll at a leisurely pace, instructing Piry and Erika to follow at a discreet distance.

Komárom seemed like a rather small city, asleep in the night, with an occasional window light still burning. Viktor led them up and down cobblestone streets with stately three-story apartment buildings along the sidewalks, closer and closer to the bank of the Danube. The closer they were the colder it got with a light wind brushing their faces.

The Danube River at Komárom served as the border between Hungary and Slovakia on its opposite bank. A wide stone bridge stretched across the water, connecting the two countries. Before World War I, the other side was also part of Hungary. Most people across the river still spoke Hungarian as their first language. But now that half of the city was called Komarno, in the Slovak tongue, and belonged to Slovakia. After World War II Slovakia became attached to the Czech Republic. Now both countries were one, under Soviet rule, as Czechoslovakia.

"Why can't we cross the border to Austria in Komárom?" Erika whispered to Viktor when they stopped for a moment to take a break in their night stroll.

"Because it's not possible to do it here. It's too well guarded, and there are mines along its perimeters. You don't want to step on one those in the dark. The Slovak border is still porous enough to get through. That's why." He playfully touched Erika's forehead with his index finger as if to impart the knowledge there. "Now let's walk some more."

It was a clear, moonless night. The snow was crunching under their feet as if they were walking on crystal sugar. All the trees lining the streets were covered with frost and stood like skeleton fingers reaching toward the night sky.

"We'll have to walk until just past 11 o'clock," said Viktor as they paced the streets.

Cold and bored, Erika looked up and was amazed. She had never seen so many stars in the sky. Her breath formed little puffs of white clouds in front of her, and she amused herself for a while by inhaling deeply and letting the air out slowly, pretending it was cigarette smoke.

The wind that occasionally swept snow dust into their faces and down their necks, also carried the sound of music. Near the river, high along the embankment, stood a row of barracks.

"Russian soldiers are housed there," Viktor whispered.

It was their singing that drifted toward them, and Erika recognized the melodies from having learned them at school. It was such a different feeling, singing them happily in the classroom or hearing them now by Soviet soldiers stationed in Komárom. The songs at school gave the illusion of happiness. The barracks full of Soviet soldiers in Hungary were the reality.

◎◉◎

They also heard the singing when they sat by the bank of the Danube, waiting for the boatman who was to row them across the river to Slovakia. After walking for an hour and a half, Viktor said it was time to carefully, noiselessly inch their way down the icy slope and sit on the snow-covered sand by the water. His friend, the boatman, was supposed to arrive any minute now.

Above them, to their right, stretched the connecting bridge. The three women sat in its shadow and watched the guards on the Hungarian side walk to half the bridge and then with military precision do an about-face and return. The border patrols on the other side did the same. Guns on their shoulders, their dark silhouettes loomed menacingly against the night sky.

Viktor didn't sit with them. He said, he could see the signal better from the top of the embankment. Piry suspected that he was lying but there was nothing she could do about it. *It was safer for him to be further away from the river and from them. For what if one of the border patrols looked down? There is sure death peeping at us from above, for if we were sighted, how could I explain why we had traveled from Budapest to sit at this particular spot by the Danube, late at night, in December? I should have asked him what we could say, but didn't think of it,* Piry blamed herself.

Then she realized, it had all happened so fast, and Viktor certainly didn't explain the details of their trip; he just guided them to the next step as was necessary. It's too late to worry now, we just have to go along and trust him, she shrugged to herself.

A rising wind was running through their coats and all three of them were shivering as much from the wind as their fear. Above their heads the gust carried the drunken voices of the Russian soldiers. Suddenly, a light flashed on the other side of the Danube. It was gone in the blink of an eye, and Erika wondered if the others had also seen it. Viktor had told them not to talk, so she couldn't ask them. As they sat there in tense silence, they could hear the splashing of the water against the bank grow louder.

They could not see the man rowing, and it was just as well, for if they couldn't, neither could the guards on the bridge. Time passed in anxious waiting. The snow started to softly crunch behind them, and they turned in fright. But it was Viktor, descending carefully, practically on all fours. The women sat waiting, without uttering a sound. Viktor silently crouched down beside them, also waiting. Then slowly, slowly, a dark moving bulk approached the shore, making the water lap faster against it. They peered into the dark. A small rowboat was gently bobbing in the water with a man keeping it still by pressing an oar into the wet sand of the bank.

"You two go first," whispered Viktor, pointing at Piry and Erika. "I'll come with Judith on the second round."

There was no time for debate or discussion. In fact, Piry thought, how smart he is. *He knows Judith needs a man to control her, whereas Erika is easy to handle.*

The tiny rubber boat swayed precariously as the oarsman, in a black coat, his head covered with a black cap, reached out a black gloved hand to help the two passengers into his dinghy. They had barely slipped onto the back plank when the man, sitting in front of them on the middle plank, started silently dipping his oars into the dark water.

Erika watched as the shoreline of Hungary melted into the night. She was struck by the irrevocability of the moment and her stomach contracted with fear and pain.

Where are we going? Toward what? Why? Tears rolled down her cheeks, the wind blew on the wet furrows they left, her face felt frozen. *Why am I so upset to leave Hungary?* Her mind raced over sun-filled summers, loving relatives, friends, schools, all that had formed her life up to this point. She realized that with the deliberately torn ties with her homeland the cords of her childhood had also been cut.

Piry sat silently beside Erika, and thought, *had I known how dangerous this journey would be, I might not have risked it.*

The boat docked smoothly on the dark bank across the river. "My name is Bálint," the boatman whispered as he helped Piry and Erika to climb out. "Wait there," he pointed at some bare bushes just above the bank.

They stood shivering in silence behind the shrubbery while the man returned for Judith and Viktor. It seemed like hours had passed by the time they docked and emerged from the night, pebbly sand crunching under their feet.

"We'll go to Bálint's house for a few hours' rest," Viktor explained, as he came over to Piry and Erika. Then he and Judith walked ahead, following Bálint.

His house was nearby. It was small, and clean, with an entry through the well-scrubbed kitchen. Once they were inside, Erika took a quick look at their guide. He was a short, stocky man with a broad, kind face. He pointed at a coat stand by the door.

"Take your coats and hats off, it's warm in here," he smiled. He also removed his gloves, his coat, and black knitted cap."

He probably covered his head so well, not just against the cold, but also to hide his blond hair from the bridge, Erika thought. She noted that his bushy eyebrows were as fair as his hair.

His wife, Maria, also a blonde and equally short and stocky, greeted the guests warmly. She offered bread, butter, and cheese, tea or coffee, and they gratefully accepted the modest dinner. As soon as they finished eating, a visible exhaustion came over all three of them. Maria led them into a bedroom, most likely their own. It was customary in Hungary, and evidently across the border as well, to offer guests the best room in the house.

"I'll stay up a while," Viktor informed them with a smile as he settled at the kitchen table with Bálint, a carafe of wine and glasses set before them.

Twin beds pushed together stood in the middle of the simply furnished room. Judith and Piry each took a bed, while Erika lay down between them with a blanket rolled flat to fill the crack between the mattresses. They removed their shoes and lay fully dressed under the big goose-down comforters, slowly relaxing in the safety of the room.

As she was falling asleep, Erika could hear the branches of a tree beating in the wind against the window as if someone were knocking to be let in.

◎◉◎

At 5 a.m. next morning Viktor knocked on the bedroom door and opening it a crack, called in: "Piry, girls, wake up, we must continue our trip as soon as you can get ready."

It was freezing cold in the room and dark outside. But Piry rolled out from under the duvet and tapped both her daughters to do the same. There was a blue zinc pitcher on the floor next to a stand holding a white enamel bowl. They hurriedly washed their faces by pouring cold water from the pitcher into the bowl. They shared the small hand towel that hung on a rod by the side of the stand.

Down the hallway was a small room with a regular flush toilet. They had used it the night before, and now, as they left the room, they stopped by it one by one.

"At least they have an indoor toilet," Judith grinned at Erika while they waited for Piry to come out.

"Just come to the kitchen when you're done," Piry instructed her daughters.

The hallway led to the kitchen, which felt cozy with the stove burning. On it sat a pot of hot coffee. Maria offered them bread and cheese again, and milk, along with the coffee.

"You must eat, even if you're not hungry," Viktor insisted. "Or make a sandwich, wrap it in a piece of paper and bring it with you," he suggested, looking at their sleepy faces. "We have a ways to go and there may not be food available on the train."

All three of them cut their bread in half, placing a slice of cheese in the middle, and wrapping it in a napkin, plus newsprint, handed to them by Maria. But they gratefully drank a mug of the warm, sweet, black coffee which helped them to get going They thanked their hosts, and walked out into the snow covered, dark, December dawn.

Viktor led them at a brisk pace to a train station. "Don't talk on the train," he ordered them. "Even though this is a border town and many of the residents are Hungarian, they also speak Slovak, and you don't. Plus, your Budapest Hungarian sounds very different from the local dialect. So, unless you have an urgent problem that you need to whisper to me, just keep quiet during the trip."

As before, Viktor went and bought their tickets. They boarded the train and sat in silence during the trip. None of them had asked Viktor how long the ride will take, and now it was too late. The sun rose outside the train windows while they ate their sandwiches and then fell asleep under the hypnotic rattle of the wheels. Viktor woke them with a gentle tap on their shoulders. He indicated by tilting his head toward the exit door that they were getting off at the next stop.

The train came to a screeching halt. As they clambered down the metal stairs into the station of a small Slovak town, they saw a big sign displaying its name: Dunajska Streda.

"The Hungarian name is Dunaszerdahely, but no one calls it that anymore," Viktor whispered to them, flashing his quick, charming smile as he led them out of the station. Once on the street, he quietly said, "We're going to my brother's house. Just walk with me as if we were a family. But now it's even more important that you don't talk. Unless you speak Slovak," he added with a grin.

"Do you?" Erika asked, and it earned her a pinch on her arm from Judith.

"Stupid," Judith hissed so only Erika could hear.

"Of course, I speak Slovak," Viktor smiled at Erika. "I speak four languages." So, relax, and follow me."

Striding to keep up, Erika was busy thinking about which languages Viktor was likely to speak. Obviously, he spoke Slovak and Hungarian, and probably Russian and German. She decided she would ask him once they were able to talk again.

Walking ahead with Piry, the girls following closely, Viktor led them through what seemed to be most of this small town. It had tree-lined streets, one-story houses, and dogs that barked at them as they passed by. Viktor didn't pay any attention to the racket they made. He just strode ahead, clearly eager to get them to their destination as fast as he could. They turned onto yet another tree-lined street, and Viktor pushed open the gate to a small garden with a white- washed house in back of the yard.

Before he could knock on the wood front door, it was opened by a young man. He was taller than Viktor but strongly resembled him though he didn't have a mustache. He pulled Viktor into a bear hug. "You're back!" he exclaimed in Hungarian. Then Viktor stepped aside, and his brother gestured for Piry and her daughters to enter.

"Welcome to our humble little home. I am Štefan -- that's my Slovak name. My Hungarian name is István, but it's better for me to use the Slovak version. We Hungarians are not very popular with the Slovaks." He grinned, and went on, "My wife Ibolya will be with us in a minute. She is feeding the baby." Then he added, "Please, make yourselves at home."

They hung their coats and hats in the hallway, and Štefan led them into the spacious, warm kitchen. "Please, sit down, sit down," he pointed to the carved wood chairs that had colorful flowers painted on their back support. Just like Hungarian folk art, Erika thought. The familiar design made her feel at home.

"How was the trip so far?" Štefan asked, sitting down with them.

"We're all here," Viktor smiled at him.

"First thing I must tell you is that our guides recommended we cross on the 8th" Štefan responded.

Viktor was taken clearly aback by the news, "Today is only the 6th! What are we supposed to do till then?"

"Be our welcome guests," Štefan grinned at him.

The kitchen door opened, and a very pretty buxom young woman entered. "You made it!" she exclaimed, with a broad smile, her eyes traveling from face to face around the table. She wore an embroidered green apron over her white blouse, and a blue-green flower-patterned pleated skirt. Her hair was neatly pulled back into a smooth bun, and she showed even white teeth as she smiled at them. She had a round face with warm brown eyes which contrasted nicely with her blonde hair.

Viktor rose, gave her a hug, then introduced Piry and the two girls.

Ibolya studied her guests as they sat stiffly at the table. "You must be exhausted. Would you like to have a bite, then take a nap?"

Without waiting for an answer, she started putting glasses and plates on the table. As if on cue, Štefan opened a cupboard and took out a sizeable leg of ham and a large cheese round and arranging them on a wooden board set it on the table. Ibolya added a loaf of home-baked rye bread, and a pitcher of water. Štefan put out a bottle of red wine.

Piry was too embarrassed to say they couldn't eat ham because it wasn't kosher. Because she had said nothing, she watched as her two daughters happily accepted slices of buttered bread, topped with ham and cheese. She remembered Elek's words about the laws of kashrut being lifted when one's life depended on it. She recalled the bacon and bread she had eaten on the train after the war, when she first met Paul Miko. That was not kosher either and lightning hadn't struck her. In fact, her acceptance of Miko's food was a lifesaver—not only because she was starving but because it had resulted in a friendship and a profitable business for both of them. So, she hid her qualms and ate with the rest of them.

"We took the baby's crib into our bedroom and set up her room for the three of you," Ibolya explained, as she led them to the room that was to be theirs during their stay. The bathroom, equipped with a sink and a tub, was at the end of the hall. Next to it was a small, separate room with the toilet. *They have indoor plumbing,* Erika thought gratefully, recalling the outhouse at Dunakeszi, the Hungarian village, where she had spent such wonderful summers.

"Our bedroom is on the other side of yours," Ibolya explained.

Catching Piry's questioning look, she added, "Viktor will sleep on the living room couch. It's only for a couple of nights. Besides, he's done that on his visits ever since the baby has taken over the guest room."

During the following two days Piry made herself useful by helping Ibolya with meal preparations for the suddenly increased household. Erika happily played with the baby girl, Sofia, who was only six months old. She smiled a lot, loving the attention. Judith sat quietly, most of the time reading a Hungarian novel she found in the couple's bookcase. Viktor and Štefan chopped wood for the fireplace and went food shopping for cold cuts and loaves of bread which they planned to take along when they continued their journey.

"As I told you at the start," Viktor explained to Piry over dinner, "this trip will be my last for some time, if not forever. So, my brother and his family will be coming along as well. Now you know how important it is for me to make it a safe and successful crossing."

"Life for Hungarians, even if they're born in Slovakia, and their families go back centuries, is becoming increasingly difficult," Ibolya added, when she saw the look of surprise on her guests' faces.

"I thought all nationalities were treated equally under communism," Erika piped up.

"That's the story," Ibolya replied, smiling. "The reality is quite different. As you may have studied in geography class, after the war Czechoslovakia had been cobbled together from three different nations. The Czechs, the Slovaks, and the Moravians. Our languages and customs are similar but not the same. However, under the Soviets we're considered one nation.

"I don't know if you know this," Štefan added, "but during the Austro-Hungarian Empire, and for centuries before that, Hungarians occupied a part of Slovakia as their domain. The Slovaks, belonging to the Slavic nations, hated the Hungarians' rule."

"Why?" Erika asked wide eyed, "I was taught in school that the conquest of the land between the Hungarian tribes and the Slovak king Svatopluk had been a peaceful one, based on a treaty."

Štefan smiled at her. "Want to hear the story from the Slovak point of view?"

"Isn't it a bit late for stories?" Piry asked Viktor.

He smiled and shrugged, "It won't take long, let them learn."

So Štefan began: "Originally, the Hungarians were warrior tribes who came into Europe from Mongolia during the 9th century. To survive, they constantly raided European nations that had long established borders among each other. However, at times when these nations fought each other, they would hire those wild Hungarian warriors to help them win their war.

During one of these wars the Hungarians, in alliance with Svatopluk I, king of Moravia which included Slovakia as well, invaded the territory of Pannonia, in central Europe. The Slovaks won the war with the help of the Hungarians. When the fighting ended, the Hungarians tricked Svatopluk into giving them the land that is now Hungary.

"The story goes that a representative of the Hungarian tribes, called Kusid, was sent to Svatopluk with the following gifts: a great white horse wearing a bridle and a saddle made with gold from Arabia, with the request to let the Hungarians settle in Pannonia. Seeing this noble horse carrying such precious gold, Svatopluk rejoiced, thinking that they were sending gifts of homage in return for living and working on his land. Therefore, Svatopluk replied, "In return for these precious gifts I will let your tribes have as much land as they desire."

Then the Hungarians sent another envoy to Svatopluk to deliver the following message:

"Árpád and his people say to you that you may no longer stay upon the land which they bought from you. For with the horse they bought your earth, with the bridle the grass, and with the saddle the water. And you, in exchange, granted them the land to live on, and the grass and the water to use."

"King Svatopluk, recognizing his mistake, knew he could not chase the Hungarians off the land. So, he made a treaty with them. In exchange for the land on which they would settle and cultivate, the Hungarians would stop attacking their neighboring countries. The treaty was sealed by sharing a loaf of bread and a jug of water between King Svatopluk and Árpád, chief of the seven Hungarian tribal leaders."

"That's why, it's still a Hungarian custom to take a loaf of bread and not water but wine when visiting someone's house for the first time," added Piry.

"Things have improved since the 9th century," grinned Viktor.

"That's an amazing story," Erika exclaimed, wide eyed.

"Wait, it doesn't end there," Štefan said. "When Svatopluk made the treaty, he had also sent a messenger to the Pope who then sent a Bishop to convince the pagan Árpád to convert to Christianity. Once Árpád was baptized, the other tribal chiefs had to follow suit, and each of their tribes also converted. That is how the Hungarians became Catholics in the 9th Century and settled in the middle of Europe as a new nation."

Viktor added, "That is why amidst their Slavic and Romanian neighbors the Hungarian language remains a totally unrelated tongue. Also, despite all their so-called peaceful co-existence, the Slavs and the Hungarians went on fighting each other. And the victorious Hungarians occupied Slav territories, till the end of World War II."

"Is that why the Slovaks hate the Hungarians?" Erika asked, thinking, that Hungarians hated the Soviets, who occupied their country.

"Pretty much," Štefan replied. "You're a smart kid. You'll do well in the West!"

CHAPTER 17

ON THE 8TH OF December, after two cozy days and nights, Viktor and his charges were ready to go on. It was mid-afternoon when Štefan locked the front door and the gate of their home, taking only a small suitcase with him. His wife, Ibolya, carried the baby, Sofia, all bundled up against the freezing cold weather.

Piry and her daughters followed them with Viktor. They walked to the train station, careful not to slip on the icy snow that covered the streets. Viktor went inside the station building and returned with tickets for them.

"Take a separate compartment and meet us in Bratislava," Viktor instructed his brother.

On the train, the seats were comfortably padded. They sat opposite each other, Erika and Judith by the window, Viktor facing Piry on the isle. They were all silent, as instructed earlier. Erika watched the trees and meadows, buried under a thick coat of snow, disappear as the train sped by. An infinite gray sky covered the world. Then it turned dark blue, dotted with stars which seemed to sit still as they left them behind.

Erika tried to sleep but couldn't. The yellow lights of the compartment made everyone look sad and lonely. *Or is it just my own feelings of loneliness that I see reflected on Anyu's and Judith's faces?* Erika wondered, observing her silent family's empty gazes. Viktor was asleep, his head tilted against the seat back.

The monotony of the chugging train was in sharp contrast with the turbulent feelings Piry had about the upcoming border crossing. *What if we don't make it? No, we will make it, we must.* She looked at her daughters and envisioned a home for them somewhere in America.

They will finish high school, go to university, and learn a profession unlike me. I wasn't allowed to study because I was a woman. Of course, they will get married as well, and have children, and all this will be well behind them. She couldn't picture what her future would be like in the new country. *Would Feri follow me? Would I want him to follow, considering what a bad husband he turned out to be? Maybe not. We are divorced; nothing obligates me to live with him again. Maybe I will meet someone new in the new land. Someone who will be good to me as Zoltan had been.* Her musings were interrupted by Erika's whisper:

"Look, there are more and more lights coming up."

Viktor heard her, opened his eyes and stared out the window.

"Hey, we're coming into Bratislava!"

A tremor ran through Erika hearing that they had arrived in the capital of Slovakia, the city that bordered with Austria. They were coming closer and closer to their destination.

The main railway station, Hlavna Stanica, as a sign read, was a two-story building, large and busy. *Just like in Budapest*, Erika thought, *people are rushing back and forth carrying suitcases, hugging each other good-bye or welcome.* Strange syllables filled the air—everyone was speaking Slovak. Here and there Erika understood a word that was similar to Russian. But she knew better than to comment on this to her companions.

Štefan and his family appeared by their side, and they walked out of the station together, onto a crowded avenue, Predstaničné Námestie. It was well lit, store windows glittered, coral-colored streetcars clattered along with the ting-a-ling of bells, warning people of their passage. A light fog hovered over the city; everything glistened with the moisture. The sidewalks reflected long streaks of colorful lights from the shops, intercepted by shadows of hurrying pedestrians. Viktor led his small group to a side street that was relatively dark and far less crowded.

He said, "We shall have to take a bus over the bridge to the other side of the city. However, because the Austrian border is on that side, the security police occasionally raid the buses. So, for greater safety we'll have to form pairs with one person fluent in Slovak. But please avoid talking. This is a risky ride."

Piry got on the bus with Ibolya and the baby, Erika and Štefan went together, followed by Judith and Viktor. The twosomes sat apart from each other, aware where the others were but avoiding eye contact. Other people on the bus did not seem concerned and Erika envied them. She sat with her gloved fingers clutching the handle of the small briefcase on her lap, feeling butterflies in her stomach.

Finally, they rolled across the bridge. After a couple more stops, Viktor rose, indicating that they will be getting off. They avoided looking at him but followed him into the street. This part of Bratislava looked completely different from the heart of the city. It was a suburb of two-story homes with shuttered windows. The sparsely lit streets were covered by high snow which had not been cleared. They trudged through it, following Viktor in silence. He led them into a nearby grove alongside what seemed like a major highway.

"Each of you get behind a tree that's big enough to cover you from being seen from the road. I'll be back to give you the signal to continue," Viktor instructed them and disappeared into the night.

The grove was thick, the ground and the trees were covered by snow that reached mid-calf. They stamped it down around their feet and stood hiding from the road, each of them careful to fit behind the tree of their choice. Erika pressed herself against the trunk in front of her. She did not see the others but sensed their presence behind the trees around her. The headlights of sporadically passing cars seemed to shine directly into her eyes, and she thought she would faint if she had to stand there much longer. Finally, Viktor returned. They could hear the snow crunching under his feet. He hissed, "Follow me!"

As each of them emerged from behind a tree, Piry was shocked to see that Viktor was surrounded by a large group of people. Furiously, she whispered to Judith and Erika, "Viktor has deceived us. He is taking far more people than he had told me."

Judith shrugged philosophically, "There is nothing we can do about it now. Unless you want to turn back?"

"We can't, we're stuck. Let's just make sure that we stay close to him as we go on," Piry responded.

Judith, perhaps recalling their march with Erika during the war, made sure that she and her sister walked with their mother and that they kept Viktor and his family in sight, right in front of them as they trudged across the forest, and then what seemed like endless white fields.

Behind them the snow crunched and squeaked under the feet of the rest of the group. Piry counted about 25 people. She was enraged and felt cheated by Viktor, but this was not the time to dwell on her anger. *Once we're in Vienna I'll make sure I spread the word about him, she thought, but right now we just need to move along to make sure we'll get there.*

To advance, they had to cut paths in the virgin snow which in places reached up to their hips. Their shoes, slacks, and stockings became soaked, then froze into icicles softly clinking as they cautiously placed one foot after another. The heavy panting of some elderly members of the group lingered in the air. Clouds of their increasingly labored breath floated ahead of them.

"Let's move faster," Piry urged her daughters as they struggled to advance in the tall snow. They seemed to be falling behind, the distance increasing between them and Viktor, who was speeding ahead with his family.

They've been trudging for hours through the snowfields when the group came upon a narrow bridge over a rapidly flowing brook. It was not a solid bridge but mere planks with wide gaps between them, held together by a frame that lay along the brook's shores. Several men, who had walked ahead with Viktor, now stood by to help the others over the bridge. Piry and Judith walked across it fine, but Erika felt dizzy as she glanced at the rushing water between the planks and stopped midway.

"Be brave, little one," Viktor whispered into her ear, as he reached for her hand and guided her across to solid ground. He then quickly turned to help others, but his words flooded Erika with a sense of warmth and trust. He'll get us through, she thought, as she joined Piry and Judith.

They all stood waiting for the last of the people to traverse the bridge, when a woman screamed, and Erika saw one of her legs disappear into the opening between the planks. The helping men rushed to her and pulling her leg up, carried her across the planks to safety. The woman stopped near Erika, panting as she collected herself. Then, with everyone across the bridge, the group went on.

The snow got even deeper, and people moved slower and slower as they struggled forward against the frozen white wall. The wind rose and Erika moved with her head bowed to prevent the snow from blowing into her eyes. Her kerchief slipped off her head to her neck, collecting the drifting snow. It felt icy wet on her skin, but she couldn't do anything about it. She became too tired to carry her briefcase and put it down.

Judith, keeping an eye on her, grabbed it up. "Just move. I'll take it for a while" she whispered.

Erika remembered another night like this, struggling against the wind— in rain at that time—with Judith carrying both their briefcases. *But that was the war, and mother had rescued us then. Now it's different; we're not marching toward death but toward a new life,* she reminded herself. Obviously, it was hard for all of them, but everyone knew the goal—freedom! So, they marched on.

As the people in the group painstakingly put one foot after another into the deep snow, the icicles around their ankles chafed like iron manacles. Bent into the wind, they pushed ahead or lagged behind the others. The journey seemed endless, and occasionally plaintive voices called to Viktor who was striding ahead, "Are we far yet? How much longer?"

He would respond angrily, "Hush! Keep quiet and just keep moving!"

After countless hours, Viktor suddenly ordered the group in a low voice to stop. "Everybody lie down flat and don't move or make a sound!" he commanded.

People fell like logs onto a snowy railroad bank, numb with cold, pain, and fatigue. A train's whistle could be heard in the distance and Erika longed for the warmth of its compartments. Piry was keenly aware that the group was a dark mass over the white slope on which they waited for the train to pass just above them on the tracks.

Lying there, she recalled overhearing a comment by Viktor to Štepan, that they were supposed to cross the railroad tracks way before the train came passing by. She felt the ice reach into her depth as she marveled at their luck that none of the passengers looked out and noticed them. It would have been so easy, especially for the conductor, to spot them. Another miracle, she thought.

Then the group dragged onward. The older couples among them called to Viktor time and again to stop so they could catch up.

"We can't stop, just follow," Viktor whispered impatiently.

Obediently, they fell silent and trudged along as best they could. Suddenly, way in the back, an elderly man fell.

"Hey, people wait for me, I can't go on! I think I broke my ribs! Wait for me!" His plaintive cry carried in the silent night.

Viktor rushed back to him, speaking in a low, angry voice, "Are you mad to shout like this? You want us all to get killed? If you can't go on, stay! But don't hold everyone else up!"

Erika was shocked by Viktor's ruthlessness. She now understood, more than ever before, the risk they had taken. *It was everyone for himself. If you fell, you stayed, while the others marched on. No one could give you a helping hand. If they did, they too could be left behind.*

Yet she saw her mother and a man rush to the old man. They put their arms under his and helped him go on. Erika felt enormous relief and pride that her mother was one of the people who cared. She was aware that they could fall behind the others but what did it matter? They would not let the old man die in the snowfields.

On and on and on the group struggled forward. Despite the dark of night, the snow glowed with an eerie light. With eyes nearly blinded by the freezing air, and legs collapsing with fatigue, they moved on. Then, slowly, from behind the black dome of the sky they saw the moon slip through. It was full and brilliant. The snowy meadow lit up with a thousand sparks and the group appeared on the infinite whiteness like a black centipede.

Piry and her girls knew that it was more dangerous to go on in the moonlight. Viktor had told them at Štepan's house that by the time the moon came up they would have to have reached Austria. The reason he had chosen this night to cross was that they could do it in the dark, because the moon rose so late that night. But perhaps they were still all right. A few hundred yards ahead of them the iron curtain loomed.

In the bright moonlight the barbed wire of the Slovak border cast a long black grid on the snow. They all saw it and rushed toward it with renewed energy.

"We forgot the wire-cutter," Erika heard Štepan whisper to Viktor.

"Never mind," Viktor hushed him. "Let's just make an opening."

With the help of several men, they forced the barbed wires apart, making a sufficient gap for a person to double over so as not to get caught in the sharp wire tips, and carefully crawl through. Viktor and several younger men in the group held the wires open and helped people manage. One leg first, then the head and body, finally the other leg.

"Come, come quickly," urged Viktor, as he grabbed Erika's shoulders to help her crawl through the wire.

Judith and Piry came right after her, both rejoicing and thanking Viktor. *We made it, we are free*, Piry thought, wild with joy.

"Hurry, hurry, go on," Viktor implored everyone, "we are only in 'no-man's land'."

They all rushed ahead with strangely lightened feet, not thinking that danger could still lurk behind them.

What could happen when the Austrian border is just a few hundred yards away, and a truck is waiting for us there to take us to Vienna, Piry thought, confident in their success as she pushed forward in the snow to keep up with Viktor and the younger adults, making sure her daughters were alongside her.

The older people behind them also moved with renewed energy, for the success of leaving the communist border behind gave them strength. Even the old man with the broken ribs stopped moaning and hastened along.

It was a few minutes later, about midway to the Austrian border, that they heard a sharp hissing sound as something whizzed by the group.

"Down everybody!" Viktor shouted, "They're shooting at us!"

The group, as one, threw itself face down on the snow.

Piry, Judith, and Erika lay next to each other. Filled with fear and apprehension, they lay and listened as bullets whizzed over them.

"We can't just lie here, let's crawl forward," Erika whispered to Piry.

"Stay still or you'll get shot," Piry hissed back, and Erika, against her better judgment, had to obey.

Flares lit up the sky. They could hear men shouting and dogs barking, and they knew for sure that their escape had failed. Erika lifted her head just enough to see the black mass of their group in the white snowfield illuminated by a shower of multicolored flares, and she could hear the bullets whistling around them. She knew that crawling forward would now be truly impossible. She buried her face in the snow and waited for what would happen next.

◉◉◉

It wasn't long before the shouting, gun wielding border guards and wildly barking huge German shepherds reached the group in the snow.

"Vstavat, vstavat, davaj, davaj!" The border guards shouted repeatedly and, as they spotted the women in the group, added, "Davaj, Kurvi! Kurvi!"

Although the Hungarians did not understand the language, the Slovaks in the group and Erika, did. "Vstat and Davaj" in Russian meant, "Stand up! Move!"

They were being ordered to get up and move. Piry, hearing the word "kurvi," knew they had used the Hungarian pejorative for prostitutes. Pointing at her daughters she shouted in German, "Kinder, Kinder, nein Kurvi," without even understanding why she spoke in German. But it stopped a border guard for a second. He looked at them, then responded angrily, "Kinder, nyet! Kurvi!" (not children, whores!) and waving his gun urged them to join the others, "Davaj, davaj!" (Move, move!)

The many guards quickly lined up the group and pointing back toward the Slovak border, aided by their wildly barking large German shepherds, herded them at gunpoint in that direction.

No one in the group uttered a sound as they shuffled their way toward an open gate in the barbed wire fence. Surreptitiously searching the faces, Piry saw that Victor, Štefan and his family, and some group members were not among them. *They must have gotten through,* she thought bitterly. *I was a fool not to insist that we keep up with Victor, staying right by his side. I should have known that he would wait for no one when it came to getting across. Maybe Erika had it right, we should have crawled forward.* She glanced at her daughters and felt infinite guilt and regret for having taken a chance with their lives.

"Don't forget we were going to Israel," she whispered to them under her breath.

"Are they going to walk us back to Hungary?" muttered one of the men ahead of them. A guard next to him responded by striking his back with the handle of his gun, shouting, 'Ticho!' (Quiet!)

After a short march along a well-trod path in the snow, the captive group arrived at a guardhouse in the midst of the barbed wire fence. A guard shouted before the entrance "Prestat!" (Stop). The guards then stopped by each person and showed them to put his or her hands together in front of them. They handcuffed everyone. Then directed their captives forward into the building, using the Russian word, "Davaj! Davaj!" (Move! Move!)

Erika was frightened and looking at Judith she knew that her sister was too. Their mother's face was inscrutable, she was staring straight ahead as if in shock by their arrest.

The guards stopped them after entering a hallway and blindfolded them one by one with a black cloth that blocked out all light. Again, they shouted "Davaj, davaj," and guided each prisoner across a threshold by putting their hands on the captives' back or arm. They were walked forward, and guided to the left, then pushed forward again a few more steps. The guards shouted "Stop!" and the prisoners stood still like frozen statues. Quiet ensued.

After a few minutes, Erika cautiously moved her cuffed hands forward to explore what was in front of her. Her fingers touched a wall. Slowly, she slid one foot forward and confirmed that they had been placed in front of a wall. Young as she was, she knew what that could mean.

"They're making us stand facing a wall," she whispered to Piry next to her. "Are they going to shoot us?"

"If they are, we'll just join your father sooner," Piry whispered in a soothing tone.

Her mother's answer made Erika to totally relax. She had seen dead people during the war. She thought of death as the ultimate peace; no more problems, no more tasks to deal with, no more plans for the future. No life. *It doesn't matter whether there is life after death. We will find out right after we are shot dead.*

There was total silence in the room, perhaps the others were thinking the same thing. After a while, they could hear a noise that sounded like furniture being pulled into the room and wondered what was going on. They didn't have to wait for long.

The guards took the prisoners arms and turning them around, led them forward.

Then stopped them and turned them around again till the back of their legs touched the edge of a bench. The guards pushed them down, saying, "Posadte za," (sit down).

"I guess they're not going to shoot us," Erika whispered to Piry with a sigh of relief.

"Shut up!" hissed Judith from Piry's other side, clearly upset and afraid.

Piry quietly hushed both her daughters. She did not want to call attention to themselves.

They all sat in silence for some time, so close, they were touching in each other. Because they were blindfolded, they could not judge whether minutes or hours were passing. They could hear heavy boots coming and going from the room and conversation in Slovak among the border guards, but that was their only reference to where they were.

Then, suddenly, Piry felt a tug on her handcuffs, and a gruff male voice commanded her to get up. She rose and now felt a hand on her right shoulder pushing her forward, indicating that she should walk, saying, "Davaj, davaj". He led her out of the room and down a hallway into another room. She heard a chair being pulled out and was pushed down into it. The guard removed her blindfold, and she blinked rapidly as the bright light of a lamp assaulted her eyes.

She found herself sitting at a desk but could barely see beyond the light to the shadowy figure sitting opposite her. He pushed across the desktop Piry's Hungarian identity book. Clearly, they had recovered her briefcase from the snowfields and searched through it.

"Is this you?" The uniformed man behind the desk asked in accented Hungarian.

"Yes." Piry whispered.

"Louder!"

"Yes!" she nearly shouted.

The man leaned forward: "What were you, a Hungarian citizen, doing at our border and how did you get here? Who brought you here? Who are you with? I want to hear the whole story. Everything. I have all the time in the world."

Piry realized that there would be no point in protecting Victor or his family. She had to tell the truth, leaving out only self-protecting details, such as the fact that Feri, her husband, knew of their escape. As she told her story, she painted a picture of a woman who was left a widow after the war, divorced from a mean second husband, and had been seduced by dreams of taking her daughters to Israel, where their uncle would be a caring father substitute for them.

Piry could not see her interrogator's face but figured by the stars on his epaulettes that he was a high-ranking officer. Judging by his questions, he was intelligent, and hard as nails. Periodically, he scribbled notes on a sheet of paper in front of him, but most of the time he sat leaning back in the shadows, listening, and interrupting only for details, and then asking the same questions over and over again. Piry knew that repeating the questions were designed to rattle her, to catch her in some lie, contradicting her own story. They had to do with Piry possibly breaking down and confessing to being an American spy, or Victor being one.

But Piry held to her story and refused to be ensnared by any questions implying her spying for the Americans or being part of any type of conspiracy. She was asked about her communication with her ex-brother-in-law, Tibor in America.

"Yes, I do have a brother-in-law in America as well. He is a Rabbi there, and sends used clothes for my daughters, donated by members of his congregation. But we don't have any other contact with each other. No, we did not want to go to America. After the horrors of the war, I wanted us to go to Israel. We're Jewish and that's where we should live."

"Were you, as a Jew, mistreated by the Hungarian Socialist Government?"

"No, of course not. But having gone through the war, and losing my children's father, I felt that their uncle, who is a teacher in Israel, would help me bring them up," Piry repeated steadily.

No amount of questioning was going to make her change her story. She just hoped her daughters will answer the same way.

After what was a very long and repetitious interrogation, she was blindfolded again and led back to her seat in the room with the benches. Piry was exhausted. *It must be three or four in the morning by now*, she thought. She could not feel either Judith or Erika next to her, so she assumed that they, too, had been taken for interrogation. She wondered how they were holding up. While waiting for their return, she leaned her back against the wall and felt herself drifting into sleep. No sooner did she doze off, than she was shaken awake and led to be interrogated again. Each time it seemed to be a different officer, same questions, and the same procedure of taking her back to her seat and then taking her to be questioned again.

Judith and Erika were going through the same experience. Their interrogation had been staggered so as to isolate them from each other. When they were led back to their seats, neither of their other family members were there. They had to trust that each of them confessed only to what Piry had told them to say about the goal of their escape.

They were taken back and forth throughout the night, and both Judith and Erika were exhausted. But Judith held her own. She did not volunteer a single piece of information; it all had to be pulled out of her slowly and painstakingly. She was terrified that she might blurt out something she wasn't supposed to say, so she was deliberately difficult during the interrogations, answering as if she were the injured party.

"The Nazis killed my father, took away our home. My home-room teacher was an anti-Semite. Why wouldn't I want to go and live in Israel with my uncle who would treat me like a daughter?" she insisted righteously.

"You had a stepfather!" the Interrogator snapped at her. "And a new home. And the Socialist regime does not permit anti-Semitism. So, what was wrong with all that?"

"My stepfather was a bastard, and we lived in his house, but that was no home. My teacher hated me because I am Jewish. Everyone at school knew it!"

Over and over the Interrogator questioned her but Judith, like her mother, kept repeating the same reasons, and the same events of their attempted escape. The interrogators were particularly interested in the families that hosted them during their brief stay in Slovakia.

But all three of them insisted that Victor and his family escaped along with them, and they didn't know their hosts' last names and the address where they had stopped overnight in Komarno.

When Erika was taken for the fifth time to be questioned, she felt such anger that she was barely able to keep it under control.

The officer sitting behind the bright light that mercilessly shone into Erika's eyes, but not into his, held up Erika's Pioneer membership booklet, and said, "You are a pioneer, aren't you ashamed of what you did? Don't you know your duty as a pioneer? As soon as you learned what your mother was planning, you should have gone to the police!"

"I didn't know what she was planning!" Erika protested for the umpteenth time. "She just told me we were taking a trip to relatives, and I should pack in my bag only what I needed for a few days!"

"So, you put "The Last of the Mohicans," an American novel in your bag?"

"That book was a birthday present! And it's the story of how the invading whites waged war against the poor Indian natives. We studied that at school. What's wrong with my taking that book with me?"

"It shows that you had an interest in going to America."

Erika lost her temper. With a swift gesture she turned the light away from her face, illuminating the officer sitting across from her at the desk.

"I told you a hundred times already, we were going to Israel! To my uncle there! What do you want me to do—lie?"

Staring at him, Erika was surprised how handsome her torturer was. He must have been only in his early thirties. Had dark hair and dark eyes, movie-star straight nose, and shapely lips. His white teeth flashed as he burst into a smile. "I'm trying to get to the truth about all this. Why would I want you to lie?"

Erika's eyes bore into his, "I've been telling you the truth over and over, all night. I have nothing more to tell you." Then, with a sudden turn of genius she pretended to be sorrowful and asked, "Will I get back my Pioneer membership book?"

She knew full well the effect it would have on him. Her question implied that she was just a child who valued her communist upbringing, and it was not her fault that she had been dragged on this venture.

The officer stared at her, speechless. Then he put her membership booklet down on the desk and called for the guard, "Take her back."

Erika was not called to be interrogated again that night. Exhausted, she leaned against the wall behind her and with the blindfold blocking the light in the room she slept, sitting up.

◎◉◎

Early next morning, two guards came into the room where the prisoners were dozing sitting upright and awakened them. At some point during the night their handcuffs had been removed. Now they were told they could take off their blindfolds as well. They blinked under the bright bulbs in the room, stealing glances at each other to see who was sitting there.

Piry and her daughters noted that Victor and his family were definitely not among them. He could have gotten through or could have been shot; there was no way to know. Only fourteen of them were sitting on the benches. Piry wondered whether the other ten or so had been able to crawl to the Austrian border or had been shot by the Slovak guards. There were certainly enough bullets flying around to kill them. She would never know.

Two more border guards came into the room, wheeling carts with trays of large cups of coffee and thick slices of rye bread. "Jest, kava, egyenek," (eat, coffee, eat) they said in Slovak and in Hungarian as they nudged the prisoners to take a cup and a slice of bread.

After breakfast, they were instructed to use the toilets because afterwards they were being transported to Bratislava. Once again, they had to put on their blindfolds, and the guards led them to the appropriate toilet doors. Erika's guard held her not by the shoulders but by putting his hands over her breasts. *The pig*, Erika thought, but instinctively knew she could not react. Blindfolded, she wondered why no one noticed him doing this, but figured he was careful not to be observed. *Most men are pigs*, she thought as she walked along. Not knowing how the guard might react if she complained, she decided that if she acted as if he weren't doing it, it wasn't happening.

When all of them were done with their bathroom activities, they were told to put on their overcoats and head coverings, which most of them had removed overnight.

They were handcuffed and blindfolded again, then led outside. Erika knew they were outdoors because of the intense cold that struck her face where it wasn't covered with the blindfold.

"Davaj, go up steps," she heard the guard speaking to her in broken Hungarian. He pushed her forward slightly, and she could feel the front of her shoe bumping into a step.

"Up!" repeated the guard, and Erika understood that she was supposed to climb stairs. After three steps up, the ground became level again under her feet. She was led to walk ahead, then she heard the guard say "Stop," his hand pressing her shoulder. He removed Erika's blindfold and handcuffs.

Now Erika could see that they were inside a long van. It had a central walkway and both sides were lined with narrow metal doors. Each door had a tiny window at eye level. She also saw that there were prisoners ahead of her, Piry and Judith stood right behind her, and there were more prisoners after them. Guards were at everyone's side. The guards unlocked the doors to reveal tight metal cubicles with a narrow metal seat in each. Each prisoner was directed to go inside a cubicle. These were so small that one had to back into it and plop down on the cold, hard seat. Having the blindfold off made no difference once the cubicle door had been slammed shut and locked. The windows on the doors were covered from the outside and it was pitch dark inside, except for a narrow shaft of light under the door.

Erika sat quietly, wondering where her sister and mother were. To find out, she gently knocked on the sides of her cell. *One, two, three*. She listened and heard a faint tap from both sides of her walls. Feeling reassured, she leaned back and closed her eyes. *At least we're together in this*, she thought.

The van door slammed shut, the motor revved up, and they began to roll forward. Being in the dark, there was no way to tell how long the ride took. The next thing Erika knew was feeling the van stop, and hearing keys being turned in the cell doors. Loud voices ordered everyone out. Manacled and blindfolded once again, they were led to walk into a building.

Again, their blindfolds were removed, their wrists freed of the handcuffs, and they found themselves standing in a large room in front of a reception desk. A guard called their names one by one, and Erika once again stood with her mother and sister as the guard handed each of them a prison uniform.

"Since you're Hungarian citizens, your personal items and your clothes will be kept together and returned to you when it will be decided what to do with you," a guard explained in Hungarian to Piry and her daughters. "Now take the clothes you've been issued, and one of our Comrade Guards will show you where to change. You must not keep any jewelry, money, or even your underwear. Everything you need is provided in your clothes packet."

A female guard came up to them and led Piry and her daughters to a changing room. It was large, all the walls were bare. There were benches against the walls. They could use these during their changing clothes. The guard had provided each of them with a large cloth sack for putting in it their personal items. Once done, they stood in their green cotton prison uniforms and pulled the strings of the sacks that now held their belongings from a past life. Their new life, with an uncertain future, was about to begin.

◎◉◎

A guard escorted them down a long hallway lined with cells. Piry was led into a cell with several women already in there. One of them spoke some Hungarian, and asked why Piry had been brought in. When Piry said, "Trying to escape," the woman translated it for the others. They all shook their heads and sighed.

"That's the worst!" exclaimed the Hungarian-speaking woman. "You might get the maximum, a life sentence."

Piry, not wanting to show how this prospect terrified her, shrugged. "We'll see. Why are you here?" she asked the Hungarian speaker.

"Not for a big crime like you! I killed my husband because he was a mean sonofabitch. Got three years for it." She nodded toward the other women, "They're in for lesser sentences, like for theft, or knifing a colleague at work. But we all feel sorry for you. Being a political prisoner is really bad. It shows that you're against the regime. They get really mean about that."

Piry lowered her head with a pensive expression, as if she were absorbing their opinions. In effect she thought, *What do these women know? It will be up to the Hungarians to convict me. We will probably be transferred back to Budapest in a few weeks. Until then, I'll just listen and keep my opinion to myself. What a world we live in! A murderer thinks she is less guilty than someone who was merely trying to leave the country!* She smiled at the women, then walked over to the bunk bed assigned to her and curled up on it.

◎◉◎

Judith and Erika were placed into a narrow cell with two beds, and a bucket in the corner to be used as their toilet. Next to it a tiny metal sink with a faucet provided running water. On it stood two tin cups, presumably to be used for drinking water.

Judith sank down on one of the beds, broken both in spirit and body. She felt drained, her life deprived of all hope. Her thoughts raced wildly in her head, *Apu is dead, why am I not? Anyu is clearly incompetent to raise us. She married a horrible man—how could she remarry in the first place? And now she has botched up our escape, the one hope I had for my future. Instead of being glued to Victor, she went to help that old man who was probably shot dead anyway.*

She looked at Erika, who sat calmly on her bed, observing her sister. Judith wished she could be like Erika, taking everything in stride. But then again, Erika was young, she probably didn't understand the significance of what was happening to them. *Yet, it was she who suggested that we crawl. Maybe she was right, we might have made it to Austria had we crawled. Or, she might have gotten us shot had we crawled. So what? Dying would have been a lot better than being caught! What will happen to us now?*

The cell door opened, interrupting Judith's thoughts. A guard came in, pushing a cart into the cell with two trays on it. Each tray had a bowls of bean soup, a slice of bread, and tin cups with sweetened black coffee. He mimed eating as he pointed at the trays, and without saying a word left the cell.

"I'm not hungry, are you?" Erika asked her sister.

"I'm not either but we must eat to keep up our strength. Who knows what'll happen to us next? They'll probably question us some more and then put us into a van again and transport us back to Hungary. God knows what will happen to us there! Probably prison for life for Mom, and correctional institutes for us. A great future—just what we dreamed of."

Erika knew Judith was probably right. Yet, a born optimist, she said, "Yes, that's one possibility. But maybe they'll consider that as Jews and orphans we just wanted a different life and not punish us so harshly. Rákosi is Jewish, maybe his laws are kinder for Jews."

"Yeah, right…Eat!" Judith barked.

They fell silent, each of them forcing down the food. They were exhausted from not having had enough sleep for nearly twenty-four hours. So, after putting their trays on the floor by the door, each girl rolled on top of her bed and despite it being early afternoon, fell asleep.

They didn't nap for long. They were awakened and taken individually to be interrogated again. So was Piry. The procedure was similar to the one at the border, with an officer sitting in the dark and a bright light blinding the prisoner. The questions were also similar but asking more details about their home life and the reason for their attempted escape, trying to trap them into revealing a different story.

However, Piry and each girl kept telling the same story. By now memorized, it was easier to repeat. Then the day must have turned into evening for the interrogations had stopped and they were returned to their cells. Shortly after, dinner was brought to them. It consisted of a plate with rice and some sort of meat in a sauce. It also came with a strange kind of bread that looked like a slice of spongy dumpling, The meal was actually tasty, and once again the two girls forced themselves to eat. Piry, had no appetite. But because of the other cell mates, she felt that she had to eat in order not to show fear or weakness in front of them.

A short while after dinner guards removed all the trays. The lights were dimmed in the cells from the outside, indicating that it was bedtime. Judith and Erika didn't feel like talking. They lay quietly on their beds, aware that periodically a bright light streamed through the small window on their door; clearly, a guard was looking in on them. Slowly, they fell into a deep sleep.

◎◉◎

In the morning, after a breakfast of sweet black coffee and a thick slice of buttered bread, a guard came into their room and asked Judith to follow him. Erika found herself alone not just for the time an interrogation would take, but the entire day. After a while, feeling lonely, she knocked on the wall by her bed, and got a response from the cell next to hers. Her mother was there, knocking back. At lunchtime, along with her food tray, the guard slipped a piece of paper under her plate.

"Don't be afraid, things will work out. Anyu."

Erika felt infinite gratitude towards the guard who had smuggled in the note, and a sense of relief at the reassurance by her mother. To dispel her loneliness, she began to sing all the songs she knew. Hungarian folk songs, Russian songs of the Communist movement, and once she ran out of her repertoire, she started all over again.

When she grew tired of singing, she thought about the books she had read, recalling the stories, and of her former life at school, and her friends. Thinking of them made her wonder whether she would ever see them again. This made her sad, and for a while she just lay quietly on her bed. The day seemed long, and except for the meals that were brought to her by a guard, she saw no other person. After dinner she went to sleep wondering where they had taken her sister.

She found out in the early evening, two days later, when Judith was led back into the cell, looking deeply upset and strangely broken in spirit.

"Where were you?!" Erika exclaimed, hugging her.

Judith accepted the hug, but Erika could sense that she wasn't responding. She seemed like a sleepwalker, talking and moving but not really awake.

"They drove me to the houses where we had been when we came to Slovakia," she finally blurted out. "Of course, nobody was at Victor's brother's home, but they also took me back to Komarno, by the Slovak border and drove me around till I recognized the house and pointed it out to them. I felt terrible doing it. They arrested the couple that had helped us. On the drive back here, I broke down and sobbed all the way. I think I was actually hysterical. They tried to calm me down at first, then just let me cry."

Erika listened as Judith, her voice breaking time and again, with tears streaming down her face, described where she had been. Finally, she took Judith's hand into her own, and squeezed it, "I'm so, so sorry you had to go through this."

Judith said nothing but held on to Erika's hand as they sat on her bed.

The next morning, after breakfast, both girls were told they'd be leaving their cell. In fact, they were led next door and reunited with Piry. She hugged her daughters, holding each of them tight in her embrace. Observing that Judith was somehow emotionally distant, Piry sat with her for a while, and talked to her. She tried her best to console Judith, absolving her guilt feelings about showing the guards where they had stayed in Komarno. "There was nothing you could do differently. We're in their power and the better we cooperate the less punishment we'll get."

Judith nodded without a word. She wasn't ready to be consoled, and no amount of positive thoughts could convince her that her life was not in shambles. *Even if they released us in Hungary, where would Erika and I live? What school would accept me with my new criminal political background?* She did not bother to share her thoughts with Piry. Her mother simply wouldn't agree and wouldn't understand her. *Never did, never will. Whatever will happen, will happen. Life is not worth living or bothering about*, she thought.

After a while, Piry gave Judith a hug, and went over to Erika who was sitting on her assigned bed.

"I'm sure they're not going to keep you here," she told Erika. "You're too young to be in prison. Even Judith might be too young. But you, they'll definitely take somewhere else."

"Great. And how will we stay in touch?"

"I wouldn't worry about that," Piry reassured Erika. "They'll keep an eye on all of us, and when the time comes, we'll be taken back to Hungary."

"Let's just see," Erika shrugged, feeling emotionally drained.

The following morning, two guards came for Erika. They told her to say good-bye to her mother and sister—she was being transferred to a place for children.

"What about my sister?" Erika asked before leaving the cell.

"Your sister is fifteen years old, she will stay with your mother."

Erika said nothing. She knew that according to communist laws, a fifteen-year-old was considered fully responsible for his or her actions. Having done something illegal, he or she would be put into prison. She felt terrible as she hugged Piry and Judith, and whispered to each,

"I love you."

CHAPTER 18

Erika was led to change back into her own clothes and then was taken outside and ordered to get into the back seat of a jeep. An armed guard sat next to her, and another guard drove them into the city. They did not pass over a bridge, so Erika assumed that the prison she had been in was on the main side of Bratislava, not across the river where the border was. Indeed, as they drove, she saw that they were entering the downtown area. The streets were wide, lined with trees, parked cars, and well-kept two- and three-story buildings. All were covered in a thin layer of snow.

"Here we are," said the guard next to her in Hungarian, as the driver pulled up in front of a black cast iron gate. They got out of the jeep, and flanked by the two guards, they walked with Erika into a garden. On the left was a building that looked like a private house, and to the right stood a giant chestnut tree, its branches bare, covered with snow.

"This way," the guard with the gun pointed ahead them, and they walked down a wide path paved with large stones. At the end of it, extending the entire width of the garden, stood an elegant beige villa with a red tile roof, and several balconies on the second floor, overlooking the garden. Above the wide front door a discreet sign read: "Detska Izba Verejnej Bezpečnosti."

Neither guard bothered to translate it for Erika. One of them knocked on door. A stocky woman, in a tight-fitting police uniform, and her black hair pulled into a bun, opened it.

"Prist, prist," she said in Slovak.

It must have meant "come in", for the guards led Erika by the shoulder into the hallway.

The policewoman seemed to have been expecting them, because after exchanging a few words with the guards, she led them down the carpeted parquet hallway to the room at the end. She knocked, and a deep male voice shouted from inside, "Prist!"

It definitely must mean "enter," Erika thought, for the Hungarian speaking guard opened the door and said, "Menj be" (Go in)."

"Zdrastvujte," Erika said, not sure she used the right grammar or word, but it meant hello in Russian, and she figured that the man behind the desk might just understand it.

He stood up to receive them. He was tall, had a strong chin, prominent nose, clear blue eyes under dark bushy brows. He looked incredibly handsome to Erika in his dark gray military uniform with a captain's insignia on his shoulders. He also had a warm smile as he greeted them and pointed at the chairs in front of his desk. Erika and her guards sat down. The guards spoke in rapid Slovak and handed an envelope to the captain. He opened it, pulled out the papers from inside and read them briefly. He then turned to Erika and spoke in an accented but fluent Hungarian.

"Welcome, Erika Fábián. My name is Velitel Miroslav Lubomir, but you may simply address me as Velitel. You are in a place called the "Detska Izba Verejner Bespečnosti," the *Children's Room Security Institute*. This is where we house children who have done something against the law, or their parents have abandoned them, or in some way need help. They stay here until a juvenile court or the authorities decide their situation. You will live here until it is decided by the Hungarian authorities what to do with you. Your mother and sister will remain in prison, but you are too young for prison.

However, here you will also be under guards, so don't even think of leaving this place. We will treat you well if you behave well. The guards speak Slovak, but there will be one guard during each shift who speaks Hungarian. So, if you need something, you can go to her. There are also other children at the Detska Izba, and you will soon meet them. So, welcome, and I hope you will do just fine here."

He came out from behind his desk, spoke to the guards who had jumped to their feet. He shook hands with them, then escorted them to the door and called out to someone. The two prison guards left without as much as a glance at Erika. A female guard came in, different from the previous one. She had long blonde hair in a ponytail that reached to the middle of her back, large blue eyes, and a friendly smile.

"Erika, this is Sudruška Zofie. She will explain things to you about this place."

"Come," Sudruška Zofie said in heavily accented Hungarian, smiling at Erika.

Erika rose from the chair. "Thank you for telling me where I am," she said to the Velitel.

He smiled and nodded as Erika followed Sudruška Zofie out the door.

◎◉◎

As they walked down the long corridor, Sudruška Zofie pointed to the left, and said, "These two doors are to the guards' rooms, and these are two bathrooms, one for us, one for the children who are staying with us, like you."

On the right side of the corridor were glass doors to two large, bright rooms. Sudruška Zofie explained, "These are rooms for you children. The first one is for the younger ones, and the next one is for kids your age and older."

The younger children's room had shelves with toys, and several small tables and chairs placed in the middle. A wide bay window looked out on the garden.

"Now the garden is full of snow but in the spring and summer children can play out there," Sudruška Zofie explained.

The other room was similar, but with adult size furniture. As they peeked into the room, a uniformed female guard waived at them from a large armchair placed in the corner to the left of the door, overlooking the entire room.

"This is Sudruška Valentina." Sudruška Zofie said, then spoke to her in Slovak, and Erika heard her name mentioned. Sudruška Valentina nodded, looking at Erika, but said nothing. They left the room and Sudruška Zofie continued Erika's orientation to the place.

"You will meet all the guards as they come in for their shifts each day. Two guards are always on duty, they even sleep here, so you can all be safe." Then she pointed to the left side of the hallway, "Here are the pantry and the kitchen, where you will eat your meals with the others."

Erika saw a kitchen sink and counter against the wall, and a large table by the window, overlooking the garden. It only had a few chairs around it, and she wondered if the children ate in shifts or if there were not many children at the institute, but she didn't ask.

"Now we go upstairs."

Erika followed Sudruška Zofie up a wide, tiled staircase to the second floor. The rooms up here were all bedrooms. At the start of the hallway, Sudruška Zofie pointed out, was the bedroom where the guards slept. There were two bathrooms along that same wall past the guards' room. Just like downstairs, one was for the guards, the other for the children. On the opposite side were two very large bedrooms. One was set up with cribs, the other with five single beds in a row. Everything was sparkling clean. The beds were neatly made, and in each room lace curtains hung over the large double windows. Wood shutters behind the curtains covered the windows at night.

Sudruška Zofie stopped in the middle of the hallway and opened a closet door situated between the two bathrooms. It was full of neatly folded towels and sweatpants with matching tops in two colors: cobalt blue and emerald green. She looked at Erika, as if measuring her size, and pulled off the shelves a blue and a green set of tops and pants.

"These are what you will wear while you are here with us. We will put your clothes in storage and return them to you when you leave. You will wear one outfit for a week, then while that is being washed, you will wear the other one. You can choose which color you want to wear first."

Erika took the two bundles from her, as well as a large towel that the Sudruška handed to her.

"Now I will take you to meet your companions in the bedroom where you will sleep. You will change your clothes there before you all come down for dinner." She led the way to the end of the hall, to the room situated above the Velitel's office on the first floor. She knocked, and without bothering to get a response, opened the door.

Two young girls jumped up abruptly from the beds where they had been sitting face-to-face, and stared at Erika, while exclaiming almost in unison, "Sudruška Zofie, Dobrý deň!" (Good day!)

"Hello to you two," Sudruška Zofie said in Hungarian and smiled at them. "I bring you a new companion. This is Erika. She is also Hungarian."

With that, she pointed at the third bed in the room, and said to Erika, "That bed is for you. You have a couple of hours before dinner to get to know each other." She left the room, closing the door.

The three girls stood silently for a moment, taking each other's measure. Finally, Erika went to the empty bed and dumped her new belongings on it. Then she turned to the girls,

"My name is Erika Fábián. What's yours?"

"I am Marianne Ábrányi," said the taller of the two. She stepped forward and extended her hand to shake Erika's. She was big boned but very thin. Her straight brown hair fell to her shoulders, her eyes were not large but interestingly slanted upward and yellowish green like a cat's. She turned around to introduce the other girl.

"And this is Maria Vengersky."

"Hi," Maria said, and also went to shake Erika's hand.

Maria was a bit shorter than Erika. She had dark blonde hair, very white skin, and the most remarkable light blue eyes.

"Where are you from?" Marianne asked. She seemed a lot friendlier than Maria, who sat back on her bed, quietly observing the newcomer.

"From Budapest. And you two?"

"Also, from Budapest. How come you're here?" Marianne asked.

"We tried to get across to Austria and got caught."

As if the very air had exploded around them, both girls shouted, "Us, too! When?"

"A week ago. And you?"

"We came three months ago!"

"You've been here that long?"

"Yes. Waiting for the Hungarians to requisition us. Tell us your story!"

They pointed at their beds, and sat down, with Erika on one bed facing the two girls on the other. She gave a brief description of how they signed up with Viktor and ended up getting caught.

Listening intensely, the two girls stared at each other, then Marianne said, "Our story is almost exactly the same! What did your smuggler look like?"

Erika described Viktor's looks, and Marianne exclaimed, full of excitement, "You must have had the same smuggler as us!"

Maria spoke up, "Clearly, we must have been the victims of the same method. He recruited too many people, took some across, and let others be caught to satisfy the border guards. Probably the ones who paid the most made it across, and the rest of us were fodder for the system."

"Did he say his brother was also coming along?" Erika asked.

"No, there was no brother. We stayed with a family, like you did, but either it wasn't his brother's, or he just didn't tell us that they were."

"How old are you?" Marianne asked.

"I'm twelve and a half. And you?"

"I'm thirteen. Maria is almost fifteen. And you know what?" She turned to Maria, "Can I tell her?"

"Tell me what?"

Maria shrugged, "You might as well."

Marianne stood up and said, bowing with great flourish, "Maria is a countess! Her mother's family is the Prince Hadik line, and her father is Count Vengersky."

"No kidding!" Erika exclaimed and threw herself back on the bed as if the weight of the information so impressed her that she keeled over. In fact, she was impressed by the news. She had never met an aristocrat before since the Communist Government seemed to have killed or exiled them all. Evidently, not all. She sat up, saying, "So, do I address you as Countess?"

"No, silly. Just Maria will do."

Erika looked at Marianne, "Are you also an aristocrat?"

"No! My father is a journalist working and living in Vienna. My mother died when I was eight, and my father remarried. He went to work in Vienna as a reporter two years ago, in 1951. The Hungarian Government kept me and my stepmother in Budapest as assurance that he wouldn't defect. So, my stepmother and I decided to escape, to join him. Now she is in jail, and I'm stuck here."

"Well, I'm certainly in illustrious company," Erika declared, only half in jest.

"Are you Jewish?" Marianne inquired out of the blue.

"Why do you ask?" Erika responded, always cautious about admitting it.

"I don't know, just wondering," Marianne shrugged.

"I am. My grandmother's maiden name was also Ábrányi—are you?"

Marianne laughed, "Mine is a very bohemian family, all artists and writers. So, who knows who is what? In any case, I was raised Catholic, as was Maria of course."

"Well, just don't hold it against me," Erika grinned, secretly uncomfortable that one's religion always had to be brought up when people met.

Maria said, "We'll talk more after dinner. You had better change into our 'uniform' because pretty soon we'll have to go downstairs."

Looking closely at them, Erika noted that they were wearing the same kind of sweat suits she had been given. Maria was in blue, and Marianne wore green. Erika chose the green outfit as well.

"Our bathroom is the first door on your left," Maria pointed out, as if sensing that Erika was hesitant to change in front of them.

"Thanks."

It was a large bathroom, with a sink, a toilet, and a bathtub all made of white marble. *This place must have been taken over by the Slovak Communist Government, just like they appropriated homes and apartments in Hungary; like Uncle Laci's villa in Buda,* Erika mused, while she changed into her new outfit. *I hope these girls and I will get along,* she thought as she joined them to go downstairs.

◎◉◎

Dinner, as all their meals, Erika learned, was provided downstairs in the kitchen. Only the three of them sat at the table. Food had been laid out on a counter in the pantry window that overlooked the kitchen. Each dish was in an aluminum pot that could be stacked vertically and locked together for carrying.

"We get our food from a nearby police station," Maria explained when she saw Erika's puzzled expression. "Sometimes, during the day they let Marianne and me go to fetch it."

"Ah. So, they let you go out of this place?"

"Yes, to bring the lunch meal, and sometimes for an afternoon walk."

"They trust you?"

"With our families locked up, do you think we would risk getting them punished because we ran away? Besides, where could we go? We don't know a soul in this town," Maria whispered as they served themselves from each container.

This evening's dinner was pork chops, rice, and green beans. They even had a piece of peach preserve for dessert.

"Food is usually pretty good," Marianne commented, "and certainly enough."

"Are we the only residents here?" Erika asked as the three of them settled at the table. Even the Sudruška guarding them this evening left them on their own.

"They just took a bunch of kids away earlier today," Maria replied. "They bring them here for a couple of days, then take them away. We're the only "long term" residents, till the Hungarians ask for us to be sent home."

After dinner they placed their dishes into the sink.

"Don't we have to wash our dishes?" Erika asked.

"No, a cleaning woman comes every morning and takes care of it. Better than at home," Marianne grinned. "Come, now we go to our dayroom till bedtime."

The three girls walked into the large room across the hall from the kitchen. A Sudruška was sitting there, as if waiting for them.

"Dobri večer Sudruška Agata," the two older girls called to her, and she responded with the same greeting.

To her surprise, Erika knew it meant "good evening." It sounded just like Russian.

The three of them settled around a small table by the window, though there was nothing to see outside since the early winter darkness had set in.

"Do you speak Slovak?" Erika asked her new friends.

"Enough to get by, and every day we understand more and more," Maria explained. "But nobody is teaching us, and we don't really converse with our guards. They talk to us only when they want us to do something. So, we just chat with each other, in Hungarian."

"Do you know what Sudruška means? It seems to be attached to all their names, so I assume it's a title of some kind?"

Marianne recited in an almost bored tone, "*Sudruška* means comrade, *Velitel* means captain, and the name of the place we're in, *Detska Izba, Verejnej Bezpečnosti*, literally translated means *Public Safety Children's Room*. Maybe that means that the place is for youngsters who are a public menace, like juvenile delinquents. They are brought here until they are taken before a judge and sentenced. Or kids come here when they are rescued from bad parents."

"We seem to get all kinds. They come, stay a few days or a few weeks, then leave, and we never hear about them again. They're probably placed into juvenile correction places or foster homes."

Erika was surprised at Marianne's detailed explanation since her tone sounded as though she was bored by telling her all this. "Thank you," she grinned at Marianne to show her appreciation. "Now I know where I am. So, do you play with the kids who come here? Or what do you do all day?"

"Sometimes we talk or play with them if they're interested," Maria responded.

"But usually we just sit around, bored," Marianne shrugged. "This is what we do: we get up, bathe, have breakfast, come in here and sit around till lunch time. Then we eat, and sometimes we walk in the afternoon. Then we have dinner, and then we go to our bedroom at nine. Lights are out at ten. A very exciting life!"

"We are also allowed to go to our room during the day if we feel like it," Maria added.

"But when you're down here, you just sit?" Erika asked aghast.

"Oh, it's not as bad as that," Maria cut in. "We talk, play board games, discuss life, it's really not so bad."

"Booring…" Marianne sighed.

"Well, what do you expect, entertainment in prison? This is a prison, you know, it's just that it's for children." Maria said, in a soothing tone.

"Why couldn't we go to school?" Erika wondered.

"Because we're criminals. Besides, we don't speak enough Slovak! I hated school anyway," Marianne shrugged, "So this is like a grand vacation. It won't be much fun once we get home, since we might end up in a reform school."

"Let's talk about something else," Maria suggested. "What was your favorite subject at school?"

"Literature" Erika replied.

"You like to read?" Maria asked.

"Love to."

Maria said cheerfully, "Then I have an idea. From tomorrow on, each of us will tell the story of a book we've read. We'll take turns doing it, so we share different novels."

Marianne yawned, "I'm bored already."

"Well, you can join us or not, as you wish," Maria said gently, smiling at her friend.

Erika said nothing. She had quickly assessed that her two new companions had very different personalities. Maria was gentle and serious. Marianne was rough, rebellious, and seemed angry at the world. Maybe she had a right to be. There will be time to find out why in the days ahead. At the moment Erika was content with her unexpected luck at having these two Hungarian girls at her new institutional home.

When they were sent upstairs, while getting ready for bed, the two girls warned Erika about their circumstances.

Marianne said, "Some of the Sudruškas are nice, some not so nice. Don't ever provoke them in any way or answer back. Just obey what they tell you to do, and you'll do fine here."

Maria added, "Also, even though they claim not to speak Hungarian, don't assume it's true. They might just not admit it so they can catch you saying something bad about the regime, or them, or this place, and then they can punish you, God knows how. We can talk up here, but not downstairs."

"Thank you for telling me all this. Good night, sleep well." Erika said to her new companions as she rolled on her side in her bed. Exhausted from the long day's events, she wondered what her life will be like at the Detska Izba, which was not a 'Children's Room' but a children's prison.

◎◉◎

In two weeks, Erika had adjusted to the routine of the Detska Izba. She and her new friends rose and went to bed at the same time, ate all their meals together, and spent their days sitting around in the teenager's room or in the one for younger children. To keep busy, they conversed or sat reading the meager collection of Hungarian books.

Erika was rapidly learning the Slovak language by occasionally chatting with their guards and by studying the picture story books they kept for very young children. She figured, it was a good way for her to acquire a vocabulary. The Slovak language was quite similar to Russian, which she had studied at school for the last four years. But Slovak was easier to read because it used the Latin alphabet versus the Cyrillic one. Also, hearing a language and needing to respond daily, was quite different from studying one in the classroom a few hours a week.

One morning, a nurse, carrying a very young child, arrived at the Detska Izba, accompanied by a policeman. The little boy seemed quite ill. They were guided by Sudruška Zofie to the Velitel's office, where they stayed briefly. When they came out, Sudruška Zofie took them upstairs to the bedroom with cribs. The policeman and the nurse came downstairs without the child, but one of the guards, Sudruška Kata, stayed upstairs with the little boy.

The Velitel went to see the three girls in the dayroom. "We'll have an injured child in our care for a while," he explained to Erika and her companions. "His name is Ivánka. Please be nice to him. He'll be out of bed in a few days and will come downstairs to play. I'm sure he will appreciate some attention from you girls. He speaks both Slovak and Hungarian." The Velitel gave them a quick smile and left.

"Must be from a Hungarian Slovak family," Mária whispered to her companions. "Otherwise, he would only speak Slovak. Also, Ivánka for males is a diminutive only in Hungarian. In Slovak, Ivanka is the female version of the name. Ivan is for a boy."

Erika said to her friends, "While we stayed with Victor's family, I was explained the history of Hungarian dominance of Slovakia under the Austro-Hungarian empire prior to World War II. Victor's brother told me that when the countries had been split up after the war, there were many Hungarians stranded, living in the new Slovak ruled territory. That is why some of the Sudruškas speak Hungarian. Likely, the parents of this little boy are Hungarian. Of course, living in Slovakia, they also have to speak the local language," she added, grinning, "Just like we need to learn it to be able to communicate with the people around us."

Sudruška Kata, sitting in the guard's armchair, looked at Mária and Marianne, and said in Slovak, "It would be nice if you kept that child company when we're busy."

The girls nodded, saying, áno (yes).

As it turned out, in the following weeks it was Erika who spent the most time with Ivánka. That's because when the girls got to their bedroom at night, both Mária and Marianne admitted that they had no interest in the child. On the other hand, Ivánka reminded Erika of her cousin, Nandi, and she was glad to be with him.

She read Ivánka stories from picture books the Sudruškas had given him. After a week, he was able to go downstairs with Erika, and she played with him in the children's room. At age three, he spoke mostly Hungarian, though he easily switched to Slovak when the Sudruškas talked to him.

A few nights after Ivánka's arrival, Marianne whispered to Mária and Erika in their bedroom that she had overheard the Sudruškas talking about Ivánka. "They were saying that both his parents had been killed at a border crossing, while he had been wounded only in the shoulder. That's why he was brought here by a nurse. He had been in a hospital till now, to get the bullet out, they said."

"He must have been part of my group," Erika said pensively. "I remember a couple carrying a young child. He was on his father's back and didn't utter a sound. Probably, he had been sedated, poor baby."

The girls fell silent, each thinking of their own nightmarish attempt to cross the border.

"What do you think will happen to him?" Erika asked her friends.

Marianne shrugged, "Who knows? "

Mária said, "If he is a Czechoslovak citizen, he might be put into an orphanage or if he is lucky, he'll be adopted."

◎◉◎

One day, Erika was sitting with Ivánka in the playroom laying out dominoes with him. A couple came in, accompanied by Sudruška Blanka, one of the bilingual guards. The nice-looking man and woman were young and well dressed. They stopped just inside the door, smiled and said hello, then stood there, looking intently at Ivánka. Erika didn't rise from her chair, she just eyed the visitors, holding a domino in her hand.

"Just keep on playing," Sudruška Blanka instructed Erika.

Obediently Erika placed her domino, and Ivánka, ignoring the visitors, put one of his to match hers. But Erika could feel that the child was also aware of the adults observing him. Then the couple left, and for another week life returned to routine between Erika and Ivánka.

She ate her meals with her two friends while Ivánka ate separately under the care of the Sudruškas. But Erika spent most of her time with Ivánka, reading to him and playing games. She even told him bedtime stories after a Sudruška had bathed Ivánka and put him to bed.

In their room at night, Marianne teased Erika, "You will probably have a dozen children when you get married."

"Actually, I don't think I'll have any children," Erika laughed. "I want to be a writer and writing books will probably take up all my time."

"We'll see—if we ever get out of here and are taken back to Hungary—what our beloved government there will let us become when we grow up," Marianne responded.

"We're minors, we may not have to pay for our parents' actions," Erika countered.

"Don't bet on it," Marianne disputed.

"What's the point of speculating about this," Mária chimed in. "Let's not worry till we have to. For me, I'll go crazy if I do. I'll be fifteen in a few months. I could spend my time fearing that I'll be put in jail, but I don't want to do that. I'd rather deal with each day as it comes."

"Yes, wise Countess," Marianne bowed, her tone filled with sarcasm.

"Mária is right, it's pointless to try to guess our future," Erika pointed out. She had found even in the short time she had been at the Detska Izba, that Marianne was often angry and cynical, her outlook on life pessimistic. Whereas Mária always had a positive attitude.

Perhaps Marianne has a right to be like this, given that her father had left her with a stepmother for years, while he was out of the country, Erika thought. *By contrast, Mária's family is close knit and had taught her to be proud of her ancestry even if they were despised under the communist regime.*

"Enough," Marianne snapped at them imperiously, and turned her back on both her roommates. "I want to sleep."

Erika and Mária exchanged a look, then Mária turned off the ceiling light and the room became dark and silent as each girl curled up in her bed for the night.

The following week, the young couple returned to the Detska Izba. They spent some time talking to the Velitel in his office. Then, Sudruška Zofie came into the playroom and stopped Erika's storytelling midstream.

"Ivánka's new parents are here," she told Erika. "Say goodbye to Ivánka, they'll be taking him with them to his new home."

Ivánka listened but was too young to understand the significance of what was about to happen. Sudruška Zofie knelt down to face him and said, "Ivánka, let's put on your coat because you are leaving here. You will go home with the nice people who will be your parents from now on."

Ivánka rushed to Erika and wrapped his arms around her neck. "I don't want to leave! I want to stay here with you!"

"Sorry, my pet, you can't," Sudruška Zofie said as gently as she could. "Erika will have to leave from here too and then who will play you? The nice couple who wants to take you home will love you and take very good care of you. You will be their son."

"But I can't be their son, I am my parents' son!" Ivánka shouted. "They will come for me and take me home when they feel better!"

"Yes, Ivánka, but until then you must go and live with this nice couple." Sudruška Zofie replied, obviously shaken by Ivánka's ignorance about his parents' demise.

Erika knelt down and held Ivánka in a tight embrace for a minute, then pushed him away. "Go, darling, maybe I can come and visit you," she said, to make him feel better about leaving.

"Promise?" Ivánka asked, as Sudruška Zofie was putting on his coat.

"I will, if I can," Erika looked into his eyes, and then at Sudruška Zofie.

"Just come," Sudruška Zofie abruptly pulled Ivánka away by his arm, and he was gone.

Erika sat back on her haunches feeling an infinite sadness for the loss of her little playmate. Yet she was glad he would go to a good home. After a while she rose and went into the teenagers' room where Mária and Marianne were playing a board game. She pulled up a chair beside them, quietly watching, nursing her sense of loss.

"Did you know Ivánka is being adopted by a Jewish couple?" Marianne asked Erika.

"Really, why would that be?"

"Because he is Jewish!" Marianne's voice was full of disdain at Erika's ignorance.

"How do you know that?"

"Daahh…I heard the Sudruškas talk about it. I guess your Slovak isn't good enough yet to understand when they talk among themselves. They said, he had no family left, but they found this Jewish couple who wanted to adopt him because the kid was Jewish too."

Erika stared at Marianne, upset at the casual way she had described Ivánka's lack of family. She wanted to get back at Marianne so she responded harshly, "If he had no other family, it could only mean that they had all been killed by the Nazis. Like most of my family."

Both Marianne and Mária seemed taken aback by Erika's comment but looked away without responding to her.

No wonder I liked him so much, Erika thought, but did not share this with the other two who silently went back to their game.

◎◉◎

The following days Erika began to feel isolated by both girls. They talked between themselves but seemed to ignore her. If she asked them something, they answered briefly, but gone were their long conversations of the first few weeks of her stay. Finally, one evening, in their room, Erika could not stand it any longer.

"What's going on with you two? Why are you ostracizing me? If I've done something wrong, or said something hurtful, please tell me! But don't just treat me as if I didn't exist!"

The two girls exchanged a conspiratorial look. Then Mária shrugged and leaned back on her bed while Marianne burst out, "We're sick and tired of you! Every time we talk about anything, like our lives at home, or at our schools, you always tell us how you were the best at this or that, or how many honors and awards you got at your school. So, we got fed up with hearing how great you are and just stopped talking to you."

Erika felt as if a thunderbolt had struck her. She had never been told off like this by anyone. In fact, all she had ever received was praise and recognition. How could she have known that her simply describing events in her life would be perceived as bragging? She was shocked and hurt. At the same time, she felt a deep gratitude for being told the truth about how she had affected her new friends. *Perhaps the girls are right. Maybe my stories do sound like bragging. And maybe my self-confidence is irritating.*

Painful as it was at the moment, Erika recognized that this was the best life-lesson she could have ever received. Mária and Marianne were not her schoolmates; they didn't have to be nice for fear of retribution. Back in Hungary, a bad word by a classmate to his or her parents could end up as a word to the Secret Police. That, in turn, could lead to a whole family's deportation to a village or jail. Anyone, anywhere, could be denounced as anti-communist and end up in the hands of the secret police.

Here, the two girls had nothing to gain by honestly telling her how she had affected them. After a while, Erika quietly said, "I'm sorry if I offended you. I had no idea that I sounded like I was bragging. I appreciate your candor and would like you to call my attention to it when you catch me doing it. I'd like to learn from you how not to do it."

Mária said gently, "Just don't keep saying you're the best, or the most talented, or the top at everything. Find a way to be a bit more modest and you'll be a lot more likeable."

Marianne pointed out sharply, "Yeah. Mária is a countess, but you don't hear her saying how important her family was before the war. Her great grandfather was Count Hadik, the famous warrior but she isn't bragging about it."

"Marianne, enough," Mária stopped her softly. "I think Erika's got the picture. We'll help you to learn," she smiled at Erika.

Erika rose from the edge of her bed, "Thank you for leveling with me. I'll do my best and with your help I will learn. Can we be friends again?"

"Of course!" Mária rose as well and pulled Marianne up. "Let's hug and make peace."

They stood in a tight circle with their arms wrapped around each other's shoulders, feeling the warmth of a new bond among them.

When Erika curled up in her bed, she felt a boundless sense of relief and joy. She had her friends back, and she was about to learn how to be likeable. Recalling her school days, she realized that in fact she only had a few close friends. Others around her treated her with respect but not warmth, perhaps not even trust. *Strange, how the misfortune of our getting caught at the border might bring me a brand-new way of behaving that will make my life better. Maybe things happen for a reason.* She smiled as she was falling asleep.

◎◉◎

In the ensuing weeks, at each mealtime, Mária taught Erika formal table manners; how to hold her utensils properly. Also, how she should put in her mouth no more food than what fit on the back of her fork. "Smaller bites enable you to carry on a conversation without sounding like you've got your mouth full," Mária explained.

Marianne shoveled a chunk of meat, potatoes, and cabbage into her mouth till her cheeks bulged, and asked. "Like this?" Clearly, she was making fun of her two friends. She refused to go along with the program of higher education in good manners.

Mária smiled indulgently and ignored her. Marianne would always be contrary; there was no point in trying to tame her. Erika was different. Within a week she acquired flawless table manners and ways of expressing herself more humbly. She even managed to restrain herself and let her friends serve themselves first at dinner, or when selecting dessert after their meal.

By contrast, Marianne deliberately began to take the best of everything, just to show her disdain for these courtesies that she considered totally artificial. Erika didn't mind. She realized that the better her manners became, the closer the bond grew between her and Mária. She adored Mária. She looked up to Mária as her mentor, and a generous friend. Mária had awakened in Erika a higher self she didn't know existed within her.

In addition to teaching Erika good manners, when they were sitting in the dayroom, Mária began to narrate the stories of her favorite books. She was thus acquainting Erika with the best of Hungarian literature.

The Sudruškas, watching the girls just sitting around talking, decided that they needed some activity to keep them busy. Sudruška Zofie brought in crocheting needles and yarns and taught the girls how to make doilies. Thus, while Mária was telling her stories, all three of them were crocheting doilies of various sizes and designs. Marianne disdained doing it but knew that she had to comply. Mária had already known how to knit and crochet. Erika was delighted to acquire this new skill.

In addition to these new activities, Erika also found time to assist the cleaning woman, Berta. Erika was used to befriending the help around her home. Now, as she gained fluency speaking Slovak, she began to converse with Berta. She kept Berta company while the woman was dusting or cleaning the bathrooms. Erika learned that Berta was married, had two daughters, and her husband worked in a factory. Berta cleaned at the Detska Izba plus at the police building from where their food was supplied. She didn't have to explain to Erika why she was working at two jobs. Erika knew that in socialist countries everyone had to work really hard. First, because one salary was not enough to cover a family's expenses. Secondly, because under communism everyone had to have a job. "You don't work, you don't eat" was the well-publicized mantra in countries dominated by the Soviet Union. After a number of chats with Berta, Erika remarked, "I love talking with you, but I can't just stand here while you're working. Let me help you."

Berta sized up the girl. She obviously came from a well-to-do background. "What can you do?" she asked, smiling.

"Anything. I used to help around my home. I enjoy doing it."

"All right let's try you," Berta said, giving her a dust cloth.

Erika worked by Berta's side several times a week, dusting in the bedrooms and cleaning the upstairs bathroom that she and the girls were using. After the third week of consistently doing this, Berta pressed three korunas into her hand.

"Don't tell anyone," she whispered. "Just buy yourself something you need."

Erika, taken aback, protested, "I'm not doing this for you to pay me."

"I know, but surely you could use some money. If for no other reason than to buy a roll of cotton for your monthlies," the older woman winked.

Erika blushed and smiled at her. "That's so kind of you," and she gratefully pocketed the coins. Fact was, she hated using the pieces of cloth she had been provided by the Sudruškas. Those had to be washed and stored after each use.

"I have daughters, I know how it is," Berta patted her on the shoulder.

Erika felt deeply touched. She thought about Mária, their maid at home. She now realized that her ability to form a friendship with the help, no matter where, added a special dimension to both their lives. This woman, like Mária at home, appreciated being treated not as a servant but as an equal.

"Thank you again," she smiled at Berta, and went back to polishing the bathroom fixtures.

Secretly, she was proud of herself. Proud of being useful and being able to earn pocket money. Above all, proud of being appreciated for what she was doing. She also knew that she was not going to tell her girlfriends about her new income, lest it make them envious. She knew how to keep secrets.

CHAPTER 19

Soon the routine of the girls' lives was interrupted by the arrival of three boys. Caught while attempting an illegal border crossing, they had been brought to the Detska Izba early one morning. They were to stay here while awaiting their court appearance. Velitel Stavinsky received them. He interrogated the boys and then checked them in. They were given breakfast and shown to their bedroom upstairs. It was next to the baby's bedroom, catty corner to the girl's room. Once they dropped off the small bags each had carried during their escape, they were escorted into the teens' dayroom. They were told to stay there during the day, under the vigilant glare of the Sudruška on duty.

At this time, it was Sudruška Valentina's shift. The boys greeted her with the customary "Dobrý deň," (Good day) and were sitting huddled together when the three Hungarian girls walked in, after their breakfast. Sudruška Valentina pointed at the new arrivals, and said to the girls in her gruff voice, "You've got companions for a while. You can talk and play together, provided you behave."

The boys rose, and one by one, introduced themselves. Lubo, the oldest at fifteen, was a tall, handsome boy, with sandy brown hair and warm brown eyes. He had a friendly but commanding personality. Štepan was fourteen, clearly at the awkward age when his mustache was sprouting but his height had not caught up with his muscular build. His dark brown hair was short cropped, and his piercing brown eyes under bushy brows spoke of a strong personality. The third boy, Jaro, was the "runt" of the group. He was also fourteen, but short and slender, delicate looking, with blond hair and blue eyes in a narrow face.

The girls, speaking Slovak reasonably well by now, told the boys their names and that they came from Hungary. After the somewhat formal introductions, they all sat down in a small circle and began to chat. The boys were curious how three girls from Budapest ended up in Bratislava. It didn't take long for them to discover that all of them were there for the same reason: trying to leave the country illegally. This immediately established a trust among them.

With Sudruška Valentina listening nearby, they could not say that they wanted to escape because they hated the regime under which they were forced to live—but then they didn't have to say it. The mere act of their attempted border crossing was proof enough of where they stood politically. Casting a quick glance at Sudruška Valentina sitting in her corner armchair in the room, they all knew, the less they said the better.

Dropping the subject, they began to discuss their school systems, similarities and differences. But then Sudruška Valentina left the room, and they quickly returned to their escape story.

None of the boys' families had been aware of their intention to escape when they had snuck out of their homes the night before.

"Of course, by now they all know," Lubo shrugged. "My parents won't punish me for it, though they will surely make a scene, 'how could I do such a thing, leaving them!' But I'm sure secretly they're sorry that I didn't make it," he added in a whisper.

"Mine will be horrified and scold me till I'm blue in the face," Jaro grinned. "My concern is whether or not the Judge will allow us to go home. Or stick us into some correctional institute to make us turn into good little pioneers."

"And you?" Erika turned to Štepan who sat morosely, staring into space.

"Oh, his father will kill'im when he finds out," Lubo jumped to reply.

Štepan looked at him darkly, "So? Let him. See if I care."

"Why?" the girls asked in chorus.

"My father is a Colonel in the Security Police. How do you think he'll feel about his son trying to leave illegally the country he serves so devotedly?"

They all fell silent. They understood the horror of what Štepan had just told them. It was bad enough for the other boys to try to escape. But the son of a high-ranking Security Police officer? Not only the son but the father might also be held responsible for this. His superiors might ask, 'Didn't you teach your son right?' Or worse, they might accuse the father of sending his son abroad so through him he could be supplying the West with confidential political information. Young as they were, they all knew the trouble Štepan might be in.

"We'll see," Štepan shrugged, either pretending not to be worried or being truly fatalistic. It was hard to tell since he kept up a closed façade.

Sudruška Valentina returned to the room and settled in her chair again.

"Let's play a game." Lubo jumped up and grabbed one of the boxes off the shelf that had board games on it. He looked at the box and laughed, "Ladders and shoots is just right for us. We go up or slide down, at the toss of the dice."

A week passed, and none of the boys' parents came to visit them. The six teenagers fell into a pleasant routine of spending their days talking, having meals together, and playing a variety of games. Lubo taught Erika chess, Jaro played dice games with Marianne, while Mária continued to crochet. Štepan sat apart, glumly staring out the window, refusing to join in any of their pastimes. They kept their conversations light and inconsequential in the dayroom. But at night was a different story.

When they went upstairs to their rooms, they got ready for bed and waited for the lights to go off downstairs. They made sure the Sudruška on duty was also in her room behind closed doors. Then the boys snuck into the girls' room to talk. They spoke passionately about the hopelessness of their futures.

"You girls at least can blame your parents for dragging you into this. But what is our excuse?" Lubo would ask.

"No excuse, we'll be put into some sort of institution and re-educated," Jaro shrugged.

"I don't want to sit around to find out," Štepan muttered.

"Strange, that none of your parents have come to visit you," Marianne commented.

"Not strange at all," Štepan countered, "it's the system. They are probably not allowed to see us till after we go to Court. The police don't want us to tell them our stories before we are interrogated by the authorities."

"But they haven't taken you for questioning and you've been here a week," Mária said.

"They did debrief us quite extensively the night we were arrested, so maybe that was enough. Now we'll just have to sit tight till our court date." Jaro explained.

"That'll be too late," Štepan suddenly blurted out.

They all looked at him, wondering what he meant, but before they could ask, Lubo stepped in, "It's late, let's let the girls get some sleep. See you in the morning."

◎◉◎

A couple of evenings later, sitting on the beds in the girls' room, the boys informed them that they had decided to make another escape attempt.

"The Velitel told us this morning that the Court date is set ten days from today. It will be a new moon in seven days, so the night will be totally dark. We'll leave that night," Lubo said.

The three girls were silent, absorbing the portent of this information.

"We'll help you in any way we can," Marianne suddenly declared, knowing her friends would go along.

"That's a very generous offer but what if the Sudruškas see you doing something unusual, or you are questioned, and they make you confess? You could be severely punished," objected Lubo.

"We are Hungarian, what could they do to us? We're underage, so they can't put us in jail. And can't send us back to Hungary till the government there requisitions us." Mária replied.

"How about no food and solitary confinement here?" asked Štepan.

"That's not such a big deal," Marianne shrugged. "We'll survive it. Let us know what we can do for you when the time comes."

"Thank you," Lubo said, and suddenly reaching forward pulled Mária into his arms and kissed her passionately on her lips.

The other two boys, following Lubo's action, also grabbed for a girl. Štepan went for Erika, and short little Jaro drew Marianne's face down to his level, to kiss her.

Although Erika wasn't attracted to Štepan at all, she did not protest. Fact was, she had a secret crush on Lubo, but accepted that he had chosen Mária, since they were both the leaders of their own little circle. So, Erika closed her eyes and let Štepan's large, soft lips touch hers. She didn't find his kiss unpleasant, but it was not exciting either.

"Wait a minute," Marianne ordered, when she came up for breath after Jaro's kiss. She reached over to the light switch and counted aloud, "One, two, three," and suddenly they were plunged into darkness. "Kiss," Marianne commanded, and they all obeyed. With the same authority, when she finished kissing Jaro, Marianne called out, "One, two, lights!" and she switched on the ceiling light, while the others quickly pushed free of their partner's embrace.

They looked at one another and laughed, both out of embarrassment and a sense of fun. Marianne said, "Let's do this again; "One, two," and switched off the light on the third count.

This kiss is lasting longer, Erika thought, as she felt one of Štepan's hands gently slide to her breast, cupping it. She pushed his hand away but stayed in the kiss. Štepan understood and didn't try again. Instead, he wrapped his arms tightly around Erika's waist, holding her close to his body. Erika didn't protest. He was leaving. This was like a gift she was giving him before he put himself into harm's way again.

When Marianne switched on the light, they all stood a little dazed, flushed, clearly aroused, and wondering what was coming next.

"It's late, go to your room, we'll talk tomorrow," Mária commanded, breaking the magic threads that invisibly bound each couple together.

◎◉◎

Over the following days, they all pretended that nothing was brewing among them. They sat in the dayroom and played, or talked, and joked during their meals about the food. But at night things were different. They spent time planning but mostly holding each other tight and kissing. The boys accepted the limits the girls set—kissing but no groping—although, who knew where their hands wandered in the dark.

Erika did not allow Štepan to touch her breasts or put a hand between her legs. She acquiesced to his kisses because he was the one allotted to her in their pairing off. But that was all. Had it been Lubo, she wasn't sure how she would have reacted. Štepan did not excite her. It was like a game to her, "Lights off, kiss, lights on, stop." It was just fun.

Cleverly, Mária always stopped them from having the lights off too long so things would not get out of hand. Oddly, the girls did not discuss their activity after the boys left, and they settled in their beds. Somehow, because the boys were leaving, it seemed sacrilegious to comment or criticize the way they kissed or behaved. They were counting the days till the new moon when their "kissing game" would come to an end. Until then, they felt they should live to the fullest for there was no telling what the future might bring.

Today is the day, Lubo whispered one morning when he ran into Erika on the staircase. She was coming downstairs while he was heading up to their room. As he had leaned close to her ear, he also extended his left arm and for an instant reached with his middle finger between her legs. Erika was so taken aback she froze mid-step, staring at him. She couldn't believe he had deliberately touched her so inappropriately. *He is Mária's boyfriend, why would he do this to me?*

He flashed her a quick, conspiratorial grin and continued up the stairs.

What's wrong with all these men, Erika wondered, *or what's wrong with me that they all think they can make sexual advances to me? Did Lubo sense somehow that I am not as innocent as the other girls? Or what is it? Was Lubo trying to tell me that he is as attracted to me as I am to him, but he couldn't do anything about it anymore than I could?*

Erika slowly descended the stairs, realizing that she had to stop thinking about what had just happened, and appear perfectly composed by the time she entered the common dayroom. This was certainly not the time nor the day to figure out her personal issues. It was the day the boys were going to escape.

Late afternoon, the Velitel left the building. Sudruška Olga, on duty, was in her usual corner in the dayroom. She knew she could relax while awaiting the arrival of her shift change in a short while. So, she didn't worry about having only Jaro in the room with her. After all, the youngsters were allowed to go to their rooms during the day, even take a nap if they wanted to.

Jaro sat calmly reading, then stopped and started talking to Sudruška Olga. He had to keep her occupied for at least half an hour. The best way to do that was by pestering her with questions about their future. Such questions always elicited from most of their guardians long lectures about their misdeeds and dark future.

Meanwhile, the other two boys were in their bedroom, putting their coats on and waiting for the girls to give them the signal to go.

Marianne had snuck into the Velitel's office while Mária loitered in the hallway watching out for her. Inside, Marianne opened the tall cabinet where the staff always kept a couple of guns, and grabbing one, she deftly hid it under her sweatsuit, holding it steady with the elastic of her pants. She calmly came out and silently closed the door behind her. She walked down the long hallway and heard Jaro talking with Sudruška Olga. Grateful to be able to avoid the Sudruška's eyes, Marianne went upstairs. She entered the boys' bedroom and quickly removed the gun from under her blouse. Lubo grabbed it from her with a nod. Marianne, backed out of the room without a word and went to her own bedroom. She threw herself on her bed and put her hands over her wildly beating heart to calm down.

Mária, observing Marianne safely go upstairs, now noiselessly entered the Sudruškas' downstairs bedroom off the hallway. She knew she had just minutes before the new shift would arrive and likely first come into their room. Mária quickly found the building's phone line and switched it to the guards' bedroom upstairs. Due to the scarcity of available telephone lines, even institutions like the Detska Izba were allocated only one line. It rang in the Velitel's office and had an extension in the downstairs bedroom used by the Sudruškas on duty. Additionally, the building was wired so the line could be switched upstairs. The girls knew that on nights when the Sudruška on duty came upstairs to sleep, she would transfer the phone line to her room there.

During preparatory discussions, Lubo told the girls that one of them would have to cut the phone wire so when their escape was discovered, the Sudruška on duty would not be able to report it quickly. Mária felt uneasy about cutting the wire. She thought it was sufficient to switch the line upstairs. Because by the time the Sudruška on duty figured out from where to report the missing boys, they would have gained time getting away. Besides, having the line upstairs could look like it had been done the night before and then forgotten to be switched downstairs in the morning. She snuck out of the Sudruškas' bedroom, carefully shut the door, and headed upstairs.

Erika was waiting for her in their room. When Mária told her the phone line was now upstairs, without a word, Erika left. She tiptoed to the wall cabinet where the phone system was housed, and softly opening the door, pulled the main wire out of its socket. Not completely, just enough to disconnect the phone line. She disagreed with Maria about merely switching the phone line upstairs.

Lubo had been very clear about this. "It's critical for the phone to be disconnected to prevent a swift call to the police station when our escape is discovered. We need all the time we can gain before the police come after us. There is no question that they will, but before they do, we must get as far away as we can from the Detska Izba and hide out somewhere till dark."

Štepan cut in, "We'll need to cross the river before our pursuers begin their hunt. It would be easy for them to catch us crossing the bridge. Once on the other side of Bratislava, we can hide in the forest. Once it gets really dark, we'll find a spot at the border where we can crawl under the wires without touching them. Then we will make a run through no-man's land to the Austrian border."

When they explained this to the girls, the night before their escape, Erika had the distinct feeling that though Lubo was their leader, it was really Štepan who had masterminded the plan. *Maybe I misjudged him merely because he isn't as good looking as Lubo*, Erika thought as she listened to him. She felt a lot more respect for Štepan and even enjoyed their "kissing game" more during their last evening with the boys. Their farewell kisses had an added intensity as a sense of loss had cast a shadow over their "fun". They were all painfully aware that most likely they would never see each other again.

And now it was time for the boys to leave. They quietly scratched on the girls' bedroom door. The three girls jumped off their beds and ran to face Lubo and Štepan in their doorway. They locked eyes but did not touch or kiss goodbye. Lubo and Štepan were tense and preoccupied with their escape.

With Mária leading, the girls went downstairs to the dayroom. They sat down pretending to listen with interest to Sudruška Olga's lecturing of Jaro. As they sat, they also caught a glimpse of Lubo and Štepan sneaking by their room, down the hall to the Velitel's office.

The boys' plan was to climb out his office window that faced the back of their building. Then scaling a brick fence, jump into the yard of the next villa. From there, they hoped they could easily get out to the street.

About a half hour later Sudruška Olga, done with her rant to Jaro, sat quietly, awaiting her shift change, and watching her charges playing a board game. She looked at her watch and asked no one in particular, "Where are the other two boys?"

The three girls and Jaro looked up and shrugged their shoulders.

"Maybe they're sleeping," Jaro suggested.

"They won't be able to sleep at night if they're napping all afternoon."

Again, the four youngsters had no answer. They just stared at the Sudruška, secretly wondering what she was going to do next.

"Jaro, go wake them up if they're asleep. Or tell them to stop whatever they're doing, and come downstairs," Sudruška Olga ordered.

Jaro obediently rose to go upstairs. Except that he didn't. Instead, he surreptitiously crept down the hall to the Velitel's office where his coat was waiting for him. He had known all along that he would go with his friends. But the three of them had decided to play it safe and not tell the girls about it. Their concern was that the girls would be worried about Jaro while he was keeping the Sudruška occupied, and their guard might sense the tension in the air.

Jaro looked out the Velitel's office window and saw that their building was actually on the edge of their property with a brick fence separating the neighbor's yard. Lubo and Štepan were huddling by the fence, waiting.

"Throw your coat to me, you'll put it on outside," Lubo whispered. "We must get going."

Jaro tossed out his coat and pulled himself up into the open window frame.

"Jump," ordered Lubo.

Jaro went out the window feet first and was caught by his friends before he landed on his face in the snow. Even as Jaro was pulling on his coat, the three boys scaled the fence that separated the neighbor's yard, and running along bushes that lined that yard, slipped through the unlocked wrought iron gate. They were out in the street. It was already dark, only streetlights illuminated the sidewalks.

"Walk fast, but don't run," Štepan instructed them in a low voice as they disappeared into the night.

◉◉◉

While waiting for Jaro's return with the boys, the girls pretended to have started a game, but in reality, they sat listening for Jaro's footsteps coming down the stairs. When after about ten minutes neither he nor the boys appeared, Sudruška Olga, wondering what was keeping them, turned to Erika, "Go upstairs and tell them to come down at once!"

Obediently, Erika jumped up and ran upstairs. She deliberately slowed her steps as she went to the boys' bedroom and knocked loudly on their door. She waited for an answer, and when there was none, she knocked again, and called out loudly, "Jaro, Lubo, Štepan, what's going on with you? Come on down!"

She waited for another minute, then knocked again and opened the door. Then quickly ran down the stairs and breathlessly announced to Sudruška Olga: "They're not in their room!"

"What do you mean? Then where are they?" Sudruška Olga jumped to her feet, and without waiting for an answer barked at the girls, "Don't leave this room! I'll be right back."

The three girls remained frozen in their chairs, as though they were just obeying orders. They were in fact terrified, realizing that Jaro had also escaped. They wondered whether the boys have had enough time to get away.

But they had agreed long ago that this room may be bugged and that it was never safe to say anything in there that could not be heard by their guards. So, they were silent. They could hear Sudruška Olga scaling the stairs, and opening every door, and slamming them shut again. Then she came running downstairs, and continued her search down the hallway, looking into every room, including the Velitel's office.

Just at that moment they could hear the front door open and banged shut as Sudruška Agata arrived for the night shift. Sudruška Agata was not one of the brightest of guards. She was heavy-set and slow moving, had pasty white skin and small brown eyes beneath bushy brown brows. She wore her mousy brown hair in a bun and frequently reached up to smooth back any nonexistent stray strand.

The girls liked her because she had a sweet disposition. When on day duty, she allowed them to walk to the police station at noon to pick up their lunch. Though the station was only a few blocks down the street, being in the outside world was always a treat for the girls. Now Sudruška Agata stood in the middle of the hallway, puzzled, as Sudruška Olga shouted to her: "They're gone! Sound the alarm! Call the police!"

"Who's gone?" Sudruška Agata asked, thinking, perhaps Olga had gone mad, for she could see the girls sitting quietly in the dayroom, staring at her.

"The three boys!" Sudruška Olga's voice could cut a cord with its sharpness. She turned on her heels and ran to the Velitel's office to phone the police station. She suddenly became aware of the cold air coming into the room and saw that the window behind the desk was ajar. There was no question about it, the boys had escaped. She lifted the receiver. There was no dial tone. The phone was dead. She looked down and saw that the cord had been pulled from its socket. "The little bastards," she muttered, and plugged the phone in. But there was no line. She ran out of the office to Sudruška Agata who still stood in the hallway not quite comprehending the situation.

"Don't just stand there, ask the girls if they know where the boys might have gone!"

It was a futile hope, but Sudruška Olga thought, perhaps they were just playing a prank and were hiding somewhere in the garden. Or they really had managed to escape. Perhaps the girls might have known about it. It certainly didn't hurt to ask but not at this moment.

Sudruška Olga ran upstairs to the night phone, but that, too had been disconnected. She ran downstairs, and grabbing her coat, shouted to Sudruška Agata "I'm going to the police station, don't let any of them out of the playroom! Stay with them till we get back!"

Sudruška Agata removed her coat and asked, the three girls, "Do you know what's going on? Did the boys tell you that they were leaving?"

"No, they never said anything about leaving," Mária replied blandly.

The other two girls shook their heads and shrugged their shoulders, looking at each other, in wonder.

"They certainly didn't say anything to us!" Erika declared.

Soon they could hear the blaring of police car sirens surrounding their block. Policemen were running in their heavy boots into the yard, and all around their building. Their loud voices and the agitated barking of their German shepherds reached the playroom. It made the girls tense with the recollection of their own arrest as well as fear for the boys. They sat very still, listening to the racket all around. Taking advantage of the chaos outside, Mária whispered to her friends, "Remember, they said nothing, we knew nothing."

"Do you think we're stupid?" Marianne hissed back.

"Let's each of us grab a book while we're waiting to see what's next," Erika suggested and rose to get one.

◎◉◎

Soon the Velitel arrived, and sticking his face into the room, barked at the girls, "I'll want you in my office one by one, as soon as I send for you," and continued down the hall.

The girls exchanged looks. They didn't have to say anything; they were familiar with what may be coming their way. Heavy questioning over and over again, in the hope that one of them would break and provide some information. But as they looked into each other's eyes, they all knew, none of them would confess to a thing. It was not only for the protection of the boys; their own skin was also in this game. Should the Velitel, or any of the Sudruškas, get even a hint of their participation in this escape, heaven knows what punishment would await them.

Each girl was well trained by the totalitarian regime in which they lived to being "two-faced" by necessity; saying things they didn't mean and being able to keep their thoughts and feelings buried just to stay alive and out of prison. They were already in captivity. Should they by mistake reveal their role in this escape, their guardians could retaliate by punishing their parents who were being held in jail.

Taking deep breaths to relax, they leaned back in their chairs, awaiting the Velitel's call.

The girls didn't have to wait long before the Velitel summoned them, one by one. He was obviously nervous and preoccupied with the boys' escape. Therefore, his questioning of each girl individually, and then together, was almost perfunctory. He asked if any of them had known anything about the boys' plans. But when each girl firmly denied any awareness whatsoever, he let them go.

They were provided dinner as usual, but Sudruška Zofie told them, "Go to your room right after you've finished eating, and stay there. We want to be sure of your whereabouts," she added in Hungarian with a sly smile.

During their dinner the girls could hear policemen coming in and out of their building. They ate faster than usual and kept their voices low as they

331

made small talk. When they headed upstairs to their room, they could see that the Velitel's office door was ajar, the light was on, and they could hear male voices having a loud discussion in there.

Two Sudruškas were standing vigilantly in the downstairs hallway, and one was upstairs, watching the girls as they headed for their bedroom. All the Sudruškas were wearing a holster around their waist with a gun in there.

"They seem pretty serious about all this," Erika commented once they were in their room.

Maria grinned, "Maybe they're concerned that we'll bolt too."

"Either the Velitel believed us, or he didn't really want to know," Marianne reflected on their interrogation as they prepared for bed.

"He probably didn't want any more trouble than he was already having," Maria said. "In any case, I hope they won't come down too hard on him if the boys manage to get away."

"I hadn't even thought of what could happen to him!" Erika exclaimed. "Just think, they may blame him and remove him from this post for not being vigilant enough. That would be dreadful. I really like him. And who knows what a new man would be like."

Marianne yawned, "Let's not worry about this till we have to," and added, "though I wouldn't mind it if they removed some of the bitchier Sudruškas."

Erika grinned, "No, they would probably remove the nicer ones because they too might get blamed for not having watched the boys well enough."

"Let's go to sleep," Maria sighed. "But first, let's say a prayer for the boys."

The girls slid off their beds and knelt, with eyes closed, hands held together in prayer. Maria recited the Lord's Prayer and added at the end, "Please God, let it be your will for the boys to succeed."

"Amen," whispered the other two.

They lay in their beds quietly, hoping for their prayer to work its magic.

◎◉◎

A loud banging on the front door, followed by boots pounding downstairs, woke the girls out of a deep sleep. They bolted upright in their beds, tensely listening to the sounds downstairs.

"They've caught them," Maria whispered.

They could hear the rough commands of the guards ordering the boys to go upstairs to their bedroom.

"Don't you dare go anywhere else!" shouted an angry male voice.

Heavy steps came shuffling up the stairs. The girls could hear the door to the boys' room open, and it sounded like furniture was being moved.

"Ah, they're putting an extra bed in there," Marianne whispered. She had opened their door a crack and peaked into the hallway. "They'll have a guard sleeping with them tonight," she concluded.

"I wonder if all three of them had been caught," Erika whispered. "Marianne, can you see who is going into their room?"

"No, I can't. Shall I go to the toilet and see what's going on?"

"Absolutely not!" Maria ordered her swiftly. "Shut the door and let's go back to sleep. Time enough to learn what happened in the morning!"

She is afraid to know, Erika thought, as she obediently slid under her cover. Marianne stood by the door for a while, trying to listen for the boys' voices, then shrugged and also went to bed.

◎◉◎

It was still dark when the girls were awakened by the noise of shuffling feet in the hallway. Marianne jumped out of bed and peeked out the door.

"They're taking the boys downstairs. I'm going after them to see where they're going."

"No, don't! You'll just get yourself into trouble," Maria warned.

"Screw them!" was Marianne's response, as she bolted out of the room.

She returned a few minutes later to report, "They took the boys into the playroom, and are making them kneel on the sharp edge of a log taken from the stack of firewood by the ceramic stove. I'm going downstairs and will kneel with them, to show solidarity."

"Are you crazy?" Maria warned her.

But Marianne was already out the door in her pajamas. Erika and Maria exchanged glances.

"We can't let Marianne do this alone," Erika finally said, and got to her feet.

"Let's go!" Maria agreed.

In the dayroom, all three boys were kneeling on logs that had been chopped into triangular shapes. The wider side of each log was on the floor and the boys' knees rested on the knife sharp top edges. They looked exhausted and bedraggled, with heads down, eyes cast on the floor. They were facing the door. Sudruška Valentina stood by her chair, watching them, and turned in surprise as the three girls marched into the room.

"Good morning," the girls smiled Sudruška Valentina as if what they were about to do was the most natural thing in the world. The boys looked up for a second but immediately cast their eyes down again, refusing to acknowledge the girls' presence.

Without saying anything, Marianne boldly went to the stack of firewood and selected a piece. The other two girls did the same. Marianne went behind the boys, and placing her log on the floor, carefully knelt down on it. Maria and Erika followed suit. No one spoke. Sudruška Valentina was either so surprised or so aghast at this act of solidarity that she remained speechless, staring at them.

She probably doesn't know what to do, Erika thought. Likely, they have no precedence for such behavior and so she doesn't know how to handle it. Erika deeply admired Marianne's courage. She usually thought of Marianne as a lightweight, superficial, and totally self-absorbed. For the first time since they had met, Erika saw a whole different side of her.

This was a girl who stood for something and wasn't afraid of confronting the authorities with her position. Guessing at Marianne's reasoning, Erika figured that Marianne wanted to show the Velitel and the Sudruškas that she felt the boys had done nothing wrong. *Nothing more than what we had tried to do previously: leave the country. That's the reason for all of us being held prisoners at the Detska Izba! So, if the boys are being punished for their intention, the three of us should be too. Marianne has a lot of guts to do this*, Erika thought.

She stole a furtive glance at Maria, wondering what she was thinking, and was surprised to see that her palms were pressed together, in prayer. Maria probably thinks we're all martyrs, Erika thought, amused. She wondered whether Sudruška Valentina noticed Maria's gesture. Most likely, yes, but obviously there was nothing she could do about it. *It's kind of funny, despite the awfulness of the situation, that we are able to protest without the guard's objection.*

Erika's knees were starting to hurt, the sharp edge of the log cut into the tender part just under her knee bone. She assumed the others were also suffering the same pain but none of them gave even the slightest hint of it. So, she took deep breaths, and tried to think of something good, like the fact that all three boys were in one piece. None had been shot during their arrest. A closer look at Štepan revealed black and blue marks all over his swollen cheeks and around his eyes. But he seemed to be the most stoic of them all as he knelt holding himself upright, with a blank stare.

Just as Erika's knees began to feel like a hundred needles were pricking them, Sudruška Blanka entered the room and barked, "Get up, all of you. Boys, go to your room. Girls, go get breakfast."

With sighs of relief, they all scrambled to their feet. They exchanged quick, furtive glances as they all put the logs back by the fireplace. Then the boys left the room, followed by Sudruška Blanca.

"Move!" Sudruška Valentina ordered the three girls toward the kitchen.

"You could cut the tension in the air with a knife," whispered Marianne, as after breakfast the three of them sat in the playroom, unable to concentrate on anything but the boys upstairs. The boys were guarded in their room with a Sudruška present at all times. The guards took turns every hour or so to keep them alert. There was also a Sudruška stationed in the hallway, in case one of the boys needed to use the toilet.

"What do you think they'll do with them?" Erika whispered, knowing, whatever the answer was, it would be pure speculation.

"Who knows?" Maria shrugged.

"They'll probably keep them here till their trial, and then off they go to be re-educated," Marianne said, in bitter tone.

◎◉◎

That afternoon, a short, stocky Secret Police Officer arrived, marching down the hallway to the Velitel's office, nervously guided by Sudruška Olga. Then Olga went upstairs to fetch the three boys and led them into the Velitel's office.

Although all the doors were closed, the girls could hear the man shouting in the Velitel's office. They could also hear sounds of furniture being thrown about. Then the office door flung open, and the Velitel and Sudruška Olga led Lubo and Jaro down the hall into the dayroom, where the girls were sitting in frozen silence. The Velitel cast a quick glance at them and left the room without a word.

"Sit!" commanded Sudruška Olga, settling in her corner of the room.

Erika, who was sitting closest to Yaro, asked whispering, "What's happening?"

"Well, it's either Štepan flying against the walls, or chairs are flying at him, or his father's fists are beating him to a pulp," Yaro whispered back with all the cynicism he could muster to hide his feelings of helplessness and despair about what was happening to his friend.

Lubo leaned back in his chair and closing his eyes, muttered, "That bastard!"

"No talking!" bellowed Sudruška Olga.

The room became silent. Laden with the uneasy, heavy air of the pain and concern of the youngsters, they sat motionless, staring blindly ahead, listening.

◎◉◎

In the Velitel's office, Štepan let his body become limp as he was knocked about by his father. General Solovič, a short, muscular man, struck Štepan where he could, shoving him around the room, slamming him into the furniture and the walls. As he grabbed Štepan by the arm and twisted him around, the boy fell forward, and Comrade Solovič kicked him viciously in the ribs with the sharp tip of his boot.

Solovič was livid, his fury growing as Štepan yielded to the beating without resistance. *Why was the boy not fighting back? He should at least make excuses for his behavior, or apologize, or something! Anything!* Solovič thought, as his son flopped about like a limp sack of wheat. Yielding when he was pushed, submitting to each fist striking his face, his back, his shoulders, and arms. Frustrated at not getting a reaction out of Štepan, Solovič began to shout, as he continued to pummel Štepan.

"You scum, you miserable swine, you filthy traitor you! So, this is what you do to me! Once was not enough! You had to go and do it again! What the hell were you thinking, you bastard! That I'll save your neck, no matter what? Hadn't it occurred to you that your political sabotage is putting me, your father, in danger?! Damn you! My own son! Here I am, protecting the safety of our country, sworn to eliminate all counterrevolutionaries, to seek out and punish all enemies of our people and whom do I find as Enemy Number One? My very own son! Oh, hell, you can't be my flesh and blood! Who knows who your mother paired with—but sure as hell you're not my son!"

"Leave my mother out of this!" Štepan shouted angrily.

"Ah, you've found your voice! Well, you haven't got the right to defend her, you miserable cur!"

Furiously, he kicked Štepan's back, but the boy just rolled and remained motionless where he landed from the force of the boot. His father, leaning over him, continued his rant that could now be heard down the hall through the slightly ajar office door.

"Haven't I given you everything? The world could have been yours! With my position in the Party, you could have become anything you wanted! You could have joined the Party and become a great builder of our socialist society! And what do you do instead? Drag my name into the mud where you and your bourgeois friends grovel! But why?! Why did you do this to me?! What was lacking in our life that you had to escape from? What?! ANSWER ME!"

"I don't have to explain anything to you!"

"Oh, yes you do!" shouted Solovič, kicking Štepan again, in blind fury.

But Štepan remained silent. Frustrated, Solovič picked him up and shook him, grabbing him by the shoulders. Štepan offered no resistance, his limp body further infuriating his father.

"You will damn well explain yourself, you little bastard! Answer me or I'll beat you to death with my own two hands!"

Štepan, despite his aching body, couldn't help retorting with a wry smile, "Go ahead. It wouldn't be the first time you've beaten someone to death."

Solovič exploded, "How dare you!! You miserable runt! I'm breaking my back working for our country, and what do you do?! How dare you to sit in judgment of me!!"

"I don't have to…history will…"

Solovič pushed his face close to his son's so Štepan could feel his hot breath on his cheeks.

"History is what I make! The Party makes! Listen, you rat! When I was your age, I had to grovel before the factory supervisor; I had to lick his boots to be kept on the job. My wages were not enough to support my mother and me! My father died in the First World War, and my mother died of illness and malnutrition.

"She died because there wasn't a doctor I could afford to call to her! There wasn't a thing I could do! I couldn't even give her a burial! The city came and put her in the public cemetery where one carcass was no different from another. And I swore, I swore when I became a member of the Party, to hunt down and kill every capitalist pig that ever grew rich on my mother's misery."

"All right, you're doing it! But why do I have to be a part of it?"

"Because I fought for you, too! You're my flesh and blood and I fight daily battles so you could grow up having what I never had! So, you wouldn't have to die in a factory filling the pockets of capitalist pigs!"

"Now I can fill the wallets of communist dictators!"

Solovič slapped his son hard, "How dare you!"

"That's it! Beat me! That's what you do best! Kill me because we disagree! Is this the way I'll find the truth?"

"There is no other truth but mine! You are misled by your bourgeois friends. You only see the immediate reality before you, and not the grand plan. The ideal for which we are all willing to die...and KILL! Kill everyone who stands in our way!"

Štepan retorted, "Why kill? Why not just let go? Why keep the people who refuse to cooperate? Why not just let them leave the country?"

Solovič stared, taken aback by his son's logic. Then, as if he were talking to an equal, he explained, with great intensity, "People are children...and stupid... like you. They don't know what's good for them! They don't understand what it means to work for an ideal. They must be taught. They must be forced to learn for their own good. Even if it means a period of great hardship, till they come to recognize the value of the end results.

"And you? You are the future generation! Our pride and hope are vested in you! You should be the true builder of socialism! You, my own son, you should have comprehended that the higher the goal, the more sacrifices it requires. But you are not my son. You can't be! Understand this: your trial is coming up and I won't lift a finger for you. Not one little finger to save you!

"Had you been brought to me, to my Office of Interrogation, I'd had you shot as a traitor for what you have done. You are just lucky that you were not caught by my people. And I hope you'll get a sentence that will teach you to understand what we stand for. I'll be the first one on the witness stand to accuse you and ask for no mercy for you! You have betrayed me! You have failed me, but I won't fail you! One way or another you'll learn to cooperate."

His voice trailed off as he stared at his son with hatred and pain in his eyes. Then he reached toward Štepan and grabbed him by the arm shoving him toward the door, "Now get out of my sight. I'll see you in court!"

◎◉◎

Štepan, barely able to stand up, slowly shuffled out of the Velitel's office. He held on to the wall as he painfully paced down the hall. Sudruška Eva, standing at the other end of the hall spotted Štepan and quickly came to him.

"Come, I'll help you up to your room." She put her arm around Štepan's shoulders and slowly walked with him. "You look awful. But I'm sure you deserved what you got."

◉◉◉

In the dayroom, the others caught a glance of Štepan passing by. By now it was dark, they have had their dinner, and it was getting close to their bedtime. Sudruška Valentina said to them harshly, "All of you too, go upstairs now, and don't let us hear a peep out of you."

Pretending that they were feeling fine, the three girls and two boys politely said good night, then ran upstairs as fast as their legs could carry them.

As they headed toward their bedrooms, Lubo and Jaro whispered to the girls, "Don't worry, we'll take care of him," and disappeared into their bedroom.

The girls did not feel like discussing the events of the day. Depressed and silent, each got into bed.

"At least they're alive," Erika finally whispered in the dark.

"Today, they are," Marianne replied.

"Let's pray for them," Maria suggested.

Kneeling by their bedside, they recited the Lord's prayer, at the end of which Maria added, "please Jesus, look out for those three boys, don't let any more harm come to them."

"Amen," echoed the other two.

Even Marianne prayed, Erika thought, once she was under her cover again. *She must be as upset and scared for them as I am.* Silently, she recited the most ancient of Hebrew prayers to allay her own feelings of sadness and concern for all of them, including her mother and sister in prison.

S'mah Israel, Adonai Elohenu, Adonai echad. "Hear, O Israel! Adonai is our God, Adonai is One," and for the first time since she left the prison, she recited the entire night prayer her mother insisted that they always say at bedtime.

Erika had abandoned praying when she was separated from her mother and sister and brought to the Detska Izba. She realized only now how angry she was at God who was supposed to have helped them and instead abandoned them. It didn't matter that Maria was a devout Catholic and said the Lord's Prayer nightly before falling asleep. Marianne disdained religion, and for the first time in her life, siding with her, Erika was able to do the same. She was able to question, *What good is a God, if he exists at all, who allows all the misery in the world? Why would God put us into our current situation if he was a loving god? Where was God when the boys got arrested again?"*

Maria's answer was always the same, "We can't know or judge God's ways".

Marianne would always respond, "What God? I hate the communists, but in this one thing I agree with them: religion is the opiate of the masses. Religion is how the Church was able to keep people in line—by having them confess every sin, so the priests would know everything about them. Then put the fear of God into them while collecting their pennies for their so-called salvation. What a racket!"

Now, lying in bed, despite agreeing with Marianne, Erika couldn't help but pray. There was no hope for any of their futures but praying made her feel better.

◎◉◎

In a few days' time, the three boys were taken from the Detska Izba in a prison van, similar to the one that had brought Erika to the place. Because the boys had been so closely watched during those two days, the girls never got a chance to ask them how they had been caught. While sitting mostly in silence in the dayroom, they did find the opportunity to exchange home addresses, promising each other to write when they had a chance. And then they were gone.

"They probably took them to a higher security place," Maria suggested when they were in their bedroom.

"Yeah, the Sudruškas here got tired of doing double shifts," Marianne's voice was brimming with sarcasm.

"Let's face it, this place is not set up for high-risk kids," Erika pointed out.

The weeks before the boys escaped, she seemed to have finally gained the trust of the staff, and they allowed her to go along with the other two girls to bring their meals from the Police Headquarters.

"We need more food since the boys arrived, and you're the extra hand they can use to bring it," Marianne laughed, as the three of them set off twice a day to bring their lunches and dinners back to the Detska Izba.

Erika loved going down the street with her friends. The Police Headquarters were just two long blocks away, but she could see so much life during their brief walks. Cars were whizzing by on the wide avenue, people were walking on the sidewalks in all directions, totally unaware that the three girls in their jump suits and heavy overcoats were actually young prisoners, on duty to deliver food to their jail.

Then it was March, still very cold, but it didn't matter whether it snowed, rained, or the sun was shining. Erika inhaled deeply the fresh air outside the gates of Detska Izba and loved feeling normal by walking on the street just like everyone else. She knew, as did her friends, that their time for these daily outings was measured; they had to return to their residence within a reasonably brief time, which included waiting to have their carrying dishes filled and stacked up.

Nevertheless, it was time away from the watchful eyes of the Sudruškas, away from having to be careful of every word they uttered. Yet oddly, they seldom discussed anything "taboo" along the way. As if by silent agreement, they just wanted to enjoy their freedom. After the three boys had been taken away, Erika wondered whether they would be once again kept inside. To her joy, the Sudruškas created a schedule for them, whereby the three girls rotated the collection of their meals, so each got an equal chance for a walk, still in pairs.

A week later, a small gang of boys was brought in along with their leader, Peter. They had been skipping school and were caught shoplifting. Five of the boys seemed to be around twelve to fourteen years old but Peter was nearly fifteen. A head taller than his gang, he had an athletic built, a broad face under a mop of blond hair, large blue eyes, a strong straight nose, and wide, shapely lips. He exuded masculinity, rare in a boy his age, and Erika found him very attractive. He, on the other hand, seemed to be more interested in Maria, who was closer to his age. She also had a better figure than Erika.

Shortly after Erika had been brought to the Detska Izba, she stopped having her period. Each month that she had missed, she seemed to gain a couple of pounds, and she was becoming noticeably rotund. The Sudruškas never commented on her weight gain, and only her two girlfriends knew of her missing periods. They speculated among themselves that because Erika had been menstruating since she was ten years old, perhaps her body just felt like stopping for a while. They did not discuss it with the Sudruškas because they made nothing of it. They sometimes joked that the food was too good, and Erika should eat less, but that was all.

Erika was not self-conscious about her weight gain; she made nothing of it. Her sister Judith had gained weight when she turned thirteen, and slimmed down by fifteen, so Erika figured, the same thing was happening to her. But she did wish for Peter to pay attention to her, and it happened in a totally unexpected way.

One day, when it was Maria and Erika's turn to pick up their lunch, on their return Marianne did not show up in the kitchen. They went to look for her, and Maria discovered her lying in the waterless bathtub with her wrists slit, her blood streaming into both sides of the tub. Maria screamed at seeing all the blood, but Marianne spoke to her quite calmly since she had cut herself only minutes before, with a stolen knife.

"I thought I might bleed to death while you're out, but miscalculated the timing," she explained serenely to Maria.

Maria, without replying, darted out of the bathroom shouting "Help! Help!" and Sudruška Olga, as well as Erika ran upstairs, with Peter in tow.

"Grab some towels and tie up her wrists," Sudruška Olga shouted to the girls while she ran to the phone in the guards' bedroom upstairs.

Within minutes they could hear the police sirens and ambulance arriving. Two big male nurses ran upstairs, lifted Marianne out of the tub, wrapped her into the blankets provided by Sudruška Olga, and carried her to their vehicle. Sudruška Olga instructed the girls and Peter to go downstairs and take care of serving lunch to the others, while she grabbed her coat and left in the ambulance with Marianne.

The other Sudruška on duty, Zofie, came into the kitchen and told Erika and Maria to eat fast, because the Velitel would be arriving shortly to question them. Neither girl had any appetite for lunch. They asked Peter to serve his group and left the kitchen. They sat in the dayroom, stunned.

"Did you have any idea she was planning to do this?" Erika asked, because Maria was so much closer to Marianne. Perhaps she had talked about it.

"Not a word," Maria shook her head. "I can't imagine why she would do such a thing!"

"I can," Erika sighed. "Think about it: you know she doesn't have a real mother, her father is in Vienna, and she'll probably never see him again. Most likely, her stepmother blames Marianne for this whole escape fiasco, while Marianne probably feels like she has no future whatsoever."

"You're right. Who will she live with when we're taken back home? Her stepmother may be in jail for years. I don't think they have any relatives to take her in. And since her father, the big reporter, is suspected of being a CIA agent in Vienna, she won't be accepted to any high school. Still, life is too precious, and anything could happen. She shouldn't have lost hope to this degree; wanting to kill herself." Maria shuddered. "This comes from her lack of faith. I must pray for her." She looked at Erika, "We both must pray."

Erika stared at her friend. Faith must be amazing, she thought and shrugged, "I'll pray with you, if you think it'll do any good".

Maria whispered, "I discovered a place where we can go to pray. I'll tell you later." She stopped abruptly as Sudruška Zofie entered and asked them to follow her to the Velitel's office.

Seeing the two girls quite upset, Velitel Stavinsky questioned them briefly but realized that they knew nothing about Marianne's plan to commit suicide. Instead, they seemed to need reassurance from him.

"Will she live?" Erika asked.

"Yes, of course. They'll keep her in the hospital for a while and then will bring her back here." He smiled at them. "But she will need to be watched very closely once she is back. And I'm afraid you two will be as well. So don't you try anything as foolish as she did!"

"Of course not," they protested.

◎◉◎

Surprisingly, during Marianne's absence, the Velitel seemed to feel sorry for the two remaining girls and gave them permission to take an hour-long walk each afternoon, weather permitting. Walking toward a hillock, where local children were using toboggans to slide down the snow-covered slope, Maria led Erika to an indentation in the stone wall of the hill. A lovely marble statue of the Virgin Mary stood there on a pedestal, decorated with flower placed by her feet in vases and buckets.

"How did you know this was here?" Erika was astonished.

"When Marianne and I first came to the Detska Izba it was early fall, and they let us go for walks just like now, and we discovered it."

"How come you never mentioned it before?"

"Because we weren't allowed to go for walks till now. I guess it was too cold during the winter months. Let's pray."

Quietly repeating after Maria, Erika said both the Lord's Prayer and a Hail Mary. To her amazement, she felt an inner joy and lightness on their way back to the Detska Izba. She did not share her feelings with Maria, but she willingly accompanied her on their daily walk to pray. At night, before they went to sleep, Maria often spoke to Erika of her deep faith in Jesus.

"He helps me cope with whatever is happening to me. I feel he will help me when we are taken home. That's why I can keep so calm."

Erika listened attentively and thought, I'd love to convert but it would kill my mother, so she said nothing to Maria. Christianity had always been a part of Erika's childhood. She had pretended to be Protestant during the war; she had read the Catechism along with her Catholic friends in grade school; thus, going to pray with Maria was not something out of line with her belief system. She didn't really have a belief system. At school, she had been taught that religion was the way authorities controlled people. The confession to the priest, the fear of God, were there to keep people in line. Hebrew classes taught her about her ethnic origins, but she could never accept God's miracles on faith.

Communist dogma at school gave logical explanations, even for the parting of the Reed Sea during the Exodus of the Jews from Egypt. Erika liked the rational explanations of religious events. But for the first time in her life, praying felt good. Maybe there was a God after all because praying to him had brought her a sense of inner peace.

◎◉◎

Their walks stopped when Marianne was brought back by ambulance a couple of weeks later. Her wrists were still wrapped in white gauze, and she was ordered to stay in bed for at least a week.

She seemed very depressed. Not wanting to leave her alone in the room, Maria took it upon herself to stay with her. Occasionally, Erika took over but clearly, Marianne preferred to have Maria with her. Maria was calm and soothing, and Marianne felt more at peace in her presence.

Erika spent her time in the teen's room along with the boys. She either read or crocheted and occasionally played games with the boys. Peter discovered that she knew how to play chess, so he would frequently ask her to a game. He was a good player, and Erika enjoyed the challenge he presented. She was also good at strategy, so often they would sit for a couple of hours, feeling the tension between them as each tried to win the game. The other children would gather around them, watching, and trying to prompt Peter or Erika to a make a move, but they were quickly hushed. The players didn't need or want any help. They seemed to enjoy the competition between them, and each worked hard to win.

Erika also felt a different kind of game growing between them. Whenever Peter walked by her, either down the hall or up and down the stairs, he'd come so close that she could feel his body heat. At times, he'd actually bump against her and grin without any apology.

She understood his approach, his growing interest in her as a girl, and enjoyed his flirtation. She smiled at him at such times but did not physically respond in any way. She was all too familiar with how his teasing could progress and had no intention of going there. He must have sensed that she was not encouraging him but not discouraging him either, for he continued his physical contacts.

A week later Marianne was able to come downstairs. The incipient attraction between Peter and Erika became hidden before the observant eyes of both Marianne and Maria. Soon, a major event grabbed all their attention.

◎◉◎

It was early morning on March 6, 1953. Since the young captives at the Detska Izba didn't know what was happening in the outside world, they were surprised to see the Velitel, and his entire staff arrive in full armor. They all settled in to stay, not only for the day but the night as well.

Then they heard the news, blasted by a radio announcer throughout their building and out in the streets, repeating over and over in a solemn voice: "*The heart of the comrade-in-arms and continued genius of Lenin's cause, the wise leader and teacher of the Communist Party, and of the Soviet Union for nearly 30 years, has ceased to beat."*

Stalin, the beloved leader of the Soviet Union was dead. He had died of a massive stroke and heart failure the evening before, on the 5th of March. He was 73 years old.

Erika and all her captive companions were stunned.

"I thought he would live forever," Peter muttered under his breath.

"He looked ageless," Erika commented. "Now what's going to happen?"

"Yeah, what will happen now?" they whispered to each other with eager anticipation, hoping for the collapse of the hated Soviet Empire.

"Nothing at the moment," Maria announced soberly as she peered down the hallway and saw Sudruška Olga standing with a pistol in a holder at her hip on duty by the main entrance.

Marianne, always the most stoic among them, simply said, "Let's just act like nothing has happened, and have breakfast."

The following days the tension was palpable among the guards at the Detska Izba. Sudruškas sat in pairs or walked on both floors fully armed and vigilant, constantly listening to the news on radios set up for them. The radio stations broadcast nothing but the events around Stalin's death. The announcers described step by step the funeral procedures taking place to honor the beloved dead leader.

First, Stalin's body was embalmed and then put on display for three days in the Hall of Columns in the Kremlin. Although people knew that he was responsible for the death of millions through famine and purges, that he had everyone whom he mistrusted or disliked put on trial and killed, still, when he was lying in state, thousands lined up in the heavy Moscow snow to pay their respects to the leader who had saved them from the German invasion during World War II.

Hard as their lives had been under his rule, Stalin represented the father figure they loved, feared, and hated but uniformly accepted as the ruler of their lives. Now, he was gone forever.

"Maybe one of his people caused his death," Marianne speculated when they were alone in their room at night. They all knew that this could easily be the truth. But at this point it made no difference. Stalin the dictator was dead. Now the question was: will the communist system continue or *hopefully* collapse.

While the staff at the Detska Izba continued to listen on their radios to the funeral procedures in Moscow, their young prisoners also listened as much as they could, secretly hoping for a miracle.

On March 9th, the pallbearers placed Stalin's coffin from the Hall of Columns onto a gun carriage. In a solemn procession by all the Soviet government dignitaries, Stalin was transferred to Lenin's tomb on the Red Square. There, his coffin lay in front of the mausoleum, and all the officials stood facing the enormous crowd that had gathered for this last rite in honor of their leader. Yet only three top officials addressed the public, Georgy Malenkov, Vyacheslav Molotov, and Lavrenty Beria.

Being a high-ranking officer, Velitel Stavinsky already knew why only these three men gave eulogies at Stalin's burial. He had been informed by his superiors that on March 6, the day after Stalin's death, at a top-level Soviet leadership meeting, Malenkov had been selected as Premier and First Secretary of the Communist Party. Molotov was to be the Foreign Minister, and Beria the Minister of State Security and Internal Affairs. This put Beria in control of both the regular and the secret police, as well as the head of a small private army of infantry divisions. This new leadership, all close comrades of Stalin, ensured that the Soviet Union would remain a Communist Empire and continue its domination of its satellite countries.

But Velitel Stavinsky was not about to share this information with his staff. These were volatile days and until Stalin was actually placed in the Mausoleum next to Lenin, and the new Soviet government was announced, he and his staff had to stay on high alert.

Finally, when the official radio stations broadcast the new leaders of the Soviet Union, the entire staff at the Detska Izba could relax. There was to be no change in their political system. They could put their guns away and return to the routine of their lives.

The news hit the Erika, Maria, Marianne, and Peter's group real hard. They were desperately hoping that after Stalin's death things would change. Now they knew that there was no hope for their future.

They were wrong. Stalin's death had created a crack in the Iron Curtain.

CHAPTER 20

IT WAS APRIL AND spring was in the air. The days were sunny and warmer, leaves began to sprout on the giant walnut tree in the front yard. Tender shoots of grass were covering the ground where snow used to be. The young captives at the Detska Izba were allowed to play in the garden since the gate to the street was always locked.

Erika and her companions enjoyed running around in the garden, playing ball and chasing each other. She and the boys even climbed the thick branches of the walnut tree. Maria was too dignified to do so, and Marianne was simply not interested. Being able to climb and play "catch as catch can" with the boys made Erika feel free. She could ignore that in reality she was living locked up and under constant vigilance. Instead, it reminded her of the summers she spent at Uncle Ede's home in his village. Playing outdoors made her feel inexplicably happy.

One sunny morning, after finishing her usual chores with Berta, the cleaning woman, Erika slipped out on the balcony of the infants' bedroom on the second floor. Overlooking the green garden suffused her with a joy like she had never experienced before. She watched the billowing white clouds floating in the infinite blue sky and knew that someday she would become a writer. Then she would be able to describe her feelings of elation at just being alive. Her life at the Detska Izba always had an undertone of oppression and hopelessness. Thus, she was aware that this was a rare moment, when the beauty of life itself filled her with hope for the future.

Since such moments were virtually non-existent under her current circumstances, Erika waited for her mood to calm down before going downstairs to join the others. She thought, they would not understand her joyfulness. None of them had been told anything about their parents during their time at the Detska Izba. The three of them lived in the bubble of the Detska Izba's routine, anticipating that one of these days the bubble will burst, and they will have to face the prison system of Hungary. But until then, the arrival of spring brightened at least Erika's life.

◎◉◎

One morning, after breakfast, the Velitel called Erika to his office.

"Is there anything you'd like to tell me about yourself?" he asked in Slovak, since he knew that by now Erika spoke the language like a native.

"Like what?" Erika responded, wondering what the Velitel was driving at.

"I know you're close friends with Peter. We all know you have physical contact with him. Is there anything going on between you two in secret?"

"What are you talking about?"

Everyone at the Detska Izba had watched Erika and Peter get into a wrestling match after each one of their chess games. Regardless of who won, they would accuse each other of winning by cheating and end up rolling on the floor wrestling wildly. Eventually, Peter would manage to pin Erika down so she would lie under him on her back with her arms pressed to the ground till Peter would decide that he had won the battle and let her go.

Erika found these scuffles exciting and knew that Peter did too. She liked to feel the muscles of his arms as he tried to overpower her, his body against hers, his weight on top of her once she gave up and he pressed her to the ground. Her girlfriends just laughed off these fights as Erika's craziness. But the young boys in Peter's gang would surround them while they were fighting, and once Peter held Erika down, they would chant, "Kiss her, kiss her!"

Peter never did. Erika often wondered what made him hold back. Perhaps it was the very public way they conducted their fights. Or he was older and knew what a kiss could lead to and didn't want to endanger either of them. After all, Erika was only thirteen years old, and he was nearing sixteen.

At his age, he could be convicted for sexual assault of a minor.

Oddly, none of the Sudruškas who watched them fight, ever interfered. Maybe they found it amusing to just let them be children and work off their pent-up feelings with these tussles. Actually, no one ever commented about them once their fight was over. It was as if everyone had accepted their behavior as entertainment.

And now, here she was, with the Velitel asking her what else might have been happening between Peter and her. Erika knew full well what he wanted to know but she chose to respond as if she were totally ignorant.

"I have no idea what you're talking about."

"I want to take you to a doctor. The Sudruškas tell me you haven't had a period for a few months now."

Erika blushed to the roots of her hair. How did they know? "I can assure you we haven't done a thing and I'm not pregnant!"

"Listen, we have girls younger than you get pregnant and not even know it. I've made an appointment for tomorrow morning. I'll come for you after breakfast, at ten."

◉◉◉

The next day, Velitel drove Erika to a gynecologist. The doctor was an amiable middle-aged man, who asked the Velitel to stay in the waiting room while a nurse led Erika into the examination room. The nurse stayed there and told

Erika to remove her pants and underwear. She then instructed her to lie on her back on the examination table with her knees spread apart, her feet in the stirrups at the table's end. The doctor came in and sat down between Erika's legs. With the nurse standing by his side and shining a light at her pubic area, the doctor gently spread open Erika's labia with gloved fingers, then said, "You can get up and dress now," and left the room.

The nurse helped Erika off the examination table and left as well.

While Erika was putting on her clothes, she remembered her mother taking her to see a doctor after that weekend at Uncle Laci's house. She felt the same sense of humiliation and anger now as she did then. *Peter and I had done nothing wrong. The Velitel and the Sudruškas instead of dragging me to the doctor should have just asked us about it. How should I know why I haven't had my period? Maybe I could ask the doctor.* But by the time she got dressed and walked out into the reception area, the doctor was gone and the Velitel was waiting with a broad smile on his face.

"You're just fine and I'm glad" he said.

"I'd like to ask the doctor why I don't have my period," Erika responded.

"He is seeing another patient, and I must get back to my office. It's just the way it is," the Velitel shrugged, and taking Erika's arm, gently led her out of the doctor's office.

"Will I ever be able to see my mother and sister?" Erika asked in the car on their way to the Detska Izba. "I don't even know where they are."

"In jail, of course. I'll tell you what. I'll make some inquiries to see if you could go to visit them."

"Thank you," Erika said, her anger and resentment vanishing, feeling grateful. *Maybe this humiliating experience made the Velitel feel sorry for me, and he'll try to do something nice for me as a result,* she thought. *In that case, it was worth going through it.*

Life continued at the Detska Izba with the routine of meals brought by the girls from the Police Station, playing in the garden, and even Erika and Peter's daily wrestling. Spring melded into early summer, and the girls wondered whether their warm winter jump suits would be changed to a lighter fabric. Before it came to that, the Velitel called Maria and Marianne into his office.

"You are going home," he informed them. You will leave here in a week, on May 29th. You will join your parents for a few days in jail, and then you will all be transported back to Budapest."

"What will happen to us then?" Marianne blurted out.

"I don't know. But I wish you the best."

That week before Maria and Marianne were to leave, seemed to the three friends like the hardest days of their lives. On Erika's part, the anticipation of losing her friends, and the overwhelming fear Maria and Marianne felt about their future, made them huddle together late into the nights, speculating on what might happen to them back in Hungary.

"I'll be sixteen in a few months. They might keep me in jail for years. Not just for the escape attempt but because of being an aristocrat," Maria frowned.

For the first time since Erika had known Maria, she heard her friend divulge feelings of fear and concern. Erika tried to cheer her up, "Maybe some miracle will happen, and they won't put you in jail. I'll pray for you," she added, bringing a weak smile to Maria's face.

"Naah, even though Stalin is dead nothing seems to have changed in this damned totalitarian regime in which we live," Marianne pointed out bitterly. "I will probably be put into a reform school."

"Don't you have any relatives who could take you in?" Erika asked.

"Yes, I've got some aunts and uncles and even grandparents on my father's side. But because my father is politically undesirable, a journalist who defected, the Secret Police will probably take it out on me and not let me live with any relative. My poor stepmother will be locked up for who knows how long, just for being my father's wife."

Their fears and worries put special emphasis on Maria's usual evening prayers. Erika prayed with her, and even Marianne joined in, with tears running down their cheeks.

"I don't know how long they'll keep me here either," Erika said, a couple of days before her friends' departure. She was trying to show that they were sharing a similar fate, and it was merely a matter of time before she would be faced with the same situation. "Here is my address, please memorize it in case the guards take the paper away from you, so you can find me once I am also taken home."

The other two girls also gave Erika their former home addresses and the names of their relatives.

Maria said, "Maybe the relations who had moved into our apartment after we escaped, are still there. They will know how you could find us once you are also repatriated."

Even with all these preparations for eventually reconnecting in Hungary, nothing could ease the gloom that hung over them. Filled with anxiety and the pain of separation, they prayed and lay awake in the dark most nights.

Then the day came when the girls were to be collected by the prison van. After a tension filled breakfast, Sudruška Zofie handed Maria and Marianne the clothes they wore when they first came to the Detska Izba nine months ago.

"You look so different," Erika grinned through her tears, seeing her friends wearing "normal" clothes for the first time since she had met them. "You look nice in your own dresses," she complimented them, trying to ease the pain all three of them were feeling.

"Time to go" declared the uniformed, rifle-bearing guard.

The three girls looked at each other through tears, and hugged one last time, forming a circle with their arms around each other's shoulders as if trying to gain strength through their love for each other.

"I wish you all the luck in the world," Erika whispered as they parted.

She followed them in the garden at a distance as they were being escorted with one gun bearing guard in front, another behind them as if they were dangerous criminals. Sudruška Zofie unlocked the front gate. Erika watched her beloved friends walk through the gate and clamber into the windowless police van parked by the sidewalk.

One guard climbed in with the girls, the other went to the driver's seat. He started up the van. Sudruška Zofie locked the gate. Erika had walked up to it and watched through the bars as the van took off. Maria and Marianne were gone. Erika felt paralyzed. She stood rooted to the ground, staring at the vacant sidewalk beyond the gate.

"Come in, come in," Sudruška Zofie urged her, then taking Erika by the arm, led her into the house.

Pulling her arm away, Erika walked into the younger children's dayroom, where she used to play with Ivanka so long ago. She went to the bay window and folding herself into a child's low wooden chair, sat, staring out the windows into the garden, seeing nothing. She felt a great void in the deepest core of her being. As though her heart had been ripped from her, she felt totally vacant inside. She felt like the world had become an empty glass globe and she was encased in the middle of it.

Peter came into the room at some point and asked if Erika wanted to play a game of chess. Erika shook her head. "Go away." For emphasis, she turned her face away to lock him out of her presence.

Rough-hewn as he was, he could see that Erika needed to be left alone with her grief. He silently withdrew from the room.

Erika spent two whole weeks in mourning. The Sudruškas excused her from fetching food from the police station, but she was ordered to show up at mealtimes though she hardly touched any food. She was told to go to bed and was awakened in the morning by a knock on her door. She continued to help the housekeeper, Berta, but she spoke to no one beyond the necessary communication. She did not cry but did not smile either. When done with her chores or meals, she sat in the small chair by the bay window in the youngsters' dayroom; motionless, staring at nothing.

The Sudruškas let her grieve, they did not suggest even that she go for a walk. The boys also left her alone. Once in a while a conversation with Maria or Marianne floated into Erika's mind but most of the time she just gazed vacuously out the window. She felt dead inside and barely looked alive on the outside. She moved like a robot, and most nights cried herself to sleep towards dawn. She feared that she would never see her friends again.

◎◉◎

After two weeks of utter desolation, Erika began feel her life-force returning. Still sad but no longer filled with the hopelessness she has been feeling, now and then Erika joined the other children in the common room. Three new girls had been brought into the Detska Izba. One of them, Nella, was a very pretty brunette, Peter's age. She had been arrested for prostitution and was now awaiting a court date for sentencing.

Peter took great interest in her, and Erika saw that Nella liked him too. Erika was surprised to feel a pang of jealousy. This was the first emotion she had since her friends had left. Erika realized that she was beginning to recover from her state of mourning. She made no attempt to compete for Peter's attention. But she began to enjoy again the sun in the garden, and even her work with Berta, cleaning alongside her.

Then Nella was taken away from the Detska Izba. Peter went into the children's playroom where often Erika still preferred to sit. He grabbed Erika out of her chair and wrestled her to the ground. Erika fought back as she had never done before, fueled by all her pain and anger.

They wrestled fiercely in silence. There was no sense of fun between them as in the past. It seemed that Peter was just as upset and angry as Erika. They rolled around wildly on the floor, as if trying to take out on each other their distress over the recent events in their lives. And then it was over. They lay on their backs next to each other, on the floor, exhausted, panting.

"Welcome back," Peter grinned at Erika.

"Welcome back to you, too," Erika returned his smile.

◎◉◎

A couple of days later, Sudruška Valentina popped into the older children's room where Erika was now sitting, quietly reading, and called to her, "The Velitel wants to see you in his office."

Erika jumped up, asking, "What am I being summoned for?"

Sudruška Valentina just gestured for her to go right away.

The Velitel shouted "Enter" when Erika knocked on his door. He was seated behind his desk and gave Erika a warm smile as he pointed at a chair opposite him, "Sit down. I've got some news for you."

Erika's heart gave a large thump. Was it news about her friends? She sat up straight, her hands on her knees, eagerly looking at the Velitel.

351

"I've got you permission to visit your mother. You will be picked up tomorrow morning at 10 a.m. by a police van and transported to the jail. After your visit the same van will bring you back."

Tears of gratitude welled up in Erika's eyes. "Thank you," she whispered, barely able to get the sound out, she was so taken by the news. For the first time since her friends had left, she actually felt a joyful anticipation.

The police van was similar to the one that had brought Erika to the Detska Izba. It had a small cell inside a windowless interior, with a wall separating the driver's section. The main difference was that this time there was no guard sitting with her in the back. On arrival at the imposing gray building, Erika was escorted by a gun bearing guard into a reception area and signed in by another guard at the front desk. Then the guard who had received her led Erika down narrow hallways into a room full of cubicles that were partitioned with glass walls for privacy.

"Sit here" the guard instructed her and left. Erika sat down inside a cubicle, facing a small table opposite which was an empty chair. Within a few minutes a guard ushered in her mother. Her heart beating wildly, Erika stood up and leaned forward, so they could hug across the table since there was no room to go around it.

They kissed each other on their cheek and the guard on Piry's side shouted, "Sit down, both of you!" They did as they were told.

"You cut your hair," was Piry's first comment, looking at Erika, "It suits you," she added with a smile.

"You look thin," Erika responded, "Tell me how they are treating you."

In the half an hour that was allotted to them, Piry explained how she survived in prison.

"I told the officers early on that I can iron beautifully so they put me in a room alone, where I'm spending all day ironing their shirts. I told them I eat only kosher food, so they are bringing me meatless dishes, like cabbage, potatoes, and eggs. I can heat up my food on the iron turned upside down, so I'm quite all right."

Erika shook her head at her mother's ingenuity. It was good to hear that she was taking care of herself adequately. Then she asked, "How is Judith doing?"

"We're in the same cell, so I see her in the morning and evening. She is working in the laundry room, sorting clothes. She doesn't say much, has become kind of a recluse. I don't blame her. There is nobody her age in our cell, or probably in the entire prison. I feel for her but there is nothing I can do. Except, now listen to me very carefully." Piry smiled, then leaned forward and lowered her voice.

"Since we're lucky enough to see each other, here is the most important thing I need you to do. It came to my mind that your father had a cousin living in Prague. He is some sort of a journalist. I want you to contact him. His name is Feri Shatz. Maybe he can do something for us, like take you and Judith to Prague to live with him while we're waiting for the Hungarians to requisition us."

"Mother, I have no idea how to find him in Prague. What are you thinking of? I'm not free to contact anybody! I couldn't even write to you! I'm a prisoner, like you, it's just that it's a prison for kids."

Piry stared at Erika as if seeing her for the first time as the child that she really was. Then she said, "Try to do it, somehow. Find a way." And she asked Erika to memorize his name and an address in Prague, where she thought he could be reached.

The guard watching them now approached and shouted, "Visiting time is over!"

Piry quickly leaned forward and kissed Erika's cheeks. "Do it," she whispered.

Erika felt helpless as she watched her mother being escorted by the guard back to the depth of the prison. She felt like their roles had been reversed. It was now her mother who had made childish demands, and Erika was the adult, saying, it couldn't be done.

Although Piry seemed content with the conditions of her captivity, Erika sensed that her spirit had been broken. Perhaps it wasn't her spirit. Maybe it was just the knowledge that she was a prisoner and saw Erika as being free simply because she wasn't in prison with her.

But Erika knew better. *There is no way I'm going to contact this cousin of my long dead father. I'm not going to jeopardize the trust I had built at the Detska Izba. They allow me to take walks freely in the city. I'm not going to lose that privilege for some dream about this cousin getting me out of there.*

Back at the Detska Izba, she went to the Velitel's office to thank him for arranging the visit.

"How was it?" he asked.

"It was great to see my mother; didn't get to see my sister."

"Maybe next time," he smiled encouragingly.

Erika had the gut feeling that she shouldn't mention to him her mother's request to contact her father's cousin in Prague. So, she just thanked him again and left his office.

However, that evening in her room, Erika jotted down in a small notebook she had, the name of her father's cousin and the address her mother had given her. Even though she did this, she knew she could get into a lot of trouble were she to follow up on her mother's request. Therefore, despite keeping his information, she had no intention of contacting the man, ever.

◎◉◎

Peter and his cohorts were taken from the Detska Izba in mid.-July. Before leaving, Peter had given Erika his home address and wrote down her address in Budapest.

"One never knows, maybe one day we'll be able to get in touch," he told her. They smiled at each other, and then even without a hug Peter turned on his heels and left.

Once again, Erika felt totally withdrawn emotionally. She missed Maria and Marianne, and now she also missed Peter. But not with the sharp pain she had experienced during her weeks of mourning her girlfriends' departure. She felt as if her emotional core had died in her or at least went into a deep coma.

She followed an established routine of getting up at the same time each morning, and helping Berta, the cleaning woman. Then sitting in the dayroom or outside in the garden, reading or crocheting, talking to no one. Children came and went on a weekly basis, but Erika no longer had any interest in getting to know them. She was friendly but did not get into conversations or games with them. Peter's departure seemed to have put the final seal on her heart. She allowed no one in or to get close to her.

The summer was warm and beautiful. She did enjoy bringing their food from the police station and was allowed to walk in the city on her own a couple of afternoons a week. During those times she went to the Madonna statue in the cove on the hillside, to pray. She prayed that Maria's and Marianne's lives should be all right in Hungary, prayed for her mother and sister in jail, and for herself to be soon re-united with all of them. Hers was a lonely existence, but Erika didn't care. She felt as though her life had been put on hold. She was like a hibernating hedgehog who during winter would periodically come up for nourishment but most of the time just waited for a more clement climate to return.

Then it all exploded on the day the Velitel ordered Erika into his office and angrily demanded, "How dared you contact this journalist in Prague!"

Erika was shocked. "I didn't contact anybody! What are you talking about?"

"Here., I got a letter asking me to allow him to visit you."

Erika shrugged. "My mother told me we had a cousin in Prague. I told her I couldn't write to him, and we left it at that. She must have gotten in touch with him."

The Velitel grunted. "All right, you're probably telling the truth."

"I certainly am!"

"You can go for now. I'll let you know what will happen next."

Erika could hardly believe that her mother managed to send a letter to this cousin, but obviously, she did. A few days later, she was called once again to the Velitel's office. He wasn't alone. A handsome, dark haired, slim young man was standing next to him.

"Erika, this is your father's cousin, Comrade Shatz," the Velitel said.

"Call me Feri," he said, extending his hand to Erika.

He has a firm grip! Judging by his handshake, he must be a man of strong character, Erika thought.

The Velitel invited them to sit down, and Feri explained to both him and Erika: "I have appealed to the authorities to allow you and Judith to come to Prague with me. To let me take care of you until the Hungarian Government asks for your return. Legally, both of you are minors, and shouldn't be held in captivity."

"I don't know what to say," Erika responded, knowing her reaction had to be as diplomatic as she could make it. She didn't want to upset the Velitel by revealing how thrilled she was at the possibility of leaving the Detska Izba and being free again.

"I will come back for you as soon as my request is granted," Feri said.

Erika noticed his phrasing. There was no uncertainty about his returning for her. Keeping a pleasant but expressionless face, Erika simply thanked him.

◎◉◎

A week later, Erika was taken to the prison, to visit her mother again.

"I got a letter out to Feri," her mother explained to Erika. "And now, in a few days, he'll be taking you and Judith with him to Prague. But I must ask you or rather warn you about something: he may have a way of getting you and Judith out of the country to Israel. Don't even think of going. If you and Judith leave, I'll be locked up for life. My treatment here, in fact my life, depends on your remaining in Prague till the Hungarian authorities take us all back. So, promise me that you'll stay put."

"Mother, of course we will! You don't even have to ask! I wouldn't go anywhere without you! And I'll make sure Judith doesn't either."

Piry, more at ease, smiled at her daughter. "Enjoy being in Prague. I'm glad I could arrange this for the two of you."

Erika's eyes filled with tears. "Thank you. I'm so sorry you must stay in jail. I miss you."

"We'll have time to be together again when we are taken back to Hungary" Piry gave Erika a bittersweet smile.

Both of them knew the truth: once they were taken to Hungary, there was no way to predict what sentence their government would mete out for their attempted escape.

Piry could face years of imprisonment. Judith could be locked up as well since she had turned fifteen a few months before their escape. That was the legal age for being tried as an adult in their criminal justice system. And what would happen to her? Erika shuddered to think that the courts might send her to live with her stepfather.

Or they might put her into a reform school where her companions would be juvenile delinquents. Their lives might be in shambles once they were taken back to Hungary. Yet, as they bid good-bye with a tight hug, Piry said, "I have a feeling it will all work out."

Erika could only hope that her mother's prediction would come true.

◎◉◎

The day finally arrived when Feri showed up at the Detska Izba, with Judith in tow, to have Erika released to him. The Velitel signed the paperwork with a gracious smile. The Sudruškas, on duty, said good-bye to Erika with a hug, wishing her a nice time in Prague.

Then Erika went to say farewell to the housekeeper, Berta, and the woman warned her: "Just be very careful living among the Czechs. They are all liars and a phony people. They'll say you're their friend and then stab you in the back."

Erika didn't know what to make of this warning, so she just smiled and thanked Berta for her advice.

Prior to leaving, her clothes were returned to Erika but having gained so much weight, she no longer fit into them. The Sudruškas allowed her to leave wearing the "uniform" of the Detska Izba, her green double-knit gym suit, which was now of a lighter, summer fabric.

"It doesn't matter," Feri shrugged, looking at her outfit. "As soon as we get to Prague, we'll buy you some nice clothes that fit."

Erika looked at him surprised at his consideration. "Thank you," she whispered.

Walking out with Feri and her sister, Erika wondered what her new life will be like. If Feri's promise to buy her new clothes was any indication, it might be great.

◎◉◎

Feri took his nieces to the train station and once again Erika and Judith were heading on a fast train toward an unknown destination.

"My wife and I live in a tiny apartment, so we are unable to have you stay with us," Feri explained to them on the train. "But a good friend of mine is on vacation, and she graciously offered for you to stay at her place while I look for a home for you. I promise you'll be settled in no time, and I'll make sure you'll enjoy your life in Prague.

"Besides writing for a newspaper, I often write magazine articles about the history of Prague—its important buildings and districts. So, I can show you the city with some expertise." He smiled at his two nieces, "You'll get to know Prague better than the natives."

"That'll be great," Erika responded. She began to feel at ease and happy. She liked Feri.

Judith just smiled. She wasn't sure she was interested in Prague or anything else in life. But she knew better than to say so. She sat complacently in her seat and after a while closed her eyes and dozed off to the clacking rhythm of the train.

It was late evening when they arrived at Hlavni Nádraži, the main train station in Prague. Feri said, "The locals call the city, Praha, and it is the capital of the country, Czechoslovakia."

It was dark outside. Feri hailed a taxi and directed it to their temporary home.

It was a charming, one-bedroom apartment. Feri walked through it with them. He pointed out the clean towels left for them in the white tiled bathroom, which contained a sink and a tub. The toilet was right next to it, in a separate little room. The bedroom contained a narrow single bed, with a duvet inside a white cotton cover, and two large pillows, set up for a guest.

"My friend also left sheets and another duvet for one of you to sleep on the sofa in the living room," Feri explained. He reached for the bedding piled at the foot of the bed.

"I'll sleep there," Erika offered quickly, thinking Judith would be more comfortable in the bedroom. She felt that Judith needed extra care and consideration. Somehow, Judith's usual dominant behavior was gone, as if her inner self had been broken. *Perhaps eight months in jail will do that to a person,* Erika surmised as she observed her sister.

"I'll just go to sleep now, if you don't mind. Thank you for bringing us here," Judith said to Feri, standing by the bed.

"Of course, you must be exhausted," Feri said warmly. "I'll show Erika around so she can show you the rest of the apartment in the morning." He gave Judith a quick peck on her cheek.

Then Erika and Feri carried her bedding to the living room and together made her bed on the sofa. Next to the sofa was a coffee table with a lamp on it and a crystal ashtray. An armchair stood at the end of the table, and there was a large landscape painting on the wall. A Persian carpet covered most of the parquet floor. A tall bookcase stood against the far wall, and Erika thought, *if we stay here a couple of nights maybe I'll find a book to read—but not tonight.*

Feri showed her the kitchen, where inside the small icebox was a bottle of milk, bread and butter, a jar of jam, a wedge of cheese, and slices of ham on a plate.

"I asked my friend to leave these for you so you could have breakfast. There is no rush for you to get up in the morning. I'll come by with my wife, Jarka, to pick you up around noon."

"Thank you for everything," Erika gave him a grateful hug, and he left.

She quickly shed her clothes and pulled her Detska Izba pajamas out of the small briefcase she had brought with her. Then she snuggled under the duvet on the sofa and turned off the lamp. She was exhausted, and soon fell into a deep, dreamless sleep.

When Erika awoke, the sun was streaming through the lace curtains of the double pane windows. No sound came from Judith's room. Erika quietly rolled out of bed and went to the window. She pulled the curtains apart, opened the windowpanes and for a moment her breath stopped she felt so overwhelmed by the beauty of the scene before her. The Vltava River flowed just below the windows. Its blue-green water sparkled under the profusion of boats gliding along in both directions at a leisurely pace. Bridges traversed the river as far as she could see, and across the river soared the former Royal Castle glowing in the early morning sun. *Praha, City of my Freedom*, Erika thought, inhaling deeply the intoxicating fresh scent of the morning.

◎⦿◎

Later that day, Judith and Erika met Feri's wife Jarka. She was an attractive woman, had curly blonde hair, blue eyes, and a sweet, quiet disposition. She seemed totally devoted to her husband. Being a native Czech, she did not speak Hungarian. Since Erika spoke fluent Slovak, and the Czech language was closely related to Slovak, she and Jarka had no trouble conversing with each other. Even Judith knew enough Slovak to try to communicate with Jarka.

Feri and Jarka took the sisters for lunch to the very elegant Grand Hotel's Europa Restaurant in the center of the city, on Venčeslav Square. Then they spent the afternoon on a sightseeing walk around Venčeslav Square and the streets around it.

"Venčeslav Square is the heart of Prague," Feri explained to his nieces. "When people arrange a rendezvous, this is where they come to meet, by the statue of Saint Venčeslav.

Both Judith and Erika admired the dynamic equestrian statue of the saint, facing the square that was lined with hotels and shops, and well-maintained buildings. Erika particularly liked Wielhouse, with its facade painted full of medieval figures in faded orange and red colors.

"At some point we'll visit the National Museum." Feri pointed at the large, golden building across from the hotel.

Erika found the old buildings beautiful and marveled at the crowds that filled the streets. How free they are, she thought, then reminded herself that thanks to Feri, she and Judith were walking there as freely as the people of Prague.

In the early evening, they headed for Jarka and Feri's apartment in the Nusle District, a ten-minute streetcar ride from Venčeslav Square. It was a hilly part of Prague, with elegant villas along Linden tree lined streets.

"These villas had been subdivided by the government into apartments of various sizes," Feri explained as they walked toward his home. "We have a small apartment but in the same building a large apartment is occupied by the Police Chief of the Nusle District. The former owners of the building, an old Czech family, also live there. They now manage the building. We pay rent to them, and I suppose they give a portion of the rents they collect from all the apartments to the government housing authority," Feri went on, as they climbed the stairs to their apartment on the second floor.

Theirs was indeed a tiny flat. It had a small living room and a miniscule kitchen. In the bedroom a double bed took up most of the space. A tightly designed bathroom had just enough room for a sink, a tub, and the toilet.

"Now you see why you can't stay with us," Jarka explained apologetically to the girls. In her teeny kitchen she heated up a typical Czech dinner of pork chops, sauerkraut cooked with bay leaves, and the unique Czech bread, "knedlik". They squeezed together for dinner at the table usually fitting only Jarka and Feri.

"Knedlik is quite simple to make," Jarka explained to both girls. "You mix flour, milk, eggs, and stale bread cubes and form the dough into a loaf or a tube-like roll. Boil it in water for about 45 minutes. Then take it out and wrap it in a clean towel to cool. Serve it sliced with the meal, as if it were bread."

"We had this in jail, too," Judith said, and added, "but yours tastes a lot better."

"I imagine everything tastes better when you're free," Jarka smiled.

Erika thought it odd that this was the one and only reference from either Feri or Jarka to their captivity. They asked no questions and didn't seem to want any description of how the girls survived in detention. *Maybe they are afraid to ask,* Erika thought. *Probably, it's politically safer for them not to discuss our jail time lest we say something that would reflect badly on their government.*

Indeed, Feri turned the conversation to their lives in Prague. He explained that he was officially a Hungarian correspondent, reporting for the Hungarian News Agency, MTI, (Magyar Távirati Iroda). His office was located inside the Hungarian Embassy in Prague.

"I write articles about the important landmarks of Prague or other parts of the country. I also report about significant people and events to other Hungarian publications, as well as write for a variety of Czech magazines. Because I'm always roaming to find material to write about, I can take you along and show you the city," he promised during dinner. "My work has given me a chance to really get to know Prague," he grinned.

"Františku is known as an eminent historian of our city," Jarka added, smiling at Feri with admiration.

Erika did not hesitate to translate for Judith Feri's offer and Jarka's comment.

When they returned to their apartment in the evening of their first Sunday in Prague, Judith commented to Erika, "Jarka is a bit buxom, looks like a stuffed pigeon,"

Erika laughed, "You're spot on." She had to admit, Judith had a sharp eye and even sharper tongue when it came to describing people. Pretty as she was, Jarka was not just buxom, but chubby as well. However, she was also warm, and caring, a new aunt for them to get to know.

◎◉◎

It was clear to Judith and Erika that Jarka and Feri truly loved each other. Therefore, it came as a big surprise the next day, when Feri picked them up at their apartment, that he came accompanied by a beautiful young woman. He introduced her as Ivanka, a dear friend, and asked the girls, in Hungarian, to never mention her in Jarka's presence.

"Jarka is at work, so she can't accompany us. Thus, I wanted you to meet Ivanka because when I'm busy, at times she can take you around on her own," Feri explained. "You understand," he continued in Hungarian, with a conspiratorial wink, "I don't want to hurt Jarka's feelings. But Ivanka and I are close friends."

Ivanka did not speak Hungarian either, only Czech. *So likely she has no idea how Feri explained their relationship*, Erika thought.

Ivanka was a bit taller than Jarka, and a lot slimmer. She was also a blonde with blue eyes, had a charming smile and a lively personality.

"I am glad you speak Slovak so well," she said to Erika. "This way I won't feel left out while Feri is busy explaining things to Judith in Hungarian."

Although Ivanka and Feri spoke in Czech, the Slovak language was so similar to it that Erika had no trouble understanding them and translating for Judith. At times Ivanka pointed out the difference in vocabulary, or in pronunciation, between the two languages. At some point she said, "I'll help Feri find you a teacher who can give you lessons in Czech. You speak Slovak without any accent, so I'm sure you'll do the same in Czech. When you start school in September, you'll have an easier time if you speak Czech instead of Slovak. There is no great love between the two nations, even though politically we are now one country. The teachers and students will accept you more readily if you speak Czech. Just between us, the Czechs consider Slovaks as an aggressive and uneducated people."

"Thank you for your offer to help finding me a teacher. It's really thoughtful of you," Erika responded. She felt very grateful to Ivanka for even suggesting this. She did not divulge that Berta, the Slovak housekeeper at the Detska Izba, had warned her about the Czechs as "a bad, deceitful people." Erika figured, given time, she would form her own opinion of the Czech people just as she learned in Slovakia that their being nice depended on the individuals.

"We must get to the Orloj on Venčeslav Square just before noon," Feri said, and rushed them through the city by taking a taxi. "I had an article published about the history of the Orloj which you can read later. It is a fascinating and unique masterpiece of clock making," he explained along the way.

"It was made in the 15th century but after a while it stopped working. In the 16th century a man named Jan Taborsky repaired it and made some improvements to it. However, it stopped working again until 1865, when a clock maker, Josef Manes, modernized its system and put a new calendar dial on it. In 1945, almost at the end of World War II, the German army damaged the clock and burnt some of its statues. Our current government made replicas of the old figures; thus, it looks as it did originally. We're here, so you'll see the rest for yourselves."

Feri paid the taxi driver, and they all tumbled out of the car to join the crowd that had already gathered in front of the Orloj, looking up at it.

The big round clock was encased on top of a tall tower that was part of the façade of the Old Town Hall at the Old Town Square (Staroměstské Náměsti). When the Orloj's both handles rolled unto the number 12, just beneath the clock several windows opened in the tower and out came the figures of Jesus' twelve apostles. As if that weren't fascinating enough, more windows opened, and more statuettes appeared.

Feri explained to the girls, "That one on the left is Death, holding an hourglass to remind man of his mortality. The Turk next to him is shaking his head as if to say, 'I am not ready to die'. Then you can see a figure looking into a mirror, representing Vanity, and the last character is the Miser, holding a moneybag, representing greed or usury.

"Who are those statues that are not moving?" asked Erika.

"Oh, they are an Angel, a Philosopher, a Historian, and an Astronomer. There are many more things you can view below the clock but right now, just watch."

The twelve apostles finished circling around the clock and stopped. At that moment a golden rooster on top of the tower crowed loudly and flapped its wings while the deep, sonorous bell in the tower chimed twelve times.

"It always chimes just the current hour. But the figures come out only at noon. That's why I wanted you to be here at this time," Feri explained. "Now we can continue touring."

CHAPTER 21

IN THE ENSUING DAYS, Feri and Ivanka took the sisters to see the former Royal Castle of Prague; they walked across the magnificent Charles Bridge, (Karlovy Most), lined with thirty statues of Catholic saints as well as the Madonna and Christ. They visited the beautifully restored street called The Golden Lane, (Zlatá Ulicka), where in the 15th century the king's goldsmiths were housed.

"They were mostly alchemists, who were trying to convert ordinary metals with chemical compounds into gold," Feri explained. "It seems none of them ever succeeded, but the street remains a curiosity to this day."

Indeed, it was, because the houses were so tiny that even Erika, who was only 5'2" inches tall had to double over to go inside. The one house, open to tourists to visit had only a kitchen and a "main room." But attached to it was a laboratory where the alchemist was supposed to have concocted his magic potions, hoping to turn them into gold.

"Look," Feri led them down the street to house number 22, "Franz Kafka the writer lived here from 1916 to 1917. Being in the shadow of the Royal Castle must have been the inspiration for his book, The Castle."

For the last tour of the week, Feri took his nieces to the old Jewish Quarter of Prague. As they walked down the narrow, cobble stone streets lined by truly tiny houses, Feri commented, "During World War II this used to be the Jewish Ghetto. Even today, some Jews live here. Originally, it was simply the Jewish district in the city. The two most famous inhabitants were Franz Kafka, who lived here when he wasn't residing in the Golden Lane and the even more notorious resident was Rabbi Löwe, the 'Golem maker'. You know his legend, don't you?"

"Who doesn't," Judith shrugged and went on to say. "As usual, the Jews were being harassed with pogroms, and this Rabbi sculpted a statue out of mud. Then he wrote the sacred and secret name of God on a piece of paper and put it under the Golem's tongue. With that the Golem came to life and fought and killed the men who came to harm the Jews. Then at some point the Golem went on a crazy killing spree, and the Rabbi had to remove God's name from under his tongue and destroy the statue."

"Not bad," Feri exclaimed. Actually, there are stories and books with a great many variations on how and why the Golem was destroyed. I can lend you some of those stories. But what you just told us is good enough for now. Let's go to the old Jewish Cemetery to visit Rabbi Löwe's grave."

They didn't have to walk far to get to the cemetery's gate. Beyond it gravestones were leaning every which way, many piled on top of another. There was hardly any room to walk among the graves.

"This looks really abandoned," Erika commented, amazed at the unkempt state of the cemetery.

"It's not that it's neglected," Feri explained, "It just has too many graves. The cemetery was established in 1439, and Jews have been buried here until 1787. In fact, so many had been buried during those nearly 350 years that coffins had to be piled one on top of the other for lack of space. It is estimated that the coffins go 12 layers deep. There are about 20,000 gravestones here."

"That's amazing." Even Judith was impressed.

Feri continued to inform them, "As you know, Jews are not allowed to put faces on graves. So, if you look carefully, you'll see carvings which symbolize who that person was or what his occupation was. For example, look here: this violin indicates that a musician lies here. The scissors there are for a tailor. Now look here, this grave has a lion on it, and this is the one I especially wanted you to see."

They stood in front of a tomb that was partially above the ground. Its walls of thick, gray stones were constructed into a rectangular box. Its cover was a heavy one-piece stone that lay slightly askew.

"This is the grave of the famous Rabbi Yehuda Löwe Ben Bezalel, the Golem maker," Feri said.

"Oh!" both girls exclaimed, surprised that there was an actual grave.

"So, the Rabbi had really existed, whether or not the Golem story is true." Judith mused.

Erika noticed that the opening between the cover and the interior of the tomb had lots of small pieces of rolled up paper stuffed into it. "Why does it have all those papers?" she asked.

"Oh," Feri smiled at them, "That's another part of Rabbi Löew's power. Legend has it that if you write a wish and stick it into his tomb, it will be fulfilled."

"Can I write a wish?" Erika asked.

"Of course. How about you, Judith?"

"Nah...it's silly," Judith shrugged. "I am not superstitious."

"Neither am I," Erika countered, "but I do want to put a wish in there anyway."

Feri took out the notebook he always carried in his pocket and tore a sheet out of it. He handed Erika a pen as well. Erika covered the paper while writing her wish. She rolled it up and carefully stuck it inside the grave, deep enough among the other wishes for it not to be dislodged. She smiled at Feri and her sister, "Done."

"What did you wish for?" Judith asked.

"Can't tell you, or it won't come true," Erika replied. "But if it comes true, I'll tell you."

The owner of the apartment on the bank of the Vltava was returning in a few days. Feri had found lodging for his nieces in the Vinohrady district of Prague, an upscale neighborhood of the city.

Their hostess was a Jewish widow, Pani Novotna, glad to have the extra income. She had a spacious apartment with an extra bedroom which she rented to the girls. She also provided their meals.

The building was in a quiet residential neighborhood near a school.

Feri said to Erika, "This is one of the best districts in Prague. I chose it to be sure that the school you'll be attending would be a good one."

He took Erika there to register, since classes were to start in a mere three weeks. "We'll tell the principal that you're visiting me," he told Erika on their way to the principal's office. "Not a word about your escape or where you mother is. Since Judith is over 15, she can't go to this school so don't mention her either."

Erika learned that this particular school taught children only up to age 14. It was an elementary and middle school, with the same "Soviet System" as in Hungary. After 14, students could continue either in High School or at a Trade School, until graduation at 18.

"Unfortunately, Judith doesn't speak Czech, so she can't apply to a high school," Feri added. "Which reminds me, Ivanka found you a terrific Czech teacher. You'll have classes with her in the mornings. Hopefully, by the time school starts, your Czech will be as good as your Slovak. And if it isn't, we'll just have you continue with that teacher till it is. What do you think of that?"

"I think it's great! I can't thank you enough for doing all this for us. What will Judith do while I'm in school?"

"Don't worry about her. I'll invite her to be with me, or with Jarka, or even with Ivanka. She'll be fine. Also, she likes to read, and I can bring her Hungarian books. She doesn't seem to need a lot of entertainment. Has she always been so quiet?"

"No. I think being in prison had changed her a great deal. I find her subdued and kind of lost. She used to be very bossy with me. Now she just goes along with whatever we're doing."

"She probably needs time to recover. Prison couldn't have been easy for her." Feri concluded.

◎◉◎

Erika's registration at school went smoothly. Feri explained to the principal that she had spent time living in Bratislava and spoke fluent Slovak and was now living in Prague as a visiting student. With Feri's credentials as a journalist, the principal did not ask for details, just accepted the story at face value. Erika wondered whether the principal had thought that it was better not to ask why she was in the country in the first place.

As a journalist, Feri likely had Party connections and so it was none of the principal's business why Erika was in Prague, with Feri as her guardian. Everybody is afraid in Prague too, just like in Hungary, Erika thought.

The principal assigned her to a classroom. He then told her to show up for school at 7:30 a.m. on September 5th. She will receive orientation and be taken to her classroom at 8 a.m. sharp.

◎◉◎

The teacher Ivanka had found for Erika lived within walking distance to their new home. Pani Kratohvila was a woman in her fifties; small and lively, with curly graying hair and bright brown eyes. She was patient and almost motherly in the way she tutored Erika.

They sat at her small, round dining room table with a cup of tea for each of them, and she engaged Erika in ordinary, day-to-day conversation. She asked about Erika's activities or had her talk about books she had read. She taught Erika by pointing out the words that were different in Czech from Slovak. She asked Erika to repeat in Czech what she had said in Slovak. For Erika, this was like a game, and she learned the new vocabulary quickly.

"You sound just like any Czech kid," Pani Kratohvila complimented her.

"Maybe I won't even have to tell at school that I'm not Czech" Erika probed.

"Could be. Unless you give yourself away by telling them where you really come from."

"I don't think I can keep that a secret," Erika said pensively, "All they have to do is ask what school I went to before. I can't name a local school since I don't know any in Prague."

"True. But you sound really good, so it won't matter."

"Can I come to see you even after I start school?"

"Of course. And I'll continue to help you as much as I can."

Erika hugged her as she left. "Thank you. I'll be back, at least for a visit."

◎◉◎

Erika's first surprise at her new school was that all the hallways were lined with tall, narrow metal closets. Blanca, a teacher's assistant assigned to Erika at the Principal's office, opened one of the closets and explained, "We take our coats and street shoes off when we come in the building and put them into our assigned cabinet. We keep "indoor" shoes here for school wear. This way we don't bring the dirt in from outside and keep our school clean."

365

How very civilized, Erika thought but did not say it. Instead, she said, "I wasn't told to bring special shoes for school so is it all right if I walk around in my socks today?"

"Yes, of course," Blanka responded smiling. She waited while Erika placed her coat and shoes into the cabinet assigned to her. Then she led Erika to her classroom. Again, Erika was surprised to see that it was similar to her Hungarian classroom; three rows of double desks lined up from front to back.

"Here, you'll sit next to Zora," Blanka pointed to the middle seats of the front row. On one side of the desk sat a girl, who looked at Erika, and tossed her blonde pigtails unto her back.

"Zora, this is our new student, Erika. We chose you to sit with her because you're the best student in this class, and can easily help her to get oriented," Blanka explained to the girl in a tone that was more of an order than an explanation.

Zora nodded, "Yes, Sudruška Blanka," and gave Erika, a small, appraising smile.

Then class started and Erika was able to understand with ease Sudruška Pavlovna, the instructor and home room teacher. Since this was the first day of classes, it consisted mostly of orientation. They were given their schedule for their various subjects for the semester and sat through introductory classes by each of their teachers. In between, they had a ten a.m. snack break and school was over by one p.m. Two days a week classes were longer, and they were provided a noon lunch break in their schedule.

Zora patiently guided Erika through the day, showing her to the lunchroom for the break, and to the chemistry lab as part of their day's orientation.

Within a week Erika had adapted to the routine of classes and made friends with several classmates. Perhaps the biggest difference between her school in Budapest and the one in Prague was the level of politeness among the students. Czech students seemed to have gentler, better manners and less antagonism toward those who were top students. Still, there was the normal competition for being considered "the best student."

Erika found that despite her lack of a great Czech vocabulary, she still managed to be among the top five students in her class. Her desk-mate, Zora was by far the best. She excelled in both math and composition. Erika easily gave up top rank to Zora in math but when it came to writing, she worked extra hard to have her compositions selected for excellence by their literature teacher. What stood in her way at times was her lack of perfect language skill in Czech. After all, she had only been speaking Czech for a few weeks! Time and again she returned to Pani Kratohvila for help, and in fact improved to the point where the composition teacher would frequently choose her work to be read aloud.

Zora had become a close friend and instead of resenting this, complimented Erika. She would smile and say, "It makes me strive to be better because of you. I had no competition before you came, so I had it easy. I like the challenge you provide." And she would give Erika a hug.

Erika had never felt happier in her life than during these days in Prague. Her school life was a success, her friends there were fun and helpful. When she got home from school, she would do her homework while Judith sat quietly, reading. Then they would chat, Erika about her school day, Judith about the book she was reading or the outing she had been invited to by Feri. He had also introduced Judith to some of his friends, and they too invited her out. The only times Judith's old meanness would surface was on weekends when they went to see movies together.

Judith's Czech vocabulary was still extremely limited. Thus, when they went to see a film, she demanded that Erika translate the dialogue for her while they were watching the story. If she did this too slowly, or too quietly, Judith would pinch her arm and demand that she speak faster or whisper louder. Erika, would get angry but feeling helpless, would double her efforts.

When they first began to do this, people around them hissed and ordered them to stop talking. So, Judith came up with what proved to be a foolproof device to make Erika's whispering to her possible. Before going to see a show, they would stop at a deli and buy a piece of cheese. But this would be no ordinary cheese. Czech cuisine seemed to have an endless variety of cheeses and some of these had such a strong odor that even to take it out of the store the shopkeeper would wrap it into three layers of wax paper.

"You can't take these unto the streetcar," he would comment, "unless I wrap them up really tight. But oh, how delicious they are to eat!"

Once inside the movie house, after the lights were dimmed and the newsreels that always preceded the feature were running, Judith would carefully, silently unwrap the cheese. The odor emanating around them made people move away to other seats, as if the girls had the plague. Judith also figured out that the best times to do this was during matinees, when people could easily find other seats. They never went to see a movie when the theater was crowded as they could be in danger of people complaining and their trick discovered.

Much as Erika hated Judith's occasional cruelty, she didn't mind going along with her demand for instant translation. She felt that quickly understanding and translating increased her Czech vocabulary and that was good for her. After the movies both girls enjoyed eating the cheese for dinner with bread, boiled potatoes, and stir-fried red cabbage on the side, all provided by their landlady. Oddly, Pani Novotna never complained about the smelly cheese the girls brought home for dinner, and never asked why they ate this same cheese at least one day every weekend.

Another big change in Erika's life came at the end of their first month in Prague when she felt cramps in her lower abdomen. After six months of hiatus, she got her period again. Feri had learned about it through Judith's comment to him.

When Feri next saw Erika, he said to her, "I've heard that during the war women in concentration camps stopped menstruating. So maybe that is how your body reacted too, while you were in captivity at the Detska Izba."

"I wonder," Erika nodded pensively. She also noticed that despite not curtailing the amount of food she was eating, she began to lose weight, a couple of pounds each month. Maybe, that, too, is connected to my newfound freedom, she thought.

◎◉◎

Each year on November 7th there was a celebration of the Great October Revolution which had created the Soviet Union. It was also observed by all the satellite countries, that is, the "Socialist Democracies," as they were called. Weeks before the event, students at Erika's school were preparing various performances for the big assembly that was to take place in the gymnasium.

The school band rehearsed patriotic Soviet songs. Students were being selected to recite poems or read compositions praising the great Soviet Union and all its achievements since the revolution of 1917.

Erika knew that because she was not Czech, she would not be chosen to recite or to read anything. But she desperately wanted to be a part of the show. All those years back in Hungary she always had been, and she kept wondering what she could do in Prague to also perform. Then she came up with an idea. She sought out her homeroom teacher, Sudruška Pavlovna, in her office, and asked as sweetly as she could muster, "If I could gather a small group of students to do a Hungarian folk dance with me, would you allow us to do it on stage as part of the celebration?"

Sudruška Pavlovna stared at Erika. "That's a novel idea! How would you go about it?"

"I'd ask my fellow students, who would be willing to rehearse for the next couple of weeks. We'd come in an hour before classes began, to do it. I'm sure it would work. And if not, we just won't perform! You can check us out as we go along."

Sudruška Pavlovna laughed, "You are certainly enterprising! Well, if you want to put in the work, give it a try. Report back to me when you get a group together, and I'll ask the principal to give you permission to get into the building early, to rehearse."

It didn't take long for Erika to recruit nine of her female classmates to form a dance group with her. They were all intrigued with the idea of learning a Hungarian dance. Zora was presenting a poem she had written to honor Stalin and Lenin, the now deceased leaders the Great Soviet Socialist Revolution, so she could not be part of the dance team. Both Erika and Zora agreed that it was great that they could perform their own work.

Erika chose one of her favorite Hungarian folk songs that had a good rhythm. She had learned some folk dances at school in Budapest, so had no difficulty inventing dance steps for the song she had selected. Because she could not provide musical accompaniment while her group was learning the dance, she first taught the girls the song in Hungarian. They sang it together while she trained them to take the right dance steps in unison. Erika chose the best dancer of her team to be her partner in the lead, with the others easily following them *in case they forgot a step*, Erika told herself.

Her dancers all seemed to love this new experience and showed up promptly every morning at seven a.m. for their rehearsal. After the first week, they knew well enough both the song and the dance for Erika to ask Sudruška Pavlovna to come and see them.

Erika was a bit nervous about her home-room teacher's opinion, so before they got started, she explained, "Sudruška Pavlovna, you know we are only mid-way into the rehearsals. The dance will look a lot better after another week's practice. We'll speed up the tempo and it will have a lot more energy. Right now, we're still coordinating all our moves."

"I understand," Sudruška Pavlovna reassured Erika.

After watching the rehearsal for a while, Sudruška Pavlovna stood up. "Looks promising. I think we can work it into the program. Keep practicing, and I'll talk to the show director to position your performance." With that reassurance she left them to continue.

Sudruška Pavlovna's approval got the dance team truly excited. They worked hard, making sure they got all the steps right and in rhythm with their singing.

"I want you to know the steps so well that if I woke you in the middle of the night and sang you two bars, you'd know which steps to take," Erika told them. "Also, there is a big difference between counting steps and just dancing. At this stage, three days before our show, you should no longer have to think of what comes next. You should just be able to sing and dance and put your heart into it, like you're really enjoying it. If you enjoy singing and dancing, your audience will enjoy watching you."

"How do you know all this?" asked one of her dancers and added, "I know you're right because my ballet teacher says almost the same thing to us before we give a performance. But she is a teacher."

Erika laughed, "I don't know, I just know it. I started acting and dancing at age four, and I used to be in plays at my previous school. So, I guess I just learned. Anyway, let's do it once more, shall we?"

The day of the show arrived. Erika and her dance team stood backstage, awaiting their turn. The place was packed with students, faculty, and parents who were able to come to the assembly because it was an official holiday. Feri, Jarka, and Judith sat somewhere in the back, and Erika was glad they were there. She and her group heard one of the students recite a poem and then it was their turn on stage.

A couple of hours before the assembly began, Sudruška Pavlovna informed Erika that they had a pianist to accompany them. She asked if Erika had any sheet music of the song to which they were dancing.

Erika said, "No, but I could sing it to the pianist to see if he could pick up the melody."

The pianist was a crusty middle-aged man with deep lines by his lips and dark, piercing eyes that matched his dark brown, thinning hair, plastered to his skull. He stared at Erika with disapproval. "How can you not have sheet music?"

Erika smiled and shrugged. "I didn't expect to be performing here. But I can sing it to you if you could pick up the melody!"

She did so and the pianist seemed to have gotten the song, at least he was hitting the keys in tune with Erika's singing.

Now the stage manager waved to Erika. It was their turn to perform. Erika gracefully skipped with her dance group onto the stage, leading them center stage. They lined up by twos behind Erika and her partner, facing the audience, ready to start. The pianist was already at the keyboard, looking for the cue from Erika to begin playing. She nodded to him, and he hit the first notes. As he did, all the dancers, including Erika, froze. He was playing a tune none of them recognized. There was no way Erika could start their dance to his music.

"Sing!" Erika hissed to her group, and started to sing as loudly as she could, taking the first dance steps, the same way as they had been rehearsing it for the past two weeks. Her dancers quickly picked up on her idea and sang with her. The pianist froze at the keyboard without a sound. The dancers could hardly suppress their laughter as they effortlessly sang and danced, bowing to the audience at the end.

A thunderous applause followed, as though the audience had realized the initial faux pas of the accompanist and was now rewarding the dancers. Not just for their performance but for their quick salvaging the situation.

The assembly was over, and Erika was leaving backstage to join her family. She spotted Sudruška Pavlovna heading toward her and stopped to face her with a grin.

"What happened with the pianist?" Sudruška Pavlovna asked.

Erika explained that he had not remembered the tune, so she had to take quick action.

Sudruška Pavlovna patted her on the shoulder, "Erika, you'll make it, no matter where you land."

The compliment filled Erika with joy and hope. *She has no idea what her words mean to me,* Erika thought. After all, her teacher couldn't have known that Erika's daily concerns included the uncertainty of her future when she and her family would be taken back to Hungary. She worried about what punishment and other consequences their attempted escape will have.

She could be free in Prague, participate in school activities, and live a "normal" life. Once back in Hungary, she might end up in a reform institute instead of at home. Or were she to be sent home while her mother and sister were kept in jail, life with her stepfather would be a nightmare. But here in Prague they didn't know any of this about her. They had no idea that she was 'an enemy of the people,' for having tried to escape from their socialist paradise.

She smiled at her teacher and replied, "The credit goes to you for letting us do the dance. Thank you."

Taken a bit back by Erika's compliment, Sudruška Pavlovna merely said, "See you in class on Monday."

◎◉◎

Life continued. Erika's school had stopped for the "winter holidays" on December 18th. Judith and Erika spent Christmas with Feri and Jarka and enjoyed seeing with them the holiday decorations all over Prague.

It was a few days before the New Year when Feri brought Judith and Erika the news: they had to return to Bratislava. The Hungarian authorities had requisitioned them to be returned to Hungary.

Judith and Erika had a few days in which to pack and say good-bye to Jarka, Ivanka, and other acquaintances they had befriended in Prague through Feri. Erika visited Pani Kratohvila to say good-bye. Apart from her, she told only her friend Zora that she was returning to Hungary. The two girls exchanged addresses and promised to keep in touch.

"I suggest that you leave your diaries with me," Feri told to Erika when he saw her packing the four notebooks, she had filled over the year into the small suitcase he had bought for her. "I promise I'll send them after you as soon as possible. But it's not wise to carry these, written in a code, while you'll be in the custody of the security police."

Erika's heart sank but she knew Feri was right. When in captivity, she, Maria and Marianne decided to keep diaries, each of them invented her own unique code. This way they could leave their notebooks around without others being able to read them. The Velitel and the Sudruškas were well aware that the girls were keeping diaries. Yet they never asked about these little notebooks in their night table drawers.

Perhaps they weren't as thorough as we had thought and had not searched our rooms periodically. Or they did but didn't care. But now it's a different situation. As Feri said, we will be in the security police's custody, in prison. I will probably be interrogated again. Surely, they would want to know the content of my diaries, Erika contemplated.

She had been careful not to express any political opinions, despite her feeling safe by writing in a code. But there were important events, like Stalin's death, and the severe devaluation of the Czechoslovak currency, the Kronor. That happened shortly after a new Soviet leader, Georgy Malenkov took over. Erika simply had to write about these events in her diary.

Waiting to see whether or not the Soviet government would crumble after Stalin's demise was not something anyone would bring up in a conversation. Losing two-thirds of the value of her meager savings, earned by helping Berta, the cleaning woman, deeply upset her. Since she couldn't share her thoughts and feelings about these events even with her friends, she wrote about them in her diary. The Hungarian secret police, the ÁVO, would probably demand that Erika give them the code to her diaries, and due to her private comments, she might be sentenced. They might send her to a reform school. Sighing, she handed the notebooks to Feri.

"Please, please you promise to send them to me?"

"I will, cross my heart."

He also told Judith and Erika that he was going to send their mother's jewelry along with Erika's diaries, rather than have the girls carry these with them.

"When I brought you to Prague, your mother asked the prison officials to hand over to me all the jewelry she had carried with her that was now being stored in the prison with her belongings. She told me, she didn't expect me to finance your stay in Prague on my salary. So, when I needed money for you, I was to sell some pieces. Now, going through the Hungarian ÁVO, I don't think it's a good idea for your mother to carry any jewelry. I'll find a safe way to send it, along with the diaries, to your home in Budapest."

Both girls could see the logic of this, so they were grateful for his consideration. There was no need to ask Feri by what means he was going to send these items to Hungary. He was a journalist, he probably had friends traveling between the two countries. He would ask one he trusted to bring those things to them.

Feri accompanied his nieces on the long train ride from Prague to Bratislava. They spent overnight at a hotel, "our last free night," commented Judith.

Erika was quite concerned about her future once they were in the custody of the Hungarian authorities. She hoped they would not keep her mother and sister in jail and send her home to her stepfather. The very thought of living with him on her own terrified her. His difficult nature, combined with his sexual abuse of her, would make her life sheer torture.

Perhaps I could talk about my problem with Aunt Lilly, and she would know how to solve it. In any case, it's useless to worry until I am faced with the actual situation, she told herself.

It was snowing in the late morning, when Feri delivered his two nieces to the prison authorities. Both girls hugged him and tearfully thanked him for all he did for them. Erika couldn't help asking, "What made you go out of your way to get us out of prison and take such good care of us in Prague? Was it just because we're family?

Feri smiled and said, "When I was growing up, my father taught me that Jewish tradition dictates "If there is one Jew in trouble and he comes to you for help, you must give it to him. So how much more I felt this obligation when your mother wrote to me from prison, and you are my close family!"

Both Judith and Erika nodded, deeply moved. Once again, they hugged him, and he reassured them that he would be in touch. Then he was gone.

The two girls were escorted to change into prison garbs, and then to the cell where their mother was being held. Piry was overjoyed to see her daughters again. Judith let Piry hug her, responding with a tepid smile. Clearly, being back in prison, even though it meant reuniting with her mother, did not make her happy. She, too, must have been worried about her own future, though she had said nothing about it to Erika on their way to the prison.

By contrast, Erika told her mother how truly happy she was to be back with her, even if it was in a cell. They spent the evening talking about their lives over the year till the lights were shut off and silence had been ordered by the guard.

Lying next to each other in the dark, Piry whispered to Erika, "I had a very strange dream some months ago. I dreamt that my cousin Laci came to visit me wearing his ÁVO uniform, and said, 'Don't worry about being taken back to Hungary. Everything will turn out fine.'

Then he vanished and I woke up feeling strangely elated. The thing is that I dreamt it way before I was told that the Hungarian Government requisitioned us to be sent back. But somehow this dream makes me feel like we'll be all right."

"I hope so," Erika whispered back.

◎◉◎

On January 5th, 1954, they were provided an early breakfast. Afterwards, Piry and her daughters were ordered to change back from their prison garbs to their own clothes. They were also handed back the original briefcases they had carried during their escape, and any other items they had accumulated during the year.

Then, along with several other Hungarian prisoners, they were driven in a police van to the train station. They were led into a third-class compartment with hard wood benches and told to settle down for the trip. At each end of the compartment a Slovak secret police guard sat by the door. Each man displayed his gun visibly on his hip.

None of the prisoners felt like talking. After a few hours the train stopped at the border. The Slovak guards got off and tough looking Hungarian guards took their place. They nodded to the prisoners but did not talk to them.

It took most of the day on the train to reach Budapest. No food or drink had been given to the prisoners during the trip. When they were escorted off the train, a gray, windowless van stood by their train door. They were ordered to get into it, each person occupying a single compartment. Their doors were locked as soon as they sat down on the metal bench inside. It had barely enough room for their legs to fit in front of them.

◎◉◎

To Erika, it seemed like it was a short ride to the prison. It was a large imposing looking gray brick building. They were led into the reception area where they went through the registration procedure but were not given a prison garb to change into.

They were simply escorted to the prison's dining room for dinner. The food served to them was surprisingly good; sausages sautéed with sauerkraut and boiled potatoes, as tasty as any home cooked meal. After they finished eating, two guards escorted them to their cells.

Piry and Judith were placed in a cell where there were two other women already. Erika was led by a guard into a neighboring cell. A thin woman in her mid-thirties lay on one of the cots. She raised her head when Erika entered but then turned to face the wall, without a word. She clearly did not wish to bother with the young girl they had just brought in. The guard handed Erika a bar of soap, a towel, and a cup, and left.

Erika tried to settle in as quietly as she could. She put her small suitcase under the cot, amazed that it had not been taken from her. At one end of the room was a small sink and a toilet. Erika washed her face, and used the toilet, which had no seat cover but could be flushed. There was no privacy using the toilet, so Erika was glad that her cellmate had her back to her. She removed her shoes and lay down fully dressed. She even kept her overcoat on because the cell was cold and the blanket that had been left on the bed was paper-thin.

◎◉◎

The next morning, Erika was taken for interrogation. The guard escorting her was friendly and treated her with the proper handling of a young girl. The officer questioning her appeared cold and tough but was in fact quite mild mannered. He asked Erika about the details of their attempted escape, and she told him the same story she had already repeated so many times in Bratislava. After the interrogation session she was escorted back to her cell.

Her cellmate was more relaxed this day. She told Erika that her name was Vikki and asked Erika why she was there and how they had treated her during the interrogation.

Then Vikki said, "There seems to be a change. Since Stalin died some sort of thaw has been happening in the government. Our esteemed leader Rákosi is gone, and the new leader, Nagy Imre, seems a lot more humane. I was brought here a week ago from a maximum-security prison, and for all I know, they plan to release me."

"Why are you in here?"

"I was a Social Democrat, active in my party. That was my big sin."

Erika nodded. She didn't tell her cellmate that her mother's friend, Irén, had also disappeared from her apartment one day, probably for the same reason. Maybe she'll be released, too, Erika thought. Instead, she asked Vikki, "How long have you been in prison?"

"Four miserable years. Enough to pay for a political affiliation. If they let me out, I'll never join another damned thing, that's for sure!" She laughed.

Erika laughed with her. Good tip for me, she thought.

A week passed with pleasant conversations in the cell with Vikki and knocking on the wall to communicate with her mother. Treatment by the guards continued to be kind, they even brought Erika a couple of books to read. There was no more interrogation. Erika wondered what would happen next. Sentencing?

None of them, not even Piry's prison mates could guess.

CHAPTER 22

A FTER BREAKFAST ON FRIDAY morning, Erika was instructed to collect her things and follow the guard. He took her to an Officer's room, where her mother and sister were waiting.

The Officer smiled at them, "Good, you're all together now." He pushed some papers in front of Piry. "Sign these and you're good to go." Then he added, "You will receive a letter with the court date for a hearing and judgment, in due time. Until then, go back to your lives."

Piry was handed a copy of their release papers and then she and her daughters were escorted out the prison gates. They were free, and free to go home. It was a freezing January noon, and to their amazement, instead of being somewhere at the edge of the city, they were standing in the in the middle of a suburb in Buda. They had even been told which streetcars to take to Ùjpest, to their home where they had lived prior to their escape.

They had also been given sufficient Forints to pay for their ride home. Piry even received a telephone token from the Officer, so she could make a call. Piry decided to call her sister. Thus, before getting on the streetcar, they found a phone booth. Judith and Erika were waiting outside, tapping their feet on the snow to keep warm, while their mother dialed Lilly's number. The girls could hear even through the closed glass door of the phone booth Lilly's shouting with joy.

Then Piry came out of the phone booth, saying, "Lilly and Donát will visit us this evening."

It took changing to three different streetcars to get home. When they rang the bell at the front gate, it was Maria, the maid, who came to open. She nearly fell over upon seeing them. Then she quickly pulled them inside, locked the gate and hugged each of them, full of joy.

"That was a long visit with your relatives!" she exclaimed, "You could have sent me a postcard, you little stinkers! You must have had a really fun time! Feri is not home; he is vacationing in the Mátra Mountains. He'll be back Sunday night. Come on in, make yourselves at home! I'll make lunch for you."

Piry and her daughters walked in, carrying their little cases, feeling enormous relief and an odd sense of apprehension. What will their lives be like at home again?

Piry thought, *it's a good thing Feri isn't here. It will give me a chance to put myself together, so I look good when he arrives. Knowing him, I wonder how many women he's slept with during my year of absence. For all I know, he isn't vacationing alone either.* But she wasn't going to dwell on these thoughts. She assumed their relationship would resume as it had been in the past. And if not, she'll handle it.

Judith felt it was a blessing not to have to face her stepfather on their first day at home. She hated him for being an uneducated, emotionally primitive man and didn't expect to improve her past relationship with him in the future. *I'll just have to avoid him as much as I can,* she thought, taking pleasure in walking through the house. She loved looking at their beautiful furniture, the paintings on the walls, the Persian carpets everywhere. Above all, she was happy to be back in her room, with the white varnished "children's furniture".

Erika, too, was glad that her stepfather was away. *I'll have to figure out how to set new rules between us,* she thought. She carried her little case into the 'children's room' following her sister and saw with great pleasure that all her books were intact on the shelves and her clothes were hanging in her side of the closet.

"It's great to be home," she commented to Judith.

Judith had thrown herself on top of her bed, and grinned at Erika, "Would be even greater if that rotten beast didn't come back to live with us."

After lunch, Piry insisted that they go next door and say hello to Feri's brother Imre, and his wife, Magda. It being a workday, only Magda was home. She was truly surprised to see Piry and her daughters. After offering sympathy for their failed attempt, she simply said, "You're welcome home. I hope you'll settle down and stay content."

◎⊙◎

Early evening, Lilly and Donát arrived with Nandi in tow. He was six years old by now, and had become a polite, quiet little boy.

"You're now old enough to babysit him," Lilly joked with Erika as they hugged and settled down in the warm dining room.

"I will, too. Just call me. Any time," Erika responded.

Maria served a sponge cake, apples, and coffee as they sat warmed by the fire in the ceramic stove and conversed about the year's events.

"I'll tell you our story in details later," Piry promised after a brief description of what had happened to them and how each had spent the year. "Right now, I want to know what miracle caused our unexpected release."

"You explain," Lilly urged Donát.

Donát's large brown eyes were serious. He looks like a wise owl, Erika thought, as he started to talk.

"Soon after Stalin died, we felt like the walls of the Party were cracking. Not falling down, just cracking. Our valiant leader, Comrade Rákosi went to Stalin's funeral, and rumors had it that he had been chastised by the new leaders of the Soviet Union. We don't know whether that was true or not, but fact was that he was called back to the Soviet Union just a couple of months later, in July of last year.

That same month, in 1953, we got a new head of state, Nagy Imre. Shortly after Nagy took office, he began to release political prisoners. He had also ordered many ÁVO officers arrested, accusing them of abusing their power and of being "bad communists." In fact, my brother Károly came home about four months ago, along with Klara, his wife. But that's another story."

Piry suddenly had a bad feeling in the pit of her stomach. "How is our cousin Laci doing during this ÁVO purge?"

Donát and Lilly exchanged glances and shook their heads. Finally, Donát said, "Very badly, I'm afraid. As I said, after Stalin's death there was a huge purge of the ÁVO. Péter Gábor, the head of the ÁVO was ousted and jailed. Though rumor has it that he had been released and sent to live in the Soviet Union. Along with his demotion, many of his men were arrested, and even executed.

I'm afraid Laci also became a victim of the purge. They came for him at his villa in Buda in the middle of the night, and also took his wife, Kató, Péter Gábor's sister. Kató was jailed but not long ago we heard that she had been released and is now working in a state-run laundry facility.

But poor Laci was executed and then buried as a "Hero of the People." Probably Kató had something to do with this, convincing the authorities that Laci never really did anything as an ÁVO officer, because he was studying engineering at the Technical University."

Piry closed her eyes and thought of her dream. She then told about it to Lilly and Donát.

"He must have been dead when he came to me in that dream."

"You're weird," Lilly said, staring at Piry.

Piry shrugged. "I wish I had a premonition about our escape a year ago. Oh, well. We're here, together again, and I'm truly grateful for that."

◎◉◎

Sunday evening Feri came home. There were tears in his eyes as he embraced his newly regained family. They spent the evening telling him of their lives for the past year. He in turn told them how much he had missed them. When it came to bedtime, Erika was told to sleep on a mattress in Judith's room, while Piry and Feri locked themselves into the master bedroom.

I hope our lives will remain this happy from now on, Erika wrote that night in her newly purchased notebook as her diary.

Two days after returning to their home, Piry and her daughters had to go and register again with the local police department as residents of Ùjpest. They were not asked why they had been away—the police officer already knew. Piry was given her identification booklet, and Judith was issued one as well, since at sixteen she was considered of legal age. Erika was told she needed to get a new Pioneer identification booklet once she started school again.

After a couple of weeks at home, the joy of their return seemed to have worn off and their daily lives had settled into its former ways, if not worse. Feri was once again his usual taciturn self. Piry found it hard to buy food for the family on the budget Feri was able to provide. Maria, their loyal maid, had gone to work two days a week for another family, and decided not to give up that job so she could have some additional income. Her absence made Piry's life even harder.

For Erika, there was one truly bright spot in their return home. The day after they got back, she had sent postcards to the addresses that Maria and Marianne had given her prior to their departure from the Detska Izba. She let her friends know that she, too, was back in Budapest, and asked them to come and visit her. She had not heard back from either girl. But then again, Erika did not have a telephone at home, so there was no way her friends could have called her.

There was no mail response from them either. But, a week after their return, late on Sunday afternoon, the bell rang at their gate. Erika went to open and there stood her two friends grinning broadly. Erika was overjoyed. She ushered the girls into the house, introduced them to her mother—Judith was away visiting her own friends, and Feri was also out somewhere—so they could settle comfortably in the living room and talk.

To heat up the living room for the girls, Piry put extra coal on the stove in the dining room and opened the door between the two rooms. As a gesture of hospitality, she also put kindling wood into the big ceramic stove in the living room and lit that as well. Once the wood in there turned into a lively fire, Erika added some coal, so they were comfortably warm while they sat catching up with the events in their lives since they got back to Hungary.

Both Maria and Marianne were living with their grandparents for the time being. Marianne's stepmother, as she had expected, was still in jail, and so were Maria's parents. Both girls were hoping that with the new, less strict government, their parents might be released after completing a year in jail.

After a while Piry offered the friends dinner. The girls continued talking over platefuls of gulyás, the typical Hungarian beef and potato stew. Evening fell and they had just finished eating when both Judith and Feri had arrived home. After introductions, the two girls were ready to leave.

Maria and Marianne both had phones at their current homes, and before leaving, gave their numbers to Erika. She could call them from any public phone and arrange to meet again in a couple of weeks.

"We could go ice-skating," Marianne suggested. "The lake at the Városliget Park is frozen and it's fun to skate there."

"I don't have skates, and don't even know how to skate," Erika objected.

"You can rent skates there cheaply, and we can teach you how," Maria responded.

Erika looked at her mother, who nodded, "It's all right with me if you want to go."

◉◉◉

In mid-January, winter break was over at schools. It was time for Judith and Erika to return to their respective classes. However, having left without prior notice, now Piry had to accompany each of her daughters to make sure that they would be accepted back.

After the Hungarian Socialist Government came into power, they had shut down all parochial schools in the country. However, to prove that there was religious freedom under the socialist system, they kept one High School to run under the auspices of each of the nation's religions. There was one Catholic, one Protestant, one Lutheran, and one Jewish High School, all located in the capital, Budapest.

When Judith finished middle school at age 14, she was not accepted at any of the state-run High Schools because her grades were not good enough. Only students with grades "5," the top grade under the Communist school system, combined with only a couple of 4's, were eligible for a High School education. Solely students who had graduated from High School with all 5's could apply for university studies.

Judith was getting mostly "3's and therefore was told she could attend only a trade school. But Judith had no interest in studying a trade. Piry knew that her older daughter was smart enough to study at a High School despite her lack of better grades. Looking for a way to get Judith into a High School, Piry learned about the Jewish High School from the Rabbi at her temple. For sure, Judith would be accepted there. The only drawback was that it was located in the center of the city and Judith would have to take two different streetcars to get there, spending nearly an hour traveling back and forth. But at least she would be attending the right kind of school for her.

So that is where Judith had gone to High School prior to their escape, and was now able to return to it, after Piry went to register her. The only setback was that Judith had to continue classes in the second year, where she had left off at the time of their escape.

Erika was accepted back into her middle school in their neighborhood. When Piry went to the principal of the school to re-enroll Erika, she did not reveal the true reason for her daughter's absence. She said that she had been "transferred" very suddenly to Czechoslovakia and took both her daughters along. But now they were back. The principal knew better than to ask the reason for the transfer. If it was for a political motive, it was better for her not to know. Instead, she welcomed Erika back. However, even though she had continued her schooling in Prague, she also had to attend the same year that she had left off in Budapest. Seeing the disappointment on Erika's face, the principal said to Piry, "If Erika stays an all 5 student as she had been before, maybe she could go to summer school and make up the year. I will look into it and let you know."

◎◉◎

Piry felt like their lives were getting back on track despite the failure of their attempted escape. She also knew that when she went to visit her old friend Elek, to let him know that they were back, she would have to tell him how wrong he had been to suggest that it was all right for them to start their journey on a Friday evening, the start of the Sabbath. Never will I make that mistake again. God obviously had not sanctioned our escape, Piry concluded. She was now secretly praying for the government's judicial system not to give her and Judith too long a sentence. She couldn't even think about who would take care of Erika if she went to jail.

Despite attending classes with students who were a year younger than herself, within a week Erika had made new friends. She found that even her old classmates were glad to see her back. She also noticed that boys began to take an interest in her. They came to talk to her during class breaks and walked with her after school towards her home.

At times, some of them teased her by trying to grab her school satchel off her shoulder as they walked but they didn't count on Erika's ability to fight back. Having spent considerable time wrestling with Peter at the Detska Izba, Erika was quick to strike a boy who tried to grab at her or at her satchel. She would get into a real skirmish on the street, acquiring a reputation as a fierce fighter. But instead of deterring her followers, she attracted more of them.

She realized that the boys were drawn to her because she had a curvaceous figure and more prominent breasts than the average fourteen-year-old girls at school. Plus, they felt challenged by her brashness. But she was not attracted to any of them. She found even the good-looking ones too naïve compared to her recent experiences.

She longed for the hard-edged, danger filled, conspiratory friendships she had developed with the boys at the Detska Izba. She especially missed the wrestling matches with Peter which she knew both of them had found thrilling. Oddly, now that she was back in her own home in Budapest, she missed Peter and Lubo more than when she lived in Prague. Thinking it over, she realized, that the school and her living circumstances in Prague had left her no time to pine for 'the boys'. But now that she was surrounded by would be suitors, she felt their absence acutely.

In fact, when she compared her school in Prague with the one in Ùjpest, she had to admit that she was happier abroad than in her own hometown because the school in Prague was cleaner, the students better mannered.

Two weeks after she started school, Piry gave Erika with a wristwatch. "You're old enough to have one," Piry smiled, "and maybe it'll help you be on time."

Erika was thrilled by her mother's generosity and ignored her comment about being on time. Her whole family knew that Erika tended to be five or ten minutes late with being ready whenever they went to visit a relative or for temple services.

"I'm always on time for school and a stage performance," Erika retorted.

They both laughed.

Erika showed up at school the next day, wearing her new watch. During their morning break her classmates, eager to see it since none of them had one, stormed her. They pushed her against the hallway wall, grabbed at her wrist, twisting the watch around. It fell on the tile floor and broke. Erika burst into tears. Her classmates froze, feeling sorry and apologetic, but there was nothing else they could do.

Erika dreaded going home and having to tell her mother about it. She feared getting punished for being careless, even though this was clearly not her fault. When she got home, Piry was busy preparing dinner. Erika watched her working while she related what had happened. To her amazement Piry just shrugged and said with empathy, "Sorry about this, I guess it was too soon to give you a watch."

Erika did not know that Piry had other, bigger issues to deal with.

◎◉◎

Before their attempted escape, shortly after Piry graduated from the knitting school, with Maria's consent they set up the workshop in her bedroom. Then

Piry asked Maria to quit her second job and offered her the same additional salary she had been earning there, to help her knit. Erika was also recruited to work at least an hour a day and more on weekends, so Piry could meet her production quota.

The only person who avoided any involvement, was Judith. Since their return to Hungary, Judith seemed to have changed personality. While in prison, and in Prague, she was quiet and cooperative with everyone around her. Now, she has become hostile and contrary about almost everything that was asked of her. After school, and during weekends, she spent as much time as she could outside the house, with friends. When she was at home, she was rude to Piry, and put Erika down as often as she could, by mean comments. She totally ignored her stepfather when they were in the same room.

Erika wondered why her mother tolerated such bad behavior by Judith, when she knew she could never get away with it. One day, while Judith was out, and Piry was ironing bed sheets, she asked Erika to come to her.

"I want you to learn how to iron. Observe how I'm doing it and then I'll let you try it," Piry said to Erika. "Knowing how to iron well made my life bearable in prison. One never knows when you might need to make use of such a skill. Besides, you should know how to do it so you could teach your maid when you grow up and get married." She smiled at Erika.

Thus, Erika stood by, watching her mother's hands smooth out the sheet as she pressed the iron over it, making all the creases disappear. After a while Piry looked up from her work, and said to Erika, "Just because a mother loves her children, don't think for a moment that she doesn't see the differences between them. Or that she can't appreciate one more than the other. But as a mother, one can never say this, and must treat all her children with equal love. Do you understand?"

Erika nodded, realizing that the lesson her mother was teaching her was not only about ironing.

A few weeks later, Judith's behavior had changed radically. She had crying spells that wouldn't stop, and no amount of consolation by Piry or Erika helped. Judith shooed them away, or shouted at Piry not to come near her, and not to touch her.

Then after a few days, Judith packed a small bag with her nightgown and toothbrush, put her schoolbooks into her satchel, and said to Piry, "I can't stand you or this house for one more minute. I'm going to Aunt Lilly's house."

Piry called her sister while Judith was en route. "I think there is something drastically wrong with Judith," she explained to Lilly.

"We'll take care of her here," Lilly promised. "If things get worse, I'll take her to a doctor."

With deep gratitude Piry thanked her sister, and hung up the phone in the glass booth, feeling heartbroken and seriously concerned about her older daughter.

Within a week, Judith was hospitalized with what was diagnosed as a nervous breakdown. Piry explained to the admitting neurologist that her daughter had spent eight months in prison at age fifteen. Plus, she had been just old enough to understand the danger she was in during World War II, and the loss of her beloved father when she was merely seven years old. All these events must have contributed to her current mental state.

"Don't worry, Mrs. Haydu, we'll take good care of her. We have ways of helping. She'll be as good as new when we release her back to you," the doctor assured Piry.

◎◉◎

Erika hated to admit to herself that during Judith's absence she felt a great sense of relief about their home-life. There wasn't the usual tense atmosphere when Feri came home after work, and they would all sit down to dinner together. Feri still spoke in terse sentences when Piry tried to converse with him. But now and then he would even tell a joke or smile as he asked how Piry's knitting business was progressing. Erika could now disappear after dinner to the bedroom which she and Judith shared without her sister's ordering her around. She could sit quietly at the desk usually occupied by Judith and do her homework or read late into the night with a flashlight.

On weekends, she could spend time drawing dresses she was inventing for her paper dolls. She even began to write what she hoped would become a novel about a group of children who got lost in a forest and had to survive on their own.

Six weeks later, Judith returned home. She seemed normal, but rather withdrawn and subdued. She told Erika one night that the doctors had given her 'shock treatments' as a cure.

"They applied little wet patches to various areas of my skull, temples, and spine." Judith pointed at the places with her index finger. "They handed me a thick piece of rubber and told me to put it between my teeth to protect them. Then they turned up the electricity that was connected to the patches on me to such a high voltage that my whole body was shaking uncontrollably. They did this repeatedly, with days of rest in between. But they weren't really rest days because on those days I was taken to an office to talk to a doctor about my feelings. They also made me take pills, which I suppose were tranquilizers, because most of the time I felt like sleeping, and even when I was awake, I was like a zombie."

"How do you feel now?" Erika was terribly sorry for her sister.

"All right, I guess. Actually, I feel kind of indifferent about everything."

"Are you going back to school?"

"What else would I be doing—daahhh" Judith mocked her.

Though taken aback by Judith's sudden nastiness, Erika was relieved that her sister seemed to be back to her old self indeed.

◎◉◎

During the entire month of February Erika's school hours were severely cut back due to the lack of coal for heating the classrooms. Students were told to come in at 9 a.m. instead of at 8 a.m. and stay only two hours instead of the usual six. They were given brief lectures in the different subjects of their curriculum, plus homework, and then sent home.

Erika overheard her mother commenting to her stepfather one evening, "They would have plenty of coal to heat the classrooms if it weren't shipped to the Soviet Union."

"I hope I'm the only one you're saying this to," was Feri's response.

"Are you kidding me? I'm not even commenting to Erika about this," Piry protested.

Erika used her free time to read, and go ice-skating with her school friends, and was able to meet with both Marianne and Maria on Sundays. When Maria mentioned that she would only be free after Church services, Erika asked if she could attend church with her. She loved the scent of incense, listening to the choir, and the tinkling of the bells while the priests walked down the isles holding out collection baskets for contributions. Neither she nor Maria had any money to give but Maria said, "It doesn't matter. We're here for the Lord, not to maintain the Church."

After services, Marianne, who declared, "I wouldn't be caught dead inside a church," often joined them at the skating rink, or at its café house. Provided each of them had bought an espresso and a piece of pastry, they could sit as long as they wished. Since the shop was state-owned, and the waiters were paid a fixed salary by the government, employees didn't care how long customers stayed. Waiters were not allowed to receive tips, because according to the slogan, "Tipping would offend socialist dignity." Yet each girl managed to leave a Forint or two at the end of their visit.

During their meetings the three girls talked about their current lives, and how much each of them missed "the boys". They felt that their home conditions were mundane compared to the excitement of being at the Detska Izba. The boys they met now were neither as interesting nor as adventurous as their friends in Bratislava. Marianne and Maria expected their parents to be out of jail in a few more months and hoped that their lives would become better then. Erika shared little about her own home life.

At Piry's request, after doing her homework, Erika spent some of her time in the kitchen, learning how their meals were being prepared. Piry taught

Erika how to cut up a whole chicken, separating the parts they would not eat, and then "making kosher" the remaining pieces. In fact, they had to do the same procedure with any meat before cooking it. The meat not used was usually given to their dog, Maczko, who gobbled it up, and whether it was kosher or not.

"All blood must come out of the meat by sprinkling salt on every side of it and leaving it on for an hour so the salt could soak up the blood. After this we must soak the meat in water for half an hour, to get the salt and any leftover blood out of it before we can cook it," Piry explained to Erika, then added, "That's why all those accusations throughout history that Jews use blood in the preparation of their Passover matzoh are so absurd. We're not allowed to eat even a drop of blood. It was just an excuse to kill Jews."

Erika recalled that before their escape, her Uncle Imre had collected the pig's blood after they had slaughtered it in their very own yard. Later she watched as he and his wife Aunt Magda made blood sausages by mixing the blood with ground pork meat, and how delicious it was when after cooking it they had offered her a taste.

Of course, she kept these thoughts to herself. By now she realized that people did all sorts of things in the name of religion and that all believers thought theirs was the purest and truest faith. Personally, she enjoyed all rituals which went with the services, be it Jewish or Catholic. To her, they were all just ceremonies like shows that made people feel good.

◎◉◎

One afternoon, when both Erika and Judith were at home from school, Piry joined them around the table in the winter dining room. She said to her daughters, "I've got something to share with you. I am pregnant. How do you feel about this? I just found out and must decide whether to keep the baby or not. If I decide to keep it, I'd have to marry Feri again."

"You'd be crazy to keep it," Judith burst out indignantly. "Look how that man treats you! Why on earth would you want his child?"

"I think it would be great to have a little sister or brother," was Erika's response.

"Thanks for telling me how you each feel," Piry hugged her daughters. "I'll think it over."

A week later, because Erika still didn't have school in the afternoons, Piry asked her to accompany her to a gynecologist. While Erika waited, sitting just outside the doctor's examination room in the hallway, she overheard her mother crying out, "It hurts!"

Then she heard nothing more and sat reading her book for over an hour while waiting for her mother. Eventually, Piry came out smiling, moving slowly, as if she were in pain. They left the doctor's office, and Piry locked an arm into Erika's as they walked to the streetcar. They sat silently during the ride but on the way home Piry told Erika that she was no longer pregnant.

"Judith was right. There would be no point in bringing another child into the world."

Erika hid her surprise and disappointment and said, "In theory it would have been nice to have a little brother or sister. But what if it turned out to have Apu's personality? I'm sure you've made the right decision."

They both laughed, for the truth could be painfully funny.

◎◉◎

Since their homecoming, Feri had no opportunity to approach Erika privately. One evening, Piry took Judith with her to the dressmaker to have a new dress made for her. Erika went to her bedroom to get ready for bed, when she heard her stepfather calling her name. He was asking her to come to him. She was too afraid to disobey his command but determined to stand up to him.

He was already in bed, and patted the mattress, saying, "Come here."

Erika stood stock-still, looking at him, and then said politely but in the firmest tone she could muster, "I'm sorry, I won't lie with you anymore. Ever again."

He froze and did not respond.

Erika turned on her heels and hurried back to her bedroom, wondering whether Feri would follow her or what he would do. He did nothing. He stayed in his own room, and Erika cowered under her duvet, tense and awake till she heard her sister's and mother's voices in the house. She felt a great sense of relief and an even greater sense of victory. *I will never have to deal with his disgusting use of my body again*, she thought, full of joy. She fell into a deep sleep, proud of her courage to refuse him. She knew that from that point on she always could and would.

◎◉◎

Piry and Judith received a letter to appear on Monday, March 7th at 8 a.m. before the Judicial Court of Citizenship Concerns. This was the hearing Piry had dreaded. Since Stalin's death the political oppression in Hungary seemed to have mellowed somewhat. But they continued to live under a tyrannical and terrifying government. They still could not openly comment on their lack of freedom of speech. Their food supply was still sparse, and salaries inadequate. Uttering a word of complaint or dissatisfaction with their circumstances could mean arrest, torture to extract an anti-government confession, and possibly being sent to a labor camp or prison.

Piry and Judith could be facing a five-year to life prison sentence for their attempted escape. It was up to the Judge to decide. As a minor, Erika was not allowed to appear in court. However, she didn't have to be there to be sentenced and be placed into a reform school for not having reported her mother's plan to escape. Under communism, children were taught that if they overheard their parents, or any adult, say anything negative about their regime or the government, they were to report it to the police.

In fact, there had been cases where teenagers, raised by the socialist government, did report their parents' comments. The parents ended up with a jail sentence or were sent to a forced labor camp. The children were placed into good communist foster homes or orphanages. Thus, Piry was worried not just about their possible sentence but also about the fate of her daughters who neglected to report their plan to escape.

Weeks before the hearing, Piry could hardly sleep, lost weight, and had secret crying spells in the middle of the night. Feri, observing Piry's agony, admonished her, "Stop anticipating and wait till the judge actually sentences you. What's the point of worrying in advance?"

"It's not your life that's hanging in the balance," Piry retorted. "Whatever happens to us won't affect yours."

He smiled bitterly, "Why, I won't care if you and the girls are locked up? What's the matter with you?"

"I am not sure you do," Piry replied.

They both fell silent. They were aware that their living together now was not any better than it had been before Piry's escape. Feri's heavy, morose nature did not allow for much pleasure or fun in their lives. Piry knew he must love her and her daughters for he wouldn't have been so happy when they returned. But now he took them for granted again and they had fallen back into the same tense atmosphere when he came home from work, as they had before their escape.

The only time he showed any tenderness was when he and Piry made love. But since her abortion, he had approached her less often. She had the feeling that when he did, it was a mere physical need without much love for her. He never commented about her abortion, but she knew he resented her decision not to have his child. Yet his very silence and coldness made Piry feel that she had made the right decision. Had she had that child, he would have likely doted on his own to the exclusion of her daughters. His fatherhood to them wasn't great to start with. Having his own child likely would have created further detachment from them.

They had not gotten married again because of Piry's political situation hanging over their heads. When Piry told Feri that she had terminated the pregnancy, she used this issue as the reason for it. "We can always make another baby," she consoled him, "provided I won't spend the rest of my life in jail."

Judith had never expressed concern about their upcoming hearing. Inwardly, she dreaded the possibility of more jail time. But she was so unhappy about her home life, due to her hatred of her stepfather, and resentment of her mother for their failed escape, that she also thought, *maybe jail wouldn't be such a bad place to be.* Thus, instead of moping about this possibility, she spent her time after school with her friends and returned home only around bedtime.

Actually, Piry was having a hard time coping with the disappointing relationship between Feri and herself. Thus, she was glad that at least she didn't have to put up with Judith's moroseness. Erika was easy to have around since she spent most of her time either doing homework or reading a book. Also, Erika had a sunny disposition which helped Piry ease her own concern about the upcoming court hearing.

Erika was very concerned about their future. But observing her mother's mood, she thought it best not to share her own worries. For once, she liked Feri's point of view, telling herself not to worry about things before she had to.

◎◉◎

"Good luck," Feri grunted at Piry and Judith as he took off for work the morning of their court appointment. Not being her spouse, he couldn't go with them even if he had wanted to.

Piry knew Feri loved her and her daughters. He simply could not express his feelings., Feri's father never did, and his mother was a difficult, bitter woman. She worked hard raising four sons, running their household, and helping her husband at his grape and fruit orchard business, without ever getting a word of thanks or praise from him. Thus, Feri and his three brothers had not learned how to show their feelings. As a family, the brothers cooperated but there was never any open display of affection among them. Even their wives had taciturn personalities.

Piry learned all this about Feri and his brothers only after she had married him. Now, she simply thanked him for his good wishes and watched him walk out of the house. She hoped that she and Judith will be able to return to this home—the only one they had—and continue their lives as a family, despite its difficulties.

◎◉◎

Piry wore a black skirt and jacket with a white blouse under it. Judith put on a dark blue skirt and a light blue sweater. Blue was her favorite color because it emphasized her large cobalt blue eyes. Secretly, she hoped that looking nice before a male judge might help soften his verdict. They topped their outfits with black wool coats, since the weather was still cold at the beginning of March.

Since Erika was not allowed to go with them, while getting ready for school, she asked, full of apprehension, "Will they let you come home even if they convict you or will I have to search the city to find out which jail you're in?"

"Frankly, I have no idea," Piry responded. "Just pray for us and hope we'll be at home when you get back from school."

"I sure hope so!"

The three of them hugged tightly, then letting each other go, Erika headed for school on foot, while Piry and Judith took the streetcar to the People's Court in the center of Pest.

◎◉◎

Erika was almost too afraid to go home that afternoon. She worried about finding the house empty or with only Maria at home, knitting. She wondered what will happen if her mother and sister are held somewhere, and she would have to be alone with Feri till the authorities came for her as well. These thoughts made her consider calling her aunt Lilly and asking if she could spend the night at their place. Then she decided to brave going home. *After all, I can handle Apu's advances, and that's all that really worries me about being alone with him at home*, she encouraged herself as she trudged through the rain-soaked streets, carrying an open umbrella as well as her school satchel.

She unlocked the gate, locked it again, and slowly walked to the front door and opened it.

"Here she is!" Piry and Judith shouted happily as Erika entered. They rushed to hug her, smiling broadly.

"You're home!" Erika, shouted, with surprise and joy, embracing them as if never wanting to let go.

"You're not going to believe what happened," Piry told her as she gently disengaged them from the hug. "Come, sit down, we'll tell you about it while you're having lunch.

As if on cue, Maria came out of the kitchen, carrying a plate full of chicken paprikash and nokkedli, the Hungarian version of the Italian gnocchi. In her other hand she had brought a small plate of very hot yellow peppers cut into strips, knowing that Erika wouldn't eat her meal without these. The fierier the peppers tasted the more Erika loved them with her meal. Maria also placed a tall glass of water in front of Erika, and then smiling, disappeared into the kitchen. She had heard the story already and could hear it again anyway through the open kitchen door.

"So? What happened?" Erika asked while she started her meal.

"You tell it," Judith nudged her mother.

Piry gave a little shrug, and began, "We were met by a lawyer in front of the courtroom—he was waiting for us there, a middle aged, stocky man in a dark blue suit. He introduced himself as our defense attorney, provided by the State. He said, "I don't think I can do much for you since clearly you are guilty of trying to leave the country illegally. But it's all up to the Judge. So, let's go in."

"With that kind of encouragement, it was hard to walk into the courtroom and not be even more terrified than we were already. We were instructed by the guard inside to sit in the first row, reserved for criminals and lawyers. Our lawyer sat down next to us. Then the Judge came in and we all stood to attention till he bade us to sit.

"He looked at us, called out our names, and asked the lawyer if he had anything to say in our defense. The lawyer stood up and repeated what he had told us, that we were clearly guilty, we had broken the law and needed to be punished. However, he finished by pleading with the Judge that since we had served prison sentences in Czechoslovakia, perhaps the Judge would take that time into consideration in his verdict. Then he sat down.

"The Judge turned to me," Piry continued, "and asked if I had anything to say in our defense. I stood up and told him, we loved Hungary, we loved living under the socialist system. We tried to leave strictly for personal reasons—I had divorced my abusive second husband, and my two daughters and I had no place to live after that. And my children's uncle, their dead father's brother who lived in Israel sent for us so he could help me raise my daughters. So, it was truly a family situation, nothing political. 'And now, Comrade Judge, I'm worried about my younger daughter. Who will take care of her if we are given prison sentences?' I ended by asking him. There was a big silence when I stopped talking.

"The Judge stared at me and Judith and then read some papers in front of him on his dais. Then he looked up and said, "Indeed, you deserve to be punished for not trusting our socialist government to help you bring up your children. And your daughter, Judith, deserves to be punished for not reporting your plans to the police, as a good pioneer should.

"However, hearing the reasons for your escape attempt, I believe that you are telling the truth. You also have a younger daughter and you're correct to be worrying about her future if you are not around to raise her. For all these considerations, I have decided that you and your daughter Judith had served an adequate prison term for what you have done. I will grant you both pardon of any further charges. You are both free to go home and know that our government and our socialist system is fair and just. You are both herewith dismissed."

"With that he closed the folder in front of him, stood up, as did we all, and he rushed out of the room with us thanking him loudly before he shut the door behind him. And here we are, at home again." Piry concluded opening her arms as if to embrace the world and her daughters within it.

"There really is a thaw," Feri commented that evening when he heard the story from Piry. "Even at work, people don't seem to feel the same awful pressure they did before, to meet a production quota. We're working just as hard but for some reason with far less fear."

"Maybe the new Soviet leaders are softer than Stalin was," Erika piped up.

"Don't you dare open our mouth and say such a thing to anyone!" Her stepfather jumped down her throat harshly.

"C'mon you think I'm dumb?" Erika countered. "We're only among us now."

"Just be careful," Feri grunted and without further comment dug into his dinner.

CHAPTER 23

THE FOLLOWING MONTH PIRY went to her family physician and asked him for a letter stating that her health had been affected by the year she had spent in prison, and she could no longer sustain the knitting quota required of her.

When she explained to the doctor that she felt physically weak and incapable of the fast production of the sweater parts expected of her, she also gave him a letter stating this fact. Under the letter she handed to him was a separate envelope with his name on it. He read the letter and slipped the envelope for him into his desk drawer without opening it. He knew Piry had put enough cash in there to make it worth his while to submit an official letter on her behalf to the local labor office.

Within a few weeks Piry received a "Letter of Release" from her work duties. She was to return the machinery to the local labor office along with any leftover materials.

Additionally, in recognition of her health issues, she was allotted a small monthly pension to live on.

"Things have really changed for the better" Piry commented with delight as she showed the letter to her family during their dinner.

"Now you can go back to your old business," Feri grunted.

"I'll try," Piry grinned. "It might take a while. I'll have to contact my old sources and hope that they're still in business."

They both knew that she could make more money by selling things on the black market, and dealing with the private transfer of funds, than by working for any government owned business.

With their freedom granted, their lives slowly returned to their old routine. Feri left for work early mornings, as did the two girls for school. Piry kept house with Maria's help and was also able to re-connect with many of her previous contacts in the black-market business.

Once again, she was receiving and selling nylon stockings from the West, as well as exchanging Hungarian currency for dollars in Canada through her correspondence with her Aunt Vica.

◎◉◎

The most pressure adjusting to their life back in Hungary fell upon Erika. She knew she had to get top grades in all her subjects so she would be allowed to study the following year's curriculum during the summer. If she passed, she could graduate from middle school at age fourteen, as she was supposed to.

At the end of the school year, in mid-June, the Principal called Erika to her office.

"Your grades are excellent, so we are giving you official permission to take accelerated courses during the summer. You'll have to take all the tests in mid.- August and if you pass, you'll graduate from middle school. If you pass with high enough grades, you'll be able to start High School in September."

Erika was thrilled. She knew that all her school friends would spend their summer going swimming at the city's great public pools, and having fun, while she would be getting private classes, and cramming at home. But she didn't mind. She desperately wanted to enter High School with kids her age, instead of being a year older than everyone else.

In the summer heat hovering around 38 degrees Celsius (100 degrees Fahrenheit), she went to school every morning to study with the teachers designated for the day. Then she walked home and sat in the cool bedroom she shared with Judith and studied one subject after another till it was time for her to go to bed.

Piry, knowing how hard Erika needed to work, arranged for Judith to spend her summer at Lake Balaton, vacationing with friends at a government run youth resort. Judith was pleased to be away for the summer. She left in early July and wouldn't be back till the end of August, just after Erika's exams.

All went according to plans till the third week of July, when Erika woke up one morning with a sharp pain in the lower right side of her belly. Since they had been back in Budapest, Erika had experienced this same kind of pain twice, but Piry had always said, "Take a laxative and go to the bathroom. You're just constipated." And she had always been right. But this time, Piry took one look at Erika's pale face and her body doubled over in pain, and said,

"I'm taking you to the hospital."

She called a taxi because Erika was in too much pain to go by streetcar. As soon as they arrived at the emergency room, while Piry explained Erika's condition and was instructed to fill in the paperwork, Erika was whisked away for an exam and x-rays. Within the hour she was operated on for appendicitis.

"You made it just in time," the doctor said when he came to check up on Erika late afternoon.

By now she had been transferred into a bed in the infirmary room, with six other patients in a row with her.

"Had you been brought in even an hour later, your appendix would have ruptured, and you might have died of blood poisoning. Now you'll be here a couple of weeks, and you'll go home as good as new."

Erika, still dazed from the anesthesia, didn't protest or say to the doctor that she had a year's schoolwork to finish. She just thanked him for saving her life. Later in the evening, when Piry came to see her, Erika told her what the doctor had said, and asked, "How did you know that this time a laxative wouldn't have done the trick?"

Piry smiled. "Mother's instinct."

◎◉◎

The first few days after the surgery Erika felt like the right side of her lower abdomen had a sharp knife stuck in there. It cut deeply into her with even the slightest motion she had made. She was given pain medication and was told to lie still on her back till the incision of the surgery sealed and her skin would grow together.

She had asked Piry to let her teachers know what was going on with her. She also asked Piry to bring in her schoolbooks so she could at least study. And she tried but couldn't concentrate. Instead, while she lay there like a beached whale, she observed closely the male and female nurses and the interns who came to the bedside of the patients several times a day. They were checking on everyone's healing progress and bringing medication and meals.

Erika often struck up conversations with a young woman, Ildi, who lay in the bed to her left. Ildi had broken her ankle and was in a cast, but otherwise she was perfectly healthy. Erika noticed that the young doctors and male attendants who came to see them on their rounds stood by Ildi's bedside chatting with her longer than with any other patient.

One of the young male nurses seemed devilishly handsome to Erika, and she tried to keep him in conversation by her own bedside when he came to check on her. But pleasant as he was to her, he spent twice as much time with Ildi. For the first time in her life, Erika felt ignored by the males around her and this shocked her. Being viewed as a child frustrated here, and she was jealous of Ildi who was only ten years older than she. Erika liked Ildi, enjoyed their chats about themselves, the books they've read, and their career aspirations. But watching men flock around Ildi instead of her, perturbed her greatly.

I am at least as pretty as Ildi, or even more so, she told herself. *Ildi has such ordinary brown hair and brown eyes. And although she does have a cute face, I'm far more striking with my auburn hair and green eyes. So, what's wrong?* Then Erika figured it out. She may have been more attractive than Ildi, but she was only fourteen. For the first time in her life, she was being treated by men as young and off-limits to them, whereas Ildi was a grown woman, available if she wanted to be.

Contemplating this new discovery, Erika found that she actually felt lucky that her being attracted to a young man was not reciprocal. It was much safer for her to be still in love with Peter who was far away in Bratislava. Once she could sit up in bed, she wrote in her diary, which she had brought with her to the hospital: *Being in love with a male so close to me would be a bit dangerous.*

I'm not ready for more than holding hands, perhaps a kiss, yet I know full well that men eventually want a lot more. I don't quite know what makes them want more but for sure they do. My own stepfather had taught me that. Since I've found what he wanted, and him, disgusting for it, I am certainly not interested in getting any man that close to me.

It's just my vanity that makes me suffer for being ignored as a woman. Likely, I just need to get a few years older, and things will change. Right now, I should be spending my time studying instead of flirting, she concluded, and felt a lot better about her situation. She started reading her textbooks during her second week of recovery. Assessing how much work she had to do to pass the exams, she concentrated on studying.

In mid-August, fully recovered from her appendix surgery, she took all six tests required of her to graduate from middle school. She passed them flawlessly and received an "all five" report card. Now she could apply to any High School for her continued education.

Erika knew that her choice of school would also be a decision about her future. She thought very carefully about the school she should apply to. There were a number of High Schools in the city with very good reputation. There was also the Jewish High School her sister was attending.

Erika was drawn to this school, not for any religious sentiments but by a contrariness she had never experienced before. After all the years of dealing with anti-Semitism at her schools, she thought that perhaps now she should attend a school where being a Jew wasn't an issue. She also felt that by going to the Jewish High School she was defying the government, the communist system, and all that it stood for.

She figured, since she wanted to be an actress, after high school she wouldn't be going to a university anyway. She would try to get into an acting academy. So, it was pointless for her to worry about attending a state-run high school.

"I want to go to the same school Judith is attending," she informed her mother.

"Why, when you could choose the best High School in town," Piry asked, surprised.

Erika did not want her mother to know her real reason. Instead, she replied, "They may not take me at a state-run gymnasium, considering my criminal record. I'd rather go to a school where there is no question about my getting accepted."

Piry could see the logic of Erika's thinking and the first week in September went with her to register her. As Erika suspected, they didn't ask the reason for her unusual way of finishing middle school. Impressed by her grades, they welcomed her.

◉◉◉

For the first time in her life, Erika didn't feel uncomfortable about being Jewish in a classroom-full-of-students. In fact, Erika had a sense of belonging she had not experienced before in any social situation. This was a different feeling even from her living at the Zionist boarding school or the Jewish orphanage or being at the temple her family had attended. Those were religious organizations and not having any religious sentiments, Erika always felt like an outsider.

The atmosphere at her new school seemed different, even though it was just like any other school, full of ordinary students. Their curriculum was exactly the same as in all the other state-run High Schools. The main difference was that there was no need for her to feel apart for being Jewish because everyone there was Jewish too. Being a Jew was not a topic of conversation; their studies and their lives were. Some of the students came from orthodox families with strict dietary and religious observances. Others, like Erika, were conservative, with moderate adherence to the religious rules. Many were reform and did not observe any Jewish traditions. It didn't matter how observant they were. Only that they all belonged to the same "tribe."

The main distinction between public and their school was that they honored the major Jewish holidays by giving students time off. Also, boys and girls attended separate classes. Girls were taught on the first two floors of the building and the boys' classes were on the third and fourth floors.

But there were many school sponsored programs for all the students to attend and meet each other. To Erika's great delight, there was a co-ed. choir she could join, and social dance parties with live bands. Most importantly, there were plays presented several times a year with open auditions for the entire student body.

Since Erika's classmates were also freshmen, they were all interested in getting to know each other. By natural instinct for compatibility, they soon divided into small groups that stuck together in and out of school. Erika, as usual, ended up with a circle of friends who were the top students, yet they all had different abilities and fields of interest.

The girl who became her closest friend, Zsuzsi, was soft spoken, artistic, and lived just two blocks from Aunt Lilly's apartment building. Another friend, Ági, lived on the Nagykörút, (Grand Boulevard) along their daily streetcar route to school. A third friend, Kati, was more science oriented than humanities, which was just fine with Erika. Science subjects seemed to have become her weakest point, and she and Kati helped each other with their homework.

In fact, later in the semester, the hour before classes started, became a veritable "exchange market" in their homeroom. They got into the habit of arriving early and while Erika wrote one composition after another for their literature class assignments, those for whom she wrote were busy doing her math, algebra, and chemistry homework. Erika knew that eventually she would have to understand and learn the materials of her science classes, otherwise she would not be able to pass the tests in those subjects. But on a daily basis all she cared about was getting her homework done and having fun with all her extra-curricular activities.

She was often asked to be a soloist in the choir because of her vocal range from soprano to mezzosoprano, and her clear phrasing. She also performed during assemblies, reciting poetry, and got a role in a play that was to be presented in the Spring. But throughout this first semester her favorite activity came to be the evenings of social dances.

Piry, as she had done for Judith three years earlier, enrolled Erika in a social dance school for her to learn the waltz, the tango, the fox trot, and other current popular dance forms.

Every Thursday night she accompanied Erika to her dance lessons. They were held from six to seven p.m., and were followed by a "dance practice" social hour, till nine p.m.

On Saturday nights there was just social dancing from seven to ten p.m., and Piry and Erika went to those as well. Except that while Erika was at dance school, Piry used the evenings to visit friends, relatives, and clients of her re-established black-market business. She would come for Erika just as her social dancing ended, and they would go home together.

During the forty-minute streetcar ride Erika gave enough details of her dance sessions for her mother to be able to comment about it to Feri, if needed. Piry never told Erika to keep their arrangement a secret. Erika just knew not to reveal that Piry wasn't sitting around with the other mothers during her dance evenings. She and Piry had a deep, nonverbal understanding and trust between them. Erika loved it, though it was totally one-sided. She could keep Piry's secrets, but she could not reveal to her mother any of hers.

She could not tell her mother that she had fallen in love with a senior boy at school. Nor that she was developing a close friendship with one of her dance partners at the social dance school. Piry would have told her to cut off her feelings immediately at her high school and not even dream of meeting her dance partner outside the scheduled classes.

Erika knew that Piry was more worried about her losing her virginity than about her emotional life. Thus, she kept her feelings about boys to herself or shared them only with her closest girlfriends at school as well as with Marianne and Maria when they met a couple times a month on Sundays.

◎◉◎

At school, she was completely infatuated with a senior whose name she had abbreviated to Z, thinking, only her girlfriends knew about her feelings.

Actually, all the students knew about it because of what happened during the first social dances held by the school.

As soon as the music began, Erika started tapping her feet and she was asked to dance by a freshman she knew from her own social circle. It was quickly noticed by other boys that Erika was light on her feet and had good rhythm. Thus, as long as the musicians were playing, she was kept dancing.

The rules of the dance floor were that a boy could request a girl to switch and dance with him by tapping her current partner on his shoulder. Erika was asked by nearly all the freshmen and juniors in the ballroom, often being requested to switch more than once during the same dance piece.

Then, in the middle of the evening Z asked for a dance. He was an excellent dancer, and Erika was thrilled. She thought he was as sexy as Peter and as attractive as Lubo had been at the Detska Izba. He had black wavy hair and dark eyes that seemed to penetrate into her very soul. When he smiled at her, he showed a row of even white teeth. He was slim, and just tall enough for his chin to be above Erika's head. He wrapped one arm around her waist, pulling her close, while his right hand held hers with a firm grip and guided her securely through the complex steps of the fox trot.

He held her a lot closer than was customary at these dances, and Erika wondered whether others noticed it but shrugged off the concern. Dancing with Z was the best part of the evening. Then, on one of the turns Z's lips brushed her cheek and Erika felt as if a thunderbolt had run through her. Yet she said nothing as he held her even tighter in his embrace because she was at a loss what to say.

Should I protest or just pretend I didn't feel his lips? Should I ask him to behave, or continue to enjoy this electric current coursing through me? She has not felt this kind of excitement since her wrestling matches with Peter, and she decided to just go along with it. This was the last dance before a brief intermission, and when the music ended, Z held on to her hand and led her to sit down with him.

Since this was a Saturday evening Jewish High School dance, Piry had stayed around, sitting and chatting with the other mothers. Erika shot a quick glance at her mother's face, and knew she was in trouble, but she felt powerless to stop what was going on between her and this boy. So, they sat holding hands, and he asked her about her classes, and what she wanted to be when she finished high school. He didn't seem to disapprove when she told him "An actress," and Erika was pleased.

"What about you?" she asked.

"I had applied to medical school after my graduation this coming June."

It struck Erika that once he was at a university, it will be hard for her maintain contact with him but at the moment she didn't care. Nearly the whole school year was ahead of them, and she wasn't going to worry about anything beyond this evening.

After the intermission Z danced with her again, and when other boys tapped him on the shoulder to dance with Erika, he let them have a few steps with her but asked for her back. Erika was floating with the fun of it all.

Of course, Piry chided her on their way home. Erika explained that she didn't know what to do, plus promised to behave in the future. They both let it go by the time they walked through the front gate of their home.

◉◉◉

For a while, her classmates teased Erika a lot, but she simply shrugged it off. Then the gossip stopped because Z hadn't asked to date her. During the school year she often ran into him either on the streets to and from school, or at dances. He didn't always ask her for a dance. But when he did, they often ended up talking about themselves and their lives.

Erika had heard through her classmates that Z had a reputation for being a womanizer and a liar. Someone said, he had seduced a woman many years older than himself when he was merely fourteen.

Others said, he actually had a girlfriend, she was a senior at their school. Occasionally, Erika spotted Z walking with a very attractive girl on their way to school or away from it. None of this changed her feelings of being attracted to him.

She longed to catch sight of him during class breaks, when the girls were allowed into the courtyard, and many of the boys stood at the upper floor's windows, looking down. She often did spot him, and assumed Z must be watching her, for when she looked up, he immediately smiled at her.

She wrote in her diary: *In a way, it's good that he has a girlfriend, for knowing myself, and how hot-blooded I am, who knows what I'd be capable of doing with him if I were his girlfriend.*

Concurrently with her infatuation with Z, Erika was also fond of her regular partner at the dance school. Erika's closest friend, Zsuzsi, also attended the same dance school. The two girls befriended two brothers who became their most frequent dance partners. The older brother, Henri, was twenty, and was interested in Zsuzsi. Both he and Zsuzsi were tall and seemed a good match on the dance floor.

The younger brother, Pali, was eighteen. He was also tall with chestnut brown hair and dark brown eyes. He clearly liked Erika for both dancing and conversation. They looked forward to seeing each other twice a week and spent as much time together as they could, dancing and chatting during the breaks.

Erika wondered whether she was going to continue seeing Pali once dance school was over. He was a senior at his high school and Erika a freshman at hers, so for sure their schedules would not allow much free time for meeting. A week before their six week course ended, while on a break, Pali asked Erika, "What is your religion?"

"I'm Jewish, but not observant," she replied without hesitation. "And you?"

"Catholic."

"You go to church on Sundays?"

"Yes."

"I do too, at times, with my Catholic girlfriends."

He seemed to have registered this information but said nothing. They went back to dancing. The following Saturday evening, though it was their last dance session, he said nothing about continuing their friendship, so Erika asked:

"Are we going to meet ever again?"

He shook his head: "I am sorry, I don't think so."

"Is it because we have different religions?"

"I'm afraid so. It's been lovely to know you, but it won't work in the long run. I hope you understand."

Erika did. Painful as it was to face facts, she had to. She was a Jew in a Catholic country and would never be accepted by the majority of the population as their equal. She was glad she didn't have to feel like an outsider at the Jewish High School.

◎◉◎

When the school year was over, Judith asked Piry if she could arrange for her to spend a few weeks vacationing at Lake Balaton, with her school friends. Piry was able to do it, and then, not to leave Erika without a special vacation, wrote to her cousin, Marta, asking if Erika could go for a visit. Marta and her husband, Tibor, were a young couple, living in the town of Debrecen, where Piry grew up.

Marta's mother, Sara, was one of Piry's aunts on her mother's side. She survived concentration camp in Auschwitz and returned home to Debrecen. Her husband died in the concentration camp. Her daughter, Marta, then 10 years-old, survived by being hidden by a Christian family. Now at age 22, Marta was not only married but had a two-year-old son. She and Tibor replied that they would be delighted to have Erika spend some weeks with them.

Piry helped Erika pack her suitcase, "Don't forget your bathing suit," she said, as they selected outfits for the summer. "Debrecen has a great public pool. I used to go there to swim when I was your age. You'll have lots of fun, you'll see."

◎◉◎

The train rushed through the Hungarian countryside for nearly the entire day. Erika sat by the window, staring at the sunbaked summer landscape, marveling at the beauty of the golden wheat fields, tall corn fields, and green expanses of grass where cows, lamb, and geese were grazing. *How magnificent this country is. I hope I'll never leave it again*, she thought, touched by the scenery rushing by.

Márta and Tibor were at the train station when she arrived in Debrecen. *They are a handsome couple*, Erika assessed, as they came up to greet her after she clambered off the train, dragging her suitcase down the stairs.

Márta was a slim, pretty young woman of medium height, with light brown shoulder length hair and large brown eyes. Her husband, Tibor, was tall and slender, had curly black hair, dark eyes, and a charming smile flashing even white teeth.

After they had exchanged hugs, Tibor said, "Just call me Tibi." He grabbed Erika's luggage and led the women to the nearby bus stop. "One of the bus lines here makes a stop within walking distance to our home," he explained.

They lived in a one-story housing complex. The main gate led into a courtyard where a u-shaped building contained two apartments. Each consisted of a mid-size living room, two small bedrooms, a bathroom and a toilet room off the hallway, plus a kitchen, with a large pantry.

During Erika's visit they moved their two-year-old son's bed into their own bedroom, so Erika could have a room of her own. For her arrival, however, their son, Robi, was staying at his grandmother Sara's house. Robi, as Erika found out later, often stayed at his grandmother's home so Márta and Tibi could have their evenings free. As a young couple, they liked to go out, and now that Erika was visiting, they planned to take her out almost every night, either to a movie or to dinner at local restaurants. The day she arrived, they let her settle in, and dined at home, getting acquainted with each other. But the next night Márta and Tibi took Erika to the Arany Bika, (Golden Bull) the best restaurant in town, part of the fanciest hotel in Debrecen.

"The Arany Bika has a long history," Tibi informed Erika while they were walking toward the building. "Located in the city center, it dates back to 1699, when the city purchased the land and the properties on it. It included a stone building, owned by a local farmer, András Bika."

"Is that why it's called Bika?" Erika asked.

"That's right, but the name has been embellished a bit," Tibi continued, smiling. "This stone building was re-designed by the city, to be a guest house, with four guest rooms, an inn, and an apartment for the innkeeper. Then, over a hundred years, the place became so popular, that in 1799 it had to be expanded with a second story for more rooms, and a ballroom.

"It was at that time that a design, depicting a butting bull was put on its facade, and the hotel's name was changed to Arany Bika (Golden Bull). The new building became a center of intellectual and social life in Debrecen, with many famous writers, artists, and even politicians staying there during their visit to the city.

"But gradually, the building needed renovation, and it was replaced by a new one in 1915. Designed by Alfréd Hajós, Hungary's first Olympic champion who was also a famous architect, the new building has 192 rooms, two restaurants, and a ceremonial hall that is now used as a dance hall for us 'common folk'. Tibi had just finished his story when they arrived at the impressive lobby of the hotel.

They went straight to the casual dining room, and after a quick dinner they proceeded to the dance hall on the first floor. A section of this room had small tables set up so guests could sit and order drinks and desert. The center of the room had a large parquet floor where guests could dance to a live band till midnight. It was customary for men to come to the tables where women were seated and ask for a dance. Even a woman sitting with a man could be asked by a stranger, and it was up to her and her male companion whether to consent or not.

Erika was asked for a dance by several young men. She felt flattered and enjoyed dancing but had no interest in the men. After each dance, as they escorted her back to her table, many of her partners asked if they could see her again on another night. She explained that she was merely vacationing in Debrecen and didn't know when her cousins would bring her back to the Bika. In truth, these men seemed too unsophisticated to Erika. They were all right for a dance but not for dating.

A couple days after her arrival, Erika's favorite cousin, Györgyi, came to vacation in Debrecen as well, staying with her family's relatives nearby. Erika also ran into a schoolmate from the Jewish High School, Csillag Jutka. Her parents actually lived in Debrecen.

"While studying at the Jewish High School, I live with relatives in Budapest," Jutka told a surprised Erika.

"We had spent a whole school year together, and I had no idea," she responded to Jutka.

"Why would you? I didn't mention it to anyone so I wouldn't be treated like a country bumpkin," Jutka smiled.

I must invite her to my house, or better yet to Aunt Lilly's place when we're back in school, just to make her feel included, Erika noted to herself.

Here, in Debrecen, the three girls spent their days together, going to a large public swimming pool at a nearby town, Hajduszoboszló. It was easily accessible by a streetcar ride. Several local boys, childhood friends of Jutka and Györgyi, met up with them at the pool. Erika found the boys' interest in her flattering and the swimming fun, but it was the frequent dinners at the

Arany Bika, with Márta and Tibi, and spending the evenings dancing that she enjoyed most.

◎◉◎

One evening at the Bika's fancy restaurant, she heard Czech being spoken at a nearby table and got all excited.

"Mind if I go say hello to them?" she asked Márta and Tibi.

"Go head," they smiled at her.

Erika walked over to the group of young men sitting with a couple of young women, nursing large glasses of beer. She said in Czech, "Sorry to disturb you but I've lived in Prague and was thrilled to hear you speaking Czech." She gave them a bright smile, "I wanted to test how much I can still speak the language."

"Oh, you are speaking it fluently," said one of them, and they all laughed. "Come join us," they urged her.

Erika pointed at her table, where Márta, Tibi, and her cousin Györgyi were seated. "I'm with my family here."

"Our dinner will be served in about half an hour. Would you like to go dancing till then?" one of the young men offered. "By the way, my name is Rudi."

"I'll check with my family." Erika returned to her table and explained the situation.

"What a great idea," Márta laughed.

They all rose and went to the Czechs' table. During introductions Erika learned that the men were in town for a motorcycle race that was taking place the next day. Rudi invited all of them not only to join them at their table but also to attend the race. Tibi said, he and Márta were unable to attend. Györgyi couldn't make it either.

"I'd love to go" Erika quickly offered.

Rudi introduced Erika to Jana, the wife of one of the racers, and suggested that Erika sit with her in the stalls the next day.

When the band started to play in the dance hall, they all walked over there. The head of the team, a tall, handsome young man, Špinka, asked Márta to dance with him. Tibi graciously took Györgyi's arm, and Erika went with her new friend, Rudi. They all danced near each other, so Erika could act as their interpreter. Although it periodically halted their dancing, while Erika listened to their comments and translated for the others, she was happy that she could do this. It made her feel important and she liked being the center of attention. During her own conversation with Rudi, she found out that he was married and had two small sons.

"So, should I feel guilty for dancing with you?" Erika quizzed flirtatiously.

"Why, we're not doing anything forbidden," Rudi smiled at her, loosening slightly his tight embrace around Erika's waist.

The musicians now began a slower tune and Rudi once again pulled Erika close. She thoroughly enjoyed his muscular arm holding her, thinking, *he is my first dance partner since Z, whom I find truly sexy.* She liked feeling his hard body pressed against hers, and clearly, he too enjoyed holding her tightly.

His eyes sought hers but when their gaze met, he leaned back slightly and said, "I just wanted to see the color of your eyes."

"And?"

"They're brown."

"I'm told they're green," Erika laughed, "but they do change color under different lights."

Rudi looked into Erika's eyes again. Each felt the electric current between them, and to diffuse it, Rudi said, "I see them as brown. In any case, I'm twenty years older than you."

"So what?" Erika shrugged. "We're just dancing."

A half hour later, they all went back to the dining room for dinner. However, Tibi and Márta excused themselves, as they had to go home. But they allowed Erika and Györgyi to stay, provided the men would escort the girls home at the end of the evening.

After dinner, Rudi and Špinka returned with the two girls to the dance floor. During a slow tango two Russian soldiers approached Erika and Györgyi, asking them for a dance. Clearly, they were not quite sober, and the girls, looking at their Czech partners, politely said that they did not want to switch. The two Russians nodded, and slightly swaying, walked out of the dance hall.

As promised, shortly before the girl's curfew at midnight, Rudi and Špinka left the Arany Bika with them. It was fortunate that they had accompanied the girls. For just as they started down the street, the two Russian soldiers suddenly appeared, lurching away from the wall of the building. Confronting the girls, they stammered in halting Hungarian, "So you wouldn't dance with us, but would dance with these Czechs?" One of them reached out to grab Erika's shoulder.

"Hold it now," Rudi said to him in Russian, and removing his hand from Erika's shoulder, confronted the soldier. "Let's just keep it friendly, shall we?"

Špinka pulled to his full height, and facing the two soldiers said, also in Russian, "These are just teenagers, so be decent."

Though the tone of both Czechs was calm, the Russians, sensing that they were facing formidable men, backed away. Murmuring under their breath, which reeked of alcohol, they stood still, letting the four of them go on.

Erika couldn't help noting that none of them commented on the incident while the men were hurriedly walking them home; first Györgyi and then her. Even under this more lenient, post-Stalin political era, it was wise not to say anything bad about Russians. But the very fact that they did not discuss it spoke volumes of their socialist system's indoctrination. Instead, the men said, that they hoped to see the girls at their dinner, after the race.

Erika was overjoyed to see the Czech motorcycle team win the competition. They were all in a celebratory mood that evening. Both the Hungarian and Czech teams sat together at the dinner table, assessing the fine points of the event. They also discussed their next race, and the Hungarians promised to win, much to the merriment of all.

This was the last evening for the Czech team's visit, they were leaving early next morning. After dinner, Rudi accompanied Erika home. They exchanged addresses along the way and promised to keep in touch.

It was on the narrow and unlit Jókai Street, not far from Márta and Tibi's house, that Rudi fingers thread through Erika's. With his other hand Rudi turned Erika's to face him, and his lips softly touched hers.

Later, Erika wrote in her diary, *I almost swooned when I felt his hot lips on mine. I knew for sure this is what a real kiss feels like, making me weak and sensing a current race through my body. It makes me wonder whether I still have feelings for Z or is it now Rudi who holds me under his spell. We'll see how I feel when I get a letter from Rudi and when I get back to school and see Z again.*

CHAPTER 24

WHILE JUDITH AND ERIKA were vacationing, Piry and Feri were observing with curiosity and amazement the significant political changes that were happening in Hungary. They were wondering how it will affect their lives.

Earlier in the year, during the 20th Communist Party Congress, the new Soviet leader, Nikita Khrushchev, gave a "secret" speech denouncing Stalin. The secret did not remain that for long, and Hungarians eagerly anticipated political changes.

The first big change was that with the new leadership of Nikita Khrushchev, the Soviet Union and Yugoslavia had formally reestablished diplomatic relations. An article in the official newspaper, Népszabadság, reported that on June 2nd of 1955 an open the border had also been established between Hungary and Yugoslavia.

At the end of June, Radio Free Europe brought news of an uprising in Poland. On June 28, industrial workers in the city of Poznan, staged a strike, demanding wage increases, lower work quotas, and reduced food prices. They marched through the city, and their numbers swelled to 30,000 demonstrators, brandishing banners with slogans calling for "bread and freedom." They attacked local offices of the secret police and party functionaries, lynching a secret police officer.

The following day, Konstantin Rokossovsky, the Minister of Defense, ordered the Poznan military commander to suppress the uprising. Within a few days, killing sixty people and wounding over 200 rebels, order was restored in Poznan. Had the uprising continued, the Soviet army was poised to come and help reestablish peace. But the Polish leadership assured Khrushchev that Poland would remain within the Warsaw Pact (The Soviet Military Alliance of Socialist European Countries) and thus averted a military invasion of their country.

On July 27, a small article in Népszabadság carried the news that Austria had become an independent, neutral democracy. Therefore, by the following year, in the fall of 1956, the post-World War II occupying military forces, Soviet, French, British, and American, would leave Austria.

Also in July of 1955, Cardinal József Mindszenty, the beloved religious leader of the Hungarian Catholic Church, had been released from prison. He was now merely under house arrest, living in Felsőpetény, a tiny town, at about 45 km (28 miles) north of Budapest.

The biggest news of all was that Nagy Imre, Prime Minister and Chairman of the Council of Ministers of the Hungarian People's Republic since 1953, had resigned. His post was taken over by Hegedüs András, a relatively minor political figure. According to rumors, as well as Radio Free Europe, Nagy Imre had been forced out because he displeased the current Kremlin leader, Nikita Khrushchev.

"If it weren't for Nagy Imre's more lenient policies, Judith and I would still be in prison," commented Piry, as she listened to the news on the radio.

"You lucked out with Nagy being in power. We'll see what Hegedüs' rule will be like," mused Feri, and added, "I wonder whether Hegedüs had anything to do with the deposition of Rákosi".

The whole country noted that concurrent with the change in Prime Ministers, the dreaded former dictator of the country, Rákosi Mátyás, had also been removed by Moscow from his post as head of the Hungarian Communist Party.

"The whole system seems to be cracking at the seams," Piry remarked to Feri.

"It might be cracking but not breaking," Feri replied.

"With the opening of the Yugoslav Hungarian border, I wonder whether that would now be a way to leave the country," Piry pondered.

"You haven't spent enough time in jail?" Feri gave Piry his wry smile.

"You're right," she chuckled, and dropped the subject.

As if all these governmental changes had not been enough, another amazing development was the sudden release of political prisoners. Donát's oldest brother, Károly, and is wife Klára, showed up one day at Lilly and Donát's front door. They had been released from their work camps and miraculously allowed to return to their old apartment and jobs. Whoever had been living there during their years of imprisonment was gone without a trace.

Shortly after Erika and Judith returned home from their summer vacations, the whole family got together to celebrate Károly and Klára's freedom.

Back at the Jewish High School in early September, Erika was more interested in getting cast in a play during the fall term than in her studies. Although Z had graduated during the previous school year, he still seemed to be involved with activities at the school. He came to the Saturday night social events and often asked Erika to dance with him. Afterwards, he would lead her to a seat and ask about her classes. In turn, he told her that he had been refused admission to the medical school but had started to work at a medical laboratory. He was hoping this would help with his application for the following year.

Then, one of these dance evenings, he unexpectedly turned to Erika, "I'll be directing and acting as the lead in a play about the life of King David. It will be presented at the school in December. Would you like to be in it? I'm thinking of casting you as King David's wife, Abigail. She was beautiful, intelligent, and somewhat of a seer. There is a really good scene between King David and Abigail. Are you interested?"

Erika was shocked that he should offer her this important role and flattered by his comments. She replied eagerly, "Of course I am! I'd love to be in a play with you!"

"So, it's done," he said, patting Erika's hand which was grabbing the seat by her side. "I had to give the lead role, Batsheba, to a senior student. But I think you'll be good in this one. Rehearsals will start next week. They'll be Tuesdays through Thursdays, and later on also on weekends. Will you be able to stay after school? I know you live quite far.'

"I have an aunt who lives close to the school. I can stay at her home during rehearsal days."

"Great. I'll get you the rehearsal schedule next week. Let's go back to the dance floor."

Although he went off to ask another girl to dance with him, Erika felt as if she were floating on air. She hardly cared which boy she was dancing with through the night because she was dancing for joy.

◎◉◎

On Monday, Erika received a note from Uncle Martin, the history teacher, who was the co-director of the play. It detailed the rehearsal schedule that was to start the following week. Piry was none too pleased when Erika told her that she had been cast in an important role in the school play and would need to sleep over at Aunt Lilly's home after rehearsals.

"It would be late evening by the time I got home, and I would still have some homework, so I wouldn't get enough sleep for school the next day," she rationalized to her mother. Actually, after Erika had received the rehearsal schedule, before going home, she had stopped at Aunt Lilly and Uncle Donát's place. Both said, it was fine for Erika to come and stay with them.

"How about if some nights, when you're here, you would babysit Nandi, and we could go out?" Aunt Lilly suggested.

"So, we'd all benefit," Uncle Donát added, smiling broadly.

"I'll be more than happy to do that." Erika responded.

She loved spending time with her little cousin Nandi. He had recently turned seven and was fun to be with. She also realized it would be nice for her aunt and uncle to have a free evening. She had been babysitting for them over the last couple of years on Saturday evenings, and sometimes even during weekdays. So, she knew the routine of taking care of Nandi. Now, during weekdays she would have to do homework after he went to sleep but she figured that would work out just fine.

Her best friend, Forbát Zsuzsi lived just a block away. She could get permission from her parents, as well as from Erika's aunt and uncle, for Zsuzsi to come over and do homework together.

Erika felt that the greatest bonus of this arrangement was that she didn't have to go home to the tense atmosphere created by her stepfather the moment he stepped through the front door.

◉◉◉

Erika was surprised not to see Z at the first rehearsal. Instead, Uncle Martin introduced a senior student, Imi Goldstein, who had taken over the role of King David. He was a slim boy, nearly six foot tall, with curly brown hair. His lips were large and very full, his eyes small and deep set. He was more interesting looking than handsome.

When the cast questioned why, Uncle Martin simply said, "Zsigmond resigned because of differences of opinion about directing the play."

Erika had recalled friends' comments about Zsigmond (Z to her) being a difficult person. But she did not mention this to Uncle Martin or the cast members. She was disappointed but not enough to also resign. Acting was a favorite part of her life, and she wasn't about to give it up for anyone.

A couple of days into the rehearsals, while Erika was sitting in the hallway, awaiting to be called into the rehearsal hall for her scene, Imi came to sit by her. He started a conversation about the play, then quickly turned it personal. He asked, "Are you very disappointed that I'm playing the role Zsigmond was supposed to?"

Erika shrugged, "I was a bit surprised, but you're fine in the role. Why do you ask?"

"Rumor has it that you have a crush on Zsigmond."

"I like him, but that's all. He is a friend."

"Just a friend?"

"That's right."

Imi remained silent for a while, then continued the conversation asking Erika what she wanted to be when she finished high school.

"An actor, and writer," Erika replied.

There was a bright smile on Imi's face. "That's funny, so do I."

◉◉◉

Fall turned into early winter. As rehearsals continued, it was dark outside by the time they ended. Imi offered to accompany Erika to her aunt's home. They enjoyed getting to know each other. Thus, to spend more time together, instead of taking the streetcar, they walked along the broad Szent István Boulevard, discussing the rehearsal, and talking about their lives.

Imi's mother died when he was merely three years old. He had been brought up by a stepmother and had a half-brother and a half-sister. He loved his stepmother but admitted he was painfully aware that she was not his real mother.

Gradually, Erika began to confide in Imi and tell him about her unhappy home-life. She had found his reaction full of empathy. The care he showed made Erika feel close to him. Thus, it did not surprise her when a few weeks into their growing friendship he asked if she would consider becoming his girlfriend. He confessed that he had recently ended a relationship with a girl.

"She wasn't nearly as profound a thinker as you. In fact, you are the first girl I've met whom I find attractive, talented, and smart all in one package. So, I'd love to have it all," he grinned.

Erika was flattered and agreed to go steady with him. In her deepest heart of hearts, she didn't find him as attractive as Z, but his other qualities compensated for this. He was there for her, she could tell him when she was upset or happy, and she felt protected by him. Much as she loved to dance, she even accepted his dislike of social dancing. She was willing to just sit and talk during the social dance evenings at their school.

His family was orthodox, and Erika acceded to his deep-seated need to observe the Sabbath. When due to early Sunday morning rehearsals, she stayed in town over the weekend, she would meet Imi after he had attended Saturday morning's temple services with his family.

They would walk around the city talking till it was time for them to go home for dinner. This was the main meal of the day, usually served at late afternoon. Imi went home to his family, and Erika to her aunt's house to babysit.

Finally, the play was presented at their school on a Saturday night in early December. Each of them received accolades for their performances from teachers and fellow students alike. Parents also attended the show, and Erika was greatly gratified to hear Piry say, "Now I can see why you want to be an actress. You were really good."

Even Feri grunted in approval, and Judith said, grinning at her little sister, "You were better than the lead actress".

Erika introduced Imi to her family, and they congratulated him too, joking that he looked much better as a young man, than the aging King David he had played in heavy make-up and a long white beard.

To celebrate their success, Erika met Imi on Monday afternoon, after school, and they went to a small café on St. István Boulevard. It was an intimate place, with the entry door and windows covered by lace curtains. It had just a dozen small round tables where two people could sit comfortably and order an expresso and a variety of pastries. The name of the café was Ibolya, (Lilac) and the entire color scheme was that of the small blue flowers.

Imi slowly twirled his tiny spoon in the espresso cup to dissolve the three cubes of sugar he had put in there. "Now that we won't have the excuse of rehearsals, how will you stay in town?" he asked.

"I don't know. Let's celebrate and worry about that later. I'll figure something out," Erika shrugged.

In the ensuing months, Erika and Imi often met after school at the Ibolya café. Or Imi would accompany her almost all the way to her home in Ùjpest. While walking, they talked about their classes and shared the poetry and stories each had written. Sometimes, Erika mentioned how unhappy she was at home, putting up with her neurotic sister and taciturn stepfather.

In response, Imi would hug her, kiss her cheeks, and comfort her saying, "You only have to live two more years with your family. After you graduate, we could get married. You'll be eighteen and I twenty, and our parents would not be able to interfere."

Deep down, Erika wasn't sure she would want to marry Imi. But his words and arm around her shoulders or waist calmed her and enabled her to endure her home life. One of the reasons she had qualms about their future together was his possessive nature and extreme jealousy. Whenever they attended a school function, he made sure Erika paid attention only to him. At times, he reluctantly conceded to dance with her although he was not a good dancer and clearly did not enjoy it.

But if someone else tried to cut in and ask Erika for a dance, he insisted that she should say, "Sorry, we're going steady," and refuse. If Erika so much as smiled at another boy, Imi became morose and walked out of the room. Erika had to run after him and appease him, reassuring Imi that her smile was meant merely as a gesture of friendliness. She was not interested in that other young man.

A more important qualm about their relationship was that at times Imi told her he would want his wife to be a mother and a wife, not a career woman. And certainly not an actress.

When he said such things, Erika would fall silent, and Imi, knowing that she had serious career plans as an actress, would laugh and say, "I didn't really mean that, just wanted to see your reaction."

But Erika suspected that he was merely trying to keep the peace between them. Because of his orthodox religious beliefs, likely, he did mean it. At the same time, she felt so emotionally dependent on him that she could not leave him. *Things will work out somehow*, she told herself. *No rush to break up. Right now, I really need him.*

◎⦿◎

Imi often asked Erika to go to a movie with him after school. They went to mid-afternoon matinees at least once or twice a week.

"You can always say you've stayed at school to study with friends," he suggested, when at first, she protested that she couldn't do it.

Not wanting to upset him, she went along. Soon, Erika realized that his real purpose in taking her to the movies was to get physically closer to her. He chose seats in the back of the theater because in the afternoon that section was usually sparsely filled. Then, as soon as the lights went off, his hand reached for hers. As the show progressed, his hand would wonder down to Erika's knee, then glide higher onto her thigh and he would lean over and kiss her. At first on the cheeks, then a couple weeks and several movies later, he finally kissed her for the first time on her lips.

Erika knew she shouldn't be letting him touch her, even less kiss her, but his slow advances excited her. While her head warned her to stop him, her body eagerly accepted his exploring fingers.

As Spring warmed the weather, instead of going to the movies, Imi would ask Erika to go with him to the beautiful Fisherman's Bastion on the Buda side of the city.

This popular tourist attraction, designed by architect Schulek Frigyes, was built between 1899 and 1905, and renovated after WW II. The original structure was built at the site of an old rampart which had been defended against the Turkish invasion during the Middle Ages by a fishermen's guild, hence the name, Fisherman's Bastion. In fact, at that time, the guild had a fish market at the foot of the hill, and its members lived in a nearby town, called Vizivaros (Water Town).

The all-white marble bastion had seven towers, each representing one of the Magyar tribes who settled the land at the end of the 9th century. The style of the bastion was a combination of neo-Gothic and neo-Romanesque architecture, but its turrets, parapets, and winding staircases made it look more like a fairy tale castle.

Here, among the intricate marble passages, Imi could always find a private nook where his passionate kisses and attempts at fondling Erika held her in his power. Actually, it was like a game between them. Embracing Erika tightly with one arm, Imi's free hand would slowly glide up from Erika's waist to below her breast, then ever so gently, while kissing her, his fingers would start encircling a breast. But just as they cupped it, Erika would stop his kiss and push his hand away.

"No, don't" she would protest.

"I'm sorry, I got carried away," he would apologize, and lean down to kiss her again, slowly inching his hand higher and higher on Erika's body to her breast again. After many attempts, there came a moment when Erika finally let him hold her breast over her clothes because she could no longer resist the exquisite pleasure his touch aroused in her.

In order to spend time with Imi, Erika had created an intricate web of lies about her whereabouts. Thus, if her mother called her at her aunt's, and did not find her there, and then called any of her friends, asking for Erika, each would refer Piry to a different friend or location. Even her three most trusted friends, Zsuzsi, Mari, and Agi, did not quite know at whose house Erika was claiming to be studying in the afternoons when she had arranged to be with Imi.

On weekends, when Aunt Lilly asked Erika to babysit, Erika gladly did. She had been given permission for Imi to come to see her late in the evening, after she had put Nandi to sleep.

At this point, Erika had her own room in their apartment. Lilly had given up her job claiming ill health, and since she no longer used the former maid's room for work, she reestablished it as a guest room. It was furnished with a single bed, a closet, and a small night table with a lamp on it so Erika could read in bed before falling asleep.

It was here that in the couple of hours between the time Nandi had fallen asleep, and her aunt and uncle would still be out, that Imi continued his increasingly passionate exploration of Erika's body. Little by little, she let his hands roam but would stop him when she felt it would get out of her control. Each time he apologized, then started kissing and caressing her again.

◎◉◎

Erika's sixteenth birthday fell on a Wednesday. In the morning, she had final exams, which she felt had gone quite well. School ended around 1 p.m. and because it was a warm June day, Imi and Erika went swimming at the Palatinus public pools on Margit Island. Knowing how much she loved to read and recite poems, for a birthday present Imi gave Erika a book by the eminent 19th century poet, Petőfi Sándor. His gift suffused Erika with a deep love for him.

After what she considered a perfect day with Imi, Erika went home in the early evening, not expecting her family to even remember that it was her birthday. But she was pleasantly surprised. Judith hugged her and wished her happy birthday; Feri gave her a book, and Piry went to see her in her room where she was studying for next day's exam. After a hug and good wishes, Piry handed Erika a 20 Forint bill to spend as she wished.

A perfect birthday, she wrote in her diary.

To top off her birthday celebration, the next day a package arrived from her real father's brother, Uncle Tibor, the rabbi, who having survived Auschwitz, had emigrated to America. After Stalin's death, the Hungary's new government, headed by András Hegedüs, permitted 'care packages' from the West to family members in Hungary. Tibor took this opportunity to help Piry and his nieces by asking his congregation to donate clothing they no longer needed. He would bundle these up and mail them to Piry a couple of times a year.

They were beautiful American dresses for girls. They looked brand new, and whatever didn't fit Judith or Erika, Piry could sell through her business contacts, or at state-run consignment stores that specialized in selling items for private vendors. This shipment contained six dresses that fit Erika perfectly. Four were light outfits for the summer, and two wool dresses for the fall. Erika was thrilled. For the first time in her life, she had dresses that were not "hand-me-downs" from Judith. They may have come from some other girl in America, but to Erika they looked and felt new.

The following week, when she met Imi after school, she wore one of these dresses. It had a white, sleeveless top embroidered with tiny pink flowers. It was tightfitting at the waist but had a full skirt that allowed Erika to climb. The day before, Imi told her he'll be taking her on a picnic to Hüvösvölgy, a small hill on the outskirts of Buda. Erika was excited about exploring with Imi this popular excursion site. She knew the skirt would allow her to move freely.

They took a streetcar from their school and a then bus across the Danube. They then changed to a special cable car that climbed a narrow hillside road and stopped at the last station on top of the hill. This building had been painted a lovely aqua color and had a latticed wood porch that made it look more like a vacation home than a streetcar stop.

Imi had brought along a blanket and a picnic basket.

"Can I help you carry something?" Erika asked.

Imi glanced at the stylish white leather sandals Erika was wearing and said, "I'll be glad if you can climb uphill in those shoes. I'll carry these."

He led Erika away from the road where tourists gathered for their exploration of the tree covered hillside. Instead, they entered the forest, with Imi leading the way through the tall grass, thick bushes, and giant birch, oak, and fir trees all around them. They walked till the forest got even denser and there were no other people in sight.

"Here," Imi said, stopping and spreading the blanket under the shade of a large oak tree.

They settled down and Erika helped Imi unfold a couple of napkins so he could put on them the food he had brought. Wrapped in different colored napkins out came slices of rye bread, kosher salami, and pickles. He even brought a small milk bottle filled with water.

"You're a genius," Erika laughed. "This is the most perfect picnic food."

"My mother helped," Imi admitted with a grin.

"She knows about us?"

"Yes."

"Does your father?"

"There are no secrets in our family."

"Unlike at mine," Erika sighed.

"Just wait for me," Imi said, making a sandwich with the bread, salami, and a piece of pickle. He handed it to Erika. "In a few years I'll be a doctor and marry you."

Erika took the food. "Thanks. Will you marry me if I am an actress?"

"I thought you wanted to be a writer!"

"That, too. But writing takes time. I could earn a nice living as an actress while I'm also writing stories or a book."

Imi took a bite of his sandwich and grunted, "Hm. I'm not sure I'd want an actress for a wife. Let's just see what the future will bring."

Erika heard him clearly and knew that even though he was putting the subject on the back burner, he meant what he said. She also knew that no man was going to stop her from the career she chose. But he was right, this was not the time to decide. We love each other and things will get resolved as we go along, she assured herself.

When they finished lunch, Imi leaned over to kiss Erika. Within minutes they were engulfed in a passionate embrace. Time and the world around them disappeared as they wrapped arms and legs around each other. Erika had no will to protest when Imi reached under her skirt and pulled off her panties. He rolled on top her and Erika was unable to move as she felt Imi pushing up her skirt, forcing her legs apart, and then a sudden thrust of his hard membrane followed by a sharp pain between her legs.

"Stop" she cried out, but he wouldn't let go of her for a few more minutes. Then he rolled off of her but leaned over, showering her face and forehead with kisses. Erika pushed him away and he stopped, surprised. Erika moved just enough to get off the wet spot she felt under her. She glanced there and saw a bit of blood on the blanket. It was not yet the time for her period, and she thought, Imi must have injured me when he thrust himself so roughly against me. But she felt no pain, just a bit of disgust about the mess on the blanket.

"Let's go before I get into trouble at home," she said, and reached for her panties.

Imi, lying on his back, was smiling broadly. "That was wonderful. Did you feel anything?"

"What was I supposed to feel? I felt you poking hard at me. Real hard, that's what I felt."

"I'm sorry," he said, sitting up. "I didn't mean to hurt you."

Erika shrugged. "It's all right. We probably shouldn't have come here. Or at least should have had better self-control. Let's just go."

He obediently got up, poured some water over the blood on the blanket, and then folded it. "I guess I'll have to launder it when I get home," he grinned.

Erika was smoothing her dress down and combing her hair. She wanted to make sure that apart from the wrinkles on her clothes there were no signs of her lying around outdoors. She was feeling strangely uneasy about what had happened between them but decided not to say anything about it to Imi. She just wanted to get home and take a bath.

◎◉◎

At the end of the schoolyear, two weeks before Imi's graduation, Erika began to beg Piry to let her attend his graduation party. Judith decided to help Erika, by explaining to Piry that "All the kids will have their special friends with them. It would be a once-in-a-lifetime experience for Erika to go".

After a week of daily discussions, Piry finally gave in. "But you must get to Aunt Lilly's apartment by midnight," she warned Erika.

"I will, I will" Erika promised, jumping with joy.

For the party, she wore a dress sent by her uncle from America. A circular, grape green cotton skirt with a design of tiny white flowers scattered on it, topped by a white nylon blouse. It had a low-cut neckline with ruffles around it, revealing just a hint of her breasts. A couple of spaghetti straps held it on her shoulders. The colors contrasted nicely with Erika's shoulder length auburn hair. Her stiletto heeled black sandals made her a few inches taller. Thus, instead of looking up at Imi, they enabled her to face him almost at his eye level. She had tossed a light beige raincoat over her shoulders since the weatherman forecasted rain for later that night.

Imi met her at the door of the Palack Bar where the celebration was being held.

"You look stunning," he exclaimed, and Erika was overjoyed by the compliment. She felt full of confidence as they entered the bar where his friends had already gathered.

As the evening progressed, Erika felt increasingly disappointed. Imi's friends seemed rather boring from her point of view. They drank beer and talked of nothing but sports and their recent exams. They lacked the intellectual discussions Erika was used to having among her own friends. She felt relieved when midnight approached, and she needed to leave. Yet, out of consideration for Imi she said, "I'm sorry I'm making you the first one to leave."

"He shrugged, helping Erika into her raincoat, "I don't mind."

Rain was pouring in sheets outside, so they took the streetcar as far as they could. Then began to walk briskly the few blocks toward Lilly's building. Neither of them had brought an umbrella and they were rapidly getting soaked.

Imi had hardly said a word since they left the party, and Erika observed that he seemed to be in a rather sullen mood. So once again, she apologized for taking him away from the party.

"It's not that," he shrugged. They were passing by a phone booth, and he grabbed Erika's arm, "I need to tell you something, let's go in there."

With the rain pelting the glass walls of the phone booth, it felt cozy inside. Erika looked at Imi wondering what he had in mind.

"I don't know how to tell you this," he began, "so I'll just come right out with it. We must break up."

Erika stared at him as if he had hit her. "What are you talking about?"

"I didn't get high enough grades in a couple of subjects so I must spend all my time cramming for the university entrance exam next month. Until then, I can't have any distraction. We must stop seeing each other."

Erika broke into an uncontrollable sob. *The bastard,* she thought, *for all I know, he might have taken my virginity in Hüvösvölgy. And I won't know whether I'm pregnant or not for another week and half when I'm supposed to get my period. And now he wants to leave me? I can't let him. At least not till I get my period!*

Through her cascading tears, she stuttered to Imi, "Don't leave me, I can't live without you!"

Suddenly Imi became contrite. He put his arms around Erika, and said, "I'm so sorry, I don't know what came over me! Why would I even think such a thing? Truth is, I can't live without you either. You're my everything, my world. Please forgive me! I'll manage my studies. They don't even matter, only you do!"

Erika listened to his words, snuggled into his arms, and gradually stopped crying. Imi kissed the tears off her cheeks, her lips, and her eyes.

Suddenly they were both smiling.

"You forgive me? He asked.

"Yes, and I'll help you study, if I can," Erika gave him a faint smile.

I won, she gloated when she finally curled up in bed in her aunt's guest room. *But no matter how much I need Imi for the emotional support he gives me, and no matter how much I love him, I can never again trust him completely.*

CHAPTER 25

IN APRIL OF 1956, Dr. Scheiber the Director of the Rabbinical School, housed in the same building as the Jewish High School, invited Erika and Judith to his home. He told the girls, "Your Uncle Tibor and I had studied at the same Rabbinical Seminary and became close friends. He recently wrote to me that you two were attending the Jewish High School. So clearly, I have to get to know you."

They set a date, and Judith and Erika went to visit him one afternoon, after school. He lived in a lovely apartment in the center of the city, on Kun Street. He introduced the sisters to his wife, Lilla, a warm and charming woman. She brought a plateful of honey cookies to the coffee table in their living room, then left them to ogle over Dr. Scheiber's library. The living room, his office, and all other walls in their home were covered with bookcases full of books.

"Your book collection rivals a public library," Erika exclaimed, as she marveled at his crammed bookcases.

"Someday you might have the same," Scheiber responded warmly.

"I wish," Erika laughed, watching her sister walk around slowly, reading the titles of the books.

"These are not novels," Judith commented.

"No, they're books supporting my literary and Judaica research," Scheiber explained. Then he pointed at a couple of shelves, "And these are my published works."

"You wrote all these?" the girls exclaimed as they counted over twenty publications on the shelf.

"Who knows, Erika, you might write this many books too when you grow up," Scheiber smiled at her. Clearly, he had done some background check on the girls and knew of Erika's talent for writing and performing.

"I wish, or maybe I should say, I hope I will," Erika responded wistfully.

As they were leaving, Scheiber said that he wanted Erika to stay in touch with him, asking her to phone him at least once a week. "I might have some small jobs for you," he explained with a mysterious smile.

Erika followed up on his request, and within two weeks he had asked her if she would be willing to do a reading of a short story at an old age home. "Come to my office at the Rabbinical Seminary, and I'll give you the details."

Erika gladly went, because it provided her with an excuse to also meet with Imi after she had seen Dr. Scheiber. He gave Erika the address and the name of the contact person at the old age residence. Then he handed her a typed version of a short story. It was eight pages long.

"Read it for me please." Sitting behind his desk Scheiber pointed at a chair facing him. "Take your time; read it for yourself first, and then aloud to me."

Erika sat down and followed his instructions.

Scheiber listened to her reading the story aloud, then gave her some pointers about which words and phrases to emphasize, and how to produce the right overall emotional effect.

"Don't lower your voice at the end of sentences. Raise it a bit if you're going on. Use a middle tone to show that you're not finished, just pausing for effect. Only lower your voice when you're done with the whole story," he coached her.

Erika followed his instruction, and after several readings Scheiber was satisfied.

"You'll make a great actress someday," he told her. "By the way, you will get paid for this performance."

"I will?" Erika was surprised.

"Yes, they'll hand you an envelope when you're done."

Erika, grateful that Scheiber had arranged this for her, gave him a big hug. "You are so wonderful! Thank you!"

The first week in May, when Erika checked in with Scheiber by phone, he told her that he had arranged for another reading at a different old age home in Buda. Once again, with pay.

Each of these performances earned Erika one hundred Forints, which for a sixteen-year-old girl meant a fortune.

She could now buy rolls of cotton for her monthly period. She could also get her eyelashes dyed at the beauty salon a permanent black color, without having to beg her mother for the money. When dyed, she didn't have to use a daily mascara for her lashes to frame her eyes. But they faded after a while, so the money she earned to redo them, was a blessing. Erika was at the stage of her life when she wanted to look her best, and that took care and sometimes cash.

As if this had not been enough, when school closed for the summer, Dr. Scheiber notified Piry that he had arranged for Judith and Erika to go on a two-week vacation at a resort hotel in Balatonfüred. This was a favorite resort t on the northern shore of Lake Balaton, the "Hungarian Sea" as it was affectionately called for being the largest lake in Central Europe.

Erika was quick to let Imi know about her upcoming vacation. "Now you'll be able to dedicate all your time to studying for your exams," she consoled him about her leaving for a couple of weeks.

But he was not happy. "Maybe my cousin and I will visit you the weekend after my exams."

Erika was flattered that he didn't like being apart from her even for two weeks. "Do that," she said and added, "I'll give you the hotel's name before I leave so that you can let me know that you will be coming indeed. And by the way, I got my period."

◉◉◉

Balatonfüred had been first written about in 1211, in the accounting books of the Tihany Abbey, a neighboring settlement. However, even before that date, archeologists had found objects in this region showing that the Romans had lived here during their occupation of Central Europe between the 4th and 7th centuries.

In the 1700's, Balatonfüred was frequented by Europeans as a great spa with curative properties, due to its many carbonated water springs. In 1717, historians mentioned for the first time its "sourwater," a sour tasting water that bubbled up in certain springs. By 1722, the "sourwater" had been analyzed and based on its chemical composition, declared curative.

As a result, spas with accommodations for guests had been created. At first, these were modest houses, but soon new larger buildings offered rooms to visitors who came to get cured by the "magical" properties of the sourwater spas. In the 19th century the whole region surrounding Lake Balaton was developed into resort towns. During the summer season they offered swimming and sailing. In the winter, when the lake froze, ice-skating was the sport.

Along with the building of luxury hotels and vacation homes, a large state hospital had been established. A local yacht building facility was set up in the new town of Füred. At various locations, including Balatonfüred, red and white grapes were cultivated for excellent wine production.

Many successful Hungarian writers owned homes around the lake. Among these, the best-selling novelist, Jókai Mór wrote in his villa the famous novel, "Arany Ember," (The Man with the Golden Touch). The prominent poet from India, Rabindranath Tagore was invited to Hungary in 1926, to read his poems in Budapest, but ended up as a patient at the Balatonfüred State Hospital. He had spent several weeks there, recovering from a heart condition.

He was so grateful for the treatment he received, that he planted a Linden tree as a lasting gift. Other donors added more trees, till the walk grew into the Tagore Sétány, (promenade), lined with Linden trees along the shore of Lake Balaton. The local government erected a statue of Tagore in his honor. Carved into the base is a poem by Tagore which he had written for the guest book of the hospital:

When I am no longer	Leaves of thy spring,
On this earth, my tree,	Murmuring to the wayfarer:
Leth the ever renewed	The poet did love while he lived.

◎◉◎

Judith and Erika loved being at Balatonfüred. They were staying at the large, elegant Lido Hotel. Salaries were low in Hungary, but the government provided other bonuses, such as inexpensive vacation packages in the nationalized luxury hotels and converted residences of the formerly affluent class. Judith and Erika were sharing a pleasant room with two single beds and its own bathroom.

Although at some point they had gone on an excursion to see the Tagore Promenade and his statue, this was not nearly as important for them as their other activities. Both girls had friends vacationing at Balatonfüred at the same time as they did. Thus, during the day, they would meet with their own friends and go swimming and sunbathing by Lake Balaton. At times, the sisters would go with their friends to the same restaurant or nigh club, but usually they saw each other only late at night, in their room.

The first evening of their stay, Erika and a school friend, Leah, went dancing at their hotel. They met two boys there, Gabi and Iván, who, in Erika's opinion, were 'adequate' dance partners. Later she wrote in her diary: *I was missing Imi, but it was fun to be dancing with boys who liked to dance.* The second night, Judith and Erika went dancing with their friends to a nearby hotel, called SZOT (Szakszervezetek Országos Tanácsa) (National Council of Trade Unions), which was set up for office executives and had a night club with a live orchestra.

Erika, Leah, and the two boys were sitting at a table near the orchestra. Erika noticed that the drummer kept looking toward them, and when his eyes met hers, Erika felt as though he was playing for her only. He was a handsome young man, and reminded Erika of Z, because he looked so sexy while drumming. He was tall and slim and had dark curly hair. He often smiled while drumming, displaying a set of even, white teeth.

The next day, Erika spotted the drummer on the beach, but even though their eyes met, he did not say hello to her because it wasn't proper manners for people to greet each other if they hadn't been formally introduced.

Erika had befriended one of the desk clerks at her hotel, Frida, and mentioned to her when she went back to the hotel for lunch, that she would love to meet "the drummer". Frida was a small, slim woman with brown hair and a quick temper, around thirty years old. She seemed to have taken a liking to Erika. Now she smiled and said, "Come with me this afternoon to the five o'clock tea and dance at the SZOT hotel, and I'll introduce you."

Erika was totally taken aback, "Are you serious? Just like that?"

"He is a friend of mine. Actually, he had asked me about you, and whether I could introduce you to him," Frida explained.

Erika was sitting with Frida near the orchestra at the SZOT Hotel later that afternoon, and during intermission the drummer joined their table. His name was Robert. He said to Erika, "When I'm not playing, I would like to spend time getting to know you. Maybe when I'm not working, we could spend some time together?"

Erika was thrilled. Missing Imi became a background notion compared with her interest in Robert.

He was a great dancer. When Erika went to his club, she loved listening to his mesmerizing drumming but enjoyed dancing with him even more. During the following days, when they were both at the beach, they sat together, but on their own towels, and talked about life. Robert told Erika that he had recently broken up with his girlfriend and asked if Erika would be interested in taking her place.

Uncomfortable as it was for Erika, she admitted to Robert, "I actually have a boyfriend in Budapest, but who knows, perhaps as you and I get to know each other, that might change." She gave him a promising smile.

Robert smiled back, "Let's see where our friendship will take us."

In her diary, Erika wrote *I'm getting confused about my feelings. I love Imi but being around Robert is more exciting; I'm not sure why. Perhaps because he is in is twenties and more mature? Or because I find his talent as a drummer electrifying? Or maybe I just love the gentle way he escorts me home after I've gone to dance with him at his club. We talk, he sometimes takes my arm, or hand, but never pushes. Not even for a kiss. Imi wrote that he will come to visit me just for the day this coming Sunday. Let's see how I will feel then.*

Sunday morning, Erika and Robert spent time at the beach by the Balaton. As they were about to leave, Robert said to her, "My father is arriving on the train from Budapest in the early afternoon, so I'll be showing him around and won't be able to see you for the rest of today."

"That's fine," Erika replied, "I meant to tell you, my boyfriend is arriving later this afternoon with a couple of his friends, so I wouldn't be able to see you either."

"There is only one train coming this afternoon so they must all be on the same one. We could go to the train station together. I'll take you there on my motorbike," Robert offered.

Erika knew, this would give Robert a chance to take a look at Imi, as he seemed to be coming on the same train as Robert's father. She would also be able to compare the two men in her life. "That would be great," she smiled brightly at Robert.

Imi arrived with his best friend, Tomi, and the latter's girlfriend, Juli, and the four of them went straight to the beach. Erika did not spot Robert and his father at the train station, but at this point she didn't care. She was happy to be with Imi and rekindle their love for each other. But instead of talking about love, Imi chose to talk about politics. He seemed to have acquired a new interest in a Writers Organization whose members were keen on political discussions. Erika listened to Imi although actually she had no interest in politics. After a couple of hours, Imi suggested that they go for a walk. They left Tomi and Juli at the beach and headed into the nearby woods.

While walking, Imi continued his account to Erika about the increasing activities of the Writers Association. "It seems that all over the country, university students are establishing Writers Associations and are demanding freedom of speech in newspapers and magazines. Something is brewing on the political scene."

"Are you taking part in any of this?" Erika was concerned.

"Not at the moment but maybe later. Right now, I am thinking of something totally different," he grinned at Erika.

He led her deep into the forest and spread their beach towels under a tree. Erika let Imi make love to her, although she felt nothing apart from his pressure against her. When she put her panties on again, she noticed that she had been bleeding slightly unto the towel.

"It's nothing," Imi said, "you're just very sensitive there."

Erika didn't like the casual way Imi dismissed her bleeding. *He should have at least apologized for causing me to bleed*, she thought but said nothing to him. She couldn't help feeling that his main reason for coming to visit her was to get laid, and she didn't like the idea. But accepted that it was a part of their relationship. They returned to the beach to meet up with Imi's friends for dinner. After a light meal at Erika's hotel, the visitors returned to the train station and took the last train back to Budapest.

Erika had two more days left of her Balaton vacation. Monday was Robert's day off, and he offered to take Erika on his motorbike to the nearby village of Füred. It was a lovely, small hamlet, and they strolled around its beach, its parks, and gift shops. For Erika, the most exciting part of their excursion was that she had to sit on his motorcycle close behind Robert and put her arms around him during the rides.

That evening, they went dancing, accompanied by her friends, Leah, and the two boys, Gabi and Iván. Although Erika also danced with the boys, her partner was mostly Robert. He had great rhythm and Erika loved swaying with him in total harmony.

When the evening ended, Robert walked deliberately slowly with Erika to her hotel. The two boys and Leah went ahead of them, and Erika found herself and Robert alone along the narrow lane that led to a side entrance of the hotel lobby.

"Hold a minute," Robert said, and stopped Erika by putting his hands on her shoulders, turning her to face him. "You'll be going home tomorrow. Can I get a kiss before you leave?"

He leaned down, and cradling Erika's face between his palms, gently touched her lips with his. Then kissed her again, more fervently. Erika truly enjoyed his lips on hers, and they stood embracing and kissing with increasing passion, till Erika gently pushed him away.

"We must stop," she asserted, then added, "When we meet tomorrow, if you give me your mailing address, I shall write to you from Budapest. How much longer will you be staying at the Balaton?"

"Throughout the summer. Then I'll be going back to the Music Academy in Budapest, for further training. Ultimately, I want to put together my own dance band as well as play with classical orchestras around the country," Robert explained.

"That will be an exciting career!" Erika smiled at him and asked, "Will we see each other again in Budapest?"

"Yes. And also, tomorrow when you leave. My band and I will be taking the same train you'll be on for just one stop. We'll be playing at Almád, the next town. So, we can say good-bye then."

Before going to bed, Erika wrote in her diary, *Perhaps I am infatuated with Robert, but Imi seems to be my permanent mate. He and I know each other well, and he gives me emotional support to be able to tolerate my family till I finish high school and can leave. But who knows what the future will really bring.*

Before Erika returned to Budapest, she had phoned Imi and asked him to come to her aunt and uncle's apartment. They were away on vacation and had left a key with the concierge for Erika to spend the night there. She was getting into Budapest late in the evening, and it would have taken her another hour to get to Ùjpest, including walking to their home alone, past midnight.

Thus, for the first time, Erika and Imi were alone in a place where they could be naked during their lovemaking. Imi was gentle and attentive.

"You are so beautiful," he whispered, caressing Erika's breasts, kissing her nipples, then slowly sliding his lips down her belly to between her legs.

"Let's shut the light," Erika requested, feeling shy about Imi's exploration of her body.

Imi stopped and looked at Erika, "Are you sure? I love seeing all of you like this."

"Yes, please." Erika turned her face away.

Imi quickly jumped up. Earlier, they had pulled the blinds down and now as Imi had shut the lights off the room became pitch dark. He snuggled back to Erika's side and continued caressing her body, his fingers roaming freely, touching all her sensitive spots. Then slowly, gently, he rolled on top of her. Erika could feel his member sliding into her and moving in and out of her at first slowly, then with increasing speed.

His movements felt better than in their previous encounters. Suddenly, Erika was inundated by an intense pleasure bordering on pain in her loin. Imi moved faster and faster, and cried out along with Erika, then collapsed over her, burying his face in Erika's neck. They stayed motionless for a while.

During this calm spell Erika analyzed what had just happened to her. *Through our lovemaking my whole being had been suffused with a pleasure I had never felt before. For the first time in all my years of being abused by my stepfather, or even during our prior lovemaking with Imi, I had never known what these men were after, until now. I have finally discovered and understand the magic power that draws a man and a woman together in this union. Nothing can compare with the extasy that overwhelmed my entire body and mind in those moments.*

Imi must have figured out what Erika had just experienced, because he held her close till she finally said, "That was fantastic. But I'm afraid you will have to go home now."

Imi gently kissed her on the cheeks, and they rolled out of bed. Erika got into pajamas and Imi put on his clothes. She was opening the front door to let him out when Imi said to her, "My temple is sending me on a two-week vacation to Lake Balaton."

"How can you be leaving when I just got back? And you're only telling me this now?" Erika was furious.

"I didn't make a scene when you went on vacation, so just give me the same right!" Imi was indignant.

"Fine. Go!" Erika pouted. Pushing him out the door, she slammed it shut.

As she lay in bed, waiting to fall asleep, Erika reconciled her feelings of anger by telling herself, *his absence will allow me to figure out whether to stay with him or break up and try a new relationship with Robert, the drummer.*

Two days later, Erika wrote a note to Robert. But she had no word from him. By the time Imi returned, Erika figured that she would stay with Imi, and that was just fine. It seemed that they were meant to be together.

◎◉◎

During Imi's absence, and even after his return, the entire month of August, Erika was working for Dr. Scheiber. After her return from Lake Balaton, she had asked Scheiber if he could find her a paying job, and he offered one to her. She was to go daily to the Országos Széchényi Könyvtár (National Széchényi Library), and scan through newspapers, dating back about 50 years to the present, searching for poems by famous Hungarian poets that perhaps had not been published anywhere else. Scheiber knew that Erika was familiar with the most renown poets, due to her love of reading and excellent literature classes at her schools, so she would not miss a work by them.

"How would I know whether they had been published in other places or not? Erika asked.

"If you find a poem, copy the name and date of the publication, the page number it is on, and the work itself. I'll find out the rest," Dr. Scheiber instructed her.

Erika loved the job. She enjoyed entering the huge, beautiful building near the Parliament, and the palpable quiet of the reading rooms. She was immensely grateful to Dr. Scheiber for providing her with some income. During her research she did find a few poems by a well-known writer, Ady Endre, and wondered whether these had also been published elsewhere. But this was for Dr. Scheiber to determine after she had given him all the information he requested.

◎⦿◎

School started on September 3rd, and much to her regret, Erika had to stop working at the Széchényi Library. She had plenty of homework, plus she got a role in the school play that required her to stay at her Aunt Lilly's place after rehearsals. Actually, she loved the arrangement, for it enabled her to continue meeting with Imi, before or after rehearsals. He had not been accepted at the Medical Faculty, and was working at a photography studio, learning to develop film, and to print photos in the darkroom.

Two weeks after school started, on September 17, Imi met Erika after her rehearsal. While accompanying her to her aunt's house, he told Erika, "Today, the Writers' Association demanded the re-installment of Nagy Imre into the Communist Party, as well as giving him back his position as head of the government."

"Have you become a member of the Writers' Association?" Erika asked.

"No, but news gets around. You know I am also a writer; I've got my ear to the sources."

"So, what do all those demands mean? They'll just get the members in trouble."

"No, listen, something is stirring in this country. During the summer, the Petőfi Circle, a literary organization, was shut down by the authorities for saying some 'wrong things'. But now it's reopened again. They'll be holding a meeting on September 26th to discuss 'Issues of the Economic Leadership.' All this is highly unusual."

"I'm not going to concern myself with politics," Erika declared. She stopped on the sidewalk, dropped her school briefcase and reaching up pulled Imi's lips to hers. After their kiss she laughed, "This is what I'm interested in."

Imi just smiled.

Piry and Feri heard on the evening news by Kossuth Radio that Rajk László, a former Minister of the Interior, and three others, who had been tried and executed in October 1949 for allegedly betraying their country and the Party, will be rehabilitated and reburied.

"The government is really going crazy," Feri grumbled. "First, they forced them to confess crimes they had not committed. Then killed them for the crimes they did not commit. And now they'll rebury them as heroes at the Kerepesi Cemetery, where the nation's most revered are laid to rest."

"There is something definitely going on with the government," Piry agreed. "Let's see where they'll lead us."

◎◉◎

The reburial took place on October 10th. The Kerepesi Cemetery, located in the 8th district of Budapest, known as József Város, (Joseph City) was in a neglected, rough neighborhood. Although the event had been barely publicized, it was attended by over a hundred thousand people. The crowd stood in silence and watched, even though there were no speeches accompanying the burials.

Afterwards, the main newspaper of Hungary, Szabad Nép, (Free Nation), carried a front-page article entitled "Never Again," praising the deceased Communist Party members who had been unjustly accused and executed.

◎◉◎

While this was happening in Hungary, in Poland the leadership demanded the removal of two Soviet members from their government. They also reinstalled Wladyslav Gomulka as the First Secretary of the Party, in effect the leader of the country. Alarmed that the Poles were trying to leave the Soviet Block, a high-level delegation of the Soviet Central Committee, headed by Nikita Khrushchev, flew to Warsaw. The delegation put the Soviet troops stationed in Poland on the alert in case they were needed. After tense negotiations, the Soviets accepted that the Poles wanted more autonomy in their internal affairs. In turn, the Poles assured them that their country would remain within the Soviet bloc. The delegation returned to Moscow satisfied, having no notion that they were on the verge of losing Hungary.

The politically aware Hungarian intelligentsia, and university students around the country, learned via Radio Free Europe of the reforms that were taking place in Poland. They wanted similar changes in Hungary. Students at the Technical University in Budapest held a meeting and drew up a 16- point summary of their demands. Included in the list were *Freedom of Speech, Multi-Party Elections, National Independence,* and the *Withdrawal of Soviet Troops Stationed in Hungary.* They decided that the next day, on October 23rd, they will go on a peaceful march in support of the political victory in Poland. They will end the march at the main radio station, Magyar Rádio, where they will request to have their 16-point demands broadcast.

At mid-day on October 2 nd, the Party leadership forbade the march. But by 2:30 p.m. they decided to allow it. Starting at 3 p.m., three different groups took to the streets. One headed for the statue of a Polish general, Josef Bem.

During the previous century, in the year 1848, the Hungarians revolted against the Habsburgs' rule of their country. General Josef Bem came from Poland to fight alongside the Hungarian rebels. He obtained legendary status in Hungary when he defended Transylvania with a small unit against overwhelmingly large Austrian troops. The Hungarian Socialist Government had a statue erected in Bem's honor in Budapest, with a large plaza in front of it. It was to this location that the first group of demonstrators arrived and were joined by the second group.

The second group of demonstrators first went to pay tribute to the statue of Petőfi Sándor, the preeminent poet who lost is life fighting during the 1848 Hungarian uprising. Here, a well-known actor recited the "National Song," a poem written by Petőfi. They also read aloud the 16-point demand to an enthusiastic crowd. When this group joined the first one at the Bem statue, they took a Hungarian flag and cut out the Soviet designed hammer and wheat stalk emblem from its center and held it up for the crowd to see.

The people went wild, shouting "Russki Go Home!" and "Freedom for Hungary!" Perhaps this was the true starting moment of the 1956 Hungarian revolution, when they took their ancient tricolor flag and cut out the Soviet imposed emblems from its center.

By this time the crowd had swollen to about two hundred thousand people, and decided to march to the Kossuth Lajos Plaza, where they demanded to hear Nagy Imre give a speech. After a two hour wait, instead of encouraging words, András Hegedűs, the current Prime Minister, came to face the crowd asking them to disperse and go peacefully home.

The third group of demonstrators marched to the Hungarian Parliament building where they wanted to read their list of demands.

Imi, having witnessed the march to the Petőfi statue, did not follow the crowd. He rushed off to meet with Erika.

Not suspecting anything about the day's impromptu events, after school Erika had gone to get a haircut and was now waiting for Imi at their usual meeting place, the Ibolya Café. He was late and she became quite concerned.

Nursing her espresso, she could see through the café's windows that the Nagykörút (Grand Blvd) was filled with people marching and waving flags along with truckloads of men and women who were racing down the broad avenue, shouting slogans against the Soviets and demanding freedom for Hungary. People also kept rushing into the Café, bringing news of marchers heading toward the Magyar Radio Station on nearby Brody Street to have their 16-point demands broadcast.

Hearing these unimaginable demands and news, Erika wrote into her notebook, *I can feel the heat in the air, the energy, the passion, like something big is about to happen.*

Finally, Imi arrived, panting, as if he had been running. "I don't want any coffee. We'd better start you on going home, who knows what may happen later," he advised.

So many people were roiling around on the streets that they could barely advance. A truck rolled out from behind the National Theater, filled with youngsters shouting slogans.

Erika saw broad smiles on people's faces, and from many apartment windows the tricolor Hungarian flags fluttered in the wind with a hole cut in their center. A light fog moistened the sidewalks, enough for all this color to reflect on the pavements.

Erika felt a strange elation as she observed people's wild energy all around her. *This is what freedom must feel like*, she thought, as she and Imi slowly wound their way through the masses down Dózsa György Avenue toward the Városliget (City Park).

Erika knew that Imi's reason for walking her home across the park was to have a bit of a necking session with her in a private spot there. But this was not the night for it. Throngs of people were moving alongside them toward the Stalin statue that dominated the entrance to the park at the end of the avenue.

"Let's watch," Erika suggested when they entered the park. She pulled Imi over to a bench just a little way off the 'main event'. They stared, fascinated, as the huge crowd milled around the Stalin statue and chanted for its demolition. Just down the street from the Stalin statue was the headquarters of the ÁVO, the secret police. Surprisingly, not a single ÁVO man seemed to be present as people showed up with tools to topple the statue.

Created by the sculptor Mikus Sándor during the height of the "socialist realism" style of art, the 8-meter (26 feet) tall bronze statue stood on a 10-meter (29 feet) plinth. It portrayed Stalin as a speaker, standing tall, with his right hand on his chest. For added height, the statue had been placed on an eighteen-meter wide (59 feet) pedestal that displayed in relief the Hungarian people welcoming Stalin, their leader.

Erika and Imi watched as the demonstrators climbed up the pedestal and placed a thick steel rope around Stalin's neck. Others, arriving in trucks with metal-cutting blowpipes and oxygen cylinders, set to work above the bronze boots. Erika and Imi stared mesmerized as an hour later the huge statue slowly fell off its pedestal.

"Time to leave," Imi said emphatically and walked Erika to the next streetcar stop.

◎◉◎

Piry and Judith had been visiting a relative and got home shortly after Erika.

"People were handing each other pieces of the Stalin statue," Piri told Erika with amazement.

Erika said nothing.

The next morning, Piry woke her daughters at five a.m. "There is fighting in the center of Pest. You can't go to school. Get dressed, we don't know what may happen next."

Erika wrote in her diary on October 24, 1956: *I will never forget this day; our cold dark rooms with all the shutters to the street closed, and in my vivid imagination hearing the rumble of crowds and gunfire in the distance. It's a good thing that Imi and I postponed our meeting till tomorrow! I hope he got home all right.*

Erika thought, it was eerie for all four family members, as well as for Maria, the maid, to be sitting in the darkened dining room. As usual, only this room was heated, and they all sat around the table listening to the official Hungarian Radio. It was repeatedly asking citizens to calm down and return to their homes. It claimed that the 'insurrection' had been stopped. When Maria left to do her work around the house, Feri tuned in to Radio Free Europe.

This station had an entirely different story. First, it described how the fighting started: "On the night of October 23, students from the Technical University, along with a large crowd, marched from the Ben statue to the Hungarian Radio Station on Bródy Sándor Street, to have their Sixteen Point declaration broadcast. They were refused entry to the station. Fully armed ÁVH men, (Domestic State Authority) confronted the students and the crowd in front of the building, ordering them to disperse. When they did not, at 8 p.m. Gerő Ernö, First Secretary of the Communist Party, delivered a rigorous party-line speech over the radio. He finished by menacing that those who were not with the current government, were enemies of the country and will be dealt with accordingly.

From many apartments near the radio station residents placed their home radios into their windows, so the crowd below could hear the amplified rhetoric by Gerő. His message so enraged the crowd, that they attacked the radio building, trying to gain entrance. When the students forcibly got inside, the ÁVH men used tear gas and machine guns to fire at the crowd outside, wounding many and killing several people. The students inside the building were arrested and taken by unmarked cars to an unknown destination.

In response, the demonstrators attacked the gun wielding ÁVH men, grabbing their guns and shooting back at them. A unit of the Hungarian Army from a nearby barracks was quickly dispatched to the scene. But when the soldiers realized that the ÁVH was attacking unarmed demonstrators, they turned their guns on the ÁVH soldiers."

"That's why they're called it Néphadsereg, (People's Army) because they're defending the ordinary citizens," Erika commented to her family, bringing a grin from Judith and Piry.

But Feri was not amused. "Young lady keep your mouth shut or you'll be sent to bed," he growled at her.

Erika nodded to him in silence, and they all continued to listen to Radio Free Europe.

"News of the shooting at the Magyar Radio Station quickly spread across the city. Demonstrators raided ammunition depots and were supplied with weapons by soldiers of the Hungarian Army. Soon riots erupted in other cities around the country and by morning the whole nation was embroiled in the uprising. The government had moved its broadcasting to the Parliament building. While radio announcers urged the protestors to calm down and disperse, Soviet tanks had surrounded the Parliament, ostensibly to protect it. Stay tuned for more news. We'll bring it to you as it happens."

The fighting continued throughout the week, not only in the capital but the rest of the country as well. In the quiet residential area where Erika's family lived, there was no fighting, only the noise of gunfire from the center of Újpest. During this period Erika and Piry were able to walk down the street a couple of times to a nearby phone booth. Piry was calling her sister, Lilly, anxious to know how she and her family were doing. Lilly assured her that they were fine, staying at home and hoping that the fighting would stop.

Erika phoned both Imi and Dr. Scheiber. Both reassured her that they were all right.

Dr. Scheiber promised to come and visit as soon as the fighting stopped, and normal car traffic was allowed to resume. He said, when he'll come, he will take Judith and Erika into the city, to visit their friends. The anticipation of eventually being able to go into town enabled Erika to stay calm and suppress her longing for Imi.

She occupied herself by helping Maria and her mother with household chores. Because they had no homework, both Erika and Judith used their free time reading books lent to them by their Aunt Magda next door.

By October 27th, a new government had been formed. On popular demand, Nagy Imre was nominated as the Prime Minister. He announced a cease fire and started negotiations for the withdrawal of the Soviet troops from Hungary. There was a euphoric atmosphere in the country at the notion that Hungary might be freed of the Soviet occupation. Nagy also declared the abolishment of the one-party system. Within a few days a half a dozen different parties sprung into existence.

Piry and Feri, sitting in the dining room late that evening, were listening to these news, and Feri commented, "Many of these new parties are close to being fascists; and even if they're not outright fascists, they're certainly antisemitic."

"Yes, probably the only advantage to living under communism has been that it isn't openly antisemitic." Piry responded, then sighed, "Let's see what will happen. If the country really manages to get rid of the Soviets, maybe it will open the borders, and we could be able to leave."

"I doubt Hungary can win against the mighty Soviet empire," Feri declared.

"You're probably right." Piry sighed and added, "The Western countries certainly won't help us, despite all the encouragement by Radio Free Europe to keep on fighting.

As if Piry's words were prophetic, on October 29th, just two days after Hungary announced its negotiations for independence from the Soviet Union, the world had another international crisis to worry about.

"Radio Free Europe" reported, "On October 29, the Egyptian president, Gamal Abdul Nasser, blocked ships from going through the Suez Canal. Likely, he did it under Soviet influence, to divert the world's attention from Hungary's revolution to this far more important issue: the transportation of oil to Europe through the Suez Canal.

In response, Israel, England, France, and even the U.S. attacked Egypt, hoping to take control once again of the Suez Canal, this vital waterway for Europe."

Hearing the news, Piry commented, "Who cares about Hungary when Western Europe might be deprived of its precious oil supply?"

"Russians are the world's best chess players. I wouldn't be surprised if they indeed created the Suez crisis s they could handle Hungary without attention. So, let's just sit tight and see what happens. It's late. Coming to bed?" Feri asked coyly.

◉◉◉

Despite the Suez Canal crisis, the Soviets did seem to be withdrawing their troops from Hungary and there was a feeling of elation in the country. *We had won! The Russians are leaving!*

On October 31st, Premier Nagy broadcast that Hungary would withdraw from the Warsaw Pact. This was a move totally contrary to the way the Polish government had handled their uprising in Poznan during the summer. The Poles had assured their Soviet partners that even though they wanted more autonomy, they would remain within the Warsaw Pact.

According to Radio Free Europe, Kádár János, the General Secretary of the Party, was in complete disagreement with leaving the Warsaw Pact and broke with Nagy. He gave up his government post and left Budapest. Secretly, he established a rival government in Eastern Hungary, supported by the Soviet military that was still stationed there.

CHAPTER 26

ON SUNDAY, NOVEMBER 4ᵀᴴ a pale faced Piry awakened her daughters at dawn. "Get dressed! The Soviets attacked Hungary; tanks are rolling into Budapest, and fighting had broken out all over the country again. There is no telling what will happen now."

Erika burst into a sob. She had such high hopes for living in a free democracy and now saw it all crushed under the Soviets' boots.

"Stop bawling," Judith snapped at her. "That won't help a thing. Hurry, get dressed."

As soon as the sisters changed into their daytime clothes, they joined their parents in the dining room and listened to the radio broadcast that kept repeating the same message in Hungarian and in English:

Itt Nagy Imre beszél, a Magyar Népköztársaság minisztertanácsának elnöke. Ma hajnalban szovjet csapatok támadást indítottak fővárosunk ellen azzal a nyilvánvaló szándékkal, hogy megdöntsék a törvényes magyar demokratikus kormányt. Csapataink harcban állnak! A kormány a helyén van. Ezt közlöm az ország népével és a világ közvéleményével!

"This is Nagy Imre, President of the Council of Ministers for the Hungarian People's Republic. Today, at dawn, Soviet forces attacked our capital, clearly with the aim of toppling the legal, democratic Hungarian Government. Our troops are fighting. The government is in place. I am informing about this event our people and the whole world."

The message was repeated in several languages, followed by playing the Hungarian National Anthem.

Erika and her family sat by the radio, stunned by this announcement.

"It's over," Piry said. "Back to communism as before."

"I guess the factory won't open for work tomorrow," was Feri's response.

Piry rose and went to prepare breakfast for the family. Judith returned to her room, and Erika sat unable to move. She was wondering whether Imi and Dr. Scheiber were safe during this new attack in the center of the city. Feri tuned to Radio Kossuth to hear more news. There was no news, only classical music.

Radio Free Europe reported that Nagy Imre had fled to the Yugoslav embassy, but the fighting was continuing between the Hungarian freedom fighters and the Soviets troops. Kádár János had returned with the Soviet army and was declared as the new President of the Council of Ministers. Under his new government all Hungarian radio stations began to broadcast again, incessantly asking for calm and peace. But the fighting went on for a couple more weeks.

"Perhaps the freedom fighters are hoping that Radio Free Europe is telling the truth, and the West will come and give the Hungarians some military support." Feri commented to Piry.

But it had not happened. Gradually, the rebels realized that the West was not coming to help them, and they stopped fighting. Order was restored in Budapest and the rest of the country.

Erika was finally able to call Imi, on Sunday, November 18.

He told her, "The Soviets are rounding up the young people they had captured during the fighting and transporting them to work-camps in the Soviet Union. They're also just grabbing young men off the streets and taking them. My parents decided I need to leave the country. I almost left with a guide a couple of days ago, but the deal fell through so I'm still here. But please, please, try to come into town so I can see you before I have to leave."

"What do you mean leave? You want to step on a mine at the border?"

"Haven't you heard that during the revolution the mines had been removed from the border between Hungary and Austria? That was one of the first things our border guards did as an act of freedom. Freedom to be able to cross from our country to the next, like they can in Western Europe."

"Don't go before I see you," Erika pleaded with him. "Dr. Scheiber visited us last Friday and told us, now that traffic is allowed again, he'll come to take Judith and me to Pest, to stay with our Aunt Lilly."

Indeed Dr. Scheiber showed up with a car at Erika's house on Monday and promised Piry he would take good care of her daughters.

"This is history in the making," he explained to Piry over a cup of espresso. "I want Judith and Erika to see the end result of the revolution. It is now officially called the Anti-Revolution, because it was fought against the socialist system which the Soviets established after deposing the Czars."

"I just hope they don't go to places where they can get into trouble," Piry sighed.

"They'll be fine. Even the streetcars and buses have started to run. They'll stay a few days and come home," Dr. Scheiber promised.

It was a sunny but cold day, as early winter had sat in. Pulling her winter coat and her scarf around her neck tighter, Erika asked Scheiber to drop her off at her friend Marianne's apartment building. Judith went on with

Dr. Scheiber to see her friends. Erika happily raced up the three flights of stairs and practically fell through the door when Marianne's aunt opened it.

"I kiss your hand," Erika used the formal greeting between a young person and an adult, "is Marianne home?"

"Come in, you must be Erika," the aunt said, and quickly closed the front door behind them. "Marianne is not here. She disappeared three days ago."

Erika leaned against the hallway wall in shock. "Where could she be?"

"Hopefully in Vienna by now, with her father."

"So, you think Marianne was able to cross the border?"

"Her mother had been freed from prison, and I have a feeling they left together," the aunt replied.

Erika took in this information and sighed. "Thank you so much for telling me this. May I come by again or call you in a couple of days, to find out if you know for sure that Marianne had made it to her father in Vienna."

"Just call me" the aunt smiled and jotted down her phone number on a piece of paper.

Erika stumbled down the three flights of stairs as if her shoes had suddenly been filled with led. She looked for a phone booth on the street, and anxiously dialed Imi's number. *What if he had also left already?* But Imi answered, and they agreed to meet in front of his house. Within twenty minutes Erika ran into Imi's arms.

He kissed her, and said, "Let's go for a walk."

While they cruised around the narrow streets of his neighborhood, Imi said gravely, "You came just in time. Two of my cousins and I have arranged to leave tomorrow. But frankly, I don't want to leave without you. I can't. You are my life! Please come with me."

"How can I?" Erika countered.

"Because you hate living at home, and once we're in Vienna we could lie about your age and get married. We could start a whole new life together in the West! We could go to America and become whatever we want. This is our only chance! I can't live without you, and I can't stay here, so you've got to come with me!

Erika listened, argued, but after a while decided that Imi was right. She thought, I can't live without him either and if he left, my home-life would be unbearable without him.

"I'll go," she said simply.

"Fantastic! Meet me tomorrow morning at ten in front of the Opera building."

On her way to Aunt Lilly's apartment, Erika saw buildings destroyed by canon fire and streets torn up by tanks. Many building facades were peppered with bullet holes. As Erika observed the impact of the Soviet forces that crushed the Revolution, she realized that Imi was right. They had to leave. She stopped along the way at her friend Zsuzsi's apartment, but no one was home. *I hope they haven't left without Zsuzsi saying goodbye to me! I'll stop by their place again tomorrow before I meet Imi*, Erika thought.

She had a hard time sleeping that night on a mattress on the floor, next to Judith's bed in the guest room. She kept mulling over her decision to leave, wondering how her mother and sister will be affected by her disappearance. Erika knew she couldn't tell anyone about her intention to leave because they would prevent her from doing it.

Thus, she tossed and turned most of the night, alternately feeling terrible about not telling, and apprehensive but excited about leaving. Finally, it was time for her to get up. She told Judith and her aunt that she was spending the day with a school friend, Fisk Agi, and hurried off. Much to her relief, when she stopped by Zsuzsi's apartment, she and her family were at home. Erika whispered her good-bye to Zsuzsi and got on a streetcar to make her rendezvous on time with Imi.

◎◉◎

We'll be meeting my cousins at the Keleti (Eastern railway station)," Imi explained after hugging her.

Erika noted that Imi carried only a small briefcase with him for the trip. She had only her handbag. As they traversed by streetcar across the city, with each familiar street they left behind, Erika felt an increasing sense of detachment. As though she were traveling into the future, discarding the past along the way. When they got to the Keleti train station, there was no sign of Imi's cousins.

"Let's go there," Imi pointed to a small café house near the station. He ordered two espressos, and they settled down to wait. When no one showed up in the next half an hour, they went to a phone booth where Imi could call his cousins.

When he got off the phone, he told Erika, "They couldn't make it today and suggested that we meet at 8 o'clock tomorrow morning at the Keleti train station. That's the train that goes toward the Austrian border".

"So, what should we do, go home?" Erika asked.

"If we do, will you be able to get away and be at the train station that early in the morning?" Imi asked.

"I'm not sure," Erika replied pensively.

"Then I suggest that we find a hotel for the night. That way they'll think you've left already, and we won't have a problem in the morning."

Erika thought this as perfectly logical, so they started leafing through the phone book. They called several hotels in the area, but none answered the phone.

"They're probably closed, due to the situation," Imi said. "Let's try some others."

Finally, the clerk at the front desk of the Vörös Csillag Szálló (Red Star Inn) in Buda answered the phone.

"They're open and have rooms available," Imi said.

They had to take a streetcar and then cross the Danube from the Pest to the Buda side by bus and take the *fogas*, a cog wheel railway, up the hill. They couldn't help noticing that they were the only passengers on the fogas; perhaps because it was getting dark, and this was an excursion area of the city.

"Here you are," said the ticket collector, as he they reached the last stop of the train. It's just a short walk from here," he added, as he watched the young couple descend from the train. *No doubt honeymooners*, he thought, but of course he wouldn't ask.

The sight of the Vörös Csillag Szálló took Erika's breath away. Its facade had the grandiose architecture of an old, huge Hungarian manor house, with front porticos and balconies overlooking the city. But inside, it was totally modern. It had twenty-three rooms of which nine contained two beds, and the rest had single beds. The desk clerk asked for their identification booklets. Seeing that they had different last names, he assigned two single rooms to them, though with a connecting door between the rooms. Each room had central heating and its own bathroom with running hot water, which Erika thoroughly appreciated.

"Let's go have dinner," Imi suggested.

There were no other guests in the elegant dining room, and the headwaiter plus a waiter attended the young couple as if they were important visitors.

After dinner, each went to his and her room. Erika showered, then slipped into Imi's room. He was already in bed, waiting for her.

They held each other and made love most of the night, pouring into passion their unspoken fears about leaving their families and home forever. Finally, they slept a couple of hours and woke at dawn. They dressed, and watched from the terrace on their floor the sunrise paint the entire city red.

"Budapest is so beautiful," Erika sighed, her eyes moistened by tears.

"It's a great way to remember it," Imi consoled her.

After coffee and croissants in the dining room, they left the hotel and took the fogas downhill. Although order had been restored, not too many people seemed to be going to work. Imi and Erika observed the lack of passengers on the bus they had to take across the Danube, on Margit Bridge to Pest. Even the other bus toward the Keleti Pályaudvar (Eastern train station) was half empty.

"I'll run ahead to make sure the boys don't leave us," Imi suggested as they got off the bus a few blocks from the train station. "Meet us there," he ordered Erika and took off.

When Erika entered the station a couple of minutes later, to her great shock she did not see any cousins with Imi. It was his father who was standing in front of Imi. When he spotted Erika, he burst into a furious tirade.

"How could you do this?! Have you lost your mind? Your mother had attempted suicide, and your sister and father have been looking for you at all your friends' homes! Don't you know that you can't just disappear?!" Turning to Imi, he shouted, "What were you two thinking?! That Erika could just run off with you? She is under-age!"

Erika and Imi remained silent, looking at the raging man.

He continued, "Imi, your cousins are waiting for you on the train, here is your ticket, now get moving! And you, Erika, are coming with me! I'm taking you home where you belong!"

Erika looked at Imi and knew that there was no way she could leave with him. His face showed it. She threw her arms around his neck and pulled his face down for a last kiss. "Have a safe journey," she murmured and tore herself away from him.

"Bye Dad," Imi kissed his father's hand, and after one last glance at Erika turned and headed for the stairs up to the train.

Erika and Imi's father watched Imi disappear into the compartment. Reaching a seat by a window he stuck his face against it and waived as the train emitted a loud whistle and started to roll out of the station. Erika thought, *there goes half my soul with him. But not forever. I will find a way to leave, and we shall be together again.* Turning to Imi's father, she said, "My home is in Ùjpest, too far to go there. I'll go to Dr. Scheiber's house, he is a close family friend. He'll take me home by car."

Imi's father accompanied Erika all the way to the apartment building on Kun street and watched her walk up the staircase before heading home with his own concern about his son's escape from the country.

Erika had no idea how she managed to drag herself up the three flights of stairs to the Scheibers' apartment. But just before collapsing, she rang their doorbell. Aunt Lilla opened the door, shouting, "Here you are, you rascal!" She caught Erika in her arms and pulled her inside.

As though a damn had broken in Erika, she burst into a howling sob, her mind racing, asking herself, *Why am I screaming, oh yes, I know, Imi is gone, he is gone, he is gone, what am I going to do now?!*

Lilla, as well as Scheiber, held Erika and let her sob, while they gently led her into the living room and made her sit on the sofa. From another room Erika saw Judith appear, and thought, what is she doing here?

Then the realization hit her, *it wasn't my stepfather who was looking for me with Judith, it was Dr. Scheiber who was with her.* She suddenly felt better. Gradually, she controlled her sobbing by taking deep breaths and stopped crying. With a tear-stained face she looked at Scheiber who was sitting opposite her, watching her.

"Will you help us escape?" Erika begged.

"You know, until this morning, when Judith and I searched for you at every friend's house and train stations, I had no idea of the throngs of people leaving. It was a real eye opener, and I agree with you. This is a great opportunity to get out of the country. I will help you and your family to leave. And if you'd like, you and Judith can stay with us till I find a way. I'll contact your mother about it."

Erika sighed with relief and sank against the sofa back. "Thank you. May I go to sleep now?"

Lilla led Erika to the guest room which she would share with Judith. Erika slept through the entire day. She woke up refreshed, trusting that sooner or later with Scheiber's help, they would be able to leave.

◎◉◎

It took time for Dr. Scheiber to find a feasible plan for their escape. Piry came to stay with her sister for a couple days, visiting the Scheibers and her daughters several times. Then she went home, trying to convince Feri to escape with them. But as before, he remained stubborn and refused.

"I'll follow you if you make it. And if you don't, you know where you can come home to," was his determined response.

While waiting to leave, Erika and Judith visited Aunt Lilly and her family, and their friends, to say good-bye. They found that many of them had left already.

"We'll go legally," Donát told Piry when she asked them to come along. "We have a young son, I won't take a chance with my family's life," Donát explained. "You're much braver than me."

"Or more foolish," Piry grinned. "But everyone says, they have removed the mines from the border between Austria and Hungary. And even if you get caught, they just take your identity book information, and let you go, warning you not to try again."

"What if you try again and they catch you again," Lilly asked.

"Let's hope we won't have to find that out," Piry closed the discussion.

After a week, Scheiber had found a way for them to leave. Piry came to the apartment and sat along with her daughters listening to the plan.

"You will leave the day after tomorrow at mid-afternoon, along with another family, in two private cars," Scheiber began to explain. "The others are a couple with three small children and the wife's parents. They will be in one of the cars, and the three of you in the other, accompanied by a Soviet officer.

He and both drivers are from the Soviet High Command. The cars you'll be traveling in belong to a Soviet general. He is the one who had arranged the trip for you. Ostensibly, you'll be going to a family wedding at a border village."

Scheiber also told Piry that the trip will cost five thousand dollars per car. Piry was thankful that during the past two years, since her return from the Slovak prison, she had been able to save that sum because she had not been sending it to her aunt in Canada. Now it would buy their freedom.

Two days later, on December 10th, Erika was looking out the car window as their two black Mercedeses rolled through Budapest. Each street brought back a memory of walking there with Imi, and she thought, *I wonder whether you sense that I'm coming, coming to you. We must succeed because you're waiting for me!*

Along the highway, toward the Western border, their cars were stopped several times. Rough looking Soviet soldiers, accompanied by uniformed Hungarian ÁVH men, (Állam Védelmi Hatóság (National Defense Authority) asked for identifications. Each time, the Soviet officer sitting in the front seat with the driver in Erika's car calmly handed over the paperwork for both cars' passengers.

These soldiers look Asian, Erika thought as she observed them at each check point. Fearing that their driver and officer spoke Hungarian, she did not comment about this to her mother or sister. But she recalled hearing back in Budapest that the soldiers who had been sent to crush the revolution were from Mongolia. They had been told that they were fighting German Nazis. Now she could see with her own eyes that the rumors might have been true.

It was early evening when they arrived at a border village and parked the cars in front of a small peasant house. The Soviet officer led them inside and told them in broken Hungarian to sit and wait there while he went with his men to find the guides who would lead them across the border.

This "best room" of the house was smelly and dirty. *So, this is where we await our fate*, Erika thought. The other family was friendly and their children well behaved. But except for some small talk about the trip, none of them felt like chatting. They were offered water and coffee by the woman of the house, and not having eaten since noon, they gratefully accepted it.

They didn't have to wait long before the officer returned with his men and informed them, "You can't leave till tomorrow afternoon. We've found places for you to spend the night. We'll take you there now and come for you tomorrow when it will be time to leave. You'll have an ÁVH man as your guide."

With that, he escorted Piry and her daughters to a nearby farmhouse and took the rest of the passengers with him somewhere else.

Erika felt they had lucked out. The house hosting them was spotless, their room comfortable, with a large double bed. Down the hall was a bathroom and toilet.

"Surprise, surprise," Judith mocked the place, "they have indoor facilities!"

While their hostess served them dinner at the spacious oak wood kitchen table, their host entertained them unexpectedly intelligently about the political situation. He predicted that the new communist government would make several concessions, and life will improve from what it had been, thanks to the uprising.

He told them that besides Hungarian, he also spoke fluent German, "We spent more time in Vienna before the war than at home," he explained. Plus, he spoke Slovak, since periodically this part of the country belonged to Slovakia; and Czech, from having lived in Prague as well. Thus, instead of a stressful night in anticipation of their border crossing, Erika found the evening most interesting, feeling a great deal of respect for their host.

Next morning, shortly after breakfast had been served to them by their hosts, their Soviet officer showed up. He informed them in his halting Hungarian that they will be driven to another village, where they will meet their guide. Their car arrived to another peasant house, where a handsome young ÁVH man came out to greet them and invited them inside. The other family was already there.

"Please make yourselves at home, we won't leave till dusk," their host informed them.

They sat around making small talk for most of the morning. At 2 p.m. they were offered the customary main meal by the ÁVH man's mother, who seemed to live with him. The Soviet officer and the two drivers also stayed around till it was time for the families to leave.

They started from the house at six o'clock in the evening. Besides the ÁVH man, whose name was Pál, an older peasant from the village had also come to accompany them. The two families said goodbye to the Soviets and started their journey toward a new life.

It had been raining all day, and even now it wouldn't let up. Undaunted by the soft, steady downpour, the two guides led the little group across ploughed fields that had turned into soggy, sticky mud. Erika felt her shoes become twice as heavy as thick, wet clumps of earth covered them. The rain was relentless. Her kerchief slipped off her head down to her neck, and her hair stuck to her forehead dripping rain into her eyes. She watched Piry and Judith walking beside her, all three of them closely following their leaders, determined not to stop for anything this time.

They had advanced quite a distance when without warning rockets zoomed into the sky and lit up the terrain behind them. Although it did not seem to light up the fields where they were, terrified of getting caught again, Piry, Judith, and Erika urged their guides to go faster, not caring whether the other family could keep up with them. It seemed as though they did.

There is no way we're going to get caught again! Piry and her daughters thought as they sped up, lifting their feet out of the slush and mud, and sinking them into it again, rushing ahead in the night. Rain and sweat mingled on Erika's face, her coat and her clothes beneath it were soaked, but all she cared about was moving forward, moving forward as fast as she could, making sure her mother and sister were by her side.

It was close to midnight when the guides led them unto an asphalt road adjoining the fields they had been crossing. They followed the guides just a bit further and then were instructed to stop.

"This is where Hungary ends. We are not allowed to go any further," Pál told them, "But you just continue straight ahead on this road. See those lights about a hundred meters in front of us? He pointed ahead of them along the road. "Keep going towards them and you'll make it. That's Austria."

They all hugged the two men who had gotten them this far. Erika was the last one to do so, and as her arms went around Pál he embraced her and pressed his lips on hers in a passionate kiss. "I wish you lots of luck with your new life," he murmured as he let go of her.

Erika felt that his kiss meant far more than the lust of a young man for a pretty girl. It conveyed his regret because he was not able to leave, and his hope for her success in her future. *It was like kissing Hungary itself good-bye,* Erika reflected, as she rushed to catch up with her mother and sister.

Just a few minutes before reaching the well-lit gates of the Austrian border, they all had to stop to let a truck coming up behind them go by. The truck slowed down and halted beside them. For a moment Erika froze, the thought flashing through her mind, *the Hungarians sent a truck after us to take us back.* But then she heard the driver asking them in German, "Ungarn?" and tears of joy welled up in her eyes. She would have liked to run with arms outspread into the night, shouting *Imi, I'm here, we made it!* But she didn't run or shout. Dragging their mud-laden feet, their small group, exhausted, reached the red and white gate where the guards were already waiting for them.

The Austrian border guards knew where the group had come from. By now, refugees were a familiar sight at this border. Speaking German, which Piry actually understood, they let them through the gate and directed them to a nearby barn.

A table was set up in front of the large, gray double doors, and despite it being midnight, a woman was sitting at it. She asked them in halting Hungarian where they came from and wrote down their names. Then, handing each of them a bottle of water, she pointed at the barn. "You can get some rest in there before going on."

They entered, and saw that it was filled with people, sleeping in rows throughout the huge room. The golden hay on the ground right by the entrance was empty. Piry and her daughters practically collapsed on it and fell into a deep sleep.

Piry and her daughters woke early next morning, feeling stiff after having slept on a thin layer of hay strewn over the cement floor of the stable. They stood up, shook the hay off their clothes, and went outside. A friendly woman, sitting at the desk by the door explained that a kitchen had been set up near the stable where they would be provided breakfast. Also, there was a bathroom facility next door. Piry and her daughters went there first. They felt a lot better after being able to use the toilets, wash their faces, comb their hair, and in general make themselves look and feel presentable. Then they went to the dining room where they were offered bread, butter, a small variety of cheeses, and coffee.

While eating, Piry told her daughters, "We need to get to Vienna."

The Lonti family was also having breakfast there. They came over to Piry and suggested that they travel together. "I will contact my brother once we get to Vienna, and maybe he can help you and your daughters as well to get settled there," Mrs. Lonti offered.

They walked to the train station together. Then the Lontis went ahead to the ticket office while Piry and her daughters stopped so Piry could check her wallet for money. She had only Forints, the Hungarian currency, and wondered whether the ticket office would accept that. The few hundred dollars she had managed to save after paying for their escape, were carefully hidden under the insoles of her shoes. She wasn't about to get them out on the street.

A nice looking, tall man in an elegant gray wool coat stopped by them, and looking at Judith, asked in Hungarian, "Jewish?"

Piry answered, "Yes," wondering whether she should have admitted it.

But then the man asked whether Piry had any money for the train tickets, and a contact person in Vienna. When Piry replied that she had only Hungarian currency and just a couple of addresses there but nothing else, he handed her some Austrian schillings and wrote a name on his business card, handing it to Piry.

"The cash will tide you over, for a couple of days in Vienna," he said, "and the name on my business card is that of a friend of mine. I will phone him and ask him to pick you all up at the train station on your arrival in Vienna and take you to where you wish to be dropped off."

Piry and her daughters thanked the man profusely but waving off their gratitude he quickly got into his waiting chauffer driven car. It was this unexpected kindness by people that amazed Erika. Being helped by total strangers when they got to Austria and now by this man, who simply came over to them because he saw that they were lost. Still, as they headed for the train, Erika had a great sense of rootlessness, as though they were walking on the moon.

The villages the train passed along their route didn't look that different from Hungarian villages. When their train arrived in Vienna, there were two men on the platform, holding up signs with their names on it. One of the men spoke Hungarian and told them he and his friend came with two cars so they could take both families into the city center.

"Do you have an address to go to?" the Hungarian speaking man asked.

"My brother told me to go to the Europa Café, and wait for him there," replied Mrs. Lantos. She turned to Piry, "Why don't we all go there first, and then you can call your contacts from the café."

The two men dropped them off at the Europa Café, which seemed to have become the gathering place of Hungarian refugees. After many thanks from their passengers, the men drove off.

The two families entered the coffeehouse which was full of people. They were all sitting around small marble tables on small leather chairs under elaborate chandeliers and by other cone shaped lighting.

Mrs. Lonti's brother was already at the coffee house waiting for them. With a surprisingly quick good-bye, the Lonti family left, not bothering to ask whether Piry and her daughters had a place to stay—which they did not.

One of the contacts Piry had brought with her was the phone number of a couple who had come to Vienna legally earlier in the year. The other was the name and address of the uncle of one of Piry's close friends in Budapest. Erika had her friend Marianne's father's phone number given to her by the aunt. She also wondered where Imi might be but that had to wait.

Several phone booths were just outside the Café Europa. Piry and Erika were trying to figure out how to make a call on these unfamiliar pay phones but couldn't. Judith stood by, not even trying. Suddenly, a very pleasant male voice just behind them asked in Hungarian, "May I help you?"

Erika turned to face the handsomest young man she had ever seen. He had dark brown hair, soulful brown eyes, and a somewhat upturned nose. His shapely lips revealed perfect white teeth as he smiled at her. He was slim, a head taller than Erika, and was wearing an elegant black wool coat.

"Yes, please," Erika could barely get the words out she was so taken by him. She handed him the paper with the first number. Pulling a coin out of his coat pocket, he showed Erika how to make a call. The number he dialed for her was for her mother's friends. The person answering the call said, the couple had left a month ago for America. The next number was the uncle of Piry's friend. His phone just rang and rang, no one answered it.

At this point, the young man said, "I must go on. Do you think you could handle calls from here on? You can buy phone tokens at the Europa's cash register."

"Yes, I think so, thank you so much for teaching me how," Erika gave him her warmest smile.

Piry went into the Café and brought out several tokens. She continued to dial the uncle's number, without any success, while Erika called Marianne. Her stepmother answered the phone, informing Erika that Marianne was living at a boarding school, but will be home on the weekend. She gave the address of the school, suggesting that Erika could visit Marianne there.

For a few minutes Piry and her daughters stood by the phone booths feeling lost. Then Piry said, "Scheiber had also given me the address for the main synagogue of Vienna. The rabbi there is a friend of his. Let's go there."

Studying the city map they had been provided at the border, they strode through the slippery, sludge-covered sidewalks, reading the street names posted on buildings at each corner. Erika had no idea how, but by sheer miracle she thought, they got to the synagogue's address by mid-afternoon. Being winter, it was dark by then and the doors were locked. No one was there. Cold, hungry, and exhausted, they stared at each other, wondering what they could do next.

On their way to the synagogue, they had passed by a police station and now Piry said, "Let's go there and ask where we could stay."

They dragged themselves the few blocks down the street. The policemen at the station were amiable and clearly feeling sorry for the refugees who looked obviously at the end of their endurance. One of them suggested in broken Hungarian that they could go to a lager (warehouse used for refugees) not far from there, where they could get food and a place to sleep. Piry and her daughters took off, following the street-by-street directions by the policemen.

When they arrived at the right street, Piry checked the house number, Gonzage Gasse 7, and she exclaimed, "Timár Robert, my friend Betti's uncle, lives on this same street, at number 14! Let's go there first, maybe we'll find him at home."

Judith and Erika could only roll their eyes and sigh. They had no idea what their mother's expectations were, but they had no choice, so they trailed after her. If that didn't work, the lager was just down the street. They entered a stately apartment building and climbed the staircase to the second-floor apartment. Piry rang the doorbell, and a stately older man opened the front door.

"Pardon us, do you speak Hungarian?" Piry asked.

"Yes, I do," the man replied in Hungarian.

Piry quickly explained that she was his niece Betti's friend in Budapest and that she and her daughters had just arrived in Vienna that morning.

"Come in, come in," Robert said. He was an amiable short, slim man in his sixties, with a broad smile and a shock of white hair.

He settled his unexpected guests at his kitchen table. While asking about his niece in Hungary, and about his visitors' escape, he prepared a plateful of cold cuts, rye bread, and apples. They gratefully accepted what seemed like a feast by now.

"I don't have room for you to sleep here, but will find a hotel for you," Robert told them. He called around and was able to reserve a room for them at a nearby hotel.

As they were leaving with profuse thanks, Robert insisted on giving Piry money for the hotel room.

◉◉◉

It was a small, clean room, and much to the relief of the three women, the attached bathroom had running hot and cold water. They took turns bathing and then exhausted, fell into bed.

The hotel staff had set up a cot so Erika could sleep in her own bed. As she was falling asleep, Erika's last thoughts were, *Imi, we're in the same city again. I wonder whether you sense that I'm near you.*

The next morning, refreshed by a good night's rest and breakfast at a nearby Café, Piry said, "First thing, we must get our Gray Paper."

This was an identity document issued to refugees. They had been told by the border authorities that once in Vienna, they must register as refugees in order to continue to receive help. Following the border authorities' instructions, the three women headed for the police station that issued the Gray Paper.

Along the way, as Erika was reading the street names on each corner, she suddenly shouted, "That's the street and house number Imi's mother gave me! That's where he lives now with a Mrs. Klein!" And despite Piry's objections, Erika took off with Judith in tow, looking for Imi. They ran up the three flights of stairs and rang the doorbell at the designated apartment.

An amiable older woman opened the door. She spoke Hungarian, and panting, Erika explained that they were looking for Imi.

The woman said, "Sorry, he just moved to a hotel a couple of days ago. But he has been visiting me daily, so I'll tell him you are looking for him. He goes for dinner nightly at a kosher kitchen, set up for refugees. Why don't you go there too this evening? It's at Weissburg Gasse 10. If he comes today, I'll tell him to look for you there."

Erika thanked Mrs. Klein, and with hope in her heart, she and Judith rejoined their mother, who had been waiting for them in the cold, by the building's entry door. Standing on the sidewalk, in her limited German, Piry asked a passerby whether he knew where the police station was that handed out the Gray Paper. Another passerby overheard them and said in Hungarian, "I've got my car parked just there," he pointed at an elegant gray sedan, "I can take you to the police station where you can get documented."

Gratefully, and greatly relieved, the three women clambered into the man's car. They all thought that it was amazing how total strangers offered them help. After a short ride, the man stopped in front of an imposing looking police station and cheerfully said,

"Here you are, good luck to you." Not wanting to hear their thanks, after they got out of the car, he took off.

Inside the station a Hungarian speaking policewoman took their personal data with great efficiency. She filled out the necessary paperwork and handed each of them their own Gray Paper.

"Use this for your identification everywhere you need to show one," she told them and turned to the next set of clients already lined up behind Piry and her daughters.

With obtaining their identification papers accomplished, they headed for the kosher kitchen Mrs. Klein had told them about. They managed to find it using their map and arrived there just in time for lunch. No one asked them any questions at this place. It was full of Hungarian Jewish refugees. They were simply offered to join the line that led to the buffet tables.

Being a refugee brought back memories of the war to Piry. At least now they could be assured of getting meals, but she had no idea where they would sleep. The hotel where they had spent the night informed Piry in the morning that they were fully booked for the night. While eating, and thinking of their situation, Piry suddenly got an idea.

"Wait for me here," she commanded her daughters with a broad smile."

She went to the door where volunteers were bringing out the food from the kitchen. Slipping by them, she entered the kitchen and asked, "Where is your Chief Chef?"

"Is something wrong?" a female cook in a white apron asked, alarmed.

"Oh, no, I would just like to talk to him" Piry reassured her.

"There. The man with the white cap" the cook pointed out and returned to her work.

Piry strolled over to the Chef and stopped in front of him giving him a broad smile.

He looked up from studying the evening's menu and asked, "Can I help you?"

Piry, using all her charm replied, "Maybe I can help you. I see that you have a lot of people to feed and not enough help. I'm an excellent cook. My family owned a restaurant in Hungary. Would you be able to hire me? I've got two daughters to feed and no money."

The Chef sized Piry up, thinking over her surprisingly direct appeal. Finally, he said: "I can't pay much but you and your daughters can have all your meals here. When can you start?"

Piry happily grabbed his offer. "I can start today."

Piry informed her daughters of her new job and asked them to stay in the dining room till they could figure out where they would sleep that evening. Then she disappeared into the kitchen to help cut vegetables for the evening meal.

Not knowing where else they could go, Judith and Erika hung around in the dining room. To their delight, they ran into a number of their schoolmates from the Jewish High School in Budapest. They too had come to this haven for refugees. So, they all passed the day exchanging stories and wondering what their future will bring.

Evening set in. Judith and Erika had eaten dinner and were waiting for Piry to join them after her work. They still had no idea where they would sleep that night, and were hoping that while working, Piry would have been given some ideas.

One of their male school mates came to their table and said to Erika: "Someone is waiting for you outside,"

Erika shrugged, saying to Judith as she left, "I'll see who it is."

She stepped outside, and Imi stood there, smiling at her. Erika ran into his arms laughing, with tears in her eyes, feeling the same elation and love that she did when they first met in Budapest after the fighting stopped during the revolution. Inside the restaurant, they quickly caught up with each other's escape stories, then Imi offered to help Erika and her family to find a hotel room for the night. But they couldn't find one. Imi had to go back to his quarters because he had an early morning appointment. They agreed to meet the next day again at the kosher restaurant.

Erika, her mother, and sister went once again to ask for help from Timár Robert. But it seemed that all of Vienna's hotels were full, there was not one room available anywhere that evening. They ended up going down the street from Robert's place to the nearby refugee shelter.

Later, Erika's only note about it in her diary was: *Awful.*

The following morning, bad as it had been sleeping in the fully packed lager on mattresses on the floor, and using a crowded, not too clean women's bathroom, they gratefully accepted the coffee and a "kifli," (a crescent shaped roll) graciously offered to them by volunteering women at the shelter. After their quick breakfast, Piry headed for her new job at the kosher kitchen. By now, her daughters had addresses and phone numbers of former school friends, and each went her own way to meet with their own buddies.

Meanwhile, Piry didn't work full days. She would leave the kitchen for several hours between meal preparations to take care of their future. Her first priority was to find lodgings for her daughters and herself. By sheer luck, she ran into a former suitor of hers, whom she had met after the war in Budapest. He was a Hungarian born Englishman, who in Piry's view was 'ugly but super-rich'. She asked if he could help her get a room somewhere, at least for the night. He did and even paid for their room at the hotel where he was staying. In exchange, he asked Piry for a date, and she happily went out for dinner with him after her work at the kosher kitchen. Sher daughters settled into their new hotel room, and then they also went out with their friends.

◎◉◎

Piry knew that their situation was temporary. During the ensuing days, taking time off from her work, Piry visited with her daughters two Jewish agencies that had set up offices in Vienna. Both the HIAS (Hebrew Immigrant Aid Society), and the JOINT (Jewish Joint Distribution Committee), were there to register Jewish refugees, and to help them find a new country to live in. Piry asked for their help in gaining asylum in America. She also tried to promote their move by going to the American Embassy and listing her daughters and herself for admittance to the United States, as part of their government's refugee program.

She had heard that the USA, in consideration of the Hungarian political crisis, issued a "Refugee Relief Act," and will accept an additional five thousand people over their usual quota for Hungarians. She wanted to make sure that she and her daughters were among those five thousand. She was informed at the embassy that they needed a sponsor who would be responsible for them, so as not to become welfare cases in America.

Piry figured, that her former brother-in-law, Tibor Fábián, the rabbi, would sponsor them. Thus, she gave him as reference. She also sent a message to Tibor through HIAS, alerting him that they were in Vienna, and asking him to sponsor their immigration to the States.

One day, a man approached Piry at the kosher kitchen, and told her that her deceased husband's brother, Eli Fábián had sent him to offer Piry and her daughters a home in Israel. "Eli would take care of you there," the man said.

Piry was far more interested in going to America. Israel's involvement in the recent Suez Canal crisis made her think that because Israel always seemed to be at war, living there would be a last resort; only if they couldn't get into America. Thus, she did not say 'no' to the envoy. She wrote down his contact number and promised to look into it and get in touch with him.

Through Timár Robert, who by now had become a friend, Piry found yet another hotel, the Regina, where she and Erika could stay as long as they needed to, while Judith had been invited to lodge with friends.

◉◉◉

Apart from the official visits to the offices where they had registered for help with their repatriation, Piry was busy working at the kosher kitchen. Thus, Judith and Erika were pretty much on their own during the day. They spent their time with friends, and Erika and Imi roamed freely, exploring the city. Usually, they ended up either sitting by the shores of the Danube, or in his room, making love.

It was somewhat tricky for Erika to go to Imi's room because his cousin, Frigyes was also lodging at the same hotel and often stayed in. On one occasion, the three of them went together to Imi's hotel. Using the excuse of needing to rest, Imi told Frigyes to leave him alone. He whispered to Erika "Wait five minutes and then sneak up to my room. I'll leave it unlocked."

Erika succeeded in doing so, and they made love. But just as they lay there glowing satiated, feeling the closeness between them, there was a knock on the door.

It was Frigyes, asking Imi, "Is Erika in there with you?

"What's it to you?" Imi shouted through the door.

"Have fun," he yelled back, and they could hear him laughing as he left.

Erika was furious. "Why did you admit that I was here?" she demanded.

"He knows. The other day he asked me, 'Is Erika still a virgin? Or was she before she started going with you?' Imi told her.

"And what did you say?" Erika asked tensely.

"I told him, "She is not anymore, that's for sure!"

Erika was livid. She jumped out of bed and began to throw her clothes on. "You had no business telling him that! You humiliated and disgraced me!" she burst out. "I'm going home!" Looking at the dark sky through the window, she turned to Imi and asked in a milder tone, "It's late, will you escort me?"

Imi suddenly grabbed his forehead, and rolled off the bed, collapsing on the floor seemingly in a faint.

Alarmed, Erika shook him, "Imi, Imi, what's wrong with you?"

He opened his eyes and muttered, surprised, "What am I doing on the floor? I must have passed out." Then clenched his forehead moaning, "Oh, my head! I've got a beastly headache! You go on, I'll let Frigyes take care of me once you leave."

Erika put on her coat, saying "I hope you'll feel better," and snuck out of his room. On her way to the hotel room she shared with her mother, she felt a bitter resentment toward Imi.

The bastard was pretending to be sick so he wouldn't have to escort me home. I wonder if he still loves me or is merely using me. But what am I to do? I still love him and need him. But who knows what will happen with us in the future?

◎◉◎

Next morning, Imi didn't show up for breakfast at the kosher kitchen. Thinking that he might be sick, Erika went to his hotel but neither he nor Frigyes were there. Now seriously concerned, she looked for him at the Europa Espresso house, the Hungarian refugees' gathering place, but he wasn't there either. Giving up, she decided to stop by the HIAS office, to see if there might be news about their acceptance to America.

The office was crowded with petitioners, and suddenly she spotted Imi talking to a group of people. Erika walked over to him. As she stood by, waiting for him to finish talking, she realized that he was translating between Hungarian and German mixed with Yiddish. He noticed Erika and excusing himself, came over to her.

"I got this job as an interpreter and had no way of letting you know. Come back around five, when I get off." Giving her a quick smile, he went back to work.

Erika wondered when Imi had gotten this job and why he hadn't let her know last night. *Surely, he knew*, she thought. *Maybe he was afraid to tell me because it clearly meant that he won't have time for me during the day. The bastard, he just wanted to get laid. To hell with him. I'll find things to do on my own.*

Without spending so much of her days with Imi, Erika used her time to go visit Marianne at her school. She called ahead, and the headmistress allowed Marianne to meet with Erika at a nearby café house. They discussed their current situation, and their future.

Marianne explained, "I'll finish the gymnasium (high school) at this school, then will study chemistry at an Austrian or German university. I probably won't get great grades this year, but next year I'll be more serious about studying and will get into a good university."

"I didn't know you were interested in science, I thought you wanted to paint," Erika wondered.

"I can paint on my own, but to support myself, someone will have to pay me a steady salary," Marianne laughed. "What about you?"

"I'll be an actress and a writer, no matter where we end up," Erika replied, then asked, "Do you know where Mária is?"

"No idea. She must have escaped with her parents, but as far as I figure, they must have reconnected with their fellow aristocrats, and dumped us, commoners."

They sat in silence for a few minutes, as if mourning their lost friend.

CHAPTER 27

"LET'S GO TO THE Danube," Imi suggested one evening when Erika came to meet him after his work at the HIAS. They clambered down to the riverbank. As soon as they settled on the stone steps by the Danube, Imi burst into a sob.

"I'm so lost," he stammered between tears, "I have no future and no past, what am I going to do with my life? Where will I be going from here? Where will you go?"

Erika hugged him, wiped his tears, and calmed him down, assuring him, "Life has a way of working itself out. All you must do is work on the path you choose, and you can make it happen."

He smiled at her through his tears, and said, "Both Frigyes and I have applied to go to America, because we have relatives in Brooklyn."

"So, we'll both end up in America, and we'll find a way to be together after we settle there," Erika smiled back, smoothing the tears off his face.

"Women keep flirting with me here. What if I yield to temptation and go to bed with one of them? You'll leave me, won't you?" he was crying again.

Erika, taken aback by his question thought for a moment. She too, had been tempted by others, and yet returned to him, so she replied, "I can understand the desire to explore others. Do it now, while we're both young and free. If we do eventually marry, I'd want you to be sure it's me you want. At that point I want us to be faithful to each other. I don't want you to feel like you've missed out on something when we're husband and wife."

Her words seemed to have a curious effect on Imi. He wrapped his arm around Erika's shoulders, and smiling through his tears, said, "Let's renew the vows we gave each other a year ago today, that we will never leave each other."

Later, Erika wrote in her diary: *We were sitting in a different country, under different stars, on different steps by a different shore. Yet, by the same Danube, where we first kissed and promised to stay together. This Danube will touch the shores and the steps where we first swore to be together. Our love is old but tonight it has become new again.*

◉◉◉

A few days later, Erika went to inquire again at the HIAS about the progress of their application. To her overwhelming joy, she ran into her friend Forbát

Zsuzsi and her entire family. They had arrived in Vienna just a few days earlier and were there to register for repatriation. Erika waited till they were done signing up. Then Zsuzsi's sister and parents left for their hotel, and she and Erika fount the nearest café house to sit and catch up with their stories.

Zsuzsi told Erika, "My parents donated our beautiful three-bedroom apartment to a woman employed at the same company as my father. She had a brother working as a guard at the frontier, and in exchange, he was to guide us across the border to Austria.

"We knew we'd never go back," Zsuzsi shrugged, "so why not buy our freedom with the apartment? But you know what? The guide took us across fields full of mud, then he stopped when we got to a paved road and said, "If you just continue straight, you'll get to the Austrian border. They're expecting refugees so they'll receive you." And he left.

We started to walk, and my father looked up at the sky—it was a very cold, bright night—and he said, "Judging from the position of the moon and the stars, we're going in the wrong direction. Let's turn around." We did, and that's how we reached the Austrian border."

"Was the guy guiding you to turn back toward Hungary?"

Zsuzsi shrugged, "Who knows? Maybe. But we made it. What about you?"

Erika briefly described their escape, then went on to disclose to Zsuzsi her intimate relationship with Imi.

"I think you're wrong to do it," Zsuzsi responded, "but it's your life. Just don't get pregnant."

"He started using protection since we got here. I told him I wouldn't go to bed with him without it."

"At least you're smart," Zsuzsi laughed. Her boyfriend was also in Vienna, and so were several other close friends of theirs. Thus, before parting company, they set up a time to meet with them all while Imi was at work, and Erika was free.

But all the fun and gatherings were coming to an end. Erika and her family had been called for physical exams at the American Embassy, and another one at the HIAS. Passing those, they had to go and register at ICEM (Intergovernmental Committee for European Migration), the office which handled travel arrangements for repatriated refugees.

They stood in line on a sunny day in bone chilling cold on an icy sidewalk, along with a long line of refugees, all there to register. They were barely inching forward. Finally, Piry and her daughters got to ascend the stairs leading into the building.

Suddenly, there was a flurry of activity from inside, as several men in black coats and hats rushed out, followed by a tall, nice-looking man in his mid-forties.

"The American Vice-President, Richard Nixon," people whispered all around them. "He had come to personally assess the Hungarian refugee situation, and what better place than at the ICEM! He can see us standing in line, hoping to get into his country," a man commented on their line, laughing.

Erika wrote in her diary, *Nixon walked right by us, I could have touched his coat sleeve. It was a good omen for what happened next. Once he left, we were able to get inside. While waiting there, Judith and I decided to look at the lists of refugee repatriation schedules.*

I was especially concerned because Imi told me this morning that he and his cousin were on the immigration list, they just had to choose a departure date. He told me, if at all possible, they won't leave without me. So, as Judith and I were studying the lists, we discovered that we had been put on a list two weeks ago! So, it was a turn of fate that we missed that and now Imi's got his date so we could all leave together for America!

◎◉◎

The following days were a flurry of registrations for departure and saying good-bye to friends still awaiting their fate. During the final preparations, Erika was at the ICEM office with Imi, when they ran into her former flame, Z. He was there, scheduling his departure to Sweden, where he had been accepted to a medical school on a full scholarship.

Erika felt good standing next to Imi, chatting with Z in a friendly, detached way. She thought, *my hurt vanity might never get over the fact that he did not chose me for his girlfriend. But aside from that I'm no longer drawn to him either emotionally or physically.*

"Adios, I wish you all the luck in the world," Erika smiled at Z as they shook hands, likely, for the last time in their lives.

ICEM had set their day of departure for the afternoon of December 23rd. That morning Zsuzsi came to Erika's hotel to say good-bye. Marianne came as well, driven by her father to make sure that she would get there in time.

Painful as these farewells were, none of the girls felt that they were final. No matter where fate may toss them, they were now living in the free world. They could stay in touch and even visit each other in the future.

At three p.m. Piry and her daughters, Imi and his cousin, Frigyes, and many other refugees, lined up in front of the ICEM building. They were instructed to board the buses waiting for them in front of ICEM. Each bus had a preassigned passenger list and Imi and Frigyes were not listed on the bus that Erika's family was to get on. Boldly, Imi and Frigyes just got on it on their bus.

When all seats were filled and the last two passengers assigned to this bus had no seats, the supervising officer from ICEM did a roll call and promptly discovered the impostors. Erika was devastated when Imi and Frigyes were ordered off the bus. They didn't even have a chance to say good-bye to each other. Neither had any idea when and where they would see each other again.

◎◉◎

Driven by a handsome American soldier, after a short trip their bus pulled into a refugee camp in the small, picturesque town of Kaisersteinbruck. All passengers were instructed to get off the buses and line up outside the building to be assigned quarters.

Erika and her family were led by a woman soldier to their barrack, and she found herself facing Imi at the entrance. She was suffused with joy at seeing him again. Inside, they were told to make themselves comfortable on the mattresses provided in adjacent but separate rooms for men and women. Meals were served in a common dining room at a different building, walking distance from their barrack. After a few of days, they would be transferred to another location.

But it didn't take that long for them to be moved. They spent the night at the barrack but early next morning the Catholic Hungarian refugees started grumbling to their American hosts. They were claiming that Jewish refugees were being moved to their destinations faster than they were. Their temper was getting out of hand, and they had threatened to "Kill all the Jews."

Afraid of violence breaking out in the camp, the American officers who were managing the transportation of the refugees, went to every barrack and asked the Jewish refugees to gather their things. After a quick breakfast, they were going to be moved to another location.

Piry, Judith, and Erika were quite upset by the announcement. Imi and Frigyes quickly came to their side.

"This time we'll insist on traveling together with you," Imi assured them. "We'll claim to be cousins."

"Just look at our Hungarian compatriots," Piry responded with bitter sarcasm. "No wonder we want to leave and never see Hungary—or them—again!"

By eleven o'clock in the morning, all Jewish refugees were boarded on buses. But it seemed that there had been no decision as to where to take them. So, they were instructed to just stay on the buses. It was cold inside, and periodically soldiers came and turned on the motor to heat up the buses inside. It was four o'clock in the afternoon by the time the refugees were informed that they'll be driven to a different camp back in Vienna.

During their wait on the buses, they had been provided lunch. Sandwiches, sodas, and coffee but were instructed to stay on board. Even trips to the buildings' bathrooms were discouraged, although allowed, and watched over by the American military personnel on duty.

Erika was sitting with her mother and sister, but periodically she got up and walked forward to chat with Imi who was seated with Frigyes two rows ahead of them. After she did this a couple of times, the female soldier on the bus asked her to go and sit down. Erika obeyed, though not without resentment. Everyone seemed to be tense on the bus, awaiting their next move, and apprehensive about the delay. Seat partners conversed softly or tried to doze off.

Piry quietly talked about their relatives in America, assuring her daughters that they'll be taken care of by them once they get there. "We have my mother's aunts and uncles there as well as your father's brother, Tibor."

"How will they know that we are there?" Erika asked.

"The HIAS organization will let them know. Your uncle Tibor will be notified of our arrival and the place where he can pick us up."

Reassured, the two girls fell silent, awaiting their next transportation.

Finally, the drivers came on board, and their caravan of buses took off. After about an hour they had arrived in Vienna. As they were rolling through the city streets toward the central district, looking out the window and recognizing buildings, Erika was thinking, it's almost like coming home.

But it was not to be. At the new camp they were instructed to rest as best they could on cots provided to them in several large barrack dormitories. They were told, that after some rest they will be moving on. Anticipating their next journey, Erika and her family found it hard to sleep. They lay quietly on the cots, just resting. Imi and Frigyes were in an all-male dormitory. But before Imi and his cousin were told to go there, he assured Erika that he'll make sure they'll be put on the same flight to America.

After a couple of hours' rest, once again they were given sandwiches and drinks. With their meal finished, they were instructed to board the buses. By this time, it was around eleven o'clock at night, and extremely cold.

It is December, Erika thought, as they trudged through the slippery, ice-covered parking lot to the waiting buses. They had been informed earlier that first they will be driven to Salzburg and from there to München where they will board U.S. military planes to America.

This time on the bus, Erika sat by the window with Imi by her side. She was looking at Vienna as they drove across the city. When they arrived at the refugee camp in Salzburg, before lying down on her cot, Erika wrote in her diary: *My last memory of Vienna is the Mariahilfer Strasse (Maria's Help Street). What a strange coincidence is the name of this street as we're heading toward our future! It made me recall going to the Maria statue in Bratislava with Maria and praying. Maria, my dear friend, where might you be?*

Imi and I held hands as the bus raced down the avenue with us. Tonight is Christmas Eve, and the streets were deserted. Thousands of Christmas lights had been strung high above the street, illuminating the night. It was an overwhelming feeling to be speeding down the road under their glow toward more lights ahead as though they were an omen of the future that is awaiting us.

At the Salzburg military base, the refugees disembarked and were provided cots to rest on. They were awakened in a few hours and served breakfast in a cafeteria. It was filling food, scrambled or soft-boiled eggs, croissants, and coffee with milk. Then they were instructed to get on the buses again.

◉◉◉

When they arrived in Munich, almost at dawn, once again they were told to go and rest, this time on very comfortable military beds of the American army. With all this moving around, Erika and her family were exhausted and welcomed getting several hours' sleep. They were awakened late-morning, and after using the bathroom facilities, were ushered into a large cafeteria for breakfast. Again, it consisted of buttered croissants and jam, hard boiled eggs, and coffee, black or with milk.

Despite all the sporadic rest periods, Erika felt energetic. Looking at her mother and sister, they too seemed to be filled with anticipation. Imi and his cousin, Frigyes, sat with them during breakfast, and Imi reassured Erika again that they'll be on the same flight.

At noon, all the Jewish refugees were transported by small buses to the tarmac where three military planes stood waiting. They were told to go up the stairs and settle into their assigned seats to be flown to their new homeland.

On the plane, Erika sat with her mother and sister. Imi and Frigyes were two rows ahead of them. Erika would have loved to sit with Imi but accepted that she couldn't. At least he was there, sitting not far from her. It was to be a long flight, and Erika thought, *surely, we'll have a chance to switch seats and be together.* For the moment, she listened to the instructions to fasten her seat belt. With a broad grin, Erika said to her mother and Judith, "It took a revolution, and a second escape, but looks like we'll make it this time."

As soon as the plane leveled off and they could unfasten their seatbelts, Erika pulled out her diary to jot down her thoughts:

The plane set off with enormous jolts and roar as it ascended into the sky. It is such an odd feeling to be flying. It's as if we're gliding on solid blue air. Just under our plane, billowing white clouds are spread like a thick, fluffy blanket above the earth.

I'm floating on air to America.

THE END

ACKNOWLEDGMENTS

No book is created by a writer without the input of many others. My thanks go to the following people:

to my sons, Dan Reinstein, who sponsored the writing of the book, and Anthony Fabian Reinstain, for his editorial suggestions.

The various editors, including Sharon Daly, Maria Giribaldi, Amelia Stone, and Frank Shatz, who tirelessly read the manuscript making text and spelling corrections.

Special thanks go to Hailie Johnson, the book's designer, for her hard work and infinite patience while formatting the pages of *Liars' Paradise*.

And all other friends and professional acquaintances who encouraged me to write this story.

DICTIONARY FOR *LIAR'S PARADISE*

Anyu (Anyuka)	Mom
Apu (Apuka)	Dad
Apucika	Daddy
ÁVO	Állam Védelmi Osztály –Homeland Security Division
Kapish	Understand (Russian)
Kashrut	Kosher–law that governs foods Jews can eat
Komondor	Hungarian sheep dog
Kulák (kuláks plural)	Wealthy landholder or farmer with large land holdings
Maczkó	Bear cub (common dog's name)
Népszava	People's Voice
Neolog	Conservative
Palack Bár	Flask Bar
Proletár	Working class person
Proli	Hungarian abbreviation for Proletár
Puszta	Prairie, the Hungarian flatlands
Rózsa Domb	Rose Hillock
Status quo	Current State of Things
Sziget	Island
Ushanka	Russian style fur hat
Ùt	Road
Utca	Street

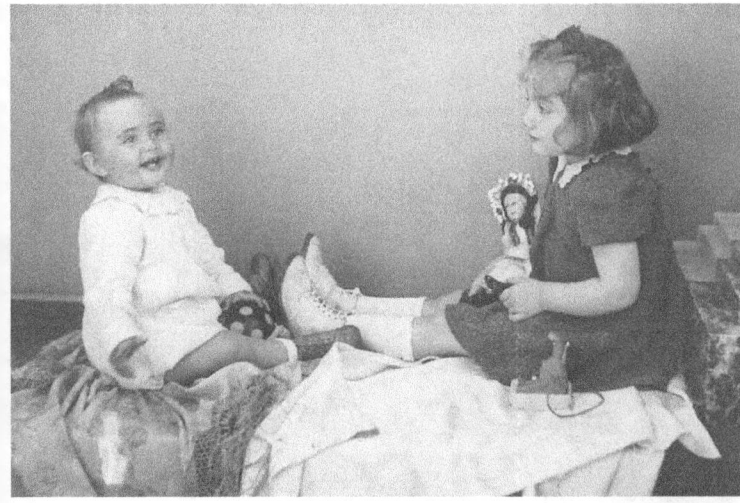

Erika age one
Judith age five

Erika with paternal grandparents

Judith and Erika
at the park

Judith age six

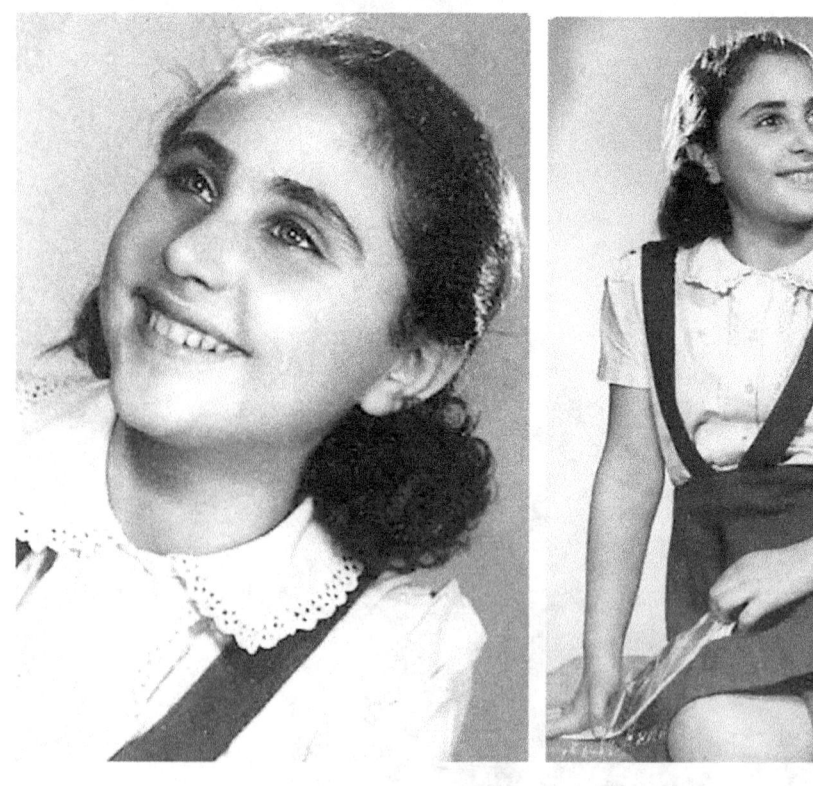

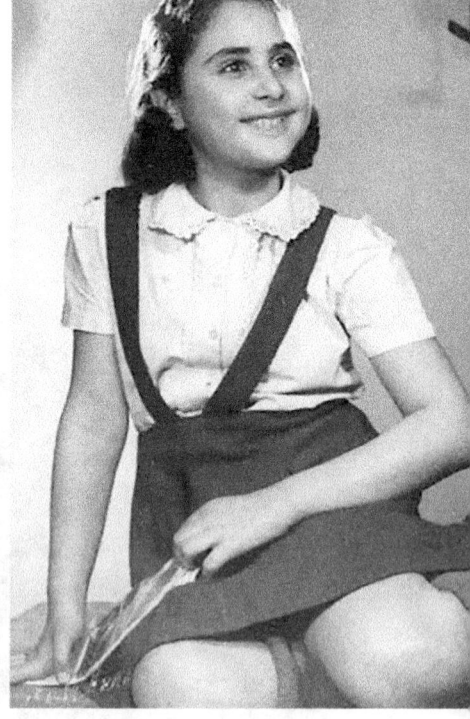

Erika at fourteen years, 1952

Erika 1966 bedroom

Erika in profile 1956

Erika 1956 living room

Judith 1956

Judith 1956 portrait

Piry in 1948

Piry and Zoltan pre-war

Piry 1956

Zoltan student photo

Zoltan as a young man

Feri Haydu,
Piry's second husband

www.ingramcontent.com/pod-product-compliance
Lightning Source LLC
Chambersburg PA
CBHW070151120726
47909CB00001B/72